THE CURSE OF HURLIG RIDGE

World Tree Online: 1st Dive

M.A. Carlson

M.A. Carlson

Visit my website at https://macarlsonauthor.wordpress.com/

Printed in the United States of America

First Printing: Aug 2018
M.A. Carlson

ISBN-978-0-692-15000-9

For Dad, thank you for the encouragement to pursue writing.

CONTENTS

Prologue..1

Chapter 1 6

Chapter 2 30

Chapter 3 53

Chapter 4 71

Chapter 5 95

Chapter 6 113

Chapter 7 128

Chapter 8 144

Chapter 9 165

Chapter 10 186

Chapter 11 215

Chapter 12 232

Chapter 13 249

Chapter 14 266

Chapter 15 282

Chapter 16 305

Chapter 17 323

Chapter 18 345

Chapter 19 363

Chapter 20 381

Chapter 21 402

Chapter 22 415

Chapter 23 436

Chapter 24 453

Chapter 25 473

Chapter 26 496

Chapter 27 512

Chapter 28 528

Chapter 29 544

Chapter 30 559
Chapter 31 576
Chapter 32 592
Chapter 33 611
Chapter 34 630
Chapter 35 647
Chapter 36 665
Chapter 37 689
Epilogue 702
Stats, Equipment, Skills and Spells 715
Author's Note 728

PROLOGUE

Welcome to the World Tree

I can't even begin to express how happy I was to be reading those words on the little screen of my new Seedpod just a few inches away from my face.

System initializing . . .

The screen updated with a little progress bar that was quick to fill. I was so happy I spent the money to update my internet connection to a 100-terabytes upload and download speed. I know the Seedpod only required a 10-terabyte connection, but I didn't want any lag.

What is the Seed? So glad you asked. The Seed is the first of its kind, Full Immersion Virtual Reality (FIVR) pod. Virtual Reality (VR) had been around for a long time, well before I was born. FIVR has been around for about 10 years and met with a good deal of success but nothing compared to what the Seed promised to deliver.

Previous FIVR systems would allow short-term dives, limited to about 4 hours at a time due to biological needs such as food and bathroom. Part of the safety requirements, enforced by the government, made it a necessity after a few idiots wet themselves playing too long and caused a surge in the equipment, which in turn fried their brains, stopped their hearts or both. Following the unnecessary deaths, the systems all had a 4-hour automatic cutoff installed with a mandatory 2-hour cooldown, which severely limited the playability of most games.

The Seed promised a two-part solution to the problem. First, the fact that people needed food and water at specific intervals while playing was solved with an injection system, which sounds much worse than it is. Second, and most complicated, was the implementation of nanotech, or microscopic machines. The nanomachines were able to monitor and control your bodily functions to prevent muscular atrophy and handle waste. As a result, it was now not only possible but entirely feasible to FIVR dive for up to a month at a time.

Best of all, you come out of the machine fit and trim after a month due to the machines being programmed to optimize your health in every way possible. As a husky guy myself, someone who had little interest in exercise or sports, this was a Godsend.

Initialization complete. Prepare for a message from Mitchell Dawson . . .

Mitchell Dawson was the chief software and hardware designer and largest stakeholder in Seed Inc. Apparently, he turned down the offer to become the CEO stating he enjoyed building things more and was happy to be able to continue to do so.

"Hello and welcome to the World Tree," greeted an image of the man himself on the little screen. "First let me thank you for your purchase and especially for your patience in the delivery of your Seedpod."

Patience probably wasn't the right word for it. Patience would have meant I was understanding of and accepted the delay of my Seedpod. I can honestly say I was not patient. Especially after the three rotten months, it was on backorder, despite my being one of the first to preorder a unit, and a deluxe model, no less, with a significant price mark up.

You'd think, after spending almost half a mil for my unit it would have been here on the promised delivery date. And yet, my unit was only delivered in the last week and finally setup over the last two days by the company's technicians. I understand they severely underestimated the demand for the Seedpods but 3 months, really? Three months in which I couldn't play. Three months of not leveling. Three horrid, hellish, long drawn out, boring months!

But it was going to be okay, it was finally here, I was finally going to be able to log in and play. Not just play but play nonstop for the next 30 uninterrupted days.

If you're curious how a 20-year old such as myself can afford such an expense, I suppose you could say I was an overachiever in high school. I wrote a phone app, which I ended up selling for a cool 50 million. While it wasn't a huge amount of money these days, after several smart investments including purchasing a large shareholding in Seed Inc., I was in a situation where I would never have to worry about money again, provided I wasn't epically stupid in my spending.

"As an apology for the delay in delivering your unit, we'll be giving you an experience boost for your first 10 levels, to help you catch up with other players. Thank you again for both your participation and patronage. I sincerely hope you enjoy your time exploring the World Tree." His statement was brief, and the screen faded to black immediately after. I honestly felt angered by his statement. Ten levels . . . what was that? And how much of a boost? I know from the various forums, there were several people already in their 50's. The highest leveled gamer, Titan Beast, was Lvl 66 and was exactly that, a beast. Boosted experience for 10 levels, such bull.

Okay, so maybe I was more than a little angry.

A moment later, the screen faded back into an image of a room again, this time with a young digital woman on the screen. I say digital cause no woman could sound so angelic. Wavy blonde hair with an unnatural shine to it. A perfect heart-shaped face with a small nose and pouty lips. Totally unrealistic for someone to look this good, but man, if she wasn't the hottest thing I'd ever seen.

"Good afternoon, Byron, I am Maggie, your digital guide. It is my job to help with the first login and calibration of your Seedpod. First, my sensors indicate your armband is slightly low on your right arm, please shift it above your bicep."

I couldn't help but blink in surprise, both at the instruction and just how lifelike the Artificial Intelligence, or AI as it was usually referred to, was. I blinked again and then as instructed, I reached across my body and nudged the armband a little further up my arm.

"Perfect," Maggie said, once the band was where she wanted it. "Now, you are going to feel a pinch but not pain as the armband has already released a mild numbing agent. This is how we will manage your health while you are in your full immersion dive. Are you ready for the lid to close?" When I first got into the Seedpod, the lid only closed part way allowing a good deal of light to filter in from the side, as well as placing the small screen just far enough away for me to see it clearly. Once the lid closed completely, it would be too close to comfortably read or watch.

Focusing on the task at hand, I ran one more, quick, mental checklist. My brother and his wife were taking care of my cat for the next month. My internet, water, electricity and condo association bills were paid up for the next 6 months or turned on to auto-debit my bank account. Additionally, my bank account was linked to my World Tree account, so I could deposit any money I made while in the game or withdraw money from my account if I needed it. My doors were all locked up tight and the security system was activated. The fridge was emptied so no food would go bad and the trash was taken out.

4

My stomach was empty because I hadn't eaten in 24-hours per the Seedpod's full immersion requirements. I couldn't think of anything I may have missed so I stated it clearly and simply, "I'm ready."

"Great, the lid will close, and you will be in darkness for what will feel like a few minutes before you wake in the character creation center. We will be putting you to sleep first though so please do not resist or the process will take longer," she explained briefly.

"Can do," I replied, I felt a little nervous but also very excited.

"Great, speak to you soon," she said, smiling in a way that could be nothing less than supernatural.

With the lid closed, completely sealing me in darkness. I closed my eyes and within moments the beta wave transmitters put me into a deep sleep.

CHAPTER 1

When I woke up I was laying down comfortably. I wasn't sleepy, per se, but I did feel sluggish.

"Take your time acclimating, there is no rush," said the unmistakable voice of Maggie, though it sounded more as if she was in the room with me now instead of speaking to me through the pod's speaker.

I opened my eyes and had to blink a few times to adjust to the brightness of the room. I took a few deep breaths. The air smelled off to me, maybe a little stale or musty. I'm not sure why but it reminded me of a museum or one of those old libraries, the kind that used to have books printed on paper. It wasn't until my eyes started recognizing the objects in the room, I understood why.

The walls all around me were covered in bookshelves from floor to ceiling and the shelves themselves were covered in books. As for me, I was lying on a small cot in the center of the round room. Then I noticed, the room had neither doors nor windows, yet it was lit perfectly. Then I saw Maggie sitting in an armchair near the end of the cot, staring at me with a polite smile.

"Hello," she smiled and gave a small wave to me, coming across as both friendly and a little condescending at the same time.

"Hi," I answered, not sure what else to say.

"Before we begin this next part of the process, please try to remain calm. I understand you may feel awkward being in the buff with me present, but I assure you, you do not have anything I have not seen on the other male divers," she stated unabashedly.

It took my brain a moment to process she was talking about. I was naked as the day I was born.

"Which is fitting, as you are about to be born again," she commented, her smiling widening as she said it.

"Did you just read my mind?" I asked, feeling slightly uncomfortable with having my privacy invaded.

"Yes, I did, and I will again. It will help me assist you in selecting the character that best fits you. You will only get to be born into the World Tree once," she answered succinctly.

That was the only major complaint people had so far, you only get one chance to make a character. There were no do-overs. You also only got to select one class, which would develop based on how you played the game. It was truly about you and who you were as a person that determined how you would develop in the game. However, it should also be noted, most classes also had advancements or evolutions, but they were not easy to come by.

"You are absolutely right. So, let us start with you telling me what name you wish to play under. Please note Players are strictly forbidden from using their real names while in-game," she stated, beginning the process of creating my character.

"Bye-bye Jacko," I answered. It was the name I always used in Massively Multiplayer Online Role-Playing Games (MMORPG). As long as they allowed two names. My name is Byron Jacobs. When I was in grade school, one of my tormentors would always taunt me 'Bye-bye Jacobs' before he punched me or pushed me into someone. On the advice of my older brother, I tried to own the name. It wasn't until, said tormentor, tried to trip me going up some stairs, only for me to turn the tables on him . . . read 'accidentally' tripped him instead. He tumbled backward, falling halfway down the stairs at which point, I stated clearly and loudly for everyone to hear, 'Bye-Bye Jacko'. This earned me a good laugh and a week of detention, but it was totally worth it. Since then, my nickname, within my limited circle of friends, was 'Bye-Bye', which caused confusion and humor in equal measure.

"Excellent, the name is available and now it is yours alone. Next, in order to be supportive of the transgender community do you wish to play as male or female. Please bear in mind, if you choose to be female you will feel female in the game, including all that goes with it?" Maggie asked but also warned.

"Male," I said quickly, maybe a little too quickly. I am a guy and prefer to remain a guy.

"Moving on, what do you enjoy about Massively Multiplayer Online Role-Playing Games (MMORPG's) and we'll go from there?" she asked.

"Can't you just read my mind?" I asked. Admittedly, my response sounded snarky. I didn't intend to be, but there it was.

"I can only read your surface thoughts, so I suppose you could think about it to me, might be excessive though, yes?" she answered.

"Right, sorry. I guess I'm just feeling a little out of sorts so far," I replied contritely.

"It's understandable. It will take a little time to acclimate. It is also part of this process," she explained.

"I'm an explorer at heart. I love dungeon crawling and even raiding. I loathe Player versus Player (PvP) more than you can imagine," I started telling her. I hate PvP gameplay because it was unfair that a high-level player would kill someone weaker than them, just because they could.

"What kind of exploring?" she asked. It was then I noticed she was sitting perfectly still, she wasn't fidgeting or shifting in her seat, it felt unnatural, but given she was a computer program I suppose I shouldn't have been too surprised.

"Well, in other Massively Multiplayer Online (MMO) games I've played, I love finding hidden Easter Eggs. Secret quests and the like," I answered. An Easter Egg is just as it sounds, but for games instead of finding actual eggs, plastic or otherwise, your goal is to find hidden quest lines, secret events, and other gaming fun.

"I see, and dungeons and raiding?" she asked.

"What's not to love there? You get to explore tombs filled with challenging and unique monsters. You have to work as a team to clear it and more importantly, you have to know what you're doing."

She nodded thoughtfully. "I suppose then I should ask why you dislike Player versus Player? As I'm sure you know by now, there is only one server and it is all PvP eligible."

I stayed silent for a minute as I thought about my answer. "I hate when other people take pleasure in hurting others, it disgusts me to be honest. Most of them are bullies, real life or game doesn't matter. They pick on people and players weaker than themselves. I've encountered PvP fanatics in the past and I personally think most of them should be put behind bars or banned from games like this. To enjoy killing another person is just wrong and as lifelike as this FIVR is . . . well, let's just say I would never trust a Player Killer (PK) in real life. PKs are the worst."

"Okay, can you tell me about your play style?" she requested.

"I usually play a paladin or similar class. I find they have so much versatility, I can heal with them or tank or even be a damage dealer," I answered.

"So, you prefer close range? Or staying at a distance as a healer?" she asked.

"I'm good with either. They each have different aspects I find enjoyable," I answered.

"Have you ever played as a mage or hunter type class?" she asked.

"Not really. I usually played with a group of friends and they needed me to fill one role or another, so I usually go with the one giving me the most versatility," I answered honestly.

"Are you opposed to trying such a class?" she asked, continuing to probe at my gaming preferences.

"Not at all. Does it matter? I mean, doesn't our play style determine our class?" I asked, wondering if maybe all the gameplay research I had done previously was for naught.

"Absolutely it does, but some classes are more magically gifted, while others are more physically gifted, thus getting increased gains to the stats aligning with their class," she explained, reassuring me.

"Makes sense," I mumbled. It was interesting, and I would have liked to ask more questions, but we were getting off topic and I wanted to get into the game to start playing as soon as possible. I chose to redirect the conversation back to the purpose for being here. "So, what race do you recommend?"

"Based on what you have told me, I believe a half-High Elf and half-Human, or half-Mountain Dwarf and half-Human would suit you best," Maggie advised confidently.

"Why them?" I asked, curious about her choices for me.

"High Elves have bonuses to Lore, which is a big part of exploration and discovery in the World Tree, they also have bonuses to holy magic and ranged attack damage as well as gaining +2

Intellect with each level. The Mountain Dwarves are also blessed with Lore bonuses, but they don't mix with the High Elves and therefore do not produce children together. The Mountain Dwarves get +2 stamina with each level and have improved ax and mace skills, as well as mining and blacksmithing crafting bonuses. The Humans are blessed with the ability to use any weapon with training and gain increased experience in learning weapons skill, where the others are limited by either race or class. It will allow you to fight in melee or shoot from range and they also get +2 Charisma with each level. Their versatile racial ability also allows them to learn up to 4 different professions, where all other races are limited to 2. Now, as a halfling, the bonuses are cut in half, but you can still benefit greatly," she elaborated on her recommendations.

"What other Elf and Dwarf races are there? And why is there only one race of human?" I asked. I sure did seem to be asking a lot of questions.

Maggie smiled, she appeared to be thinking about the answer to my questions. I would have thought the question about the Elf and Dwarf races was easy, so it must have been the question about the Human races taking her a while to answer. Eventually, she did answer, but the answer surprised me. "It is a delicate subject and not something I've been asked before, regarding the Humans at least. Originally the game did offer 3 difference races of humans, but it caused a big uproar with the higher powers and was quashed rather brutally."

I wanted to ask more but figured it was probably something more to do with the race difference outside of the game than inside the game. "So, about the Elf and Dwarf races?"

"Good, so there are Wood or Brown elves which gain boost to nature magic, herbalism, and alchemy. They also receive +2-

Intellect per level the same as their High Elf cousins. Dark Elves get a boost to dark magic and enchanting with the same intellect boost. Actually, all the elven races get the intellect boost, just different magical boosts and profession boosts depending on where they are born," she explained.

"Okay, do any of the elven races get a general magical bonus?" I asked.

"No," she answered simply. "As for the Dwarves, they all pretty much get the same stamina boosts, but depending on where they are born, they will get different weapon expertise or a +1 bonus to another stat, and all dwarves get some manner of crafting skills efficiencies."

"Are there any other races you think would be worth looking at? I know from the forums, there are some crazy offshoot races, which can only be halflings," I said.

"There are, such as the aquatic, reptilian and mammalian halflings. They can look very pretty, but the racial abilities are rather specific to a single style of play and from your previous statements in preferring more versatility I do not believe they would be a good fit," she explained.

"Could you elaborate anyway? Just for my own edification?" I requested. I couldn't help but be curious.

"For example, the aquatic races will get natural water breathing and bonus to dexterity, stamina or endurance, as well as one strong gathering bonus. The Mammalians can get bonuses to anything, as there are so many kinds of animals. They get some race specific attacks and skill bonuses and a single stat bonus gain per level, but again, it is a +1-bonus similar to the aquatic halflings, and then they also get one strong bonus to a gathering skill. As such, the people who usually select these do so to either make a specific class of character or just to earn money exclusively gathering and selling their goods though there are those who choose the mammalian halflings strictly for social purposes," she answered, more thoroughly than I would have expected.

"So cool, but you're right, I do prefer more versatility," I replied.

"They do boast some of the most interesting characters and gameplay. For example, a water breathing privateer in one of the oceans and sea provinces can be effective to a devastating degree. Likewise, a cat halfling with a high level 'Stealth' skill, can be an outstanding assassin, due to their dexterity bonus and their bite and claw skills. There are several Bear halflings that make excellent tanks, due to their strength, stamina and endurance bonuses. However, based on your play style and preferences in gaming, I did not feel these would fit you. However, I cannot prevent you from choosing any race you wish, as I can only make recommendations."

"Any others?" I asked, more out of curiosity at this point.

"There are also the Orcs, Goblins, Ogres, and Trolls with all their variants. They are all tribal races so while they seem primitive compared to some races they have some great combat bonuses, especially the Orcs and Ogres if you want to play a melee class. The Trolls get some bonuses to magic and Lore like the Elves. There are the Fae races, which include fairies, sprites, brownies and harpies, all gifted in the magical arts but weak physically. Is there a particular race you would care to know more about?" she answered and asked.

"No, but, thank you for the explanation," I answered. In truth, I had done some study on the various races before, but it never hurt to gather a little more information and get another opinion. I also realized I was getting distracted yet again.

"It is what I was created for. Please take a moment and consider your options. Let me know if you need more information," she stated.

"No, I think you've explained everything perfectly well. I do believe I will go with the Half-High Elf, Half-Human race," I stated.

"Okay, so as a Half-High Elf, Half-Human, you will get +1 bonuses to holy magic power, +1 Intellect, and +1 Charisma. This will be added to each additional level automatically. You will start with the profession Lore at level 2 and earn +25% experience in leveling Lore using one of your two profession slots. You will also have the racial ability Lesser Versatility, which will add a third profession slot in addition to increasing weapon skill experience gain by 10%. Please confirm," she stated, reviewing the specifics of my soon to be new race.

A system message appeared in front of me with the details she'd just explained.

Race:	Half-High Elf, Half-Human	
Elven Racial Bonus:	+1 Holy Spell power per Level, +1 Intellect per Level, +1 Level to starting Lore profession and +25% Lore Experience Gain	
Human Racial Bonus:	+1 Charisma per Level, Lesser Versatility grants 1 additional profession slot for 3 total and the ability to learn all weapon skills and +10% Weapon Skill Experience Gain.	
Do you accept?	Yes	No

"Confirmed," I said clearly, the 'Yes' flashed and the system message closed. I also took notice, it didn't require me to say 'Yes' or

'No' to accept the quest, it would be much more organic once I started accepting and completing quests.

I reviewed the message one more time, it was a solid build. I'd never been much into crafting professions, but from what the forums had said, there were some phenomenal bonuses from certain crafting skills, and increasing the rate I could level my weapons skills would be huge in the long run.

"Great," she said. She then gestured to her right side causing a mirror to appear. She then motioned for me to approach the mirror. "Now for your appearance."

I finally stood from the bed, very thankful the room wasn't cold or drafty. I couldn't help but subconsciously cover a certain part of my anatomy, regardless of what Maggie said earlier. I took a few stumbling steps at first as I approached the mirror. It took a few steps more before I got used to walking in this world. Looking into the mirror, I was staring into my own image, or rather, mostly my own image. I was just as tall as I was in the real world, just over 6'2", maybe I was slightly taller now, but I couldn't really tell. My face was thick, matching the thickness of the rest of me, spare tire and all. The only real difference from my usual appearance was the long, pointy elven ears, they were at least 6 inches longer than my normal ears, and my eyebrows, which extended a good 2-inches out to the sides of my face. I also noticed, as an afterthought, my green eyes now had a faint glow to them.

"Wow," I said, peering closer at my face, studying the eyebrows and ears. I loved the eyes but wished the ears were smaller and the eyebrows didn't stick so far out.

"Just touch the mirror to select an aspect of your image to adjust your appearance as you prefer. Let me know if you require any assistance," Maggie offered, still sitting comfortably in her armchair, paying no attention at all to my state of undress.

I put a finger on the mirror touching the eyebrow, it instantly froze the image and highlighted the eyebrows or rather greyed everything else out. On the right side, there was a color palette, but nothing to change the size.

"Just drag your finger along the mirror, it will change the eyebrow accordingly," instructed Maggie from behind me. I never saw her move, which sent a chill down my spine. Creepier still, she had no reflection in the mirror which was both spooky and ghoulish.

Trying to ignore her presence behind me, I put my finger to the end of the eyebrow and dragged my finger across the mirror causing the hair there to become shorter and shorter until it just barely stuck out but wouldn't let me make it any smaller. It was good enough. I then looked at the color palette. I'm a halfling now, might as well make myself look different. I tried the blue first, but it clashed with my green eyes. My natural brown didn't look right either. Green was just too much green. I ended up torn between black or white. Black ended up looking too unfriendly for my tastes so white it was.

Next, I touched the ears, once again everything but the ears turned grey. For these, I only wanted to make them smaller, so I dragged from the tip to the smallest possible size and the face looked more familiar. I was mostly myself again.

I selected the hair last and changed it to the same white as my eyebrows. However, the right side of the mirror offered several different hairstyles. I smiled a little, I knew exactly what hair I wanted. I could never pull it off in real life, but in the game, it should be more than doable. Military Undercut, last option available. It looked a little odd in white, but still awesome except for the chubby face.

"Maggie, can we make me thinner?" I asked.

"Of course, just select the body part you wish to change," she answered, though not the answer I wanted.

"Is there a way to do it all at once so it comes out even?" I pressed.

"I can assist you, how do you wish to appear?" she asked, much to my relief.

"Healthy? Can you do that?" I asked.

"It depends on your definition of healthy," she replied.

"How about how I should look once I exit the dive? I'm supposed to lose a ton of weight and build a bunch of muscle, right?"

It only took a moment for the image to morph and shift to match my request. My face thinned as did the rest of me. I now had a good amount of muscle and definition to my arms and chest, but my stomach still had a little gut to it. "Can you give me a six-pack? Same definition as my arms?" This might have been a bit of wish fulfillment on my part, but I figured I'm allowed. I was pleased as the gut shrunk until it was gone, replaced by the faint outline of a developing six-pack. Overall, I looked good.

"Are you satisfied with your appearance? You will not be able to change it once you finalize it," she stated clearly, maybe a little louder than I had come to expect from her.

"Can you give me a tan?" I asked.

Maggie answered by darkening my skin-tone a couple shades.

"I'm very satisfied." If I could look this good in real life I don't think I'd spend so much time in games . . . Oh, who was I kidding? I would still spend the same time on games that I do now.

"Very well then," she said, which was followed by the mirror digitizing and vanishing.

"So, is it time to play?" I asked, starting to feel excited.

"Almost, before you enter there are some things we must review, then you can select one of fifty starting areas and a set of starter equipment, including a weapon in the style of your choice," Maggie answered.

I nodded.

"First, all points to stats must be earned. Other than the points your racial bonuses give you with each level you must work to increase your other stats through hard work and dedication. If you want strength, you must work on building strength, so lift heavy things repeatedly or put more effort into swinging your weapon. Nothing in this world will be given to you. Please also note, due to your racial improvements to Intellect and Charisma, your level cap is 50% higher than all other stats," she began.

"Second, respect the Gods. The system governing the Gods and Goddesses is very fickle, as it should be. A God could bless you one day and curse you the next, so be careful not to offend them. It is also possible, you might never interact with the Gods, so do not get upset if you do not," she continued.

"Third, World Tree citizens are just that, citizens. They each have their own feeling and beliefs as well as backstories. Do not assume, a citizen does not have a name just because he or she is identified as a Peasant of Burke. They each have a story of their own, or a quest to be shared with you after some form of conversation. The World Tree will provide you with unlimited opportunities to find those Easter Eggs, you so love if you are patient," she continued still, making me curious. I wanted to interrupt and ask her questions, but she wasn't having it.

"Forth, PvP is allowed everywhere, even in the towns and villages, with the exception of the inside of Root City itself. If you are killed by another player within 10 levels of you, they will steal the experience you've earned for your current level and 5% of the money on your person. This incentivizes an active PvP player base without risking your hard-earned gear or loot as they say. This does not prevent them from stealing items and money from your bag, and only your bag, excluding items bound to you, before they kill you. But, once you are dead, they cannot touch you. Please keep in mind, if you do engage in PvP while in a town or village, you will instantly be declared a criminal to be hunted down and killed by the guards," she added.

"Finally, remember this is a game, you are there to have fun and enjoy yourself. Yes, the World Tree has proven to be lucrative for some and may be so for you but do not count on this to gain instant wealth and fame," she finished.

"Any final questions?" Maggie asked.

"No ma'am," I answered, unable to stop the grin splitting my face.

"Then let us select your starter gear and weapon," she said.

Even as she said it I could not help but feel a sense of awe as the bookshelves that surrounded the room kind of folded into the wall allowing new shelves and racks to fold out of the wall and even the floor revealing weapons in all kinds of styles and classifications.

"All of these weapons and armor are rated for a level 1 character with a base strength, dexterity, stamina, and endurance of 5. Please choose carefully. Whichever weapon you choose will give you a free level 1 skill in the weapon. All other weapon skills will have to either be trained by a professional or developed through practical application," explained Maggie. "I recommend starting with the style of clothing you would prefer to start with." She pointed to the only wall with armor, taking up one small section of the room.

The first thing I noticed, it was all light armor, which I suppose makes sense given she said it was based on my level. As a side thought, probably my current state of undress too. Looking at the options, it seemed I could choose a shirt, shoes, and pants in any style I want or a robe, shoes, and pants in any style I want. I've never been a big fan of robes, so the shirt won out.

"Do not forget your undergarment," Maggie warned me with a hint of amusement in her voice. She then gestured to a shelf I had clearly skipped over. Naturally, I blushed a little.

"You have briefs here?" I asked, slightly surprised upon looking at the shelf she had pointed to.

"There were complaints from customers during beta testing about itching and discomfort, too many complaints. Hence, this one, and only one, leeway from the modern world. Please note only you, or someone with your explicit permission can remove those. It is one of our anti-rape protocols. Additionally, do not ever try to rape someone or blackmail someone, to have sex with you. Neither a citizen of the World Tree nor another player. It is an instant character deletion and permanent ban, as well as instant jail time for the attempt. It is one of the few gamer rights laws the supreme court has upheld," Maggie explained. I was surprised by the edge in her voice, then again, maybe I just perceived an edge because of how serious the topic was.

I could only nod and grabbed a pair of black boxer briefs which instantly resized to fit me perfectly. Then I pulled on a pair of black burlap pants and a white burlap short-sleeve shirt. Followed by a pair of sandals, socks were not available, and I didn't appreciate the feel of the shoes on my feet without them.

"You may also select either a traveler's cloak or a vest," she offered, pointing at the next shelf over.

"Is there a difference?" I asked.

"They both provide the same armor but fit a different equipment slot," she explained.

"Does one give me more benefit for the quests in the starting province?" I asked. I didn't figure she'd tell me, but it never hurt to ask.

"You're right, it does not hurt to ask," she answered.

It took me a minute to puzzle out she had read my mind again. The exasperated sigh escaping my mouth was ignored. I didn't particularly care for any of the traveling cloaks, so I took a green vest.

"And finally, a weapon. You may choose either a ranged or melee weapon. Ranged weapons will be supplied with a small stock of ammunition," she explained, motioning to the numerous racks of weapons.

Here is where I took my time. I had played so many MMO's in the past, I could identify almost every weapon. I could also honestly say, I had never used most of them before. In the past I always kept it simple, a sword, a dagger or a mace. Simple weapons of this nature are common enough and can reliably be leveled up without much fuss. But here, I was presented with an opportunity to do something wildly different.

"Eliminate all but the least used weapons," I requested, instantly all the normal bladed weapons, maces, staves and even bows vanished. "No ranged weapons either." All the slings, crossbows, dart guns and a dozen other weapons vanished. It left me with just 6 different weapons to choose from.

Flail	A threshing tool consisting of a wooden staff with a short heavy ball swinging from it. Base Attack Speed 3.50 – Weapon Damage 5-8

Brass Knuckles	Pieces of metal shaped to fit around the knuckles. Base Attack Speed 1.20 – Weapon Damage 3-4
Sickle	A hand-held agricultural tool designed with variously curved blades. Base Attack Speed 2.20 – Weapon Damage 4-5
Spear	A pole weapon consisting of a shaft, usually of wood with a pointed head. One-Handed Base Attack Speed 2.4 – One-Handed Weapon Damage 4-5 – Two-Handed Base Attack Speed 2.00 – Two-Handed Weapon Damage 7-9
Bullwhip	A single-tailed whip, usually made of braided leather, designed as a tool for working with livestock. Base Attack Speed 2.20 – Weapon Damage 5-6
Three-section staff	A flail weapon consisting of three wooden or metal staffs connected by metal rings or rope. Base Attack Speed 1.80 – Weapon Damage 3-4

So difficult! So many cool weapons! Why? Why did I have to choose just one of them?

Admittedly the Bullwhip was so very tempting. With my interest in the Lore of the game, I could be the next in a long line of adventuring explorers, I just need a fedora. I don't care if the movie is older than dirt or whatever, it was still awesome, even in this day and age. Unfortunately, it wasn't very practical. It was also more of a ranged weapon than not.

There was one weapon that made more sense than any of the others. The Spear. I would have thought it was a common weapon but then if I hadn't considered it as a common weapon option before I'm sure many others didn't either. Plus, it had one-handed and two-handed usage.

With a heavy sigh, I picked up a simple spear.

You've learned the skill 'One-Handed Polearms'

One-Handed Polearms	Level: 1	Experience: 0.00%
Current Damage Modifiers	Damage: +0.50	Critical Strike Chance: +0.05%

You've learned the skill 'Two-Handed Polearms'

Two-Handed Polearms	Level: 1	Experience: 0.00%
Current Damage Modifiers	Damage: +0.50	Critical Strike Chance: +0.05%

"Oh, hell yeah!" I exclaimed. I got two different weapon skills at once.

"A wise choice. Very few people ever look at the spear. It is the only weapon in the current starter catalog that offers both One-Hand and Two-Handed usage from the beginning," Maggie gave me a small nod of acknowledgment.

I couldn't help but grin. "If I use it one-handed does that mean I can equip another weapon in the other hand or a shield?"

"A spear user may only equip a Phalanx Shield or a Net in the offhand," she replied.

"What's a Phalanx Shield?" I had an idea of what she meant but I felt it would be best to get clarification from her first.

"A Phalanx Shield is a classification of shield within the World Tree. This shield has a notch cut into the side to support the spear increasing both the accuracy of the spear and providing a forward guard to the user," she answered.

"Does this mean I can get a Phalanx Shield or a Net to go with my spear as it is part of the one-handed usage?" I asked, doubting it would work. Still, it couldn't hurt to ask.

Maggie paused again as if searching for the answer. After a few minutes of silence, which honestly worried me a little, she finally started speaking. "You are without a doubt the biggest troublemaker I've ever encountered," Maggie spoke, but it was no longer Maggie's voice. It was a voice I recognized as the lead developer from the short video, Mitchell Dawson.

"Mr. Dawson?" I couldn't help but ask to confirm.

"Yeah, that's me, I've temporarily hijacked Maggie here. I just had to speak to the colossal pain that found himself a giant hole in our character creation process. And here I thought just putting in the spear was enough of a hidden Easter Egg, to begin with, given it would provide two weapon skills from the start. Then you just had to go and scramble my egg by pointing out the shield and net usage," he explained.

"Am I in trouble?" I asked, feeling cautious. It wasn't too much of a stretch to imagine him taking my new skills away from me already.

"Trouble? Of course not," exclaimed Mitchell. "If anything, I'm happier than a kid on Christmas morning. Anytime a player finds a bug I missed it gets me fired up."

"So, I can keep the spear?" I asked, not sure what his 'fired up' would entail.

"Yeah, you can keep the spear. You can keep the weapon skills too. I'm even going to give you a little bonus. I'm going to create a new skill and even let you have it as part of your starting weapon kit. But first, choose, shield or net," he replied with a grin in place, it just didn't look right on Maggie's face.

"Shield," I answered without hesitation.

You've learned the skill 'Phalanx Shield'

Phalanx Shield	Level: 1	Experience: 0.00%
Current Defense Modifiers	Block Chance: +0.05%	Critical Block Chance: +0.025%

"Sweet! Is this a unique Skill?" I asked.

"Not at all, but it is specific to using a phalanx shield where all other shields fall into a single category. Anyway, great job finding this hole in our programming. Maggie will rejoin you in a moment and let you select a shield. Unfortunately, now I have to go and remove the spear as a starting weapon option. I was able to sneak in 2 skills for one weapon, but three skills will never fly once the game forums pick up on it. Which reminds me, I have just given you a significant starting bonus, I'm going to have to ask you keep your mouth shut about this, or your skills and weapon may just disappear n'est-ce pas?" he finally asked.

I understood fully what he was saying. He just gave me a massive boost. One he could easily take away from me later. So of course, I answered, "I completely understand, my lips are sealed."

"Good, in that case, enjoy the game," he said with a friendly smile. Maggie's eyes closed, and her head nodded forward as if asleep.

"Hello again, I am back," said Maggie, perking right back up again and back to her usual self. "So, we need to select a phalanx shield for you."

"Before that, what do +0.50 Damage and +0.05% Critical for the current damage modifier mean, or the defense modifiers?" I asked, always trying to get just a little more information.

"Your skill with one-handed polearms, two-handed polearms, and the phalanx shield is very primitive and relatively unskilled. You are just competent enough to not stab yourself on accident," she answered.

"So, if I had no skill with the weapon there is a chance I could stab myself?" I asked, I was trying to be funny, but it clearly didn't work.

"Yes," she answered seriously. "However, the chances of that happening are low."

Talk about a critical failure roll just waiting to happen. I had heard plenty of stories about old tabletop games, where players used a 20-sided die to determine success and failure. The best stories were always the unique and interesting ways a game master would completely screw over a player when they rolled a natural '1' and the critical failure that followed. They always made me laugh.

I shook my head in disbelief. "Okay, weapon and clothes have been selected. Show me the phalanx shield choices."

A single weapon rack appeared with 4 styles of shields to choose from. I took the simple, round phalanx shield, matching my simple spear.

Once all the equipment racks vanished, Maggie spoke again. "Next you will select a starting province. As you do not have a racial ability granting heat resistance, cold resistance or water breathing, you have 34 provinces to choose from. Do you have any preference in the type of environment?"

Now, this would be important. If I chose the wrong environment it could hurt or even destroy the development of my skills. A desert environment might reduce my ability to learn stealth and I could also have problems with food and water. Although, I imagine a desert environment would be good to build up poison resistance.

I had to shake my head to get that thought out of there. I needed someplace with a fair climate and good environmental skills available to learn.

"Based on your line of thought, I would suggest either a jungle or forest environment. A mountainous region would also suit your purposes." Maggie suggested.

"Jungle is too hot and I'm not big on mountains but not completely opposed either. So, Forest or maybe a mountain forest?" I requested.

"Excellent, I narrowed your choices to these two," said Maggie.

Suddenly, my view was invaded by two large windows baring the system description for the two suggested provinces.

Piper Forest – Level 1-5
Piper Forest is inhabited by common critters of all sorts from bears to wolves and an abundance of small caves for them to hide in amongst the hills and trees of the area. There is also a large rat population beginning to give the locals no end of trouble, just waiting for some young fool adventurer to deal with them.

Or.

Hurlig Ridge – Level 1-5
Hurlig Ridge is a forested area with a mountain ridgeline bordering the northern edge of the province. It plays home to a number of dangerous fowl and their natural feline predators, as well as a healthy wolf population. If the wolves are not enough, the ancient ruins in the area have sparked many ghost stories among the local residents.

"Hurlig Ridge, that's got to be it. There's a ruin there, which would probably be perfect for me to build up my Lore profession." I said excitedly. It was finally time for me to get my game on.

"Excellent, I hope you felt this time was productive and I have done everything I can to prepare you for the adventures ahead?" she asked.

"Thank you, Maggie, you were very helpful," I replied.

"In a moment, you will close your eyes and when you reopen them you will be placed at random in Hurlig Ridge," she explained briefly.

"Wait, random? Don't I start in a safe zone?" I asked, feeling slightly confused.

"It will be a level 1 area near the province village. We have found it disturbs the citizens when people just suddenly appear," she clarified.

"How odd?" I wondered aloud. I supposed the game was just that advanced. "Anyway, I'm ready when you are."

"Enjoy your adventure," she said her parting word with a vibrant smile.

My eyes suddenly felt heavy, closing on their own. Once they closed I felt a kind of rush of wind and everything felt so much different. At first, I could hear water rushing in the background, some kind of river and maybe a waterfall not too far off. A screech above told me there was a bird nearby. The gust of wind made the branches of the trees around me rattle and the leaves on the bushes rustle. The wind had a cold bite to it but not freezing. My eyes opened once more to see I was indeed in a forest surrounded by tall pine trees and a smattering of bushes nearby, ripe with blackberries.

"Oh wow," I couldn't help the sigh of contentment and enjoyment. Everything felt so real, smelled so real, hurt so real.

Pwn Star69 Lvl 37 does 368-damage to you with a thrown pebble.

Pwn Star69 Lvl 37 has murdered you. You will be automatically transported and revived at the nearest graveyard.

CHAPTER 2

The line of explicative statements spewing from my mouth upon respawning is not something to be repeated for civilized ears. Let's just say, my rant could have made the devil blush.

"Take it, easy kid, you're going burst a blood vessel in your head if you keep ranting," offered an old man I just realized was there to hear my little episode. I looked at him closer to see a player nameplate reading <Old Benji Lvl 3>. He appeared to be wearing simple brown pants, sandals and a white shirt, nothing too special about it. He was bald with a few tufts of silvery-grey hair around his ears. He also looked the part of the kind and friendly grandfatherly sort. Not someone deserving of the snarky retort I was about to unleash on him.

"I was just PK'd, Benji. I'm not happy," I stated as calmly as I could though I could easily feel the rage and wrath bubbling just below the surface. How could I have been player killed already? I had only just logged into the World Tree.

"Pwn Star69?" he asked.

"Yes," I replied. "Did he get you too?" I felt slightly mollified knowing I wasn't the only one.

"Yes, he did. No big deal. I just hope I didn't have a big one on the line. That would be disappointing," grumbled the old man.

It took me a second to puzzle out his statement. "Fishing?"

Old Benji nodded and grinned with a little grunt to it. "I used to go fishing with my dad when I was a young boy. But with the damages to the environment and the restrictions on such activities now I haven't gotten to do it in more than 50 years. This world lets me fish to my heart's content . . . except when a PK'er gets it in his head to boost his kill count with an easy target."

"Has he killed you before?" I asked, feeling anger on behalf of the friendly old man, someone who just wanted to enjoy some fishing, but totally approved of in here. Fishing was basically illegal in the real world unless you knew someone with enough pull to get you a license. A lot of pull.

"Several times. Eventually, I'm sure he'll hit his kill count number he needs to join whatever PK guild he's trying to get into and he'll leave the province behind. Still, with your death, that makes it his sixth kill of the day. He'll be banned for the next 24 hours."

"Banned? I don't understand? I thought PK'ing was totally approved here?" Now I was truly confused. PvP is encouraged in the World Tree from what Maggie had said during my orientation and yet the guy who just killed me got a 24-hour ban for killing another player.

"You must be new. PvP is encouraged. However, killing players more than 20 levels lower than you is highly discouraged. As such, after killing 6 players more than 20 levels below your own in a 24-hour period, results in a 24-hour game lockout."

"Okay, but why would he keep killing low-level players if it gets him banned for a day?"

"He does it to inflate his kill count. In PvP, kill count matters, especially death to kill ratio. So, players will artificially inflate their kill count this way. It helps them get into PK guilds."

At that moment, something in me kind of snapped . . . maybe broke is a better word for it. "I haven't even been in the game for 5 minutes and this . . . PK'er killed me for the sake of an inflated kill count. I didn't even get a chance to check my stats and this clown, one-shot my brand spanking new toon. I swear . . . I swear on whatever Gods or Goddesses might be listening, I will have retribution . . . no, I will have justice!"

Apparently, my vow was heard, as a rumble of thunder and a flash lightning in the perfectly clear sky symbolized . . . I suppose the system message appearing before me, was more compelling.

Attention: *The Goddess Issara has heard your vow demanding justice.*		
A unique class has been offered to you by the Goddess Issara, Goddess of Retribution and Justice		
Warrior Priest of the Goddess Issara - +20% to holy spell damage, -25% to holy spell healing		
Do you accept this great honor?	**Yes**	**No**

I had to blink several times to understand what just happened. "Did that really just happen?"

"Did what happen?" asked Benji.

"You didn't hear the thunder?" I asked, not sure if I wanted to share the details with the old man.

"No, no thunder," he then paused to look up at the bright clear sky. "Nope, no thunder. Not even a cloud in the sky, just you suddenly halting your vow of revenge to stare off into space," he answered.

"Okay, then please ignore me. I'm having an off day." Okay, so it probably wasn't very convincing, but the old man didn't seem concerned.

"Well, feel better young fella. So long as Pwn has hit his quota, I'm going back to fishing. Good luck on your revenge," he offered with a tip of his fishing hat which he must have just equipped, he also now had a fishing rod and tackle box in hand.

Back to the more important matter at hand. A unique class. There were rumors on the forums about this kind of thing, but no one had ever confirmed them as true. There were stories of all kinds of things in the World Tree, but the most exciting were always about the unique classes and the amazing abilities they had. But once again, they were never confirmed as they were so coveted. If anyone had one, they would hide it. No matter what. And it wasn't as if a person could see your class if they inspected you, only your gear could be inspected, and the level was displayed right next to your name, but you couldn't ever see their specific stats or abilities which made it easier to hide.

But still, I'm only level one and haven't killed anyone or anything. But then again, I didn't even have the chance to do anything before I was killed. Immediately following which I made a vow to the Gods and Goddesses.

It then occurred to me, there were probably several unique factors required to occur for this to happen. First, to be murdered or rather PK'd. Second, to vow to the Gods I would get retribution or maybe justice . . . both? Third, and this was just a guess, the circumstance of the death had to be exactly correct, in my case, murdered with zero experience, murdered by someone more than 20 levels above me or maybe 30 levels above given Pwn Star was level 37. I'm not sure what other factors applied, but it was probably along those lines.

"What am I doing?" I asked myself. Why was a thinking about all of this when the golden goose just laid a big fat golden Easter Egg right in front of me? I quickly directed my thoughts to a big fat 'Yes, I accept'.

33

Congratulations! You have become a Novice Warrior Priest in service to the Goddess Issara.

Your new class grants you the following base spells. Use them well and advance through the ranks.

You've learned the Holy spell 'Holy Smite'

Holy Smite	Level: 1	Experience: 0.00%
Spell Damage: 5-10	Spell Cast Speed: 1.50 seconds	Spell Mana Cost: 10
Spell Effect (Active): *Smite a single target with holy damage*		

You've learned the Holy spell 'Lesser Heal'

Lesser Heal	Level: 1	Experience: 0.00%
Spell Heal: 5-10	Spell Cast Speed: 2.00 seconds	Spell Mana Cost: 10
Spell Effect (Active): *Heal a single target*		

You've learned the Holy spell 'Lesser Holy Imbuement'

Lesser Holy Imbuement	Level: 1	Experience: 0.00%
Spell Duration: 10 minutes	Spell Cast Speed: Instant	Spell Mana Cost: 50
Spell Effect (Active): *Imbued Weapon now deals holy damage causing an addition 1-2 damage per hit*		
Spell Effect (Active): *Imbued Shield now deals holy damage causing 2-3 damage per block*		

You've learned the Holy spell 'Lesser Combat Blessing'

Lesser Combat Blessing	Level: 1	Experience: 0.00%
Spell Duration: 10	Spell Cast Speed:	Spell Mana Cost: 50

minutes	*Instant*	
Spell Effect (Active): *Increase Stamina +2, Increase Strength +2, Increase Dexterity +2, increase Endurance +2*		

You've learned the Holy spell '???????'

???????	*Level: 1*	*Experience: 0.00%*
Spell Duration: ?? *minutes*	*Spell Cast Speed: ?????*	*Spell Mana Cost:* ??
Spell Effect (Active): *??????*		

I so wanted to scream in joyous ecstasy. I was even more curious about the mystery holy spell. I'm sure it was something unique to my class, something to make it worthwhile and then some. Of course, with my naturally curious nature, I wondered what I needed to be able to use the spell. I would find out eventually, but I wanted to know now, not later.

Frowning, I checked the next system message.

Class: Novice Warrior Priest of Issara
Armor Restriction: Light Cloth, Light Leather (50 Natural Strength Required), Light Mail (200 Natural Strength Required), Light Plate (400 Natural Strength Required)
Novice Class Effects: +20% to holy bonus spell damage, -25% to holy bonus spell healing

My arms shot straight up into the air in celebration, followed by my own little happy dance, but I refused to let any noise escape. The last thing I needed was to get killed again for celebrating.

Class Quest Alert: Novice Warrior Priest of Issara – Your Goddess' Path Lies Ahead
You have been charged by the Goddess you now serve to mete out punishment on the murderer you vowed to bring to justice. Time

Limit: 28:00:00			
Reward:	Hidden		
Do you accept this Quest?	**Yes**		No

I hesitated.

I couldn't decline the quest. I don't think I would have anyway, but I couldn't help feeling troubled by this quest. How was I supposed to kill the Player Killer that killed me in 28 hours? How could I win, when he was level 37, and I was only level 1? Assuming I could even find him again. Worse, if he saw me first and decided to throw another pebble at me to kill me again, I wouldn't put up much of a challenge. But the quest didn't say I had to kill him, just punish him. Still not sure how to complete the quest considering the level difference but I had to at least try, I accepted the quest with a mental 'Yes'.

Okay, so planning first. If I had to dish out some punishment on Pwn Star69 then I'd better put forth the best effort I could. I had at least 24 hours, well slightly less than 24 hours before Pwn Star69 would be able to play again. I had 24 hours to try and level as much as possible . . . well, more along the line of 16 hours because I would still need to sleep at some point, or else I'd incur massive penalties starting with a fatigue reducing all my stats and ending with reduced experience gains.

However, if I do it right, I can work hard to level tonight until around 10, then crash at an inn and get an early start in the morning and get maybe 6 more hours of questing and leveling time. Therefore, I needed to be efficient which ultimately meant stacking quests to the best of my ability.

And as luck would have it, there was a little village just a stone's throw away from me, undoubtedly brimming with quests for a starter noob such as myself. I had to budget my time searching for those quests, I couldn't afford to spend more than a few hours tracking them down.

Second, I still hadn't even looked at my stats and with a thought, I was presented with a new system window showing my current gear and stats.

Equipment Slot	Name	Armor/ Damage	Bonus Stats
Helm:	Empty		
Head Accessory:	Empty		
Shoulders:	Empty		
Back:	Empty		
Chest Armor:	Light Vest	+5 Armor	
Chest Cloths:	Burlap Shirt	+0 Armor	
Wrists:	Empty		
Hands:	Empty		
Arm Accessory 1:	Empty		
Arm Accessory 2:	Empty		
Finger Accessory 1:	Empty		
Finger Accessory 2:	Empty		

Waist:	Rope Belt	+0 Armor	
Leg Clothing:	Burlap Pants	+0 Armor	
Leg Armor:	Empty		
Feet:	Light Sandals	+1 Armor	
Weapon:	Simple Spear	4-5 Dmg	
Off-Hand:	Simple Phalanx Shield	+5 Armor	
Charm:	Empty		
Bag:	20 lbs. Sack		

Level:	1	Experience:	0.00%
Class:	Novice Warrior Priest of Issara		
HP (Health Points):			15/50
MP (Mana Points):			60/60
SP (Stamina Points):			50/50
Strength:			5
- Melee Damage Modifier			+5
Dexterity:			5
- Melee Critical Strike Chance			0.50%
- Hit Chance			60.25%
- Dodge Chance			0.50%
Endurance:			5
Stamina:			5
Intellect:			6
- Spell Critical Strike Chance			0.60%

Wisdom:	5
Charisma:	6
Health Regeneration per 10 Seconds:	3
Mana Regeneration per 10 Seconds:	3
Stamina Regeneration per 10 Seconds:	3
Holy Spell Damage Bonus:	4.20
Holy Spell Healing Bonus:	2.63
Carrying Capacity in Lbs.:	25

Okay, so I have generic stats and was fairly well balanced for a starting character. Because I chose two races, each having decent bonuses without significant penalties, it was as much as I could hope for. My gear was again very basic, but the spear and shield gave me more versatility than any of the other weapons offered.

My bonus spell damage was solid and would only improve with time. I didn't care for the low regen values much but hopefully with some more stat points and better gear it would improve in time. Carrying capacity did not please me either, only 5 lbs. per point of strength, even at level 1, such a thing was just sad.

Not much I can do about it now, so I opened my bag next to see if I was given any starter food or money.

20 lbs. Sack (Capacity 20 lbs.)	Gold: 0 Silver: 0 Copper: 50
5 Adventurer Tac – Food Stuff will restore 20 HP if completely eaten.	
1 Empty Water Canteen (0/5) – Can be filled with water (various effects)	

Great, I was also poor but then I suppose 50-copper should have been plenty to start with. Plus, I can always get more from the World Tree bank once I leave this area.

With a rough outline of a plan in place and having taken stock of my situation, I took my first step outside the tiny graveyard onto the rough dirt road, leading to one place. As I walked toward the village I had hoped to come across some kind of mob to fight for a little experience but no such luck.

It was maybe a 10-minute walk from the graveyard before the village came into sight. I counted just 15 buildings of various sizes, but I was sure there were more. They all appeared to be made of wood but lacked any color beyond the basic wood grain of whatever tree they used. Once I got closer to the village, I saw a small moat surrounding it, but no wall. I guessed it was more to direct traffic and keep the critters out, than serving any actual defensive purpose.

The entrance in front of me had a single guard hut with an armored guard sitting inside it, snoring rather loudly. The man had the simple description <Village Guard Lvl 8> hovering above his head. Looking closer at the man, he looked as though he forgot to shave this morning, maybe a few mornings in a row. The dark black stubble was more akin to a beard than a shadow of one. His armor was dented and dinged and hadn't been polished in a long time but appeared perfectly serviceable. Leaning on the wall of the shack next to him was a sword and sheath and on the back wall of the hut, a crossbow hung at easy reach.

Now, I knew it was probably okay to just enter the village and ignore the guard, but at the same time, I also knew it could possibly cause me some trouble if I didn't at least check in. By the same token, it could cause me some trouble with the guard if I woke him up.

I sighed, knowing my luck I'd be screwed either way. Best to choose the option least likely to get me branded a criminal, I serve a Goddess of justice now and I can't imagine she'd be too pleased with me if my first act after getting her blessing would be to break a law, even unknowingly.

"Excuse me, sir," I called out to the snoozing guard in a normal voice.

The guard didn't even twitch.

This time I knocked on the guard post door frame. "Hello, sir."

His snoring paused for a moment only for him to shift slightly and snore even louder.

I kicked the side of the guard post hard which cost me -2 HP for damaging my toe, but it was sufficient to stir the guard who was now suddenly awake and brandishing his sword at full alert.

"Wha? Whose attacking? I'll kill you rotten animals!" he shouted, not quite aware of his surroundings yet after being woken so suddenly.

"Hello, sir," I greeted the man again, trying to pretend there was nothing strange about the man's reaction.

"What's this? A traveler? Why did you not use the main entrance?" he all but demanded.

"I didn't know there was a main entrance. I've just come from the graveyard back yonder," I said, motioning behind me.

"Oh great, another sad sack adventurer. And I suppose you too want me to give you some grand quest to kill and kill and kill some more?" he asked, more than a little sarcasm dripping into his voice.

"While I would love a quest, I would just be happy to be allowed to enter the village," I met his sarcasm with some of my own.

This time the man laughed. "At least you are honest. My name is Gavin Bryant, but it is Guard Bryant to you, at least while I'm on duty. As for entering the village, it is fine. Just do not cause trouble or I will have to thump you and if I fail to thump you then the sergeant will thump us both." As soon as he said his name the nameplate above his head that previously read <Village Guard Lvl 8> changed to <Guard Gavin Bryant Lvl 8>, it was awesome.

"Any special rules or regulations I need to follow?" I asked.

"You have to hop on your left foot through the village. If your right foot touches the ground it is a 10-copper fine payable in pints from the tavern," Guard Bryant stated in as serious a voice and stone-faced as I'd ever heard or seen.

"You're messing with me, right?" I asked.

Bryant apparently couldn't keep up the act as he snorted a laugh. "Cannot blame me for trying. Some of you adventurer types are just so gullible."

"Someone actually fell for that?" I asked, struggling to believe anyone would be that gullible.

"More than one," he replied, a small grin working onto his face.

Now it was my turn to snort a laugh. "Sir, I believe I owe you a pint anyway. That's freaking brilliant."

"Now we are talking. My shift ends at late bell, I will meet you at the tavern for a pint a little after. If you are staying in town, I would recommend the Dog House Inn. Just tell Dogson I sent you, he will give you a discount on a room," suggested the guardsman.

"Thanks, Guard Bryant, much appreciated, now I owe you two pints," I promised, it never hurt to make friends.

"Well now, fast to make friends, are you?" said Bryant, appraising me closer now. "You know how to use that spear and shield of yours?"

"Only how not to stab myself with the spear or knock myself silly with the shield," I answered remembering what Maggie told me about my skill level. Given how quickly Bryant's attitude seemed to shift, seemed my charisma was already paying dividends and better I might just be getting a quest or training . . . or a training quest, now that would be awesome.

Bryant, of course, laughed again. "Honest indeed. Go 'round back of the barracks, the Sergeant is always drilling back there, he can probably show you a thing or two. Once again, let him know I sent you."

Quest Alert: Training with Sergeant Butters		
Your new friend Guard Bryant has suggested you seek out the Sergeant for some weapons training.		
Reward: Experience, Weapon Subskill		
Do you accept this Quest?	Yes	No

"I'll go see the man right away," I answered, verbally accepting the quest.

"Oh, and do not call him Sarge or Sir, he hates that. It is Sergeant or Sergeant Butters," he warned me.

"Got it, thanks for the tip. Mind if I ask a few more questions about the village?" I asked.

"Sure, you are only interrupting my valuable nap time but what the heck, why not?" joked Bryant. At least I hoped he was joking.

"First, where is the Inn? Second, where are the Barracks? And third, where is the library?" I asked, then as an afterthought I added, "If you have one?"

Bryant once again laughed. "Walk down the street to the only crossroad and turn right. You will see a big building at the end of the street, it is hard to miss. That is the town hall, closest thing to a library we got. The longhouse on the right of the Town hall is the town barracks. The three-story building on the left, just before you get to the Town hall is the Dog House Inn."

"Thank you, I'll see you tonight for that pint," I said, ready to venture into the village.

"Two pints," he reminded me.

"So, three then?" I asked, laughing with the man.

"Go on, let me get back to sleep so I can prepare my constitution for a night of boozing it up," joked Bryant, making a shooing motion with his armored hands.

The walk was fine, the roads in town were cobblestone, so it was easier than the dirt and mud road from the graveyard. Looking around as I walked I could see the town didn't boast a huge population, but there were plenty of citizen going about their business, children playing here and there, all in all, a normal village from what I could tell.

No one was rushing up to me asking for help and there were no giant indicators above people's heads telling me they had a quest for me, which I kind of loved. It meant, that to get a quest I would have to talk to the citizens, have an actual conversation.

I decided to stop at the inn first to get my room accommodation sorted out. I was honestly surprised when I entered the inn. Not because it was almost empty but because of the Bartender. This was the first mammalian halfling I'd seen, and it was rather extreme and very realistic. The bartender <Bartender Lvl 6> and I'm guessing owner was a dogman, half-dog, half-something else, but based on his posture the way he moved I would say man or elf. He had the head of a hound dog with long floppy ears. Oddly he had black hair on top of his head styled formally, parted down the middle and combed flat. He also wore a pair of thin wire-rimmed spectacles.

"Hello, are you Dogson?" I asked the dogman bartender.

"I am, and who would you be?" he asked.

I still enjoyed the novelty of his nameplate changing from <Bartender Lvl 6> to <Dogson Lvl 6>. "Bye-Bye Jacko but my friends just call me Bye-Bye," I introduced myself.

"Nice to meet you Bye-Bye, what can I get you?" asked the dogman.

"Guard Bryant suggested I come to talk to you about a room," I answered plainly.

"5-copper a night, 20 for the week," he stated. I could now see behind the bar he was washing glasses in a modern sink, but I wasn't about to complain about a lack of authenticity. I personally preferred clean dishes and well-cooked food.

"I'll take the week," I said, putting the 20-copper on the counter. I was sure to get more eventually as I gathered and completed more quests. Still, parting with almost half of my funds hurt.

Dogson slid the coppers from the counter and slid a key with a tag with the number '8' on it in their place. "Breakfast and dinner are included with the room. We serve breakfast from sunrise to mid-morning bell. Dinner from dusk to late bell," he said.

"Excellent," I replied. It really was excellent. I could eat the tac if I needed it while questing and still get a good meal twice a day to satisfy part of my health requirements. "I'll be back for dinner then."

Dogson just nodded, still busy with his dishes.

Next, I headed for the Barracks or rather the back of the barracks. There I found what I could only describe as the most grizzled, toughest looking old man, I'd ever laid eyes on. The man wore chain-link leggings and heavy plate sabatons over his feet and a white tank top shirt. His arms were covered in scars as was what could be seen of his chest. Even his face was covered in scars which made his grey beard and mustache appear to be a shaving mishap, the only bit of which wasn't scared was covered by an eyepatch which I didn't doubt covered up more scars. Mirroring me, he also bore a military undercut on top of his head, his hair was grey to my white. I looked up at his nameplate to make sure I had the right guy, <Sergeant Butters Lvl 38>.

"And what does a piss-ant adventurer want with me?" asked the Sergeant, knocking me out of my stupor.

"Sorry, I was just surprised," I answered.

"Scars scare you little girl?" he asked, eyeing me up and down.

"No, I was just thinking you might be the toughest old man I've ever seen," I replied.

"Good answer. So, what can a military man, such as myself, do for an adventurer such as yourself?"

"I was speaking to Guard Bryant-" I started.

"He was awake? At the sleeping gate?" he asked, disbelief on his face.

"I may have had to wake him up," I answered, feeling pleased to have earned at least a little of the old soldier's respect.

The Sergeant cackled with laughter for a good minute before finally calming down enough to talk again. "Oh, I would have paid to see the look on his face. Anyway, you were saying?"

"Right, so I was talking to Guard Bryant and he mentioned you might be able to train me to better use my spear," I finally finished explaining.

"A polearm user," He nearly shouted in surprise. "I have not seen any of you adventurer types with a spear before. Good on you son, it is an excellent weapon choice, lots of versatility. I think I can give you some pointers, but we have not got much time left in the day. My shift at the main gate starts in a few hours. So, I can help you with your two-handed polearm skill or your one-handed polearm and phalanx shield skills. Your choice." The Sergeant offered.

"I believe I would benefit more in the immediate to improve my one-handed polearm and phalanx shield skills," I answered. As a low-level toon, it would be best if I could use the shield to defend myself and attack at the same time, given my low mana pool.

"Right then, let us get started. First, let us get you a usable attack. Are you right or left handed?" he asked.

"Left-handed," I answered, for the first time I considered there might be an impact gameplay.

"Okay, shield goes in your right hand then, spear in the left," he ordered.

I did as he instructed. A look at my character sheet showed my equipment was set to a right-handed by default. Simply switching my spear and shield switched them in my character sheet too.

"Now, the shield should always be in front of you. The top of the shield needs to be held so it is just below your line of sight," explained the Sergeant, who was also now holding a spear and shield. He stood across from me holding the shield exactly as he'd told me I should be holding it. His eyes were just visible above the top of the shield.

"Good," he said, nodding in approval as I adjusted my round phalanx shield. "Now, you will notice your shield has round notches cut into it at equal intervals for four in total. It mirrors the four sub-points on a compass. We're going to work with the northwest notch so rest your spear shaft on it."

I rested the tip of the spear just as he told me, but it kept bouncing off the notch in my shield, teeter-tottering against it. "What am I doing wrong?" I asked in frustration.

"How long is your spear?"

"About 8-feet," I answered.

"Right, and how much of your 8-foot spear can you use right now?"

"Ah," I said seeing the problem. I barely had 6-inches of the spear past the notch of the shield. I would hardly get any reach out of it. "How far back should I grip the spear?"

"Generally speaking, you want to grip the spear about a foot back from the half-shaft. There, the spear can rest comfortably on the shield and not tip backward. It will also give you plenty of reach and retreat," he explained. He now gripped his own spear, the arm holding the spear was cocked way back with his hand up near his ear and perfectly in line with the shield, putting the spear tip a good 2-feet ahead of the shield.

Once again, I mirrored his hold, admittedly it felt much more natural. I felt as if I was prepared both to block and attack.

"Good, now you are holding your spear and shield properly. Let us give you your first attack. Now watch me," he ordered. A moment later his spear and arm suddenly jolted forward and back again, his hand not going past the shield and the shield not moving in the slightest. "Watch again, I will slow down this time." It was still very fast to me, but I was better able to follow his movement. "Now you try."

And I tried. It was slow, my arm went way past the front of the shield and the spear slid from my grip shooting forward a few extra feet.

"Reset and try it again," ordered the man. He didn't seem angry or amused by my blunder and was in fact very patient.

I reset my position and held onto the spear. This time I went as slow as I could, and my hand still hit the shield edge rather painfully.

"Better, again," he ordered.

So, I did it again, this time I didn't hit the edge of the shield. The next time I hit the edge, but it was just a touch. I did it seven more times before he halted me.

"Good, get yourself a drink, your stamina looks to be depleted," instructed the Sergeant. "There is fresh water in the barrel."

I hadn't even thought about my stamina, it was indeed down to just a few points.

I took out my empty canteen and dunked it into the aforementioned barrel and filled it to the brim.

Full Water Canteen (5/5) – Freshwater restores 5 stamina per mouthful.

I didn't take long to drink enough to fully restore my stamina and get right back to it. It took another hour, including a few more stamina breaks, before I completed the quest.

Quest Alert: Training with Sergeant Butters – Completed!
Your new friend Guard Bryant has suggested you seek out the Sergeant for some weapons training.
Reward: +500 Experience, Weapon Subskill 'Jab'

You've learned 'One-Handed Polearms' subskill 'Jab'.

One-Handed Polearms	Level: 3	Experience: 28.76%
Current Damage	Damage: +1.5	Critical Strike

Modifiers		Chance: +0.15%
Subskill: Jab	Damage: +1.5	Skill Stamina Cost: 13

The second window was much more important to me.

Congratulations! You've reached Level 2!
+1 to bonus Holy Spells, +1 Intellect, +1 Charisma

Getting the level was awesome, but I didn't even notice I had gained levels with the 'One-Handed Polearm'. There was no system message letting me know, like the one that popped up for the quest completion, for the new subskill and character level. Then I noticed several shaded exclamation points at the bottom left of my peripheral vision. I guessed this was part of my User Interface (UI). As soon as I focused on them, several messages were displayed rapidly.

Working hard. You earn +1 Stamina
Breaking your limits. You earn +1 Strength
Aiming, who knew? You earn +1 Dexterity
No pain, no gain +1 Endurance
One-Handed Polearms has gained a level. Damage +0.5, Critical Strike Chance +0.05%
Working harder. You earn +1 Stamina
Breaking more limits. You earn +1 Strength
Aiming, pointy end goes in the other guy. You earn +1 Dexterity
Pain, Gain. You earn +1 Endurance
One-Handed Polearms has gained a level. Damage +0.5, Critical Strike Chance +0.05%
Working even harder. You earn +1 Stamina
Breaking all the limits. You earn +1 Strength
Slippery fellow. You earn +1 Dexterity
More pain, More gain. You earn +1 Endurance

One-Handed Polearms has gained a level. Damage +0.5, Critical Strike Chance +0.05%
Ladies must love you. You earn +1 Stamina
Don't break yourself. You earn +1 Strength
Dodge, dip, duck, dive, and dodge. You earn +1 Dexterity
Ouch! You earn +1 Endurance
One-Handed Polearms has gained a subskill Jab. Damage +5 Skill Stamina Cost 10

"Hell yeah!" I exclaimed happily, I could feel myself grinning from ear to ear. New level and subskill plus some huge stat gains. I know stat gains eventually slow down drastically, but I was so happy to gain so much for just a few hours of work. Don't get me wrong, questing and leveling pay bigger dividends in the long run, due to the new spells and abilities requiring higher levels. But anything I can do to improve my stats now can only help me to be able to level later. Also, "Ugh!" Why the wall of text? I'll have to check later to see if there is a summary option.

"Nice work and just in time too. I have got my shift starting soon but if you want to come back and train again tomorrow, you are more than welcome. I have no doubt got a good number of skills squirreled away you might benefit from learning. Just make sure you come prepared to work for it," he stated, a small grin at the corner of his mouth and a glint in his eye, dare I say he looked prideful.

"You can count on it. What time should I be here?" I asked.

"Show up whenever you choose, just keep in mind I have a day job and other recruits to train so I can't give you more than two or three hours a day," he advised me.

I understood immediately, it was to temper my advancement and to ensure I wasn't just sitting in this training field all day. The game wanted to make sure I also got out and did quests and actually explore the game, you know, be an adventurer. "I understand completely. I just appreciate you offering the time to me."

"Well, then, I would say we are done for the day," he said with a sense of finality.

"Thank you again, Sergeant Butters. I'll see you tomorrow then," I said.

"See you tomorrow. Keep up the good work," said the Sergeant, he then turned and marched himself into the barracks without another word, just a small salute as he entered.

"What a great day so far and I'm only getting started!" I exclaimed   excitedly.

CHAPTER 3

So much to do and so little time left to do it. Okay, so I had time still, but I had to get about 8 hours of rest in there somewhere.

Class Quest Alert: Novice Warrior Priest of Issara – Your Goddess' Path Lies Ahead	
You have been charged by the Goddess you now serve to mete out punishment on the murderer you vowed to bring to justice. Time Limit: 24:47:16	
Reward:	Hidden

After the extremely valuable training session with Sergeant Butters, I had about 16 hours left to get my justice. So, my next stop was to hit up the town hall and see what I could uncover with my lore skill, and maybe see if there are any bounties or quests available.

The Town hall looked more akin to a barn, but with a normal door. Inside was simple looking as well. There were two doors on the right wall, I guessed they led to offices. The left wall had a bulletin board with a sparse number of yellow papers tacked up. On either side of the board, were bookshelves, one of the main reasons I was here. Books are filled with knowledge and if you're careful you can pick out a good amount of game lore and hidden puzzles and quests. The Easter Eggs I love so much. The rest of the room was dominated by rows and seats and a podium at the back of the room.

First, I needed to check the bulletin board. I needed some easy experience, and quests where you didn't have to do much searching, were great.

Quest Alert: Harvest Help (Recommended Level 2-4)		
Farmer Johnson needs help with is his corn harvest.		
Reward: Experience, Fresh Corn, 20-Copper		
Do you accept this Quest?	Yes	No

That one was easy to accept.

Quest Alert: Clothes Line (Recommended Level 2-4)		
Mrs. Johnson needs help with a clothes thief.		
Reward: Experience, Variable Piece of Gear, 10-Copper		
Do you accept this Quest?	Yes	No

Another easy one.

Quest Alert: Pack Wolf Bounty (Recommended Level 2-4)		
Standing Village Bounty for Pack Wolves frequently encroaching on the village.		
Reward: Experience per Paw Collected, 2-Copper per Paw Collected, Chance of Variable Piece of Gear		
Do you accept this Quest?	Yes	No

Accepted.

Quest Alert: Leader of the Pack Bounty (Recommended Level 3-5)		
Standing Village Bounty for Alpha Wolves frequently encroaching on the village.		
Reward: Experience per Paw collected, 10-Copper per Paw Collected, Chance of Variable Piece of Gear		
Do you accept this Quest?	Yes	No

Accepted, more dangerous I'm sure but hopefully, the experience balanced out the danger.

Quest Alert: Blackberries Wanted (Recommended Level 1-3)		
Rita Dogson needs a bushel of Blackberries to make pies.		
Reward: Experience, Blackberry Pie x2, (bonus experience and Blackberry Pie x2 for an additional bushel)		
Do you accept this Quest?	Yes	No

Not difficult and probably a good idea for me to find the blackberry bush where I died the first time. If I could find it there was a good chance I'd have a lead on finding Pwn Star69. What I would do when I did find him was yet to be determined.

The other notices all required going and meeting one person or another, several miles from the village with vague directions on where to find the quest giver. Seeing as there was little chance the requests would disappear overnight, and I was pressed to get as many quick quests as I could, these seemed to be the right choices for the time being. Especially since the wolf bounties were limitless.

Next, I turned to the bookshelves. Now, I know I won't have a ton of time to read, but I would have downtime once the sun had set, allowing me to read and study.

"Well, how about that Margie?" said a voice behind me just as I was about to reach up and grab the first book from the shelf. "An adventure has bothered with our little collection of books."

I turned to face the voice to see a bald man with a few wisps of hair on his head and a portly belly, his shirt could hardly contain. Next to him, an arm gripping his at the elbow was an older woman with dark grey hair and where the man was portly she appeared thin as a rail.

"Oh, leave him be, Homer," she said. "See, now you have gone and interrupted him."

"Sorry, young fella. Please don't hold back on enjoying our little collection there," he said motioning back to the bookshelf. "I imagine you will find quite a few useful skills in there if you are patient enough to actually read the books."

"These are skill books?" I asked, unable to hide the surprise in my voice. Forums said skill books were very rare.

"I suppose you might call them that, but it is up to you, whether or not, you find the skill in the books," he replied.

"What do you mean?"

"Books hold knowledge, not everyone is capable of gleaning actual knowledge from a book let alone a real usable skill," he explained.

Now there was a thought. Had no one else bothered to ever read these books? Or had they read them and just not found a skill in them. This definitely warranted looking into. I seemed to have two willing resources right in front of me if I could get them to help me out.

"I don't suppose you'd recommend any of these books more strongly than others?" I asked.

"By the Gods, we have got a smart one on our hands Margie!" exclaimed Homer, the man was practically beaming. "Well then lad, my name is Homer Simper. I am the Mayor in his here town and this is my wife Margie. She also happens to be my secretary."

"Pleased to meet you both," I replied, trying hard to contain my excitement. "I'm Bye-bye Jacko but you can call me Bye-bye."

"You poor boy," said Margie. "How could your parents give you such a ridiculous name? Did they hate you or something?"

I couldn't help but laugh. "It's more of a nickname, it stuck as a kid. I like it now anyway."

"Good on you lad. Now, as for the books, you should read. And I mean read, as in study them until you get a skill out of them." He walked with a purpose to the bookshelf to the right of the bulletin board and pulled out two books. Then to the left side bookshelf where he pulled out another book. He turned to me and pushed all three into my waiting hands.

You Receive three books for study. Books must be returned in 14 days.
World Tree Bestiary – Common and not so common beasts and where and more importantly how to find or avoid them.
The Trained Eye – Techniques for building acuity and accuracy.
The Greater Outdoors – Survival in the wilderness made easy.

If I had to guess, the Bestiary would give me some kind of tracking skill. The Trained Eye, a perception or observation skill, maybe night vision which would become essential eventually. The Greater Outdoors was obviously survival skills, maybe herbalism, campsite setup or similar skills.

"Now, before you go running off to complete those tasks from the bulletin board, let me ask. Are you planning to go hunting the wolves' bounty?"

"Yes, I was, but after I helped Farm Johnson and his wife, why?"

"I thought so. I would ask you to take this next bit of advice as seriously as you can. Take an hour and read the Bestiary before you step outside of town. It's not a thick book but if you can learn from it, you will have a much easier time of it.

Quest Alert: Read World Tree Bestiary and learn from it

Mayor Simper has strongly recommended you read and study the World Tree Bestiary before you leave the village on some fool adventure.		
Reward: Experience, New Skill		
Do you accept this Quest?	Yes	**No**

I'm not so stupid as to look a gift horse in the mouth. "I can do that. It is a reasonable request and suggestion. I suppose I shall head over to the Inn and give this a read then."

"Good on you lad," said Homer, sagging a little in relief. He seemed to actually care. "Now, get on out of here so I can lock up for the day. You're welcome to come back as often as you can, between the midmorning bell and midafternoon bell." As if his words called the bell to action, the ringing sounded from above me. As expected, the sound drew my attention upward where I saw a large cast-iron bell, not unlike those found in old European churches.

"Right, out with you lad and good luck," said Homer, ushering me from the building.

"Thank you again for the help," I said before going my own way from Homer and Margie.

Entering the inn, I went straight to the bar which was now starting to fill up.

"What can I get you?" asked Dogson.

"I picked up a request from Rita asking for a bushel of blackberries. I don't suppose you could tell me where to find them?"

"Sure, go northeast from town, past the Johnson farm until you hit the river then follow it east for about an hour. You should start finding the blackberry bushes as you get closer to the waterfall. Cannot miss them. I hope you get a lot of them berries. Maybe the missus will make enough pies for me to sneak one," he said as the man's tongue gave an exaggerate lick of his lips and snout.

"I'll do my best, I don't suppose you've got the bushel baskets here?"

"You will find a few laying around by the bushes. We have around 20-bushel baskets, they are delivered out there as soon as they have all come back to us. There should be at least 10 of them still laying around out there."

Interesting, they built-in a quest to replenish the baskets occasionally. "Thanks for the tip. I'll be in my room reading for about an hour. Can you send up some tea in about 30 minutes?" I requested.

Dogson nodded before returning to cleaning the counter. The game definitely needed to improve the way the citizens ended conversations. Or maybe I was just socially inept.

It was a short climb up the steps and a short walk down the hall to my room, number 8. The room was small, just a single bed, an armoire and a desk with a simple wooden chair. There was a large window which let in plenty of light.

I moved the chair next to the window, slipped off my sandals and propped my feet up on the bed. Getting as comfortable as I was able to, I opened the book and started to read.

The book was straightforward. It would give a classification of a beast, a list of common traits and attacks, images of their tracks, then more information about their hunting patterns and preferred environments before it went into additional subclasses. They were mostly the same, but with a few minor differences, from environmental to subtle track differences.

It was robust in the number of species it covered too, dozens of bears, wolves, big cats, birds, boars, bats, all animal based. Of course, nothing on goblins, orcs or the undead. I didn't exactly expect it from a bestiary, but I was still curious. The last section was the most interesting to me. It went into rumors of legendary beasts and where to find them, the history of the creatures. I was so engrossed in reading, I wasn't expecting the system notification.

I was so startled by the message popping up, I tipped right back in my chair, my head banging on the floor, a little -2-HP floating away from my body. I half expected to see stars or little tweety birds flying around my head as I sat back up. Instead, I was confronted with a system message following my movements.

Quest Alert: Read World Tree Bestiary and learn from it – Completed!
Mayor Simper has strongly recommended you read and study the World Tree Bestiary before you leave the village on some fool adventure.
Reward: +200 Experience, Beast Tracking

You've learned a new skill 'Beast Tracking'

Beast Tracking	Level: 1	Experience: 0.00%
Skill Effect (Passive): *Enables you to see animal tracks to better hunt them.*		
Skill Range: 10 yards	Chance to See: *10%*	Chance to Track: *20%*

"Sweet," I said to myself excitedly, I hadn't even finished reading the book and gained the skill in addition to completing the quest. Then I saw a bunch of shaded exclamations points faded in my peripheral. "Sweet!" I reiterated more exuberantly.

You learned something. You earn +1 Intellect
You understand something. You earn +1 Wisdom
You learned something else. You earn +1 Intellect

You understand more. You earn +1 Wisdom
Lore knowledge has improved and is now Level 3.
New Skill has been learned 'Beast Tracking'

"Now how long was I studying?"

Class Quest Alert: Novice Warrior Priest of Issara – Your Goddess' Path Lies Ahead
You have been charged by the Goddess you now serve to mete out punishment on the murderer you vowed to bring to justice. Time Limit: 21:23:44
Reward: Hidden

Just over an hour and a half, not bad. I've still got about three hours of daylight. I could probably get to the Johnson farm and back, but I felt my time might be better served hunting wolves, they were guaranteed experience, both for killing them and for the repeatable quest items.

It didn't take me long to get outside of town, this time through the main gate. I made sure to say hello to Sergeant Butters who warned me not to do something stupid.

The first time I spotted a track of some kind it was just a little glowing footprint. I had to study it closely to determine it was made by a deer. The next set of tracks was a rabbit, as was the next one. But the fourth track turned out to be a wolf, just a pack wolf by the size of it. Unfortunately, I lost the trail after about ten yards, which was disappointing.

I found another wolf paw print about 10 sets of tracks later. It was another pack wolf which was probably good to start with. This time I successfully found the wolf, or he found me, either way, we found each other and one of us met a violent end. It took four 'Jab' attacks to kill the level 1 animal. I gained 15 experience points for the level one enemy and had to use my spear to cut off the paw which thankfully came off with a simple stab at the ankle. Unfortunately, I didn't have any skill to be able to remove the skin or harvest any meat or organs, so the carcass was left to rot or de-spawn, not sure yet how the game handled it.

I guessed it had around 60 HP given my spear only does 4-5 damage and 'Jab' adds +3 to damage and my Strength adds another +9 on top. All told, if it takes four strikes from me assuming the wolf has no or only a little armor at level 1 meant I was doing 16-17 base damage per strike. Not too shabby.

The wolf wasn't exactly a dangerous or complex opponent. It was kind of a just go forward and attack until it died, ignoring the minor damage it dealt in return. The strategy would be fine for now, but eventually, I would have to start fighting smarter.

Next, it was time to try some of my magic. Time to try 'Lesser Holy Imbuement' on my spear.

Lesser Holy Imbuement	Level: 1	Experience: 0.00%
Spell Duration: 10 minutes	Spell Cast Speed: Instant	Spell Mana Cost: 50
Spell Effect (Active): Imbued Weapon now deals holy damage causing an additional 1-2 damage per hit		
Spell Effect (Active): Imbued Shield now deals holy damage causing 2-3 damage per block		

It was surprisingly easy to cast. I just looked at my spear and thought 'Lesser Holy Imbuement' and the tip started to glow with a yellowish-white flame. Then I slapped myself in the head, it might take more than 10 minutes to find another wolf and the spell wasn't cheap for my limited mana pool.

As luck would have it or bad luck would have it, I found a wolf about 8 minutes later. Still, four hits to kill it, but the last hit was more putting it out of its misery, as the animal's health bar showed barely a sliver of life remaining.

Two wolf paws in thirty minutes. I needed to get better at this tracking thing. By the time the sun started to set, and it was time to head back to the village, I had collected 13 more paws from pack wolves and 1 paw from an alpha, which nearly sent me for respawn.

Still, I made some good progress for my efforts. 'Lesser Holy Imbuement' only gained a little experience, I was only able to use it two more times, the mana cost was very inefficient right now. I made a mental note to investigate getting some mana restoratives tomorrow. Where I did gain big time was in my other stat points.

Stab that wolf. You earn +1 Stamina
Don't bite me bro +1 Endurance
Hurt that wolf. You earn +1 Strength
Hit that wolf. You earn +1 Dexterity
One-Handed Polearms has gained a level. Damage +0.5, Critical Strike Chance +0.05%
Why is he still biting you? You earn +1 Endurance
Keep stabbing. You earn +1 Stamina
More damage. You earn +1 Strength
Cut it out already, that hurts. You earn +1 Endurance
You don't want to die, do you? You earn +1 Endurance
Ha ha, you dodged. You earn +1 Dexterity
One-Handed Polearms has gained a level. Damage +0.5, Critical Strike Chance +0.05%
More stabs. You earn +1 Stamina

How are you not dead yet? You earn +1 Endurance
Bring the hurt. You earn +1 Strength
Right in the eye. You earn +1 Dexterity
One-Handed Polearms has gained a level. Damage +0.5, Critical Strike Chance +0.05%
Isn't your arm tired yet? You earn +1 Stamina
Don't bite me there. You earn +1 Endurance
Stab harder. You earn +1 Strength
Yelp! You earn +1 Endurance
Woohoo! You dodged again. You earn +1 Dexterity
One-Handed Polearms has gained a level. Damage +0.5, Critical Strike Chance +0.05%
Bite marks aren't a fashion accessory. You earn +1 Endurance
Is it nap time yet? You earn +1 Stamina
Oh Goddess, you're gonna die. You earn +1 Endurance
Your death is imminent. You earn +1 Endurance
Meet the Grim Reaper with dignity. You earn +1 Endurance
Yes! You live! You earn +1 Endurance
Lesser Heal has gained a level. Spell Heal 5-15, Spell Cast Speed 2.00, Spell Mana Cost 12
Wolf Kabab anyone? You earn +1 Strength
Not the cleanest kill. You earn +1 Dexterity
One-Handed Polearms has gained a level. Damage +0.5, Critical Strike Chance +0.05%
You just keep stabbing. You earn +1 Stamina
Don't bite me bro . . . again. You earn +1 Endurance
Now that's power. You earn +1 Strength

Hit 'em where it hurts. You earn +1 Dexterity
One-Handed Polearms has gained a level. Damage +0.5, Critical Strike Chance +0.05%

"Ugh!" again with the wall of text. I needed to find a way to fix that if I could. I took a minute to look at my options menu only to find my only option was to either turn off all notifications or turn them on. I made a note to bring it up if there was any kind of feedback or survey when I logged out.

While 'Lesser Holy Imbuement' may not have gotten much stronger my 'Lesser Heal' did gain a level. This was mostly due to the fact I've decided I don't enjoy getting bitten by wolves, especially not those of the Alpha variety. Still, 12 points to Endurance is more than a little useful. What would be more useful is if I knew how to block with my shield when the rotten beasts go for the legs and not the chest or head where my shield was fixed to defend. I'd have to ask Sergeant Butters to teach me how to block tomorrow.

The walk back to town was uneventful, no wolves to speak of, nor anything else trying to make a snack out of me. I greeted the Sergeant again on my way back into town where he greeted me with a little bit of a snicker when he saw my current state. I didn't appreciate the amusement on his face when I looked back after entering the village. It suggested he knew I was going to have problems protecting myself from the wolves and didn't bother to inform me.

Having no other plans to work in the dark, mostly due to a lack of night vision skill, I headed back to the Inn. Once there I was more than happy to sit at the bar and eat the hearty meal Dogson provided his guests. It would be a while before Guard Bryant came in, so I opened one of the other books the mayor recommended to me, 'The Trained Eye'.

This was more involved than the Bestiary. This was all tricks and techniques for seeing everything around you all at the same time. The idea was to relax the eye to an extent, you want to see everything at the same time, then focus on a single target in an instant. And that was just the first exercise. I flipped ahead a bit and saw there were techniques for improving my ability to see in the dark, increasing the range of my vision, and a few others looked interesting. I was getting the feeling this book was filled with several skills I could learn, if I practiced each of the techniques. I would have to read through and prioritize the sight abilities I think would be most useful. So rather than trying the techniques as I read through I just read through the book trying to figure out what each technique would allow me to do if I could turn it into a skill.

"Ugh, not the eye book of doom," complained a voice from next to me interrupting my reading.

Looking to the source I was surprised to see Guard Bryant. "Hey, you're here? Is it already late bell?" I asked, looking briefly at my game clock to see it was just after 10:00.

"An hour past late bell. The Sergeant spent an hour jawing on about you. Never seen the old goat so excited about getting pestered for training. Apparently, he loves the spear training cause so few ever bother learning it. He wants to start drilling all the guards now on how to use a spear," complained Guard Bryant.

"Sorry, Guard Bryant, I didn't intend-" I started.

"Forget it and I am off duty now, so please, call me Gavin. Now, I believe you promised me a few pints," he suggested, waiving for Dogson.

"Right you are my good man," I said, happy for the distraction. It would be good to cut loose tonight and have some social fun. "Dogson, two pints for Gavin and I if you please."

Dogson rolled his eyes but smiled all the same as he poured two pints from one of the barrels mounted on the wall behind the bar. "Two Delger Dwarven Stouts," he said setting the dark ale in front of us. "2-coppers."

I paid the man happily then picked up my glass. "Cheers," I said, offering my glass toward Gavin who tapped his glass to mine before he took a long draft off his beer. Foolishly, I tried to follow suit and nearly choked to death for the effort. The beer was as thick as molasses and probably had enough alcoholic content to peel paint.

"Oh yeah, we are gonna have some fun tonight," said Gavin, grinning and swatting me on the back, as I coughed and tried to swallow the thick beer down.

~

The crowing rooster the next morning met an unfortunate end as my 'Holy Smite' destroyed the far too loud bird without a second thought. How could I have a hangover? How did I even get drunk? This game at this moment was just too real.

"Oi!" came a loud pounding on my door. "Do not go killing my chickens!"

It was Dogson.

"So loud," I complained, pulling my pillow over my head.

"Get dressed and come downstairs, we will get you some breakfast and a hangover curative," Dogson shouted through the door.

Now that sounded promising. It was with great reluctance I crawled out of my bed pulling on my shirt and vest as I seemed to have slept in my pants. I slipped on my sandals as I exited the spinning room and stumbled my way to breakfast.

Rather than sitting at the bar this time, I dropped into a seat by a corner table, the one with no direct sunlight hitting it. Sadly, it didn't seem to provide much if any relief.

Dogson appeared a minute later setting a pint on the table. "Drink first," he ordered.

"Your hangover curative is more of the beer I drank last night?" I asked, not completely believing Dogson was suggesting 'hair of the dog'. The irony was not lost on me.

"Just drink it, you will feel better, then we can get some food in you and you get off to doing whatever it is you need to get done today," the dogman ordered.

I shuddered, as soon as I caught a whiff of the stout beer I wanted it to be as far away from me as possible. I swallowed thickly, bringing it to my lip and taking a drink. I immediately wanted to put the mug down and vomit but Dogson had a hand on the mug preventing such an action. Before I knew it, I was more or less chugging down the entire beer in one go.

When the pint was empty, and I sort of slammed it down on my table. Dogson collected it and walked away ignoring my swearing.

It took a moment for me to realize, while I was swearing, the room had stopped spinning. I no longer felt the need to vomit and every little noise was no longer an anvil hammering in my head.

When Dogson returned with a hearty plate of breakfast a few minutes later, he ignored me when I tried to ask him about the curative. I wondered if he didn't add something to beer.

With my hangover relieved, I made short work of breakfast, it was just what I needed.

It was then, I saw a few exclamation points waiting for me. What exactly did I do last night?

Your ability to tell a tall tale gains you some new friends +1 Charisma
Your successful flirting gains you some amorous attention +1 Charisma
Your alcohol tolerance improves +1 Endurance

Nice I thought and chuckled to myself. I'll have to remember to get drunk more often if I wake up with more charisma and endurance for my troubles.

Eventually, I walked up to the bar after giving the meal a few minutes to settle in my stomach. "Thanks for breakfast and the cure. What do I owe for you for the rooster I smote?"

"It is fine, the missus is turning it into potpie for dinner tonight, just do not let it happen again," he answered.

"Thank you, and sorry again about the rooster," I said. I didn't feel too sorry, the rooster had it coming as far as I was concerned.

"You are not the first and certainly will not be the last. Though I cannot say I have seen a rooster die by holy smiting before, so that was new," joked Dogson.

"In my defense, the noise was unholy," I retorted with a little laugh. "Anyway, where can I pick up some mana restoratives this morning before I head out?"

"The general store should be opening soon. If you head over now, you should only have to wait a couple minutes for Ned to open the shop, just do not let him draw you into debating the Gods or you will never leave," warned Dogson. "He is a good man but . . . well, you will see when you meet him."

"Right, and where is the general store?"

"Oh, just head for the crossroad, it will be on the corner closest to my Inn."

"Great, thank you," I replied. "Um, by the way, you wouldn't happen to know who I was flirting with last night would you?"

Dogson let a few loud barks of laughter ring out before he shooed me away.

I frowned, my curiosity wanted to demand I press for answers, but I had things to do today. Time to get moving.

Class Quest Alert: Novice Warrior Priest of Issara – Your Goddess' Path Lies Ahead	
You have been charged by the Goddess you now serve to mete out punishment on the murderer you vowed to bring to justice. Time Limit: 7:59:01	
Reward:	Hidden

CHAPTER 4

'Ned's Sundry', the sign over the shop door read. Doors which were firmly closed. I could see a wooden sign in the window, also stating plainly the shop was still 'Closed'.

With a sigh, I sat down on the steps in front of the shop to wait.

"Hey Mic, look, we got a new guy in town," said a voice to my right in a British accent, easily drawing my attention. What I saw was a man probably at least dozen years older than me. He also had to be at least half-ogre based on his size alone, maybe full ogre, but with their intellect penalties it was rare one could even speak.

"Blimey, it is a new guy," said a decidedly more female voice, also with a British accent. This character was also very tall, only a head shorter than the other ogre, maybe she was a female ogre, they had those right?

"Hello," I greeted them both with as friendly a wave as I could muster. The pair were tall as I mentioned before but seeing them both close up was even more impressive. They were both at least a good two feet taller than me. Ogres were generally identifiable by their single eye and a small horn in the middle of the forehead which both had. While the man was bald the woman had short spiky hair colored hot pink. They were both muscular, looking similar to professional bodybuilders and they both wore blue coveralls and a white shirt.

"Nice to meet you, mate, I'm Olaf Crushhammer and this is my wife, Micaela Crushhammer," said the man.

"Nice to meet you both, I'm Bye-bye Jacko," I introduced myself.

"Ooh, good one," said Micaela. "I make all the baddies say Bye-bye. Hasta la Bye-bye. You've got a built-in catchphrase, love. I totally approve." She ended by giving me two thumbs up.

"Thanks, I think," I said laughing a little. This chick was an original character. I took a closer look at them, they were both level 3. Just guessing based on the mining picks hanging from their belts, they were professional miners, still, it was polite to ask. "You guys professional miners?" I asked.

"Picks gave it away, didn't they?" joked Olaf, patting the pick at his side almost lovingly.

"Might have," I answered.

"Yeah, we're miners. We make more in a week mining ore for 40 hours than we did in our jobs working between 50 and 60 hours each. The economy in the World Tree is so much better, regardless of the initial expense to get the two Seed pods," explained Olaf.

"Um, no offense but . . . how are you able to . . . you know . . . speak? I thought ogres took big intellect penalties, which left them illiterate and unable to talk for several levels," I asked, not sure on the best etiquette here.

"They are, but there is a little exploit we found, it let us get our intellect up to 4 so we could talk," he answered.

"Can you share?" I asked, my curiosity getting the better of me. I knew it might have been rude, but I just had to know more.

"Sure, we met in the army," started Micaela.

"We learned a shorthand sign language from when we served. It let us talk to each other, which gave us intellect points the more we used it," answered Olaf. "We've shown others, but it only seems to work for races with big intellect penalties and it only gives you just enough to be able to speak in complete sentences, then it cuts off."

"Which royally bites," complained Micaela. "It left us both short of being able to read. Now, any book we look at just blurs horribly. It's a right bother."

"It's still impressive, the way you both were able to boost your intellect enough to talk," I complimented them. "How long have you two been playing?"

"We've been playing since day one," answered Olaf.

This created a disconnect for me. How were they only level 3?

"How . . . Um, why . . ."I asked, confused by how they could only be level 3 after almost 3 months in the game.

"Why are we only level 3?" offered Olaf. "We spend all day mining, haven't done anything but mine. The low-end copper we mine stops giving experience once you hit level three."

"So, why not go somewhere with better ore? Or just go kill some monsters and level?"

"It's all about supply and demand. Right now, the game is still new, only three months old. There are so many people starting and dropping professions in rapid succession, all in the search to find the one they enjoy. As a result, the demand for copper is through the roof. So, we bought ourselves an ore broker AI. Then we ship our weekly ore intake to it. It then takes a 10% commission on any ore it sells for us to pay for its maintenance. It then mails 10% back to us for our expenses here and deposits the rest in our World Tree bank account. I figure we've got three more months before the copper demand starts to fall. But, we've only got a month to go before our Seedpods are paid in full then we can mine part time and actually play the game the rest of the time."

"Very nice, it sounds like you two have got all your ducks in a row," I complimented them.

"We try," said Mic, grinning.

"So what classes are you going to go for once you switch to mining part-time?" I asked. I hadn't read much on Ogres after I read about the illiteracy penalty they start with, so I didn't know what all was available to them.

"I'm going shaman all the way. It's the only caster class an Ogre can have because it relies on the wisdom stat which doesn't get penalized as an ogre. I'm totally gonna get a spirit wolf," said Mic excitedly.

"I thought I read about an Ogre mage a few days ago on the forum," I countered. I truly had read about one.

"Ha! Yeah right!" Mic jumped. "How could an ogre get their intellect stat so high? You would have to have a minimum of 50-Int to become a mage. Because of the ogre intellect penalty, you'd have to be at least level 10 with the maximum intellect to pull it off."

"Hey now, don't forget I have to hold out until level 30 for my class," chided Olaf. Seeing my confused look, he answered the unasked question. "I'm going Ogre Artillery, it's a rare class," said Olaf, with what I can only assume was a smug grin, it didn't look quite right on his face.

"I'm just telling you what I read on the forums, I didn't honestly look too deeply into it. Now, what's an Ogre Artillery?" I asked, my curiosity peeking out.

"It's an Ogre restricted class. Think warrior with a cannon mounted on his shoulder but you have to have 750 natural strength to do it."

"Ouch!" I said appreciatively. Some firearms existed but they were prohibitively expensive because they were so powerful, other than the cost the only downside was they are stupid slow to reload and fire. But to have a freaking cannon.

"Yeah, it's a pain. I have to get to level 30 before I can even start on it. Being unclassed to 30 is gonna be a bloody nightmare of a grind. Plus, the grind to 750-Strength, ugh! Then, I have to enslave a pair of dwarf, gnome or goblin engineers to work as my cannon crew, which is an additional pain, cause if you take the wrong pair of NPC's it can turn the entire race against you," Olaf groaned.

For most classes, the stat point cap per level is 10 points, except for endurance which allowed 20. The game designers did this, so they wouldn't end up with a level 1 player with a 1000 strength going around one-shotting everything in existence. Various races had an increase to various stats level caps, such as my own 50% increased cap for intellect and charisma. This meant I could gain 15 points to those two stats per level. As for the strength, only ogres could get that kind of strength. One of their racial bonuses more than doubled their strength cap per level. So, where I was capped at 10-strength points per level they had a cap of 25 points per level. On the other side, was their massive Intellect penalty. They could only gain 5 points of Intellect per level. Oh, and an NPC is a Non-Player character or citizen as they refer to themselves.

"Can't you just hire a crew? Offer them profit sharing or something?" I asked, curious about the enslaving a crew of engineers, it felt wrong to me.

Olaf blinked a few times looking at me as if I'd grown an extra head. "I have no idea. The forums only say you need to force them to work for you. I wonder if anyone has ever bothered to offer to hire them on? Maybe there is a charisma component?"

I shrugged. "It might be worth looking into."

"Ooh Babe, we're totally friending this guy," said Mic.

You've received a Friend Request from Micaela

Crushhammer!		
Do you accept?	**Yes**	**No**

"Sounds good to me," I said accepting, only to get a request from Olaf too which I also accepted.

"So, what about you?" asked Olaf. "What class you planning to get when you can?"

"I'm a priest already," I answered. There was no need to hide it, I am a priest and my spells would make it obvious once I start casting. They didn't need to know I was a unique class of priest.

"Nice, healzor, now you're an even better friend to have," chattered Mic excitedly.

I let it go, no need to disappoint them with my awful healing penalties.

"Your age is showing Mic, no one says healzor anymore," laughed Olaf.

"He heals, therefore healzor, don't try your logic on me," stated Micaela firmly.

"Howdy folks, I will have this door open in just a moment," said a muffled voice from inside the store behind me.

Looking over my shoulder a saw a thin man with an odd mustache and glasses working on the locks inside the store.

"Take your time," I called to him, standing from my seat on the steps.

"So, what are you here for today?" asked Mic.

"I need some mana restoratives," I answered.

"Ouch, potions are expensive at this level," cringed Mic.

"Just looking for mana replenishing water or juice or something. For after combat and between pulls," I explained.

76

"Oh, I hadn't even considered that," chatted Mic excitedly, earning a roll of the eye from Olaf.

"I won't bother with potions until I start doing dungeons which won't be for a long time. I'm a lore hound, so I won't leave this province for a long time," I explained further.

"Ugh, you're actually trying lore? All the forums say its complete garbage, mate," stated Olaf.

"I got it as a natural profession with my race, half-high elf and I don't mind cause I'm also half-human which gives me an extra profession slot. I doubt Lore is as useless as people say, I just doubt anyone has put the time into it. When I checked the forums before I started my dive yesterday, it said the highest level anyone had got lore to was level 3 and that was a pure High-Elf who started with Lore level 3. I started with Level 2 yesterday, I'm already up to level 3. If I get it to level 10 and still haven't found anything useful for it then I might drop it, but for now, I'll keep plugging along," I answered.

"He's got a point, hon," Mic added. "What was the game you used to play? The one where they said shamans were a complete waste of time? Who was the guy? You know the one, he completely wrecked the myth of shaman's being bad and shocked the entire player base?"

"Yeah, yeah, whatever. I'll reserve judgment for now," said Olaf, a chagrined smile on his ugly mug.

"Alrighty folks, come on in," said Ned, finally opening the door to his shop.

I entered first followed by Olaf and Mic, both of whom had to duck to get through the door and continue ducking while inside. "Mind me asking what you two are here for?"

"Don't mind at all. We both hit the level 3 cap of 75 strength yesterday so we're getting better picks and bigger bags. Probably a few stamina potions too," answered Olaf.

"We wanted miner's bags, right?" asked Mic loudly. I could see her hunched over a shelf or rack to the side of the shop.

"I better go help the wife before she buys me a hot pink bag," joked Olaf.

"Right, you two want to get dinner tonight? I'm staying at the Dog House Inn over by the Town hall," I offered.

"Sure, we'll meet you there around 6:00 or evening bell as they call it here," said Olaf.

"Later then," I said, watching only for a moment as Olaf went to wage shopping war with his wife. I made a beeline for the register and Ned as I could see foodstuffs and bottles of stuff on the shelves behind the counter he currently manned.

"Morning and welcome," greeted Ned. "What can I do you for?"

"I need mana restoratives," I answered.

"Potions or food based?"

"Food-based, water or juice if you've got it?"

"I can fill you up with mana-rich water, just need your canteen," he said which caused me to cringe. My current canteen was filled with stamina restoring water.

"I guess I need to buy a second canteen then," I said. I was a little worried because I was down to my last 15-coppers.

"Sure, a basic canteen will run you 5-coppers and the mana-rich water is another 5," said Ned.

I handed over the coppers cringing at my remaining 5. Hopefully, I wouldn't need to buy anything for a while now. I would replenish my money shortly when I turned in the wolf paws and completed some of the quests I picked up.

"Can I get you anything else?" asked Ned.

I checked my bag one more time. I still had 3 of the tac foodstuffs and I'd refill the stamina water canteen when I trained with the Sergeant. "No, I think that'll do it. Thank you."

"Have a blessed day," said Ned in his seemingly natural friendly manner.

"You too," I said, stashing my new canteen away and heading out of the shop. I spotted Olaf and Micaela still looking through the bags, the poor man looked ready to jump off a cliff. I could only shake my head in pity for the man even as I left the shop, leaving him to his misfortune.

It was still early, but I had a few things I had to take care of this morning. First things first, I need to see the Sergeant about learning to block.

I found the Sergeant in the back of the barracks, already hard at work. Jabbing at a practice dummy with a pair of daggers, doing a dozen different strikes, flowing from one to the next effortlessly.

"Back for more, are you?" asked Sergeant Butters, not breaking his stride as he continued to attack the dummy.

"Right you are, Sergeant. I found out I need some training in how to block with my shield," I answered.

"Alright, I will give you a choice of skills then. First, is what I call aggressive blocking or the 'Shield Slam'. You hit your target interrupting their attack or spell. If you get good enough with it, you will eventually be able to stun your target. The second skill is a block and counter-skill or 'Shield-Counter'."

"Given my current skill with the spear, which would you recommend?" I asked, hopeful the village weapon master would be willing to impart such wisdom.

"Either is fine, it just depends on how you fight. Are you defensive or offensive?"

He had a point. Yesterday I had no choice but to be aggressive since I didn't have any defensive skills. But how would I fight in the long term? My class was a warrior priest, but should I fight up close and personal or sit back and cast or did it even matter? How did I want to fight? If I thought back on how I played games before, I played Paladin's which I guess could be similar to a warrior priest. Which meant I was usually up close and personal. But there I also had heavy plate armor, giving me protection to fight so up close and personal.

Here I needed to rethink how I would fight going forward. So, I have magic to do damage from range, but I also had spells able to enhance my ability to fight in close. So, both were viable. *Both* were viable. I needed to be able to fight both at a distance and in close and switch between the two flawlessly.

Forgetting where I was and what I was doing, I was brought back to reality by the Sergeant clearing his throat rather loudly. "I'll need to learn both techniques eventually, but for now I need abilities to help me hunt the local wolf population," I finally decided.

"In that case, I would go with the 'Shield Slam' to start," said Sergeant Butters, nodding his approval of my decision. "As I said before, this is aggressive blocking. When you see your opponent about to swing or attack, you need to close the distance and slam your shield into them. If you cannot figure out how to time their attack, you will be in for a long and painful morning. Now, we have got 2 hours before my first training group arrives. Let us get to work."

I moved into the stance the Sergeant showed me the day before with practiced ease. Across from me, the Sergeant was now wielding a large wooden club.

"So, the club is slow, it will help you get used to timing an attack. As you get better we will move to faster weapons, ending with daggers, the fastest weapon I can use effectively. First, you do not want to slam into me at the start of my swing with a slow weapon. Second, you do not want to slam into me at the end of my swing because I will still smack you pretty good. Third, depending on the strength of your opponent versus your own strength you may not be able to slam them effectively if their strength is more than twice your own. Fourth, the only exception to rule three is spell casting, slam always interrupts casting no matter how far into the cast they are. The only thing to keep in mind, if you interrupt too soon they'll be able to start casting again right away, so the closer you can get to the end of their cast bar the better. Plus, it will really make them angry." The Sergeant's grin as he finished his explanation made me feel like the canary before a hungry cat, or maybe a ravenous tiger. "Now, I know I am stronger than you by a large margin, but for the sake of training if you slam me with the right timing I will stop my attack."

"Got it, can you show me first?" I asked.

"Kid, I am of the school, you learn better by doing," he said seriously. "Let us get started."

I focused as hard as I could on watching him start the swing of his club. When the club got about halfway through his swing, I tried to step forward and attempt to interrupt the attack. But it was already too late, the club had full momentum by the time I got to him. It hurt when the club slammed into my side, lifting me from my feet and sending me rolling bodily across the training ring.

"You need to already be moving when my swing starts. The actual act of slamming the shield into me should occur mid-swing," coached the Sergeant.

I nodded painfully and climbed back to my feet. I took a moment to cast a couple of quick 'Lesser Heal' spells on myself, restoring my HP from the damage done.

"Again," ordered Butters.

And again, I tried. He slammed me to the ground six more times before I finally got one slam, even if it was pathetically weak. I couldn't figure out what to do with my spear.

"Better, you got to me that time, but your spear got in the way. Let me ask you this, what were you planning to do after you slammed me with your shield?"

What was I going to do? I was going to turn him into a pin cushion. What did he think I was going to do? And there was the answer. My spear needed to be in a position to attack after I used 'Shield Slam'.

"Good, seems you figured it out. Again," ordered Sergeant Butters, starting his wind up.

This time I moved forward quickly, drawing my spear back as I moved in. My shield slammed into him mid-swing interrupting the attack and without thinking my spear shot forward in an attempt to impale the sergeant.

The man's movement shocked me as he effortless dodge my attack. "Well done!" he shouted, grinning from ear to ear. "I think you are the first adventurer I have met with the fortitude to actually attack me."

I was about to stutter all manner of apology, but the man was positively beaming with joy. "You keep this up and I will make a soldier out of you yet."

"Thank you, Sergeant!"

"Right then, I think you are ready for a faster weapon, right?" A moment later, the club was replaced with a dulled great-sword. "This baby is blunted so it will not cut you in half, but it is a fair bit faster than the club," he said, his grin doubling in size.

I swallowed thickly. The sergeant's sword may well kill me even blunted as it was.

"Get to it," said Butters.

Thankfully the man only slammed me to the ground with the sword twice before I got the timing and managed to 'Shield Slam' followed by an attack.

Next, he switched to a small two-handed battle ax, which didn't knock me to the ground. It still hurt when it hit, and I got hit more often than I would have preferred. Learning the timing of the swing was difficult because it was much faster. Eventually, I understood, it didn't have as much reach, which meant I had to close the distance much faster and shorten up the movement of my 'Shield Slam'.

I had a similar issue with the long sword he used next.

By the time we got to the short sword, I was getting used to the timing of faster weapons. I also figured out they didn't need as much strength to interrupt the attack. Daggers prove to be the easiest to slam despite my earlier worries, having seen him work with them the way he did.

"Right, so long as your opponent stays in front of you, you are good to go," said the Sergeant. It was something in the way he said that made me worried.

"Fights don't happen in a straight line," I said, followed by a heavy sigh.

Sergeant Butters just grinned and nodded. "Good, figured it out on your own. Now, on to phase two of your 'Shield Slam' training. Shifting and pivoting. Sounds easy right?"

"But it's not is it?" I asked, concern in my voice.

"Actually, it is pretty easy. It will just take some practice to get used to it," he stated confidently.

"So, what do I do?" I asked.

"As a lefty, you should have noticed by now, you need to keep your right leg forward and your left leg back. When you move forward to attack or use your 'Shield Slam' you push off your back leg. I have not said anything about it because you were just getting comfortable with the stance, but you should never take a full step forward, or it will cause you balance problems. So, you need to be able to lunge, or more accurately shift forward, keeping both feet close to the ground while covering as much distance as you can. It should never take more than one shift to close on an opponent," the man explained, showing the footwork as he did so. It was impressive to watch. I found myself even more impressed with just how much effort was put into the weapon skills in the game. "Give it a try," he ordered.

The first few times I tried, it definitely came out as more of a hop than a lunge or shift to close distance. It took a good twenty or thirty tries before the Sergeant was satisfied.

"The same applies to creating distance from an opponent, except you're pushing back with the front leg. There is such a thing as someone being too close for comfort, you try it."

Just as in learning to shift forward, it took a while to learn to shift backward.

"Last, is pivoting. Take your stance and try to keep me in front of you," he said then began to circle me. I tried shifting at first, failing completely.

"Keep your back leg planted and rotate using it as your axis. Your front leg should always be pointed toward your opponent," explained Butters.

It took time again before I grasped the concept of pivoting. When I finally had a handle on it, a handful of messages popped up.

You've learned the skill 'Shift'.

Shift	Level: 1	Experience: 0.00%
Combat Movement Skill	Range: 1 yard	Skill Stamina Cost: 5

You've learned 'Phalanx Shield' subskill 'Shield Slam'.

Phalanx Shield	Level: 4	Experience: 32.55%
Current Defense Modifiers	Block Chance: +0.20%	Critical Block Chance: +0.10%
Subskill: Shield Slam	Damage: 2-4 Effect: Interrupt	Skill Stamina Cost: 14

A new skill and a new subskill in one go. Alright! And according to the exclamation points in my peripheral another parade of stat points.

Don't you ever take a day off? You earn +1 Stamina
Muscles, grrr! You earn +1 Strength
Can't touch this. You earn +1 Dexterity
Pain now, pleasure later. You earn +1 Endurance
Pain now, pain later. You earn +1 Endurance
Phalanx Shield has gained a level. Block Chance +0.05%, Critical Block Chance +0.025%
Seriously? You earn +1 Stamina
So strong . . . NOT! You earn +1 Strength

Hit 'em high. You earn +1 Dexterity
Masochist. You earn +1 Endurance
Sadomasochist? You earn +1 Endurance
Phalanx Shield has gained a level. Block Chance +0.05%, Critical Block Chance +0.025%
You keep going, and going, and . . . You earn +1 Stamina
Break on through. You earn +1 Strength
Hit 'em low. You earn +1 Dexterity
You can take it. You earn +1 Endurance
Phalanx Shield has gained a level. Block Chance +0.05%, Critical Block Chance +0.025%
And going, and going . . . You earn +1 Stamina
Keep on trucking. You earn +1 Strength
Did you miss? You earn +1 Dexterity
Might not want to take it. You earn +1 Endurance
Phalanx Shield has gained a subskill Shield Slam. Damage 2-3, Effect: Interrupt, Skill Stamina Cost 5

"Not bad at all," said Sergeant Butters. "I think we are out of time for today. Good work."

"Thank you very much," I said as graciously as I could.

"You are very welcome, come back tomorrow if you want to learn more," offered Butters again.

"You can count on it."

"Right, off you go then. I'm sure you have other things you need to accomplish today," said the Sergeant. Without any other formalities, he waved toward the other half-dozen guards, all gathered for their daily drills.

Class Quest Alert: Novice Warrior Priest of Issara — Your Goddess' Path Lies Ahead

> You have been charged by the Goddess you now serve to mete out punishment on the murderer you vowed to bring to justice. Time Limit: 5:31:12
>
> | Reward: | Hidden |
> | --- | --- |

A quick check of my class quest told me I still had about an hour and a half before Pwn Star69 would be able to log in. Then, I'd have just four hours to hunt him down. But it also told me, the midmorning bell would be chiming soon, and I needed to turn in those wolf paws.

It was barely a five-minute walk to the Town hall, where I took up residence on the steps to wait for the Mayor and his wife to arrive. In the meantime, I contented myself with opening the book, 'The Trained Eye'. I didn't get to finish reading it the night before due to Gavin's timely arrival, and the binge drinking that followed. Right now, I was determined to finish reading the book. I would prioritize which techniques to practice later. First, I needed to figure out what those skills might be and how useful they would be in the long term. I only got through about two more chapters before the mayor showed up, though his wife was absent.

"Morning Mr. Mayor," I greeted him.

"Back for more books already?" he asked, a genial smile on his face.

"I wouldn't say no to another book. I finished the Bestiary you gave me. It gave a nice skill. I'm sure I will get more than enough use out of it too, so thank you," I replied.

"Glad to hear it. Have you given any thoughts to what profession you intend to take up?" he asked as he fiddled with his keys to open the door.

"I already have Lore as a Half-High Elf and because I'm Half-Human, I can pick up two more professions, but I haven't given it much thought," I answered. Truthfully, I lied to the mayor. I had spent copious amounts of time investigating the various professions and what they had to offer.

For example, First Aid could evolve into Medicine which was supposedly a prerequisite to getting the class, Doctor, it was even more useful if you were primarily a healer. It was something I considered, given my healing penalty, as it would give me a way to hide my true class. I probably won't, but it was worth thinking it over. The one I knew, I was going to take was Writing. It offered multi-tier evolutions, including Enchanting and Runes. Both skills would be beneficial to my Lore Profession.

"You should look into the Drawing and Writing professions, in my opinion, if you intend to keep Lore. There are just too many complimentary skills for you pass up," suggested Homer as if he'd just read my mind.

"Do you have any skill books for it?" I asked. As I said, I knew I was going to take writing, but drawing was new to me. I hadn't read anything useful about it, except you could get map making, which was mostly useless.

"We've got books for the evolutions of the professions but if you want to gain the writing and drawing professions, it starts with buying a blank book and writing and drawing in it. All your adventures, a fantasy novel, whatever you desire, should be written down. The skill can only be gained by actually writing. Drawing pictures of an animal you fought or a pretty flower you saw will help you learn drawing. Now, as far as evolving the professions goes, if you have those two professions, you should take Cartography and

Runes, both of which can make you rich if you develop them," he explained.

"Why them?" Again, I had done research but maybe he had some insight I did not.

"First, cartography is very useful. Have you even bought a local map yet?" he asked.

"Not yet." I didn't even know that was an option.

"Well, if you had, you would know the local maps, you can buy here in town, are not very good. It will point out the town, the road, the portal to the World Tree, a few other points of reference but the detail is poor. If you were to take on cartography, you would be able to note down all manner of things. If you join the cartography guild, your map of Hurlig Ridge could then be mass produced and sold here in town and in Root City for the benefit of everyone in the World Tree . . . if the quality is high enough. Anyway, a good map sells for good money, 2-5 silvers for a map of this province. Maybe 1-2 gold for higher areas. And do not get me started on what you could make if you discover or get the chance to map a dungeon. Anyway, if that does not explain it nothing will," he finished.

He'd given me more information and even added a few details I didn't know. The fact this province had not been mapped very well yet, and the currently available maps, were probably all low-level maps. Maps no cartographer ever bothered to detail. It is possible no adventurer even bothered to attempt to discover much of the province. However, the mayor still didn't tell me how it benefited Lore.

"But how does Lore benefit from cartography?" I asked, hoping for more.

"Are you really that daft? Lore is all about history and finding lost knowledge. I would think, many of the clues you will find while you are researching might point to landmarks or important details about a province? And would it not be helpful if you had knowledge enough of maps to be able to find those locations?" he explained and asked.

"Okay, that makes perfect sense," I replied, feeling slightly stunned. He was absolutely right, if I was going to pursue Lore as a profession, then cartography would be paramount.

"As for Runes. Runes are power lad, no two ways about it," said Homer, the shuffle of keys prominent as he tried yet another key.

"What do you mean? I know it's different from enchanting but how is it power?" I had honestly wanted to get enchanting if I could only pick one evolution, it would be nice to be able to enhance my gear with bonus stats and abilities.

"Runes communicate power, which makes it one of the hardest professions to learn and develop."

"Sorry for so many questions, but what do you mean 'Runes communicate power'?"

"Correct me if I am wrong but, you have read a couple of those books you referred to as a skill book we offer right?" he asked, still fiddling with his keys, which was become comical at this point.

"I have," I answered, his comment pointed to Runes being linked to skills in some way.

"So those are not true skill books. A true skill book or scroll contains knowledge, something a person can learn instantly and those use runes," he replied simply.

I was stunned by his response. The town's books weren't true skill books, but they were books capable of teaching skills . . . if you had the patience to study them. Which meant, a true skill book would be able to instantly impart the knowledge of a skill, probably applied to spells too.

All of this led me to the idea, if I learned Runes, I would be able to create and sell skills and spell books. But again, I came back to the question of how this would help me with lore. I looked at him again, but as soon as I opened my mouth to ask my question, him he cut me off.

"Some runes have been lost to time," he answered my unasked question.

Lost runes meant lost skills or spells, things unable to be recreated otherwise. And Lore was all about the lost. I suddenly felt an overwhelming need to drop everything I was doing, and rush to learn these two professions, but I knew better than to forgo anything, I still had plenty I needed to get done before the day ended.

"Any other profession you think might help me?" I asked, interested to hear his opinion, but I knew my mind was made up. I'm pretty sure he knew my mind was made up too, but it was worth asking anyway.

"It depends on you I guess. Crafting professions are always helpful, it is nice to be able to make your own armor and weapons, but the choice is up to you," he answered, finally getting the door open, a smile of achievement and jubilation on his face.

Once inside I followed him to his office. "Now, what can the Mayor do for you?" asked Homer, his tone of voice slightly different from the friendly older gentlemen. It was now more akin to that of an authority figure.

"I've collected 15 pack wolf paws and 1 alpha wolf paw," I answered.

Homer went to his closet and pulled out two buckets and placed them on the desk. "Deposit the paws in the buckets."

As I made my deposit, Homer watched me and counted as each paw entered the bucket, mumbling as he did.

"Good work," he said, going to a cabinet and fiddling with his keys again. It took a minute for him to open the cabinet. When he came back to the desk he was carrying a black metal lockbox. More fiddling with his keys. "Here you are, 40-copper and it looks like you could use a pair of gloves, please choose one.

Please choose one pair of gloves as part of your bounty:
Light Burlap Gloves +2-Armor, +1-Intellect
Light Leather Gloves +5-Armor, +1-Stamina
Light Mail Gloves +10-Armor, +1-Endurance

Sadly, I didn't have the strength for anything but the Burlap gloves. My stamina was in a good spot anyway, but my intellect was a little behind, so the lighter gloves made more sense.

You've selected 'Light Burlap Gloves'		
Are you sure?	**Yes**	**No**

Yes, I am. The mayor held them out to me and I slipped them on right away. The gloves were fingerless, and a perfect fit as expected.

Pack Wolf Bounty – 15 paws collected
Reward: 30-Copper, 60 Experience

That was one.

Alpha Wolf Bounty – 1 paw(s) collected
Reward: 10-Copper, 30 Experience

That was two. So, not great experience or money, but it was a steady income. Thankfully, nothing in town was prohibitively expensive yet, so copper was more than sufficient for the time being.

"Also, please feel free to keep collecting the bounty on the wolves, the more help we can get with this scourge the better," the mayor added.

"I'll bring you more when I can, for now, I'll be heading toward Farmer Johnson's. He needs help with his harvest and his wife needs some help with a clothes' thief. Then I'll be going for some blackberries for Rita Dogson," I told him. I've found, sometimes, if you let an NPC know your plans, you'll trigger an extra quest.

"Excellent, don't suppose you would mind picking up a case of mason jars from the sundry and delivering them to Duke for me? I will give you the money for the jars now, and Duke will pay you when you deliver.

Quest Alert: Shiny Delivery Service 1 (Recommended Level 2-4)		
Mayor Homer Simper has asked you to deliver a case of mason jars to Farmer Johnson's		
Reward: Experience, 50-Copper		
Do you accept this Quest?	**Yes**	**No**

For 50-copper? You bet I accept. "Can do."

"Excellent," said the mayor. "Just uh, let us keep this between you, Duke and I. No need to let the missus know, if you catch my meaning."

"Sure," I answered, not at all sure why he would make such a request. I looked again at the quest name 'Shiny Delivery Service 1' which indicated this was part of a quest chain which usually leads to a good amount of experience. But why 'Shiny'? I was missing something here.

"Great, here's 2-silver to pay for the jars. Please be careful not to break them," the man held out the coins, he took them not from the lockbox, but from his own pocket.

I took the coins, still not completely sure about the quest, but the experience and copper would hopefully be worth it.

CHAPTER 5

I actually had a chance to enjoy the scenery outside the village, during the short jaunt from town to the Johnson farm. The ground was uneven and covered in loose rocks, but the tall pine trees were beautiful and smelled fantastic. I wasn't sure what kind of farm could succeed in this terrain, but I would find out soon enough.

As I emerged from the forest I could finally see the farm. It was stepped and looked similar to Japanese rice patties but with corn stalks growing tall instead of rice. At the top of the corn patties, was a small farmhouse parked right next to a large barn.

I found a trail that was easy to follow, leading around the patties up to the house. As I approached, I saw a smokestack on the roof and a thin line of grey smoke steadily rising. The roof was thatched, and the walls were made of cobblestone. It was the first building I had seen in this style, where all the houses back in the village were made of wood. The barn next to the house had a cobblestone base about four-feet high, which then turned to wood the rest of the way up. It all looked rather quaint.

It did lead to a stray thought though. I was simply referring to the village, as the village. I hadn't even bothered to find out if the village had a name. Hurlig Village? I'll have to ask when I get back.

"Ho there, young fella," called a man, exiting the house. My guess would have been Farmer Johnson.

"Hello there," I greeted him. I couldn't help but notice he seemed rather guarded. "Mayor Simper sent me. I also picked up the request to help you with your harvest and to help your wife with her lost laundry."

The farmer seemed to study me for a minute. "What does Homer want with me?"

I took out the box of mason jars from my bag and presented it to him. "I was asked to deliver some mason jars."

"Well why did you not say so," said the man, his previous suspicion of me completely forgotten. He stepped forward and happily took the box of mason jars.

Quest Alert: Shiny Delivery Service 1 - Completed		
Mayor Homer Simper has asked you to deliver a case of mason jars to Farmer Johnson's		
Reward: +300 Experience, 50-Copper		

"I will have these ready for pick up tomorrow around midday bell. Would you mind coming back and picking them up then?"

Quest Alert: Shiny Delivery Service 2 (Recommended Level 2-4)		
Return to Farmer Johnson in one day.		
Reward: Experience		
Do you accept this Quest?	Yes	No

"I can do that," I answered as it suddenly dawned on me what 'Shiny' meant. Farmer Johnson was a moonshiner.

"Good lad," said Duke. "Now, you mention helping with the harvest and looking for the missing bedsheets?"

"Yes sir," I answered. "Where should I start?"

"See the empty bushels," he pointed to a stack of empty bushel baskets. "Fill a few of them up to help me out, you can leave the filled bushels at the end of the row."

"Can do," I said. I tried to sound cheerful about it, but I hated gather quests. They were always annoying, tediously so and hellishly time-consuming, despite being rather simple.

But, there was no sense putting it off. I would have to head toward the waterfall soon, hopefully, find Pwn Star 69, get my justice, and hopefully live long enough to do it.

Thankfully the quest was easy, and I was done inside of 30-minutes. I just had to pull down on the ear of corn and it broke from the stalk and dropped into the waiting bushel.

Quest Alert: Harvest Help - Completed
Farmer Johnson needs help with is his corn harvest.
Reward: +150 Experience, Fresh Corn, 20-Copper

I was rewarded a moment later with a new level.

Congratulations! You've reached Level 3!
+1 to bonus Holy Spells, +1 Intellect, +1 Charisma

The corn was a cooking ingredient or could be eaten raw for a few HP.

"Thank you for the help, sonny," said Duke, sneaking up on me and causing me to nearly spear the man.

"Happy to help," I replied, my heart still hammering in my chest. I hate when NPC's just appear when you've completed a quest. It was just unnatural, and as in this case, heart-stopping.

"My wife's clothesline is behind the house, feel free to check around for any clues," suggested the farmer. He then bent down and picked up the filled bushel and headed toward his barn, obviously planning to make a little moonshine.

The back of the house did indeed have a clothesline, but it was currently bare. As luck would have it, my 'Beast Tracking' skill popped up right away, with prints going back and forth under the clothesline. I knelt down next to the prints to see if I could identify the animal. It appeared to be some kind of wild boar, its hoof prints eventually went northeast toward the river and based on the spacing of the steps it was running fast.

I supposed I was to follow the prints. It surprised me when I didn't lose the hoof prints even once, but even if I did lose the tracks, I think I could have just followed the trail of destruction. Everywhere I looked there were broken branches, strips of torn cloth, trampled bushes and grass. If I didn't know I was tracking a boar, I would have thought a small tornado touched down here and kept going. Eventually, I heard squealing, I assumed had to be from the boar.

I was not prepared for what I found. The poor boar had managed to tear a hole in the sheet and put his head through it. If that wasn't enough, the stupid animal had run into a bramble adding tears and more holes in the sheet, and worse still, he'd managed to get himself all wrapped up and suspended in the bramble with his little piggy hooves desperately trying to find traction with the ground, despite the inch gap between the two.

On top of that mess, and what I was dreading dealing with most, was the 5 wolves biting at each other, trying to be the first to get to the easy meal. Did I mention it was 5 Alpha Wolves? Cause it was.

Quest Alert: Piggy in Peril 1 (Recommended Level 5+)		
You've found the thief, a portly piggy that is about to become wolf chow.		
Reward: Experience		
What will you choose to do?	**Protect the Boar**	**Leave the Boar to the wolves**

I wanted to sigh, this would be trouble, I could already tell. I'll try to save the little porker.

"Troublesome," I grumbled softly anyway. Now, the good news was the wolves weren't exactly being gentle with each other, all of them only had about half of their hp left. Even though their hp pools were not dropping any lower. Hopefully, it wouldn't take as much to kill them. It was still going to be tough. So, I thought it was time to break out the 'Lesser Combat Blessing' and 'Lesser Holy Imbuement', even if it did only leave me with 10 mana, it was worth the extra damage, stamina, and HP.

"Please let my first shot be a crit," I sent up a small prayer to Issara and charged in, slamming my shield into the closest wolf and driving it into the next two closest wolves, and then driving my legs harder, trying to push all three of them into the bramble in hopes of at least slowing them down. I'm sure the sergeant would have been on my tail for the bad form and sloppy footwork, but right then, I didn't care too much. I started attacking with my spear even as I drove on, using 'Jab' every time my arm came back, attacking in quick succession.

A painful bite to the back of my back leg had me shifting away and pivoting quickly, trying to put the wolves in front of me. I risked a glanced back and was pleased to see my attack had been successful, two of the alphas were dead and pinning a third. Just two left, both in front of me, at least until the third struggled free.

I thought back to my training with Sergeant Butters as I faced the two wolves. The one on the left barred his fangs and lowered slightly, I shifted forward and slammed my shield into the wolf just as it was about to attack. It interrupted the attack and I struck immediately with two rapid 'Jab' attacks. I shifted back again to ready myself for the next attack. I expected the wolf on the right to attack while the one on the left recovered but it just growled at me, actually taking a few steps back.

Meanwhile, Lefty was back on his feet and rushing headlong at me. I used 'Shield Slam' again and two more quick 'Jab' attacks to finish it off.

I should probably have paid more attention to Righty. He suddenly howled loudly which was echoed through the woods around me with three matching howls. "Oh, you stupid . . . evil . . . wolf," I complained even if the wolf couldn't understand me I hope my 'Shield Slam', 'Jab', 'Jab', 'Shield Slam', 'Jab', and 'Jab' made my displeasure clear upon his death.

I could now hear the bushes around me rustling more loudly, backup was getting close. I decided to quickly finish the still pinned alpha as he was about to break free.

The reinforcements were thankfully just Pack Wolves, but there were still three of them and they were all at full hp. It took three attacks each to kill the pack wolves, unfortunately, I wasn't as flawless as fighting the Alpha wolves. I was able to 'Shield Slam' the attack and 'Jab' the target but one of the other two wolves would always attack at the same time. I had yet to get an ability to deal with multiple targets at once. When the last wolf died, I was nearly out of stamina and my health was hanging on by a thread.

Thankfully, during the course of the fight, I had regenerated a good chunk of my mana, enough to cast 'Lesser Heal' three times, bringing me back almost 30 hp. At least I was no longer in the red, near-death state, I had been, but still not very good either.

I at least felt comfortable enough to drink my Mana Rich Water from my canteen, restoring most of my mana and then spending most of it to heal up the rest of the way. I finished off the water in my canteen then started on the stamina water to bring my SP back up to full.

I took a minute to collect the paws from all 8 wolves, glad I would make a little money on this deal. I really needed to learn some kind of scavenging skill, until I did I was literally leaving meat on the bone of the monsters I kill.

Finally, I looked back to my terrified and squealing objective. "Now, what am I supposed to do with you?"

Quest Alert: **Piggy in Peril 1 - Completed**		
You've found the thief, a portly piggy that is about to become wolf chow.		
Reward: +200 Experience		

I do love me some experience points.

Quest Alert: **Piggy in Peril 2 (Recommended Level 2-4)**		
You've found the thief, a portly piggy that has gotten himself into quite the predicament.		
Reward: Experience, Variable Piece of Gear		
What will you choose to do?	**Save the Boar**	**Kill the Boar**

After I just fought off the wolves what did the game think I was going to do. Of course, I'll save him.

It took a while to work my way through the bramble to the trapped boar, who seemed to thrash more, as I got closer to him.

"Oh, calm down you brat, I'm here to help you," I shouted at the boar after he nearly gored me with his tusks. If anything, the boar squirmed and squealed more.

I tried to get a better look at the situation. There was no way I was going to save the bedsheet. I could get it free of the brambles but then the boar would just run off again and probably get itself stuck again, or worse. I had to free the pig from his blanket.

"Hehe, pig in a blanket," I chuckled at my own joke.

I was forced to try to use my spearhead to cut the animal free. Hopefully, the boar wouldn't kill me once I did get him free. "Okay, Boris, let's get you out of this mess. I would appreciate it if you didn't kill me once I do set you free."

I cut the cloth around the boar's legs first for which, the little pig thanked me by running his suspended legs as fast as he could, kicking me several times for my troubles. "Boris, relax, you're almost free." Next, I started to cut away the cloth under him starting from his chest and trying to work back in a single cutting motion. As the last of the cloth cut free, the boar bolted and charged through the rest of bramble unhindered, disappearing from view quickly.

"You're welcome," I called after him. I picked up the scraps of cloth to return them to Mrs. Johnson and stuffed them in my bag.

I really wished I hadn't turned around just then. I was met by yet another boar, this one staring intently at me. I should also mention, this was far and away the biggest pig I'd ever seen, it was easily 10'-feet tall at the top of its shoulders or maybe taller. It had dark grey bristles covering its body and the snout was just inches away from my face was covered in scars. Don't even get me started on the tusks.

"Um, hi?" I said, my voice quavering slightly.

The boar snorted, seeming amused by my intelligent greeting.

MY THANKS! SON SAVED! GIFT!

It wasn't speaking but I felt the words were spoken into my mind or something. I unconsciously put my hand forward, open and palm up. The boar's snout covered my palm which was followed by a flash of light between my hand and boar's snout, blinding me for a moment. When my eyes cleared the boar was gone and in my hand was a little blue boar made of glass or maybe a gemstone on a short metal chain which was also blue in color.

Quest Alert: Piggy in Peril - Completed
You've found the thief, a portly piggy that has gotten himself into quite the predicament.
Reward: +500 Experience, Boar Charge Charm

Huh, how about that. I turned it over and there were symbols carved into the back of the charm, but I couldn't make out what they were. Thinking back to my earlier conversation with the Mayor, I figured they must have been runes.

Boar Charge Charm (Unique) - +10 Stamina, +10 Endurance – Equipping will teach skill 'Boar Charge' 0/100

I whistled in appreciation. I didn't hesitate for a second to equip it to my charm slot. The stats alone made it worth it, add in the skill it will eventually teach me and this was a fantastic piece of gear.

With the boar gone and my new charm equipped, I took notice of the exclamation points lining the bottom of my view.

"Ugh! Again?" I exclaimed, why the wall of text? I could only sigh in exasperation. Despite the wall of text, there were some excellent skill development, +7-levels to 'Phalanx Shield', +6-levels to 'One-Handed Polearms' and +1-level to 'Lesser Heal', and big stat gains, +7-Stamina, +7-Strength, +7-Dexterity, and +11-Endurance.

Since I had a minute to rest while I waited for my health, mana, and stamina to recover, I decided to review my current stats. In looking at my stats now, I found I had neglected my Intellect, Wisdom, and Charisma. I made a vow to work on those if I made it through the day.

Level:	3	Experience:	0.50%
Class:		Novice Warrior Priest of Issara	
HP (Health Points):			176/420
MP (Mana Points):			110/210
SP (Stamina Points):			54/360
Strength:			26
- Melee Damage Modifier			+26
Dexterity:			26
- Melee Critical Strike Chance			2.30%
- Hit Chance			61.15%
Endurance:			42
Stamina:			36
Intellect:			11
- Spell Critical Strike Chance			1.10%
Wisdom:			7
Charisma:			10
Health Regeneration per minute:			21
Mana Regeneration per minute:			4
Stamina Regeneration per minute:			18
Holy Spell Damage Bonus:			10.20
Holy Spell Healing Bonus:			7.50
Carrying Capacity in Lbs.:			130

I still need to take the scraps of the sheet back to the farm. Thankfully, it was on my way back to town, after dealing with the berries, of course. I started walking toward the river, I could hear it nearby. Following the river was supposed to lead me to the blackberry bushes, provided I followed it further east toward the waterfall. That also meant trying to find a way to punish my killer, which I still hadn't figured out how to do yet.

It was about an hour of walking to find the blackberry bushes and the place of my death.

Right away I found one of the empty bushels and started collecting the blackberries. This was considerably more difficult than the corn, the berries were smaller and hard not to crush on accident, the bushes had thorns too, cutting up my fingers and forearms, and due to their size, I had to gather many more of them to fill the bushel basket.

I was about halfway through filling my first bushel of the two I intended to fill when the world took on a red tinge.

Enemy of Issara's justice is nearby and must be punished!

I looked around wildly at first, spinning in place when suddenly I could see an outline of a person surrounded by a red glow or aura. I couldn't tell you what I thought I was going to accomplish against a level 37, but I felt compelled to confront him directly.

You've unlocked the holy spell 'Justice Bringer'

Justice Bringer	*Level:* ∞		*Experience:* ∞	
Spell Duration: 1 hour	*Spell Cast Speed: Instant*	*Spell Mana Cost: 1*	*Cool Down: 24 hours*	
Spell Effect (Active): All Adventurers and Citizens within 100 yards have their effective level lowered or raised to match your own. Does not work on enemy Citizens, Beasts or Monsters.				

Now I understood. It wasn't a God mode spell, but it made things fair. Gave me a chance to fight on equal footing. It was lucky too, I saw him before he saw me. It was then I also saw a debuff symbol next to his name. It was a red icon shaped in a mirror image of the symbol of Issara and had a counter of 139 under it.

I tried to look closer to understand when I got a system message explaining it.

> **Divine Judgement of the Goddess Issara** – Earned by dishonorably killing the Citizens of the World Tree and its adventurers 20 or more levels below their own.
>
> Only visible to the servant of Issara. The afflicted player takes +20% damage from the servant of Issara. Afflicted player deals -10% damage to the servant of Issara. Upon death all judgments are removed at the cost of 100,000 Experience per Judgement, will reduce levels until all experience penalties are removed.

And there it was, the answer to all my prayers. I knew there was still a chance I could lose but I felt emboldened.

"Pwn Star69, the Goddess Issara has judged you guilty of 139 counts of murder against the citizens of the World Tree and Adventurers more than 20 levels below your own," I stated loudly and clearly.

"Eh? What are you blabbing about noob?" he asked rather crudely, finally taking note of my presence. The man stood, not bothered by me in the slightest. He had to have about 5 years on me based on his looks and as he looked at me he snorted in laughter. I studied him trying to guess who he was, what class and such. The mages robes and a cloth headband he wore suggested he was a caster of some kind, but nothing screamed, mage, priest or warlock or any of the dozen other caster offshoots. Based on his skin tone and exaggeratedly pointy ears I guessed he was a dark elf which did suggest darker magics.

It seemed he grew tired of waiting for me to answer, he drew back his arm with a lazy kind of deliberateness, it irked me. Before he could throw I cast my newly unlocked spell 'Justice Bringer', which erupted in a wall of light all around, passing through everything harmlessly.

I wasn't sure what to expect, but to hear Pwn laughing at me was not it. For a moment I feared the spell had failed, or maybe my cast had missed. So, I was fully expecting to die, just as I did the first time. When the small pebble was released and traveling on a straight line directly for my forehead, I fully expected instant death.

I only took -1-HP of damage. Both Pwn and I were dumbfounded. Then I saw the new debuff next to the 'Divine Judgement' stack, this one had the appearance of a small balance scale and was described as 'Scaled Justice'. Now I understood, he couldn't see it and apparently didn't notice the reduction of his level.

Another pebble hit me then hit the ground doing only -1-HP damage again.

"What the hell kind of messed up hax is this?" Pwn demanded. He started chanting and this time a fireball flew from him hitting me in the face and doing -33 HP damage. Suddenly I was all too aware, a few more hits and I would be dead again anyway.

It was no longer time to talk, I needed to act. I opened up with casting Holy Smite, which hit him for a whopping -22-HP, but not as much as I would have hoped. I had to assume he had more HP than I did, and at level 3 he probably had the maximum HP without any gear buffs, which was 600.

"How the hax is a level 3 doing three hundred points of damage?" complained the mage, his face reddening in anger.

I had to move fast now because I couldn't see him letting me get any more free shots. I charged ahead as he began to cast again. I interrupted him with a 'Shield Slam', just in time to stop the spell and doing 8-damage, but more importantly, it also knocked him off balance. I follow up with a 'Jab', knocking off another chunk of his health, even though I only saw a mark of -26-HP. It was hardly any damage. I needed to do more. I used 'Jab' twice more doing -24-HP and -41-HP, the second hit a critical.

Pwn was back on the attack, this time swinging a previously hidden staff at me. I missed my timing on interrupting the swing with my 'Shield Slam' and took 35-HP, but still dealt 6-damage to him. His health was now down by a third, but I had to keep pressing the attack.

I attacked again with my spear doing -22-HP, but this time I received a nasty shock, literally. It was some kind of electric shield skill, zapping me for as much damage as I dealt. It must have been an instant cast spell, I never saw him cast it.

The shock left me slightly stunned giving Pwn time to start casting another spell, one I couldn't interrupt in time as the stun only faded just before he finished his cast, hitting me for 33-damage. He must have thought he'd have more time because he started casting again but this time I was able to hit him with a 'Shield Slam' dealing 8-damage to him and myself, but no stun effect this time. As the reflect damage seemed to be equal to the damage I dealt, I smacked him again with my 'Shield Slam', but this time there was no shock. It opened him up to three rapid 'Jab' attacks for -22-HP, -26-HP and -21-HP.

Pwn grit his teeth, anger clearly building, he swung his staff again but this time I had the timing of the attack and shifted in close hammering him with 'Shield Slam' for 20-damage, another critical and leaving him with a stun effect. I laid into him with as many 'Jab' attacks as I could muster before the stun wore off, dealing enough damage to send him to barely a flicker of health left when the stun faded.

Something changed in Pwn. I saw something new in his eyes. I now saw fear. I almost pitied him . . . almost.

"You have dishonorably murdered 139 citizens of the World Tree and Adventurers more than 20 levels below your own. Issara, the Goddess of Justice and Retribution, has judged you guilty. I 'Holy Smite' thee per the judgment of my Goddess!" I exclaimed loudly, enjoying the sight of him getting hit by the flash of holy light.

Pwn Star69 has been killed with 48- damage from 'Holy Smite'. Pwn Star69's level has been reduced to Level 1 as divine punishment and has been banished from this province.

"Holy!" I exclaimed in shock. "I love my Goddess!" It wasn't an easy fight by any stretch of the imagination, but to be able to deliver divine punishment to PK'ers was a dream come true for me, one who so hated them. It wasn't insta-jibbing, but it was a way to make things fairer. And there was nothing PK'ers hated more than fair play.

Of course, I was still curious about the judgments and how they worked, but I could honestly say I was just happy I could now do something about them and do something I would. PK'ers everywhere would pay and pay severely.

I suddenly felt as if I'd been doused in freezing cold water, shocking me, waking me up maybe. Where my previous thoughts were of revenge, feeling suddenly doused in cold water made me realize, if I did seek revenge, I would become just like them. It also made me think about what it meant to become a warrior for a Goddess of justice. It made me take a step back and truly thinking about the situation I was now in.

Over the next few minutes of self-reflection, I came to realize a few things. It seemed to me this wasn't just about stopping Player

Killers or just getting revenge on them. It was about getting justice. It was also about citizen killers as well as the unfair player killing. Players who kill the NPC's and other weak players were the targets of divine punishment. The game wants to encourage PvP, but if I had to guess the developers, or Devs for short, got tired of people complaining and created warriors of the Goddess to combat this menace to encourage fair gameplay. I would guess too, the Devs got tired of having to reprogram the murdered AI's that make up the citizens in the game.

I was worried too as the gravity of my class hit me. My class is unique, meaning only one in the entire game. How could I be expected to carry out justice all on my own? Something bound to become increasingly more difficult over the course of the next year or two. Projections already had the game set to grow from the half million players, currently enjoying all the World Tree had to offer, to millions of players, overwhelming this world as more and more Seedpods get shipped out. There had to be more to it. It was then the quest completion notice popped up, distracting me from further reflection.

Class Quest Update: Novice Warrior Priest of Issara — Your Goddess' Path Lies Ahead - Completed	
You have been charged by the Goddess you now serve to mete out punishment on the murderer you vowed to bring to justice.	
Reward:	Collect your reward from the Temple of Issara in Root City. You may also find the answers to your questions.

Okay, so, some of my concerns were answered or promised to be answered. I suppose I'd just have to wait until I got to Root City to learn more, but it was still frustrating.

Mission accomplished, what's next? It was only then I realized, I had to . . . do nothing. I no longer had any pressing or immediate concerns. I was now free to explore everything this game had to offer. No pressing time limits to complete quests. Nothing standing in the way of me learning anything and everything there was to learn, in the village from Sergeant Butters, or from the books in the Town hall. I could take my time. Spend a few weeks or even a month exploring the province and building up my skills. Finally, I could game the way I wanted to game.

I felt as if there was this giant pressing burden taken off my shoulders. I actually laughed. If anyone had seen me just then, I'm sure they would have thought I was off my rocker, but I didn't honestly care.

Eventually, I stopped my laughter. I was pretty much standing right where I had died on my first day, my first minute in the game. I couldn't help but close my eyes and breath in deeply and just appreciate this world. The fresh pine trees, sweetness from the berry bushes all around me. The sound of the river nearby filled my ears as did the bushes rustling leaves, and the birds chirping in the sky.

"Okay, let's finish collecting the berries and get the bushels back to Dogson's," I said, more to myself than anything.

****

Bye-bye Jacko Lvl 3 does 592-damage to you with 'Holy Smite'.

Bye-bye Jacko Lvl 3 has delivered divine judgment upon you at the behest of the Goddess Issara. Your level has been reduced to Level 1 as divine punishment and you have been banished from Hurlig Ridge.

You have been placed in Ash Hills – Level 1-5 province

"That's impossible," Pwn Star69 whispered, as the world came into focus around him. The ground was covered in grey ash and the few visible trees were burning. There was no sign of any wildlife and the air was rife with smoke. He was in the graveyard, apparently sent there by a complete noob. Worse, a quick check of his character menu showed his level had indeed been reduced to a lowly 1. "This is impossible!" he screamed as loud as he could.

Pown Powny Lvl 44 does 687-damage to you with a throwing needle.

Pown Powny Lvl 44 has murdered you. You will be automatically transported and revived at the nearest graveyard.

CHAPTER 6

There was a skip in my step as I made the return trip to the village. I stopped at the Johnson farm and talked to Mrs. Johnson about her bedsheet. She asked me to buy a set of new bedsheets in town for her and to drop them off the next day.

I was attacked by 4 sets of 3 Pack Wolves at different times, which eventually I realized must have belonged to the other Alpha Wolves I killed earlier while protecting the boar. It reminded me of something I once read, it said wolves are one of the only creatures known to seek revenge for members of its pack.

It was unpleasant dealing with so many at once. But after the earlier experience, I had a better handle on the process, and more strength and stamina to deal with them requiring fewer 'Shield Slam' and 'Jab' combos. Still, free stat points and a couple more skill levels to 'Phalanx Shield', 'One-Handed Polearm', and 'Lesser Heal' were appreciated.

I will say this, I was never so happy to see the village again as I was coming back. I had been in the game for less than 2 days, but it could have been 2 weeks for as much as I had accomplished. Entering the gate, I greeted Gavin, the man still looked hungover, maybe it was a permanent debuff. Remembering my earlier thoughts regarding the name of the village, I took a moment to look at the sign hanging by the village entrance 'Hurligville'. I'm not sure what about the little town warranted a 'ville' in its name, but it didn't matter enough to me to ask.

I looked at my game clock and it was still before the midafternoon bell, but not much before, if I wanted to turn in the paws. I got to the Town hall in short order and knocked on Homer's office door and went in after he called for me to enter. I deposited the 15 Pack paws and 5 Alpha paws, more than a little happy for the bounty I was about to receive.

Pack Wolf Bounty – 15 paws collected
Reward: 30-Copper, 60 Experience

That was one.

Alpha Wolf Bounty – 5 paws collected
Reward: 50-Copper, 150 Experience

And that was two. I felt a little sad I didn't get a piece of variable gear, rotten random number generator. It seemed the God of RNG still existed, even in this realm.

Okay, so as I mentioned earlier, I had fallen behind on my Intellect, Wisdom and Charisma development. It was time to get reading and see if I could catch those up. I grabbed a book, 'Trapology' before I left Town hall.

From Town hall, I went back to Ned's Sundry to refill my Mana Water and ended up buying four more canteens. Two got filled with Mana Water and I was planning on filling the other two with the stamina water from the Sergeant's training circle.

I also picked up a handful of other items that today's adventure made me realize I could use. I got a blank journal and some pencils, so I could start working on the writing skill. I also picked up a common utility knife, as I wanted to be prepared if I ever had to cut something free again. I wouldn't be struggling to use my spear to do so, thankfully there was no skill required but it was also not usable as a weapon. Finally, I picked up a stack of Adventurer's Jerky which restores +100-HP when eaten.

It cost me 55-copper for everything, but I also knew, as I progressed in the game, things would just get more and more expensive.

My final stop of the day was back to the inn to turn in the berries and retire to my room, hoping to read until dinner. I was looking forward to socializing with the locals to boost my charisma later. Other than visiting Sergeant Butters to get spear training I had no intention of leaving town until my Intellect, Wisdom, and Charisma hit their caps for level 3. Except for my trip back to the Johnson farm tomorrow, of course, but nothing there should prevent me from coming straight back to my room in the inn to continue reading and studying.

Was it boring to grind stat points? Certainly, but I also knew from reading on the forums, past level 5 and the base of 50 stat points and 100 endurance, every point was a nightmarish grind. I might have to kill a hundred monsters 3-4 levels above my own to get even one point of strength. You could run a hundred miles for a single point of stamina. I had also read on the forums, there were quests starting at level 5 rewarding +1 to a stat of your choice, but those were few and far between. I know the counter-argument, I can just level up and then the stat points will come easier, well they don't. Stat points get their own experience bars, each level requiring more experience than the last. At least, according to the forums.

So, I happily sat in my room, reading 'The Trained Eye', which I had yet to complete. That said, I did start over, but this time I made notes in my new journal. I noted what the technique was in a condensed format, as well as what I thought it might do for me. I did this for each training technique as I read through the book and before I knew it I had reached the end of the book and had a list of twenty-one training techniques. I also received system messages informing me I had gained +3 Intellect and +5 Wisdom. The Wisdom increase honestly surprised me, I'm not sure why I gained more Wisdom than Intellect. However, I wasn't going to complain about the mana regeneration boost, I did need it. If I wanted to make any real progress leveling up my, albeit limited, selection of spells, I would need to either increase my mana pool or mana regeneration.

I set the book and my journal aside, it was about time for dinner and I was looking forward to the chicken pot pie and the blackberry pie, I had been promised for dinner tonight.

"Good evening, Dogson," I greeted the proprietor and bartender.

"Evening, Bye-bye, you have still got about 20 minutes until dinner will be served," he added.

"Sure, can I get a pint. Something not as strong as what you served me last night," I requested.

Dogson smirked a little, then filled a pint, this time the ale was a reddish gold. This beer, I knew only too well as an amber ale, my favorite. He set it before me, "Clan Rashisa Amber Lager."

"Clan Rashisa?" I asked.

"An Orc clan from the Rashisan Highlands," answered Dogson

Orc's make beer? I was admittedly curious about how it would taste. I was not disappointed. It might have been the best amber ale I'd ever had and even if it wasn't it was still delicious. Orc's don't just make beer, they make good beer. Who knew?

"Started without us I see," said a voice, drawing my attention away from my beer. I turned to look, it one of the two ogres I had met outside of Ned's Sundry. For some reason, whenever I heard her

116

speak, I couldn't help but imagine a pink-haired pixie on a sugar high, which did not fit with the image of the ogre before me.

"Can't fault me for having a beer before dinner. Especially not a good beer," I retorted before turning to face the pair.

"I suppose not," she replied grinning. Though the grin was a little distorted as her head was cocked to the side as she was too tall for the room. Just behind her, I could see Olaf had it worse.

"Why don't we sit," I motioned to the open couches around the fireplace.

"Oh, thank God," said Olaf. "Was expecting to have to use 2 chairs, one for each cheek." The man sat heavily upon the couch, easily covering half of it. Once Micaela sat next to him, there was no more couch to be had.

I laughed as did Micaela. "Where do you guys usually stay if not at the inn?" I took my own seat in an armchair just across from the pair.

"The mine has a bunkhouse for its workers," answered Olaf. "They have oversized cots and chairs designed for the larger races. Food too. It's kind of . . . meh but it beats trying to stay at an inn where we just don't fit. I heard Root City has inns with accommodations for all the races."

"I heard the same, I also heard every store and shop is built to accommodate all the races too," I added in.

"All the dungeons and large group dungeon raids are supposed to be large enough for all the races, and then some," Micaela added. "I'm sure the designers thought of almost everything. Unfortunately, there are just some provinces that weren't given the same level of design thought. I've even heard some provinces are hostile toward certain races."

"It makes it all very realistic," I said, sipping at my beer, trying to make it last until dinner. "So how goes the mining?"

"Not bad at all," said Olaf, who was now grinning broadly, looking just a little too pleased with himself.

"And just why do you look so pleased?" I asked curiously.

He leaned forward and motioned for me to do the same. "I hit a geode today," he whispered.

"What's that?" I asked. I honestly knew nothing about mining.

"It's a rock egg, filled with a bunch of rare gems," he answered, then leaned back again.

I leaned back again. "So, it's valuable?"

He grunted and nodded slightly. "I've already dropped what was inside it in the mail to our broker. I don't know the going rates for gems, but I suspect we won't have to mine again if we don't want to."

"That valuable?" I asked.

"Oh yeah," said Micaela. "Anyway, best not to talk of such things too loudly. We won't know anything for certain for a few days."

"Well congratulations then," I said happily.

"Can I get you folks something drink?" the only waitress asked. "How about you, sugar? Need a refill?" she turned and asked me, leaning in way too close and pushing her cleavage into my face.

I think I just solved the mystery of who I was flirting with the night before. "You bet, doll," I tried to flirt.

"Oh, you stop," she said, playfully swatting my arm. "I will be back with your refill in a minute. You want your dinner too?"

"Please, thank you. Can I get a couple of extra-large servings for my friends too? Two flagons of Rashisa Ale for them as well?" I asked, possibly ogling her a little too long.

"Alright, sugar," she said in a sultry voice, giving me a wink before she sauntered off.

"Oh, you dog," said Olaf, barely containing his laughter.

"Hey, +1-Charisma from flirting," I defended myself, though I had to admit. If the opportunity truly presented itself, I'd be a damned fool not to indulge.

"All men are pigs," said Micaela, trying to look affronted but failing. I could see the corners of her mouth twitching trying not to smile and join her husband in laughing at me.

"Yeah, yeah, yeah, what else is new?" I asked, a chagrined smile on my face.

"So, flirting builds charisma?" asked Olaf, finally getting his laughter under control.

"Yeah, just about any kind of positive socializing. I guess I got pretty hammered last night with one of the guards. From what I hear, I flirted, told a few entertaining stories and when I woke up the morning I'd gained a few points of charisma."

"So, you're saying getting drunk is a good idea?" asked Olaf, a mischievous spark behind his eyes.

"If I say yes, will I be waking up hungover again?" I asked. Honestly, I wasn't in the mood to get so drunk again.

Micaela and Olaf both laughed loudly, clearly enjoying themselves.

"I'd love to get good and pissed with you. but we have work in the morning. I promise though, as soon as we've paid off our Seedpods we'll get well and truly pissed together," offered Olaf.

"Deal," I replied. I do love the British, good accents and fun expressions.

Eventually, dinner turned up, I flirted more with the waitress, who thanks to Micaela, I learned was named Trish. We all drank a few beers, enjoyed conversation. Eventually built up a crowd as we started sharing stories and past exploits.

"Alas, late bell has tolled," said Olaf, hearing the chime. "It is about time the missus and me got back to the mine."

"So soon?" I asked. I was having a grand time. I had a good buzz going, I was drunk for sure, but not too drunk. I wouldn't forget everything in the morning.

"Yeah, sho shoon?" echoed Micaela. The poor girl was completely sloshed and would definitely be feeling it in the morning.

"I blame you for this," said Olaf, sighing loudly.

"Harsh but fair," I said with a small laugh.

"Still, it was a good night. Even got a few points of charisma myself. I'm sure the wife did too but . . . well . . ." he sighed, exasperation apparent.

"I understand," I replied.

Olaf carefully guided his wife out of the inn. Once outside the man lifted her into his arms. "We'll have to do this again soon."

"You know where to find me," I said, motioning to the inn behind me.

"That we do," he replied, then gave a final wave and started his walk home.

Back inside the inn, I went back to the bar to settle up with Dogson before turning in for the night.

I was awoken again, by a new miserable rooster cock-a-doodle-do-ing, right outside my window. Through sheer force of will, I refrained from executing it, as I wasn't nearly so hungover. Just a pinch of a headache. I dressed and made my way downstairs for breakfast.

Dogson presented me with a pint again. I didn't feel the hangover was severe enough to warrant hair of the dog, but I drank it anyway. Another hearty breakfast and I was out the door.

"Morning Sergeant," I greeted the man, as I came around to the back of the barracks.

"Morning," he said in his standard gruff manner. "So, what are you looking for today?"

"Training as usual," I replied.

"I kind of figured that part out already. I meant what do you want to learn?" he asked.

"Oh," I said dumbly. "Well, I need a technique for dealing with multiple opponents at the same time."

"I have just the skill," he said with a grin.

I was beginning to dread this man's grin. I had already gotten the impression, his grinning meant bad things for me, well, not bad but certainly not good. "How do we start?" I asked, a little reluctant.

"Well, this one is pretty easy as you already know 'Jab'. This skill uses the base skill of 'Jab' and escalates it," he explained.

I had a feeling I knew where this was going. "Multi-Jab?"

"More or less," he replied. "So, this is a purely offensive skill. You're going to 'Jab' multiple times as rapidly as you can, creating a cone of damage directly in front of you. Now, each 'Jab' will not do as much damage as your regular 'Jab' attack, but it doesn't matter. You will be striking so many times so quickly, you will make up for the damage loss. As I said, this sacrifices defense for all-out offense, this is one of the few skills I will teach you that does so."

I nodded, picturing what he wanted in my head.

"So, the only thing to do is to start doing it," instructed Sergeant Butters. He motioned to a pair of dummies placed next to each other. "Get to it."

I started out standing at attack range and used 'Jab' once to test the range.

"Do not start in range of the targets. In real combat, you will always have to shift in or out to attack. Do not get lazy now."

I shifted back away. I shifted in and used 'Jab' then triggered it again.

"Stop!" ordered Sergeant Butters. "Do not use 'Jab'. I told you this is similar to 'Jab', but not 'Jab' itself. If you use the existing skill, then all you're doing is using your skill. You need to start by jabbing, then continue jabbing repeatedly. Not with the skill, but with your own arm. Also, accuracy with this technique is actually a detriment. You are not trying to hit the same point on the target. You are supposed to be trying to cover an area with damaging spear thrusts your targets will have no way of a dodging or predicting. Now, try again."

Okay, so I wasn't supposed to use 'Jab'. I shifted in again this time I attacked, moving as if I was going to 'Jab', but instead I used my arm alone to do it. Then I thrust again, and again, but on the fourth attack my hand hit my shield with a meaty thud, followed by me dropping the spear and cradling my hand, which now carried a debuff 'crippled'.

"I told you to sacrifice defense," warned Sergeant Butters.

I took the liberty of casting a few 'Lesser Heal' spells on myself, then I tried to target my hand directly which successfully remove the 'crippled' debuff to my great pleasure.

"Try again," ordered Butters.

And so, I did. This time as I shifted in, I pulled my shield back, still partially covering my face, but giving the arm holding the spear, free range of motion. I attacked the dummies, arm forward, all the way back, arm forward, all the way back. It was ridiculously slow. No way was this going to get to a rapid speed. I need to shorten my thrust, either not go so far forward or not pull back as far.

I shifted back again, my body reclaiming my natural spear and shield stance automatically. I thought it was cool. It had only been a few days, and I was already building muscle memory.

I shifted forward again, my shield arm already pulling back as my spear arm shot forward hard when it reached full length my arm naturally bounced back but I couldn't allow my arm to come all the way back, so I thrust forward again just as my elbow started to bend. Thrust, rebound, thrust, rebound. I had found a rhythm to my attack. I was so close. Unfortunately, my stamina quickly approached depletion, so I shifted back.

"Better," said Sergeant Butters. "Get some water, recover a little and then get back to it."

I filled my canteen and the two spares I had picked up the day before. Once my stamina had refilled I went back to it. It didn't take very long to get back into the rhythm of the attack.

"Good, now you need to start moving faster. Do not worry about being accurate here. You need to be fast and attack with reckless abandon. Create a cone of damage in front of yourself," the sergeant instructed.

I tried to give up control as instructed, but it wasn't easy for me. It was hard to stop focusing on a target and just attack recklessly, trying to push as much speed out of my arm as possible.

You've learned 'One-Handed Polearm' subskill 'Rapid Striking'.

One-Handed Polearms	Level: 19	Experience: 64.22%
Current Damage Modifiers	Damage: +9.5	Critical Strike Chance: +0.95%
Subskill: Rapid Striking	Damage: -2 Strikes: 10 Cone: 30^0	Skill Stamina Cost: 49

I love this game so much right now. Yeah, it bites that 'Rapid Striking' reduces the damage of each spear thrust, but the 10 attacks in a row more than make up for it, especially an attack capable of hitting multiple targets.

"Good work," said Butters. "Now, one last tip. Always aim for the center of your group of targets. Do not aim for center mass but attack the center of your target area. You have two dummies in front of you, right? Aim for the space between them. If there were three and they were spaced equally from each other, then aim for the one in the middle. Got it?"

"Yeah, got it," I answered.

"Good, now get out of here. I have more work to do and I am sure you are just itching to test out your new skill on some poor, unsuspecting woodland critters."

"Those wolves have it coming," I joked with him.

"Maybe they do, maybe they do not. You ever consider, maybe we have it coming? We are invading their home turf, no? Just food for thought," he offered.

That was very philosophical. I hadn't expected that from the sergeant. If I were honest with myself, I don't even think I would have expected that from any other NPC either. It also got me wondering about the wolves, where did they come from? Why were they such a problem for Hurligville?

Without giving it much thought, I returned to the Town hall and sat on the steps to wait for the building to open. I wanted to ask the mayor about it. It shouldn't have been a mystery, wolves have got to eat too, but why attack humans? Wasn't the forest full of easier prey? Did something happen to agitate the wolves?

Before I knew it, the mayor had arrived.

"Morning Mayor Simper," I greeted him.

"Morning Bye-bye, having a productive morning already?"

"Somewhat, I got in some training with Sergeant Butters."

"Good man, we are lucky to have him. You know, he used to be a knight in service to King Leopold the 8th?" asked Homer, pride beaming on his face.

"I had no idea," and I truly didn't. To think, the sergeant was actually a knight. Shouldn't he be an officer? If it is true, why is he a sergeant now?

"I do not know his whole story, so do not ask. What I do know is not for me to share, so again, do not ask," said the mayor, cutting me off, clearly seeing I had questions. "Now, I am just guessing, but you did not come here to discuss the sergeant's past, so why not see what I can do to help you this fine morning?"

He was right, the mystery of Sergeant Butters could wait. I had another mystery just clawing at me. "I was wondering about the wolves."

"What about them? They are a menace. What more is there to know?" asked the mayor, confused by my question.

"I don't know, they just seem way too aggressive. Wolves don't usually encroach upon a settlement this large the way these do," I explained my reasoning for being curious.

125

"Huh," said the Mayor, a thoughtful look on his face. "I cannot say I know either. It has been this way since before I was born, as far as I know anyway. Maybe the town history will give you a clue." He gestured toward the bookshelf.

Quest Alert: Breaking the curse of the Wolves 1 (Recommended Level 4-5)		
Mayor Simper has suggested looking into the town history for the source of the wolf problem.		
Reward: Experience		
Do you accept this Quest?	Yes	No

"I'll definitely look into it," I said, accepting the quest. This was the kind of thing I gamed for. A mystery to be solved. And the way it was worded, could there be an actual curse placed upon the village?

"Good luck to you. Let me know what you find out. Have a good afternoon," he said his farewell, leaving me to the bookshelf, while he went back into his office.

That was something I had noticed as well. The NPC interactions were smoothing out. On the first day, I couldn't help but notice how choppy and incomplete they seemed. I wonder if the AI was learning the more it interacted. I wondered, if the first-day behavior was learned based on their interactions with other players, then it might make more sense. It was a fact, most players talk to NPC's only long enough to get a quest before they bolt from the room to go do it. My first day here, it seemed the NPC's expected me to bolt the instant I got the quest, so they had no frame of reference for how to end a conversation, or maybe they were just surprised I stuck around. It was just a thought and one I couldn't prove but still . . . more food for thought.

Snapping out of my internal thoughts, I looked to the bookshelf for the town history. I found the book on the third shelf from the top, it was 'Hurligville Vol I: The Founding' and 'Hurligville Vol II: Years 5-10'. There were at least twenty more volumes each covering a 10-year time span. This might take me a while to read through all of it.

I looked at the game clock to figure out my next move, it was just about 10:00 already. I stuck the first two volumes in my bag. It was time to head for Farmer Johnsons to pick up the mayor's moonshine. Why did I feel a hangover coming to me in the near future?

CHAPTER 7

The walk to the farm was quiet. No wolf attacks or other little critters giving me troubles. It wasn't until I was about halfway to the farm I noticed the sky was darkening ahead of me as if a storm was brewing. Then I smelled smoke and started running. When I emerged from the woods, Duke's fields were on fire as was the barn and house.

"Oh, no," I whispered in shock. I started sprinting for the house, hoping to get there in time to help. I found Duke dragging his wife out of the house and ran to help him.

"Duke," I called to him, as I got closer.

"Help me move her!" he called back as he worked to drag his wife clear of the burning house.

I immediately lifted his wife's feet and helped him carry her away from the house and the burning fields. There was so much smoke, it was hard to breathe in the suffocating heat. I have no idea how Duke was able to run into the house and pull his wife out. I was especially shocked as I got a closer look at Duke. His shoulder was bloody, a stab wound was steadily leaking blood. Then I checked his wife. She had a bloody gash on her forehead and cut across her stomach bleeding profusely. I was surprised either of them survived as low as their health bars appeared to be.

Once we set her down, Duke simply held on to her, whispering assurances.

I started to chain cast as many 'Lesser Heal' spells as I could, targeting the cut in her stomach, unsure if targeted casting even worked. I had tried a few times to target a specific injury while training with Sergeant Butter when I got hurt training. It seemed to work, but I just wasn't certain. When my mana pool emptied, I drank mana water and started again. After completely emptying two of my canteens I'd finally stabilized her. She was weak but didn't appear to be in danger of dying.

Once I knew she was going to be okay, I cast a few on Duke as well, at least until the bleeding had stopped. I finally had a chance to look up from my work. How hadn't I noticed the look on Duke's face? He stared at me with such gratitude. I can't recall ever seeing such gratitude from someone, not in real life. "You never told me you were a priest."

"It didn't matter," I said.

"I can never thank you enough for saving her," he said, elated didn't begin to convey how happy he was. "Tell me, what God or Goddess you serve, and I will offer her prayers of gratitude for the rest of my days."

"I serve Issara, Goddess of justice and retribution," I answered.

Duke seemed genuinely surprised by my answer then I saw a dark look cross his face. "Priest of Issara, I charge you, seek justice for what transpired here today. Hunt down the two bandits who burned my farm and tried to murder my wife and I. Please, I beg you, bring us justice," his last words more of a plea than the charge he started out.

Class Quest Alert: Seek Justice for Farmer Johnson and his wife (Recommended Level 4-5)

Duke Johnson's farm has been sacked by a pair of bandits. You have been charged to serve justice and capture or eliminate the criminals. Time Limit 02:00:00		
Reward: Experience, Bounty Marker, Hidden		
Do you accept this Quest?	**Yes**	**No**

I felt this man's pain, he may have been an NPC, but I only saw a person asking . . . begging for justice. "Of course, I will see Issara's justice done, I could do no less."

"Thank you, priest," he said, head bowed reverently.

"Can you tell me anything about the bandits? Which direction they went would be very helpful" I requested, it wouldn't do me any good to run off without some idea where to go.

"They were trolls, both ran south toward the road. I would bet they are making a run for the portal to the World Tree. If you hurry, you can catch up to them. They did not have horses or those weird lizards' trolls are known to ride on, so they will be on foot I think," answered Duke.

"Did you see any weapons?"

"One had two daggers, the other a big sword."

"What did they steal? I'll be sure to bring it back if I can."

"They took what little money we had and my wife's jewelry. And worst of all, they stole all my moonshine," Duke answered. He didn't look upset about the lost items until he spoke of the lost hooch. I badly want to shake my head in disbelief.

Quest Alert: Shiny Delivery Service 2 - Complete
Return to Farmer Johnson in one day.
Reward: +200 Experience

I couldn't believe this quest was still going, let alone considered completed. I suppose I shouldn't have been too surprised it was then followed up.

Quest Alert: Shiny Delivery Service 3 (Recommended Level 3-5)		
Farmer Johnson's moonshine has been stolen and asks you to recover it from the thieves.		
Reward: Experience, 2-Silver, Variable Piece of Gear		
Do you accept this Quest?	Yes	No

"I'll get your booze back if I can. Will you be okay to get back to town?"

"We will, as soon as the missus awakens, we will make our way there," he answered.

"Okay, I'll be going."

"The road is to the south but if you go southeast you might be able to cut them off sooner," he advised, seeing me already in motion.

"Thanks, I'll meet you in town shortly," I replied, already starting to pick up some speed as I ran southeast. I didn't know if this was the work of other players, or if this was an area event, or if it was simply part of a quest chain, and I'm not sure I even cared. Right now, I just wanted to get justice for the farmer and his wife.

I had to stop after about 20-minutes of running to drink from one of the stamina canteens. Then ran again for another twenty until I hit the road. I know 'Beast Tracking' only works on animals, but it did give me knowledge enough to be able to check the road for recent activity. As far as I was able to discern, the road hadn't been touched, except by a few wolves running across it chasing a deer and none of their prints were broken by anyone else tracking through them.

I kind of grinned a little, I had beat them here and had a chance to set up an ambush. Unfortunately, I had no skill in setting up traps and I probably wouldn't have had time as I could now hear voices coming up the road. I had very few choices for an ambush. If I could find a tall tree with a branch that extended over the road, I could drop on top of them. I just had to hope they wouldn't notice me, which meant the objective tree needed to have plenty of leaves for coverage if I was going to surprise them.

I ran up the road, continuing easterly looking for just the right tree. I found the perfect tree about 500-yards up the road. I climbed the tree, which wasn't as difficult as I expected it to be. My original assumption was that it would require a skill of some kind, but it didn't.

Once I had climbed up the tree and out clambered out on a limb overhanging the road, I tried to focus on slowing my breathing, moving as little as possible, waiting for the two bandits to approach.

I saw the two trolls coming up the road, laughing and joking as they passed a mason jar back and forth between them. They were NPC's both labeled accordingly, <Troll Bandit Lvl 4> and <Troll Cutthroat Lvl 3>, both baring the debuff 'Inebriated'.

Inebriated – Earned by consuming too much alcohol. Causes -10 Dexterity -10 Intellect

I knew I would need to kill the bandit first if I wanted any chance of surviving this encounter.

It was an agonizing two minutes of waiting for them to walk under me. Two minutes of not moving or twitching. Two minutes of willing myself not to sweat or even breathe heavily. And finally, the moment was here, I simply fell forward with my spear right in front of me, lancing forward as I fell. I speared the <Troll Bandit Lvl 4> through the back of his neck causing him to drop to the ground. With his spinal column severed from one perfect strike, he was little more than a puppet with its strings cut. I didn't pay any attention to it when I was notified of the critical strike and bonus damage for ambushing the target. Nor did I pay attention to the +60-Experience killing the troll had just awarded me.

Instead, I was quickly scrambling back to my feet and desperately pulling my spear free of the corpse. The cutthroat looked shocked, but only for a moment before he was reaching for the large sword strapped across his back. I shifted into the cutthroat and used my 'Shield Slam' preventing him from even drawing his weapon. I then followed up with a pair of 'Jab' attacks hitting his left arm and shoulder causing a crippled limb debuff. I was about to finish him when the unexpected happened.

"Wait, stop, I surrender," grunted the troll, his only good hand, and arm trying to stop the bleeding from his other arm. As he said it, he dropped to his knees with his head bowed.

I was sorely tempted to just finish him off but refrained. I served justice, not revenge even if you could argue retribution was the same as revenge. "Drop your sword, armor, bags and anything else you may be carrying except for the clothes you're wearing." I kept my spear ready to strike if he tried anything. I saw then the troll gained a debuff 'Captured' which was followed by giving me another +60-experience.

The troll moved slowly but eventually dropped everything I could see. "Now, face down in the dirt," I ordered. I didn't have anything to tie him up with so, for now, I'd have to improvise and hope the captured debuff was sufficient to hold him.

With the trolls face firmly planted in the ground, I picked up everything the troll dropped. Then I looted the other guy clean, except again for his clothes.

"Has your arm stopped bleeding?" I asked, giving the troll a prodding with the tip of my spear.

"Looks like," he replied. I know trolls get a regeneration bonus, but I wasn't sure how strong it was. I checked him again, the health was still in the yellow and he still had the crippled debuff on his arm but there was no longer a bleed effect.

"Okay, get up, pick up your buddy's body with your good arm. We're going back to the village where you will face justice," I stated clearly. The troll looked afraid, he was resigned to his fate. He hefted the dead body up over his good shoulder and started trudging back down the road.

It took about an hour and a half to make the walk, taking one short break for some water. I was met about a hundred yards from the village by six of the village guards including Sergeant Butters.

"Well now, this is quite the surprise," greeted Butters, his grizzled mug grinning from ear to ear.

"Did Duke and his wife make it to the village?" I asked, worried about the farmer.

"Aye, he and the missus showed about fifteen minutes ago, both of them pretty banged up but alive. From what they said, without you, they certainly would have perished."

I nodded, feeling relief. "Thank goodness. These two were the ones responsible," I said, prodding the still living troll for good measure, making him stumble forward a step.

"Good man," said Butters, then turning to his men. "Grunk and Teve, take the prisoner and the corpse into custody. Put the survivor in the stocks and lay out his partner next to him. We will have Duke identify them later." He then turned back to me. "Did you take their stuff?"

"Yeah, here it is," I removed all their stuff from my inventory and handed it over to him. Everything except for the stolen hooch, which was a quest item and wouldn't let me hand it over. He motioned for his remaining men to collect the stuff. "I have an item Duke asked me to retrieve for him, is it okay if I give it back to him directly?"

"Yeah, should probably give him back these too," Sergeant Butters passed an item back to me, a quick look and I put in my bag. "As for the rest, you will get your share once we have fully dealt with the situation," he said, confusing me slightly.

"What share?" I asked, confused by the statement.

"Spoils, son. You captured them, you get a share of the spoils from the things they had in their possession," he explained. "But first we have to go through it all and see what they had, and what was stolen, or at least reported stolen, then see about returning it. Should take about a week, maybe two. It all depends on their bounties if they have any, but I am sure a fine upstanding pair of bandits such as these two has at least one or two of them apiece. Just have to wait for a runner to go to the Root City bounty offices and gather the necessary information."

"Oh," was my eloquent and intelligent reply. I hadn't heard anything about this, it certainly made for an interesting aspect of the game. Bounties on bandits was an old idea, but it usually required you just bring back proof of death in such games. The idea of being able to capture an enemy combatant was completely new.

"Don't worry about it, kid. For now, I'm sure Duke and his wife will be more than happy to see you are alright. They are in the

Town hall now with Mayor Semper and Priestess Trinico who was working on healing them up last I saw," explained Butters.

Suddenly, I was feeling drained as the adrenaline, which had been coursing through me just moments before, had suddenly dropped off. I really just wanted to return to the inn and take a nap, but I had a pair of quests to finish first.

It was a short walk back to town with Butters and the other guards and after a few quick farewells and promises to get drinks later I trudged through the streets to the Town hall.

Immediately, I was greeted by Margie who escorted me to the mayor's office. Inside, every seat was filled, mostly by people I recognized but there were two I hadn't met yet.

"Ah, Bye-bye, you are back," the mayor greeted me boisterously. "Did everything go well? Were you able to catch the brigands?"

"Yes sir, killed one but captured the other. I've already turned over the prisoner and body to Sergeant Butters and his men. I also turned over all their property," I answered. I felt it would be best to be thorough.

"All the property?" asked Duke, he sounded slightly unsettled.

"All but the personal item you asked me to collect for you, but we can go over that in private later if you are alright with waiting a little while," I answered, hoping it would be sufficient, I still didn't know the other two people in the room.

"I am afraid I will have to insist you return the personal item now," said one of the two people I hadn't met yet. This <Guard Lieutenant Lvl 9> was a soldier, but different from the guards I'd been dealing with. This man had an arrogance to him I didn't care

136

for. This must have been the much-ridiculed Lieutenant, the guards had complained about.

"Bye-bye, this is Lieutenant Graves. He oversees the garrison," explained the mayor, I couldn't help but notice the man looked slightly crestfallen.

"Very well," I said, pulling the two wedding bands Butter had me hold onto, I guess he was thinking Duke and his wife would want them back immediately. Or he knew what I was bringing back to Duke and felt the need to protect them and me. "Here you are Duke, Mrs. Johnson," I presented them both with the rings.

"Please Bye-bye, I think you can safely call me Mary now," said Mrs. Johnson, happily taking her ring and slipping it back on.

"I see," said Graves stiffly. I could see he was expecting something entirely different. Meanwhile, both the mayor and Duke looked the parts of a pair of cats just ate an entire opera of canaries. "I will go question the prisoner. Good day gentlemen." The man said nothing further and left, but not before giving me the stink eye.

I wasn't sad to see the Lieutenant go.

"I suppose I should move on as well," said the last person, an older woman in white robes, I assumed she was Priestess Trinico, her nameplate changed instantly from <High Priestess Lvl 34> to <High Priestess Trinico Lvl 34>. She gave a few farewells to everyone in the room and nod of respect to me before she too departed.

"You brilliant boy," said the mayor, positively giddy.

"I have the other item but again, we can deal with that once we can be sure Graves isn't going to suddenly pop back in. Are you two alright?" I asked, concerned for both Duke and Mary.

"We are fine, you patched us up just enough to get back here and Trini patched us up the rest of way," said Mary, reassuring me

137

and lightly squeezing my forearm in a surprisingly comforting manner.

I couldn't help but sigh in relief. "Before I forget," I began as I removed the bedsheets from my bag and handed them to Mary. She snorted in amusement once then she began to laugh heartily, wiping at a few tears in her eyes.

Quest Alert: Laundry Service - Complete
Mrs. Johnson has asked you to buy a new set of bedsheets to replace the sheets destroyed by the boar.
Reward: +40 Experience, 10-Copper

"I do not get it," said Duke, looking from Mary to me and back again. "You know our house just burned to the ground, right? Bed and all?"

"Oh, he gets it, Duke, it is what makes it funny," said Mary, wiping away a few tears of laughter.

"Well then, I will start to organize some volunteers to help with rebuilding your farm. I am afraid there is nothing we can do about the lost crops but not all is lost. At least you still have what was retrieved to sell, it should be enough to rebuild the house, but the barn may take some time," stated Homer, trying to provide solutions to their problems and offer hope. "For now, I will arrange a room for you at Dogson's, it is the least I can do."

"Mind me asking about Graves? Why did I get the feeling he was looking for the moonshine?"

"Because he was. He does seem to have a hatred of anything alcohol related, even the beers and spirits Dogson has. Now, Dogson acquires his through legal and licensed means, and as such Graves cannot touch him. So, when he had a chance to nab Duke for making a less than legal beverage the man jumped at it. I should warn you.

You have probably made an enemy of him now, too." The mayor's explanation was clear enough. However, to me, it meant Graves might have an interesting and unique backstory worth investigating.

But that could come later.

"Duke, would you agree justice has been served?" I asked.

"Assuming you got the right guys and given you have returned our wedding rings, I think it is safe to assume you got the right guys. As such, I would say yes, justice is served."

Class Quest Alert: Seek Justice for Farmer Johnson and his wife - Completed
Duke Johnson's farm has been sacked by a pair of bandits. You have been charged to serve justice and capture or eliminate the criminals. Time Limit 02:00:00
Reward: +500 Experience, Bounty Marker, Collect your reward from the Temple of Issara at Root City.

That was well-earned experience.

Congratulations! You've reached Level 4!
+1 to bonus Holy Spells, +1 Intellect, +1 Charisma

So much for a quiet day of reading. And of course, there were a bunch of exclamation points in the corner which I had ignored earlier.

I wasn't sure what to expect as the stats I usually raised were already maxed out for level 3. So, when I opened the messages I was pleased. Very pleased. This was different from what I thought it would be. There were no stat increases except for two new levels in 'Lesser Heal'. What was surprising was the two new skills or rather skill and subskill, 'Stealth' and 'Ambush'

Stealth	*Level: 1*	*Experience:* 0.00%
Non-Combat	*Chance of Being*	*Skill Stamina Cost:* 2 per second

Movement: Speed Reduced by 80%	Revealed: 60.00%	
Subskill: Ambush	Critical Strike Chance: 100.00%	Skill Stamina Cost: 20

Now that was awesome.

I stayed in the mayor's office for a little while as they conversed, asking the occasional question, taking in some of the town gossips and getting a few names of people I should probably talk to as they may lead to a quest or two or just have interesting lore to them.

"Alright, it is about time to close up the office," Homer finally said. "I am sure Graves is long gone so if you do not mind completing your delivery, I am sure Duke and his wife would appreciate a good meal and some real rest."

So, I handed over the moonshine to Duke.

Quest Alert: Shiny Delivery Service 3 - Completed
Farmer Johnson's moonshine has been stolen and asks you to recover it from the thieves.
Reward: +200 Experience, 2-Silver, Farmer's Ring of Stamina

"Thank you again," said Duke. "I want you to have this," he then dropped a ring in my hand, not his wedding ring either. I'm not sure how he held onto it with the recent robbery but figuring it was just one of those game things, I was happy to accept the ring. I was even happier when I saw what the ring gave me, Farmer's Ring of Stamina which gave me +2 Stamina and +4 Stamina Regeneration.

"I was happy to help," I replied. I was happy to help, the ring was nice, but I had actually helped someone. It didn't feel as if it was just another NPC for a quest, but a real person. I knew then if I wasn't careful, this place could become more real to me than the real world and that would be a slippery slope into bad places.

A few more farewells and I walked over to Dogson's with the Johnsons in tow. I said farewell to them as they went to talk to Dogson himself. I, in turn, went straight to my room intent to take a nap.

I was woken from my nap by a knock on the door and Dogson advising me dinner would be starting soon. I didn't remember setting a wakeup call, but I was happy for it, the growl of my stomach agreed.

Dinner was good, a roast of some kind of meat, potatoes, carrots and another slice of pie. I had a few pints of the Orcish ale I fell in love with the day before. I ended my day recounting the day's adventures for the patrons willing to listen. I flirted more with Trish but made no progress but did earn a few more points of charisma for my efforts.

As I was about to head upstairs to sleep, Dogson signaled me over.

"How can I help you, my good man?" I asked a bit more gregariously than I normally would, thanks to the liquid courage I had consumed.

"Before you head off to bed, might I suggest you take a bath or shower, you have begun to ripen," he advised me.

In the three days since I'd been here, I hadn't used the bathroom once which was normal for games for the most part. However, I hadn't given a single thought to cleanliness. I sweat plenty with all the training I do. I had killed animals and been splashed with blood, I could still see some of the stains on my clothes. So, I did the one thing I hadn't considered, gave myself a pit check and nearly choked.

"Do you do laundry too?" I asked.

"Thank Sirius, you asked. I was thinking about simply stealing your clothes while you bathed," he said, a clear look of relief on his face.

"Do you have some spare clothes I could use for the night, while these are washed?"

"If you were to look in your armoire you will find a robe, pajamas and fresh towels," he answered, and boy did I feel stupid for not looking earlier. "You can put your dirty clothes in a basket in the washroom and they will be returned to your room first thing in the morning clean. We can patch up any damages for anything cloth or leather, but anything chainmail or heavier will have to be sent out to a blacksmith and they have a 48-hour turnaround for the most part."

"That would be great if they could be repaired."

"Excellent, washrooms are the end of each floor hallway, only one occupant permitted at a time, so you do not have to worry about anyone walking in on you or walking in on someone else," he explained.

"What if I wanted company in the bath?"

"This is a hotel, not a brothel. Everyone uses those washrooms, so any kind of activity other than bathing is strictly prohibited. And if you are thinking about trying to sneak someone in, do not bother. I paid a mage to put a barrier on each door only allowing one person in at a time."

"I wasn't going to, I was just curious, I swear," I said, trying to sound as innocent as I could.

"I am sure you were," said Dogson flatly, but I could see the corner of his mouth twitching a little trying not to laugh.

"Well, then, off to the bath I go," I stated. I was quick to my room to grab a towel, pajamas and a robe which I took with me to the bath. It was thankfully unoccupied. I could have taken a quick shower, but the bath was appreciated. I could feel the hot water seep into my joints and muscles. I hadn't noticed just how sore they were from all the constant running around and training.

This game was something special.

After soaking for a good while in a nice hot bath, I was happy to put my clothes and armor into one of the baskets and return to my room. My head hit the pillow and a few minutes later I was dead to the world.

CHAPTER 8

ROOSTER MUST DIE! I wanted so badly to smite the demon fowl, but Dogson would probably get angry with me. Angry Dogson could lead to bad things happening with regards to my current home and I don't want to be evicted over a chicken. These were the thoughts dominating my sleep addled brain as I slowly awoke. At least today would hopefully be a lazy day or a lazier day.

I had no urgent quests to worry about. The one quest I did have required research, but there was no rush to research the town history. So, I returned to my original hopes of a lazier day. The only non-lazy thing I had planned, was training with Sergeant Butters.

I suppose I did have one other major objective today, reading or maybe writing and drawing. I had so much reading to do, my pile of books hadn't diminished at all since my first day. If I didn't get it in gear and start devouring these books, I'd be in for a world of hurt later on. Especially if I didn't do my utmost to learn as many skills as possible, while they were so freely given.

On the other hand, I would love to start working on Writing and Drawing, the sooner I got them both up to level 10, the sooner I could evolve them to Runes and Cartography. I guess I would just have to see what the day held for me before I decided anything.

After breakfast and some conversation with Dogson and the Johnsons, I sought out Sergeant Butters for our morning training session. Walking toward the barracks I saw the troll trussed up in the stocks looking rather pathetic, his partner's corpse still laid out next to him and starting to gather flies from the look of it.

Leaning against the barracks' wall just behind the prisoner was one of the town guards I hadn't met yet. He gave me a polite nod which I returned.

"Hey, spare some water," the troll asked, seeing me walk closer.

I looked to the guard first who just shrugged, he didn't seem to care one way or the other. I frowned but saw no reason not to give him some water. I pulled out my canteen and walked closer to him. "Open up," I ordered.

The trolls mouth opened, his lower jaw stuck forward naturally due to the two large tusks he had instead of lower canines. I poured some water into his mouth, which he swallowed thirstily. "Thank you," he said softly.

"Why'd you do it? Was it worth it to rob the Johnson farm?" I demanded.

The troll looked hesitant to reply before simply looking at the ground. Clearly, I wasn't going to get an answer. So, I resumed my walk to meet up with Sergeant Butters. Just as I was turning the corner I heard the troll grumble, "We should never have taken that job."

My eyes widened slightly even as I kept walking. The bandits were hired to torch the farm and kill the Johnsons. But by who? And why?

Quest Alert: Shiny Delivery Service 4 (Recommended Level 4-5)
Conspiracy? Who hired the trolls to attack the Johnson's Farm and why?

Reward: Experience		
Do you accept this Quest?	Yes	No

Of course, I accepted the quest. It was just too good of a mystery to pass up. This was starting to get interesting and I was only on day 4 in the game. I couldn't wait to see what kind of mysteries I uncovered the rest of the month.

"Morning Sergeant," I greeted the man. The sergeant was doing pushups in the middle of the training ring, and as such barely acknowledge me with little more than a glance. I waited a few minutes for him to finish and when he stood, he finally greeted me in return.

"Morning," he damned near shouted. "Ready to get to work?"

"Yes, sergeant," I answered.

"Good, so what will it be today?"

"I was thinking it might be good to learn the other shield subskill you told me about, 'Shield-Counter'," I answered.

"Let us get to it then," he said pulling out a one-handed sword. "First, you will only need your shield to start so set your spear in the rack," he motioned to the weapons rack he usually kept his own gear in.

I set my spear next to his own, pausing a moment to admire the intricacy of his spear, even if his training spear was blunted. I quickly joined him in the center of the training ring, the spear would soon be forgotten.

"Now, you need to learn to block. Left!" he shouted suddenly, swing the sword toward my left side.

On reflex alone, my shield moved left in an attempt to block and I was successful in doing so. I was proud of my success for all of about two seconds. It was extinguished as soon as the sergeant spun back around to the right and struck a painful blow to my overextended arm, causing me to lose my grip and drop my shield. A moment later the sergeant unceremoniously knocked me to the ground and held his sword to my throat then shouted, "Dead!"

"Ow," I groaned in pain.

"Get up, let us try again," said the sergeant. "Now, assume your stance."

I took up the stance he'd drilled into me the last few days.

"Right!" he shouted, swinging for my right side, again my arm moved and blocked the attack of the sword, but did nothing against the steel covered boot. The sergeant's armored foot nearly caved my chest in when it went unblocked. The kick knocked me to the ground, pushing all the air from my lungs and leaving me in pain. Pain sucked in this game. Yes, I felt pain, I've mentioned it before when things have hurt me, but this time felt more potent. As to the pain itself, the game certainly reduced it, any kind of painful death was very muted.

When asked once, Mitchell Dawson said, feeling pain was an important teacher in real life, so should it be in the game. Now, torture was forbidden obviously, there was nothing to be done about emotional pain and some physical pain was good for us, even if unpleasant. Right now, I could have done without this particular pain.

"Come, up you get," coaxed the sergeant, nudging me with his boot.

It was painful climbing back to my feet. "Rather than just beating me to death here, think you could give me some instruction?"

"Take your stance! Overhand!" he yelled, a swing already coming.

I moved my shield again on reflex, blocking the attack and was treated again with another kick, this one catching me in the gut.

"Up and take your stance," ordered the sergeant.

I didn't understand what he wanted from me here. I was blocking his first attack, but the second kept crushing me. I clambered back to my feet still in pain.

"Low!" he called, his sword swing for my feet.

I slammed shield down, trapping the sword on the ground only to catch the sergeant's fist in my face. I swear I saw a flash of lightning when his fist struck.

"That really hurts! What am I doing wrong here?" I asked, anger starting to get the better of me.

"Take your stance," he ordered simply.

Three more attacks and blocks, each followed by me getting knocked to the ground rather painfully. And the only thing he said to me was "Take your stance" as if saying it again would explain what I was supposed to do.

I took my stance again.

"Left!" he called.

It was time to try something different. Every time I had to move my shield I would get thumped pretty hard and it was getting to be more than irritating. This time I didn't move my shield from in front of me, this time I moved my whole body to align the shield with the attack. I blocked and suddenly it made sense. I only had to pivot this time to intercept the second attack. I was so pleased with my success, I didn't see the third attack coming until I was once again on my back and looking skyward.

"Take your stance," he ordered again, except this time he was grinning a little bit. The man was a sadist, no doubt about it. But boy, if he didn't know his weapons training.

It took almost another hour of getting used to shifting and pivoting into blocks when attacks came from the left or right. Then to figure out I needed to retreat from an overhead strike and a low strike had to be shifted into, which naturally led me to use 'Shield Slam'. This even got a nod of approval from the sergeant. It was definitely the most brutal training session so far.

"Good, grab a drink then pick up a staff, you might actually hurt me with this training if you were to have a sharpened weapon," ordered the sergeant, backing off and giving me a little room to catch my breath.

I was only too happy to gorge on the water, even pouring some over my head and bruised arms. Healing spells took care of the lost HP and could mend broken bones, but it still took time for the bruises to vanish, another one of Mitchell Dawson's brilliant ideas. However, I couldn't say the man was wrong. Pain was a great teacher and an even better motivator.

"Now, you know how to block the attacks coming at you. Counterattacking, just like the 'Shield Slam' skill, is all about picking your moment. Wait too long, and I will just keep attacking. Attack too soon, and you open yourself up to even more pain," he explained, finally providing at least a little instruction.

The staff was slightly shorter than my spear and thicker around, but the weight was almost the same. It took me a second to adjust to the length but otherwise, I had myself in my stance and ready to start within a minute or two.

This time there was no call out of an attack direction. There was no way for me to expect what was coming. I had to react on instinct and the muscle memory the training had imparted to me.

It took practice to get adjusted to blocking while holding the 'spear' but after a few attacks and blocks I gained a level of comfort, I started looking for the opening to counter. My first counter came on an overhead strike, I shifted back away from it and as soon as the arc passed, I shifted in and struck, the 'spear' striking the sergeant in the shoulder spinning him slightly, but not enough to distract him for long.

I was quick to reset my stance even as the next strike came, this one from the left. I shifted to put my shield in front of it, then attacked before he could spin the attack into my right side.

It continued for a while before the sergeant called it a day. "Not bad work today. Same time tomorrow?"

I was about to protest, as I hadn't learned a skill yet, then I notice the flashing exclamation points. The system hadn't told me the previous day when I had learned 'Stealth', so maybe it was going to stop popping up certain notifications. It must be some kind of setting for the game, maybe a tutorial mode I had unknowingly completed, and therefore wasn't going to be told about every little change, unless it was urgent. And it seemed anything related to skills was no longer considered urgent.

"I'll see you tomorrow, same time," I agreed. I took a minute to fill all three of my empty stamina canteens then sat down to rest for a few minutes. Today's session had been brutal, I felt achy all over from it. Mitchell Dawson, you are a real piece of work.

I finally checked the system notifications, and a long list it was. Apparently, my brutal training session yielded massive rewards. My Strength, Dexterity, and Stamina had all hit the level cap of 40 points, and my Endurance had increased to 68 points out of the 80 possible. And I had learned the subskill 'Shield-Counter', almost thirty minutes ago. This was in addition to several level increases to both 'Phalanx Shield' and 'One-Handed Polearms' skills.

Phalanx Shield	Level: 19	Experience: 15.44%
Current Defense Modifiers	Block Chance: +0.90%	Critical Block Chance: +0.45%
Subskill: Shield Slam	Damage: 8-9 Effect: Interrupt	Skill Stamina Cost: 39
Subskill: Shield-Counter	Block Chance: 29.50% Cooldown: 30 seconds	Skill Stamina Cost: 44

'Shield-Counter' was costly but for almost a 30% chance of blocking it was worth it even with the cooldown.

On my way back to the inn, I stopped at Ned's Sundry again. I bought another notebook, this one much larger, to use as a sketchpad and hopefully later as a map book. I also refilled on enriched mana water, as I was still empty from the previous day's excursion to the Johnson farm.

It was just before noon when I returned to the inn. I asked Dogson for some lunch to be brought to my room which he agreed to with a simple nod.

I sat once more with the chair by the window and my feet propped up on the bed. I had thought about this for a while, or at least since the mayor first told me about writing, thought about what I would write. I could write my strategies and game plans. I could simply write a novel or maybe a short story, but I didn't have any ideas for something original.

Then it struck me, there was a story I could write. A personal story, my story or rather my game story. I put pencil to paper and I started writing. I wrote first of my arrival and immediate death then continued from there. Lunch arrived just as I finished writing the first paragraph on Day 1, I was just about to begin my introduction to 'Old Benji'.

Lunch was a simple sandwich, ham, lettuce, and tomato with a spicy mayo. Happy for the simple flavor, reminding me of the real world, I sat and savored it. It also gave me a little time to reflect on the old fisherman, I could picture him, sitting happily along the river bank, just casting and reeling back in, smiling contentedly.

Without meaning to, I'd drawn an image of the man fishing on the next page, a portrait of his face smiling just as I'd imagined. Now, I'm not much of an artist in real life, I couldn't draw a portrait to save my life, but this was a good drawing, in my opinion, thank you game assist. Giving it a moment more thought, I couldn't help but smile, it was a good idea.

I went back to writing my Day 1 entry. Once I got to the bottom of the page and continued on the page after Old Benji's picture and continued my story. When I got to Gavin and my first meeting, I couldn't help but draw a smaller picture of the slumped over guard in his little hut, little cartoonish snot bubble coming from his nose showing he was asleep and not dead.

My story continued, my meeting with Dogson, his image, my first training session with Sergeant Butters, meeting the mayor and his wife, all with portraits included.

By the time I finished Day 4, today, it was already dark outside. My game clock told me it was 8:38 pm. Realizing I only had about 20 minutes to get dinner before they stopped serving, I closed my book and rushed to dinner.

While I ate, I reviewed my system notifications for my two new professions and the several levels they had both gained.

You've learned a new profession 'Writing'

Writing	Level: 8	Experience: 97.99%
Professional Skill: *Writing is the ability to communicate through the written word.*		

You've learned a new profession 'Drawing'

Drawing	Level: 9	Experience: 16.55%
Professional Skill: *Drawing is the ability to communicate through drawn images.*		

Somehow, I got the feeling the only reason they both advanced as much as they did is because I was telling my personal story, sharing my personal memories and feelings. At this pace, I'd be able to evolve both Writing and Drawing soon. Things were getting interesting now.

I finished dinner, took a bath and went to bed happy with my day's progress.

***

A new day and same problems. Mostly the same cursed bird. I could feel I was losing the war to not execute the demon fowl. I'd have to talk to Dogson about this before there was another incident.

Breakfast was lighter than I've had the last few days. Of course, it helps I didn't get drunk the night before, so no hangover cure required. I also didn't stay up and socialize so there were no gains to charisma either. It didn't take long before I was out the door and, on my way to meet with Sergeant Butters.

I was content to enjoy the short walk from the inn to the barracks, only to halt when I saw the stocks. The same stocks that held the troll I had captured two days prior.

The stocks that still held the troll I had given water to just the day before. The stocks that were now holding a headless troll, or at least mostly headless. The lower jaw with its two large tusks and neck were still there, which was a disturbing sight to see, more so with the greenish-blue blood sprayed everywhere. I looked for the guard that was supposed to be watching the prisoner, but he was nowhere in sight.

"Sergeant Butters!" I yelled as loudly as I could, hoping he'd hear me from around the back of the barracks. It only took a moment for the Sergeant to come tearing around the building, his armor-clad boots and legs clanking the whole way.

Butters saw the same thing I did, but ran for the barracks, instead of halting as I did, to stare in shock. The barracks doors opened with a loud bang, followed by more loud banging as Sergeant Butters hammered at the door with his boot. "Up, all you worthless knuckle-draggers, you sorry sacks, get up right now!"

Less than a minute later, the entire garrison, or those not currently guarding one of the gates, had assembled in front of the building, in various stages of undress.

"Gunderson, why in the name of all the Gods and Goddesses were you sleeping?" demanded Butters, getting right up in the guard's face.

"Davies relieved me. Told me you sent him," he answered, his voice shaking slightly. It was obvious to me he was terrified.

"Are you kidding me?" demanded Butters, his face turning slightly red, his eye seemed to develop a twitch, it reminded me of an old anime trope. If it hadn't been so serious I may have laughed. As it was, I was afraid to say anything. I could only imagine how the man being stared down felt. Butters was just inches away from Gunderson's face already glaring into the man's eyes. "In the five years you have been under my command, have I ever sent in a relief guard?"

"No, sergeant," he answered, his voice quavering slightly.

Butters glared at the guardsman harder, his forehead now pressing into the uncomfortable guard's forehead. Eventually, he relented only to glare at the rest of the platoon. "Now where is Guard Davies?"

The other guards looked around at each other before one of the men I hadn't interacted much with yet answered. "He is not here."

"Well then, do you not think you all better find him?" Butters asked, but after a few seconds of inaction, he yelled. "Now!"

It was a mad dash for the guards to get back into the barracks only to emerge moments later with their gear, some of it equipped but mostly the pieces were tucked under an arm as they were trying to finish equipping the armor as they ran off to start the search for their missing comrade.

"Bye-bye, I am afraid we will not be able to train today," said Butters, turning to face me. I'd never seen the man look so grim.

I knew I would regret asking this even if it would lead to a quest, I could feel it in my bones. "What can I do to help?"

Butters looked appreciative of my offer, his mouth curving just slightly before turning grim once more. "You are a good lad, see if you can help the men find their missing compatriot." He then handed me a green not-quite candle thing. My prompt told me it was a 'Green Smoke Beacon' and I had to pull the string to activate it.

Quest Alert: Missing in Action 1 (Recommended Level 4-5)		
Guard Davies has gone missing under suspicious circumstances. Help the garrison locate the missing guard. Activate the green smoke beacon if you find the missing soldier.		
Reward: Experience		
Do you accept this	Yes	No

Quest?		

"I'll get started right away," I replied, accepting the quest and the smoke beacon.

"Do yourself a favor, go pick up the book 'Bounty Hunting for Fame and Fortune' from the Town hall and give it a read before you get started. It will help," Butters suggested.

Quest Alert: Read Bounty Hunting for Fame and Fortune		
Sergeant Butters has strongly recommended you read and study Bounty Hunting for Fame and Fortune before joining in on the search for the missing guard.		
Reward: Experience, New Skill		
Do you accept this Quest?	**Yes**	**No**

"I'll do that, but the Town hall doesn't open for a few hours, isn't this more urgent?"

"Here, take my key," said Butters, pulling out a key from his pouch and tossing it to me. "Just be quick in there and bring the key right back. I will be here dealing with this mess," he motioned to the corpse still suspended in the stocks.

"Okay, I will," I replied, accepting another quest. Any plans I had for the day going up in smoke, not that I had anything planned for the day.

I ran quickly over to the door for the Town hall and opened it with the key from Sergeant Butters. It took a minute to find the book and another minute to exit the building and lock it back up again.

I could see Sergeant Butters was still in front of the barracks. He was busy with removing the corpse from the stocks and laying it out next to the other dead troll. I quickly returned the key, promising to join the search just as soon as I finished the book. For the time being, I would hole up in my room at the inn and get to reading.

I wanted to speed through it, so I could get out and help search, but I also knew it was possible I could miss something important in the book if I did. Slow and steady won the day, no matter how much I disliked it. It took a good hour and a half to read 'Bounty Hunting for Fame and Fortune'. Similar to the Bestiary, it went through the various humanoid and other intelligent races, it talked about traits and even their tracks, with the disclaimer stating many races wore boots or shoes able to obscure the footprint. Where this one was more complex, is in the habits of these races.

Many of them had habits they couldn't control, it was a compulsion they couldn't refuse to see through. Most of which, revolved around their needs for food, sex, religion or some combination of all three. The latter part of the book went into more of the money side of it, talking about famous bounties, and how much they were worth. By the time I finished the book, I had gained another 2 points to both Intellect and Wisdom along with the new skill 'Humanoid Tracking'.

Humanoid Tracking	Level: 1	Experience: 0.00%
Skill Effect (Passive): *Enables you to track humanoids.*		
Skill Range: 10 yards	Chance to See: 10.00%	Chance to Track: 20.00%

It was actually kind of annoying it did the same thing as 'Beast Tracking', but for humanoids. Why couldn't it just be a skill for tracking period? I shook the thought away, it was time to return to the scene of the crime.

I also got the notification of the quest completion.

Quest Alert: Read Bounty Hunting for Fame and Fortune –

Completed!
Sergeant Butters has strongly recommended you read and study Bounty Hunting for Fame and Fortune before joining in on the search for the missing guard.
Reward: +200 Experience, Humanoid Tracking

When I returned to the stocks, the body had been removed, as well as the body of the dead partner, and Sergeant Butters was nowhere in sight. First, I needed to check the footprints going to and from the stocks. It hadn't rained recently so the ground was dry, so nothing could have been washed away. Unfortunately, the cobblestone streets made it pretty much impossible for there to be any footprints to follow.

I needed a different way to track the killer as footprints weren't going to work here. Or so I thought until a footprint did light up my vision. It was mostly covered in dust at this point, but when I used my utility knife to scrape at it I found a layer of blue-green blood. The killer had stepped in blood. I now had a trail to follow.

I followed the trail and it kept getting smaller as the bloody footprints got smaller and smaller, until they vanish altogether. I ended up in a part of town I hadn't visited yet. There were only a few homes in the area. I saw a shop sign for a leatherworker's shop. I also saw a larger building with a sign, 'Butcher', which explained the awful smell I was just now taking note of, as well as the large fly population dominating the area.

I looked further down the street and there was nothing ahead except for the small moat surrounding the village. There was a good chance, the probable killer had business in this area. I would have to knock on every door and question the occupants.

The leatherworker's shop and the butcher didn't appear to be open yet and my game clock showed the time 8:13, meaning it would probably be too early in the day to start knocking on the doors of people's homes. I had little choice but to wait. Thankfully, I had a book and there was a large shade tree next to the leatherworker's shop that looked just about perfect to sit down under.

I don't know if it was good luck or bad luck, choosing the tree I did, but I couldn't help but notice an increase in flies as I got closer to the tree and further from the Butcher's, as well as an increasingly foul stench. I wish I hadn't decided to try to find the source.

What I found was a dead guard. The only reason I knew it was a guard was due to the uniform, though calling the strips of cloth and rent armor a uniform would have been a stretch. I couldn't even say the man was butchered, as that would imply some kind of skill was used to bring about his death. The man had been eviscerated, his throat was more or less gone, looking as though a large animal had taken a bite out of it. Meanwhile, the chest and stomach were torn right open and appeared to be missing several bits, also apparently eaten by something. I focused on his face, despite being bloody I recognized him. He was the same guard I'd seen on duty the previous morning. It occurred to me, maybe he heard the same thing I did, regarding the trolls being hired. Could that information have gotten him killed?

It took a minute for me to take my eyes away from the scene. I pulled the smoke beacon from my bag and pulled the string, then tossed it toward the street to signal the other guards.

I knew it would be a few minutes before anyone arrived. I couldn't help but go back to what was left of the guard's body, the man's eyes were wide open, but was it in shock or was it in disbelief . . . agony?

For some reason, I couldn't stop looking. I also couldn't stop thinking about the book 'The Trained Eye'. There was an exercise in it, I couldn't help thinking about. It talked about seeing a scene and seeing what happened there. It talked about looking at the evidence, at the whole picture and trying to pick out the details and reconstruct the story.

I found myself doing exactly that. Based on the footprints it appeared the guard had been waiting for someone. He'd been pacing a little, but mostly he seemed to be bouncing on his feet in excitement, or was it anticipation, maybe even nervousness?

There was a second set of footprints, booted, possibly armored, they walked up facing the guard. So, the man knew his attacker. There didn't appear to be any signs of a struggle either. The man's sword was still in its sheath. Had the guard let himself be killed? Was he poisoned maybe? Paralyzed by a spell? Was there even a way to check those things? I frowned but continued trying to reconstruct the event. The person who met him also took a bite out of him, but how could a man do that? Maybe it wasn't a man, it could have been a mammalian halfling, a bearman or something similar. It would have to have a very large mouth on it with even sharper teeth.

What else? I could see there were boot prints next to the body, the toes of the boots dug into the ground slightly, the killer crouched down to eat. A small clump of dirt highlighted in my vision next to the boot print, I'd have to ask about the dirt, but I dare not touch it. I know this isn't the real world, but I'd seen too many shows about crime on TV, I knew well enough to not get too close to the body, lest I become a suspect of the crime. It also occurred to me, I was able to reconstruct the scene partly because I had seen as many crime shows, as I have.

"Call out," called a voice I didn't recognize. I looked and saw a guardsman by the smoke beacon a short distance away.

"Over here," I called back, getting his attention.

The guardsman started toward me, freezing when he saw the dead man. He quickly turned away and ran off out of sight. I heard retching a moment later.

"Get ahold of yourself, Watts," shouted a voice I did recognize.

"Sergeant Butters, over here," I called to him.

The man jogged over to me, a deeper frown than usual marring his face. There were two more guards just behind him, each paling upon seeing the state of the body.

"Those cursed wolves," hissed one of the guards with Sergeant Butters, his previous pallor shifting a few shades darker and redder with anger.

"It was not wolves," said the Sergeant and I at the same time.

"What do you mean it was not wolves?" asked the same guard. "Do you see the state of his body? I have only seen the wolves do something like that."

"Do you see any paw prints? Also, the moat is just there, and you know well enough the silver essence we lace the moat with, prevents the beasts from crossing," Butters stated, giving his loose mouthed guard a good stare down.

The guard decided to keep his mouth shut, his eyes looking down. Meanwhile, it appeared the other guard was simply trying not to lose his lunch by looking anywhere but at the body.

"What else do you see?" asked Butters, looking at me now.

I relayed my theory to the sergeant, pointing out the various foot traffic patterns also asking him if there was a way to check the body for poison and magic.

"I agree with your reconstruction. We will have to take the remains to Trini to check for the presence of poison or magic," said Butters about to turn to his men to start barking orders.

"One other thing," I interrupted him before he could start. "I notice a small spot of rock that looks out of place." I moved around the body and crouched to point it out.

The sergeant didn't look the least bit miffed that I'd interrupted him. Instead, he was quick to join me. "Looks like 'Crystal Sandstone'."

"What's that?" I asked.

"Something not usually found around these parts. In fact, I can only think of one place around here with any," said the Sergeant.

"Where?" I asked.

"The ruins," was his answer.

"Will you and your men investigate?" I asked, hoping to tag along.

"I will send a patrol to check them for any recent activity, but I would not hold my breath. Those ruins are little more than a few large stones and partial walls," he answered. "Unfortunately, that sandstone could have been left by anyone." He sighed and stood from the crouch and moved back to his men. He started ordering them about, while I thought about his answer.

Quest Alert: Missing in Action 1 – Completed!
Guard Davies has gone missing under suspicious circumstances. Help the garrison locate the missing guard. Activate the green smoke beacon if you find the missing soldier.

Reward: +500 Experience

I was glad for the experience, but it was not how I would have preferred to gain it.

Quest Alert: Missing in Action 2 (Recommended Level 4-6)
Guard Davies has been murdered. Details at the scene suggest the murderer is somehow related to the nearby ruins. There are also several questions that must be answered to progress the investigation. Meet Sergeant Butters at the Hurligville Temple at Noon.
Reward: Experience, Variable Piece of Gear

Do you accept this Quest?	**Yes**	**No**

How could I not?

"Meet me at the temple at midday bell," said Butters, finally returning to my side. "I figure you will want to hear Trini's report, same as me."

I nodded my ascent. I know it was wrong to even let the thought cross my mind, given just how gruesome this particular quest line was starting out, but this was fun. I was surrounded by mystery and an awesome quest line with good rewards.

It was pointing me toward the ruins, the very thing that drew me to this province in the first place. I was also learning all kinds of skills and given the flashing exclamation points at the bottom of my user interface (UI), I may have just learned another. I was having fun and part of me felt guilty . . . but only a very small tiny bit, like a microscopic bit. I also wasn't as bothered by the corpse as I probably should have been, probably because I knew this was just a game. It was an AI that had been killed and would be recycled into another NPC. At least, that's what I told myself.

"I'll see you then," I said to Butters. I was careful to walk around the guards, so they could focus on the task at hand. I certainly didn't envy them for the job ahead.

Leaving the scene behind, I decided it was probably time to do a little shopping. I had a feeling I would be needing just a little bit stronger gear, sooner rather than later. Plus, I hadn't done much exploring around town yet, so I was probably overdue.

CHAPTER 9

My walk took me back past the barracks and town hall and back down the main street. I came across the blacksmiths first. I could see the small forge was open to the elements and a rotund dwarf was busy hammering away on a block of orange glowing metal, probably copper or tin, as was to be expected from a starter province. <Dwarf Smith Lvl 34>. He was barely taller than four feet, maybe four and a half if you counted his topknot. He was covered in soot from head to foot, as was expected, so I couldn't be sure if his hair was naturally black or just sooty, not that it mattered. He was a stocky fellow but seeing the muscles on his arms as he swung the hammer, I would have put money on it he was more akin to a professional strongman, as opposed to overweight, as the large belly would lead many to believe. His face was angular as if hewn from rock. The image was completed with a beard cut short to the point of almost not existing.

"Afternoon," I greeted the dwarf.

Without looking up he stated plainly, "Unless you are here to learn to be a blacksmith, I suggest you head inside the shop and speak to the missus."

"Will do, thank you. I'm Bye-Bye by the way," I introduced myself to him. The more I explored the game the more I found getting to know the citizens paid off.

"Kirlan Dunkirk," the Dwarf replied, still not looking up from his hammering. "You here for training then?"

"No, sir, just thought it wise to meet the town blacksmith," I replied.

"Right, nice to meet you. Now, if you would let me get back to work, the wife will take care of you inside," he stated gruffly, a slight Scottish brogue coming out in his voice at the end. It was a common trope or stereotype, Dwarves speaking with such an accent. I was initially surprised he didn't when we first started talking. So, either the game was trying to meet my expectation of an accent, or there was a backstory, one in which the smith had worked hard to get rid of it altogether.

"Nice to meet you too," I replied before turning toward the shop. There was a little bell chime, as I entered the shop. The blacksmith's shop was bright and filled with natural light, much different than I would have thought a typical blacksmith's shop would look. In most games, they were dark and dingy, filled with soot and dirt and stank of sweat and something burning. This shop was spotless and smelled of wildflowers . . . wildflowers and steel, but still a considerable upgrade from what I had expected.

"Good morning," said a high-pitched voice, drawing my attention to the counter. There was a female gnome standing at the counter. I hadn't seen a gnome in the game yet, but I'd seen a few artist renderings from the game's website. They were typically around three to four feet tall, neither slim nor plump, looking mostly human, except for rounder heads and larger noses. They also typically sported interesting hair choices, this little lady had short and curly green hair with a pair of up-curls in front that could have easily been mistaken for horns.

"Good morning, Kirlan directed me inside," I said, hoping this was his wife.

"Sorry if my husband was gruff with you. He is a big teddy bear once you get to know him," she replied, also letting a slight Scottish brogue creep into her voice. That was not something normal for gnomes, or at least not in the common tropes.

"It's no problem, but now I have a question that may be considered odd. I couldn't help but hear something of an accent in your voice and your husbands too, can I ask why?"

"What an odd thing to ask," she said, then giggled a little. "Honestly, I probably picked it up from him. You should have heard his accent when we first met, thicker than tar. But I suppose we've both been around humans and each other so long most of his accent is gone though I may have picked up a little of his along the way too."

"Interesting," I replied. It was interesting. There was so much effort put into constructing the citizens, I couldn't help but be impressed every time, especially with such diversity in their backgrounds.

"I suppose it is," she replied, a fond smile on her diminutive face. "Now, how can I help you today?"

"I am considering replacing my spear and shield," I replied. I would maybe get a small upgrade if the price was right, but I didn't have a great deal of money to go spending willy-nilly.

"What level are you?"

Her question caught me off-guard. I hadn't been asked about my level before, I suppose because my level didn't matter for any of the things I was learning, and the quests were all within a certain range, so they weren't necessarily concerned with my level either. But this was about gear and gear had a level requirement at times.

"I'm level 4," I answered.

"Okay then, I have got a few level 3 spears and shields," she replied, walking through the door to the back of the shop. I finally looked around again at the shop. There were several sets of armor and even weapons and shields on display covering most of the shop, but there was one wall covered in rifles and pistols. I walked straight to the guns to sate my curiosity. They were all from level 1 to level 8 at the highest. However, any interest I may have had in them died when I saw the cheapest one cost 5-gold.

"Oh, found my little ones, did you?" asked the gnome, returning to the front room and setting down 4 spears and 3 shields on the countertop.

"Little ones?" I asked. I assumed she meant the weapons, but it seemed politer to ask.

"Yeah, I am a gunsmith, you know?" she asked, smiling proudly.

I took a closer look at her <Mrs. Dunkirk Lvl 37>. She was at a higher level than her husband.

"Do you sell many? They seem . . . uh . . . expensive," I was trying to be delicate but there aren't many good ways to bring up the cost.

"Of course, those are," she said. "Those are my best works, all of them top quality and enhanced with stat boosts. The cheapest there gives +2 Dexterity and has a faster reload speed."

Ah, that explained it. As I looked around the room, I assumed everything on display was their higher end equipment which explained why she went into the back room to get me stuff to look at. Did she just assume I was poor? Or was it just typical for a level 4 to have such a low amount of money?

"Anyway, come have a look. These are all pretty basic, but they are solid enough and a good upgrade from the piece of junk you've got now."

I looked at my spear and then looked at the ones she set on the counter. There was a pretty big difference between them, simply from the visible sheen on the spears she set out, versus the dulled and chipped appearance of my own spear. I suppose I hadn't bothered to have my spear or shield maintained. They did look rather beat-up, but they were just starter gear pieces, so I supposed I hadn't considered spending the money to maintain them.

"I mean, do you even have a whetstone to keep the blade maintained?" she asked.

"I do not," I answered hesitantly. "I've only been here 4 days so . . . I guess I haven't gotten to it yet."

"Not to worry, I will let it go this time, but if you ever come in here again with a weapon that has not at least been maintained, I will kick you right back out and will not let you return," she stated matter-of-factly.

"Understood," I replied. Then a thought occurred to me, I had no idea how to maintain a weapon. "Umm, I don't know how to maintain a weapon. Or a shield either."

"I suppose I can teach you but only if you buy. I am not teaching no freeloaders around here," she said with a stern look on her face.

"Deal! Now, let's take a look at my options," I replied happily. I didn't actually want to spend money today to buy a new spear or even a shield, but the chance to learn how to maintain my gear, even a little bit, was worth it.

The four spears were all the same price but had different capabilities from damage to attack speed.

Pike	A pole weapon, a very long thrusting spear formerly used extensively by infantry. Two-Handed, Base Attack Speed 2.40 – Two-Handed Weapon Damage 14-19 – Durability 15/15
Assegai	A pole weapon used for throwing, usually a light spear made of wood with a pointed fire-hardened tip. Throwing Speed 3.00 – Ranged Damage 30-40 – Durability 5/5
Hasta	A pole weapon consisting of a shaft, usually of wood with a pointed head. One-Handed Base Attack Speed 2.20 – One-Handed Weapon Damage 7-8 – Two-Handed Base Attack Speed 1.80 – Two-Handed Weapon Damage 14-16 – Durability 15/15
Boar Spear	A pole weapon that is relatively short and heavy and has two wings on the spear socket behind the blade. One-Handed Base Attack Speed 2.8 – One-Handed Weapon Damage 9-11 – Two-Handed Base Attack Speed 2.40 – Two-Handed Weapon Damage 18-22 – Durability 20/20

I knocked off the Assegai immediately, I had no interest in a throwing spear or any ranged weapon at all. If I was going to fight from range, I had magic. I also eliminated the Pike, as it was for two hands only. In the future, I might want a weapon for two-handed and one for one-handed only, but for now, versatility was more important to me. The choice was between the Hasta and the Boar Spear. As much as the higher damage from the Boar Spear was nice, it was just too slow. The Hasta was the better choice and for 1-Silver, it certainly should have been.

"I'll have to go with the Hasta," I stated, picking it up, testing the balance versus my old weapon.

"Good choice, so with the trade of your old spear its 95-copper, agreed?" she asked.

"And the maintenance training is included?" I asked. The last thing I needed was for her to charge me for the skill.

"Yes, it's included."

"Whetstone and Shield Oil too?" I asked, trying to squeeze her for as much as I could. I had a limited amount of money until I could get to a bank in Root City.

"Greedy little grub," she complained. "I suppose I could throw it in given you are buying both weapon and shield from me, but no more free handouts, you got me?"

"Deal," I replied. She removed the spears I didn't select from the counter and walked them back into the backroom while I looked at the shields.

Light Tower Shield	A light tower shield in the phalanx class capable of covering more of the body. +7 Armor – Durability 10/10
Light Round Shield	A round shield in the phalanx class offering solid protection. +10 Armor – Durability 15/15
Maasai Shield	An ovoid shield in the phalanx class that is very lightweight. +4 Armor – Block Chance increased 5.00% – Durability 7/7

I eliminated the Maasai shield right away as it was less defense than my current shield, even if it did offer an increase to block chance, it wouldn't absorb enough damage to be worth it. The tower shield was definitely tempting, but I saw one major problem right away, first being it would limit my field of vision. Having trained with the sergeant as much as I have, I've learned a great deal about the need to see your attacker. The round shield was already in the style I was used to working with and it had more defense and durability than the other two.

By the time Mrs. Dunkirk returned I was already experimenting with my new 'Hasta' spear and the 'Light Round Shield'.

"So, picked the shield you wanted then?" she asked, gathering up the other two and already walking back.

It just struck me as odd, the woman was being awfully trusting of me not to steal anything, but then I recalled Dogson's warning about his bathrooms. I could only imagine something similar had been done here to prevent a thief from leaving with anything they had not paid for. She was quicker to return this time, but she was also carrying a whetstone, rag and a bottle of what I could only assume was the shield oil.

"The shield is 50-copper, minus the 5-copper for scrapping the old shield comes to 45-copper. All told, you owe me 1-silver, 40-copper," she tallied the final bill.

I happily paid her . . . well not happily, but close enough, plus the improved gear was much needed.

"Okay, now, I am going to use your old weapon and shield to teach you, as I do not want you to start losing durability on your new toys so soon," she explained, but before she could start, I had to stop her.

"What do you mean, lose durability?" I asked.

"You are not a smith of any sort so every time you do maintenance on your equipment you will reduce your piece of equipment's overall durability. As a beginner, at most, you will only be able to restore 1-2 points of durability at a time. For example, your old spear here. If you perform maintenance on it, you might bring it up to three durability points from its current durability of one. But, the maximum durability is almost guaranteed to drop two points from eight to six. Obviously, this will improve as your skill improves, but until you improve, you will cause permanent harm to the equipment. Understand?"

"Yeah, I think I get it," I replied. Thankfully this was all low-level gear, so it didn't matter how much I damaged it in the long run as eventually, I will replace it with better and better gear.

"Now, a professional smith like my husband or even an engineer like myself can repair any equipment brought to us if it is within our specialty. So, for my husband, anything with metal, save guns, which is my specialty. Any questions before I get down to finally teaching you?"

"No ma'am," I replied. For the next hour Mrs. Dunkirk, who I learned during the training was named Giggle-Ana, drilled into me how to use the whetstone for the spear tip until it met with her standards and in the process pretty much destroyed the spear. The next hour had me polishing the old shield until I could see my reflection in the polished surface.

"Not bad," she finally said. "Now, don't be too eager to maintain the new equipment you just got. I don't want you ruining it."

"Yes ma'am," I replied, causing her to giggle again. I was beginning to understand why she was named Giggle-Ana too.

"Well, I should see about an early lunch, I have a midday meeting," I said, preparing to depart when the door opened to an unexpected but pleasant surprise.

"Olaf," I greeted the friendly mining ogre I'd befriended a few days ago.

"Bye-bye, how are you doing my good man?" he greeted in return.

"Not bad, finally upgraded my spear and shield," I answered the big man . . . ogre.

"Nice, I'm kind of envious," he replied, frowning slightly before shooting a glance toward Giggle-Ana.

I glanced back and saw her frowning and glaring at Olaf.

"What's that about?" I asked, looking back to Olaf. I was shocked by the change in the little gnome's attitude.

Olaf sighed. "It's a racial thing." Then he snorted, "Imagine that, me a white guy in the RL getting racially profiled in a game. Talk about bollocks!"

"I do not need such language in here, you can leave if you're going to talk that way, ogre," Giggle-Ana nearly spit.

I was honestly shocked. I hadn't expected that at all. Especially when Giggle-Ana was so kind and friendly to me. I couldn't help but intervene. "Giggle-Ana," I started, trying to sound as disapproving as possible. "Why are you treating my friend so poorly?"

"You are friends? With that . . . that . . . that ogre?" she asked in shock.

"Olaf and his wife Micaela are nice people. They were helpful to me a few days ago," I chided her.

"But he is an ogre, they kill people, do you not know?" she expounded.

"Some do, but so do some gnomes. I heard a story about some gnome engineer name Whiztinker the Inept the other day, he destroyed an entire town, didn't he?"

174

"Well, that is . . . it is not the same. Everyone knows ogres are dumb beasts, they only know how to smash things and kill people," she protested.

"And has this ogre ever smashed things or killed?" I asked.

"Not that I have seen, but I cannot watch him all the time," she retorted, but I could see her defenses starting to wane.

"And dumb? Doesn't he speak to you clearly and articulately?" I challenged her further.

"It is a trick," she tried to defend.

"Giggle-Ana," I chided her again. Despite the level difference I couldn't help but think of her as a spoiled little girl, so I may have treated her as such, but given it seemed to be working, I wasn't going to change my approach.

She frowned, fighting an internal debate, but I could see she'd need just one more nudge of encouragement.

"Tell you what, I'll personally vouch for him and his wife, then if they cause any damage or hurt anyone in the village, you can hold me personally responsible, sound fair?"

That seemed to do it. "Fine, but if he or his wife causes even a little trouble, it will be my husband's boot to your backside," she threatened.

"Deal!" I replied, turning to face the gobsmacked Olaf. "Stop gawking and get to talking. You're here for a reason, right?"

Olaf snapped out of his dumbfounded state after a moment, he carefully approached the counter.

"Hello ma'am," he said politely, giving a small bow of his head to the diminutive woman.

Giggle-Ana took a deep calming breath then gave a quick glance for reassurance, to which I just nodded. Finally, she looked at Olaf and spoke. "What can I do for you?"

"I wish to order two pistols and ammunition, for both," he replied. "I know they'll have to be custom made for my size, but I can pay."

Giggle-Ana studied him for a minute and though I was sure she would never admit it was there, I saw a small spark of excitement in those little eyes.

"No," she replied firmly. "I cannot and will not make a pistol for you."

For a moment both Olaf and I were going to protest before she held up a hand stopping me in place.

"A pistol would be little more than a toy for you. You would probably break it the first time you used it. What you need are hand-cannons."

Suddenly Olaf's face lit up like it was Christmas and his birthday all rolled up in one. "Thank you!" he said emphatically, the smile on his face threatened to split his head open right there.

"It will not be cheap mind you, and the ammo will cost too, but it should do you fine," she explained.

"I'll pay it, whatever it costs," he replied excitedly.

"1-gold each and another 8-gold for 200 rounds of ammo," she stated.

That sounded stupidly expensive to me, but I saw Olaf happily drop the 10-gold onto the countertop without another word, or complaint.

"Okay then, come back in about a week and I'll have your hand-cannons and ammo ready. Make sure you purchase or have an artillery-pack crafted by then for the ammo," she instructed, sweeping the gold off the counter.

"Thank you so very much, Mrs. Dunkirk," said Olaf, once again super grateful.

"Thank Bye-bye," she said, trying to act highbrow about the whole event.

"Oh, believe me, I will," said Olaf.

"Now, will there be anything else?" she asked. She still did not appear completely comfortable talking to Olaf but was at least making an effort.

Olaf hesitated a moment.

"Just ask," she said, seeing him hesitate. As much as she wanted him out of the shop, she wasn't going to kick out someone paying so well. Apparently, even she could be bought.

"I want to learn Engineering," he said in a rush.

Here Giggle-Ana growled a little, she clearly did not like his request. I could hear her grumbling to herself before taking a few more deep and calming breaths before she spoke again.

"I do not want to teach you, especially not an ogre. However, I am required to take on students willing to pay my fee. So, I will warn you now, I am going to gouge you so hard, you will be poor for the rest of your life. Are you sure you still want to learn from me?"

Olaf swallowed nervously before nodding the affirmative.

"Fine, 50-gold, and you need a minimum 20-Intellect and 20-Charisma though the last part is just so you are not so ugly to look at all the time."

"Holy!" I couldn't help but exclaim. That price was ridiculous. I could already picture Micaela strangling Olaf for doing something so stupid. And yet, Olaf looked completely relieved.

As if the price wasn't shocking enough, I could hardly believe what I was seeing when Olaf easily put another 50-gold on the counter, not even flinching. I was sure my mouth was hanging open in shock at this point.

"Fine, come back when your Intellect and Charisma are where I told you I required them," said Giggle-Ana, sweeping the gold from the counter. "Unless you need something else, please depart. Oh, and Olaf, be sure you are bathed and deodorized next time you enter this shop, or I will send you away for at least 24-hours."

"Yes, ma'am," he replied, bowing his head again.

"My mother would be turning in her grave if she found out I was teaching an ogre, of all things," grumbled Giggle-Ana as she retreated to the backroom of the shop.

"So . . ." I started, not sure what to say.

"Lunch?" asked Olaf.

"Yeah, sounds good," I replied.

"Great, just have to find the wife. Who knows where she got off to?" he wondered.

I couldn't believe neither of us were going to say anything about what just happened. It was eating at me the entire walk down the street where we met Micaela coming out of Ned's with her usual pixyish grin on her face. How an ogre could look pixyish I don't know, but Micaela pulled it off.

"Bye-bye!" shouted the woman spotting me with Olaf.

"Hey Mic," I greeted her in return.

"I was just telling Olaf we should see about getting dinner with you again soon." She was quick to speak. "We had such fun last time plus I got a few points of Charisma which was totally cricket."

"We're treating Bye-bye to lunch at the Dog House Inn," said Olaf, a content and happy smile firmly planted on his face. I was getting the feeling nothing could bring him down at this point.

"Great," said Mic, one of her giant hands patting me on the back, almost knocking me to the ground in the process.

The walk back to the Inn was mostly quiet except for Micaela jabbering a mile a minute, filling me in on all kinds of gossip from the mine, not that I had any idea who she was talking about, but it was entertaining all the same.

Dogson happily served us each a beer and a sandwich with chips, though Olaf and Micaela's dishes were twice the size of mine.

We ate in near silence, Micaela finally seemed to have picked up on the odd mood Olaf was in. I couldn't tell if he was just preparing for the storm or if he was trying to keep the suspense for his own entertainment. Maybe both.

Still, I didn't crack, just kept eating my meal. Having a second beer which I pretty much moved to just nursing as I still had a meeting to attend in a little bit.

I should have known it would be Micaela who cracked first. "Okay, what in the name of LJ is going on? What happened? Did the little witch finally agree to sell you a weapon?"

"I got a class offer," he finally said.

"You did?" asked Micaela, the surprise was written all over her face. "I thought you were going to hold out for artillery?"

"I did," he replied, his already large smile grew even more.

"What?" she shouted. "How?"

"So, I went back to visit Mrs. Dunkirk as I have every day since the first day we logged in," he began.

"What was different this time?" asked Micaela.

Olaf simply pointed at me. "This beautiful man was there."

"You're not my type Olaf, but thank you for the compliment," I replied, trying to take the focus off of myself. I was never the center of attention kind of guy.

"What did Bye-bye do?" asked Micaela, literally starting to bounce in her seat with excitement.

179

What followed was the story from his perspective in which he witnessed me bring Mrs. Dunkirk low and guilted her into letting him shop there. Then he started talking about his request for the pistols and her refusal.

"That little witch!" shouted Micaela, her face turning red with anger.

"Calm down, let me finish the story," Olaf chided her.

"Hey, just wondering, why didn't you select a gun during character creation?" I interrupted.

"It's because of our account type. Financers have to work off our pods, so we get a gathering tool to start with, but no weapons. It's also how we ended up as Ogres. There were only two choices for financers in the race category. Ogre miners and Sprite herbalists. Sprites get more choices once they've paid off their pods for classes, but herbs are super inexpensive right now. I imagine in a year or two it'll reverse but for now, the ore is worth three to four times as much. Anyway, most financers go with the ogre and then as soon as they pay off their pod, they cancel their account for a month which wipes them from the system. Then they can sign up again and start any toon they want," he explained.

"So, there is a way to change classes?" I asked, making sure I understood him correctly.

"Only on the financers account," replied Olaf. "It's some legal loophole. Seed Inc fought it tooth and nail, but because of one little miss in the financing contract, they are stuck. Not that it matters. I actually prefer my ogre. Especially now that I have my preferred Class."

"Right, so continue the story before I go squash the little witch," said Micaela.

I was sure, if Olaf didn't have a viselike grip on his wife's hand, she'd have already charged back down the street to attack the gnome.

Olaf continued on to the part where she refused then stalled any protest by saying he needed hand-cannons which prompted the artillery class.

That got us both questioning.

"That was only what the forum had said," defended Olaf. "I'm betting people only ever enslaved the work crews, which triggered the class and only then because of the strength requirement for a regular cannon. I'm starting to think most of these players are complete idiots."

"So truthfully, all you need is the hand-cannon to trigger the class?" I asked.

"Well that and 75 strength, which is the minimum required to carry them. I'll have to up my strength more still to carry the ammo plus other gear, but at least I can start working on my 'One-Handed Artillery' skill. Man, I can't tell you how excited I am. I'm just dreading her other conditions?" the ogre griped.

"What conditions?" asked Micaela. "And conditions for what?"

"So, I also got her to agree to teach me Engineering. It cost 50-gold, but we knew it would be at least that much anyway. It's the 20-Intellect and 20-Charisma I'm worried about."

"Seriously, it only cost you 50?" asked Micaela, her face looked shocked.

"Okay, maybe I'm crazy here, but 50-gold sounds like a whole lot of money to learn a profession, and I thought you still had to pay off your loan for the Seedpods?" I interjected, my confusion reaching its limit. If my math was right and it usually was, 50-gold converted to about £2,500.00

"As for the gold, well, remember that geode Olaf mentioned finding? Well, the gems sold. The rare gem made us almost a 5,000-gold alone, so we're in good financial shape right now. As for the other part, we're ogres, we get huge charisma penalties," answered Micaela. "As a result, we usually get price gouged everywhere we go, if we're even let in the door. Plus, we get a racial penalty on charisma, half of normal so the citizens, almost by default, hate us," Micaela explained.

"You guys both got a couple points the other night with me, right?" I asked.

"We did, it's actually the first time we've gotten any charisma points. We tried to go to the miners' bar the next night, and they wouldn't even let us in the front door," explained Olaf.

I honestly felt indignant on their behalf. That was ridiculous. "From now, we have dinner here, every night until you both have 20-Charisma," I stated.

"You sure?" asked Micaela, it was the first time I'd ever seen her even remotely timid.

"You bet I'm sure," I replied.

"Great, one problem solved," said Olaf, sagging slightly in relief.

"Int?" I asked, confused. "How is that a problem?"

"We're not sure how to gain it? All the ogre forums say it's impossible," replied Micaela.

"But you gained Intellect from using your sign language, right?" I asked.

"Yeah, but it stopped at four," she replied, now looking defeated in addition to timid.

"Can you read with four Intellect?" I asked.

"Need 5 to read," she replied.

I just scratched my chin in thought. Then I reached into my bag and took out my large notebook. I tore out 9 pages then tore those into quarters. I then printed the letters of the alphabet on them A-Z then 0-9.

"Okay, this may seem stupid, but just go with me," I said because it did seem stupid. It might be oversimplified on my part, but they knew how to read outside the game, their avatars just lacked the knowledge of the alphabet and maybe numbers, Olaf was able to pay earlier after all. Still, it was worth a shot. So, if their toons in the game could just learn the alphabet then maybe it would boost their intellect that last point that would let them read.

"A," I stated simply, showing them the letter.

"This is stupid," said Micaela and Olaf in a single voice.

"Just try it. What have you got to lose?"

"Fine," they said again in unison.

"A," I stated, prompting them to repeat.

"A," they replied.

"B," I started showing the next card, prompting them to repeat.

"B," they lifelessly repeated.

I went through the alphabet and numbers with them and halfway through the third time when shocked and delighted smiles split both their faces.

"Five?" I asked.

"Yeah, notification just popped up at the bottom of the UI. We gained an intellect point. We can read now," answered Olaf.

"Blimey, we can read," Micaela shouted in joy.

"Now we just need to buy some books," said Olaf, grinning.

"Why buy them, you can read the ones in the Town hall for free? And their skill books too."

Both of them suddenly looked at me as if I'd grown a second head.

"Skill books you say?" they asked together, which was starting to get creepy how often and easily they did.

"Yeah, not true skill books but if you read them and pay attention they will teach you skills," I answered.

"Hon, I think your decision to befriend this poor sop that day may be the greatest thing you've ever done," stated Olaf, wiping away a fake tear.

"Dearest, I might have to agree with you. Say, Bye-bye, are you married?" she asked.

"No," I answered, not sure where she was going with this, but feeling decidedly uncomfortable with the look on her face.

"I'd leave him for you if you want me to, just say the word. I'm sure he'd understand, wouldn't you?" she teased.

"I'm afraid I would, it would sadden me greatly, but I would indeed understand. Hell, I might just leave you for him if he swings that way," replied Olaf, adding to his wife's uncomfortable joke.

I shuddered. Now they were both creeping me out. "First, I won't break up a marriage, so you're both out of luck. Second, I definitely prefer the company of women."

"Oh, well, we can still use you though, right?" asked Micaela, leaning in closer to me, her hand gripping both of my shoulders preventing me from fleeing.

"How do you mean?" I asked, suspicious of the odd woman, wriggling unsuccessfully, attempting to get loose from her monster grip.

"Knowledge you dummy, though the offer of a threesome stands, just say the word," said Micaela, a waggle of her one eyebrow and an even more mischievous smirk in place.

"Okay, you guys are making me uncomfortable. I'll show you to the books in the Town hall, then I have a meeting to attend," I offered trying to escape the pair of them as soon as possible. And here I was just agreeing to have dinner with them every night until the pair got their charisma up where they needed it.

CHAPTER 10

After dropping the pair off in front of the bookshelves in Town hall, I booked it to the village temple. "Heh, booked."

Sergeant Butters was waiting for me inside.

"Hello again," I greeted him.

"Hello again Bye-bye, wish it were under better circumstances," he replied solemnly. "Well, come on then, Trini is probably waiting for us."

I follow the man inside the temple and was surprised to see so many altars made of several different materials ranging from stone to metal to various kinds of wood. The walls were also covered in different iconographies suggesting this really was a temple for all faiths.

Butters was steadily continuing through the temple, past the various places of worship, and led me down a flight of stairs to a large room, feeling more like a morgue than part of a temple. If not for all the different iconography on the walls, I might have thought it was one. There were also a few altars made of different kinds of dark colored stone, suggesting this part of the temple was devoted to other, less than reputable Gods.

"Hello gentlemen," greeted Trinico.

"Hello Trini," greeted the sergeant, his tone of voice somewhat softer than usual.

"Bye-bye, nice to see you again. I know we did not get much of an introduction last time we met. I'm Priestess Trinico, servant of the faithful house of all Gods and Goddesses."

I wanted so badly to ask her questions about all the altars and icons, but there were more important objectives at the moment. Namely, the corpse placed on the large stone table in the center of the room.

"Bye-bye Jacko, pleased to meet you," I replied, forgoing my class and titles and any stress that might induce.

It appeared, she too had questions but also recognized the need to get to work. Sergeant Butters and I each took a place standing around the table with the body. Admittedly, part of me was focused on not breathing, the stench was unpleasant.

"I checked the body for poison as requested, but nothing showed. I also checked for magic or curses, which also came up negative. I cannot find any reason he would have just invited death the way he did. Unless he believed he would not die after being attacked the way he was. My greater concern, what would make him believe that without leaving behind some kind of magical residue or toxin in his system? I have no idea," she reported, very businesslike.

Sergeant Butters cursed loudly and slammed an angry fist down on the stone table. The man looked truly sorrowful when he spoke again. "You know I hate to ask you to do this, but I have to. How long?"

Trinico sighed deeply, also seeming to sadden significantly. "Two weeks I think. The eve of Lunestra should be sufficient to call him back and question him," answered Trinico.

"What do you mean, call him back?" I asked, unable to keep the question back. Part of me wanted to keep quiet because both looked so sad before. I couldn't help but wonder though, could an NPC be resurrected?

"I forget you are new. While you adventuring types are blessed with unlimited reincarnation, us citizens are not so lucky. No, I cannot resurrect young guard Davies. What I can do is a small necromantic spell to recall his spirit, momentarily, that we might garner some information on his death, maybe he will tell us who killed him," explained Trinico.

"I thought you were a priest? How can you cast necromantic spells?" I asked, curiosity getting the better of me yet again. I instantly realized I sounded accusatory and apologized. "Sorry, didn't mean to sound like I was accusing you of anything. You just caught me by surprise and I suppose I'm just naturally curious."

"No worries, young priest, you have much still to learn. I am a priest not pledged to any one God or Goddess. I serve in one of the open temples or 'Free Temples', which represents all pantheons. As a protector and servant of such a place, I am granted a small boon by the Gods and Goddesses. It allows me to learn a few magic spells of their realms. Here, in this place devoted to the various Gods of death and the afterlife, I am able to cast such a spell, but only during specific times of power. The eve of the full moon is one such time, as is the actual full moon and the day after. There are more days such as the solstices, equinoxes or any annual death celebration, and a dozen more days throughout the year."

"I see, thank you for the information," I replied, the more I learn the more this world impresses me. Still, I wasn't happy she called me a priest, especially with the look I was now getting from Sergeant Butters. I guess he and I hadn't talked about much during our training sessions to even broach the subject of my class. I also thought he might already know, I assumed after saving Mary Johnson it was bound to get around. And now, I had to worry Sergeant Butters would stop training me since he found out I was a priest and not a warrior or even a paladin. The man had seen me casting healing magic, so he had to know something. I suppose I would discuss it with him soon enough.

Quest Alert: Missing in Action 2 - Completed
Guard Davies has been murdered. Details at the scene suggest the murderer is somehow related to the nearby ruins. There are also several questions that must be answered to progress the investigation. Meet Sergeant Butters at the Hurligville Temple at Noon.
Reward: +500 Experience, Guard's Light Leather Belt

I accepted the completed quest, I hoped the belt wasn't the same belt Davies had been wearing. Unfortunately, I would also need another level and ten more points of strength before I could equip it.

Quest Alert: Missing in Action 3 (Recommended Level 4-6)		
Guard Davies has been murdered. Details at the scene suggest the murderer is somehow related to the nearby ruins. Unfortunately, the Priestess Trinico found no signs of magic or poison on or in the dead guard leaving her no choice but to call back the man's spirit from the nether. Return in 14 days.		
Reward: Experience, Variable Piece of Gear		
Do you accept this Quest?	Yes	No

I accepted the follow-up, promising myself I would check the belt later, along with all the pending system messages I still hadn't checked.

"Come, let us leave this place of death, we can speak more in my office. Plus, it smells so much better than the unfortunate Mr. Davies," said Trinico darkly.

"Right you are," said Butters, leading the way, followed closely behind Trini while I followed up last.

Once in her office, Trinico served us a pleasant tea and cookies. I'd forgotten the taste of cookies, even if it had been less than a week since my internal cookie monster reared his ugly head. I enjoyed them very much, one might say they were a weakness of mine.

"Thank you, Trini," said Butters kindly. Then he turned on me, all kindness gone. "Now what the devil was she talking about, you being some stupid squishy priest?"

I was afraid of that, so I had to make a choice. Tell them both the truth or lie through my teeth, hoping neither decided they wanted nothing to do with me.

"Sweetie, how did you not know?" asked Trini, fixing a look on Butters.

"Why would I know? We train every day, building up his combat skills. It is not some silly knitting circle," answered Butter.

"David, calm down," ordered Trinico with an edge coming through in her voice.

"Yes dear," replied Butters, his face taking on the visage of a scolded child.

"Wait, dear?" I asked, confused.

"Yes, David and I are married, does this surprise you?" asked Trinico, amusement in her voice and in her smile.

"I'd be lying if I said no," I replied. Sergeant Butters and Priestess Trinico were so different from one another. Not only that, she was a priestess, were they even allowed to marry? And what about Sergeant Butters? Not to seem cruel, but how did he convince the woman to even give him a second look with all the scars and his grizzled attitude.

"We are different, but as they say, opposites attract," she replied. I actually saw a hint of a blush on the sergeant's cheeks.

"Can I ask how?" This had to be a good story. At least, I hoped it would be a good story.

"You can ask anything, I will not guarantee an answer though. However, given how much of a shine my David has taken to you I suppose I can tell you the story," she replied with a kindly smile.

"You always make it sound so overly romantic, and I am no romantic, woman," the sergeant, no, David insisted.

"So? I tell it better anyway," she retorted, her blush and smile not fading in the slightest.

"Fine, tell the story your way, but do not expect me to keep my trap shut, not when you tell it wrong," he insisted once more.

"So, years ago David was a knight in the service of King Leopold the 8th. He is royalty you know, son of an archduke no less," started Trinico.

David made a sound of disgust, "My father was not a good man and worse as a parent. He pressed me into service as a squire at 7 years old, then forced a knighthood on me at 14, and then forced me to court, just a day after my knighting, to serve the king. I may not have known better back then, but I still hated what was forced on me."

"David, you would not be the man you are now if not for your past. You must let it go," said Trinico. It seemed they had this argument frequently enough.

"Just tell the story already," the man insisted, changing the subject away from his youth.

"I met David five years after he began service to the king. I was 18 and I was aspiring to become a high priestess of Hermes, the God of medicine and healing. So of course, I knew, for what I wanted to achieve, I would have to serve on the battlefield. Looking back, I had no idea what I was getting into at the time," she paused here, and her face looked sad, lost in history. "I was such a foolish little girl back then."

"It was the demon incursion of the Western Whitelight Mountains, one of the kingdoms primary sources of mithril ore and marble stone. As you can imagine, it was of key importance. We must have thrown half a million soldiers at them in the first month alone, most of those men died, but I guarantee you, those boys took at least two demons apiece before they passed. Those were the days before the Adventurers. Boy, do I wish we had some of your ilk back then," David mused.

Trinico continued, "I had never seen such death and devastation. I remember pouring out all the healing mana I could, drinking a potion or two and doing it again and again, for days on end. Anyway, one day, the legion I was serving as support for had been flanked-"

"That rotten Montague should have held his line," groused David, I'd never heard such venom from the man, not even when he was dressing down his men this morning.

"The group responsible for holding the eastern flank of our battle-line panicked and ordered a retreat. The demons, seeing the line break, took advantage. They split their number, sending half east and half west, right at my legion. It became a massacre. We were so overwhelmed, I had said my prayers to all the Gods and Goddesses promising to become a servant of all if they would spare the people I was charged to protect. And my prayers were answered," Trinico sighed loudly, a dreamy expression came over her face.

"I tell you, I was just following orders to try and reinforce your group, after that moron's cowardly retreat," David interrupted, a deep frown marring his face.

"And I say it was the divine hearing my prayer, my version sounds better anyway, now may I continue husband?" she asked impatiently and clearly annoyed by him ruining her fanciful daydream.

"Yeah, sure, you just keep telling it wrong, but whatever," he said noncommittally.

"Anyway, here comes this young, brash knight in shining silver armor on a beautiful white steed, the likes of which I had never seen."

"The horse was gray, the armor was gray with a black and gold tabard, and I was certainly covered from head to toe in demon blood and guts," he whispered to me a little too loudly.

Trinico glared at her husband but he clearly ignored it. "His unit saved my people and me but during the fight, he was gravely injured. I made it my personal mission to ensure he was healed to full health."

"It was barely a scratch," protested David.

"Your arm was half cut off and you lost an eye," stated Trinico.

"Just a scratch," stated David, again, though his protest was not as forced.

"I never left his side again. For the remainder of the campaign, I was always there to heal his wounds and look after his men."

"I forgot how clingy you were back then. I swear you were like a little, lost lamb," David disputed her recollection.

Ignoring him again, she continued, "After the demon invasion was pushed back, and the portal to the inverse was sealed shut, I chose to continue my service to David's legion. I went with him when his father took ill."

"I told her to stay with the legion," said David sighed, defeated at this point, and simply accepting the inevitable retelling of their story.

"I healed his father, removing the disease. When it was done, I had hoped his father would be proud of all David had accomplished. All the battles won, the loyal friends he had earned. Instead, the man scorned me. He said if I was even a decent priestess, his son would not be so disfigured . . . would not be such a monstrosity," she paused here to wipe away a tear.

"He was always a complete bastard. Always favored my older brother, the more cunning one. I do not have proof, but I would bet he is the one that pushed my father to shutter me into service. Does not matter anymore, the lot of them are a complete waste of life," David hissed angrily even remembering the event.

"You would not have believed the way David leaped to my defense, tearing down his father the way he did. Belittling the old man's lack of honor or service to the crown. It was impressive to watch, David let loose every last bit of feeling and emotion he had ever felt. He let him have it for all the things his father had done to him. Then at the end, he said, and I will never forget this. 'I would rather choose her every day for the rest of my life than have anything to do with you or this family.' It was so romantic and such a powerful proclamation of love and his desire to marry me."

"His father disowned him outright, and despite his service as a knight in the incursion and all he had achieved, the king had no choice but to strip him of his knighthood. Rumors at the time said his father and brother put pressure on the court, but once again there was no proof. Still, the king did not forget about him, or me, for that matter. The king personally talked to the pair of us in private after the official proclamation. The king had said it was not much, but he could at least offer him a billet as a sergeant in this quiet little hamlet and me this church. David and I married a week later and moved here together. We've been together ever since," she ended her story looking content and happy, a dusting of blush on her cheeks.

David leaned over and whispered to me, "When she invited me to a church that day, I thought we were going to pray together for a safe journey or something. Mind you, this before the adventurers and the portals on the World Tree opened up. Anyway, I had no idea we were getting married until she said, 'I do' and gave me a look, I felt it in my bones, warning me I had better say the same thing, or else."

"So perfect," said the woman. She was suddenly giggling in a way that would make any little girl proud, her cheeks aflame with a deeper, redder blush.

"Right, so you have heard her version of our story . . ." he looked like he had more to say but chose to just let it lie, lest he ends up in trouble with the woman. "Now, I believe you owe me a story about you, young priest," the man prompted me.

Ugh! Why did they share their story with me? It was romantic, and David's interjections were hilarious, and I couldn't help feeling as if I knew these two people, and now, I had to talk to them straight. "I am a priest," I started.

"Such a waste of talent," complained David.

"Let me finish," I insisted, forestalling the man's grumblings. "I am not a normal priest. I was granted a unique class by the Goddess Issara." Even as I said it, I could have sworn a light shone down on me from above.

"Great blessings be, he is a chosen of the Gods," gasped Trinico, suddenly kneeling and bowing in reverence to me.

"Please, don't do that," I said, looking to the sergeant for help only to see him take a knee as well. "Stop it, both of you get up. You don't have to do that."

I didn't notice it at first, but both were mumbling rapidly under their breaths, seemingly in prayer. It was another minute before they both retook their seats.

"What was that all about?" I asked, not sure if I wanted the answer.

"I do not know much but I will tell you what I can," started Trinico. I was once again preparing for a long story. "When the first adventurer appeared just over 3 moons ago, the citizens of the World Tree rejoiced. The opening of portals throughout the land to join us all together was supposed to be a great and wondrous event, heralding a time of light and hope for all of us. We had no idea of the diversity that would come . . . or of the evil, some adventurers would unleash."

"The adventurers were supposed to be heroes made real. Immortal and powerful, they certainly were. Heroes many . . . most were not. In fact, I would say most were more villain than hero. We had little to no defense against them, entire settlements were slaughtered. Other adventurers tried to help, but even they would be killed as well. Despite being able to reincarnate, they could not stop them. Those adventurers just seemed to give up trying to stop the evil and moved on to other adventures."

"Thousands of citizens and adventurers alike were killed, but nothing was done to stop the suffering . . . the murders. Eventually, the holy orders came together to pray to all the Gods and Goddesses for help, and the prayers were answered. Every priest throughout the World Tree was told, Adventurers will come who will hear the call of justice, and by their words promise justice to the Gods and Goddess, above and below. And in service to the Gods and Goddesses of justice, they would bring us hope."

"So, you see, you are an answer to our prayer," added David.

"Okay, I understand this is important, and honestly, pretty freaking awesome, but I'm missing something. First, why wouldn't the other priests in service to the Gods and Goddesses of justice already be doing this? Second, why would it matter which God or Goddess you serve if it's to grant justice to the people of the World Tree?"

"You are the only priest of the Goddess Issara," answered Trinico, smiling at my apparent naivete.

"Eh?" I asked, not quite believing what I was just told. "What do you mean the only priest?"

"The Gods and Goddesses of justice are the few Gods capable of influencing the world, as such they are forbidden priests and paladins to serve as their will in the World Tree," Trinico explained.

"I don't understand, paladins are all about justice. Why wouldn't a God or Goddess of justice be able to have a paladin or many paladins in their service?" I asked.

"It is old knowledge, but in exchange for Law and Order to be used to rule over the people of the World Tree, the one thing they can still influence, the Gods and Goddesses of justice had to give up the ability to give their blessings to such men and women. As such, there are no priests or paladins in their service," she answered.

"Then how do Law and Order get enforced?"

"And this was the trick of the other Gods and Goddesses. In order to uphold the law and establish order, the responsibility was turned over to all the other Gods and Goddesses. They were to charge their paladins and priests to enforce the Law and Order but as you can imagine . . ." she paused.

"Each God or Goddess only encourages the enforcement of Law and Order according to whatever will serve them better. In other words, the paladins and priests are weapons to see who can gather more power," I finished her statement.

"Correct," said Trinico sadly. "But to know our prayers have been answered. That a priest of a Goddess of justice has appeared in the World Tree. And best of all, it is truly a blessing this priest has been placed with us, to be able to host you in our little town. Wait until word spreads, there will be such celebrations."

"Woah, hold it right there. This doesn't go beyond this room. I trusted you with this knowledge because you trusted me with your story. I know the knowledge of my existence gives you hope, but as soon as other adventurers find out, they will come hunting for me. Do you truly think I have the power to defend myself, while my own adventure in the World Tree has only just begun?" I protested, hopefully, given them both pause.

Trinico deflated slightly, bringing her hands to her mouth. The idea had apparently not even crossed her mind.

"He is right," said David, though he looked rather sad to say it. "He is growing stronger every day, but he still has a long road ahead of him."

"He is our hope for the future, we cannot let hope be extinguished," said Trinico. A fire seemed to have suddenly lit inside her. "Then we must do everything in our power to prepare him for the long road ahead."

"Hmm, true. But I have to say, it makes me a little sad. I was enjoying working with him, but as a priest, his time is better served working with you," said David.

Double ugh!

Why did I keep getting forced into a corner at every turn? First, it was my class quest, then the moonshine quest chain, and now the murder investigation, not to mention all the other quests that kept popping up. Now, I was risking losing valuable training if I didn't fully trust these two. So troublesome!

I sort of just sagged back in my chair sighing loudly. Eventually, I spoke, I couldn't hold back from these two if I want to keep up my training. "Stop jumping to conclusions, Sergeant. Didn't you listen to your wife's story? The Goddess Issara isn't allowed to have either a priest or a paladin."

"But you just said you are a priest . . . you are not just a priest, are you?" asked David, suddenly looking excited.

My own grin may have grown in anticipation. "I am a Novice Warrior Priest of the Goddess Issara," I answered, feeling smug and maybe a little happy to see the infectious grin split the sergeant's grizzled mug.

"Oh, you sneaky, wonderful Goddess," said David, his eyes shining happily.

"Yeah, she's pretty awesome," I replied, trying but failing to keep a straight face.

"If I was not already devoted to service of all Gods and Goddesses, I would have this temple converted tomorrow and swear my loyalty and service to her for the rest of my days. As it is, I will just have to give extra offerings in her name," said Trinico, grinning similarly to David.

"But boy, if you do not have your work cut out for you, you poor sod," said David. His grin turning slightly mischievous, which I really didn't care for at all.

"Why?" I asked hesitantly. What did I miss? He clearly knew something I didn't, but what?

"Do you know what the main stat attributes of a warrior are?" asked David., His grin threatening to turn into a full-blown smile from ear to ear.

"Strength, Dexterity, Stamina, and Endurance," I replied, caution in my voice and feeling a sense of dread, he was about to drop a giant bomb on me.

"And a priest?" asked Trinico.

"Intellect and Wisdom," I answered.

"And Charisma," she added.

My thought process halted on that. Why would charisma be important for a priest? I gave it only the slightest bit of thought when I realized why. Part of being a priest meant attracting followers to your God's cause. It was also necessary to get people to trust you enough to ask for help.

"Now, if you put it all together," prompted David.

Warrior and Priest classes. Warrior Priest class. I wanted to curse my Goddess just then. Curse her loudly and for all time.

"I think he gets it dear," said Trinico, the amusement in her voice was easy to hear.

"Not yet, but he is close," said David, actually smiling now. He was definitely amused.

I hate my life sometimes and this was definitely one of those times. As I've mentioned before most players are strongly encouraged to hit at least the level 5 stat cap for all stats. This is done intentionally to give all players a solid base and the ability to select from a wide range of classes. Once you hit the level five cap for a stat, the experience gained for that stat drops to 10%. As such, prior to the level five if you received +100-Experience for a stat by doing a specific action, after level five, +100-Experience turns into +10-Experience. The only exceptions to this reduction are racial bonuses. Let's say for me if I didn't already have a class, everything would drop to 10% except for Intellect and Charisma which would only drop to 50% because I am a half-high elf, half-human, but everything would remain low until I chose a class.

As to how that affects your class selection? Say I choose to become an archer. My primary stat as an archer would be dexterity, which would probably give me 100% or higher experience gains to that stat. Secondary would be stamina which would be used for most, if not all of my abilities, which would probably give me around 75% or higher experience. Tertiary would be Strength and Intellect. I would need strength to draw my bow, and some special shots, may use mana instead of, or along with, stamina, which I would guess, you'd get 50% or so experience for those stats.

However, I've already selected my class. I'm a warrior priest, what does that mean exactly? I get the bonuses for a warrior of Strength, Dexterity, Stamina, and Endurance with Dexterity probably on the low end at 50%, cause, after all, you can't kill what you can't hit, which impacts both hit rating, dodge rating and even parry rating. And I get the priests bonus experience for Intellect, Wisdom, and Charisma where Charisma is probably the lowest, around 50%, simply because it's hard to help the people who need your help if they don't trust you.

I'm sure you're thinking, why is that a bad thing? Why is it bad to be able to increase all your stats more easily than other players?

The answer is simply time.

It takes time to level stats. It takes even more time as you get to higher levels and higher stat points because each successive level requires additional experience, so do stat points.

I simply leaned forward tucking my head between my knees and tried to breathe deeply to will nausea away.

"Now he gets it," said David. The man sounded way too pleased with himself.

I got an awesome, overpowered class and it is going to be the death of me. I'm not a grinder. I hate grinding. I know early on that player characters require a good amount of grinding to build up skills and abilities and even the base level 5 stat caps. I accepted that coming into this game and was mentally prepared for it. What was a little grinding at the start? But what is being asked of me now is just not fair.

Part of me wished I could just drop my class and pick something more my speed, but I didn't want that either. I loved dishing out justice to Pwn Star69. I accomplished something when I caught those trolls. If I were to become a paladin for another God or Goddess, then I'd be serving justice best suited to them and not what I felt was justice. I don't believe in absolute justice or that justice should be blind. I guess I'm more of a moral justice kind of guy, following what I believe to be right or wrong with my heart.

Trusting my gut as my grandpa used to say.

I suppose that was the moment, I understood I had chosen my path when I first said 'Yes' to the Goddess' offer. But I hadn't truly accepted my path until that moment.

"And there is acceptance," commented Trinico as I sat back up.

"Good," said David, his hand giving my shoulder a reassuring squeeze.

"So, how do I do this? How do I build my stats across the board?" I asked.

"Okay, so there are a few skills I can teach you, one, in particular, is very useful and can be used as a stat building exercise. That should cover Dexterity and Stamina completely and give a little to Strength too. I have a plan for Strength too, but . . . well, just wait for tomorrow. Endurance you can earn out in the world fighting beasts and monsters to your heart's content," stated David thoughtfully.

"I will teach you a more difficult skill, hopefully, it will cover all three, but you will need to read this tonight," she opened a desk drawer and rummaged for a minute before producing a book.

"How to Win Friends and Influence People," I read the cover. It sounded familiar to me, but I just couldn't place it.

"It probably will not give you a skill, but it will give you some ideas for the exercise I am going to be teaching you," she said, a little caution in her voice.

"Okay, anything else? I think my brain is going to melt if you make me realize anything else today," I said, roughly rubbing my hands through my hair.

"I think we have tormented you enough for today, come to see me early tomorrow and we will get you started," said David.

Class Quest Alert: Training with Sergeant Butters 1		
Having put your trust in Trinico and David Butters, they have offered you training to develop your stats as quickly and efficiently as possible.		
Reward: Experience, Skill		
Do you accept this Quest?	Yes	No

"And come to see me when you finish with David," said Trinico with a kind smile on her face.

Class Quest Alert: Training with Priestess Trinico 1		
Having put your trust in Trinico and David Butters, they have offered you training to develop your stats as quickly and efficiently as possible.		
Reward: Experience, Skill		
Do you accept this Quest?	Yes	No

"Okay, see you both tomorrow." I accepted both quests, partly excited, partly terrified of what was to come. For now, I needed to get back to the inn and read this new book.

The return to the inn was slow and quiet. I had a great deal of information to digest. Specifically, regarding my class. I was unique, being the only Warrior Priest in service to the Goddess Issara. There would be no others. That was more responsibility than I probably wanted. It also made me wonder, was I unique as a Warrior Priest or was I unique in service to the Goddess? If I was the only Warrior Priest, then the workload to keep up justice would be beyond me. However, if I was simply unique to the Goddess, then there would be others for the other Gods and Goddesses of justice. That also made me wonder how many other Gods and Goddesses of justice were there?

Eventually, I returned to the inn as planned, but rather than hide in my room like I should have, and wanted to, I took a seat next to the fireplace in the lounge area, taking one of the big squishy chairs. I popped open the book and started to read, trying to ignore all the other noise still running around in my noggin. I had a task to complete before the next day. Thankfully, the book wasn't thick, less thankfully, it was more than a little complex. Parts of it seemed to be outright manipulation to me, but it also gave so many ways to improve relations with the people around me. I couldn't not see the benefit. I wasn't sure how this was going to help me with boosting my Intellect and Wisdom, but it would definitely help with my Charisma. Maybe that was the point. I'd find out the next day when I met with Trinico for training.

Before I knew it, it was nearly time for dinner and I still hadn't bothered looking at the overwhelming number of system messages, I would no doubt be inundated with as soon as I hit the button. Still, I was going to put it off until I have my evening bath. I had the perfect bathtub reading material and was not going to let it go to waste.

Instead, I went back to my room and sat down with my journal and started writing about my day, parts of it in painful detail, adding drawings to bring life to the memories I couldn't adequately describe in words. I have to say journaling in this manner proved to be very therapeutic.

When I returned downstairs, I was greeted by the sight of Micaela and Olaf seated comfortably on the couch, waiting for me. Both of them looked exhausted and tired too.

"Evening," I greeted the pair, taking a seat in the same large chair I had sat and read in earlier.

"Hey Bye-bye," grumbled Micaela, her head resting on Olaf's shoulder.

"What's up with you two? Why so exhausted?" I asked, looking at Olaf as he seemed to be a little more awake than Micaela did at the moment.

"Too many books," they grumbled in one voice.

I tried not to grin but couldn't hold back. "Oh, do tell."

"Met the mayor, he came out a few minutes after you left and gave us a few books, he said they were worth reading. I learned 'Beast Tracking' while Mic read a book that gave her a 'Scavenging' skill. It allows her to get meat and trophies from animals or parts from machines. It's not a gathering skill so she can't use it to get leather or metals or even herbs. I think it's mostly just a way to loot things without pockets or some kind of magic. Still, a good skill to have. Then we traded books."

"What book did you read for the 'Scavenging' skill?" I asked. That one would actually be useful out in the wilds.

"The book is called 'Let NO-Thing Go to Waste'. Mayor said you might want it and asked us to give you the book when we were done, so here you go," added Olaf, tossing the book to me. I added it to my ever-growing list of books.

"Then Micaela found a book called 'Way of the Spirits', which she just had to read."

Micaela perked up for a moment to cheer loudly, pumping one of her massive arms in the air, "Worth it!" Only to slump back over again.

"She's a Shaman now, which is exactly what she wanted to be," explained Olaf.

"Not yet I'm not," protested Micaela. "Not until I carve my first totem and enter the spirit realm."

"You have the class babe, you're a shaman, stop sweating the details," Olaf attempted to reassure his wife.

"While she read through that, I picked up a book called 'Steady Hands', which turns out is the name of the skill. It's a dexterity training skill which is awesome, because that is an important stat for me, you know, for aiming," he continued, smirking.

"Nice, so I take it you both had a productive afternoon?" I confirmed.

"Yeah, just mentally wiped I think. Still, +5-Intellect and +5-Wisdom each," he smiled happily at the end. I could see he felt a real sense of accomplishment.

"Congratulations," I said, honestly happy for the pair to have proven to everyone that 'knew' ogres were a crap class, they didn't know what they were talking about.

"We owe you Bye-bye," said Olaf seriously.

"And I'll be sure to collect one day, but that day is not today. Today we celebrate, so wake up. We're gonna party tonight!" I cheered, attempting to rouse them both from their brain stupor.

"Fine," groaned Micaela. "I suppose I can muster up a little enthusiasm, but only because it's you asking."

"Right then, Dogson," I called looking toward the bar. "Three Delger Dwarven Stouts if you please!"

Dogson quirked an eyebrow, surprised by the loud request, but nodded anyway.

"Are you two working in the mine tomorrow?" I asked, looking back at my friends as an idea came to mind.

"I think we can miss a day in the mines," said Olaf.

"Yay!" cheered Micaela.

So, we celebrated, the booze restoring life and animation to both Olaf and Micaela, as they started to have a little fun.

"I've been meaning to ask," I started, trying to change the subject away from my flirtations with Trish, the barmaid. "You guys mentioned you financed your pods, right? I'm sure you weren't the only ones. So how come I don't see a whole bunch of ogres and sprites running around all over the place?"

"Day one, mate," answered Olaf, as if that would make everything clear.

I waited a moment for him to expand but he didn't. "Please, tell me more," I prompted him, a little sarcasm leaking through.

"As it was explained to us by Maggie, the ogre were designed to be the best mining race and the sprite the best herbalism race. I guess the high up mucky-mucks predicted there would be a high demand for resources and as such, a very lucrative opportunity. Lucrative to them especially, the percentage our broker keeps and the percentage the auction house keeps, goes straight into Seed Inc's pockets, as pure profit. Because of that, they reserved 20% of the first wave of pods for those who were willing to finance their pods."

"After our first month, we did a little research during the mandatory seven-day break. We found out they did the same for the second and planned to do the same for the third wave. They'll probably do the same for every wave of pod shipments. Keeps a workforce providing supplies, while they pay off their pods, and keeps bringing in a new labor pool as we pay off our pods."

"Anyway, back to the original question. Most of the miners are idiots. They figure that since they've leveled, they would move provinces, so they can mine higher level ores which theoretically should sell for more, except most ores don't sell well because there is still such a high number of people choosing professions, only to drop them to try something different. Demand on the low-end ore stays high while high-end ore stays low, for now at least. So, there are plenty of ogre miners and sprite herbalist running all over, but most of them have stupidly moved on to the higher-level provinces," explained Olaf.

"I also read they were going to open up two more races," added Micaela. "Treant Herbalists and Knocker Miners. I get the Treant Herbalist, you're basically a walking tree but Knockers are tiny little blighters, how can they be any good at mining?"

"What's a knocker?" I asked. I'd never heard of such a creature.

"It's a little cave gremlin with a pointy head and razor-sharp teeth," answered Olaf.

"Huh, how about that?" I was genuinely curious. I'd have to look them up when my first month of emersion ended. Still, playing a treant sounded fun.

"It was only a rumor, probably not true," added Micaela. "But yeah, it could be fun."

"Time for another round, I think," said Olaf, staring the bottom of the keg he called a beer mug.

I signaled Trish for another round of beer getting a wave and smile in return which I took to mean 'yes'.

"Oi!" shouted a voice from the entrance, calling everyone's attention. There stood Guard Gavin Davies pointing a finger at me.

"Who? Me?" I asked, surprised by the pointed finger. I guess I shouldn't have been too surprised, given everything I'd done that day. Still, I'm not sure what exactly I could have done to get Gavin this worked up.

"You, what did you do?" demanded Gavin as he marched straight for me.

"I have no idea, but I'll bet it was something awesome," I replied, feeling rather gregarious. Clearly, the beer was going straight to my head.

I could see I threw Gavin with my reply, but it didn't last. "What did you do to the sergeant?"

"David? Nothing, why? Did he say I did something?" I asked. I had no idea what I could have done to the sergeant, but I had a feeling it would affect me more than I would want it to.

"He is smiling," answered Gavin.

"And that's bad?" asked Micaela.

"Yes!" shouted Gavin. "But that is not the worst of it. He was humming . . . I think he might have been . . . I think he is . . . happy. What in the name of all the Gods and Goddesses did you do?"

"Nothing, I swear. I had tea with him and Priestess Trinico," I replied, slightly perplexed, first by Gavin's pale complexion and what I could only guess was panic. Second by the sergeant's odd behavior.

"What was this sergeant doing while he was smiling and humming?" asked Micaela, she seemed to be as curious as I was.

"He was building something by the training area. He had all the guards cutting back the forest near the barracks all the way to the mote. We had to cut them down to the root too and burn out what we could of the stumps," complained Gavin.

"Did anyone bother to ask him why?" asked Micaela.

"Ours is not to reason why ours is to do or die," replied Gavin automatically.

"So, what is Sergeant Butters building?" I asked.

"Would not say," answered Gavin. "But he did say, and I am quoting here, 'Bye-bye is gonna love this'."

Suddenly I was regretting sharing anything with Sergeant Butters about my class. I was suddenly terrified and had no idea what to expect.

"So, I ask again, what did you do?" asked Gavin again.

"We talked about training, that's all," I replied. I had my secrets to keep.

"Fine, do not tell me, but I swear, if I get pulled into any crazy training because of this I will feed you to the wolves myself, understand?"

Thankfully any further conversation was forestalled by Trish bringing our next round of beers, which also seemed to make Gavin forget any anger he may have had for me.

I stayed with them for a while, chatting, drinking and flirting with Trish at every opportunity, but called it an early night but not before eliciting a promise from Olaf and Micaela to meet me at 8:00 in front of the barracks.

Once I had finally sat in the bath and let the stresses of the day fade away. I opened the many system messages, I hadn't bothered with yet. First, between the shopping, talking with David and Trinico and finally, drinking with Olaf, Micaela, and Gavin I had gained +10 Charisma. That made today's adventures alone completely worthwhile.

I did gain +5 Intellect and +5 Wisdom from reading the two books today. After tallying my stat increases the remaining messages were all related to skills. First, regarding the two books I read today, my 'Track Humanoid' skill gained a few levels but the 'How to Win Friends and Influence People' yielded an amazing skill called 'Influence'.

Influence	Level: 5	Experience: 16.77%
Skill Effect (Passive): Increases your Charisma by 0.50%		

Skill Effect (Passive):	Increases your Charisma Experience Gain for successful interactions by 5.00%	

I'm not sure if it was what Trinico had in mind when she gave me the book, but I was not going to complain at all. While the boost to Charisma was terrible right now, it would eventually get much better. But to go along with 'Influence' I picked up a skill 'Barter' from when I was haggling with Giggle-Ana in the weapon shop.

Barter	Level: 3	Experience: 19.54%
Skill Effect (Passive): Reduce purchase cost by 0.04% (0.15% of Charisma)		
Skill Effect (Passive): Increases your Charisma Experience Gain for successful transactions by 3.00%		

Once again, not very strong to start, but will improve with time and practice. I also got the 'Maintenance' skill from Giggle-Ana.

Maintenance	Level: 5	Experience: 0.54%
Skill Effect (Active): Allows basic repair of equipment restoring 3 points of durability at the cost of 2 durability capacity.		

My favorite by far was the next skill I learned, probably from trying to reconstruct the crime scene earlier that day.

You have learned the skill 'Eye for Detail'

Eye for Detail	Level: 1	Experience: 0.00%
Skill Effect (Passive): Enables you to see details that would be missed otherwise.		
Skill Range: 10 yards	Chance to See: 10.00%	Chance to Identify: 10.00%

Congratulations! Having learned a third ocular skill, you have unlocked the Advanced Skill 'Perception'. 'Beast Tracking', 'Humanoid Tracking' & 'Eye for Detail' have become subskills of 'Perception'.

Perception	Level: 5	Experience: 18.90%
Skill Range: 10.50 yards	Chance to See: 11.25%	Chance to Identify/Track:

		13.00%
Subskill: Beast Tracking	**Skill Effect (Passive):** *Enables you to see animal tracks to better hunt them.*	
Subskill: Humanoid Tracking	**Skill Effect (Passive):** *Enables you to track humanoids.*	
Subskill: Eye for Detail	**Skill Effect (Passive):** *Enables you to see details that would be missed otherwise.*	

It was awesome. And it combined all of my other skill levels for 'Beast Tracking' and 'Humanoid Tracking', making it start at level 5. As an added bonus all three of my professions had leveled up.

Lore	**Level: 4**	**Experience:** 87.50%
Professional Skill: *Lore is the study of the history of the World Tree and its denizens.*		

That must have been from hearing David and Trinico's story, at least the parts regarding the Demon Incursion and Sergeant Butters family history.

Writing	**Level: 11**	**Experience:** 45.35%
Professional Skill: *Writing is the ability to communicate through the written word.*		

From journaling.

Drawing	**Level: 11**	**Experience:** 38.65%
Professional Skill: *Drawing is the ability to communicate through drawn images.*		

And drawing the images to go with my journal.

I was most excited about the last two. I only needed level 10 to get a specialization in 'Writing' and 'Drawing'. I just needed to see the mayor tomorrow, to speak to him about the books for it.

Eventually, I hit a point where I knew it was time to leave the tub and go to bed. One last check of my stats and I was set to sleep off the beer and mentally prepare myself for the days ahead.

Level:	4	Experience:	23.75%
Class:	Novice Warrior Priest of Issara		

HP (Health Points):	780/780
MP (Mana Points):	230/230
SP (Stamina Points):	520/520
Strength:	40
- Melee Damage Modifier	+40
Dexterity:	40
- Melee Critical Strike Chance	4.00%
- Hit Chance	62.00%
- Dodge Chance	4.00%
Endurance:	78
Stamina:	52
Intellect:	23
- Spell Critical Strike Chance	2.30%
Wisdom:	19
Charisma:	26
Health Regeneration per minute:	39
Mana Regeneration per minute:	10
Stamina Regeneration per minute:	30
Holy Spell Damage Bonus:	18
Holy Spell Healing Bonus:	13
Carrying Capacity in Lbs.:	200

CHAPTER 11

New day, same dead fowl clucking . . . if only. Breakfast and hair of the dog, at Dogson's insistence, had me out of the inn a little before 8:00 am. Thankfully it was a short walk to the barracks and to meet the waiting Olaf and Micaela.

"Morning you two," I greeted them, cheerfully.

"What did you make us drink?" moaned Olaf, looking more than a little pale.

"Dwarven Stout. I suppose I should take you back to the inn for the cure," I volunteered.

"Cure?" the pair asked in a singular and still creepy voice.

"Yeah, come on," I motioned for them to follow me back to the inn. Thirty minutes later all three of us were on our way back to the barracks.

"I still can't believe we went back to the Dog House Inn for Dogson's cure, which happened to be hair of the dog," joked Micaela, more pep back in her step.

"Is she going to keep saying that?" I asked looking to Olaf for some kind of relief. The woman must have repeated the same statement at least a dozen times in the last ten minutes.

"She'll get it out of her system when something new distracts her," offered Olaf, chagrin clear on his face.

Once around the back of the barracks, I found the Sergeant going through some weapon routine or other, but beyond the training circle he was using, I saw the construction Gavin had mentioned the previous day. It appeared the man had built some kind of training equipment, it looked familiar to me, but I couldn't exactly place where I'd seen it before.

"Ooh, gymnastics equipment," cooed Micaela excitedly.

Now I recognized the equipment from the now defunct Olympics. The games used to represent the best in athletics the world had to offer, until it became far too expensive to maintain, combined with a huge number of scandals involving bribery of judges and performance-enhancing drugs. Eventually, no country in the world wanted to host them, so they went the way of the dinosaur and the desktop PC. There were still sporting events, but most of them were now digital and actual sports like gymnastics were scarce.

"Right, you are, lass," said the sergeant as he approached. "That there is for Bye-bye. I will get him started in a few minutes. The real question is, what can I do for a pair of ogres such as yourselves?"

"David, these are my friends, Olaf and Micaela. I was hoping you'd be willing to give them some weapons training," I explained, the man didn't seem put out by their presence, and I was hoping he wouldn't be prejudiced toward them due to their race.

"Sergeant or Sergeant Butters while I am at work if you please," he barked harshly. Then he turned to Olaf and Micaela, both of whom suddenly looked rather small next to the powerhouse former knight. "I do not see any weapons on either of you, so we might have something of a problem here," snarled Sergeant Butters. The man finally took a calming breath. "I am not unwilling to train you both, but you need a weapon to learn a weapon skill."

"I'm an Ogre Artillery, my hand-cannons won't be ready for a couple weeks," explained Olaf without needing to be prompted.

"Okay, I can help you with your weapons when you get them but for now there is not much I can do for you. Now what about you lass?" the sergeant asked.

I was a little sad to see Olaf deflate, looking so small.

"I'm a shaman," said Micaela proudly.

"Very nice, do you have a totem yet?" he asked.

"Not yet," answered Micaela sheepishly.

"Right, so neither of you have weapons yet," said David.

"No sir," they answered together.

"But you can still teach them to move right?" I asked. I knew it was a long shot, but I couldn't have just brought them here only to let them down.

"Yeah, but it seems wasteful . . . then again, maybe it is not a bad idea. Alright, I will help them, but it will not be much." Micaela and Olaf perked right back up again, seemingly much more excited.

"But first, I need to get you started on your training," he motioned for me to follow him.

I followed him past most of the gymnastics equipment until we were standing before a large square metal frame with an equally large square of cloth suspended in the air by metal springs.

"This here is a trampoline. It is where we are going to start training you in 'Acrobatics'," he explained.

I knew what a trampoline was, but I'd only ever seen them in old circus vids, never in real or digital life, not until now.

"So, what do I do?"

"Shoes and armor off, rack your weapon and shield then climb on. Then, just start jumping around to get a feel for it. I will be back in a few minutes, need to get Olaf and Micaela's training started."

I walked back with him to rack my spear and shield with his gear before walking back to the trampoline. I didn't have much in the way of armor, just my vest and gloves which I set atop my sandals next to the trampoline.

It wasn't hard to climb up onto the surface of it, but it was odd to stand on. Every step I took sank in, like walking on sand, but then pushed back when I stepped off, causing my step to bounce. It was kind of fun, to be honest. Eventually, I jumped, surprised by how it caused me to jump to a great height and land in a way that allowed me to jump even higher still. Before I knew it, I was jumping two and three times my height straight into the air, it was awesome.

"Good," called the sergeant from the side of the trampoline. "Now, try to toss in a flip."

A flip, really? I'd never done anything like that before. But then again, with this kind of height in my jumps, why wouldn't I be able to flip. So, this time when my feet hit the surface and pushed off, I added some forward rotation that turned into a flip, then another, and then half of another before I face planted on the springy surface.

Sergeant Butters began howling with laughter, letting me know what he thought. Personally, I was just happy not to be injured or hurt.

I affixed the best glare I could and leveled it at the sergeant, who just waved it off.

"Oh relax, you are fine. Now you know you can try anything you want on the trampoline and not worry about getting hurt so long as you do not go off the side," he defended, still chuckling.

He was right. I could already tell, I no longer had reason to fear the trampoline. I could experiment freely, I could flip and jump all I wanted, not getting hurt if I fell or mistimed the move.

"Now, you've played around and gotten a feel for the trampoline, we can start the actual training part. 'Acrobatics' is a way of moving that incorporates jumping, flipping, rolling and diving. It is also one of the most difficult skills the learn, unless you're a ranger, archer, rogue or thief, and even they struggle to learn this. Why is this so important for them to learn? Because, it is far and away the best way to train Dexterity and Stamina with a little Strength training on top," the sergeant explained.

That sounded so awesome to me.

"I will have to tell you up front, do not expect to learn this in a day. Do not be discouraged if you have not learned it in a week. Do not panic even when you do not learn it after two or even three weeks. You need to have patience and learn all of it," he paused, motioning to the new equipment he'd added to the training area. "One step at a time. We start with the trampoline where you will find your center of balance."

"How do I start?" I asked, trying to sound determined. If this was such a difficult and rare skill, then it was one I was definitely going to learn.

"Good then. You started out with jumping up and down, trying to get higher and higher. Do not do that. This skill is not about jumping as high as you can. It is about jumping to dodge an attack or hurdling an obstacle in your path as you run. You will do yourself a favor if you start with the mindset of the 'Shift' skill."

I nodded. I had to remember, this skill was about combat and training. Not just a way to make fancy moves and look cool . . . at least not entirely.

"First, you are going to work on a simple front flip," said the sergeant.

I started to bounce to get some height before I was pelted in the forehead with a pebble, compliments of Sergeant Butters.

"No bouncing. You will not be able to bounce once you are on solid ground. A trampoline is a training tool, but it only works, if you do. Now, flip forward, try not to use the trampoline too much."

And here I thought this first step was going to be easy. I tried again. This time, I bent slightly at the knees and pushed off. Still aided slightly by the trampoline, I got a little extra height, rolled forward in the air, but came down too soon. I landed on my butt and bounced back up to my feet.

"Better, but you need to get your flip motion faster. You should be starting your flip as soon as your feet leave the trampoline," instructed the sergeant.

For the next hour I flipped and flipped and flipped some more, and even when I successfully flipped once or even twice in a row I flipped again.

"Take a breather, get some water then get back to it. I should probably spend some time with the new victims you brought me."

I jumped down from the trampoline expecting the ground to absorb my impact, similar to the trampoline but was met with disappointment and pain in my legs and bare feet. I walked for the water barrel with my legs making odd movements with every step, certain that if I'd seen myself, I'd have laughed. The laughter from Olaf, Micaela, and Sergeant Butters as they watched me was all the proof I needed.

Sergeant Butters said something to Olaf and Micaela I couldn't hear, but seeing them walking toward me, it must have been instructions to get a drink.

"You okay there Bye-bye?" asked Micaela, snickering.

"I'll be fine, eventually. My legs feel weird from that trampoline," I explained, knowing there was nothing I could do about their laughing at me.

"Good to know," said Olaf, trying to stop his laughter.

"So, what has he had you two doing?" I asked as I put the canteen to my lips to drink.

"Leaping," answered Micaela.

"Leaping?" I asked, stopping drinking for a moment.

"He said that as a caster and a gunner, range was always going to be important to us, so we need to learn to create range. The idea being to leap back away from a closing enemy to be able to keep fighting and even keep firing while leaping backward. He also said something about teaching us a dodge-roll technique next time, but for today this was more important," Olaf clarified, which made much more sense.

"Are you learning gymnastics?" asked Micaela.

"Sergeant Butters called it 'Acrobatics'," I answered, but as soon as I did I felt it may have been a mistake if the widening of their eyes was anything to go by.

"Why are you learning a Dexterity skill? I thought you were a priest?" Olaf asked, surprise evident in his voice.

"I am a priest," I answered, though I was still faced with a dilemma. These two people were my friends, but I honestly hadn't known them very long. How could I trust other gamers with my secret? How could I be sure it wouldn't end up all over the internet? "I want to tell you both more but . . ."

"We haven't known each other long, right?" asked Olaf. "I get the feeling you've got a big secret. The kind gamers of all kinds covet. Kind of like the knowledge of how I became an Ogre Artillery at level 3 is a big bloody secret. One I trust you won't share with anyone else."

Ouch, dude totally had me there. "Okay, but this is big. Just to warn you, it's huge . . . like . . . bigger than you can possibly imagine big."

"Oh, now you have to tell us," said Micaela excitedly.

"I have a unique class," I said, barely a whisper, but both Micaela and Olaf exploded in a combination of excitement and curiosity, both bombarding me with questions.

"There were so many rumors, but to actually know someone with one," jabbered Micaela before she finally made an 'Eeeee' sound in excitement, nearly shattering my eardrums.

"So, what are you then, if not a priest?" asked Olaf.

"I didn't lie about being a priest. That part is true. I'm just a different kind of priest. I'm a Warrior Priest," I answered. I didn't want to say more. Luckily, it seemed to have at least pacified the pair for now.

"Then why the training?" asked Micaela.

"He's a Warrior and a Priest," answered Olaf, seeming to have fully understood. "You poor blighter," he eventually added.

I sighed, knowing exactly what he meant. "Yeah, pretty much."

Micaela though frowned. "It can't be that bad. So, what, you have to train more stats up, big deal."

"Babe, it's not some stats, it's all stats," explained Olaf. "Warrior and priest hit all stat categories between them.

"Oh . . . Ooooh," she said finally understanding. "I agree with my husband's sentiment. You poor blighter."

"Thanks," I said agreeing with both of their sentiment. "Anyway, there is a little more to it, but that is basically the reason Sergeant Butters built the training equipment for me. I think it's some kind of special award for my class. A way to make it not so grindy. I won't know until I actually learn the skill and do all the training."

"That would actually make sense," said Olaf, rubbing his chin in thought. "But let me say up front. Your secret is completely safe with me. You helped me get a huge edge in leveling, even helping me get the class I wanted super early. You've helped us both break barriers previously thought unbreakable. We owe you, nothing else to it."

"I appreciate that, but I'd rather just continue being friends. I like you two, you're fun and you both have gotten me out of my anti-social shell. So, no owing anyone anything. We're friends. I help you, you help me, right?" I stated.

"Now, aren't you glad I made friends with him outside of Ned's shop?" asked Micaela, she seemed to be blinking back tears and grinning from ear to ear.

Leave it to Micaela to break the tension.

"Alright, enough gossiping, get back to work," ordered Sergeant Butters. "I have got about an hour left before my fat and lazy guards show up so let us get back to it. Then all three of you can head over to see Trini at the temple for training with her."

"Back to the grind, we go," I grumbled.

As promised, an hour later Sergeant Butters was kicking the three of us out of his training area.

I was happily rewarded with an unexpected quest completion.

Class Quest Alert: Training with Sergeant Butters 1 - Completed
Having put your trust in Trinico and David Butters, they have offered you training to develop your stats as quickly and efficiently as possible.
Reward: +100 Experience, Acrobatics 6/100

That was different. I'd never seen a skill show any kind of progress notification before. My mind jarred to a halt because I had seen something similar before on the charm I'd gotten from the Boar Spirit. I'd actually forgotten about the thing. I opened my inventory and looked at the charm.

Boar Charge Charm (Unique) - +10 Stamina, +10 Endurance – Equipping will teach skill 'Boar Charge' 25/100

I was saddened to see I had only gained 25 out of 100. On the other hand, I haven't been doing much fighting or questing, so maybe it wasn't getting experience. I'd have to experiment some later to find out what gives it experience.

Class Quest Alert: Training with Sergeant Butters 2		
Having put your trust in Trinico and David Butters, they have offered you training to develop your stats as quickly and efficiently as possible. Return to Sergeant Butters to continue your development of the skill 'Acrobatics'.		
Reward: Experience, Skill		
Do you accept this Quest?	Yes	No

Of course, I accepted the next quest in the chain, this was basically free experience for me.

"That was awesome," cheered Micaela excitedly, as we started our walk toward the temple and more training. She then looked at her husband with a serious expression. "Why was there never a mention of skill trainers on the forums?"

Olaf was silent for a moment before answering. "I honestly have no idea. The game is new, only three months old, not everyone can afford to buy a pod either. Even the financing options are limited right now. Still, I would have thought people would have started figuring all this out by now."

"Or people know an edge when they find one and know to keep their mouths shut about it. I mean think about it, there is considerable money to be made from being the first to accomplish anything new or finding some secret or another. You mentioned the rumor about an ogre mage before, he clearly figured out how to raise his intellect, but he never shared the knowledge, why? Because it made him more powerful. It got him attention and acclaim too. Of course, that's just what I think," I said, suddenly feeling uncomfortable with the pair staring at me. I really did believe it to be true and would be even truer in the future as more and more people started to play the game.

Eventually, someone would figure out about the skill books and trainers in the starting villages and post it to the forums. Whoever did so, would become hated by anyone that knew the secret, and loved by everyone who didn't. Either way, that person would become a target. Having the unique class I did, meant I had more than enough reason to keep my mouth shut about it.

"He may be right," said Olaf. "Just consider how limited the information is on becoming an Ogre Artillery. I get the feeling that people who have gotten the class have been spreading false information, trying to deter others from trying to get the class."

It was Micaela's turn to frown. "I don't like all these secrets. I guess some people never learned to share in primary."

"Gamers are greedy and selfish by nature. Every gamer always wants the best gear, the best quests, the best guild or clan. One of the best ways to accomplish that is to limit or reduce the competition. Create a rumor about Ogre Artillery, saying you need to have a ton of Strength stat and you can only get it at level 30, because of that requirement, suddenly the class doesn't feel as appealing anymore. Or the rumor that you have to enslave engineers to work as your artillery crew, even attempting it would cause you to be hated by several races, limiting you even worse," Olaf responded.

"Yeah, gamers can be . . . difficult at times. The question becomes, what are you going to do about it? I appreciate you promising the keep my secret, I'm not comfortable spreading it around and becoming a target. But that doesn't stop you from sharing your own secrets, telling the truth about how to become an Ogre Artillery class. You could tell others about the skill books and skill trainers. Though personally, I'd prefer to keep it secret a while longer or we'll suddenly find ourselves overrun with high-level players after skills. Which also means more PK'ers." I know I sounded selfish myself there, but we do have an edge and right now it is a big deal. I want to be able to make use of our edge a little bit longer.

"I know you don't like it Mic, but Bye-bye has a point. I want to share this too, but let's wait until we're completely set to leave this province behind," said Olaf.

"What about just sharing with the people already in this province?" asked Micaela.

Olaf and I both cringed a little.

"Let's take it on a case by case basis," I suggested. "I am not against sharing, you two are proof of that. But I also got to know the both of you before I shared. We built up a friendship and trust between us first."

Micaela seemed to be thinking it over, a frown marring her usually happy face. "I suppose I see your point. I don't necessarily like it, but I get it. I guess I can see where you're both coming from. If we share the information with the wrong person, it could cause the province to be flooded with high-level players and PK'ers. I suppose it could even bring a whole PK guild down on the province, which would wipe out all the NPC's, which would, in turn, wipe out any quest chains we're working on. Bloody hell, now I'm a greedy cuss."

"It sucks," said Olaf. "But we're also here to make a living Babe. If we can get even a little bit of an edge toward that goal, then

I'm for it. We're not just in this for us either. Da- Our daughter is at university and that bill isn't getting any smaller."

That seemed to be a massive blow to any resistance Micaela may have had. "Okay, I'm in. But we will share with any new players, if they make it through our vetting process, Q.E.D. become our friends."

"That is more than a reasonable vetting process," I added, feeling relieved we all seemed to be on the same page now.

"We should totally make an Order," said Olaf earning an odd look from myself and Micaela. "Look, with Bye-bye's awesomeness and ability to figure out all these little details, I have no interest in joining any Order that he's not a part of. I get the feeling, if we follow this guy around we're going to get into some fantastic adventures along the way. Probably get rich doing it too. I know this is coming out of nowhere, but my gut is speaking, and I'm listening."

"Are you sure it isn't the booze from last night acting up again?" I asked, feeling decidedly uncomfortable with the attention.

"It's not, I happen to agree with him," said Micaela, her smile restored and the pixyish glint in her eyes dancing in merriment.

Now it was my turn to frown. I just want to explore the game and see cool stuff, but now I'm being drawn into forming an Order. Plus, the duties, I'm going to assume, that will come with being a Warrior Priest of Issara. It would seem the game is working against my interests.

"Guys, I appreciate it. I enjoy hanging out with you two as well. I'll even be happy to join whatever Order you want, but I want . . . this is going to sound selfish, I want to be able to explore the game and find new and hidden adventures. I don't see that happening if I have to help manage an Order," I said, trying to convey what I wanted most without sounding like a jerk.

Olaf just laughed. "Goodness Bye-bye, I don't want you to lead the Order. I want you out finding those hidden adventures. I just want you to bring us along. The reason to form an Order is that I have no doubt, some of the adventures you are going to find will need a small army to navigate."

Well, that was a relief. A seriously, big relief because I don't want to lead anything. But he did have a point, there were times in other games I'd find something rare or hidden, and not been able to complete or defeat the objective by myself, which was always disappointing cause failure meant whatever I'd found would disappear, sometimes forever.

"I'm in," I answered. "But no responsibility, finding cool stuff to do only."

"Deal, I'll even create a cool title for you. How does 'Lore Master' sound to you?" Olaf offered.

"I like it," said Micaela. "I was thinking 'Cool Stuff Finder' was a good title but yours works better."

I couldn't stop the laugh coming out of my mouth, which the pair were both quick to join in on.

Once the laughter settled, I asked the next question. "What do you plan to call this Order?"

"No idea, but it will be Epic," he replied.

"Ooh, I have it," said Micaela excitedly. "As long as the name isn't taken yet, we should be the 'The Order of Epic Adventures'."

"Sounds a bit . . . um childish," I responded as politely as I could.

"It's not terrible but it could be considered . . . erm . . . kiddy," added Olaf.

Micaela harrumphed and stomped ahead of us.

"We're totally going to end up naming it that, aren't we?" I asked, looking at Olaf sadly.

Olaf just sighed. "Probably, but if we're lucky, she'll come up with a dozen more names and forget all about it."

"Where's a luck stat when you need it?" I wished.

Olaf barked out a loud laugh then shook his head. "We'd better catch up to her or she's going to terrify the priestess."

"I wouldn't count on it. Trinico is one scary lady when she wants to be," I replied. While I had no personal account of having seen her in action, the fact she not only served on the battlefield during a demon incursion but also survived, spoke volumes to me about just how formidable she might be.

"So is my wife," replied Olaf.

"So, we should hurry," I added, quickly picking up my pace.

We caught up with Micaela though she refused to acknowledge either of us, instead choosing to pout the rest of the walk.

"Welcome back, Bye-bye," greeted Trinico when I entered the temple. "I see you have brought guests, welcome to you as well."

"Hello Trini," I greeted her with a friendly smile, only for her to pelt me with her staff.

"Priestess Trinico while on duty if you please," she instructed, the kind smile never leaving her face despite me now holding my head and rubbing the spot where she bashed me.

"Greetings Priestess Trinico," Olaf and Micaela greeted her as one.

"Now, I know what the rude one is here for, how may I assist you?" she asked, ignoring me at this point.

"Sergeant Butters said we should come with Bye-bye for training with you," replied Olaf, humbling himself before the rather slight human woman.

"All are welcome for training in this temple. Are you seeking to become priests?"

"No ma'am," answered Olaf. "I'm an Ogre Artillery."

"Ah, then you are here to train your mind, same as this rude one," she said.

This time she jabbed me in the stomach with the tip of her staff, knocking the air from my lungs and dropping me to the floor, gasping for breath. I just knew this woman had to be powerful, but why did she have to make an example of me?

"How about you, young miss?" Trinico asked.

"I'm a shaman," Micaela replied nervously, her eyes wide and staring at my crumpled form.

"Wonderful, we have not had a shaman around these parts in some time. Have you crafted your first totem yet?" asked Trinico sweetly.

"Not yet," answered Micaela.

"Fantastic, let me get your mate and the rude boy on the floor started in their training, then we can go for a walk," said Trinico, her ever-present smile, still firmly in place.

Thankfully Olaf picked me up from the floor, where I was still struggling to regain my breath from whatever she had done to me.

"Please place Bye-bye in the room to the left," said Trinico, when we came to the end of a short hallway.

"I think I can walk now," I told Olaf, letting the man set me on my feet and I walked into the room to the left. It was a domed room maybe twenty-feet to the top. There was no floor, only a pool

230

of water with a path of stepping stones leading out to a small island in the center. There were no lights, not that I could see anyway, yet the room was well lit. There were no plants and I could not see any fish in the water.

"Sit in the center, I will be back in a moment," said Trinico, closing the door. I assumed she was setting Olaf up in one of the other rooms, giving him instruction first.

I was careful to walk along the stepping stones, doing my best not to disturb the completely calm water. The island in the center was small, I could probably lay across it from head to toe, but not much further. It was covered in soft well-trimmed grass but offered no other seating. So, I sat down to wait for Trinico to return.

Welcome to the Puzzle Room.		
Are you ready to begin?	Yes	No

Huh, how about that. Yes, I am.

Solve as many puzzles as possible. (Limit: 2-hours per 24-hour period)
Beginning in 3 . . . 2 . . . 1 GO!

Sweet!

CHAPTER 12

"Well now, it seems Bye-bye figured it out himself," said Trinico, feeling all too pleased with herself.

"Figured what out?" asked Micaela, nervously. She couldn't but feel nervous, seeing the doors to the rooms her husband and Bye-bye entered vanish, replaced by a smoothed-over wall.

"How to activate the Puzzle Room," answered Trinico.

"So, what will I be doing, Priestess Trinico?" asked Micaela, slightly worried.

"Please dearie, as long as it is just us, call me Trini, most everyone else does," replied the older woman.

"But didn't you just-" started Micaela.

"Bye-bye needed a good thrashing and a lesson on propriety. Truthfully, while I am fine with him calling me Trini, I need to start working on his etiquette. Especially if he is going to be in service to a Goddess," explained Trinico.

"That's right, he's a Warrior Priest, he has to serve a God or Goddess, right?" asked Micaela, her comfort with the old woman rising quickly. "Hey, you said Goddess, do you know who he pledged to?"

"Indeed, I do, and when he talks to his Goddess, he had better be polite, or she might just smite him and strip away his class. That would be bad for all of us. As to who he is pledged in service to . . . well . . . it is a secret," answered Trinico. "Anyway, they will be in there at least two hours. Assuming they do not give up before then, but as far as I can see, Bye-bye is not one to quit. I cannot speak for your husband, but if he is friends with Bye-bye, then I imagine he is much the same."

"Oh, those two are very alike in that regard. That daft fool went into the little hag's shop nearly every day for over 3 months, trying to get her to either sell him a pair of pistols or to train him as an engineer, despite her violently saying no every time. Stubborn fool, but I love him anyway."

"That is good, he will do well in there then," Trinico replied confidently, setting Micaela more at ease.

"Will I be going into the other room?" asked Micaela.

"You do not need that room dearie," replied Trini. "We are going for a walk. Do not worry, I will keep you safe. I just hope you are prepared for what it will take to become a shaman."

Micaela swallowed nervously, trying to mentally brace herself for the dirty work ahead. "I think so. I'm not looking forward to it."

Trini frowned slightly. "What are you not looking forward to exactly?"

"You know, the blood and cutting part," replied Micaela, shivering slightly.

"Blood and cutting? What dark shaman rituals have you been reading? Blood and cutting, how foul!" Trinico exclaimed in shock.

"But, all the . . . erm . . . the literature I read said you had to cut out an animal's heart, then merge it with a totem," defended Micaela, feeling hopeful Trinico knew a better way.

"Are you trying to become a Witch Doctor?" asked Trinico, looking appalled.

"Witch Doctor? Of course not, but . . . everything I read said there was no other way," explained Micaela.

"Then you are reading the wrong things," Trinico replied more harshly than she intended.

"Do you know another way? Please tell me, I would much rather do it a better way, preferably one that doesn't involve cutting out some poor animal's heart," pleaded Micaela.

"Okay, first, are you a shaman? Do you know the 'Call Spirit' spell?" asked Trinico.

"Yes, but I thought it had to be used on the totem," answered Micaela.

"It does but it is also used to create a totem. Second, do you have the 'Infuse Spirit' spell?" asked Trinico.

"Yes," answered Micaela.

"Good, then you have everything you need to create a totem, except for a willing participant and an appropriate medium, something like mana infused wood or stone," explained Trinico.

"Stone?" asked Micaela, trying not to sound as surprised. "But the literature I read said- "

Trinico sighed before replying, "Honestly dearie, at this point, I would just forget whatever you read because clearly whoever wrote it was an idiot or a liar."

"Yes ma'am," replied Micaela feeling relieved, but also a little sad. The recent discovery that her husband, and his desire to become an Ogre Artillery, was loaded with misinformation and was not a one-off, as she too had been tricked in a similar manner. She just couldn't believe how much false information there was out there.

"Now, you seemed surprised when I mentioned stone, does stone have meaning for you?" asked Trinico

"I'm a miner, my husband and I both are. We sell our ore in Root City, but most of the stone goes to waste. It just doesn't sell well because no one is building castles yet, and even then, they probably won't use the lowest level stone we can mine here."

"Do you have some on you?" asked Trinico, ignoring Micaela's nervous chattering.

"Yes, I have some Limestone," answered Micaela.

"Now we're getting somewhere. Have you learned the 'Shape Totem' spell?" asked Trinico

"Of course," Micaela answered. The spell description said it could only be used on an appropriate medium, but didn't specifically say wood, and yet she assumed that's what it meant.

"You also said you are a miner correct? Do you have the 'Infuse Mana' subskill?" asked Trinico.

"No, I've never even heard of it," Micaela replied, slightly surprised Trinico even knew about it.

"Honestly, if you adventurers are our last hope, then we are all doomed. Come with me," said Trinico, changing course toward the Town hall.

Once they arrived at the Town hall Trinico told Micaela to wait outside and said she'd be right back. The woman emerged a few minutes later but without a book, just a scroll which she held out to Micaela.

Mining Subskill – Infuse Mana – Teaches the Mining Subskill 'Infuse Mana'		
Would you like to learn 'Mining Subskill – Infuse Mana	Yes	No

Micaela didn't even hesitate to learn it. It was both a shock and an undeniable blessing to be given such an important skill. And without a quest or killing something powerful to obtain it.

You have learned the 'Mining' subskill 'Infuse Mana'

Mining II	Level: 5	Experience: 57.54%
Professional Skill: *Mining is the ability to extract usable material from rock and stone.*		**Skill Stamina Cost:** 5 *per swing*
Subskill: *Infuse Mana*	**Skill Effect (Active):** *Used to create Mana Infused Stone.*	**Skill Mana Cost:** *1,000 per cubic foot of stone with a maximum density of 2.4.*

Unfortunately, it also made her curious enough to ask, "Why?"

Trinico stopped to study Micaela for a moment before she spoke. "Why am I helping you?" guessed Trinico, pausing for a moment, "Bye-bye is special, you have seen it I am sure. I am doing what I can to help him. It seems to me, helping you and your husband will help him. By the way, what is your name? Your husband's too. I do not think we were ever properly introduced by that rude boy."

Micaela couldn't help laughing, something Trinico joined her in.

"I'm Micaela Crushhammer, my husband is Olaf, it's nice to formally make your acquaintance Trini."

"Nice to formally make yours as well. Remind me to give Bye-bye another good whack when we get back to the temple," joked Trinico.

"I promise I will. Can I ask? Where did you get the scroll?"

"I made it," answered Trinico. "I am a Rune Master. I know a great many of the true words. In there is a book, 'Earthen Ways and Means'. There is one chapter explaining the process of infusing mana into stone and how to do it. I simply translated that into the true words, placing them within the scroll for you."

"Wow, thank you so much," said Micaela. "Can you do that to all the books in there?"

"Most, but why would I? If everyone who came to this town could get all the skills in there instantly, then we would never have adventurers come for more than a few minutes to learn all the skills they can. Then what? They would all turn around and leave. They would not help the town or complete quests for the people living here, some of which, are in real need. I expect you not to share this with anyone other than your husband. You had best warn him to keep his trap shut or else," Trinico warned her.

"You got it Trini, honestly, he'll just be so happy to read that book himself," said Micaela.

"It is a good book for all miners to read, though most do not bother, the lazy sods," complained Trini. "Anyway, you can now infuse mana to stone, meaning you can make an appropriate medium for your totem."

"Trini, you are amazing," cheered Micaela happily.

"I know this, but you need to stop cheering and dancing like a child. You should make your totem already," Trinico instructed the woman, trying not to sound either harsh or irritated.

"Right," said Micaela. She opened her miner's backpack and took out the first piece of stone she'd ever mined, it was a memento of her first day on the job. The very first thing she'd gotten from the very first time she swung a pick at a greenish copper vein.

Limestone – Chunk of limestone rock. Density 2.3

"Good, first cast 'Infuse Mana'," instructed Trinico.

Micaela was surprised by the sudden drop in her mana pool, sucking away all 100 of her mana points instantly and seeming to want more.

"Drink this," said Trinico, handing her a vial with swirling blue mists inside.

> **Superior Mana Mist 3/3** – Restores full mana and 100 mana per minute for 10 minutes.

Once again, Micaela followed orders drinking a sip of the potion filling her mana back to full which the stone instantly drank away from her. Eight more times it drained her limited mana pool, taking a total of 1,000 mana, but when it was done the stone had changed.

> **Mana Infused Limestone** – Mana infused stone is a powerful crafting element useful for empowering buildings if used in construction.

"Wow," breathed Micaela, waiting for the potion to trigger again.

"Next you have to cast the 'Shape Totem' spell. I warn you, you must have a clear image in mind of your totem. I advise you avoid giving it any kind of animal motif or you may offend a spirit you wish to enlist to help you."

Micaela knew exactly what she wanted her totem to appear, or at least she did until Trinico warned her not to use an animal motif. Then she remembered the Sergeant asking her if she had a totem yet. He'd said he couldn't train her as she had no weapon, or he did until Bye-bye convinced the man to teach her and Olaf a combat movement style. Still, the original question about her totem, made her think. Didn't that indicate the totem could be considered a weapon?

"Can a totem be a weapon?" asked Micaela.

"Good girl," said Trinico proudly. "it certainly can and should be. Why do you think you are able to shape your totem yourself?"

That had just opened up so many possibilities. "You've known shamans in the past, right?" asked Micaela, shaking with excitement.

"Of course, I have known and fought with many shamans, from a great many clans. I have known shamans who use stationary totems to act as spellcasters, and I have known shamans who use weapon totems giving the weapon shamanic attributes and powers. It all depends on the shaman," answered Trinico.

"So, if I made my totem a staff, I could use it to cast ranged spells but also fight in melee?" asked Micaela.

"You could make your totem into a sword and do the same thing. Or you could go the other direction. I once knew a shaman who made his totem a throne to sit upon while he cast spells. It was not a very mobile totem, but it was quite powerful," Trinico smiled, remembering her old friend.

Knowledge was good. "How many totems can I use at once?" Micaela asked next.

Patient as always, Trinico answered, "As many as you can manage but bear in mind you can only carry so many totems and despite what many will tell you, size matters."

Micaela snorted at the joke mixed in there, but she understood. She could have a dozen totems the size of a dagger, but they would all be fairly weak or limited in their growth. She knew totems could level. What she was being told now, was she able make weapons capable of leveling up. Then she had another thought.

"What about armor? Could I make stone into armor and make it a totem that way?" asked Micaela, ideas flitting through her mind like a pixie on a sugar high.

"I find that I like you very much. You are a smart woman. Something to keep in mind though. Depending on the stone you use, the level of the spirit within will be limited. For armor, using Limestone, which is the softest stone in this world to the best of my knowledge, will only be good to about level 10 or so. It is also not very sturdy as armor goes. Then you would need a harder stone. Hopefully, you will have learned the transfer spirit spell by then or you'll have to train your new totemic armor all over again, starting from level 1. I should also tell you, totems may not be enchanted, as they are technically already enchanted items," Trinico did her best to share what she knew of shamans with the young woman.

"I'm going to be amazing," said Micaela, mostly to her own surprise, until she got a good knock to the head, courtesy of Trinico's staff.

"Do not get full of yourself, shaman. You have potential, but never forget this is a dangerous world. It is filled with plenty of things more than able to still kill you. Also remember, right at this moment, it cost you a thousand mana to infuse one rock. For an entire suit of stone armor, you'd need close to fifty thousand mana, and that is if you only use Limestone. As such, this is something you are not capable of doing just yet. You also have not yet created your first totem, which will also take a considerable amount of mana beyond what you have now," Trinico chided, bringing Micaela back down to earth from her vivid daydreams.

"Man, being brought back down to earth hurts," complained Micaela rubbing her forehead.

"Good, if it hurts, you will remember. For now, why not shape your first totem?" suggested Trinico.

Micaela sighed sadly at having her dreams dashed. She focused instead on the rock in her hands. She started by thinking about what kind of weapon she wanted. Knowing it would be a totem meant it could cast spells while in her possession. It would also get stronger the more she used it, but she was getting ahead of herself again. She needed to think about weapons. Swords weren't really her style and she couldn't picture herself using a staff or large club or even a spear like Bye-bye did. In fact, she'd always pictured herself wielding two weapons, axes with wicked crescent-shaped curves covering one side of the handle.

As if coming out of a trance, Micaela found herself looking at the very ax she'd just pictured, made completely of stone, but could have easily passed for wood and steel if not for the coloring which was completely white with a few orange striations running through it.

"Well done, a very fine ax," complimented Trinico.

"I need to make another," said Micaela excitedly.

"Duel wielding then, good for you," said Trinico. "Well, hurry along and make it."

It took a little while for Micaela to infuse another piece of Limestone. It wasn't as special as the first piece she'd ever mined but that was okay. Especially, if they were only good for around 10 levels before she'd have to replace them. After that, she already had the template for the ax-shaped totem in her memory, so it was easy to shape the newly infused stone to match.

"Good, and now we will go looking for a young spirit to bond with," stated Trinico, leading the way toward the village gates with a happy and excited Micaela in tow.

They walked for a while outside the village. Anything approaching Trinico was dealt with instantly, simply falling to the ground. It wasn't until they found a small hill with a smaller opening at the base, that they stopped.

"This should do. In that hole, you should find a wolf and two cubs. I will deal with the wolf, I want you to bring the two cubs out," instructed Trinico.

"Are you going to kill the mother?" asked Micaela worriedly.

"It is not necessary. We are not killing the cubs, only taking the young spirits that have attached themselves to the pups. You will understand better shortly once you have finished your totems," explained Trinico. Her kind smile reassured Micaela.

As soon as Micaela approached the hole, a snarling wolf sprung from the nearby brush blocking her path, but only for a moment as the wolf collapsed as if boneless a moment later. Micaela was surprised, her first thought was that Trinico killed the wolf, it looked just like all the other wolves they encountered on their way here. However, this was the first time Micaela had been close enough to see the wolf was simply asleep.

Trinico stopped her before she could touch the sleeping wolf. "Do not touch her or she will wake up. The sleep magic does not always work the second time in, meaning we would have to kill her. I would much prefer not to have to kill these poor animals, despite the standing bounty in town."

Micaela was relieved. She moved closer to the wolf den until she was at the entrance with a serious dilemma. She would not fit inside. She would have to draw the two cubs out. Thankfully, she remembered she had some Adventurer Jerky in her bag.

It was relatively easy at that point, she simply set the jerky in front of the den and the two little wolf cubs came charging out a moment later, nipping at each other playfully trying to be the first to the meat.

"Now comes the hard part," said Trinico. "Look at the pups and cast your spell, 'Call Spirit'. Do not be alarmed, do not panic and do not try to run."

Micaela swallowed nervously after that instruction, but still cast her spell, looking at the cub with darker coloring, a small cut in his ear she hadn't noticed before while the cub's brother darted around trying to steal bites of the jerky, he was a light brown, almost blonde coloring, starkly contrasted his brother.

Suddenly, Micaela was no longer in the same forest, or she was, but everything took on a grey misty otherworldly hue.

"It's mine, I got here first," said a little voice far too close to Micaela, surprising her.

"Not fair, let me have some of it," said another little voice.

This finally drew Micaela's vision down, there were the two cubs, still fighting over the jerky. Both of the wolf cubs were wrapped in something completely transparent, superimposed over the cubs but lacking any real form.

"Hello little guys," cooed Micaela, doing what she felt was natural to her.

"Hey, did that big thing just speak?" asked the pup with the damaged ear to the blonde pup.

"I think so. I did not know those things could talk, did you know?" asked the blonde pup.

"Of course, I knew, everyone knows. You are just too stupid, so no one bothered to tell you," stated the darker pup.

"Liar, you did not know either," argued the blonde pup, having lost the fight for the meat.

"My goodness, you two are just so cute," Micaela cooed again, barely able to hold back from picking the pair up in a big hug. Instead, she settled for petting both of them with one of her giant fingers each.

"Hey, stop, it tickles," complained the one with the damaged ear.

"No, do not stop, it feels so nice," said the other totally in bliss.

Micaela looked around again while the little wolves enjoyed or fought off her ministrations. She saw Trinico sitting nearby but seemingly not paying much attention. She saw the sleeping mother wolf behind her, but that's when she noticed. Neither Trinico nor the mother wolf had anything superimposed over them, just the little ones did.

"Say, do you know why she doesn't have a . . ." Micaela started to ask.

"She is old now," answered the very content blond spirit pup. "We are fragile things, we latch on to the young where we can be protected, eventually they will grow and will find another. Eventually, we too will grow and when we do, we will find strong wolves to make a pact with."

"Would you two make a pact with me?" Micaela asked, not sure if she was doing the right thing or not.

"Are you strong? Can you protect my brother and me?" asked the one still trying to fight off her finger of ticklish doom.

Micaela frowned at the question. She wasn't strong, not by this world's standards. "We can get strong together," she offered instead.

"How?" asked the one with the damaged ear.

At this Micaela took the two axes from her belt and set them before the two wolves.

"Totems," gasped the pair, a new excitement seemed to bloom in both of them.

"Why did you not say you were a shaman?" demanded the pup with the damaged ear.

"I am a new shaman. I don't know everything yet," she answered. "You two, you want to get stronger, right? Will you partner with me?"

"Happily, just promise more petting session," said the happier of the pair, his blonde fur was ruffled but the little guy looked completely content at the moment.

"I cannot leave my brother alone, I will join you as well," said the darker pup spirit.

"Wonderful, do you have names?" asked Micaela.

"We have never had need of names before. Would you name us?" asked the pup with a damaged ear, suddenly looking vulnerable.

"You're Butch," she said point to the pup with the damaged ear. "And you're Sundance."

"Hmm, I find the name acceptable. Be mindful, names have power," warned Butch. "You may cast your spell to join us to your totems.

Micaela wasn't sure what spell the little guy was talking about but the only other spell she had was 'Infuse Spirit'. Assuming that was it, she began channeling the 60-second long spell.

As the spell completed, the ethereal shroud covering the darker colored pup, Butch, ghosted forward landing on the first totem she had to create. The totem was suddenly sucked into him as if it was never there and in its place was the same wolf pup but much less ghostly. "Now we are bonded. Hurry up and join Sundance, she can poke you later."

"Fine, cast the spell," sighed Sundance, reluctantly wriggling free of her masterful ministrations.

Micaela smiled and began the spell again.

As the spell finish, Sundance too surged forward landing on the other ax, it too was sucked into his body and reformed back into that of a wolf pup. "Now we are bonded."

"Thank you, Micaela," said the pair in one voice. "You have given us a foot in both worlds to grow stronger. There are a few things to know. Do not ever let a smith try to repair us, we are not this stone nor are we metal. We live and must be healed."

Micaela blinked in surprise as she received a notice of learning a new spell, 'Heal Totem'.

"You may speak with us any time by simply holding our weapons in the other world, but do not forget, we are here in this world. There is much still for you to learn from us and much for us to learn from you," they continued.

Micaela blinked in surprise yet again as another new spell, 'Spirit Walk' was learned.

"Protect us as we protect you," they said again in a single voice.

Micaela blinked again suddenly finding herself back in the other world. In front of her were the two little wolves fighting over the piece of jerky. Smiling a little she took out another piece of jerky and gave it to the pups so they each had one.

"I take it you were successful?" asked Trinico.

"Yep, meet Butch and Sundance," she said holding up the twin axes.

"Interesting names, I take it you wish one to give you strength and the other the power of the sun?" asked Trinico.

"Nope, just like the names," Micaela grinned, hearing the pair arguing in her head about something silly.

Trinico simply shook her head and sighed at the woman's excitable nature. "We should head back. I am sure your husband and the rude boy are done by now."

"Sure," Micaela replied, grinning from ear to ear.

The return trip was as quick as the trip out had been, plenty of wolves all put to sleep by Trinico, but no real danger beyond that.

Returning to the temple they were greeted by Bye-bye and Olaf, having an excited and seemingly happy discussion.

"Hey, you're back," said Olaf, seeing the pair first.

"How did it go?" asked Micaela, skipping over to her husband, her skip causing one altar or another, to shake slightly.

"I got +2 Intellect, which maxed me out, for now, need to gain another level to get another 5 points. I also picked up +12 Wisdom and +3 Charisma, so probably the best two hours ever," replied Olaf, a grin matching his wife's. "How about you? You look awfully pleased," inquired Olaf.

"Meet Butch and Sundance," Micaela said happily brandishing her two weapons.

"Are those stone?" I asked, quirking my head to the side.

"Yep, these are my totems. I'm a fully-fledged shaman now," Micaela said proudly.

"Congratulations Babe," said Olaf, give his wife a quick kiss and hug, carefully avoiding the ax blades.

"Maybe I'm missing something here but aren't totems usually wooden statues or something?" I asked, slightly confused.

"I learned some really cool stuff today," said Micaela grinning happily and very pleased to share what she had learned.

"I call hax," I said, grinning anyway. I didn't actually believe Micaela had actually hacked the game.

"I have to agree with our boy here, hax, Babe," added Olaf, also grinning.

"At least I'm on your side," Micaela replied, smiling brightly.

"And how did your time in the puzzle room go, Bye-bye," asked Trinico.

"Not bad at all," this time I was smiling brightly.

"Well, out with it already," snipped Trinico, not liking his smile at all.

"I gained +35-Intellect, +21-Wisdom, and +16-Charisma," I answered, causing both Trinico and Micaela's jaws to drop.

"What did you do? No, how did you do it?" Micaela finally voiced.

"Have you ever heard of the app called 'Puzzle Box'?" I asked, still grinning.

Trinico looked confused for a moment before blinking away the confusion, having simply forgotten all about her wanting to question what an app was.

"I've definitely heard of it. Micaela is obsessed with it, even though she still hasn't made it past level 17. I'm level 32 myself, the room seems to have been based on it now that I think about it."

My smile got just a little wider. "I created it."

Olaf cursed and called out, "HAX!"

I only laughed loudly and happily.

CHAPTER 13

"What do you mean you invented it?" asked Trinico. "Puzzle Rooms have existed for centuries?"

"I didn't invent the Puzzle Room," I said, trying to find a way around this. The NPC's usually ignored weirdness, but apparently not this time. "I invented something similar when I was younger. It was so much like the Puzzle Room, it made it easier for me to solve the puzzles."

Trinico frown then smiled then frowned again. "How many puzzles did you complete?"

"Forty-six," I answered which prompted the quest completion notice.

Class Quest Alert: Training with Priestess Trinico 1 - Completed
Having put your trust in Trinico and David Butters, they have offered you training to develop your stats as quickly and efficiently as possible.
Reward: +100 Experience, 46/100 ?????

That was annoying. I killed it in training today and I was only 46/100 toward learning whatever skill Trinico was trying to teach me. I also took note the number 46 was kind of significant. That was the number of puzzles I had solved.

Class Quest Alert: Training with Priestess Trinico 2
Having put your trust in Trinico and David Butters, they have offered you training to develop your stats as quickly and efficiently as possible.
Reward: Experience, Skill

The follow-up quest was expected, but still annoying. I still had no idea what the skill was. It did give me a clue to another mystery I'd remember that morning. The Boar Charm.

Boar Charge Charm (Unique) - +10 Stamina, +10 Endurance – Equipping will teach skill 'Boar Charge' 25/100

It wasn't experience. The charm was looking for something specific. Some action I had done caused it to tick up. But what action had I done 25 times since I received the charm? What specifically caused it to grow? I would have to pay close attention to everything I do over the next few days and check it frequently. It was another clue.

"I still say hax," grumbled Olaf.

Micaela meanwhile seemed to just stare at me with a rather blank expression on her face.

"I am not sure of this word 'hax', but based on how he is using the word, I might just agree," said Trinico thoughtfully before turning to Olaf. "Does 'hax' mean to cheat?"

"Basically," answered Olaf, smirking.

"I did not cheat. I love a good puzzle. Why do you think I'm a lore hound? How do you think I found as many of the things as I have since coming to this town?" I was kind of annoyed that my friends, new as they were, would doubt me so easily.

"Hmm, I think I am starting to understand you better," said Trinico. "I apologize for doubting you. I should have shown more faith. It is well that you have a love of puzzles. It has allowed you to make significant strides towards learning to 'Meditate'."

Meditation? How did solving puzzles lead to learning to 'Meditate'?

"How does solving puzzled lead to learning to 'Meditate'?" asked Olaf, taking the question right out of my mouth.

"As the puzzles progress, they become much more complex, much more inward looking. Eventually, it will allow you to 'Meditate', which is thinking deeply or focusing one's mind for a period of time. It is a key aspect of training the mind."

"How does 'Meditation' help with Charisma?" I asked.

"Meditation allows you to focus on any subject considered a mental pursuit. Interactions with others is a mental pursuit," Trinico answered as if it should have been obvious.

"That kind of makes sense," said Olaf. The man turned to look at his wife only to groan. The woman was still staring intently at me. "Mic, don't go there, please."

"But he . . . he . . ." Micaela started, pointing one of her large fingers at me.

"Yes, I know he is responsible for creating your arch nemesis the 'Puzzle Box' but I'm sure he didn't do it just to cause you pain and suffering," said Olaf, trying to comfort his wife and not laugh.

"But he . . ." Micaela started again.

"I know babe, I know," said Olaf, trying to placate his wife.

"Something I should know?" I asked, starting to worry.

"I told you she's obsessed with the 'Puzzle Box' but can't get past level 17. She has cursed your name so many times without knowing your name or who actually created it. I think she's torn on what to do now," Olaf explained.

"Oh, should I go?" I asked, motioning with my thumb extended toward the exit. I didn't think she'd attack me, but you never knew.

"No!" shouted Micaela, deciding the course of action she wished to take. "You must teach me, oh great puzzle master!" she dropped suddenly to her knees bowing in supplication.

"That's just excessive," said Olaf, shaking his head and trying not to laugh, but failing miserably.

"Uh . . . what am I supposed to do?" I asked, feeling more confused than ever before.

"Just promise to help her get past level 17," suggested Olaf, starting to feel embarrassed.

"Okay, I promise to help you with your puzzle box," I said, hoping the odd scene would just go away.

"You keep strange company, Bye-bye," added Trinico, shaking her head. She then gave Micaela a poke with her staff drawing the woman's attention. "Up you get, the only worship to be done in this temple is to the Gods and Goddess. Servant of a Goddess, Bye-bye might be, but a God he is not."

"You promise?" Micaela asked, looking at me again.

"I promise," I said reassuring her. This was definitely the strangest five minutes of my life.

"Alright, enough from all of you," said Trinico, clearly at her limit for the day. "Please return tomorrow for further training."

"I think that was our invitation to go," I offered.

"Right, let's get going. I'm sure there is more we can do today." Said Olaf, trying to guide his wife out of the temple.

"Have a good day, and may the Gods and Goddesses watch over you," Trinico said with a sense of finality to their training and time in the temple, for today at least.

"So now what?" asked Micaela, once we were all back outside.

"Reading," I stated only to be halted as my world turned red.

An enemy of Issara's justice is nearby and must be punished!

"Oh no," I said softly, turning in place to look for the source. I wished I hadn't. There were at least twenty of them, all outlined in red.

"What is it?" asked Olaf, his head turning to try and follow my gaze. When he did, he mirrored my sentiments. "Oh no." While he couldn't see the red outlines, I could. I was sure he was smart enough to recognize the same thing I saw from a group that large, all with levels in the 30's or higher.

"Oh no," added Micaela following our gaze.

"It's a raid," said Olaf.

My mind was rushing through dozens of scenarios, as I watched the group enter a building. The sign above the door read 'Doc B's Saloon'. That meant they weren't starting their raid, not just yet anyway. They were going to get good and drunk first. They probably wouldn't be attacking until it was dark, so we had some time.

"What are we going to do?" asked Micaela.

"We can only run or die," said Olaf sadly.

"What if there was a third option?" I asked, as much as I liked the idea of running, it just didn't sit well with me. I could only think of one solution, 'Justice Bringer'. It would at least level the playing field, but three of us, versus twenty of them, and there was no guarantee more wouldn't show up before the attack began. And no guarantee some of them weren't out scouting the town.

"You have a plan?" asked Olaf.

"Maybe, but first, we need to get to Sergeant Butters," I said. It would have to start with him if we were even going to have a chance of winning this thing. I could see Olaf and Micaela were about to run, but drawing attention was the last thing we needed. "Walk, don't run," I hissed shortly. "Don't draw their attention."

After my warning, we walked toward the barracks, hoping we'd find the sergeant around back. As luck would have it, he was just coming around the front of the building.

"Bye-bye, Micaela, Olaf, good evening," he greeted us.

"Evening," I said calmly, not sure if anyone stealthy was around and listening. "I came to turn in the quest you gave me this morning. I found the banner you wanted for inside the barracks." I know what I said was odd and completely false, and even worse, probably as confusing as could be, but hopefully, the sergeant would understand.

"Well done you three, come on in," he replied, walking to the barracks door and motioning us in ahead of him. Once inside, he shut the door firmly behind him confusing the other guards who were currently resting in their bunks. As Butters ushered us into the office, he asked, "Now what the devil is going on?"

"The town is going to be raided," I answered.

"We saw them, around twenty or so, all level 30 or higher," added Olaf.

The sergeant cursed angrily under his breath. "We cannot fight a force so large with the power they are wielding."

"What if we could?" I asked, I was a little nervous about this, but I didn't want to see this town burned down.

"I am listening," said Sergeant Butter, looking to me with hope in his eyes.

"When I became a Warrior Priest for Issara I was given a number of spells. One of those spells has the ability to reduce or elevate the level of all Adventurers and Citizens within 100 yards of me, to my current level."

"A level playing field?" asked Butters, a new gleam in his eyes I'd not seen before. "Oh, now that is what I call a blessing. With that, we could at least have a chance. Wait here, I will go rouse the men."

"What kind of an overpowered hax ability is that?" asked Olaf, finally finding his voice.

I gave Micaela and Olaf a quick rundown of the story regarding the Gods and Goddesses of justice.

"Bye-bye, my friend," started Olaf, placing his big meaty hands on my shoulders and looking me in the eyes. "I've said it before, I'll say it again. HAX!"

"Just a little," I replied, grinning now to match his and Micaela's. It was an overpowered ability, but one we would benefit from, big time.

"What a brilliant idea! Such a simple way to encourage PvP while discouraging being a tosser," said Micaela, grinning too.

"We're in," said Olaf. "I know I don't have a weapon, but I can punch pretty hard."

It was good timing, as Sergeant Butters returned just then. "Okay, the men are gearing up and will be ready in a minute. Now, we have a few options for dealing with these brigands. You said they are all currently in 'Doc B's Saloon'? We can attack them there."

"Except they may have scouts spread around. The spell only reaches 100 yards."

"Okay, then we need to draw them to us, all of them," said Butters. "I need you three to go next door. Tell Mayor Simper 'The Bell Tolls Thrice', exactly those words."

"An emergency signal?" I asked.

"Indeed, it means a tornado is imminent, seek shelter at the Town hall. The town drills for this so it will not cause a panic. I have one of my scouts going to warn Doc B to get himself and his staff out quietly and to try not to draw attention."

"I'll be able to spot if any of the raiders follow them," I added.

"Now, how can you do that?" asked Olaf.

"I didn't tell you that part, did I?" I asked, chagrined.

"I get the feeling I'm gonna call hax again. Lay it on us," said Olaf.

"So, I suppose I should mention the Gods and Goddesses are angry. Scorched earth angry," I started.

"Maybe I don't want to know," said Olaf.

"I want to know," added Micaela.

I continued regardless, "So, these PK'ers all carry judgments from the Goddess Issara. One judgment for every citizen they've killed, and one judgment for every Adventurer killed that is more than 20 levels below them. Every stack will cost the Adventurer one-hundred thousand experience, reducing levels until the debt is paid. Some of those guys had hundreds of stacks."

"Scorched earth indeed," said Olaf.

I could see the disbelief and shock clearly on his face.

"We're never killing a citizen, not ever," said Micaela as seriously as she could.

"Divine Justice indeed," added Sergeant Butters. "Okay, we have a plan, you three get to the mayor, but be quiet about it."

"Thanks, we'll see you over there shortly," I said to the man.

The walk from the barracks to the Town hall was quick and quiet. We found the mayor in his office chatting with his wife Margie.

"Bye-bye, Olaf, Micaela, please come in," the man greeted us.

"We just came from seeing Sergeant Butters. He said we were supposed to tell you, 'The Bell Tolls Thrice'," I stated as calmly as I could.

Any jovial happiness at seeing us was quickly forgotten. "Stay here," he ordered. The man then brushed passed us rushing as fast as his portly legs would carry him. He rushed onto the stage and through a previously hidden doorway.

"We should form a group now," suggested Micaela.

I mentally opened the social menu of my user interface and accessed my friend's list. Targeting Micaela and looking to the group invite option by her name. Then I did the same for Olaf. There was an immediate change to my UI. To the left of my vision, images of Olaf and Micaela appeared. Next to their images was their names and levels. Under the names, it displayed their health, stamina and mana bars but didn't give me any numerical values.

Suddenly, there were three loud bell tolls from above us, significantly louder than usual. I'm not sure if it was because we were in the building or if there was actually a way to toll the bell louder. Either way, people began to flow inside almost immediately.

The mayor returned a moment later motioning us into his office.

"Now, what is really going on? I looked at the skies while I was up there, everything is clear."

"There is about be a raid on the town," I answered.

"What?" He shouted in surprise, his face starting to turn red. "Why would he have us get all our people here? We should be evacuating as many as we can. What is that man thinking? Does he actually think he can take an army of adventurers all on his own?"

It was worrisome, the mayor was spiraling. I knew I had to do something to reassure him, but it meant sharing my secret even further.

"Mayor Simper, calm down. We have a way," I tried to reassure him.

"How? What could a level 4 and two level 3 adventurers do against a raiding party?"

I sighed. "I am a Warrior Priest of the Goddess Issara, Justice is with us." I was so reluctant to say those words, but to watch the fear just melt from the man's face made me wish I'd done so earlier.

"At last, our prayers have been heard," said Margie before both she and mayor dropped to their knees and started praying.

"What's this all about?" asked Micaela.

"I don't know, Sergeant Butters and Trinico did the same thing when I told them about it," I replied. I really needed to get to Root City soon and visit my Goddess' temple.

The praying didn't last long before both of them stood again.

"Did you say David and Trini both know?" asked the Mayor.

"Yes, I told them yesterday. But please," and I stressed the 'please', "try to keep quiet about this. If word spreads too far too soon it could mean danger for me," I still tried to keep my secrets. At this rate, it wouldn't last long, but it was something.

"I understand my boy, I am a politician remember. I understand the danger you represent as well as the hope. Your secret is safe with me, for now at least."

"We should get out front, try to prevent any of the PK'ers from getting inside," suggested Olaf.

"It won't matter. Remember, anyone who gets inside will have their level reduced to mine. They would suddenly be surrounded and won't last long, after their first attack. We'll be better

258

off out front to fight. Plus, it gives more range on my spell," I countered, as nicely as I could.

"I'd still feel better if at least one of us stayed in here," said Olaf.

"I'll stay," said Micaela. "My boys and I will take care of anyone stupid enough to start something in here."

I could have argued with her, but I wasn't going to. She wasn't wrong to try to protect the people inside, especially with all the soldiers being outside.

"When Giggle-Ana gets here, send her to me. I will get her up to the crow's-nest to snipe these brigands," instructed Mayor Simper.

"Let's go, Olaf," I said, walking back toward the entrance.

"Be safe, my love," said Micaela, giving her husband a soft embrace and quick kiss.

"You too, babe," whispered Olaf.

When we got out front, all of the guards had assembled and were ushering citizens inside. So far, I hadn't seen any of the PK'ers mixed in with the citizens. I saw at least one some ways off, obscured by a building to everyone else but he stood out clearly to me with his bright red outline and a stack of 57 judgments.

"Is that red outline what you see?" asked Olaf, not pointing or trying to draw attention.

"You see it?" I asked.

"And the 57 stacks of Divine Judgement of Issara," Olaf replied. "At level 27 I'd guess he is just a scout or some low-rank member of the PK guild responsible for this mess."

"How many missing?" I asked Butters, walking closer to the man.

"More then 50," the sergeant answered. "The tornado warning should have been plenty to get people rushing here. Unfortunately, when dealing with civilians, they have a bad habit of grabbing personal effects and wealth."

"There is a level 27 scout just over there watching us," I said, moving to stand in front of the sergeant then pointing with a finger toward my left shoulder, my body obscuring the motion.

"Gotcha, nothing we can do about him. Just let me know when he moves," Sergeant Butters ordered.

I nodded, then went to join Olaf to wait.

I was pleased to see Olaf greeting Giggle-Ana, though she didn't look overly pleased to see him.

"Giggle-Ana, good to see you again," I greeted her.

"Bye-bye, is what this lummox says, true? Is the mayor looking for me?"

"Yes ma'am," I answered.

"Let us go, Kirlan, boys," she said, giving a small glare at Olaf and nod of acknowledgment to me. I didn't notice the two young men standing with her and Kirlan. One was built similar to Kirlan but as short as Giggle-Ana, while the other was as thin as Giggle-Ana but nearly as tall as Kirlan.

"She is one tough little woman," he commented, shaking his head at the gnome's stubbornness.

"She'll soften up once you've built up your Charisma," I offered. "Were those two boys her kids?"

"I sure hope she softens toward me. But yeah, I would guess they are their kids," he replied.

Kirlan returned a moment later brandishing a massive Warhammer.

"Big hammer," I complimented him.

260

"Nah, this is my little thumper. Did not know I would need the big thumper tonight, but I suppose this will do in a pinch," Kirlan commented, grinning excitedly.

"Good to see you, Kirlan," Sergeant Butter greeted him.

"What is the plan?" the blacksmith asked.

"When the army comes, do not make a move until Bye-bye works his magic. Speaking of, will we know it when we see it?"

"Yeah, it's a bright wave of white light, expanding all around me," I replied.

"Then you stand behind me," ordered Trinico, joining us. She looked different or rather her clothes did, she wore bright white robes and hood, both had an ethereal glow.

"Why?" I asked.

"So, they do not know you were the source. As long as they think it was a Citizen that cast the spell, maybe they will be more cautious in the future," Trinico answered.

"A bluff," Olaf said, grinning slightly. "If the PK'ers think a Citizen cast the spell, it will create a ripple doubt in the PKer community."

"Exactly," said Trinico, a comforting smile present, as always, on her face.

"Still missing 20, but Doc B and his people just entered. The raiding party will know something is up soon," interrupted Sergeant Butters.

I looked for the scout to see he was gone and cursed. "The scout is gone, sorry, I lost track of him."

"It is fine, we are pretty much ready to go now anyway," the sergeant said, trying to reassure me.

I scanned our surroundings but didn't see anyone on the peripheral. It was a few more minutes of waiting before the red aura returned. The raiding party was coming as one giant group, laughing and talking loudly as they walked up.

"Are they stupid?" whispered Olaf. "Surely they must know we have some kind of trick by now."

"PK'ers are idiots. They probably think this is our way of surrendering or something even stupider," I offered.

The group stopped about a hundred yards back. Then one man walked forward, the level 47, the highest-level player of the bunch. He stopped about fifty-yards away from us then motioned us to join him.

"I'll go," I volunteered.

"Are you sure that is wise?" asked Sergeant Butters.

"Yes, worse comes to worse, my spell is instant. If he swings on me, I'll trigger it. That close it will hit all the raiders," I answered.

"Have faith," said Trinico. "The Gods and Goddesses are with us."

As I walked toward the waiting killer, I half expected the obligatory tumbleweed to go rolling past. But it wasn't high noon or an old western and there was no tumbleweed to be found.

I swallowed once and took a few calming breaths before taking the last dozen steps to parlay with the murderous PKer. Walking toward him, I took a moment to observe my enemy. He was probably a few inches shorter than me, but between his boots and overly large hat, he was nearly the same height. He wore a bright red leather jacket and had a cutlass sword strapped to each hip. The curly mustache and small goatee finished the man's look. The more I looked, the more I was sure he was going for a pirate look, it was very cliché.

"You got guts kid, I'll give you that. Not much for brains, but plenty of guts," he greeted me, smirking as if he was ultimately superior to me in every way. He had 376 judgments against him, if I accomplished nothing else today, I would kill this man.

I shrugged, trying for nonchalance. "Probably more along the line of, I'm expendable."

The man laughed. "What's your name?" the PKer asked.

"Can't read?" I asked him, pointing above my head.

Apparently, he didn't appreciate my joke, his hand twitched toward one of the swords at his waist. "I was trying to be polite before I kill you and all the people behind you. If you don't care to observe the niceties, I can just kill you now and see if the next guy they send out will," the PKer retorted.

"Fine, calm down," I tried to placate the man. "I'm Bye-bye."

"Six Fingers," he introduced himself.

"So, why the parlay?" I asked.

"I wanted to see what was happening. What would cause the people to gather like this? Maybe, I was hoping to get a little explanation. I know you can't be planning to fight back. All you've got is an old level 38 NPC warrior and I'm guessing a level 36 NPC priest. So please, enlighten me," Six Fingers replied, his gaze directed behind me.

"We're going to kill you to the last man," I replied, smiling as friendly a smile as I could muster.

Six Fingers just laughed. "Kill us? And just how do you plan to do that?"

"The Goddess Issara is angry," I responded, trying to sound confident.

"Oh, which impotent wet blanket is that?" asked Six Fingers insultingly. Thunder boomed loudly above me before my vision was filled with white light, as lightning struck all around me and Six Fingers, but not actually hitting either of us.

"The Goddess Issara is the Goddess of Justice and Retribution. She has this thing about murderers like yourself. I mean, you have killed 376 civilians, and players whose levels are more than 20 below your own."

Six just shook his head, clicking his tongue. "Like I said, an impotent wet blanket doesn't even have the power to strike me down."

Thunder sounded above and more lightning arced from the sky this time hitting the tip of my spear causing it to glow white hot. When I saw the *Divinity's Touch'* buff applied, I wondered what it would do, but I didn't think I'd have much time to look for a description.

"Ooh, fancy light show," taunted Six Fingers.

"Huh, you have no idea what you've brought down upon yourself and the others, do you? As they say, you can't help stupid," I said finally hitting the limit of my patience. "Justice Bringer," I stated clearly, causing a pulse of white light to explode from me and spread like a giant shockwave of light, doing no damage at all but placing the debuff 'Scaled Justice' on all those present.

"And what was that supposed to do?" asked Six Fingers.

"This," I said, reaching my spear forward and gently touching it to the unsuspecting man's chest. Lightning arced from the point of contact and continue through his body, shooting into the mass of murderers behind him. His body literally disintegrated into ash as did those who were struck behind him, cutting the raid in half in an instant. There was no damage listed, the men were just dead and gone.

When the light faded I could hear cheering behind me along with the stomping of feet, the sound of a charge, but I saw the looks of utter silent shock in front of me, the murderers, for the most part, looked horrified and scared with few exceptions.

"Charge!" called Sergeant Butters, leading the way. As soon as they caught up to me I joined the charge, picking a target ahead of me and running with the pack.

The raiding party was already broken after watching their leader so ruthlessly extinguished, along with half their group in a single attack. Most of them turned to flee. A few of the stubborn ones tried to fight, only find out their level advantage meant nothing as they were fallen upon by guards and the braver citizens, like locusts to a crop.

In the end, I'd kept my word, they died to the last man.

The party following our victory would be the talk of the town for at least the next week, and the story would no doubt travel to Root City and the other provinces, spreading a wildfire of rumors. As for me, my secret, or at least part of it, was out now and there was no going back.

CHAPTER 14

"Three cheers for Bye-bye," shouted Gavin, raising a pint of beer into the air. The area in front of the Town hall had become a massive celebration. It seemed like the whole town turned out to celebrate, or at least most of it. There were torches set up and lanterns slung between buildings, lighting the entire boulevard leading up to the Town hall. A band had materialized at some point along with a makeshift bandstand. Dogson and a man that went by Doc B set up a makeshift bar. Kids were running about with sparklers and playing games. Girls flirted relentlessly with me, which was both a blessing and a curse.

"Hip-hip-hooray," chorused three times from the revelers.

"Did you shee it?" asked Micaela, yet again. "It was all like, whoosh-crackle-kaboom."

"Yes, I saw it," said Olaf. "I was even closer than you were."

"God, how aweshome was that?" she asked, giddy as can be and also getting pretty tipsy.

I could only laugh, my mug clanking against anyone that came near, not getting a chance to actually drink my beer.

"I have to say, Bye-bye," said Olaf, his voice taking a more serious tone. "That might have been the most awesome thing I have ever seen."

"It was pretty cool," I commented, trying to downplay it. "It was more my Goddess's work, than my own."

266

"Yeah, and we're never getting on the bad shide of her . . . ever," said Micaela.

"No, we are not," agreed Olaf. "Did that idiot actually say that about her?"

"Well, I don't think the man had ever truly faced off with a God or Goddess, Six Fingers had no idea what he was starting," I answered. Honestly, I hadn't given much thought to what it meant to be a God or Goddess, or what kind of power one might wield in this world. I knew I would have a healthy amount of respect toward her, or any God for that matter, going forward.

"Right, so we also will never speak badly about a God or Goddess. I know Maggie gave us that warning about being careful with what we say regarding Gods and Goddesses, but I never imagined that could happen," commented Olaf, the man then hefted his large mug and started guzzling.

It seemed to me, he also now had a healthy amount of respect.

"I'm going to take a walk," I said, standing. "I need to clear my head." I moved quickly to depart before anyone could protest. I just needed to get out of there.

My walk carried me down the street and away from the loudest of partygoers. Eventually, they carried me inside the temple. I didn't know where to look or which altar it was I should visit, but I needed to pay my respects and give thanks.

There were all kinds of statues, altars and representations of Gods and Goddess spread throughout the temple. I don't know how long I wandered around inside the temple when I stopped in front of a small altar. On the table stood a small statue of a woman, she wore armor but no helm. Her head instead bore bandages, wrapped around her head, covering one eye. She held a torch up in one hand, glowing with an otherworldly light. In her other hand, she held the pommel of a sword that had its tip stabbed into the ground.

"The Goddess Issara, I see you have found her," said a voice behind me, startling me.

"Trini, you scared me," I said, looking to her and giving her a small smile before looking again at the statue.

"Have you come to pray?" asked Trinico, stepping up beside me.

"Maybe," I replied. "I don't really know how to pray. Is there any specific format here?"

"Some Gods and Goddesses require certain niceties be observed. But for the Goddess Issara, as her only priest, only you would know if there is something you are supposed to do."

"She didn't exactly give me an instruction manual," I retorted, joking lightly. I was rewarded with a thump to my head by Trinico's staff. "Sorry."

"For you, I would just try talking to her," suggested Trinico. "I will leave you to it." With that she walked on, doing some kind of check of the temple or maybe offering evening prayers to different Gods.

"Hello," I said lamely. I did not expect a reply.

Greetings my little Warrior Priest.

That shook me, even more than Trinico sneaking up on me. The fact that I now heard a light laugh coming from nowhere and everywhere, did not make me feel any better about it. Looking around, the room also seemed brighter somehow.

"Yeah, yeah, laugh it up," I groused before realizing what I was doing. "Sorry, didn't mean to offend."

You worry too much. I chose you for a reason, it had nothing to do with your etiquette or lack thereof.

"Why did you choose me?" I asked, a kernel of self-doubt rearing within me.

I gave you a chance because you wanted justice that was deserved. I chose to keep you after you followed through and earned much-deserved retribution on that thug. I was proud of you then. Even knowing you had little hope of winning that first fight, you still went to face him. You had faith in me without knowing me or what I represented. You have earned your place as my Warrior Priest.

Sadly, my faith in you was shaken. I started to have doubts about you as you tried to keep your link to me a secret. You were even willing to put people at risk to protect yourself. I did not make you my Warrior Priest, so you could hide and watch injustice flourish.

But tonight, you proved yourself to me yet again. Tonight, you chose to serve justice and to protect the innocent. You even did so, over protecting what you felt had to be a secret.

I felt pride when she said that, but also shame. I was still worried about what would happen to me now, my being a Priest of Issara would begin to spread throughout the World Tree.

You worry too much. What will come, will come. Tonight, you dropped a pebble onto still waters. You cannot yet see the waves for good or for ill.

"So, I should just hope this doesn't backfire?" I asked, feeling heat creep into my cheeks. Maybe it was the alcohol giving me the courage to speak to her this way, but I had to speak. "What about all the people here that are now at risk? You think the Adventurers I slaughtered here won't come back looking for revenge? That some other guild won't take this as a challenge? I'm selfish you know, I just want to have a grand adventure. I want to explore and see everything the World Tree has to offer. I can't do that if I'm constantly having to protect towns and villages, or even 'villes', from raiding parties similar to what happened tonight."

You exist, that is enough. You may not understand everything just yet, but the fact you exist is a deterrent. And as you have already experienced, not only will the citizens stand with you, but so too will the adventurers.

"I think you underestimate how much hate and anger those murderers possess," I snapped, feeling angry now. I guess I was feeling trapped after everything that happened tonight. That earlier feeling of not minding that my secret got out, had long since vanished. It would have been one thing if tonight had actually been a fair fight like we'd originally planned for, but after Issara interfered the way she did, it would cause a backlash. Players would be in an uproar over this. I could hardly believe the developers hadn't already stepped in to undo it all.

I supposed I expected Issara to get angry with me now, maybe take away my class, but she didn't. She actually giggled a light tinkling laugh.

You are such a silly boy. Look upon that statue meant to represent me. What do you see?

I wanted to rage, how could she laugh at me, to make light of my fears and concerns. Didn't she understand the dangers she created tonight? Still, I indulged her. "An injured Goddess looking for a way to escape responsibility," I snarked and was rewarded with thunder rumbling around me and shaking the room. I guess I had finally pushed too far.

What do you see?

Her demand sounded much harsher this time, her humor gone. It served to stifle some of my resentment and anger, replacing it with the temporarily forgotten respect she deserved.

I looked at the statue again and tried to take it in again. To really see it. "The bandage on your head does speak of injury. The covered eye is reminiscent of the idea that justice is blind. I think,

270

maybe it means justice was hurt or injured, or that justice could not be blind to those injured by it." I felt this ring too close to my own beliefs regarding justice.

Continue.

My eyes were drawn to the armor and sword. "Justice should be used to protect others, but it must also be prepared to fight." Finally, I looked at the torch. "The torch is the light, a guiding light to follow forward. Maybe where law and order are light, and the darkness is chaos."

Close, what stands behind me?

I looked again, I hadn't looked behind the statue before. When I did, I wasn't sure what to think. There were people, droves of them stretching to the wall of the alcove. The wall was painted to look as if the line of people went on forever. "It's more than just a guiding light. It's about being the light, showing the people the way forward. You set the example for the people to follow."

Who are you?

"If I represent your power in this world, then I am also the light. I am also to set the example."

Can you?

"I don't know," I answered, my previous fear and concerns, about what she expected from me, reared up again.

Nor should you. The hero is made in the moment. Tonight, you acted as the hero, ignoring any possible consequences. When the next moment comes, will you be the hero again? Only time will tell, but know this, I have put my faith in you. I believe you can, and will, be the hero I thought you could be when I gave you that first chance.

"I'm afraid," I replied. And I was afraid. It was so much responsibility and now so many people would be gunning for me.

And those who couldn't hurt me would hurt those I've come to care about, the overly real NPC's in this village for example.

Fear not, for I am with you always. Now, I charge you, share your knowledge and protect the World Tree.

Class Quest Alert: Share your knowledge and Protect the World Tree
The Goddess Issara has charged you to share your knowledge to protect the World Tree. Speak with Priestess Trinico to begin.
Reward: Experience, Hidden

Share my knowledge, what knowledge? I'm only a Novice Warrior Priest. What knowledge could I possibly have to share?

The room seemed to dim on me and I knew Issara had gone. Part of me wanted to lash out and smash that stupid statue, but a larger more rational part of me knew it would be wrong.

I finally sighed, not defeated, but certainly worn down. I had been standing there, lost in thought, for far too long. I went in search of Trinico, hoping to resolve whatever the Goddess wanted from me with this latest quest. When I found her, she and the sergeant were sitting in one of the pews talking to each other in hushed voices. As much as I wanted to speak with her, I knew I should leave them to their time together, the quest could wait until morning, or afternoon, depending on when the party broke up.

I rejoined my friends, more subdued, but I did my best to enjoy the celebrations with them, even flirting with Trish. She was so hot. Or was that the booze talking?

The party was still going when I made it back to my room, thoroughly drunk, though not blackout drunk this time. I knew I should sleep, but I wasn't ready to, not with all the noise still going outside and in my head. So, I sat at my small desk, in my small rented room, and started writing, putting the day's events down on paper, letting out all my frustrations and fears. I ended up purging everything that had built up, when I was done and had completely unburdened myself, the first light of day was creeping in my window, I fell soundly asleep and did not wake until well past noon bell.

***

It may have become predictable by this point, but that cursed bird seemed to know exactly when to wake me. It was well past noon and that evil rooster was loudly announcing it was time for me to rise.

"Four hours of sleep, you wretched bird, let me sleep," I complained, only for there to be a knock on the door.

"Come get some lunch, you will feel better," called Dogson through the door.

"You're saved this time bird," I said, glaring through my window at the rooster, who uncaringly stood on the window box outside.

Lunch was quiet, it appeared I wasn't the only one who was just waking from all the revelry, nor was I the only one severely hungover and tired.

"Morning! So, what's the plan today?" asked Olaf cheerfully in greeting, I didn't even hear the ogre approach. He then sat heavily on the couch across from me.

"Hungover," I groused, hoping he took the hint to quiet down.

"Yeah, shush," said Micaela, collapsing onto the couch next to Olaf, laying her head on the man's shoulder. It was clear she was a fair bit more hungover than even I was.

"Don't you shush me, you boozer," countered Olaf, louder than was necessary.

I chuckled then cringed in pain. Why did laughing have to hurt?

"That'll teach you," laughed Olaf.

"Why aren't you hungover?" I asked.

"I still haven't gone to sleep. I might still be drunk actually," he answered, scratching his chin in thought.

"I hate you," I grumbled. Finally, Dogson arrived setting a pint before me along with a greasy breakfast plater laden with greasy food, despite it being lunchtime. Either way, the eggs, toast, potatoes, bacon, ham, and sausage were greatly appreciated, as was the pint which was quite successful in washing away the grogginess from a lack of sleep and a mighty hangover.

"Now then, what is the plan for today?" asked Olaf.

"Before you get off on some adventure, the mayor has asked to see all three of you," interrupted Dogson, collecting the empty plates and mugs.

"I guess that's the plan," I answered. I didn't feel up to whatever quest the mayor might want us for, but it would rude not to at least meet with him.

"Ugh," Micaela whined. "No quests today . . . too sleepy."

I agreed wholeheartedly but there was no point in fighting against it right now. "Might as well see what he wants."

At least the weather was nice today. I stopped for a minute outside the inn to simply stand in the bright afternoon sunlight and soak up the lifegiving rays. Also, this sun didn't threaten to give me skin cancer which was an added bonus.

"Afternoon Bye-bye, Olaf, and Micaela," greeted the mayor, with a beer still in hand. He was sitting rather happily at one of the tables that had been set up for the previous evening's celebration.

"Mr. Mayor," I returned the greeting.

"Hey Homer," said Micaela while Olaf simply nodded a greeting to the man.

The man stared at all three of us in silence, a good minute passed that way before he spoke. When he did speak, the words were simple but had humility and impact, ones I don't think I'll ever forget. "Thank you."

I instantly felt embarrassed, more so with the system notification that popped up.

Hidden Quest – Successfully repel a raid on a small village - Completed
Reward: +2000-Experience, +5-gold, Title: Local Hero

"You all have earned every bit of that reward. We cannot begin to thank you enough," he said, his head bowed in gratitude, his beer set aside.

"I only did what was right," I replied, knowing there was no use in refusing a quest reward, as they were immutable. I could only be grateful.

"We were happy to help," said Micaela, perking up ever so slightly. I couldn't help but notice she was wiping away a few tears. I also couldn't help but notice that both she and Olaf were now level 4.

I took a quick look at my own level and found I was close to leveling up myself.

Level:		Experience:	81.2 5%

"Anyway, I thought I should also let you know most of the town will be closed today. Far too much revelry last night. I think even David and Trini had fun. So, I suggest all three of you have a rest day. I'm sure everything will be back to normal tomorrow."

That was fine by me, at least mostly okay. "Any chance I could grab a couple books?"

"Sure," he said, tossing me a key, then one to Micaela and Olaf each. "That's your copy, the Town hall is open to you three any time. Consider this your 'Key to the City' ceremony."

"Thank you," I said emotionally, and I meant it too. This was a big deal to me, to be able to access both the job-board and skill books any time I wanted to. It was a major boon to me and my friends.

"Anyway, I suppose I should get home. I imagine Margie is fairly upset with me by now, being out all night as if I was a young man again. You three get some rest and be ready to get back to work tomorrow." With that said, the mayor stood and almost fell over, catching himself on the table. "I am fine, just a stumble," he said, righting himself and beginning a very drunken stumble home.

"Have you looked at the title yet?" asked Olaf, grinning.

"No, why? Isn't it just a title?" I asked.

"Nope, take a look, you too babe," Olaf prodded us.

I opened my character menu but didn't see anything.

"It's under your class menu," said Olaf.

I don't know if he was telling me or Micaela, but I was glad for the information.

I opened my class menu and there was indeed a 'Title:' now but it was blank until I focused on it. It presented a drop-down menu, but there was only the one option, so I selected it.

Title: Local Hero (Reduces cost of all goods and services in Hurligville by 20%. Effective Charisma tripled with Citizens of Hurligville)
Class: Novice Warrior Priest of Issara

I whistled loudly in appreciation. That was a lot of Charisma. It was also a big discount on goods.

"Nice," said Micaela, life finally returning to her.

"I like this title, I should be able to go see Giggle-Ana today and get my Engineer profession, but seeing as the town is closed up, it will just have to wait until tomorrow," said Olaf, thinking out loud.

"Wait, we can only have one title?" asked Micaela.

"Only one active one," Olaf replied. "Besides, we're always turning off the 'Miner Rank II' title, unless we're working. I imagine this will be much the same."

"Hey, does mining have any evolutions?" I asked. I had never done much research into the major gathering professions. Any kind of gathering profession to me was grinding and I hated grinding.

"No, Mining and Smelting, Skinning and Tanning and Herbalism and Mortaring, they all get subskills and Titles as you level up," answered Olaf.

"So, what does the title 'Miner II' do?" I asked.

"Miner Rank II' reduces the stamina cost of mining by 10% and increases yields by 10%," answered Micaela.

"I bet that's helpful," I appreciated the knowledge. The gathering professions in the World Tree were much the same as any other fantasy-based role-playing games, but much more advanced. As I mentioned, I hadn't done much research in the gathering professions, but the little I had read, said they were much more involved and considerably more difficult than in other similar games. "Anyway, I need to grab a couple books, so I can evolve my own professions, then I'm all in for a lazy day."

"That sounds fantastic to me. I keep forgetting to get that mining book too," said Micaela, drawing both me and Olaf's attention.

"What mining book?" Olaf and I asked at the same time.

"I didn't tell you?" Micaela asked. "I thought I told you both about Trini taking me around to build my totems."

"What does that have to do with a mining book?" I asked. "And aren't you already a miner?"

"It teaches mining subskills," Micaela explained. "I could have sworn I told you both all about this. Oh well, let's get it since we're here today." She then charged ahead of us determined to use her 'Key to the City' first.

"I love my wife, I do, but sometimes, she can be so scatterbrained," an exasperated Olaf grumbled good-naturedly.

I could only chuckle at him, I was unfamiliar with that state of being. Honestly, part of me envied him.

"Anyway, let's go before she destroys all the books," I said.

Inside I went to the bookshelf looking for anything that may reference either Cartography or Runes. I found the cartography book pretty easily, 'Legend'ary Maps'. It was an interesting play on 'Legend', you know, a map legend. The book I figured was for Runes was called 'Ruins Runes', another play on words but I was honestly amused by both book titles.

The inn welcomed us as usual, as did the seating we'd pretty much claimed as ours at this point.

'Legend'ary Maps' turned out to be fairly simple in its instructional capacity. Most of it focused on properly conveying distance and even perspective. Other than that, there was a small blurb on the map legend's construction and the Cartographer guilds map requirements. This time I was greeted with a system message.

New Professional Evolution Available, 'Cartography'. Do you accept Yes/No?

I accept, why would I hesitate when this was what I had been working towards.

278

Cartography (Evolved from Drawing)	Level: 10	Experience: 0.00%
Professional Skill: *Cartography is the ability to read and draw maps of varying detail.*		
Professional Skill: *Drawing is the ability to communicate through drawn images.*		

"Sweet, that's Cartography learned," I said to Olaf and Micaela, trying and failing to draw their attention away from their books. Then I frowned. I'd lost 4 levels to my 'Drawing' profession. Not just four levels, but it put me at exactly level 10 with zero experience. So, evolution did have a drawback. Wish I'd known that before, but there was nothing to do about it now. Then I realized I hadn't heard anything from my compatriots, which drew my attention from my new Profession.

Olaf was buried in the mining book, turning pages then going back and rereading a page or two then jumping forward only to go back again a minute later. He simply paid me no mind.

Micaela was more scratching her head and looking confused. I tried to spy the name of the book she was reading but her large meaty paw pretty much covered the whole thing.

"Mic, what are you reading?" I asked her. I should have taken an interest earlier.

She frowned for a moment before closing the book. Then she closed her eye and took a few deep cleansing breaths.

"Mic?" I called to her again.

"Sorry Bye-bye," Micaela said, opening her eye again. "I was trying to figure out this mana regeneration skill."

That got my interest.

"It's from the book I got my Shaman class from," she continued, while I deflated a little in disappointment.

"What's it say?" I asked. I may as well see if I can help her.

"Something about spirit tapping the veil and taking a sip. It's very confusing," Micaela whined.

"Okay, what's the veil?" I asked. If I was going to help I'd need some kind of background information.

"The barrier between this world and the spirit world," the ogre pixie answered.

"Okay, and you can access this spirit world?" I asked.

"Yes, but it's usually all in or all out. I'm not sure what they mean by spirit tapping the veil," she explained.

"Okay, let me think for a minute." So, she was trying to figure out how to tap into the spirit world to regain mana. But her ability put her all in or all out. So, either she was missing a spell or missing a key detail, probably the second.

"May I see the book?" I asked.

Micaela shrugged and handed it to me, opened to the page she'd been reading from. I studied the entry eventually going back a few pages to get more information.

"Hmm, from the sound of this, I believe someone or something is supposed to do the spirit tapping for you. Something in this world and that world, at the same time, has to act at your command. Does that make any sense to you?" I asked.

"Of course," she said, "I need another totem, one that has the ability to draw mana from the spirit world."

"Cool, does that mean I helped?" I asked, amused by her acting as if I had just cracked the greatest mystery of all time.

"Yep, but now I need to go hunting. Back in a while," she said quickly, dropping a quick kiss on top of her husband's bald head before rushing out of the inn.

Olaf just kept reading his book, flipping pages back and forth.

I could only shrug and open my next book, 'Ruins Runes'. From page one I knew this was not going to be an easy read.

Still, I was excited to get to work.

CHAPTER 15

"Morning," I greeted Micaela, as I took a seat across from her in the sitting area of the Dog House Inn. That rabid rooster narrowly avoided being on the receiving end of a smiting, yet again. That said, I was much more rested after taking the previous day to rest.

"Morning," she replied with a frown.

"What's wrong?" I asked curiously. I don't think I've ever seen Micaela not bubbly and happy or as I usually describe her, being an ogre pixie.

"I couldn't find a spirit for my new totem, or rather I couldn't find the right spirit," she complained.

"What kind of spirit do you need?" I asked, I still wasn't sure how her spirit and totem thing worked. She had a pair of axes that were both combat ready, which were also totems at the same time. It was weird given the history of gaming and the way in which shamans usually worked.

Traditionally, a Shaman was a caster class. They had spells that were considered nature magic and they had totems that would give certain effects, but the number of totems was limited and usually pertained to a specific element.

This system, from the little I had gleaned from Micaela, was more in line with the old hunter or ranger classes, where you would have to go out and tame a pet to work for you, and yet still wildly different from even that.

"Yesterday, I went to go hunting, knowing I needed to find a spirit. But, since I didn't know what kind of spirit I needed, I sat down and entered the spirit world to talk with Butch and Sundance about it. They said I should look for a bird spirit or maybe a fish. I went to the river, but I didn't see any fish spirits and I couldn't find any bird's nests either," Micaela explained, clearly frustrated.

Okay, so she can talk to the spirits in her weapons? Is that what she was saying there? Weird but cool, truthfully this version of a shaman was sounding cooler the more I learned. "So, you need to find a spirit to inhabit a totem? Is that right?"

"That's what I just explained," she stated. "But I had no luck."

"Well, Trini helped you last time. Maybe she'll help you this time too?" I suggested.

"I already paid her a visit this morning. She said, I would need to figure it out myself this time," she grumbled irritably.

"I see," I said, trying to placate her. "Have you asked Olaf for help?"

"He wanted to spend today mining and getting his strength stat up since we hit level 4 he wants to get his stat cap as soon as possible. Plus, he farmed seven new subskills from that book, gaining the title 'Miner Rank IV'. I didn't want to bother him with this, he was so excited to have skipped right past rank III." she explained.

"Wow, congrats to him. So, from what you said yesterday, you were hoping to get another totem, one to help with mana restoration, right?" I asked, making sure I understood what she was looking for.

"Yeah, exactly. I've been infusing mana into limestone ever since I learned the skill. It has been repeatedly draining my mana too. I've got a few infused stones now, all so I could make another totem or even a few more totems. My priority is to make one that can help with my lack of mana," she explained further.

"How do your spells work anyway? I'm just curious."

"Oh, I don't have any spells . . . well, I have a few spells, but nothing for causing damage or healing people, or anything. I have my totems. They cast the spells that damage, heal, buff or debuff," Micaela answered, sounding a little excited as she talked about her class.

"And they need your mana for that?" I asked, assuming that to be the case.

"Well, no, they can just do it. Their spells work on a GCD," she said.

A global cooldown (GCD) spell system? That was totally unfair. "So, does having more mana make them stronger?"

"Not at all, they get their strength from my connection to the spirit world, which is governed by my Spirit stat," she replied.

"Spirit stat?" I asked. There was no spirit stat as far as I knew.

"Oh, sorry. When you accept becoming a shaman, you lose the Wisdom stat and gain the Spirit stat instead. So normally, Intellect increases spell damage, spell crit and your mana pool, while Wisdom affects your mana regeneration," She explained.

Of course, I already knew this but let her continue knowing eventually she'd get to the point.

"When Wisdom becomes Spirit, Intellect only increases your mana pool, no more spell crit or spell power. Instead, we get Spirit which increases totem critical strike chance, totem damage and of course mana regeneration," she continued.

Ah, now we were getting somewhere. "Okay, I think I understand. But I have to ask again, why do *you* need a totem for mana regeneration?"

"Two reasons, first it doesn't just regenerate my mana, but those I consider allies within a certain range. Second, it will help me make more totems faster," Micaela finished.

See, now that was a perfectly reasoned explanation, and after hearing such, it was a task I was more than willing to assist with. "Now I understand. Okay, I think I can help you. However, we need to go see Sergeant Butters first. You still need to learn how to Dual Wield Axes and I need to get in my 'Acrobatics' training. Then we can go see about getting you your next totem before we go see Trini. Deal?" I offered.

"Deal," said Micaela, grinning happily.

After a quick walk to meet up with the sergeant, training began.

"Onto the trampoline you go," order Sergeant Butters.

I was hoping to do something else today but complaining would be pointless. Besides, I was sure Sergeant Butters wouldn't send me to work on the trampoline unless he thought it was necessary.

"Remember, flip, no bouncing or pre-jumping," Sergeant Butters ordered. "I will be back in a little while. I need to get Micaela swinging around those stone monstrosities."

He may have sounded harsh, but I could tell he was actually excited to work with her and her totems.

That left me standing in the center of the trampoline. I didn't want to repeat what I was doing yesterday. Three hours on the trampoline only yielded 6/100 on the progress toward learning Acrobatics.

I needed to be smarter about this.

I had to think it through. My instruction was to complete a front flip, but there had to be more to it. The way the sergeant emphasized not bouncing or pre-jumping, I assumed the goal was then to flip without bouncing, using as much of my own power and control as I could. I was trying for a perfect flip, just one perfect flip.

The only thing I could do was test my theory. I bent at the knees slowly, so as to not bounce, then I pushed off hard as I could, rotating forward as soon as my feet left the springy canvas. I landed perfectly on my feet with hardly a shake or bounce of the canvas. Out of curiosity, I checked my quest to see if I was working in the right direction.

Class Quest Alert: Training with Sergeant Butters 3
Having put your trust in Trinico and David Butters, they have offered you training to develop your stats as quickly and efficiently as possible.
Reward: Acrobatics 7/100

It changed by one. The perfect flip increased the bar. Now I had to do it again to see if it would work again.

I calmed myself, bent at the knees, and pushed off, flipping around again and landing on my feet, trying my best to stay under control.

Reward: Acrobatics 8/100

"Yes!" I cheered. Progress. It wasn't about chaining together a bunch of flips. It was about getting it done right.

I flipped again, 9/100. And again, 10/100. And again 10/100. I flipped again, thinking maybe that one was off, but it still came back 10/100. I flipped ten more times and still 10/100.

"Alright, you have got the front flip figured out," said Sergeant Butters, drawing my attention. I didn't hear or see him arrive but when I looked at him he was just nodding in approval. "Now do a backflip."

So that was it.

There would be a series of exercises I would need to complete, each providing a certain amount of progress.

It took a few tries to get the hang of the backflip but now that I had a better idea of the goal I knocked out 10 more points of progress rather quickly.

"That was quick, not bad," complimented Sergeant Butters.

"What's next?" I asked eagerly.

"The mats," the sergeant said, motioning to, and then walking to a large square area covered by some kind of padded surface. "Now then, you have gained some semblance of balance and some control over your body, we need to take that to the next level."

"Right, what do I do?" I asked, eager to begin.

Sergeant Butters actually groaned in annoyance, or was it reluctance? "Watch carefully, I will show you once, then it is up to you." The man stepped on to the mat, not bothering to remove his sabatons. He bent forward placing his hands flat on the mat, then lifted his legs straight into the air. Then he walked forward about ten steps on his hands, then his arms bent as he rolled forward in a summersault. Using the forward momentum, he sprung up and forward onto his feet and let the momentum carrying him into the air, where he flipped forward landing perfectly on his feet. Next, he cartwheeled backward three times, the last one turning into a backflip. It was all very impressive, leaving me with the impression I was about to hurt myself even trying this.

"There you go," Sergeant Butters said before walking away.

"So unfair," I complained, dreading this. The routine he showed me was simple, just four moves, but they were all difficult to pull off without significant training. Rather than get too bent out of shape over it, I paused, trying to think it through, it was four moves or rather series of moves. It occurred to me, I would have to learn

287

each series of movements one at a time. Handstand, summersault, I already knew how to flip, but combining it with the summersault would be difficult, and finally the backward cartwheel and backflip.

The handstand, it turned out, wasn't as difficult as I feared. My strength in the game made it more than manageable, the only difficulty I had with it was the balancing. Once I got the hang of balancing, I spent a good chunk of time just walking around on my hands.

The summersault was also easy, though to be honest, I did not picture the summersault as being too difficult. I was quickly able to grasp the concept of using the momentum from it to help spring me from the ground, adding more height than my normal jump probably could have managed alone. I would wait on adding the flip as that was the part most likely to end in injury.

Finally came the backward cartwheels. My first few attempts would have been hilarious to watch if not for the pain I felt. The first time I arched backward my head slammed into the square and even with its little bit of padding still hurt more than I would have preferred. The second, third and fourth weren't much better.

It was while lying on the ground after the fourth attempt, I came to the decision that this step would need to be broken down even further. Starting with a simple reverse push up and arching back and pelvis skyward was fairly easy, easier than a handstand anyway. I felt the difference in my body position immediately, starting with the bend in my knees and the placement of my hands.

I moved from this position into a handstand and back to my feet. "Much better," I complimented myself. I did this several more times before I tried again, from a standing start and when I made that fifth attempt it was much better, even though I still almost knocked my head into the ground. The fact that I didn't, suggested I was getting better. Once more I moved into a handstand and back to my feet but much faster than before.

Soon enough I was doing backward cartwheels, eventually chaining them together in groups of three, then picking up speed.

Satisfied with my progress, I went back to the summersault, this time determined to add the flip to the end of it. I was shocked when my first attempt at the flip was a success, but less shocked that I lost my balance right afterward. More practice and more successes and the occasional faceplant ensued.

Eventually, I combined the handstand walk into the summersault and flip. Once again, I practiced the motion repeatedly until I was comfortable enough to add in the backward cartwheels.

More practice, more repetition until finally, I started trying to add in the backflip. The backflip was much different from the front flip, I kept overcorrecting causing me to land either on my behind or back, the one time I landed on my head was one time too many.

Practice paid off though because eventually, I got the hang of it and was able to do it all together. Before I knew it, I'd progressed nicely.

Reward: Acrobatics 30/100

"Not bad," said Sergeant Butters, drawing my attention. I hadn't realized it, but apparently, I'd drawn a crowd. The guards had gathered to wait for their own training. I guess they chose to watch me while they waited.

"Way to go, Bye-bye," cheered Micaela.

"So, what's next?" I asked.

"That is it for today, come back tomorrow and we will start you on the next part," Sergeant Butters answered. "I have got soldiers to train, you know."

Class Quest Alert: Training with Sergeant Butters 3 - Completed
Having put your trust in Trinico and David Butters, they have offered you training to develop your stats as quickly and efficiently as possible.
Reward: +100 Experience, Acrobatics 30/100

"See you tomorrow then," I replied, accepting the completion and the next quest in the chain. Then looking to Micaela, I asked, "Are you ready to go?"

"You bet your holy behind I'm ready to go," she replied.

"On second thought," I paused, an idea coming to me. "Hey Sergeant Butters, one more question before I go. Where do owls nest around here?"

"Owls, not sure about owls but if its birds you're looking for I'd start by checking out by the wild blackberry bushes to the northeast. Plenty of mice and such for birds to prey on," the sergeant answered.

"Thanks," I replied.

"Thank you, David!" shouted Micaela, not caring that the man was on duty. And yet, I saw the man smile and give her a friendly wave. If it had been me, I'm sure I would have gotten a boot to the face, and this was while having considerably more Charisma than she did.

I ended up grumbling about 'double-standards' and 'dirty old men' the entire walk out of the village, while Micaela was humming a happy little tune. It wasn't until we were a good mile from the village that I let it go, the wolf that attacked us wouldn't have had it any other way.

It was nice to be outside of the village again. The walk was nice as was the weather. We did run across a few more wolves on the way, but they were no trouble for the two of us, sadly they barely gave any experience anymore, only +5-Experience for each of us per wolf. We took turns collecting the paws. I tried to get Micaela to use her scavenging skill on the rest of the wolves, but she refused, stating it was bad enough to have killed a wolf, then she started petting her axes and whispering sweet nothings to them.

I let it go at that.

"Okay, welcome to the Blackberry bushes," I said, making a grand gesture to the bushes all around us.

"Ooh, I have a quest to gather these for Rita too," said Micaela excitedly.

"How about I work on that for you while you look for a bird around here?" I offered.

"Thank you," she said, then wandered off.

After I filled two bushels and she still hadn't returned, I was tempted to go check up on her, but as we were partied up, and her health and mana bars displayed in my UI never fluttered, it was a safe assumption she was perfectly okay. That left me to find something to keep myself occupied.

I ended up walking around the area and doing a little bit of exploring. At first, I walked along the river following it east then northeast when it turned. At the end of it, I found a beautiful waterfall and the start of the northern ridgeline on the other side of the river. If I had to guess, I was at the northeastern most point of this province.

I found a large rock to sit down on, pulled out my large sketch pad and started creating my first map. Starting from this spot and mapping all the way back to the village. I made sure to include the Johnson Farm, the road where I fought the trolls, the blackberry bushes, and as much of the surrounding forests as I could. Finally adding Hurligville, drawing in the buildings then labeling them and the points of interest that I knew of.

"Bye-bye," called a searching voice I recognized as Micaela. She sounded pretty far away. Looking down at my own map, it appeared I had wandered pretty far from the Blackberry Bushes.

"Over here, I'm on my way back," I called back, standing from my rock seat and beginning to walk back in her direction.

"What were you up to?" she asked.

"Working on my first map," I answered, showing her the fruits of my labor.

"Hey, this is pretty good. Much better than the maps sold in town," Micaela complimented. "Are you planning to sell that in town?"

"I have to go to Root City first and register with the Cartographer's Guild. Then I can register my map and if it's the best quality map for the area it will be sold in the village," I explained to her.

"Nice, I bet you could make some good money from that."

"That is the idea," I replied. "Anyway, you get your totem sorted?"

"You bet I did," she exclaimed, pulling a large stone gourd about the size of my torso from her belt. It was smooth and perfectly shaped and even had a perfect fit stone stopper. "Cool isn't it? I can fill her with water, and Barista will turn it into mana enriched water after 30 minutes. In addition to that, she boosts mana regen to me and my party by 10 per 10 seconds. All that and she's only level one. Once she levels up, she'll make the water faster and stronger and even be able to carry more of it."

"That is seriously overpowered and more so, just clever thinking. I would never have thought to make a totem into a gourd," I complimented her.

Micaela was the surprising one in my opinion. Sometimes, she seemed so flighty, and other times she seemed far too wise. It was an interesting dichotomy, if nothing else, it was entertaining.

"For totems, size matters, so I had to have something large enough for Barista to grow into but also compact enough to carry. Thankfully, I've got more strength than most, so I can carry more. Right now, she can hold 50-drinks."

I really wanted one of those so badly just then. I would never realistically be able to carry it. I still wanted one. My canteens only carried 5-drinks a piece.

"So, did you get a bird spirit?" I asked lest I get lost in daydreams of walking around with a giant stone gourd strapped to my back.

"I found a raven," she answered proudly. "The boys like her too."

"That's a good thing. I'm sure it's good that your totems get along so well," I replied. So weird. I don't know how I'd feel about having to keep so many NPC's on me at all times, worse if I was the only one that could hear them speaking. It also made it so shamans were going to be very taxing on the game's resources if every totem had its own AI. To have so many AI's at once would probably end up being unsustainable. Then again, I had never talked to one of her totems, so I had no idea how complex the AI's were.

Still, it seemed excessive.

"You betcha!" she cheered in her pixyish way. "So, back to see Trini for more training?"

"You betcha!" I mimicked her, causing her smile to widen even further.

The walk back to town was filled with Micaela's constant chatter and relaying the comments of her totems. We killed a few more wolves along the way, but nothing out of the ordinary.

"You are late, Bye-bye, I expected you hours ago," said Trinico as we entered the temple.

"I was helping Micaela get her new totem," I replied smoothly. I didn't appreciate the accusation in her voice but complaining about it would do no good. I swear this woman was bi-polar with the way she constantly switched her moods.

"So be it. Micaela, I suggest you spend time in the spirit world. Your totems will help you train. Bye-bye, you must be close to your stat caps. Why not head into the puzzle room to finish up?" Trinico ordered.

I could only shrug and agree with her. I took a moment on my walk to the Puzzle Room to check my stats and gear. I was pleasantly surprised to see my Boar charm had gained some progress.

> **Boar Charge Charm (Unique) -** +10 Stamina, +10 Endurance – Equipping will teach skill 'Boar Charge' 30/100

I just wasn't sure what I could have done to gain 5 points of progress until I looked in my bag again, there were 5 wolf paws out of the 10 we'd killed today. Could that be it? Could it be the bounty? The boar I protected that earned me the charm was being attacked by wolves, so it would make sense. I would definitely be going back out to hunt some wolves after I finish training with Trinico today.

It took about thirty minutes to grind out the last +2-Intellect and +18-Charisma. The Charisma gain surprised me or sort of surprised me.

The Puzzle Box I created was pretty straightforward, providing a mix of puzzles and mental challenges, getting progressively harder as you advance. There was no set pattern as to whether they would be social or mechanical in nature.

The Puzzle Room seemed to be more advanced than that. It seemed to give me challenges based on what I needed to work on or what I was able to improve upon. So, after 14-puzzles solved I'd hit my cap and departed the room.

I found Trinico watching over Micaela who appeared to be in some kind of trance.

"She is walking with the spirits. How did your training go?" the priestess asked.

"Fourteen puzzles solved, and my stats all capped," I replied.

"Well done. I would suggest you try to level up before spending more time in the Puzzle Room," Trinico recommended.

Class Quest Alert: Training with Priestess Trinico 3 - Completed
Having put your trust in Trinico and David Butters, they have offered you training to develop your stats as quickly and efficiently as possible.
Reward: +100 Experience, 60/100 Meditation

"I will," I replied, accepting the completed quest and the next in the chain. "I didn't get a chance to talk to you again after you left me to pray the other night."

"Did you find the answers you were looking for?"

"Yes and no," I replied. "The Goddess is . . . not easy to understand, I guess."

"So, she spoke with you?" asked Trinico, looking both surprised and rather pleased.

"She did. It was . . . I don't know. Anyway, she also set me a quest. She said I had to share my knowledge, whatever that means.

I'm supposed to talk to you to start," I explained as best I could. I was honestly trying not to think about my conversation. I still felt like so much was out of my control.

"Such a blessing," said Trinico, positively giddy now. "I am happy to receive such knowledge."

"I still don't understand, what knowledge?" I asked.

Trinico just rolled her eyes. "Silly boy, your spell. 'Justice Bringer'."

Huh, as understanding dawned on me, most of my worries melted away. This was how I was going to be able to continue my own adventures. I could teach Trinico and then I wouldn't have to worry about protecting the village all the time. I would still have to seek justice where I could, but the friends I'd made among the citizens would at least have a fighting chance if they were to be raided again.

"Is it really that easy?" I asked only to catch a new lump to my head from Trinico's staff.

"Silly boy, there is nothing easy about teaching a God-level spell," Trinico chided me.

"God-level?" I asked.

"Yes, God-level. Did you think that changing the fabric of existence, even temporarily, would be anything less than the work of a God?" she explained.

"I hadn't thought about it," I replied, getting a much harder thump of the staff. I don't know why I kept letting her hit me, but part of me thought I may have deserved it. Part of me also became worried suddenly. If I taught this spell to her, could she teach it to other adventurers? I knew she had spells she could teach me that we hadn't even discussed yet, but would she be able to give away such a spell to other players, just how much damage could it cause.

"The Goddess does have quite the plan. If you teach me, I can spread such knowledge to the other towns and villages. It will protect us all," said Trinico.

"But players could abuse such a spell," I protested.

"Silly boy, what part of God-level spell did you not understand?" Trinico asked.

"Apparently all of it. So please, explain it to me," I answered.

"A God-level spell is one given by a God or Goddess to their chosen, either a priest or paladin or in your case, a Warrior Priest. This spell cannot be taught to anyone that has not been permitted to learn it, and that person would require the God or Goddess that gave the spell to approve such a thing. As such, if you teach the spell to me, I can only teach it to those permitted to learn it by the Goddess Issara herself. So long as she wishes to protect the citizens from the less savory Adventurers, I cannot imagine she would allow such a spell to be taught to anyone, but the local priest or priestess and only if they were a citizen. So, you see your spell will be safe from being abused," Trinico explained.

Such instant relief. A giant weight lifted off of my shoulders at her words. This must have been the developer's goal all along, Creating the Warrior Priest class would allow the game to introduce the new spell in an organic manner. The spell would eventually spread, probably through the lowest level provinces first, they were the most defenseless. Then move to the next tier and the next tier after that. Forcing a more balanced system of play on the various player killer groups. There would always be those people that continued to prey on the weak, and that was the second reason for the Warrior Priest class, I would be free hunt them down and punish them appropriately.

"I love my Goddess," I said, letting all the tension that had been building in my shoulders for the last few days melt away. "So, how do we start?"

"What do you know of runes?" Trinico asked. I couldn't help groaning. I'd tried trudging my way through 'Ruins Runes' yesterday. It was extremely complicated. It wasn't simply knowing what the rune looked like but understanding the true power that it embodied. Each line held power and meaning, every circle, triangle, square and any other geometric shape did too. On top of that, each line of the geometric shapes had power and meaning too. And if that wasn't enough, then each time a line crossed, it changed the meaning and power of that entire structure.

It was exhausting to even think about.

"Good, then you have done at least a little studying. We will have our work cut out for us if you wish to teach me such a spell," Trinico said with a grin causing my brain to already hurt.

After an hour I was ready to log off and never return. Trinico was merciless in her instruction. Similar to the book, 'Ruins Runes', she was all about teaching me the meaning between the lines and shapes but unlike the book which would only punish me by causing confusion, Trinico would thump me good with her staff. If this were not a virtual world, I would have started worrying about concussions and brain damage by now. As that was not a concern, I simply had to redouble my efforts to learn, preferably before the mad priestess accidentally sent me to respawn.

"Enough, that is enough for the day," said Trinico, sounding as frustrated as I felt. I had gained the profession, but Trinico insisted I needed to gain a great deal more levels to be able to successfully share my knowledge of the spell. Then she made me grind out seventeen painful and mind-melting levels to the skill. It was now my highest-level ability by far and only slightly useful even at its level.

Runology (Evolved from Writing)	Level: 27	Experience: 48.47%
Professional Skill: Runology is the art of communicating power.		
Chance to Learn Unknown Rune: 13.50%	Chance to Inscribe Skill: +6.75%	Chance to Inscribe Spell: +3.375%
Professional Skill: Writing is the ability to communicate through the written word.		

It was no wonder more people were learning Enchanting instead of Runology. As valuable as skill books would be, it had such a low percentage chance of successfully creating one, it was hardly worth it.

"What is the point?" I asked, my frustration getting the better of me. "Tell me, Trini, what is the point of even trying. I only have a 3.375% chance of creating a spell book."

"Modified by the level of the spell," she corrected me. That stopped me short and sent a ripple of confusion through me.

"What do you mean modified by the level of the spell I'm inscribing?"

"Bye-bye, you are a wonderful young man, but you still have so much to learn. For each level of the spell or skill you are trying to inscribe, you gain an additional 1% chance to inscribe the spell or skill into a book or scroll," Trinico enlightened me.

I could only blink. "Huh?"

"Okay, so assuming your 'Justice Bringer' is a level one spell your chance to inscribe it is 4.375%," she explained.

"But the description doesn't mention anything about that," I protested. Looking at the profession again.

"Does your Runology skill not say 'Chance to Inscribe Spell: +3.375%? It is that little '+' that should tell you," she explained.

And boy did I feel stupid. I checked my spell book for some of the other spells and skills had a 'chance' to whatever some of them had a '+' sign and some did not. "Does that mean you don't need the Runology profession to create a spellbook? Say if you had level 100 of a skill?"

"Of course, you still need Runology. Just because you understand a spell doesn't mean you can properly communicate the power of that spell," Trinico answered.

"Okay, I need a blank spell scroll or book then," I said, mostly to myself.

"Do you think you have the skill to create a book already?" asked Trinico.

"The spell is level infinite. I get the feeling the Goddess Issara wants this spell shared, the sooner the better," I explained.

Trinico couldn't help but chuckle and shake her head. "Of course, it simply must be a level infinite spell. Why would it not be ridiculously easy?" she said sarcastically. "Wait here, I will be right back with a blank spell scroll."

Maybe it was me, but she seemed upset that our task just got significantly easier. She returned a moment later with a handful of scrolls and a pen and inkwell. "This is special ink, try not to waste it," she warned.

I dipped the pen in the inkwell and put it to the top of the scroll and . . . nothing happened. I was kind of expecting to just start automatically writing but it didn't happen. "Am I missing something?"

"Cast the spell," she said as if it was supposed to be common knowledge.

300

"Justice Bringer," I chanted the short phrase to activate the spell. Except the spell didn't activate, my hand did, I was automatically writing. This was another common trope in paranormal games, often called psychography, but in any MMORPG I'd played before, they tended to use a progress bar or timer of some kind, instead of actually writing. Still, I was mesmerized as the runes began to fill the page, my hand moving precisely as it jotted each line and curve and geometric symbol, right up until the page was filled.

Class Quest Alert: Share your knowledge and Protect the World Tree - Completed
The Goddess Issara has charged you to share your knowledge to protect the World Tree. Speak with Priestess Trinico to begin.
Reward: +1,000-Experience, Collect your reward (x5) from the Temple of Issara in Root City.

Excellent news indeed plus five rewards waiting for me at the temple and it was enough experience to push me to level 5.

Congratulations! You've reached Level 5!
+1 to bonus Holy Spells, +1 Intellect, +1 Charisma

You've forgotten the spell 'Justice Bringer Lvl ∞'.

You've learned the spell 'Justice Bringer Lvl 1'.

Justice Bringer	Level: 1			Experience: 0.00	
Spell Duration : 1 hour	Spell Cast Speed: Instant	Spell Charges: 1/1	Spell Mana Cost: 100	Recharge: 23:59:59	
Spell Effect (Active): *All Adventurers and Citizens within 20 yards have their effective level lowered or raised to match your own. Does not work on enemy Citizens, Beasts or Monsters.*					

That is so unfair. They just nerfed my best weapon against PK'ers. Not only does it now cost 100-mana, but its range was knocked all the way down to 20-yards. That was nothing. A good mage would nuke me from 40-yards or more. Additionally, it now had a charge count and recharge timer as opposed to a cooldown. Did that mean I would be able to add another charge of the spell eventually? Or was there something else to it. I suppose I will have to play with it for a while to figure it out.

"Why do you look like you have swallowed a lemon?" asked Trinico.

"The spell, she took it away from me and gave me back a severely weakened version of it. Now it's level 1 in addition to only being able to cast it once a day," I explained.

"Then it is well that I have the maximum level of Runology. Also, so long as I am in town you can cast your spell every day without worry as I will still have mine available," she tried to reassure me.

It still made me feel slightly exposed now. "What level is yours?"

"Your scroll gave me level 50 of the spell. I can reproduce the spell with a 100% chance. Though at three hours per scroll I will probably not be able to make many a day."

"Three hours?" I asked confused. I looked at my system clock and was shocked to see three hours had actually passed even though it only felt as if it were only a few minutes. I looked around and notice Micaela was gone, probably to meet her husband for dinner. And thinking of dinner, my stomach gave a hungry rumble, it was almost 7:00 in the evening and I was ready for some food.

"I know, it only feels like moments, but it can be a rather long process. Not that you will have to worry over creating a scroll for that spell again any time soon. Anyway, you should go, get some food and try to have a little fun. Get a good night rest too. Now that you have gained another level we have work to do tomorrow," she stated.

"So much for my plan to hunt wolves," I grumbled. "I'll see you tomorrow then Trini. Have a good evening."

"Thank you Bye-bye, you too."

The walk back to the inn was quick, it was rather quiet when I entered, not empty, just kind of subdued. It seemed a good number of people were still feeling the aftereffects of the celebrations.

"Evening, Sugar," said Trish, greeting me immediately, her hand on my arm and her body coming awfully close to mine, closer than it ever had before. "When are you going to show me your room?" she whispered into my ear, shocking me.

Trish and I had flirted a lot, usually while I was under the effects of liquid courage, and it seemed, or at least I thought it was all in good fun, nothing too serious about it. But now, she was coming on to me very strongly.

What changed? Then I remembered my new title was amplifying my effective Charisma, so instead of 61, it calculated it as if I had 183. With my Charisma jacked up so high, it was making this girl, who'd I had previously shown interest in, much more inclined to be attracted to me. But it wasn't real. It was a mathematical equation affecting an artificial intelligence that was programmed to react accordingly. She didn't actually care for me, she was simply enthralled by the Charisma stat.

It instantly lost all appeal.

Part of me wanted to argue that this was the point of having high Charisma, but I just didn't feel that way. Trinico had pointed out to me, that Charisma was useful in getting people to trust me, to ask me for help. I accepted that it also helped with trade and convincing NPC's to help me. But using it to get lucky with a machine, something significantly better than doll but still artificial? It just felt so wrong now, made me feel dirty that I had even considered it before.

I looked into her eyes and the display of emotion was very convincing, she felt real even though I knew better. I also knew that I would have to let her down gently. I didn't want to spoil our friendly banter, our almost-friendship.

"Oh, that's sweet of you, Trish. I appreciate it, I do, but I don't think it would be a good idea. I may be living here for now, but in a few weeks, I'll be moving on. I would much prefer we keep our fun flirtations and friendship. I hope you understand," I replied, trying my best to be gentle.

Her personality flipped a switch in an instant. She didn't get angry with me, but she did giggle. "Oh, Sugar, you should see the look on your face. You are a real sweetheart Bye-bye, but I was only teasing you."

I knew that she wasn't teasing at the time, but it was the perfect out. "You got me with that one you little minx. Just remember, payback is a dish best served cold," I joked.

"Whatever you say, Bye-bye, how about a beer and some dinner?" Trish offered.

"That'd be great thank you," I replied, working toward my preferred chair by the fireplace and my waiting friends, Olaf and Micaela.

CHAPTER 16

For the first time since coming to this town, I was not awakened by the damnable rooster from hell. It was in fact, a full five minutes of being awake before the bird crowed his welcoming to the new day. So, either I had finally started to sleep through the morning noise or it was actually quiet for a change. The former seemed more likely than the latter, but I wasn't going to start complaining now.

I ate my breakfast alone for the first time in a few days as neither Olaf nor Micaela decided to join me for today, though I was sure they would join me for training, or at least I hoped they would. I had grown accustomed to their company.

My journey to the training area behind the barracks was much the same as usual, what was unusual was the angry Lieutenant Graves, storming around the barracks, looking an angry red that almost matched his armor.

"Out of the way," he snapped at me as he stormed onward, nearly shoving me from my path.

I shook my head in disbelief at the man's behavior. It also made me wonder why he was so angry? Where had he been for that matter? I don't remember seeing him when the Player Killers came to raid the village.

I found Sergeant Butters, an extremely upset Micaela and angry Olaf around back. "What happened?"

"That bigoted jerk found us training here with the sergeant and went off. He said several nasty things about us and then about the sergeant for training us, and then he went off about the sergeant training you too," explained Olaf.

"I would destroy that fool now if it was not more trouble in the long run," grumbled the sergeant. "You should not worry about anything he said. I train who I want to when I want to, and he has no say over it."

"But, won't that mean more trouble for you?" asked Micaela, fighting back a few sniffles.

"As if I care what that ponce of a lieutenant thinks. The boy is barely out of diapers and he thinks he can order me about like I am just some green recruit. Now, you do not get to worry about his stupidity. You three need to get back to training," ordered the sergeant.

Olaf punched one of his meaty hands into the other in anger, looking as if he was planning something stupid.

"Don't do it, Olaf," I tried to warn him off. "There is something else going on here," I told him, trying to hold him back with my words because there was no way I would have been able to do it otherwise.

Olaf frowned and hesitated, but it seemed to be enough to pacify him, at least for the time being. "What do you mean?" he finally asked me.

"He was missing during the raid," I answered.

It was as if a light went off over the sergeant's head. "He was not there, was he? Where the devil was he then? There were no scheduled patrols or trips to Root City. The runner to the bounty office left days ago and should be back tomorrow. There was no reason for him not to be here. So, just where was he?"

"I think he's up to something and his behavior suggests that whatever it is, is something secret and possibly dangerous," I stated.

"This will need to be investigated," said the sergeant. "I cannot, nor can my men. Bye-bye, Olaf, and Micaela, can I ask you three to look into this matter?"

Quest Alert: The investigation of Lieutenant Graves 1 (Recommended Level 4-6)		
Sergeant Butters has asked you to look into the suspicious activities of Lieutenant Graves.		
Reward: Experience, Variable Piece of Gear		
Do you accept this Quest?	Yes	No

"You bet we will," answered Olaf for all of us.

"Good, but remember, be subtle about it," Butters urged us. "For now, back to training, all three of you."

"Sure thing," said Olaf, seeming to calm at least a little. Micaela also seemed to perk up.

"Bad guy?" Olaf asked quietly as I came near.

"Bad guy," I nodded in agreement to his question. I moved to follow Sergeant Butters to the training area and back to the mat. The man now carried a training dummy under one arm.

"What's the next exercise?" I asked reaching the edge of the mat.

"Squares," Sergeant Butters answered, placing the dummy in the center of the mat. It was different from the usual training dummies that were set up around the training ring. For starters, this one wasn't driven into the ground, it simply sat stationary on a flat wooden base. Second, it had four almost bodies with four faces, one looking in each direction. It also had four arms that were angled such that they could belong to either of the bodies to its left or right. In each of the four hands was either a sword or shield.

"Watch closely," said Butters. He faced one of the body and face combinations. He then flipped or rather rolled through the air almost sideways, turning just enough so that when he landed, he was now facing the body and face to the left of where he started. Then he did it again, and twice more after that until he was facing the original face.

"Start with that," he said, then walked off the mat and back towards Micaela, who was swinging her axes wildly at her husband who was doing everything in his power to avoid getting chopped to pieces by the woman.

I could do nothing but try the new step in my training. I had a good comfort level with flipping. The airborne barrel roll should be much easier. And it was, but only to an extent. The action was easy, getting the turn just right, so I ended up facing the next dummy, was not.

I got the hang of it, only after circling the dummy four or five times. I finally saw my progress start ticking upwards, except that it froze at 35/100. I looked around for the sergeant, but he was busy with Micaela and Olaf, to the point of almost ignoring me, and he probably was, which meant I needed to figure out the next step myself.

The most obvious thing to me was that the first time I went around the dummy to left. Shouldn't I also go around to the right then? Turns out the right, was the right way to go, I got the next 5 points of progress.

"Good," said Sergeant Butters, startling me slightly, I should have expected him by now.

"What's next?" I asked.

"Squares," he replied grinning. "Watch closely."

He started the same way, an airborne barrel roll and upon landing, went straight into an actual roll, continuing around the dummy. The roll brought him back to his feet and into another barrel roll, finishing with another roll back to the starting position, all of it done quickly and accurately.

"Get to it," the sergeant stated simply. "Oh, and do not injure yourself rolling," he called back as an afterthought.

The warning made one thing clear to me, the barrel roll was not the dangerous part of this exercise as the air tended to be more forgiving than ground. I learned how true this was when I rolled the first time, my head getting rolled into the base of the wooden dummy, it was an excellent teacher.

As with the aerial only excise, once I got the hang of it and got my first 5-points of progress, I switched directions for the last 5-points for this exercise.

"Good work, off with you lot for the day then. I am sure Priestess Trinico is waiting on you," Sergeant Butters ordered before motioning for his soldiers to line up.

Class Quest Alert: Training with Sergeant Butters 4 - Completed
Having put your trust in Trinico and David Butters, they have offered you training to develop your stats as quickly and efficiently as possible.
Reward: +100 Experience, Acrobatics 50/100

"So, this Graves jerk, what's his deal?" asked Olaf, once we were clear of the barracks.

"I'm not sure. The guy just seemed off to me the first time I met him." I then told Micaela and Olaf the story of our first meeting the quest that led up to it.

"Odd, why would he care so much about a little sauce?" asked Micaela.

"I don't know, but I intend to find out," I replied, grinning just a little, which was apparently contagious as Micaela and Olaf were quick to join me.

"Man, the stuff you find and get into. I'm more convinced than ever that we need to form an Order," preached Olaf, again.

"And I'm fine with that so long as my only responsibility is to find these mysteries," I replied. "That said, how long before you two plan on leaving this province?" I had no idea how long Olaf and Micaela had been playing or when they would have to log out for their mandatory week of rest from the game.

Olaf sighed. "We'll probably still be a while. While we've made enough money to pay our debts in RL, we need to build up a surplus before we can move on. And as we've been spending so much time training with you lately, we haven't been able to do that. I'm not complaining or angry about it, just letting you know where we stand. Believe me, we're actually happy to have befriended you mate. That said, I figure we're a few weeks from leaving this province. What about you?"

"Between the outstanding quests I've got to resolve, the available training here that will only be more difficult to find later, I can't be too sure. I've got about two and a half weeks before my first month comes to an end. If I'm satisfied with what I've picked up by the time that rolls around, I figure it will be just about right to head to Root City and log out," I answered.

"We finished our week offline, right before we met you. In fact, that was only our third day back," Micaela interjected. "That means we're almost on the same schedule. We'll have to log out a day or two before you do."

"It may be too much to ask," started Olaf, somewhat hesitantly. "But what if you were to log out when we do? To get onto the same calendar as us. I understand you might want to stay a few extra days here to keep training, but you can do that just as easily when you log back in and we'll stay with you for it. What do you think?"

"I'm not opposed, not at all," I answered. I wasn't against it. It would be nice to have dependable friends to game with on a fairly constant basis. Granted, we would probably get sick of each other eventually, but as far as making progress goes, it was always best to have a steady and constant group to work with.

"Really?" asked Micaela and Olaf together, sounding surprised by my answer.

"Yeah, really, logging off a day early is not the end of the world. Besides, we'll know by then if we need more time in this province or not, so why not?" I replied.

"You're a good friend, Bye-bye," said Olaf, a gentle smile on his face.

"Nah, I'm just greedy. I am more interested in working with an Ogre Artillery and Shaman. I suppose it could have been anyone, honestly," I replied, smirking a little.

"Way to ruin a moment," complained Micaela, trying not to grin too.

"What a git," Olaf added, grinning too.

"You two should just be grateful you get to run around with a uniquely classed player," I piled on. "I mean, who wouldn't want to hang out with the fantastic me?"

"I don't know, you're awfully scrawny," commented Micaela.

"And he's a prude," complained Olaf. "Did you see the way he turned down that waitress?"

"She wasn't my type," I replied. I didn't want to get into all that. "She is just fun to flirt with."

"Awe, is our wittle Bye-bye shy?" cooed Micaela in a mocking tone.

"Is he blushing?" asked Olaf.

I could definitely feel my cheeks heating now. How did this get turned around on me?

"Anyway, we should hurry on, I'm sure Trini is anxious to get our training done and over with for the day."

"Way to change the subject," laughed Olaf before suddenly turning serious. "About Graves, what . . . why . . ."

"I don't know. If you look at his level, he's only level 9, while most of the guard is level 12 to 15 while Sergeant Butters is level 38, and Trini is level 36. Even the mayor is a higher level. Beyond that, he seems built to antagonize the players and the citizens. Every interaction I've had with him has been negative," I answered.

"Makes sense. But is there something more? Don't hold back on us now," Olaf insisted.

"I only have suspicions. For now, we should just ask around town, starting with the mayor and his wife," I replied.

"Alright, we'll trust you," said Olaf. 1I could see he wanted to press it, but I was appreciative when he didn't.

Training with Trinico went smoothly. The puzzles were getting much more personal and significantly more difficult, just as Trinico had promised. I was only able to knock out 20 new puzzles gaining +7-Intellect, +4-Wisdom, and +4-Charisma. This, plus the +4-Strength, +8-Dexterity, +7-Endurance and +9-Stamina from training to learn the 'Acrobatics' skill made for a successful day

I was also looking forward to getting to the 50-Strength mark. I needed that much to be able to equip light leather. I was looking forward to equipping that 'Guard's Light Leather Belt' I had been awarded a few days ago. It gave me +5-Endurance and +2-Stamina plus some additional armor, it made for a solid upgrade from my current 'Rope Belt'.

What most excited me about that day's training, was the new spell Trinico taught me.

Lesser Holy Barrier	Level: 1	Experience: 0.00%
Spell Duration: 10 minutes	Spell Cast Speed: Instant	Spell Mana Cost: 50
Spell Effect (Active): Create a thin barrier of Holy energy around a target that absorbs 10-points of incoming damage.		

It was phenomenal. A 10-minute buff, reducing all damage received by 10. That wasn't significant right now, but in time with enough development, it could become powerful. Unfortunately, it wasn't considered Healing or Damage, so my holy Bonus did nothing for it.

Trinico tried to teach me a bunch of other Priest spells that were in my level range too, but I was unable to. We both figured it was due to my class, maybe something along the lines of being able to learn some Priest spells and some Warriors spells, not that warrior had many spells. Skills were generally unrestricted regardless of class.

But regarding my spells, that was something else Trinico had gotten on me about. While preparing the training scrolls for the spells she wanted to teach me, she finally asked about my spells and how far I had developed any of them. She was rather cross to hear most of them were still level one. She made me promise to have all of them up to at least level 2 by tomorrow with 'Holy Smite' being up to level 5.

"I should probably go hunting before it gets dark. Trini was on me today about leveling my spells before tomorrow. Are you two good to go asking about Graves without me?" I asked.

"Yeah, I won't be much good outside of town until I get my hand-cannons. Just 2 more days and they should be ready. I should also have enough Charisma and Intellect, to start my engineering training by then too."

"I'd go, but I think a little questing with the hubby sounds fun," said Micaela, she grinned and wrapped her arm around one of her husband's, pulling it close.

"Okay then, see you both tonight for dinner," I said.

"Later Bye-bye," said Olaf with a small wave, he and his wife started walking toward the Town hall hand in hand.

My journey outside of town was nice. I took a moment as I exited to check my map to see what I hadn't explored yet to the northeast. Everything north of the river was still blank but there was plenty directly east I hadn't explored yet and the western side of the map was completely blank.

As a completionist though, I knew I wouldn't be satisfied until I finished uncovering every last inch this area had to offer. I trekked eastward, filling in whatever gaps in my map I came across as I went, killing the wolves as they attacked me. Sadly, they were now only worth +1-Experience each, since I'd hit level 5, but that wasn't important to me. It was the effort I put into using magic to kill them. Each wolf took two casts of 'Holy Smite', one cast took out about 60% of their health alone.

It also gave me practice with my 'Perception' skill, which I used to track them and pick out anything worth seeing. My vision also highlighted a number of plants now, but as I had no idea what they did or how to properly gather them, I left them alone. Still, experience was experience. The other thing I started practicing was my 'Stealth' skill. With the range on 'Justice Bringer' being reduced so significantly, I would need to be able to get close to my target to use it.

So, I was grinding, and as much as I loathed it, I persevered. At least I had a few goals in mind while I did, so it didn't feel as grindy. I cast all three of my buff spells every time they wore off to keep working on those spells. I would have to get into the habit of buffing every time I could throughout my day, buffing Micaela and Olaf too. I had plenty of mana to do so now, the water in my canteens was enough to get by for about half a day before needing to be refilled, which as long as I was in town would not be an issue. But that did bring up another thing I needed to look into, getting better canteens, better-quality water, or both.

About two hours into my exploration, I found the portal to the World Tree. It was kind of awesome to behold. It sat on a large stone platform with a giant stone ring. The portal itself was a swirling green maelstrom of energy with sparks of electricity bouncing around inside of it.

I checked my map once I felt satisfied with my exploration, I had everything East of town and North of the road all the way to the river drawn in as high a detail as I was capable of.

I looked briefly at my game clock and it was barely after 3:00 in the afternoon. I had a good three hours left to explore with before I needed to head back to get some dinner, for now, I ate some of the Adventurer Jerky to satisfy my hunger.

Next, seeing as I was already at the Eastern edge of the province, it made the most sense to me to go south.

As I journeyed south, the trees began to thin and the wolves became fewer and farther between. I took this as a good sign right up until a <Giant Condor Lvl 4> attacked me.

I never saw the blasted buzzard coming, not even a shadow on the ground. He must have dived from fairly high in the air, his first attack took nearly a third of my HP in one hit and knocked me to the ground. I got up quickly, immediately taking my stance, with spear and shield at the ready. The bird was literally flying circles around me. Thankfully, I was fairly comfortable with my ability to shift and pivot, always keeping it in front of me.

The Condor attacked again, flying slightly up, then diving toward me with its talons aimed right at me. It was disappointed to meet my shield, then angry when the 'Lesser Holy Imbuement' and my spear tip lit it up with -44-HP. Almost as if on autopilot, I then smacked the bird hard with 'Shield Slam' doing another -52-HP from both the buff and the skill combined. It was barely down a quarter of its health after those two solid bits of damage. Knowing I needed to work on my casting, I chanted 'Holy Smite' on the temporarily grounded bird. It returned to the air after two casts, but I didn't stop there, I kept casting it. It only attacked one more time. This time, I failed to block, taking damage from the bird's talons. Two more 'Holy Smite' casts after that, finished it off.

When it was done, I was surprisingly elated. That was probably the best fight I'd had in the game so far. Well, so far as in most successful. Yes, I took the initial surprise attack damage and yes, the bird got me once when I failed to block. But I did block its attack, I used my 'Shield Slam' ability perfectly, and I had cast 'Holy Smite' several times to kill it. I guess, after reviewing the fight, maybe it wasn't that successful, but it still felt improved in some way from my first fight in the game.

I also couldn't help but be excited about finding something new to hunt. Even though I still need to kill more wolves for my

Charm. The next time I was in town, I would have to check the job board to look for anything related to the giant birds.

I continued south but didn't find anything, until the forest suddenly ended and sprawling out in front of me were rolling hills with tall grass up to my waistline, which was accompanied by a system message.

You have entered 'Rolling Hills of Evermore' province.

Rolling Hills of Evermore – Level 15-20
The Rolling Hills of Evermore was once a prosperous land filled with farms and small mines owned by the Dwarven Hill tribes. This land has recently been invaded by the Gurtok Goblins and Dalrogar Kobold Alliance when the Dwarven Miners accidentally collapsed a mine on top of their deep-dwelling city of Daltok.

That sounded awesome! I could not wait to explore this new province, but it was several levels above me, for the moment at least. It meant I had reached the edge of the Hurlig Ridge province, it made me realize that I could probably go further East in Hurlig Ridge, but I would have to traverse the mountains that blocked my path. It also made me aware that I didn't have to take the portal to the World Tree to get to a new area to explore and adventure.

Anyway, I went back into the forest intending to follow its edge and mapping the borders as far as I could. It was nearly 5:00 when I stopped walking west. I had mapped another six miles of the border which put me almost directly south of the village, which I felt was kind of a perfect place to stop. I wanted to explore everything North and East of this point to complete my map.

About a mile north of where I stopped, I found the southern edge of a cliff, or rather a crevasse that looked to be about twenty feet across and filled with fog. It was so thick, I couldn't see through it. I marked it on my map and began the trek east along the border of it. Even when I reach the end of it, 2-miles later, there was no path down from the East as the crevasse ended in a cul-de-sac at least 50-feet across at its widest. I wished I could explore into it, but with the sheer edges and not being able to see the bottom suggested it would probably mean my death.

Much as I would have loved to go to the other end and find a way down, I knew I had to get back to town before it got dark out. As I got closer to the village, I saw a return of the wolves and an absence of the giant birds, as expected. I was happy to return to the village, it was getting steadily darker. If not for the torches lighting the entrance to the village and my map, I might not have found my way in the dark.

It took me almost two hours to return to the village, much to my irritation, simply because I had to detour around that crevasse. All that was forgotten when I returned to the inn and was greeted by Micaela and Olaf, both sitting comfortably on the couch they had claimed, and sipping on beers.

"Hey, he's finally back," said Micaela first, nudging Olaf with her elbow.

"Hey mate, how'd it go?" asked Olaf.

"Good . . . really good actually," I replied, grinning from ear to ear. I then told them of my exploring, finding the 'Rolling Hills of Evermore' and the valley just south of town. I even showed them my map.

"So, the area to the east of here is the mine. You went right around it. From what I heard from the other miners, that valley is the next mining area for this province, it's creepy but supposedly monster free, though I don't know any miners that have gone there, most just leave the province for the level mining camp," said Olaf, looking over my map and point to the large blank area to the southeast. "There is a split in the road here that leads to the mining camp."

I looked where he was pointing, I must have missed it before because my map didn't show it, though admittedly, my mapping of the road was not very good. I'd have to explore it more carefully next time I went out.

"How about you guys? Any luck?" I asked.

"A little, Homer didn't know much about Graves," started Micaela.

"Except that apparently Graves volunteered to be posted here," continued Olaf.

"Why would he have volunteered, he clearly hates it here?" I asked.

"We asked the same thing. Homer said, even from Day 1, Graves hated being here," added Micaela.

"Did Margie say anything about it?" I asked.

"She echoed her husband, though she did mention the man looked sick the first time he came into town," Micaela finished.

"Suspicious but not really criminal," I commented.

"So, what next?" asked Micaela. "How do we investigate further?"

"We need to get into either his office or his home, have a look around," I said. "Unfortunately, I don't have any skill for breaking and entering, which means he would know if someone went snooping."

"We need a rogue or thief, maybe even a ranger. Sadly, I haven't seen many around town. Blimey, most starting areas are still sparsely populated. I can't wait for them to open the game to the four-hour limit machines," grumbled Olaf.

"I can wait," I retorted. Expanding the player base was a good thing, but right now, the game was still rather small, which meant we had an opportunity to accomplish more firsts now than we will as the population of gamers increases. We had the chance to get out of a starting area without fighting over spawn points and quests chains.

"Greedy," stated Micaela, giving me a look.

"Yes, I am," I replied, getting a small rise out of her. "Anyway, back on task. We need to find a someone that can get in, investigate, and get out undetected."

"I'll keep an eye out for one, but maybe we could just hire someone to do it," suggested Olaf.

It was an option to be sure, but I'd been burned in the past on similar deals. You hire a guy at a set price, and when he gets the info, he jacks up the price. Or decides to sell it to anyone willing to pay the same or more. It was dirty and underhanded and completely to be expected. "Let's try and hold out on something like that. I don't feel the risk of a double-cross from whoever we hire would be worth it."

"I guess you're right," said Olaf, rubbing his chin. "I forgot that many of those types will double-cross you for the right price, or you wouldn't have been able to hire them in the first place."

"So, I ask again, what next?" asked Micaela.

"For now, nothing I guess," I replied. "We just keep doing what we do. Keep training and learning skills. I'll see if I can't find a lockpicking skill, though I doubt the Town hall book stash will have anything useful. After all, I doubt the mayor wants to invite thievery into his village. I'll ask him tomorrow anyway, maybe we'll get lucky."

"I think tomorrow, Mic and I will both spend the day mining. I think we're gonna have to do every other day if we want to have our stash built up before we leave this province," stated Olaf.

"I need more stone too," said Micaela.

"So, I know Olaf is going to be an Engineer, what are you planning Micaela?" I asked. I was curious as they were both miners and given that Micaela seemed to be able to make her own weapons and probably armor as totems she didn't need Blacksmithing.

"Construction," she answered with a grin. "I'm gonna build me and Olaf an awesome castle."

"That is so cool," I replied. It was very cool. I had read a few articles on the profession, everything I read said it was ridiculously difficult to level, no one had bothered to level it very far yet, property was super expensive to acquire.

"I know, right?" said Micaela excitedly.

"Hey, you should check with the mayor, I know he was going to be putting together a team to help rebuild the Johnson Farm. I bet you could get a ton of experience from that," I suggested.

"Ooh, Bye-bye, you brilliant man," cooed Micaela. "I'll be sure to ask him in the morning."

"Well, that's one less problem to worry over," said Olaf.

And it was. The rest of the evening passed in the usual fashion with chatting and drinking though not in heavy quantities.

At the end of the night, while happily soaking in the bathtub, I reviewed my progress. My hunting yielded nice results, 36 wolf paws to be turned in tomorrow. I also gained +4-Strength, +2-Dexterity which capped for the level, +6-Endurance, and +1-Stamina which also capped for the level. I was still 2-points of Strength shy of the level cap, but I should have that well in hand by tomorrow.

I was most proud of the progress made on my spells, I had definitely exceeded Trinico's expectations, all four spells gained some much-needed levels.

First was a nice boost in my one damage spell.

Holy Smite	Level: 7	Experience: 89.99%
Spell Damage: 17-22	Spell Cast Speed: 1.50 seconds	Spell Mana Cost: 24
Spell Effect (Active): Smite a single target with holy damage		

Lesser Holy Barrier	Level: 3	Experience: 72.43%
Spell Duration: 10 minutes	Spell Cast Speed: Instant	Spell Mana Cost: 56
Spell Effect (Active): Create a thin barrier of Holy energy around a target that absorbs 13-points of incoming damage.		

Second, my buffs grew nicely.

Third.

Lesser Holy Imbuement	Level: 4	Experience: 1.25%
Spell Duration: 10 minutes	Spell Cast Speed: Instant	Spell Mana Cost: 50
Spell Effect (Active): Imbued Weapon now deals holy damage causing an addition 2-4 damage per hit		
Spell Effect (Active): Imbued Shield now deals holy damage causing 3-5 damage per block		

And Finally.

Lesser Combat Blessing	Level: 3	Experience: 99.58%
Spell Duration: 10 minutes	Spell Cast Speed: Instant	Spell Mana Cost: 50
Spell Effect (Active): Increase Stamina +3, Increase Strength +3, Increase Dexterity +2, increase Endurance +2		

It was a good day.

CHAPTER 17

Why? Just tell me why? Why can't that bird just leave me in peace? Was yesterday just a fluke? Or was this bird toying with me?

Admittedly, I didn't start my day on the right foot. My argument with Dogson was evident of that.

"It is a rooster, that is what they do!" the dogman nearly shouted at me.

"Fine, but does it have to be doing that right outside my window, every morning?" I argued back.

"It . . . is . . . a . . . rooster!" Dogson stated each word slowly as if that would make me feel any better about it.

"I know that, and I'm still asking you to do something about it," I replied hotly.

"You could always stay at another inn," Dogson threatened.

"Woah now, let's not do anything crazy. I like this inn. I like my room. I just don't like that rooster crowing outside my window, every morning. Please, if you could just do something about it. If there's much more of this and I might just have to start smiting them on reflex," I pleaded with the dogman.

Dogson finally sighed. "I will see what I can do, but no promises."

"Thank you," I said, hoping for just a little relief.

With that settled, I headed out into the village to get my day underway. First to see Sergeant Butters for training, then Trinico for more training, then the mayor's office to turn in paws, and finally out to explore the province some more.

I hoped to finish mapping the eastern part of the province today. If I was able to get back early enough, I had a good amount of reading I had neglected, so maybe I can get some of that done today too. I could only hope.

The sergeant was again working on a training dummy with a pair of daggers, moving through a number of attack patterns, looking random, but could have been predetermined. Unlike the first time I saw him doing this, I was actually able to somewhat follow his movements. I took it as a sign that I was improving.

"Morning Sergeant Butters," I greeted him with a friendly wave.

"Morning, let us get to work. No time to waste today," said the sergeant, stopping his assault on the dummy.

"Micaela and Olaf won't be coming this morning. They needed to get some mining done," I informed him.

"I know, Micaela and Olaf informed me of their plans yesterday," he replied, walking on toward the gymnastics equipment.

"So, what's for training today?" I asked.

"Either the 'Vault', 'Pommel Horse' or 'Parallel Bars'. Maybe all three, if you get the hang of it fast enough," the sergeant answered. "You have gotten pretty used to moving on flat, unobstructed surfaces. Now, you need to learn to use the environment around you. You need to learn to use your arms better while moving too."

"Won't my arms be occupied by my spear and shield?" I asked, I wasn't trying to avoid doing the work, but I still wanted to understand better.

"You will not always be in combat when you need to move. That also reminds me, 'Acrobatics' is an offensive style of combat movement. You will be better served if you start using your spear two-handed. Flipping and moving so quickly, makes it an order of magnitude more difficult to keep your shield in position. You should reserve your shield for when you use 'Shift', which is a defensive style of combat movement. Understand?" he explained, and asked, in short order.

However, before I could reply, he continued.

"Of course, I have skills to teach you eventually, but for now, it is something to keep in mind while you are out exploring the wilds. Those wolves should not present much of a challenge, but I would recommend you start improving your skill against them without putting yourself at much risk," he finished.

I think that was the most I'd heard the sergeant speak at once in the short time I'd known the man. "I can start working on my 'Two-Handed Polearm' skill, no problem," I promised.

"Good, then I suggest you watch closely for the next exercise. We will start today with the 'Parallel Bars'," the sergeant motioned a pair of long wooden bars, about 11 or 12-feet long, that were about shoulder width apart, about 7-feet up in the air, suspended by metal poles.

Sergeant Butters walked over by one of the support bars and reached into a bag, sitting at the base. When the hand came back, it was covered in chalk, which he rubbed into both of his hands until they had a thick coating. The sergeant then walked to one end, reaching up, putting a hand on either bar.

It was awesome to watch, and slightly daunting when he pulled himself up only using his arms until he was suspended in the air by just his arms. Then he rotated at the shoulder, up to a handstand. He walked forward on his hands a few steps, then bent his legs to a 90-degree angle then rotated at the shoulders again but to a seated position, it was very controlled. I could see the muscles straining and bulging, he moved with such precision. Then he swung his legs back, this time quickly, propelling his body back into a handstand, but he kept going over, his wrists rotating with the turn, back into a handstand then he swung his legs forward again.

This time using the momentum to flip into the air, only to catch himself on the bars by the underarm. He gripped the bar tightly and did a hanging handstand, I wasn't sure what it was called, but it was pretty neat, almost bat-like. He let his legs swing backward this time, and again his hands and wrists rotated until he was upright again. He then dropped to the ground and clapped his hands, sending the excess chalk into the air.

"Okay, your turn," he said as if it was the easiest thing in the world. Now, I'm sure if this was the real world, it would take months to be able to do any of the training for 'Acrobatics' I've been doing. Thankfully this was a video game, so it would assist me with learning to move my body in just the right way.

Even with that, this looked daunting.

Once again, just as with everything else I've done during this training process, I broke it down into steps. First the strength part, then the swinging around my legs, and finally the flip and catch. It was shocking how much easier it was once I'd broken it down. Before I knew it, I had it down and got my 10-points of progress much to the sergeant's pride, at least I think it was pride.

"Not bad at all, Bye-bye," said the man, grinning happily. "You made good time too. Let us get you on the 'Pommel Horse' next."

The 'Pommel Horse' was a large squared log wrapped in leather and padding with a pair of U-shaped handles near the center of the of the log.

"This is another strength exercise," said Sergeant Butters before took hold of the two handles, in a feat of pure strength, he rotated up into a perfect handstand. He started by folding his legs forward, but this time he folded completely in half. He rotated forward, his legs extending straight in front of him again. He let his body go stiff and slightly leaned back. He then rocked slightly left to right before swinging his body parallel to the log, only one hand gripping.

His legs swung back, this time behind the log, his free hand gripped the handle once more, only for the other hand to release, the legs to swing up parallel again and coming back down in front of the bar. He did this a few more times, then he started working toward the end of the 'Pommel Horse', his legs swinging around the whole time. When he reached the end, he did another handstand, and with a massive effort, used his hand to push off the log, and flip one and half times, landing on his feet.

"And I can do that?" I asked, feeling more than a little doubt.

"Of course, you can," he replied with hardly a nod in the direction of the 'Pommel Horse'.

I don't know why I expected this to be difficult. The strength part was certainly difficult, at least at first, but then it was a matter of getting the coordination for the swing of my legs and the swap of hands. Once I got that part it wasn't bad at all. I wasn't too surprised when the progress stopped at 5-points. I switched directions and got the other 5-points in no time at all.

"Excellent," said Sergeant Butters. "Last one for the day." He then led me to a smooth runway. At the end of the runway was a square platform covered in leather and padding the same as the 'Pommel Horse', but larger, or rather, it had more surface area. On the ground, just in front of the platform, was an angled board, the purpose of which, I could not divine at this distance, but I was sure the sergeant would soon explain to me.

"Watch carefully," he warned me again. He charged forward, suddenly building up speed quickly. A few feet before the angled board, he jumped, landing both feet on the board, which compressed slightly, recoiling and springing him up and forward toward the platform. He flipped as he traveled, using his hands to push off the platform, getting him more height, which he turned into a couple of twists and flips before landing perfectly on his feet.

Now how was I supposed to do that?

"This one might take you a while to get the hang of. Just remember, it is one and a half twists followed by one and a half backflips," said the sergeant, once he was close enough for me to hear.

"Any other tips?" I asked.

"Yeah, do not miss the springboard," he added, grinning.

My first run down was little better than a catastrophe, ending with my springing clean over the platform and landing on my chest, sliding a few feet grinding my face and arms in the dirt painfully.

Attempt two was better if you consider hitting the springboard, but not getting enough height, resulting in my feet clipping the platform, halting my forward progress, and faceplanting hard.

Attempt three actually saw positive progress. I hit the springboard, rotated just enough to push off with my hands. I even flipped forward just enough to land on my feet. Progress.

The next three attempts were trying for the same goal. Two out of three successes weren't bad. I tried to add in the twist, or at least half a twist and half a flip. That part was much harder, I landed hard several times, each time requiring me to cast a 'Lesser Heal' on myself.

Step by step, I got it done, the game allowing me to quickly learn from my mistakes, gaining experience and actually learning from it rapidly, until I was sticking the landing on a perfectly mirrored vault.

It took some time, but with my persistence in grinding out the progress points, I got the job done.

Class Quest Alert: Training with Sergeant Butters 5 - Completed
Having put your trust in Trinico and David Butters, they have offered you training to develop your stats as quickly and efficiently as possible.
Reward: +100 Experience, Acrobatics 80/100

Naturally, I accepted the next quest in the chain.

"Good work today, I will see you back here tomorrow," said Sergeant Butters, already looking toward his waiting men.

"I'll be here, see you tomorrow," I answered. I would definitely be here tomorrow, as much as I dislike grinding, doing so in these early days would pay long-term dividends.

Leaving the barracks' training area, I decided to stop in and visit the mayor first.

"Bye-bye, back again, eh? What can I do for you today?" asked Homer, the mayor

"I have some wolf paws to turn in," I answered.

Once again, the mayor set a bucket on the table and I deposited the 36 wolf paws for a whopping +72-Experience gained. Still, the money was nice, but I was little unhappy that I didn't get a piece of variable gear, maybe I had out leveled that part of the quest. I needed to see about getting some slightly better gear.

That reminded me to check my system notifications, I was only a few points from the 50-Strength mark. Today's training definitely should have done it. I actually managed to cap all four physical stats for level 5, which was awesome. With that, I made a mental note to equip the Guard's Light Leather Belt as soon as I left the Town hall.

"Oh, before I forget, is there any kind of bounty for the condors to the south of the village?"

"Not really. The feathers sell well with the Fletcher, and Rita can make the most succulent condor wings you've ever tasted if you can gather them without mutilating the corpse. Have you learned that scavenging skill yet?"

"Not yet," I said, irritated with myself for not doing so. In fact, I was more than irritated with myself for my lack of progress in reading those books. I hadn't read the trap book, the survival book or the scavenging book, not to mention the town histories. These were important, but I'd been too distracted by everything else I needed to accomplish, I never seemed to have time. I think I'd have to talk to Olaf and Micaela about our nightly dinner. I would still join them for the meal but as my Charisma was almost capped already for level 5, I needed to return to my room to read after eating, not every night, just more often.

"That's too bad. Anyway, if you're feeling daring, there is one condor that is rather famous around these parts. The <Greater Condor> has been the nightmare of many a sheep, wolves, cows or anything else it has managed to nab. You kill that and bring back its head and the reward will be well worth the effort," offered the mayor.

Quest Alert: Cull the \<Greater Condor\> (Recommended Level 5-8, 3 or more Adventurers)		
There is a bounty for the elusive \<Greater Condor\>, bring back its head for a generous reward and prestige.		
Reward: Experience, Good Variable Piece of Gear, Collectable Trophy		
Do you accept this Quest?	Yes	No

"If I come across him, you can bet on it," I replied. I didn't know what a 'Collectable Trophy' was, but a 'Good Variable Piece of Gear' was awesome. Good quality gear gave great bonuses, for example, my 'Boar Charge Charm' was of good quality. Though part of me had to wonder, just how big this condor was if it could carry away cattle.

"Wonderful, I have no doubt, you and your friends will be able to get that bird."

I would have to arrange a time to go hunt it with Micaela and Olaf in a few days, once he got his hand-cannons sorted and gained a little proficiency with them.

"Anyway, Trini is waiting for me to continue my training," I said, excusing myself.

"Do what you have to, my boy. Let me know if there is anything you need," he added.

"Actually, before I forget. I need to learn to pick a lock," I said, a little nervous.

"To what end?" he asked sternly. I could see a sliver of doubt in his eyes.

"I have Lore as a profession. There will be times where that will mean working in dungeons and other unsavory places, which can mean locked doors and treasure chests, I will need to get open," I answered. It was true too, but I was also eager to break into the Lieutenant's home and office to snoop around.

"No breaking into homes?" he asked, eyeing me cautiously.

"I promise to not break into any home without a really good reason to do so." It was a compromise, hopefully, it would be enough. "Don't forget too, I serve the Goddess Issara. I can't see her being too pleased with a servant of justice, breaking into a home without just cause, can you?"

Homer laughed at that. "Aye, you make a good point there. Very well," he said, walking around his desk and scribbling a note. "Take this to Giggle-Ana, she will sell you a practice lock, picking tools and give you a crash course in lockpicking. Just . . . do not let me down, eh?"

"I won't let you down, I promise."

"Right then, off you go," he said, shooing me away.

"See you later," I said my farewell. After exiting the Town hall, I traveled the short distance down the main street to the temple.

"Late again," Trinico greeted me.

"How can I be late when we never set a specific time to be here?" I asked her, being a little obstinate, just for the fun of it. It was becoming something of a game to me now, to see what I can do to rile her up a little.

"If it takes you more than 10-minutes from the time you finish training with David to get here, then you are late," she replied.

"How do you know when I finish training with Sergeant Butters?" I asked.

"I have my ways," she replied, her normally serene smile shifting slightly into a smirk. "Anyway, into the puzzle room you go."

Not needing to be told twice I followed orders. Following the previous day's trend, the puzzles were getting more complex and much more personal in nature. Integrated NPC's that were similar to people I knew in real life, my ex-girlfriends, my brother and his wife, my parents, and cousins. Even some of the friends that I'd lost touch with over the years.

I finished the 19th puzzle of the day when the system notified me I had run out of time. Checking my progress, I was kind of annoyed that I got kicked out before I even had the chance to view the last puzzle.

Class Quest Alert: Training with Priestess Trinico 5 - Completed
Having put your trust in Trinico and David Butters, they have offered you training to develop your stats as quickly and efficiently as possible.
Reward: +100 Experience, 99/100 Meditation

"How did it go?" asked Trinico as I exited the room.

"Nineteen more puzzles solved. Just one more to go."

"Well done, and your stats?"

I check my messages again. "All capped, that's a lot of Charisma to gain." I just gained +18-Charisma. That was insane.

"Maybe it is, before you go, try to learn this spell," Trinico said, holding out a scroll for me.

Scroll of Lesser Holy Fire – Teaches the spell 'Lesser Holy Fire'		
Would you like to learn 'Lesser Holy Fire'?	Yes	No

"Yes!" I exclaimed excitedly.

You've learned the Holy spell 'Lesser Holy Fire'

Lesser Holy Fire	*Level: 1*	*Experience: 0.00%*
Spell Damage: 4-5	*Spell Cast Speed:*	*Spell Mana Cost:*

per second	Instant (10-second cooldown)	40
Spell Duration: 30 seconds	*Spell Effect (Active):* Burn a single target with Holy fire. (Stackable x3)	

So nice! I got my first damage over time spell or more commonly known as a DOT. DOT's are powerful, cast it and forget it, spells and this one lasts 30-seconds which was an eternity in a fight. This one would do between 120-Damage and 150-Damage base and with my Holy spell damage bonus it would do 171-Damage to 201-Damage over 30 seconds. And it was stackable! If I could maintain 3 stacks of the spell that would triple the total damage. On a longer fight that would add up.

"Enough drooling over your new spell. Go, get practice with it. I want you to get at least 5 levels before you come back tomorrow," ordered Trinico.

"Yes ma'am," I said grinning, this was a spell I would be using on everything I fight, no matter how quickly my target dies, it was worth it if leveling the spell increased the DOT effect.

I was quickly out the door at that point, I decided to hold off on visiting Giggle-Ana until tomorrow since I was planning to go with Olaf to pick up his weapons.

Stepping out of the village I chose to follow the road this time, looking to have it mapped properly. I did find a poorly marked fork leading south right where Olaf had pointed it out. I continued to follow the road anyway, making sure I hadn't missed any other forks or dirt paths.

I found one more fork in the road, this one leading north toward the Johnson Farmstead.

I made sure I updated my map with the details I'd missed. Eventually, I left the road to map the southern area I hadn't gotten to the day before. I found the mine and mapped all around it. I had originally planned to map inside the mine, but after talking to Olaf, I found out the mine shafts were constantly collapsing or rather filling in with new ore veins.

After mapping what I could and finishing exploring the surrounding area, I moved west again. I had been making good time, very good time in fact. As such, I decided I wanted to explore that small valley or at the very least map around it, to find the entrance.

With that goal in mind, I worked my way west, zigzagging north and south, to make sure I covered all the area on my way there, just so I could map it.

When I got to the start of the crevasse, or rather the cul-de-sac end of it, I was on the southern side. It worked just as well as the north side I supposed. I would just have to keep an eye on the sky as I went.

It was unexpectedly quiet to the south. Until I came across a few dead condors. It put me on edge, only because I didn't know if whoever killed the birds was friendly or just waiting for an unsuspecting player to kill. Still, I was a curious fellow, and this demanded an investigation.

I do love my 'Perception' skill. It made tracking the player responsible, fairly easy. Whoever it was, had small feet wearing heavy armor, plate or mail, I couldn't be sure which. Because of the boots, I was also unable to determine the race.

I followed anyway. I heard the player before I saw her, at least I think it was a her. Seeing her confirmed my hypothesis as the voice belonged to a woman. She had a full set of armor covering her from head to toe, all chainmail, not plate, which was already impressive for a low-level area such as Hurlig Ridge. It was more so when I saw that she was only level 3 and battling three condors at the same time, which was actually very impressive, considering the birds all had her by a level.

She continued to impress me the more I watched her work. Her sword and shield striking and defending in a well-practiced tandem, blocking and countering, as best she could, against three higher level opponents. Even with that, she was taking some punishment from the condors in return. Her health was dwindling steadily downward. While she was making steady progress on one of the condors, the other two were still in the green. Without help, she wouldn't last much longer.

I could have just walked away to leave her to die, but that had never been my play style. Plus, she was a damsel in distress. What guy would ever turn down the opportunity to impress a young maiden? Okay, even I thought that was cheesy, but the point stood, a player was in danger of being sent to respawn. And any girl, that played as well as she did, deserved to be saved, even if she might kill me afterward.

First, I cast a 'Lesser Heal' on her, followed by 'Lesser Holy Barrier' and 'Lesser Combat Blessing', then dropping one more 'Lesser Heal' for good measure. I put my DOT on each of the three birds. Just as I had hoped, she didn't have much threat generated against all three targets allowing me to pull two of them off her.

The first bird that approached took three 'Holy Smite' spells and a second stack of 'Lesser Holy Fire' before it got to me. When it did, I smacked it hard with 'Shield Slam' then I used 'Rapid Striking' to whittle down the last little bit of its HP, while also putting some hurt on the second condor.

I took a few scratches for that effort, but it was worth it. The next attack from the remaining condor was interrupted with my 'Shield Slam', which was a critical hit and in turn, left behind a 'Stun' effect. After that, it was fairly easy to bombard the bird with a chain of 'Holy Smite' and 'Lesser Holy Fire' casts, leaving it a smoking crater on the ground. Okay, so there was no crater nor was the bird smoking, but you get the idea.

I looked to the warrior who was done with her remaining target. She was looking at me with her arms crossed, her posture gave me the impression she was angry with me. At least she didn't attack me. I suppose I should say hello or something. I was just preparing to say something witty and charming when my plan went awry.

"Incoming!" screamed a voice from above.

Naturally, I turned to look for the source only to catch two feet to the face and get knocked to the ground painfully.

"Rosie, it's a big one, get ready to taunt it," instructed a childlike voice, I could only assume was the missile that knocked me silly. The missile that was currently sitting on my face and blocking everything from view.

"Right, I'm on it Baby, but can you heal me first. I got an extra condor with that last pull on accident, it spawned right on top of me," said a woman, who I could only assume was the warrior. An enemy repopulating in the game on top of her explained how she ended up with three targets instead of one or two.

"Mind getting off of me?" I asked.

"Kya!" screamed the child suddenly jumping away from me.

When my sight was restored, I kind of wished it hadn't been. My vision was quickly being filled with a monstrously large condor, by far the largest bird I'd ever seen. <Greater Condor Lvl 7>. It was at least as tall as I was, from crown to tail, and the wingspan at least twice that.

"Come get me big boy!" shouted the warrior woman, taunting the condor.

The smart thing would have been for me to run away and come back with Olaf and Micaela. However, seeing as the level 3 warrior wasn't running. I figured it would look rather bad on me if I ran away now. It would have also been rather hypocritical of me if I ran after I had such delusions about rescuing the damsel in distress.

I looked at the missile to see a female fairy that was blushing a furious red color and looking anywhere but at me. She had platinum blond hair that looked to be styled similarly to Micaela, short and spikey. She had six translucent wings, that sparkled in the sunlight, two short upper wings draped over her shoulders, appearing to be connected to her poufy white dress, while the other four hung behind her, as if they were an intricate cape. Her look was completed with the face of a young girl no older than 6 or 7 with dimples and a pouty scowl firmly in place.

"Sorry to barge in, but could you two use some help?" I asked it was usually polite to at least ask, but it seemed both of them were determined to ignore me.

"Baby, heal me," called the warrior woman fiercely, drawing us back to the fight.

"Right, sorry Rosie," said the fairy, focusing on the warrior that was getting pummeled by the giant bird. Its claws and beak striking at her without any discernable pattern, however, each strike took a sizable chunk of the warrior's life.

It didn't appear I would be getting an answer, but for my quest, I had to get this bird's head. This was too good an opportunity to pass. I joined in, first casting 'Lesser Holy Fire' on the condor, then dropping a pair of 'Lesser Heal' casts on the warrior, to help out the fairy. Speaking of the fairy, I buffed her with 'Lesser Holy Barrier' and 'Lesser Combat Blessing', just to be safe.

Fairies are a seldom played race in the World Tree if the forums were to be believed. Because of their size, barely two to three feet tall, they had severe physical penalties. Most barely had 250-HP at level 5, if they were lucky, to say nothing of their Strength, Stamina, and Dexterity. Fairies could only wear a dress for armor, so their survivability was limited even further. Despite their physical limitations, fairies boasted massive magic bonuses to Nature magic and lesser bonuses to water magic. They were impossibly difficult to level or, so the story goes. Seeing this level 9 fairy hinted otherwise. I'd have to wait to talk to her about it after either the condor was dead, or we were.

Focusing my attention back on the fight, I cast 'Holy Smite' three times on the bird barely making a dent. I added another stack of 'Lesser Holy Fire' then cast 'Holy Smite' a few more times. I knew I would need to start attacking this bird from melee, my magic just wasn't doing enough damage, even with the third stack of 'Lesser Holy Fire' being cast. It was time to start working on my 'Two-Handed Polearm' skill anyway. I cast a quick 'Lesser Holy Imbuement' on the spear and started attacking, making sure to renew my 'Lesser Holy Fire' every time it came off cooldown.

Now the bird seemed to finally be taking damage. Despite being able to stay safely at a range to keep casting 'Holy Smite', where it wasn't doing much damage, fighting in melee did a good deal more damage, allowing me to bring the hurt.

"Hey, slow down your DPS, you're going to pull aggro," warned the warrior.

Aggro or aggression, also called threat, is a way of saying I was about to pull the enemy away from the tank, the player built to take heavy damage, making it attack me instead of her. She must have had a skill that gave her a sense of the current threat levels. I understood and backed off, stopping my damage per second (DPS) temporarily. It would give her time to build up more threat, so the risk of me getting attacked, instead of her, was significantly reduced. I renewed the 'Lesser Holy Barrier' on all three of us, as well as the 'Lesser Combat Blessing', which took a few seconds between each cast. By the time I finished that, I felt I should have been good to start attacking again.

The fight ended after what felt like hours, but in reality, it took just over thirty minutes for the three of us to kill the condor. The warrior and I were seriously under-leveled for that fight. If not for the Fairy healing the warrior, I don't think we'd have been able to beat it. Thank the Goddess too, the <Greater Condor Lvl 7> didn't have any kind of special attack or area of effect ability or we may have been in real trouble. It hit the warrior as hard as a truck, more than once, taking half of her HP with every unblocked attack. I had honestly thought the bird would at least have some kind of wind attack, given the size of its wings.

"Whew," I grunted, wiping the sweat from my brow, slumping down against a nearby tree to rest and regain some of my mana and stamina. I took out two canteens, one for mana and one for stamina and took a few drinks before speaking. "Nice work," I said, the pair quietly talking a few meters away.

"Hey, who do you think you are, jumping in on my kills?" demanded the warrior, rounding on me hotly.

"I didn't see your name on it," I snarked right back, feeling my hackles rise at the accusation. I never did take too well to attitudes like that. "Besides, I do believe I just saved both of you from a painful death. If you hadn't noticed, your fairy friend is basically OOM," I stated. I looked again at the fairy and her mana pool was refilling quickly now, but by the end of that fight, she was basically out of mana or OOM as we gamers call it. By now I was standing, staring into her glowing red eyes, the only thing visible behind the copper chain mesh that obscured her face, while the chainmail coif covered the rest of it.

"She still had a potion," defended the warrior. "All you did was steal experience right out of my pocket."

"She used four potions, I counted. One of those right at the end of the fight. With the global cooldown on all potions used in combat, it would have been at least a minute before she could drink another." Yeah, maybe I was being . . . less than civil, but she did bring it on herself.

The warrior woman growled at me, then removed her helmet to glare at me. She had blood red hair, that once free of her helmet, cascaded around her face in loose curls. She had silky smooth dark grey skin that suggested she was a dark-elf or maybe a half-dark elf, half-human. Her glowing red eyes seemed to be threatening me with pain and violence, despite their beauty. And then she barred her fangs, yes fangs. She had sharpened and longer than normal canines in her mouth that made her look even more threatening. In spite of that, or maybe because of it, she might have been the most beautiful woman I'd ever seen.

Still, not one to back down, I added, "And I did ask if you minded the help, so when neither of you replied, I took that as the okay to help. On top of that, when I got high on aggro, why did you bother to warn me?" I asked.

"Hey, I may hate having my kills stolen but I wasn't going to let you die out of spite," she snapped.

"I wasn't trying to steal experience from you. But if its experience you're after, I know of a quest in town for the bird. I'm willing to share it with you both as a peace offering, sound fair?" I offered. It was a peace offering, I didn't need more enemies even if I was developing a strong dislike of the woman still baring her fangs at me. I had an entire PK order that I'm sure already considered me an enemy. I didn't need any more than that, despite the inevitability, that I would end up with more enemies in time. Plus, it wouldn't hurt to make some new friends.

"What do you think Baby? Can we trust this guy? You got much more up close and personal with him already, so I'm sure you know him best," asked the warrior, looking to the fairy who was now blushing atomic red.

"Rosie, don't say things like that. You know it isn't true," protested the fairy, her childlike features and voice were adorable as can be.

"Oh relax, Sis, I'm just teasing," laughed Rosie. "So, what do you think? Is your new boyfriend trustworthy?"

"Rosie," whined Baby, stomping her little foot, her blush not relenting.

I'm not one to go gaga over puppies and cuteness but if I was, that would have been the ultimate 'squee'-worthy moment.

"Alright, alright, enough teasing for now. Geez, aren't you supposed to be the older sister?" laughed the warrior.

"I am the older sister, you're the bratty sister as you're proving so well right now," said Baby, her six wings fluttering slightly and lifting her off the ground to meet her sister eye to eye. That was probably the coolest thing about being a fairy, you got to fly. Not unlimited flight, but enough to be able to enjoy it.

I tried not to laugh at the pair, but their banter was humorous, to say the least, it reminded me a little of my brother and me.

"Think we're funny, do you?" asked the warrior, glaring at me again.

"A little yeah," I replied, a grin that matched, what I imagined a dashing hero would make. "I'm Bye-bye Jacko, friends?" I asked holding out a hand.

"I suppose you might have helped us a little bit," relented the woman, her own grin forming. "I'm Rose Thorns and this is my older sister Babies Breath. Nice to meet you, Jack."

"Please, Bye-bye, not Jack," I quickly corrected her, hoping against odds she wouldn't continue calling me Jack.

"Whatever you say . . . Jack," said Rose, grinning more widely.

I could only sigh. Somehow, I knew that was coming.

"Ugh, Rosie, you're going to be the death of me. Why did I ever convince you to play with me? Why did I shell out all the money for you to play for that matter? What was I thinking?" Babies Breath whined.

"Free tank?" I asked, rather suggested, getting a grin from the fairy to match my own.

"Oh yeah, that's right," Baby said. "My very own tank slave. Thanks for the reminder Bye-bye."

"Oi, don't you go sticking your nose in, Jack," warned Rosie, she had marched up to me with a finger pointing threateningly. "My sister doesn't need ideas like that taking root."

This time both me and Baby laughed.

Rose clicked her tongue in annoyance before she smiled a little. "Anyway, you said something about a quest in town? Did they already rebuild?"

"Rebuild?" I asked, confused.

"Yeah, the town was raided a few days ago. I'm sure those blasted PK'ers burned it to the ground," explained Rose to my surprise.

"Oh, that. They lost," I said lightly.

"Say what?!" Rose stated clearly not believing me, while Baby sunk to the ground, her bottom jaw slightly agape.

CHAPTER 18

"So, you're telling me, the game introduced a new spell for the town priestess, essentially leveling the field for all players and NPC's?" asked Rose, still not believing me about the successful defeat of the Order of player killers. Player killers who recently tried to burn down Hurligville.

"It's true, I was there," I stated. Maybe I obfuscated a little, but it was still true.

"What do you think Sis?" asked Rose, looking to the fairy floating next to her.

Baby put a hand to her chin, thinking before she answered, "It's possible, I'm not too surprised the Devs would have introduced something to stop or at least slow down such things from happening. I can't imagine any player killer is happy though. I'm sure they just lost a ton of income because of it."

"I never did understand why anyone would want to raid a village, especially a low-level one," I replied. I am not much for Player versus Player, so I had done zero research into the benefits of it.

"The player killer Orders get points from it and they collect tokens from each kill they can turn in to a Black-Market dealer for gear or cold hard cash," explained Babies Breath. "I don't much care for it myself, seems awfully tasteless."

"I read about this one guy who already turned in thousands of tokens. Apparently, he's got some castle he built in a high-level province. Supposedly, he had so much money left over, he built the real thing," added Rose.

"No way." I protested. I'd been fortunate to make the money I did, but even I couldn't afford land, let alone enough land to build a castle on it. "I could see him maybe buying a castle in somewhere in the World Tree, but not in the real world."

"Probably, but it's fun to dream about it," said Rose, a faraway look on her face.

"Nah, not for me," said Baby. "Give me an awesome tree fort full of magic and wonder, castles are a waste if you ask me."

"A lake cabin for me," I added. "Nothing extravagant, just a nice relaxing place to rest after my epic adventures." That was the dream anyway, but with land in the real world at such a premium it would never happen, even with my fortunate financial state of being.

"So, the Town hall will be closed by the time we get back to town," I stated, changing the subject to tackle the business end of things. Rose and Baby both agreed to come back to town with me. Rose severed the <Greater Condor> head and stuck it in her bag, stating she didn't trust me not to cheat them. Meanwhile, I had to trust they weren't going to cheat me. "I'm staying at the Doghouse Inn, I'll be meeting some friends for dinner after 6:00, you are both welcome to join us of course."

"Works for us, we had a room there before the raid, if it's still standing, we'll probably check-in again," said Rose.

I honestly felt relieved, it would be less likely they'd cheat me.

"Mm, hot bath," groaned Rose in anticipation.

"Mm, yeah," added Baby, sighing happily.

"We usually camp out around the fireplace. The couch is the only seat big enough for Mic and Olaf to sit."

"Wait, you don't mean those two ogres, do you?" asked Rose, sounding surprised but also cautious.

"Yes, they are ogres and they are nice people. More importantly, they are my friends," I stated, probably more forcefully than I needed to.

"Hey, no offense intended. I just remember seeing a pair of ogres sitting there the last time I was at the inn. As far as I remember, ogres are supposed to be dumb brutes. I was under the impression, they can't even speak until much later in the game," said Rose defensively. I couldn't exactly tell if she was backpedaling from her earlier statement or not, so I chose to take her statement at face value.

"They are neither dumb nor brutes," I stated, feeling fiercely defensive of the first friends I made in this game . . . first friends not counting the NPC's.

"I can't wait to meet them," interrupted Baby before Rose and I could start an argument or fight over it.

Any further rebuttal was interrupted by our arrival at the main gate and the greeting of a familiar face.

"Bye-bye, welcome back buddy," shouted Gavin, looking somewhat awake and not hungover for a change, he even looked to be cleanly shaven for once.

"Hey Gavin, you feeling okay, buddy?" I asked him, not used to seeing him so . . . sober.

"I am sober and not hungover at all. How do you think I am doing?" asked the guard.

"So angry and going through withdrawals?" I guessed.

"Pretty much, and do you know who is at fault for it?" Gavin asked, looking at me accusingly.

"Sergeant Butters?" I answered, hoping he would agree and let me off the hook.

"And whose fault is it? Who is responsible for Sergeant Butters being on the training wagon? Who are the guards blaming for this?" Gavin glared at me.

"I'm gonna say Olaf and hope you let me escape," I joked.

"Hah," laughed Gavin, not a real laugh, definitely forced. Made even more clear by the way he continued glaring at me.

"Do you think I have any say over what the sergeant does?" I asked innocently.

"Just, do me a favor, finish learning whatever skill he is trying to teach you. Hopefully, he will go back to normal once you do," said Gavin, looking slightly depressed.

"Tell you what, when I finish learning the skill, drinks are on me. I'll see if I can get the sergeant and Trini to join us, how's that sound?" I offered.

"You promise?" Gavin questioned, looking at me rather pathetically.

"I promise," I said, reassuring him and patting his shoulder.

"Okay, just . . . make it soon, yeah?" Gavin pleaded.

"I should be able to finish tomorrow," I answered.

"Okay, I think I can hold it together another day. Speaking of holding on, who are the ladies?" Gavin asked, his attention now diverted away from me.

"Huh? Oh, them. Gavin, this is Babies Breath and her sister Rose Thorns," I introduced the two girls. However, when I looked at them, they looked completely stunned, but why, I had no idea.

"Pleasure to meet the both of you lovely ladies," said Gavin trying to be suave.

My laugh ruined it. His glare at me made me laugh harder.

"Really, Bro?" Gavin whined, his attempted flirtation ruined for the moment.

"Gavin, last I heard, Daisy from Doc B's was seen in the company of a certain guard, and said guard, was spotted escaping from her bedroom window," I retorted, earning a blush from the man and a good laugh too.

"Anyway, we'd best be going," I said, I wanted to make a stop into the leatherworker's and clothier's, something I had been putting off for far too long.

"Sure, sure, see you later. I might try to sneak a pint with you later," retorted Gavin.

"Looking forward to it," I said. I walked into the village with Baby and Rose just behind me in unexpected silence.

"What in the name of Leeroy Jenkins was that?" Baby finally asked, bringing our group to a halt and shocking me slightly as Baby just didn't seem the type to curse. Then again, maybe it was just because she looked the part of a child, it felt so out of place.

"What?" I asked I had no idea what she was going on about, let alone what brought on the need to invoke the name of LJ. Leeroy Jenkins is still famous, even in this day and age.

"That?" she said, one arm pointing back toward Gavin.

"What? Gavin? He's not a bad guy, he just drinks too much if you couldn't tell from our conversation," I replied.

"Exactly, you had a conversation with an NPC, how did you do that?" asked Baby.

"Um, I talked to him?" I answered, her behavior was worrying me before realization hit. "Wait, are you telling me you've never bothered talking to the Citizens?"

"Why would I? Why would anyone? You ask them for a quest and move on if they don't have one," replied Baby, which actually confirmed my earlier theory, most players just try to get a quest, and as soon as they have one, they run off.

"Okay, this could be a longer conversation. However, I do need to run a few errands before dinner, so how about this. You two, check-in at the Doghouse Inn, I'll run my errands, and I'll explain as much as I can over dinner. It will help to have Micaela and Olaf there too, they can help. Does that work for you two?" I suggested.

"Okay, I suppose so," said Baby reluctantly.

"Come on Sis, let's go get those hot baths, we know where he's staying, he can't exactly avoid us," Rose tried to reassure her sister. It surprised me, given how standoffish she had been toward me.

"Fine," Baby finally relented.

"Great, I'll see you both in about an hour," I confirmed, escaping before anything else might interfere with my plans.

'Taylor's Tailors' was a small shop in an unassuming flat-faced building. The sign over the door displayed the name, an artistically painted spool of thread between the two words.

There was a tinkling of a bell, as I opened the door and entered. Looking around the sparse shop, I saw a few mannequins displaying some rather gregarious outfits, clearly not my style at all. Otherwise, there was just a long counter with a register, manned by a nonplused teenager sitting behind it. Just behind him was a door to the back room.

"Greetings, welcome to Taylor's Tailors," said the very unenthusiastic teenage boy.

"Hello, I need to get a new shirt, pants and maybe socks, if they are good quality," I said, to the young man, trying to be positive.

"Yeah, whatever, old man," he replied.

I was mighty tempted to smack him upside the head. I am not old, not even close to old. Luckily for him, a woman came from the back of the shop and beat me to it, giving the teenager a solid rap to the back of his head.

"Angus, behave yourself. This is a customer," she chided him.

"Sorry mom," Angus replied, rubbing the back of his head where the woman thumped him. It was clear, the boy didn't truly care, nor did he seem to be sorry.

"Go . . . go . . . go sort something," the woman said exasperatedly.

The teen shrugged his shoulders, walking away from the counter and into the backroom.

"That boy, I swear . . . sorry, you had to witness that little bit of family drama. The boy has been such a . . . he's been struggling since his father went missing," the woman explained.

"Oh, when did his father go missing?" I asked perking up. I know a prompt, one possibly leading to a quest when I hear one.

"About two weeks ago, I am sad to say. He should have long returned from Root City with more cloth by now," she answered, wringing her hands in her apron.

"Maybe he just got delayed," I tried to give her a little hope.

"I'm afraid bandits are more likely. They are notorious for setting up ambushes near the portal. They grab merchants on the way to or from Root City. I believe my husband was one of them," she explained.

"I would be happy to look into it?" I offered.

"Oh, I could not trouble you with this, you are supposed to be my customer, and here I am blathering on," the woman said, trying to redirect the conversation, despite the worry on her face and the start of tears at the corners of her eyes.

"Ma'am, I am a priest in service to the Goddess Issara, this is kind of my job. Please let me help you," I gently insisted.

"Thank you, you're too kind," she said, a few tears running free now.

Quest Alert: Find the Missing Taylor (Recommended Level 4-6)		
Mrs. Taylor has requested your help in finding her missing husband.		
Reward: Experience, Clothing		
Do you accept this quest?	**Yes**	**No**

"I'm happy to help. But, I'm afraid I'll have to look into it tomorrow, it will soon be dark."

"I do understand. Thank you again, so very much. Now, how can I help you? I don't imagine you came in here just to hear my sad little story."

"I was hoping to pick up another shirt, a pair of pants and I also want to check out your socks," I answered.

"Of course, do you know what kind of quality you're looking for?" she asked.

"The burlap shirt and pants matching what I have now, are fine . . . well, maybe something a little nicer. I could do without the itch. And for the socks, the best quality you've got," I answered. There have been a great many war movies, many of them suggested one thing as being more important than anything else, socks. Comfortable, dry, clean socks. Now granted, I was currently wearing sandals, but soon enough, I am sure I will end up in boots or some other kind of footwear, and I will want socks when that day comes.

"Any preferred colors?" she asked.

"White for the shirt, pants maybe brown or black," I answered.

"Okay then, I'll be right back with a small selection for you," she said, turning and bustling quickly into the back room. Only to trundle back out moments later with a stack of boxes taller than she was, all perfectly balanced. She set the stack of boxes on the counter, then split the stack into three smaller stacks.

"Shirts, pants and socks, all tailored to fit on purchase," Mrs. Taylor said, pointing at each stack in turn with the socks stack being a solitary box. I appreciated the tailored to fit part, it was good detail and a way to explain how everything fit the players.

I started with the stack of shirt boxes, opening the first box.

"Lowest quality on top, highest on the bottom," she added without being asked.

I felt the material, it felt the same as the shirt I was wearing now. "How much?" I needed a frame of reference.

"5-Copper for that one, 5-Silver for the highest grade. Pants start at 8-Copper and end at 8-Silver. For the socks you said you wanted the highest quality, they start at 1-Silver per pair," she explained the sorting and price range.

With the pricing in mind, I knew I didn't need the highest quality shirt or pants but somewhere in the middle should suffice without being too expensive.

So, I pulled the box from the middle of the stack and opened it. This shirt was the same long-sleeve design, thankfully without any decorative flourishes, like a few of the shirts on display. The material was soft, not silky, but a considerable upgrade from my current shirt.

"How much for this one?" I asked, holding up the middle-grade shirt for her to see.

"1-Silver," she answered, waiting patiently as I went through the boxes.

"Okay, I'll take this one then," I said with finality. I didn't want to be tempted by trying a higher quality shirt.

I checked the pants next, the thickness and quality were much the same, but I didn't particularly care for them, or the pants I wore now. "Do you have anything tougher?" I asked, realizing then, I was really looking for something more similar to a pair of modern jeans.

"Certainly," Mrs. Taylor said, quickly collecting the boxes and returning to the back only to come back a minute later with just two boxes. "These are slightly more durable, all cotton though. Hope they will do."

I hoped they would too. When I opened the box, I was beyond pleased, they were jeans. No zipper, a button-fly, and thick stitched seams. It was probably as close to jeans as I would be able to find in the World Tree, and best of all, they were designed to be worn beneath any armor I might wear eventually. "Two pairs please," I said a little too eagerly.

Mrs. Taylor just chuckled a little and grinned. "4-Silver per pair," she warned me. Already this shopping trip had cost me 9-Silver and with even one pair of socks, my total price tag hit 1-Gold.

"That's fine," I said, I honestly hoped to never have to buy another pair of pants again but having two pairs was probably a good idea, this way I could send one to be washed and wear the other. Which made me realize I should do the same for the shirt. "Can I get another of the same shirt too, but in black instead of white?" Variety wouldn't hurt.

"Of course," she agreed.

The socks were plain, no designs, stripes or patterns, but they were made of the softest silk I had ever touched. I selected two pairs in white and two pairs in black. My total bill came out to 1-Gold, 4-Silver with my discount from my Local Hero title. It hurt to pay, but it was worth it if I never had to bother with buying clothes again.

"I promise, I'll look into your husband's disappearance tomorrow. I'll bring you answers," I said, reassuring her once more before I left the shop.

It was a decent walk to the leatherworker's shop. However, just being near here, reminded me of Guard Davies' gruesome murder. As if the reminder of the murder wasn't enough, the shop was still closed. It was disappointing. I would have to come back tomorrow.

With a sigh, I turned back and began my return to the inn.

After a quick trip to my room for a clean towel and to select the pants and shirt I wished to wear, I was off for a quick shower before dinner.

Stepping out of the bathroom, I felt more at home than I had since I came to this game world. I was surprised by how much difference, a new shirt and a pair of pants made to my comfort level.

"Evening," I greeted Micaela and Olaf, joining them by the fire.

"Bye-bye," cheered Micaela in her normal pixyish manner.

"Evening mate," greeted Olaf.

"I love the new threads, very posh," complimented Micaela.

"I don't know how fashionable they are, but they are so comfortable," I replied, feeling content at the moment. "I didn't realize how much I missed jeans until now."

"Yeah, Olaf and I were so happy to get the denim overalls a while back. We're probably due for some clothes too, at least something to wear outside the mine."

"Oh joy, more shopping," added Olaf, his voice as flat as possible. Micaela just rolled her one eye and shook her head a little, a light laugh included.

"How was the mine today?" I asked.

"Boring," said Olaf, pouting. "Ever since I got all those subskills, the challenge has gone out of it."

"Didn't you say there was another mining area, that valley I discovered? Why not try it out?" I asked.

"I suppose I could give it a shot," said Olaf, rubbing his chin thoughtfully. "Anyway, business for another day. How did your adventures go?"

"Interesting," I replied.

"Interesting, are we?" asked a voice I was coming to dread.

"No, I said my day was interesting," I rebutted.

"And meeting us was part of your day, therefore, interesting," Rose countered.

She had me. "Whatever you say," I said, not exactly a concession, but close enough.

"Anyway, I met this . . . woman and her adorable sister," I said pointing roughly at Rose and giving as cute a wave as I could stomach, towards Babies Breath.

"And just what is that supposed to mean?" demanded Rose.

"Why does it have to mean anything?" I asked, the start of a smirk forming at the corner of my mouth, turnabout was fair play. "Are you not a woman?"

Rose narrowed her eyes, choosing not to dignify that with a response.

Now that the battle of wits had ended, I had a chance to take in the dark-elf woman, and she was still, quite possibly, the most beautiful woman I had ever seen, especially now, she was wearing a white sundress and sandals. It was a simple look, but very attractive.

"Bye-bye, introduce us to your new friends," said Micaela, grinning.

Something in Micaela's grin made me uncomfortable. Trying to ignore the grin, I introduced my new acquaintances.

"The super cute one is Babies Breath. Doesn't she have a great name?" I asked, purposely ignoring Rose, seeing her hackles rise a little. "The less cute one is Rose Thorns, she's just as the name suggests . . . prickly."

"Jack, keep pushing me, I dare you," warned Rose.

"Ooh, I like her," said Olaf, grinning, his eye seemed to dance with laughter.

"Bye-bye, I'm so proud," said Micaela, wiping away a fake tear. "You met not one but two women. They grow up so fast, don't they babe?"

"That they do my love, that they do. So, how did you meet?" asked Olaf. Yeah, this would not end in my favor, I could already feel the deck-stacking against me.

"It's nice to meet you both," said Babies Breath, ignoring the tension between Rose and I. "Bye-bye, said you were good people, he spoke very highly of you, so I hope we can become your friends as well."

"Leave it to my big Sis to put things right after Jack's lame intro," added Rose.

It seemed Micaela finally noticed Babies Breath was a fairy. Queue the room shaking 'Squee', it also nearly destroyed my hearing.

"Oh my God, she is so cute!" gushed Micaela.

Baby blushed and pouted, her big introduction just got wiped away, mostly due to the overabundance of adorable.

Rose and I both just laughed heartily as Olaf had to hold Micaela back from glomping the Fairy and accidentally squashing her.

Tension seemed to defuse after that and we began chatting amicably, even Rose and I, though both of us kept poking at each other, now it was more in fun than with the intent to irritate the other.

"Okay, so we've all eaten and had a few drinks, now I do believe you owe us an explanation," said Rose, looking at me intently.

"Oh, which explanation is that?" asked Micaela, sending a chill of worry down my spine. "The one where he found awesome skill trainers and skill books, or the one where he single-handedly defeated a PK army?" If you hear a loud slapping sound at this point, it's me burying my face in my hands.

"Honestly, Mic, you've got to think before you speak, babe," said Olaf, shaking his head in slight disbelief.

"We wanted to know about the NPC's, but now, all of that too," said Baby, leaning forward in her chair slightly, an eager gleam in her eyes.

"She's drunk, made it all up," I stated, straight-faced as possible.

"Don't even try it, Jack. Start spilling," said Rose, calling me on my poor lie.

"Okay, it's getting late so, I'll tell you about one, you pick," I offered, trying to placate them at least for the moment.

I had to wait a minute for Rose and Baby to converse in hushed tones.

"NPC's," Baby finally said with a firm nod.

"So cute!" shouted Micaela again.

"Will she ever stop doing that?" asked Baby, looking to Olaf pleadingly.

"Eventually, the trick is to find something to distract her," said Olaf, part joking, but I was sure there was more than a little truth to it. I made a mental note of it for the future.

"I'm not sure what you want me to tell you about the Citizens," I started, wanting to get this over with as soon as possible.

"Start with how you can have a conversation with them," ordered Baby.

"You just talk to them like you and I are talking now. I guess I would start by saying hello, introducing myself, maybe asking a question or two. Getting to know them as I would anyone," I started.

"Yeah, but . . . they answer you? Like, if you ask them about their families or their likes and dislikes, they will actually respond?" asked Baby.

"Sure, why wouldn't they?" I answered.

"They are computer programs, just simple A.I.'s, right?" asked Baby.

"A.I. yes, simple, absolutely not. They are each unique in their own way. From what I've encountered and seen, there is no preset programming to any of the Citizens. As far as they know, this is the only world that exists, and they each have their own part to play," I replied.

"That is so weird," said Baby, I could hear the astonishment in her voice.

"I will say, I did notice early on, the NPC's communication was choppy. For example, they'd give me a quest, then abruptly end the conversation and walk away, almost as if they expected me to do the same. I have also noticed the conversation quality has steadily improved as the various A.I. learn from the interactions," I added.

"So, you can still just ask for a quest?" asked Rose.

"You can, but there is no guarantee they will give you one. There are a couple of factors I believe influence them, from what I can tell anyway. Most important is Charisma, the stat gives a baseline for the interaction, if it's above a certain level, you have a chance to get a quest. Today at the tailor's shop, I was talking with the shop owner about her moody teenage son. Then she mentioned her husband went missing on a routine trip to Root City. A little more probing, and she also mentioned bandits tend to set up ambushes near the portal. They attack merchants on their way to buy or on their way back from selling. Naturally, I offered to help, and she issued the quest to find her missing husband," I elaborated.

"Which reminds me, tomorrow, after you get your hand-cannons, want to join me for this quest?" I asked, looking at Olaf.

"Maybe, it depends on how quickly I can get the base skill training with the sergeant. If everything goes well, then I'm definitely in," he replied.

"Good," I said before turning back to Babies Breath and Rose Thorns, waiting to see how they would react. "Anyway, that's the best I can explain it."

Baby whistled in appreciation. "I must be an idiot . . . heck, every one of the players I've encountered since I started playing, must be an idiot."

"Yeah, said the same thing a few times myself," said Olaf, nodding his agreement. "Ever since Mic and I started chumming around with Bye-bye, we've gotten mixed up in all kinds of interesting adventures and unique opportunities. The things Mic mentioned are only the biggest things so far. For example, I'm an Ogre Artillery at level 4, only because Bye-bye treated the NPC like a person, and guilted her into treating me like a person, instead of just another ogre."

"First, I have to apologize, I thought the worst of you both without knowing you, everything I've read about the ogre race, made you seem stupid and evil, killing players and NPC's, senselessly. I'm sorry," Rose apologized, looking contrite. "Second, say what? I thought you had to be level 30 or something crazy to become an Ogre Artillery, then do some really heinous stuff too?"

"So, did I, but here I am, and tomorrow I get my first hand-cannons," boasted Olaf proudly.

"False information?" asked Babies Breath.

"We think so," said Micaela. "I'm a shaman, for which there is a bunch of information, but most of it lies. The procedure the forums describe would let me become a witch doctor, which would completely ruin my character as it is an Intellect class. There is so much misinformation out there, it's not even funny."

"Oh, I hope that isn't true," said Baby, suddenly looking to her sister with worry.

"Why? What did you do?" I asked curiously.

Rose sighed, then groaned in frustration. "I want to become a Blood Knight. It's an advanced warrior class, only available to vampires and half-vampires."

"I didn't even know vampire was a playable race," I said, blinking in surprise.

"It's not. You can only be turned into a vampire or half-vampire," Rose explained

"How does that work?" I asked, ever the curious one.

"So, there is a guy who goes by the name of Vlad Tepes on the forums. He posts most of the information on vampires in the World Tree. He said, when he was around level 40, he got a quest to clear out a vampire nest but got overwhelmed. They drained him to just 1-HP. He claimed, he got an offer to join them or die. He had a chance to become the first vampire in the game, so of course, he took it. He became a Blood Knight. Since then, there have a been a few others, claiming to have become vampires, in the same way, some becoming Blood Mages, Blood Assassins or Blood Knights. They said it was possible for half-vampires too," Rose explained.

"How does one become a half-vampire?" I asked.

"You drink pure vampire blood," Rose answered. "My sister was awesome enough to get me a vial. It was pretty expensive too. Anyway, you get most of their strengths and only a few of their weaknesses. So, I'm stronger and faster than a pure dark elf would be, and I supposedly get access to Blood magic but have yet to find a spell. Also, Blood magic is considered Dark magic, which I get a bonus to as a dark-elf. Other than that, I don't care for the sun much, and I am weaker to Holy magic. I won't get wrecked in the way a pure vampire would, but I would still take a significant bit of extra damage. Now I have to wonder if the guy was lying to everyone. This is so unfair. Becoming a half-vampire was both gross and painful, and now it may have been for nothing."

"Maybe, maybe not," I said, trying to reassure her. "I would bet we can ask Trini and Sergeant Butters tomorrow. They've been around the World Tree enough to know things."

"Bye-bye is right, we can ask them tomorrow," added Micaela. "Besides, I need some more female presence on this team."

"Okay, so we have a plan. Let's call it a night here and agree to meet here at 7:00 in the morning," I said, ready to get some sleep.

CHAPTER 19

I was up the next morning a little after 6:00, no thanks to the rooster, which was thankfully silenced in short order. Unless I was mistaken, the crowing being cut off suddenly suggested I wasn't the only one tired of the foul fowl. It's truly amazing how much an extra 30 minutes of sleep can make to your outlook on the day.

I arrived downstairs with a bit of pep in my step, and a smile on my face. My smile widened a little bit when I saw Rose getting chewed out by Dogson, while her sister tried to play peacemaker.

I sat down at an empty table and waited patiently for my breakfast. I do love the breakfast here, a pint of whatever beer I had been drinking the night before, sausage, eggs, and toast. I knew I shouldn't get used to a big breakfast because once I was back in the real world, I wouldn't be able to maintain this kind of diet, if I wanted to keep my new fit form the Seedpod was crafting me into.

"Rotten rooster, you'd think he'd have penned them up or something by now," groused Rose, sitting down across from me.

"You also broke a window throwing a chair at it," chided Baby, getting a laugh from me and Rose both.

"You really threw a chair at the demon fowl?" I asked.

"Heck yeah, I did. I wish I'd done it a week ago. I heard some guy actually smote one of them before," Rose added.

"Yeah, good times," I smiled, fondly remembering that morning. "It was totally worth it too."

"That was you?" asked Rose.

"It deserved it," I defended myself.

"You know Jack, despite being . . . well, you, you may not be a complete waste of space," Rose complimented, a left-handed compliment as the British would say.

"Gee, thanks," I replied sarcastically.

"Wow, she must like you," Baby chimed in. "I've never heard her say anything even approaching friendly to a guy."

I wondered if maybe, she preferred the company of girls.

"I've just yet to meet a guy deserving of more than a few hours of my attention," Rose defended, answering my unasked question. "Jack here just has potential to prove not to be totally useless."

"Anyway, Mic and Olaf should be here soon," I changed the subject. We continued to chat while we all ate our breakfast.

"Morning," greeted Micaela first coming in alone.

"Morning," we all replied.

"Olaf, is waiting outside, didn't want to deal with the low ceiling this morning," Micaela explained, her head cocked uncomfortably to the side. "The oaf was restless all last night and all morning. He just can't wait to get his new weapons."

"Let's go then," I said to everyone, dropping my napkin on my plate and standing from the table.

Outside was another round of 'Good Mornings' with Olaf.

"So, where first?" I teased, knowing full well exactly where Olaf wanted to go.

"Giggle-Ana's," said Olaf, ready to burst. I could almost feel the excitement roiling off of him.

"Is she open this early?" I asked.

"Kirlan starts smithing at 6:00, so Giggle-Ana opens shop at the same time," replied Olaf.

"Lead the way," I said, grinning for my friend.

"Welcome," started Giggle-Ana with a friendly smile, one quick to fall away upon seeing Olaf enter the shop. "Oh, it's you."

"Morning," said Olaf. "I'm back as promised."

"Has he behaved?" Giggle-Ana asked, looking around him, at me.

"Giggle-Ana," I chided, in as disapproving a manner as I could. "Come on now. Why are you still treating him that way? Didn't he help defend the town when it was raided? Hasn't he done everything you asked of him to train him in engineering?"

Giggle-Ana frowned at me then relented and sighed. "I suppose you have a point. Fine, Olaf, you are welcome in my shop from now on . . . until you screw up and then you are out for good."

Olaf could only smile. "Ma'am, yes, ma'am."

"I suppose you are here to pick up your hand-cannons and ammo?" guessed Giggle-Ana.

"Yes, ma'am," Olaf answered, trying his hardest to be humble.

"Do you have your artillery-pack?" Giggle-Ana asked.

Olaf opened his bag and removed another bag. This one was a large green box-shaped backpack, easily as large as Olaf's torso.

Giggle-Ana sighed. "Bye-bye, be a dear and fetch Kirlan. I will need his help with the ammo and hand-cannons, they are bit heavy for me to carry on my own," she explained.

It only took a moment to fetch the blacksmith and return. Kirlan complained about the interruption to his wife but didn't say anything further.

When the bullets and hand-cannons were set on the counter, I was more than a little intimidated by them. Each hand-cannon was as long as my arm, and three times the circumference. The weapons looked like little cannons mounted onto a very large pistol grip. The grip was molded steel wrapped in supple leather fitting Olaf's large hand perfectly.

Each round had a brass jacket with a stone bullet I assumed was packed with gunpowder and wadding. Each round was also more than three times the size of my fist.

"I would recommend you save the jackets, they can be reloaded a few times each. Be mindful of the firing pins, they need to be replaced regularly, probably every hundred or so rounds. Any questions?" asked Giggle-Ana.

"No, ma'am," Olaf replied, opening the back hatch of the cannon, the chamber waiting for a single round to be loaded in.

"Fine by me," said Giggle-Ana. "Satisfied?"

"Yes, ma'am," said Olaf, putting the weapons into a holster he had also pulled from his bag. He then put the holster around his waist, tightening the belt in place. He then slung the large pack filled with ammo around his back, slipping an arm through each loop.

"How's it feel, babe?" asked Micaela. "Too heavy?"

"It's close, with the ammo and guns, I only have 5-lbs of carrying capacity left. I need to get another level soon. I need to get my strength up to compensate for it," Olaf answered, taking a moment to test his balance and movement with the pack and cannons.

"We do have a quest today, so there is a good chance you'll level from it," I reminded him. There was also the chance, he and Micaela could get credit for the <Greater Condor> if they were with us when we turn it in, but I wasn't counting on it.

"Right you are, so, off to the sergeant?" asked Olaf, eager to start shooting.

"Yeah, just a sec, I need to talk to Giggle-Ana for a minute, and don't you want to get Engineering training?" I asked.

"Right, I almost forgot about it," said Olaf sheepishly. "So, Giggle-Ana, about training in Engineering?"

"Come back this afternoon and we'll get started," Giggle-Ana stated plainly. It wasn't friendly, but it wasn't rude either. I personally thought the neutrality was an improvement. "And what can I do for you, Bye-bye?" Now she was smiling sweetly, even giggling again.

"Mayor Semper gave me this note," I explained, handing her the note.

Giggle-Ana took a moment to read it. "Sure, come back this afternoon with Olaf and I will have everything ready."

"Thank you," I said. I turned back to my group, including the surprisingly impressed Rose. "Okay, let's go see the sergeant."

The walk was pleasant, Micaela and Baby were happily chatting. Olaf kept practicing his quick draw, then mumbling some line I didn't recognize. Rose was rather subdued though, which was unusual for the brash woman, or at least unusual for the short time I had known her.

"Hey, Jack, how do you do that?" Rose asked, suddenly next to me and speaking somewhat softly.

"Do what?" I asked.

"I've only just met you, and here you've got this entire town wired. How do you do it?" Rose asked, looking like she was trying to figure something . . . or someone out.

"I don't know. I've never been what you'd call, a very sociable person. I guess it's because I treat every interaction with the NPC's, as another game, a game within the game. I ask myself, how do I get this person to like me? How do I get them to help me? Does that make sense?" I asked, not sure if I sounded like an idiot.

"Sounds manipulative," Rose replied.

"Maybe it is, but I'm also a pretty genuine guy, or at least I think I am. If I offer to help, it's because I want to help, not just because I think I'll get something for it," I explained.

Rose just nodded and kind of drifted back.

"Morning Sergeant," I greeted the old soldier, and former knight cheerfully.

"Morning Bye-bye, what is this now? Are you bringing me an entire army to train?" the sergeant asked.

"Sure," I joked.

"I might have to start charging you for my services," Sergeant Butters joked back.

"You heard him," I said turning to Olaf. "Pay the man."

Olaf was caught by surprise by my instruction and froze, unsure what to do or say.

His wife came to his rescue. "Do you take I.O.U.'s?"

Sergeant Butters just chuckled. "I see you finally got your peashooters," he said motioning to Olaf's hand-cannons.

"Yes sir," said Olaf, perking up excitedly.

"Good, now who are these two young ladies joining us today?" the sergeant asked.

"This is Babies Breath and Rose Thorns," I introduced the sisters.

"Nice to meet you Miss Babies, Miss Rose," Sergeant Butters said politely, observing each of them in turn. Then he looked at me. "Okay, Bye-bye, do you mind waiting while I get your friends started on their training?"

"Not at all, I'm kind of excited to see what you'll have them doing," I replied. I was honestly excited, I just couldn't get enough of the variety of skills this world had to offer.

The sergeant turned to Olaf first. "Olaf, follow me to the target range. We will start with you shooting at stationary targets, just to get used to the recoil and aiming. Depending on how you do today, we might get you on the mobile range."

The sergeant led us toward an archery range with the targets set 30-yards downrange from us. He walked right past the firing line until he was just 10-yards from the target.

"Why so close?" asked Micaela.

"Hand-cannons, while powerful, have poor range. Most bullets will not go further than 20-yards at which point they are little more than paperweights. Your most effective range is in the 10-yards and under, at least for those starter cannons, your husband has got there. He might be able to get another 5-yards with different ammo. Anyway, just start shooting, one-hand then the other, try to aim each shot. For now, you don't have to be super accurate, we just want to get you comfortable with the weapons," the sergeant instructed.

"Can do, sergeant," said Olaf, hands reaching for the guns.

"Let us get clear of the range before you start shooting," said Sergeant Butters, putting up a hand to halt Olaf from shooting. "I would appreciate being able to hear later, I did not anticipate the need for earplugs today."

"I'll have to remember to get some myself tomorrow," said Olaf, a slightly worried look crossed his face.

"Giggle-Ana has a powerful mean streak at times. She did not teach you 'Muffle', did she?" asked the sergeant.

"No, she did not. What is it?" asked Olaf, looking a little annoyed now.

"A skill, you can bug her about later," said the sergeant. "Who's next?"

"Not me," said Baby. "I'm a fairy, I don't get combat skills."

"Says who?" asked the sergeant. "You have a wand, right?"

"Yeah, but it's just a focus for spell casting, isn't it?" asked Baby, studying her wand a little closer.

Sergeant Butters groaned in irritation, rubbing his face tiredly. "Idiot adventurers, all of them. Follow me," he said, moving back to the 30-yard marker on the range and few targets away from Olaf's.

Boom!

The surprise of the sound made us all jump, drawing our sight to Olaf downrange. He was 5-yards back from where he started, and flat on his back, but I could see the grin from here.

"Oh, that's going to get annoying," grumbled Micaela.

"Will not be so bad once he learns 'Muffle', it will reduce the noise of his guns to a loud bang as opposed to the ear-shattering boom you all just heard. Back to you Miss Babies, your wand is a weapon. And clearly, you have no idea how to use it. Want to learn?" offered the sergeant.

"Yes?" Babies Breath half asked, half stated.

"Trini will be able to teach you more, but I can at least give you the basics. Take out your wand," ordered Sergeant Butters.

Baby equipped her wand, a simple wooden stick, barely 5-inches long.

"Now, focus your mana into the tip of the wand," the sergeant instructed.

The tip of the wand glowed slightly.

"Now, pull back your arm. Next, do not let go of the wand, I want you to throw your arm forward," the sergeant continued.

Baby swung her arm forward and the little ball of blue light at the end of the wand shot off it, making a beeline for the targets downrange. The little light impacted the outer ring of the target two lanes to the left of her intended target, leaving a little scorch mark.

"Okay, now practice," said the sergeant, ignoring the astonished look on the fairy's face and her sister's. "Who's next?"

"Me!" Micaela said excitedly.

"Okay, follow me." Sergeant Butters led us back to the practice ring, to one of the more beat up and larger practice dummies he had. He grabbed a pair of hand axes similar to Micaela's, but scaled down to his size, he then approached a smaller dummy.

"Watch and learn," Sergeant Butters said. He attacked the dummy viciously. The first attack was an overhead strike, hacking into the neck of the dummy. The other ax slashed a clean cut across the dummy's gut, the blade sliding across the wooden surface instead of cleaving into it. He yanked the ax from the neck free and circled the dummy. He hacked again, burying the ax into the lower back then he slashed with the other ax across the shoulders. "This is the 'Hack and Slash' skill. It is not complicated, but it does take practice."

"Why not just hack and hack? Wouldn't that do more damage?" asked Micaela.

"Not every enemy will react well to just hacking attacks or just slashing attacks. By combining them you can probe your enemy for weaknesses to find out what works best," Sergeant Butters answered. "Any Questions?"

"Nope, I got it," said Micaela eager to get started.

"Now Miss Rose. I cannot begin to tell you how happy I am to train a warrior," the sergeant nearly gushed.

"Hey, I'm a warrior too . . . well sort of," I protested.

Sergeant Butters just gave me a look warning me to shut up.

"Back to what I was saying, happy to be training a warrior class. What skills have you learned so far?" asked the sergeant, eager to begin training her.

"Sword and Shield and Taunt," Rose replied.

"And?" Sergeant Butters prompted.

"Um, that . . . that's all," Rose answered.

"Gods and Goddesses above, how are you level 3 and not more skilled? Who trained you?" the sergeant demanded.

"No one," she said. I could hear the anger creeping into her voice.

"In that case . . . well done. But now you are mine. I will have you up to scratch in no time at all," said the sergeant, grinning eagerly.

"Before you start, we had a question," I risked interrupting him.

"Bye-bye, can you not see I am working here?" Sergeant Butters asked, glaring at me.

"It's important, I promise," I stated.

"Fine, what is it?" the sergeant asked.

"Rose, ask him," I said looking to the young woman.

"Have you ever heard of a Blood Knight?" Rose asked, a quiver of worry in her voice.

"I have heard of the Order of Blooded Knights. Wait, do you mean a class?" Sergeant Butters asked.

Rose took a deep breath, I could see she was trying to will back tears, so I answered for her.

"She heard of an advanced warrior class called 'Blood Knight', requiring you to be a vampire or half-vampire," I explained for her.

"Oh, you must mean a Vampiric Knight," said Sergeant Butters, relieving both me and Rose of a serious worry. "Please tell me you are not thinking of becoming one of those bloodsuckers though, it would be an awful waste."

"I already am," Rose said, I could hear a little anger creep back into her voice.

"Eh? What are you talking about? You are standing in sunlight right now, if you were a vampire, you would have burst into flames already," stated the sergeant.

"I'm a half-vampire, half-dark elf," Rose clarified.

"Oh, that is a different story. Daywalkers are not bad at all, you should have just said you were a Daywalker, to begin with. Anyway, Vampiric Knight is an advanced warrior class. A vampire or half vampire is blessed by one of the vampire Gods granting the class. It is only available after you've become a warrior," the sergeant explained. As an afterthought, he added, "I think you need to sacrifice a sheep or goat or something too, but Trini would know more than I do, I assume you are going to speak with her next?"

"I've never heard of a Daywalker," said Rose, she had a small smile on her face, but it was gone in an instant. She was back to scowling and looking tough, a true warrior. "I think I prefer it over half-vampire to be honest. Okay, I can work with that. If I become a Vampiric Knight, can you still train me?"

"Of course, you are still a warrior, just an advanced class of warrior," Sergeant Butters answered.

"I have a question," I interrupted. "Is a Vampiric Knight like a dark paladin?"

"Yes and no," said the sergeant. "Dark Paladin's use pure unholy magic. They use their martial skill to increase their magic based damage. A Vampiric Knight uses a subclass of unholy or dark magic called Blood Magic. They use this magic to increase their physical based damage."

"And I use both," I mumbled.

"Exactly," said the sergeant. "As a Warrior Priest, you have skills to increase your magic damage and magic spells to increase your physical damage. The trick for you is going to be learning to use both in tandem. Not an easy task."

"What is a Warrior Priest?" asked Rose.

I had forgotten she was there. Reluctantly, I answered after the sergeant gave me a nudge. "I have a unique class called Warrior Priest of Issara. Issara is a Goddess of Justice and Retribution."

"That is kind of cool," Rose said but seemed to be reluctant saying even that much.

"You two can chat about this later, right now there is work to be done and we have not even gotten you started yet, Bye-bye," Sergeant Butters stated pointedly.

"He's right, you'll have to tell me the story later," said Rose. "What can you teach me, old timer?"

The sergeant grinned. "To start, are you a defensive or offensive type? Based on the shield I would guess defensive, but it is polite to ask."

"Defensive," Rose answered firmly.

"Good, I think we will start you with 'Shield Slam' and 'Shift'. I need to get Bye-bye started with his training, then we can get you underway," stated the sergeant.

"Works for me," Rose said, excitement creeping into her voice.

"Okay, Bye-bye, just two steps left. Think you can finish them today?" asked Sergeant Butters.

"I think so . . . I hope so," I answered.

"First up, the rings," Sergeant Butter said, pointing to a pair of rings, suspended by a length of chain, hanging about ten feet off the ground. "This one is about control and strength. Watch closely."

He jumped up, grabbing the rings, one in each hand. He jerked his arms hard, popping up so the rings were at his hips with his arms straight. Then he let his arms drift away from his body, slowly lowering himself until his arms were perfectly out to the side, where his body moved into a rigid 'T' or cross. Then he rose back up again. Next, he leaned forward until he was rigidly parallel with the ground below. He almost seemed to relax as he let his head and arms roll forward, his legs swinging over him, continuing toward the ground, and back up into a handstand. He reversed direction, swinging around to the front twice before stopping in a handstand again. He reversed direction one more time, rotating 3 times, building up speed, and on the third time, he released his grip, flipping twice and landing.

"And you're supposed to do the same thing?" asked Rose, looking between me and where the sergeant just landed.

"Yeah," I answered, mentally preparing myself for my inevitable broken neck and respawn.

"You're braver than I thought," said Rose, it was another left-handed compliment, but I'd take it.

"Get to it, I will come back to check on you shortly," the sergeant ordered before guiding Rose back to the practice ring, leaving me to my own rings.

"Steps, Bye-bye, just remember to break it down into steps," I told myself. It was how I had managed through the other exercises, why should this one be any different?

Mirroring the sergeant, I jumped up and grabbed hold of the rings. I pulled up to test my strength and the movement of the rings. It wasn't too bad. I let myself hang, then jerked hard, pulling myself up until I was held aloft by the rings in my hands, being held to my sides. Next, I tried to lower myself the way the sergeant did, but it was difficult, more than I had originally assumed. I'd get close to just the right spot, my strength would give, and I'd be hanging again or even completely lose my grip and fall to the ground. It took a few attempts to get the position just right and find the control. Going back up was almost harder on my arms, after the strain to get to the 'T' shape, in the first place. Once I was up, I leaned forward, and immediately knew I went too far, as I ended up rolling over, swinging and hanging once more.

I dropped to the ground this time, the pain made me think I had dislocated both of my shoulders. There was no debuff nor was there a loss of HP, just the pain of straining my arms.

After resting a minute, I got right back to it. I went through the routine again from the start. The cross came easier this time. I got the parallel lean down and even managed to roll forward into the swing around, but I failed to stop at a handstand and kept going. I lost my grip at this point and fell rather painfully to the unforgiving ground below me. This time there was damage and broken bones to be mended. Thankfully, 'Lesser Heal' corrected the damage and pushed the bones back into their natural alignment in short order.

I tried again and again, eventually, I got the hang of it. There was a considerable amount of coordination required when you are swinging yourself around. I learned quickly I had to get my grip just right on the rings. I also learned I had to keep a center line, or I'd risk getting tangled in the chains or clipping one of them, then losing my grip, which usually resulted in injury. However, by the time I had gotten the 10-points of progress, I had started to have fun with this exercise. It was kind of freeing, both giving up control and taking it at the same time.

"Good work," said Sergeant Butters, just after I landed my last round.

How he knew exactly when to show up I might never know. Still, I was glad he did. "So, what's next?" I asked, eager to finish this training.

"Me," Sergeant Butters answered, confusing me.

"What do you mean, you?" I asked.

"You get to fight me or rather you get to survive me," the sergeant elaborated.

"Great," I replied sarcastically, drawing out the word long. "Just what I always wanted."

"That is the right attitude," Sergeant Butters stated grinning, either he missed the sarcasm or was choosing to ignore it.

"Aren't you still training Rose?" I asked.

"No, she learned 'Shift' and 'Shield Slam' quickly. Right now, she is working with a dummy trying to learn 'Pierce Defense'," Sergeant Butters explained.

"What's 'Pierce Defense'?" I asked.

"It is an attack meant to find gaps in defenses, the chink in the armor so to speak. It is a good skill for her if she is going to be a defender because it encourages the opponent to focus on her," he answered. I think he was saying it was a good tank skill able to generate a good amount of threat. Which was awesome!

Coming back to the practice ring, the sergeant donned a sword and shield. "The goal is to dodge my attacks using the skills you have been training in for the last week, and if possible, to get behind me to attack. Obviously, I won't be moving at full speed, due to our difference in skill, and the blade is blunted, but it will still hurt if you get hit. Ready?"

I swallowed nervously but nodded anyway. "Ready."

The sergeant was quick to attack with an overhead swing, I could instantly see the opening to the left, I dove for the gap, tucking and rolling along the ground, twisting slightly, so when I came back to standing, I was facing the sergeant again. Except, he had already turned to face me, attacking again. This time, he swung wide from the left, toward my midsection. With hardly a thought, I was in the air, cartwheeling over the blade and landing, then backflipping away as his shield swung toward me. It continued on like this for a while with me doing my best to avoid being hit. I mostly succeeded, but when I didn't, he'd hit me three or four times before he relented. I noticed too, both of us continued to increase our pace, the longer we sparred. I didn't have time to think about how to move, I just moved until suddenly, I was greeted with a system message.

Class Quest Alert: Training with Sergeant Butters 6-10 - Completed
Having put your trust in Trinico and David Butters, they have offered you training to develop your stats as quickly and efficiently as possible. Return to Sergeant Butters to continue your development of the skill 'Acrobatics'.
Reward: +1,400-Experience, Acrobatics, Collect your reward from the Temple of Issara in Root City

"Yes!" I cheered excitedly, only catch a face full of the sergeant's shield.

"Why are you celebrating?" Sergeant Butters asked. "Do not lose focus during a fight, even when you do accomplish your goals."

"You're right, sorry," I said, from the flat of my back. He hit me hard, but it drove home the lesson.

"Do not forget it. That said, congratulations, 'Acrobatics' is one of the hardest skills to learn and you pulled it off in just a week," the sergeant said.

I looked at him, he had a look on his face I couldn't place at first. Then I recognized it, it was the same look on my father's face when he found out about the 'Puzzle Box' I created. I remembered it clearly because it was one of the only times I'd heard my father say he was proud of me.

"I won't, and thank you," I replied simply. I felt somewhat uncomfortable with the way he looked at me. I'd be lying if I said it didn't also feel good. I had really accomplished something.

"Anyway, enough for today. Go ahead and sit in the shade for a little while. Your friends should be done training soon. I am sure Trini is going to enjoy training your new friends today," the sergeant said, brushing away his momentarily soft demeanor.

I was happy to take his advice. I'd been here for almost two weeks now, and for as much as I spent time outside either training or questing, I hadn't done much just relaxing. Even when I sat by the waterfall, I was working, drawing my map. I decided right then and there I needed to do this more often. There was so much to enjoy about this world, things you couldn't in the real world, not anymore.

"Done already, Bye-bye?" asked Micaela, joining me first.

"Yeah, I learned 'Acrobatics' finally," I answered.

"Congratulations, well done," Micaela said, genuinely happy for me.

"How about you? How did your training go?" I asked.

Micaela responded, "I learned 'Hack and Slash' pretty quickly, then I learned a skill, 'Knob Strike', which interrupts a spell cast and potentially stuns the target."

"What's a knob?" I asked. I guessed it was the bottom of the ax handle, but it didn't hurt to ask.

"Oh, you see the bottom of my ax here where it flares out, so it doesn't slip from my grip?" Micaela asked, showing me one of her axes and pointing to the handle.

"Yeah," I replied.

"That's the knob. I had to ask the sergeant what it was too," Micaela added, smiling bashfully.

"So tired," complained a new voice joining us. It was Baby, slowly floating toward us.

"Why so tired?" I asked.

"So little mana left, arm so tired too," Baby whined.

"I take it you learned to use your wand then?" I asked.

Baby's demeanor shifted slightly, she was now smiling happily. "Yeah, I did, I gained fifteen skill levels too."

"Wow, very impressive," Micaela complimented the little fairy woman.

"Why didn't you ask the sergeant to teach you a subskill?" I asked.

"I did, but he said he didn't know any. He said Trini, whoever that is, would be able to teach me more," Baby answered.

"Ooh, you'll love Trini, she's awesome. She's David's wife and the town priestess," started Micaela. She didn't stop there. Before I knew it. the two were gossiping at such a rapid pace, I quickly tuned out, choosing instead to lean back and close my eyes for a bit.

CHAPTER 20

"Oof," I gasped slightly as I felt the air rush from my lungs. This was not an ideal way to be awoken from my well-earned nap. I opened my eyes to see a grinning Rose sitting on my chest.

"Good morning!" Rose all but shouted. "Did wittle Jack-Jack have a nice nappy-nap?"

"It was until your fat behind sat on me," I retorted, my voice sounding strained as I struggled to breathe.

"Fat behind, huh?" Rose asked threateningly. She started to stand only to drop again, harder than the first time. Then she did it again. "Still think I have a fat behind?"

"Getting fatter by the second," I fought through the pain.

After three more drops, I surrendered. "It's a fine derriere, I was wrong," I all but gasped out.

"That's what I thought," Rose said satisfied with her victory. This time she stood up completely and sauntered off. I couldn't help wondering, as I watched her go if all armor was made to sway like that.

"You're a brave man, stupid, but brave," said Baby, fluttering through the air, following after her sister.

"I have to say, she's right," added Micaela. "Brave, but stupid."

"I'm starting to realize that," I said, rubbing my chest and stomach where her armor dug in. I could definitely feel some bruises there.

"We still waiting on Olaf?" I asked.

"Yeah, he's determined to learn at least one subskill before he leaves the target range today," explained Micaela.

"So, what are your plans for your next totem?" I asked. We hadn't talked progression plans, much beyond our initial class plans anyway. Heck, I hadn't done any planning for my own progression yet, beyond getting to level 5, which I've already done. I supposed getting to my stat caps, but that was also already done. I guess, now I needed to start thinking about how I wanted to play this character. I had more information after talking to Sergeant Butters, but I still didn't have anything even resembling a plan. I know I need to learn more spells, but the priest spells I can learn are limited. I also know I need to see about learning some of the warrior spells, and yes, warriors have spells and even a few unique skills, though limited.

"I want to make two more gourds, one for stamina and one for health," Micaela answered in her usual excited manner. "The stamina one is tough though, I need to find a boar spirit. The HP is less tough, Butch, Sundance and Barista said another wolf spirit should be able to do it."

"That sounds cool. Have your spirits learned anything interesting?" I asked.

"Sundance can light on fire to either cause a burning DOT when I hit something, or I can swing him, like Baby did with her wand earlier, to throw a fireball. Butch does increased damage, almost double what Sundance does. Butch can also give a damage buff to others, called 'Spirit of the Wolf'. I found if I use the 'Hack and Slash' skill, it's best to use Butch to hack and Sundance to slash," Micaela explained.

"And Barista?" I asked, ever curious about her totems and what they were capable of.

"She won't learn many skills if any at all. She'll mostly just keep getting stronger, replenish more mana and make stronger water," Micaela answered.

"Your spirits sound awesome," I stated honestly. It was a unique take on what a shaman was, and what their totems were capable of. Heck, it was a unique take on what a totem could be.

Any further conversation was stalled by the return of Olaf. In spite of looking as if he'd been working in a blacksmith's shop all day with the amount of black scoring covering his arms and face, he was grinning from ear to ear.

"I love the smell of gunpowder in the morning," Olaf cheered loudly, as he joined us.

"Success?" I asked.

"Yeah, learned the 'One-Handed Artillery' skill, and the subskill 'Targeted Shot', which gives me a 100% critical strike chance on my next shot. Unfortunately, it has a 2-minute cooldown. Still, it's bloody brilliant," Olaf finished, grinning happily.

"I'm so happy for you, babe," said Micaela, standing and giving her husband a kiss on the cheek.

I too stood but not to give Olaf a kiss on the cheek. "I'll go get Rose and Baby, we need to stop off at Town hall before going to see Trini today."

"Okay, we'll meet you around front," said Olaf, taking his wife's hand and walking again.

Rose and Baby hadn't gone too far. When I found them, Rose and Baby were chatting animatedly about something or other.

"Hey," I called when I got a little closer.

"Hello Bye-bye, everyone ready to go?" asked Baby.

"Olaf finished his training for today. Are you two ready to head to Town hall to turn in the condor head?" I asked.

"Sure, we'll be there in a minute, I just need to finish talking to my sister," said Rose.

"Okay, meet you in front of the barracks," I said before going to meet up with Olaf and Micaela. We were joined by Baby and Rose a few minutes later.

The short walk to the Town hall was made in comfortable silence.

"Morning Bye-bye, Olaf, and Micaela," started the mayor upon seeing us. "And good morning to you two ladies as well. I do not believe I have had the pleasure of meeting you two yet. I am Homer Simper, the mayor of this little village."

"I'm Rose Thorns, it's nice to meet you," said Rose first, shaking the offered hand.

"And I'm Babies Breath, also nice to meet you," added her sister.

"So, are you two with these three local heroes or are you here by coincidence?" the mayor asked.

"Much as I hate to admit it, we're here with them," said Rose, trying to keep a straight face but grinning a little anyway.

"Well then, you are both very much welcome," the mayor addressed the two before looking at the group as a whole. "So, how may I be of service today?"

"Remember the <Greater Condor> you told me about yesterday?" I asked, my own grin forming.

"Did you really?" the mayor asked, shock written all over his face.

I nodded, and Rose produced the head from her bag.

"Outstanding, all of you, well done," Mayor Simper said, happily taking the head from Rose.

Quest Alert: Cull the <Greater Condor> (Recommended

Level 5-8, 3 or more Adventurers) – Completed
There is a bounty for the elusive <Greater Condor>, bring back its head for a generous reward and prestige.
Reward: +1000-Experience, Well Tread Boots, Majesty of the Condor

"I will be back in a moment with your rewards," the mayor said, quickly turning and rushing into his office.

"Um, why did we get credit for that?" asked Olaf, looking a little confused.

"You got credit too?" asked Rose. "That is totally hax. We do the work and you get the credit. So unfair."

"It's not like we were trying to," defended Micaela, pouting.

"Oh, let it go, Sis, it's not a bad thing to help out our new friends," said Baby, always playing the peacemaker.

"I personally hoped you'd both get credit, but I didn't know if you would. If you hadn't, we'd just have to go hunt another one down," I added. I had noticed previously Micaela and Olaf seemed to be able to join me in a quest chain halfway completed. They wouldn't get the credit or experience for whatever part of the chain I had already completed, but they would be added to my current progress.

Any further conversation halted as the mayor returned with his arms full of equipment.

"First, for Bye-bye, I could not help but notice you were still wearing sandals, I thought you might appreciate these boots," said the mayor, handing over a pair of black boots. I gratefully accepted them. The boots would cover my feet and ankles, almost to my knees. There was nothing special about the design, but the stats were the real prize.

Well Tread Boots – Light Leather - +10-Armor, +5-Dexterity, +5-Endurance, +5-Stamina, Durability 20/20

It had more armor than anything else I owned, and those stats were fantastic. I wanted to grab a pair of socks from my bag and put them on, along with the boots right away, but I also wanted to see what everyone else got.

"Miss Micaela, I do believe you will find this scroll useful," said the mayor, presenting her with a scroll. Micaela was only too happy to accept. She opened the scroll immediately causing the parchment to crumble a second later.

"What was it?" asked Olaf.

"The Spirit Transfer spell," Micaela answered, then added, "I can now transfer my spirits to new totems."

"Olaf, seeing you finally got your hand-cannons and from all the black powder covering you, I thought you might appreciate this," Mayor Simper, handing the large man a one-eyed goggle. "The last thing anyone firing a ranged weapon needs, is to have their vision obscured."

The mayor stepped up to Baby next and handed her a little brown charm in the shape of a condor on a brown chain.

"Thank you so much," Baby said emphatically.

I'd have to ask her about it later, my curiosity never seemed to quit.

"And for you miss Rose, I hope this helps keep you and your friends here safe," Mayor Simper said finally, handing her a kite shield.

"Thank you, sir," Rose said respectfully.

I half expected her to give him a nickname. So far, nothing about her seemed respectful of others, whether that was just her game persona or who she was, I had yet to determine.

"If any of you ever join or start an Order, come back and see me again. That condor is a valuable bit of prestige for any Order to display in their hall," added Mayor Simper.

I had to guess, that the 'Majesty of the Condor' was the 'Collectable Trophy' the quest originally offered as part of the reward.

"Any other bounties laying around?" asked Rose, seemingly back to her normal behavior.

"Nothing I can think of at the moment, but I will be sure to let you know if anything comes up," the mayor answered. I kind of wondered if he would have given a different answer if I had asked given my Charisma and title.

"I think Rose and Baby could use a few book recommendations," suggested Olaf.

"Ah, an excellent idea, one can never have enough knowledge or skills," said Homer, walking over to the bookshelf by the job board.

"Skill books?" asked Baby, eyes wide in surprise.

"Not true skill books," I answered. "But they are books that have skills you can learn if you study them."

"Bye-bye," called the mayor. "Have you still got 'The Trained Eye', 'The Greater Outdoors', 'Trapology' and 'Let NO-Thing Go to Waste'?"

"Yes," I answered hesitantly.

The mayor sighed. "Honestly, you should have finished at least those first two by now."

I had read 'The Trained Eye', but I had yet to put all the exercises to use. "I've been busy," I answered reluctantly.

"Well, I want at least one of those books returned tomorrow," he stated firmly.

Apparently, I would be doing some reading tonight.

"What do those books do?" asked Baby.

"'The Trained Eye' is full of exercises for learning eye skills, like night vision," I answered. "I'm not sure about 'The Greater Outdoors', but the description says it's about survival in the wilderness. 'Trapology' is about traps, though I'm not sure if it's about setting traps or disarming traps, I figure it will be useful either way. And 'Let NO-Thing go to Waste' grants a scavenging skill, allowing you to get meat from animals or parts from mechanical automatons."

"Oh my God, those sound super useful," cried Baby. "I want them when you're done."

The mayor returned then with four books, handing two to each of them. "Babies, 'World Tree Bestiary' is one of the books I recommend everyone learn. 'Hurlig Ridge Plant Primer' should help you with your Herbalism skill."

"You're an herbalist?" asked Olaf, looking at the small fairy.

"All fairies get herbalism by default and can't get rid of it. After that, they can only choose enchanting or alchemy. I chose alchemy, so the herbs would be useful," explained Baby. "I haven't done anything with it yet though. However, with this book, I just might start."

"And for you Rose, 'The Warrior's Voice' and 'Blood Works'," stated the mayor.

"'Blood Works'?" asked almost everyone.

Homer nodded. "She is a half-vampire is she not? Would it not be good to know what blood gives her what Blessing?"

"Wait, are you saying drinking blood gives her a buff . . . erm, Blessing?" asked Baby.

"Of course," Mayor Simper replied as if it was common knowledge. "Did you not know?"

"No, I had no idea," answered Rose. "What kind of 'Blessing'?"

"I have never read the book myself but as I understand it, a wolf will give you a bonus to the health or maybe strength, something along those lines. Always temporary, but still quite a Blessing," the mayor explained.

And it was a good buff, all she would have to do is drink a small vial of blood and suddenly she'd get a bonus. That could be even more useful as she continued leveling and acquired more powerful blood samples. If it benefitted me at all, I would probably read the book myself, and I still might later to sate my curiosity, but for now, I had more than enough to read.

"How are you fairing with your reading Olaf and Micaela?" the mayor asked, looking to the pair of ogres next.

"Construction is hard, so much math," whined Micaela.

"I'm almost done with 'Urgent Equipment Care'. Have you got any other recommendations?" asked Olaf.

I wish I'd known he was trying to learn the Maintenance skill. I would have told him Giggle-Ana could teach him. Then again, maybe having him ask Giggle-Ana to teach him anything more for a while, wasn't such a good idea.

"Bye-bye really needs to finish those books. Think you can hold out until tomorrow, whatever he returns, I would suggest you read next," suggested Mayor Simper.

"Okay, I get it, I'll finish a book tonight and return it tomorrow," I said exasperatedly. I know I've been slow about reading my books. In my defense, there is always something else going on in this town. I get a quest that ends up leading to a quest chain. Or I try to help my friends get stronger, find skills, get training or any number of other things.

"Good man," said Homer, ignoring my plight.

"Anyway, is there anything we can do for you?" I asked Homer.

"Actually, there is, we've been having problems with a group of bandits ambushing merchants near the World Tree portal. Would you and your friends mind investigating? I'll pay you a percentage of whatever goods and money are recovered," the mayor offered, causing a quest prompt to pop up.

Quest Alert: Bandit Round-up (Recommended Level 4-6)		
Mayor Simper has tasked you with eliminating the bandits ambushing local merchants going to and from the World Tree portal and recover any of the stolen goods or money.		
Reward: Experience, % of recovered goods		
Do you accept this Quest?	Yes	No

"Happy to," Rose answered for us, accepting the quest.

"Excellent, I hope you all have a productive afternoon then," said the mayor. "And last, lest I forget, Bye-bye, here are the bounty vouchers for those two trolls you captured a while back." He handed me seven slips of paper, each with an official looking stamp with the letter 'F' in the center. "Just turn them into a bounty office in Root City to collect your reward. This is your loot claim," the mayor added, handing me one more slip of paper. "I can pay you cash for the goods or you can see the sergeant to have the little bit of equipment turned over to you."

I looked at the paper, the weapons and armor I confiscated, amounted to barely 59-copper in total value. The equipment was all poor quality, so not worth much.

"I'll take the money," I answered, happily accepting the copper. Hopefully, the bounties would be worth more, the vouchers didn't list a value on them.

"Now, if you will excuse me, I have no doubt Margie has been piling paperwork on my desk while we've been jabbering," complained the mayor.

"We'll let you get back to work, have a good afternoon," I said to the man.

The mayor nodded to each of us before returning to his office.

"Bye-bye, has anyone ever told you, you're awesome?" asked Baby.

"Don't go giving him a big head Sis, one quest does not make someone 'Awesome'," argued Rose, refusing to give me even a little credit.

"Three," said Micaela, coming to my defense. "Three quests. The <Greater Condor> you just turned in. The mayor mentioned a quest he'd gotten yesterday, he wanted help with, and now this one. Plus, all the skills you both learned this morning, and the skill books you just got. How can you not say he's awesome?"

"Easily, you're not awesome," Rose stated flatly, but I could tell she was trying not to smile.

Baby rolled her eyes. "Sis, you're new to this game, so I'll forgive your ignorance. Do you know how many quests I got in my starting province?"

"No, I don't think we've ever talked about it," answered Rose.

"Eight, I got a grand total of eight quests in Fairy-Oaks," replied Baby. "That was over the course of a month. We've gotten 3 in two days since hanging around this guy. Clearly, he knows what he's doing."

Rose shrugged. I couldn't tell if she actually didn't care or if she was just being obstinate.

"Enough, let's get to the temple," insisted Olaf, tiring of the bickering. "We've got more training to do today, and I want to get this quest done. I can finally leave this town and do some real damage. I'll be mighty unhappy if I don't get to shoot something today."

It was embarrassing being made the center of attention, something I usually avoided, so I was very grateful to Olaf for ending the discussion. I don't know if he noticed my discomfort, but I made a mental note to thank him for it later.

Olaf and I walked in companionable silence, while Baby and Micaela started gossiping again. Rose looked to be listening to the gossip, but not joining in.

Trinico greeted us out front of the church.

"Are you trying to show up later every day?" the priestess asked me.

"No, we had some business again in Town hall today," I defended.

"Very well, are you going to introduce me to your new friends?" Trinico asked, though it clearly wasn't a request.

"This is Babies Breath and Rose Thorns. Ladies, this is Priestess Trinico," I introduced my new companions.

"Please, call me Trini, it is nice to meet you both, Rose, Babies," she introduced herself to the pair.

"Please just Baby," the little fairy attempted to correct her.

"It would not be proper, Miss Babies," said Trinico.

Baby sighed.

"How is it the NPC's can have nicknames or shortened names, but they can't call players by a nickname?" grumbled Baby.

"What was that? I could not hear you," asked Trinico, looking at the fairy.

"Nothing," said Baby, looking slightly scolded, as if she'd just been caught misbehaving.

"If you insist. Anyway, I know why Olaf and Bye-bye are here, and Miss Micaela is never too far from her husband. But how may I help you, young ladies?" Trinico asked.

"I have no idea," said Baby. "What uh . . . what exactly can you teach me?"

"Depends on you. Might I ask your class?" requested Trinico.

"I'm a sage," she answered.

"Oh my, I am so happy to make your acquaintance, Great One," Trinico said, curtseying to the fairy.

"Great One?" four of us asked, while Baby just blushed a deep red.

"Sages are rare," explained Trinico. "I have only met one in my life. And he was the most powerful healer I have ever encountered."

Four of us were now staring at Baby in shock.

Rose snapped out her shock first. "Why didn't you ever tell me?"

"I did . . . well . . . I told you I was a sage. I guess I didn't tell you it was a rare class. And I guess, I didn't want you to get jealous of me or something," Baby explained lamely.

"Is that why you spent so much money to get me that vial of blood?" demanded Rose.

"No," Baby protested immediately. "Well, not entirely. I knew how much you wanted it, I guess I thought it might not make you jealous of me if you had a rare class too."

"Oh, Sis," said Rose, softening. "You didn't have to do that."

"Touching as this is, I'm going to the 'Puzzle Room', Mic and I just hit level 5 and I need my 5-points of Intellect and Charisma and hopefully 10-points of wisdom, not that the stat is useful to me," Olaf interrupted.

"Olaf, you clod, can't see they were having a sisterly moment," Micaela chided the man, elbowing him hard in the ribs.

"Olaf, go on, the room is open," said Trinico. "Bye-bye, wait a moment before you go in today. I need to speak to you first."

"Sure," I replied. I wanted to find out if Trinico would be able to help Rose with her class anyway.

"As for you, Great One, I have many holy spells beneficial to you. I know they are not nature spells, but you should still be able to learn them. For any water magic, you may wish to go visit Malcolm, the town Mage's Guild representative. You should be able to buy any scrolls you need from him. He may even have nature spells for sale," Trinico offered.

"Actually, what was Olaf saying about raising his stats?" asked Baby.

"Ah, the 'Puzzle Room' then. You are of course welcome to use it. If you can catch up to Olaf, he will show you," Trinico answered.

Baby just nodded. "Oh, and don't call me Great One. Call me Baby or Breath."

"As you wish Miss Breath," said Trinico, curtsying once more as Baby flew after Olaf. "That leaves you, Miss Rose. What can I do for you?"

"I am a Daywalker. I spoke with Sergeant Butters this morning about becoming a Vampiric Knight and he said I should talk to you," Rose explained succinctly.

"My David told you correctly. Now, which Vampire God did you wish to receive a blessing from?" the priestess asked seriously.

"I'm afraid I don't know much about the Vampire Gods. Can you tell me more?" Rose requested.

"Honestly, you are just as bad as Micaela, wanting to become a class without knowing how or why," chided Trinico.

"Sorry, I thought I had done proper research. I guess I was lied to," said Rose, a hint of frustration in her voice, her eyes downcast.

"Worry not, child," said Trinico, placing a comforting hand on Rose's cheek and lifting her chin slightly. "I am not angry with you or disappointed. Those that gave you false knowledge though . . . they had best pray to whichever God or Goddess they worship, I do not find them."

Rose laughed a little at that, finding it slightly humorous.

"So, the Vampire Gods," started Trinico, moving on. "There are two. Lilith and Dracula."

"I thought Dracula was a man?" I interrupted.

"He was once just a man. Then Nosferatu turned him into the first vampire. When Dracula cut Nosferatu's heart out and ate it, he took his place as a Vampire God," Trinico answered, adding something to my love of lore. It was an interesting backstory for vampire Gods.

"Who is Lilith in all of this?" asked Rose.

"Lilith was Nosferatu's daughter, the first trueborn vampire," explained Trinico.

"What's the difference?" Rose asked.

"First, you should know Lilith hates Dracula for killing her father. Second, because of the reason Dracula killed Nosferatu, he by default hates the former God's daughter, as well. So, whichever you choose, be prepared for the other to declare you an enemy. Also, be aware, if you pray to one to grant you a blessing and are refused, the other will automatically refuse you on principle. No God or Goddess would accept being your second choice. Do you understand what I have said so far?" asked Trinico.

"Yeah, they hate each other so I have to choose carefully," Rose summarized.

"More or less. Dracula is more likely to accept your request, but he believes in quantity over quality when he forges his servants. Lilith is far more selective, believing the quality of her servant matters. As a result, she usually has a much more personal relationship with her servants, giving them guidance and knowledge, where Dracula will set more challenges before you, then sit back and watch," the priestess explained.

"Why would anyone ever want to serve Dracula?" I asked. The guy reminded me of the jocks from high school that tormented me and the other nerds.

"Because there is less risk of being refused," said Rose. "But you can forget that noise. No risk, no reward. I wish to pledge to Lilith."

"I hoped you might. Dracula is considered a lothario of sorts. I would worry for your maidenhood," said Trinico, getting a red blush from Rose.

I so wanted to comment but didn't feel like getting clubbed by Trinico for it. As it was, Rose, as if sensing my desire to tease her, took on the most potent glare her blushing face could muster and directed it at me.

"So, what do I do? Sergeant Butters said I might need to bring a sacrificial goat or lamb," asked Rose.

Trinico rolled her eyes. "I will be sure to give David a good wallop later. No, no animal sacrifice is required. Just a little of your own blood to swear your oath upon."

"Good . . . that's good," said Rose, looking relieved, if her shoulders sagging a little was anything to go by.

"Bye-bye, please wait here. I will return in a moment," Trinico instructed.

"Can't I watch?" I asked.

"Are you comfortable with Bye-bye seeing you naked?" asked Trinico looking to Rose.

"No!" Rose shouted, her cheeks blushing red. I felt a little heat in my own cheeks as an image flashed through my mind.

"There is your answer," said Trinico, smirking a little as she guided Rose toward the start to the basement.

You're a cruel woman Trinico, I hope you know that.

The priestess returned a few minutes later without Rose. "She'll be a while. Now, you are about to go into what I hope will be your final session in the 'Puzzle Room'."

"Should be," I replied.

"I am sure you have noticed things have been personal of late. This last session will be the most personal yet. I hope you are mentally ready," warned the priestess.

Was that it? Is that why she held me back? To give me a warning? Or an anti-pep talk?

"I'm ready," I said confidently. It's all a game. I just had to figure out what the game wanted from me.

"Very well, proceed," Trinico said, motioning toward the hall leading to the puzzle room.

I made the familiar walk entering the puzzle room to the right. I sat on the center island and as expected received the system prompt.

Welcome to the Puzzle Room.

Are you ready to begin?	Yes	No

Yes, I am.

Solve as many puzzles as possible. (Limit: 2-hours per 24-hour period)
Beginning in 3 . . . 2 . . . 1 GO!

The room went dark for a moment before relighting. I was standing on a stage, a large audience gathered in front of me. The only defense I had was a podium in front of me, off to each side was a teleprompter.

So, this was the game, my fears. My greatest fear, public speaking. I was not okay with this puzzle if you could even call it a that anymore. Then I started hearing murmuring in the crowd, restlessness. I was just waiting for the booing to start. I didn't have to wait long. Then someone threw something, and pandemonium ensued.

The room went dark a moment later and the puzzle restarted.

"Good Afternoon," I stuttered miserably, trying to read from the teleprompter. My voice was shaky and soft, barely audible. Again, the murmuring. I tried to keep going but then the booing began. It wasn't long before the room faded to black only to restart again a moment later.

"It's just a game," I tried to tell myself. The game was to be the center of attention. The game was to face my fears. "It's just a game," I repeated.

"Good Afternoon," I started again, this time as clearly as I could. "Thank you all for joining me today." One sentence, the prompter told me to pause before it continued. "Our society is changing. The digital workplace is growing faster than ever before. It will not be long before the physical workspace is replaced by a digital workspace. This is not a bad thing."

The speech was the most terrifying thing I've ever done. I joked around in the Inn and told stories there, but there were never so many people watching, nor did I have to worry over them booing or heckling me. A healthy dose of liquid courage helped too. I don't know how I made it through the 30-minute promotion of the digital world, but I did it. I avoided the hecklers and the boos. Once I remembered it was all a game, it got easier.

When someone would start murmuring to his neighbor, I would look them in the eyes, give them a smile and they'd quiet down. The only difficulty was to keep spotting these people, so I was constantly scanning the crowd. It was only about half-way through the speech, I noticed the faces in the crowd started to take on the appearances of people I'd known. People who were mean to me or tormented me in my youth, they started appearing in the crowd at random, making my heart race a little more. I persevered, but it was still the most terrifying 30-minutes of my life.

When it was done, I was pleased with myself and also satisfied, beyond what I thought I would feel when I finished it. I faced one of my greatest fears and succeeded in it. It didn't mean I would be going out and doing public speaking engagements in the real world as soon as I logged out, but I now knew I could do it. I just had to treat it like a game. Who knew that was even feasible. Maybe that was the outlook on life I should adopt, maybe if I started treating things in the real world like they were a game, then it would get easier for me to interact with the world. Something to think about in the future, at least, maybe when I had more time.

When the speech ended, and the room faded to black, I expected to be returned to the starting area. Instead, it faded into another room and it was simply spectacular. Not the room itself, it was more of a roof held up by a number of posts with a stone tile floor and a cushion placed in the center of the room. No, it was the view that was spectacular. It seemed this room was built on top of a mountain surrounded by more snowcapped mountains. There were no stairs or path down the mountain I could see, they probably were not even present. I didn't much care, this was simply too beautiful.

I appreciated the view for a few minutes before I realized I needed to figure out what to do next. Was it a new puzzle or something else? Seeing as there was only the cushion in the center of the room, I felt to be the place to start. I sat on the cushion.

Welcome to the Meditation Mind Temple			
Select Meditation focus			
Intellect	*Wisdom*	*Charisma*	*Exit*

Was this the 'Meditation' skill? I selected the 'Exit' option. Everything faded to black and I was back in the domed room, sitting on the little island surrounded by still water.

Class Quest Alert: Training with Priestess Trinico 6-10 – Completed
Having put your trust in Trinico and David Butters, they have offered you training to develop your stats as quickly and efficiently as possible.
Reward: +1,400 Experience, Meditation, Collect your reward from the Temple of Issara in Root City

You've learned the skill 'Meditation'.

Meditation	*Level: 1*		*Experience: 0.00%*	
***Skill Effect (Active)**: Enter the Meditation Mind Temple*				
Intellect: *+1 per 60 minutes*	***Wisdom:*** *+1 per 60 minutes*		***Charisma:*** *+1 per 60 minutes*	

Now that was nice. Time-consuming but nice, 10-hours of meditation to get one stat to the level cap. Still manageable, but undoubtedly boring. I would have to play around with it later. I can't see myself sitting for 30-hours every time I level up.

"How did it go?" asked Trinico, seeing me emerge.

"Not bad . . . hated it so much more than I can ever truly express . . . but not bad," I answered.

"As long as you succeeded it was worth your discomfort," said Trinico, smiling kindly.

"I take it Olaf and Baby are still inside?" I asked.

"They are, you were barely gone an hour. Miss Rose had an errand to run. She said she would be back soon. Miss Micaela is in the spirit world," the priested ended, motioning to Micaela, who appeared to be meditating.

"Was Rose accepted?" I asked. Much as the woman annoyed me and got under my skin, I did want her to succeed.

"I did not ask, and she did not share," Trinico answered. "She did not look upset when she left though she did seem to be in a hurry."

"I hope that's a good thing. I think I will head to meet with Giggle-Ana, hopefully I can finish my training with her before Olaf arrives. I want him to get Giggle-Ana's full attention," I said.

"You are a good friend to them. I hope they will be good friends to you," said Trinico.

I smiled at her and nodded, I hoped for much the same.

CHAPTER 21

Rose was running as the timer continued to tick down. She had just an hour to collect 5 blood samples and return to the temple with them. That was Lilith's test of her. They had to be unique too. They could not come from the same race of humanoid, nor could they come from the same class of beast. One wolf was the same as any other wolf regardless of their name. Still, that was only one blood sample. And she only had an hour to collect 5. That meant she'd have to collect them from the NPC's or other players.

She knew of two right away she could visit, she just had to hope they were receptive to her request.

"Welcome," greeted Giggle-Ana. "How can I help you today?"

"Hello, you're Giggle-Ana, right?" Rose asked.

"Yes, I am, how can I help you?" Giggle-Ana responded.

"This is an odd request, but can I have a some of you and your husband's blood?" Rose asked bluntly.

Giggle-Ana seemed to freeze before pulling a gun from behind the counter and taking aim threateningly. "Foul demon, you will not harm me or my husband."

"Woah, relax. I don't want to hurt anyone," protested Rose, putting her hands in the air. "I need your help."

"And you want to take my blood to do it? I will not help a vampire bring harm to this world," the gnomish woman answered.

"I'm a Daywalker, not a vampire," explained Rose, hoping it would make even a little difference.

The pistol lowered slightly as Giggle-Ana studied her carefully for a moment. "Why? What do you need the blood for? Some kind of dark ritual I assume."

Rose cringed a little there. It was probably a dark ritual. "I am trying to pledge myself in service to the Goddess Lilith. She has set a test for me. I am to collect 5 unique blood samples and return to her. I don't know if it's for a dark ritual but . . . well, it probably is."

Giggle-Ana narrowed her eyes, boring into the young woman. "Okay, I believe you," said the gnome, her gun disappearing back behind the counter. "You are Bye-bye's friend, right?"

"I don't know if I'd say we were friends. I only met him yesterday. But I would say we are on the path to becoming friend-like," Rose answered uncertainly, a dusting of pink spreading across her cheeks.

"Oh, so it is like that?" asked Giggle-Ana, giggling merrily.

Rose's cheeks reddened further, and she scowled. "No, it's not like that. He's annoying, rude and an idiot. Everything he does seems to be done just to get under my skin. But he is . . . useful . . . for now at least."

Giggle-Ana giggled again and rolled her eyes. "I suppose if Bye-bye is willing to vouch for you, I can spare a little of my blood and I am sure Kirlan will do the same."

"Bye-bye is in some kind of training thing right now and won't be out for hours. I only have 48 minutes left," Rose stated, checking the timer again.

Giggle-Ana leaned her head to the side looking out the window behind Rose and pointed.

Rose turned to look and saw Bye-bye walking toward the shop. "Be right back," Rose said quickly, then almost sprinted outside to meet him.

"Bye-bye, I need your help," Rose said quickly, trying not to let panic into her voice.

"Um, okay?" I half asked.

"Lilith gave me a quest to get blood samples, 5 of them, and they have to be unique. Giggle-Ana said she'd give me one, but only if you vouch for me. Will you?" Rose asked, trying not to sound like she was desperate.

"I can do that," I replied. "How many have you got so far?"

"None, the shop was on the way out of town. I figure I could get a wolf for one more, then ask Trinico or the sergeant for one," Rose answered.

"That would make three," I said, counting off.

"Plus, one from Kirlan and I was hoping I could wake Micaela and get her to give me one too," Rose said, explaining her plan.

"I could give you one too," I volunteered. "I'm a half high elf so that should be unique."

Rose seemed surprised by the offer and mumbled a soft "Thanks."

"No problem," I said.

"Anyway, I need you to vouch for me," Rose said, turning and rushing back inside.

"And the verdict?" asked Giggle-Ana.

"I'll vouch for her," I said, entering just behind Rose.

"Okay then," said Giggle-Ana, producing two filled vials from behind the counter. "I took the liberty of getting them ready for you. I had a feeling Bye-bye would vouch for you."

"Two vials?" Rose asked.

"Of course, one from me and one from Kirlan," Giggle-Ana answered, motioning to one then the other.

"Thank you very much," Rose happily accepted the two vials depositing them in her bag.

"Anything else I can get you? My first born maybe?" Giggle-Ana giggled, the pair of adventures looked completely unsure of how to respond to such a statement. "You are both so serious, lighten up a little, go on a date and have some fun."

"You've got a real mean streak, don't you?" I asked, looking anywhere, but at Rose, while Rose did the same.

"Only when I feel like it," grinned Giggle-Ana.

"Where did you get the vial?" asked Rose, her attention back on the task at hand.

"I can sell you three more, so those plus the two with our blood comes to 2-gold, 10-copper," said Giggle-Ana in a businesslike demeanor.

"2-gold?" Rose and I both nearly shouted.

"1-gold per blood sample, 2-copper per vial. You did not think I gave you those for free, did you? I am a businesswoman, not a charity," the gnome answered, ever the saleswoman . . . salesgnome?

Rose reluctantly paid the money, cringing even as she set it on the counter. "Well, that's me broke, only 1-silver left to my name."

"Sorry, I'm sure you'll make more," I replied, attempting to reassure her. "And I'm sure when we finish the Bandit quest we got this morning, it will pay quite well. Especially, if we can recover all, or even most, of the goods."

"I suppose you're right," said Rose, slightly mollified. "But you better be able to carry a lot. In fact, you should probably go see about upgrading your cruddy starter bag while you're at it."

It was my turn to cringe, her statement both poignant and cutting.

"And change your shoes already. You look little better than a bum. Didn't you just get a new pair of boots?" Rose asked.

"I did, I just haven't had a minute to equip them. We've been busy, or didn't you notice?" I answered.

"I notice plenty," Rose retorted. She looked as if she was going to continue but a coughing sound from Giggle-Ana made us both realize where we were.

Recovering first, Rose held out an empty vial toward me and stated simply, "Blood."

I accepted the vial then using my spear tip I cut my hand, wincing painfully. I filled the vial in short order then cast 'Lesser Heal', causing the bleeding to stop and the little bit of bleed damage to heal.

"There you go," I said, handing the vial back to her.

"Hopefully, the Goddess Lilith accepts your blood, it looks kind of weak," said Rose studying the vial close, smirking a little.

"Do not start again. Rose, you have what you need, I suggest you run along and finish the quest your Goddess gave you." Giggle-Ana chided, then asked, "Bye-bye, I assume you are here to learn to pick locks?"

"Yes, ma'am," I replied.

"You're right, I can't waste time talking to this idiot," said Rose, looking at her timer, realizing wasted five minutes bantering with me. "How do I wake Micaela?"

"Just give her a shake, as I understand it, she's aware when she's in the spirit world," I answered, frowning at the young woman.

"See you in a little while then," said Rose, turning to rush for the door and to continue her quest, she only needed two more samples.

"We'll meet up at the temple in an hour," I called after her.

Rose heard but didn't turn back or acknowledge it, choosing to run toward the village gates. As soon as she was past the moat, she pulled out her sword and shield. She had roughly 15 minutes to find and kill a wolf, then she would have no other choice but to turn back.

The problem was, she had no tracking skills, she just had to hope she got lucky. Her eyes ever watching the timer tick downward. She moved directly south of the village and away from the road. The encounters she had with the wolves previously were always away from town and away from the road. It seemed a good place to start.

After five minutes without an encounter, she began to worry a little. After ten minutes she began to panic. When that fifteenth minute passed without finding a wolf she feared she would fail her quest. Having no choice, Rose began a hard run back to town. She had to hope Trinico and Micaela were willing to donate a little blood to her cause or she would fail.

Rose ran again, this time back to the village, straight past the guards with barely a wave and shout at them as she went. Her run took her down the main street where she nearly ran over three different citizens and had to leap over a large dog that ran into her path. When she reached the temple, she hardly slowed down despite her stamina bar being depleted severely.

"Rose, you have returned," Trinico greeted her with a kind smile.

"I need blood," Rose stated bluntly, between gasps of breath, earning a shocked look from Trinico. "Just a vial of blood. My Goddess set me a quest to obtain 5 unique blood samples. Will you help me?"

Trinico's expression quickly calmed. "Thank goodness, I worried for a moment there. Of course, I will help you."

"Thank you," Rose replied, handing a vail to Trinico. She then rushed over to Micaela. When she got to her, she looked indecisive for a moment then poked the ogre in the shoulder.

No reaction.

Rose tried giving her a little shake.

No reaction.

"Give her a slap," said Trinico, having watched the attempts.

"I don't want to hurt her," Rose replied.

"She has thick skin. You will not hurt her," the priestess assured her.

The slap rang out loudly filling the almost empty building with an echoing clap of skin striking skin.

"Owee, why'd you slap me?" asked Micaela, rubbing her cheek, now sporting an angry red handprint.

Rose also appeared to be in pain. "What are you made of? Solid stone?" she asked, cradling her aching hand.

"Rose, you may want to get to the point. You seemed to be in a hurry a moment ago," Trinico pointed out.

"Right, I need your blood," Rose stated, looking Micaela in the eyes.

"Will you die of thirst or something if you don't drink some blood? Do you have to drink blood often? How much blood do you need? Will it send me to respawn? Could I become a half-ogre, half-vampire shaman?" Micaela rattled off questions.

Rose expected shock or fear at the request, not to be bombarded with questions. "Slow down," she pleaded. "I need a sample of your blood for my class quest. I've only got a few minutes left. Can you help me?"

"Sure," said Micaela, turning her head slightly and pulling back her shirt a little to better expose her neck.

"Not like that," Rose nearly shouted. "Here, in the vial," she held out the little glass tube.

"Oh, heh-heh," Micaela chuckled. "Makes sense."

With just a minute left on the timer, Rose returned to the altar of the Goddess Lilith in the basement of the temple.

"I've returned my Goddess," Rose stated as clearly as she could, while still slightly out of breath.

"*Ssso, you have,*" hissed the amused voice of the Goddess Lilith from all around her.

Rose waited with some trepidation for whatever was to happen next.

"*I sssupposse you have potential. Are you prepared to sswear yoursself to me?*" hissed the voice of the Goddess Lilith.

"I am," Rose answered.

"*Kneel,*" ordered the voice, sounding closer now.

Rose kneeled before the altar. Then she saw the source of the voice or at least, what she thought was the source. It was a tiny little mottled green and brown snake, how it could speak in such a loud and powerful voice was strange. It was stranger still, to see the snake enlarging before her eyes. Shifting, bubbling and bending into a new form. Into that of a beautiful young girl with dark raven locks of hair, black lips, black eye-liner and a black, overly dramatic dress that seemed to be alive and moving. A closer look at the dress showed it was not a dress, but snakes of the darkest black in constant motion, covering the girl. The young girl before her was the perfect gothic Lolita if one ever existed.

"Do you sswear yourrself to sserve me and my interesstss above all otherss?" asked the Goddess Lilith, now with the voice of a young girl, fitting her current appearance.

"I swear it," answered Rose confidently, sure this was what she wanted.

"Gift the blood," ordered the Goddess Lilith.

Rose took out the five vials and offered them.

"You shall drink one ssip and I shall drink the resst. Thiss magic sshall bind uss." ordered the Goddess.

Rose frowned at the idea of drinking blood, but she had come this far. She was not about to back down now. She uncorked a vial and took a sip, then handed the vial and the remaining blood within it to the Goddess Lilith who drank the rest. By the fifth vial, Rose was fighting back the urge to vomit, but that would not be a good idea in front of her Goddess.

"The ritual iss complete. I now offer you the classs of Ssquire Vampiric Knight. Do you accept?" asked the childlike Goddess.

"I do," said Rose, a grin tugging at the corners of her mouth.

"Little Pantherophis, will you accept this ssquire as your masster? Will you protect and guide her in my sservice?" the Goddess asked, looking at her hand, confusing Rose. When Rose tried to look closer, she saw a little black snake, presumably a former part of the dress, was now coiled up in the hand of the Goddess, its eyes completely white.

"You honor thiss blind sservant, misstresss. It would pleasse me to sserve," hissed Pantherophis in reply.

"I expect great thingss from the both of you, young ssquire, young sservant," said the Goddess Lilith with finality before she began to shrink until only a single black snake remained, taking the place of

the mottled green snake. The same snake, which only moments before sat upon the Goddess's hand.

"I greet you masster. I am Pantherophis, your companion from thiss day forward," said the diminutive snake.

"I get a snake?" asked Rose.

"And if you sserved Dracula, he would no doubt asssign one of his foul batss to guide you," hissed Pantherophis.

"Guide me?" Rose asked, still unclear on how all of this worked.

"Yess, I am your guide. I will help you grow your Vampiric sskillss and blood magicss. I will allso fight at your sside, though I am sstill young and will not be of much usse for a while. As I gain in sstrength you will be able to choosse sskillss and sspellss you wish me to know," explained the little snake.

"That is so cool," Rose whispered, a smile beginning to brighten her face. "Are you a constrictor or a venomous snake?"

"I am whatever you need me to be," Pantherophis answered. "You will choosse as I get sstronger."

"Right, so I select your skills when you level up," Rose stated, confirming what she thought the snake had said.

"A blunt way to put it, but yess," Pantherophis stated, his tongue flicking the air. "Pleasse allso remember, I am blind. I cannot ssee what you cannot ssee. Your eyess are my eyess from thiss day forth."

"I'm Rose Thorns, it's nice to meet you Pantherophis," said the young woman, offering her hand palm up to the snake.

Pantherophis slithered forward onto the hand and then under the armor and along Rose's arm, causing her to giggle from the tickling sensation until he re-emerged from the neck opening in her armor. The small snake then curled around Rose's neck, not unlike a necklace, the tip of the tail hooking it in place.

"So, Panther, can I call you Panther? Never mind, I'm just gonna call you Panther. What next?" Rose asked.

"We get sstronger," Panther answered. "You are not quite ready for blood magic and your only available vampiric sskill requiress you drink blood, ssomething you sseem to dislike."

Rose cringed a little. "Yeah, I don't care for the taste of blood. I don't suppose I could mix it with something else?"

"You can mix it with almost anything you prefer. Jusst bear in mind, it will quickly losse potency and musst be drunk or eaten immediately upon mixing," Panther answered.

"That works perfectly for me," Rose said. "A vial with a little blood, mix in a little vodka and I'm good to go."

"That is alcohol yess?" Panther asked.

"Yes," Rose answered.

"Then no, think more along the line of juice or as gravy on ssomething you eat," suggested Panther.

Rose deflated with that. "Lame."

"Necesssary, alcohol killss the blood," Panther explained.

"Bumber, but it makes sense. Alcohol can kill just about anything and it dulls the senses. I suppose, I don't need to be impaired when I'm supposed to be fighting anyway," Rose reasoned.

"Indeed," the little snake replied. "Any other questionss or can we proceed with getting sstronger?"

"I suppose," replied Rose, rising back to her feet from where she had been kneeling.

"Rose, you're back," shouted Baby, seeing her sister return from the basement.

"You bet I am," Rose replied cheerfully. "And I'm a Vampiric Knight."

"Ssquire Vampire Knight of the Goddess Lilith, it is alwayss besst to be precisse when you sserve a Goddess lesst they take offensse," warned Panther.

"Sorry, didn't know," Rose replied.

"Did you just hiss at me?" asked Baby, her head cocked to the side and looking confused.

"Those who do not sserve the Goddess cannot sspeak my tongue," explained Panther, from his place around Rose's neck.

"Woah, I speak snake now," grinned Rose.

"Should we start calling you 'She who-" I started but was cut off by hissing from around Rose's neck.

"May we kill him?" asked Panther, moving slightly to glare at the man responsible for making his mistress's heart race and her blood boil.

"No," hissed Rose too quickly. "He's useful to us. He will help us get stronger."

"Very well," accepted Panther, not sounding overly pleased to have done so.

"Um, Sis, you know you've got a snake around your neck, right?" asked Baby, pointing a slightly shaking arm and finger toward the snake necklace.

"Yeah, this is Panther, isn't he awesome? The Goddess Lilith gifted him to me. He's my companion and as we get stronger, he can fight with us," Rose quickly explained to her sister.

"Panther, this is my sister Babies Breath, no biting her, scaring her is fine, but make sure she deserves it," Rose hissed, pointing to her sister.

Then she looked at me before hissing again.

413

"You can bite Bye-bye if he says or does something stupid but don't kill him," she hissed instructions.

"Why do I get the feeling, Panther and I are not going to get along?" I asked, not liking the look on either of their faces.

"Brave, but stupid, mate," commented Olaf. "Anyway, now that we're all back together again, let's get to work on that quest."

"What about going to Giggle-Ana's?" I asked.

"It's only coming up on noon. I figure if we can get through this quest by 2:00 or 3:00 this afternoon, we should have plenty of time," explained Olaf, getting a nod of understanding.

"That could work," I replied.

"Great, so we're all ready to get out of here," said Rose. "Trini, it's been fun. See you tomorrow."

"It was nice to meet you and your sister. Please keep each other safe," Trinico requested.

"We will," said Baby. "Now let's go on an adventure."

"Order of Epic Adventurers let's go!" shouted Micaela, dramatically pointing an arm and finger toward the temple doors.

"We're not naming it that," said Olaf and I together.

"But guys," whined Micaela.

"Interesting friends we've made, huh?" asked Baby, fluttering next to her sister.

"Yeah, interesting . . . And fun," Rose replied, grinning a little. "Hey, what's this Order business?" she called running to catch up to them, Baby flying along right next to her.

CHAPTER 22

"Do you see any tracks, Bye-bye?" asked Olaf, waiting, not exactly patiently, for me to find something to chase.

"Tons of tracks. But I need to find the right ones," I explained, feeling his impatience. There were too many tracks all around the portal to the World Tree. I was looking for tracks leading away from the portal dais, most of which followed the road. It was almost twenty-yards north of the portal when I finally found a lot of tracks that didn't belong. It was really odd too, they just kind of started out of nowhere, wagon tracks and a large number of footprints.

"Found them," I shouted to my group.

"That's pretty far from the portal," commented Rose, echoing my own thoughts.

"Yes, it is, I don't know why it doesn't go right up to the portal itself, but these are most likely the tracks we need to follow," I said.

"Could they have covered up their tracks? Is that why they appeared suddenly? I mean, even I can see the wagon wheel indentations," added Baby, flying nearby.

"Only one way to find out," said a grinning Olaf, his hands inching towards his weapons. Admittedly, I was kind of anxious to see what they could do too.

"Lead the way, Bye-bye, we're behind you," said Rose grinning. "That way if something goes wrong, you die first."

"She's all hugs and kisses, isn't she?" I asked, looking to Baby for help.

"Nope, I'm staying out of it," said Baby, raising her arms in surrender. "You two can bicker and flirt as much as you want, just keep me out of it."

"Flirt?" asked Rose. "Are you drunk?"

"Must be, if she thinks you and I flirt with each other," I added. "No offense, but you're not my type."

"Oh please, anything with a pulse is your type," retorted Rose.

"Vampires are undead, right? That would mean you're not my type. Besides, I prefer nice girls," I poked at her.

"Are you saying I'm not nice?" asked Rose, taking a fist full of my shirt.

I looked down at my shirt in her grip. "Case in point."

"Yeah, whatever," said Rose, pushing me back a step. "Just . . . show us where to go."

I rolled my eyes but moved forward anyway. We followed the trail north, pretty close to the mountainous eastern border. This was also where we encountered the first mountain lion we had seen.

It was slightly larger than one of the wolves we encountered near the village, and its level was higher too. The <Ridge Lion Lvl 5> attacked me from stealth, there was nothing, then there was the cat going for my jugular. It must have had the ambush subskill too because it got a critical strike on me for -943-HP, which nearly killed me. If not for Baby's healing, I'm sure I would have died from the next two attacks, they took -213-HP and -224-HP. Combined with the ambush attack, I took more damage than my total 1200-HP.

Then it was our turn. Rose taunted the lion and hit it hard with a 'Shield Slam', dazing it. I didn't even get a chance to attack, to get any measure of revenge, because Olaf finally got the chance to use his hand-cannons on a real target. It took two shots for Olaf to kill it, then he reloaded and took two more shots for good measure. When it was done, it wouldn't have mattered if any of us had the 'Scavenge' skill. The only remains, after just four shots, was pulp.

"So, I may have overdone it," said Olaf, grinning sheepishly.

"Overdone it he says," laughed Rose. "A bit understated, don't you think?"

"At least he got it out of his system now," said Micaela. "Won't happen again, will it?" There was a glint in her eyes daring Olaf to contradict her.

"No, you're right. I got it out of my system," said Olaf, wisely accepting.

"I should hope so," I replied, focusing on casting my own 'Lesser Heal' to bring my HP back up to full. "So, how are we going to proceed? That cat pretty much wrecked me."

"Obviously, I'll have to go first," said Rose. "Just, tell me where to go."

We resumed our northbound route, only encountering one more of those lions. It was dealt with in short order, between me and Olaf. This encounter also made me aware of something I had not yet encountered, friendly fire. When one of Olaf's shots went wide, it happened to graze my arm, nearly taking it off, as the miniature cannonball passed. Once again, it was only thanks to Baby that I did not lose my arm, which started another discussion of curiosity.

Would limbs grow back if healed? We also had to discuss, how we would deal with friendly fire, and how we can avoid it in the future.

It made the walk north go quicker, we had a topic of interest to discuss. Before we knew it, we were standing by the waterfall I had previously mapped. What I hadn't mapped, or even seen before, was the path behind the waterfall leading into a cave system.

"Dungeon or just a cave?" asked Olaf.

"There aren't dungeons in the starting provinces," stated Baby matter-of-factly.

"But if there were, I'm pretty sure Bye-bye would be the one to find it," said Olaf confident in me.

Baby looked like she wanted to retort but held back. Eventually, she agreed, "You may have a point."

"Anyway, I don't think this is a dungeon. There is no barrier or anything leading into the cave," I replied. The entrance was as wide as the waterfall and branched into three different tunnels, each wide enough to fit a wagon or more inside. There were also tracks and wagon indentations going down all three paths.

"Which way do we go?" asked Micaela.

"Left," said Rose.

"Why left?" asked Micaela.

"Why not left?" asked Rose, grinning. Her sword and shield were already out in front of her and leading us into the cave system taking the leftmost tunnel.

Thankfully, the tunnel was at least ten feet high, so Micaela and Olaf had no problem fitting, though the width of the tunnel didn't allow for them to stand shoulder to shoulder. Best of all, the tunnel was well lit. A little looking around and I was of the opinion, these bandits had set up shop pretty well in here. Torches were mounted to the walls at regular intervals and the floor was relatively smooth. Less thankfully, there were several blind corners.

We must have been about two or three hundred yards into the tunnel when we came across our first patrol. We were just turning one of those blind corners, when three humanoids, a male orc with a large two-handed sword, a troll female with two daggers and a human with a bow, were also turning the same corner.

Rose attacked immediately, taunting them to start. "Come get me, boys, if you're man enough."

"Get her!" ordered the archer, running away about twenty yards before he turned to fire.

"I'll get the archer, try to get them turned so Micaela and Olaf can help fight them," I ordered.

"And how are you going get around them, we're pretty much taking up the entire hallway," said Rose, grunting occasionally as she blocked, stabbed and bashed the two bandits.

"Like this," I said confidently, running forward, I jumped toward the cave wall, using it as a springboard to jump off of, and dove over Rose and the two bandits, tucking and rolling as I hit the cave floor on the other side of them. I rolled right back up to my feet and sprinted down the tunnel toward the wide-eyed archer, who clearly had not been expecting me so suddenly.

I engaged the archer in close range melee combat before he could even get a shot off. I lit him up with 'Lesser Holy Fire' with the goal of building up to three stacks, as quickly as possible. Then I started attacking with my spear. Without his bow, he was mostly defenseless, even when he pulled out a dagger to try to fight me. He scored a few glancing blows, but with my 'Acrobatics' at work, I was hard to hit. I think it was more due to him having to constantly turn and change directions. He'd barely start an attack, and I would no longer be there. Instead, I'd be a few feet to the right or left and hitting him as hard as I could with my spear, even if most of the damage was from the 'Lesser Holy Imbuement'. It was over before I knew it, the archer was dead, and I was alive.

The archer was dead.

It took a minute for it to sink in and when it did, I suddenly felt sick to my stomach. I'd just killed a man, at least it felt like I did. There wasn't a ton of blood, nor were his eyes staring at me accusingly, as I half expected him to be. He kind of just looked asleep. Still, he was dead and never coming back, even if I did kill him in self-defense. I wasn't mentally prepared for the how real it would feel. Sure, I'd killed the troll bandit on the road a few days ago, but the troll didn't look human or rather looked just monstrous enough. I didn't equate it with a human, though I should have.

I turned sharply away from the dead archer, looking for my friends. They looked the same as I felt, shocked.

"You guys alright?" I asked, trying to be strong for them.

"That felt too real," said Olaf, his voice soft and filled with regret. "Mic and I were in the army, we've even been in firefights before. That just felt too real, too familiar."

"I know it's a game, I know it but . . ." Rose shuddered.

I looked to Baby to see she was crying, two streams of tears running down her childlike face. Part of me wanted to join her. Part of me wanted to just log out and never look back. But a bigger part of me knew why I was doing this, and why I had to continue on.

I took a deep breath before I spoke. "I'm not going to lie. Taking life in here, in this game world is . . . awful. This is the second humanoid I've killed in this game, and it's weighing on me. I did not enjoy it, not this time, not last time. I will probably never enjoy it. But we came here for a reason. These men, these bandits, these criminals, have been killing and robbing the citizens of this World Tree. We have the power to stop them, the civilians have asked for justice. It's for that reason, I'm continuing, even knowing I will have to kill more people."

Rose was the first to recover, which surprised me, then again, I didn't know her all too well yet. I thought Olaf and Micaela would have been first given their military experience.

"He's right. I hate agreeing with Jack here on anything but there is a good reason for being here. Hurligville is depending on us to stop these men from causing more pain and suffering. I say we finish this quest," Rose spoke, a fierce determination in her voice.

Olaf and Micaela shared a look, their entire demeanor seemed to change. Olaf spoke, "We're with you, Bye-bye."

"Why couldn't they just be monsters?" said Baby. "I could deal with monsters. Why use people at all?"

"Because just like home, real people can cause the most hurt. But unlike home, there are no cops, no detectives or anything to stop the bad guys. Only the adventurers, only us," said Rose, putting a hand on her sister's shoulder.

"Can't we just capture them? That's what the police would do, right?" asked Baby.

"We can try," I said, I hadn't even considered the option before now. "I know it's possible, but I can't say for certain it will be an option with all of them."

"Then we try it, next time," said Rose firmly.

"Do we . . . loot the bodies?" asked Micaela, it may have been distasteful, but she wasn't wrong.

"I think we have to," I replied. "We need to at least remove the weapons and armor. We can't allow another of these bandits to take them to use against us."

"How do we divide the loot then?" asked Baby.

"We don't," I answered firmly. Part of my answer was simply me not wanting to be rewarded for killing people, but then, I also knew the procedure from the last bandit I had captured. "We turn it into the town and then they give us a share of the spoils as well as any bounties on the men we capture or kill. Just like the mayor paid me for earlier."

"We need to find a wagon to load the dead bodies onto," said Olaf. "But for now, we'll have to risk leaving them here. Hopefully, there won't be another patrol down this path."

"Okay, so we go on then, everyone agreed?" I asked.

Everyone nodded but Rose who said simply, "Let's go."

We followed Rose through the tunnel, being much more careful with the blind corners until we came to a large open cavern filled with cages. It was disgusting, to say the least, the cages were filled with men and women, most likely the missing merchants or just some misfortunate traveler, who ran afoul of the bandits. It left me feeling such righteous anger.

Baby flew quickly to the cages, shouting, "We have to free them."

I went forward quickly to the closest cage.

"Help us," begged a man inside.

"I'm working on it," I replied, hoping my lockpicking skill would be enough to open the cage. Unfortunately, as soon as my picks hit the lock, I got a nasty jolt of electricity knocking off a quarter of my HP and leaving my hands numb for 30-seconds. It was a new debuff I hadn't seen before, 'Shock Nerves'.

"It's a magical trap. You have to have the self-proclaimed Bandit King's key to open it," said the prisoner, the only one who appeared to be coherent. The others, at least, appeared to still be breathing, but in bad shape.

"We'll get the key, where can we find this Bandit King?" I asked.

"One of the other tunnels. I only ever saw him once, when he told us he planned to turn us all into slaves, once he took over the province," explained the man. He was dirty, and I wasn't sure what color his hair actually was with all the dirt and grime he was lathered in. I couldn't really see the shape of his face behind the scraggly beard either, but he had bright blue eyes, looking at me with such hope. I didn't want to let this man down.

Quest Alert: A self-proclaimed Bandit King (Recommended Level 5-7)		
Stop the self-proclaimed Bandit King and use his key to free the captured merchants.		
Reward: Experience		
Do you accept this Quest?	Yes	No

I accepted the quest for the group.

"Baby, can we try healing some of these people? The ones in red at least. I'll help." I wasn't much help, but it was better than nothing. Baby and I both replenished our mana pools at least once before we went about healing again.

Between drinking and casting healing spells it took Baby and me about thirty-minutes to heal everyone enough to be sure they weren't about to die. Twenty-two lives depended on us saving them. Now, if that wasn't enough motivation, then nothing would be.

While we were working on healing the prisoners to the best of our ability, Olaf searched the room for anything useful or treasure related. It was lucky for us, he found a large supply of shackles, something we'd need if we wanted to take prisoners.

"Middle tunnel next," said Rose, returning to the original tunnel fork. There was no conversation needed or discussion, we were following our tank. After seeing this, after witnessing the evil that exists in this game world, I didn't feel as conflicted about what we had to do.

The middle tunnel was much larger than the first, wide enough for Micaela and Olaf to walk side by side. About twenty yards from the entrance to this path we found a small tunnel offshoot, leading to a closed wooden door ten yards from the path. After a quick discussion, we decided it would be best to fully clear this place out which meant leaving no room unexplored. It turned out it was a small bunk room, just four beds and two of them were occupied by sleeping bandits, both trolls.

Rose and I introduced ourselves rather violently, a 'Shield Slam' each. Olaf shot one hitting him at the knee and taking the leg clean off. That troll was quick to surrender and get the captured debuff. Baby healed him quickly, stopping the bleed effect but doing nothing for the missing limb.

The second guy just wouldn't surrender, even after we had him down to just a few HP, he kept attacking us.

He ended up dead for it.

"Such a waste," I said sadly. It was so unnecessary, he had to have known there was no way he could win.

After taking their equipment, we used one of the shackles to chain the surrendered enemy to the dead body. It would keep him here for the time being at least. Micaela then knocked him out with the knob of her ax for good measure.

We found a few more bunk rooms as we went, some had sleeping bandits, others had awake bandits, and some had none at all. We ended up capturing just six more bandits. If there was a bunk for every bandit, then we were still missing 10 bandits.

At the end of the tunnel or what we assumed was the end, was a wooden barricade with a heavy door blocking off the tunnel behind it. We were far enough back, to not be seen, but I had to get closer to see what we were dealing with. I used 'Stealth' to creep up quietly and slowly, but also not going too far, my skill level was still rather low.

In front of the barricade stood three guards. Of the two male orcs, one was labeled as a <Bandit Archer Lvl 5> and the other <Bandit Earth Mage Lvl 5>, if those two weren't bad enough there was also a single ogre warrior wearing two spiked gauntlets on his hands, this <Ogre Bruiser Lvl 6> was going to be trouble. I didn't think it was anything we couldn't handle but we'd have to be careful.

"So, what's the plan?" asked Micaela, after I had described what we were dealing with.

"I'll have to tank the Ogre," said Rose. She was absolutely correct, the bruiser had to be contained.

"Expect slow but powerful hits. Ogre Bruiser class are top melee damage dealers right now," warned Olaf.

"The earth mage explains why there were no tracks. It also explains why these tunnels are so smooth. It means he's probably got some powerful spells and underground, he is going to be even more dangerous," I added.

"The archer is the least problematic except for one thing. If he runs for help, we could be in trouble," added Olaf.

"We need a CC," added Micaela.

A crowd control would certainly be useful.

"I wish I knew 'Pollen Burst - Slumber', it would make things so much easier," complained Baby.

"What is that?" I asked. I assumed it put the enemy to sleep.

"It's a level 10 spell. I conjure a ball of pollen that explodes in a targeted area putting everyone inside of the area asleep for 30-seconds," she explained.

"That would have been good to have, but we don't have it, so let's focus on what we do have," said Olaf.

"Kill order, mage, archer and the ogre last," ordered Rose.

"I can take the archer again," I volunteered. I seemed to have that particular enemy's pattern down already.

"That puts me and Mic on the mage," said Olaf.

"Okay, I'll pull the ogre away from the others, try to fight the mage and archer at the door. Baby, position yourself between us for healing," Rose laid out a basic positioning strategy for us.

"I think we're good to go," I said. "Pull when ready."

Rose nodded and started forward. "Yo, fat, dumb and ugly, come at me!"

"She has such interesting taunts," said Olaf, grinning a little.

"Do I look fat?" asked Micaela, looking at herself and getting a small laugh from the rest of us. It definitely lightened the mood.

The <Ogre Bruiser Lvl 6> took notice of the taunt and charged at her, while the mage began chanting, and the archer nocked an arrow.

I sprinted forward myself, in an effort to close the distance and start my assault on the archer. I put two stacks of 'Lesser Holy Fire' before I even got to the archer due to having to dodge a wild swing from the bruiser. When I did get to him, I had him good and angry with me. I approached this the same way I did with the first archer I fought. Once I closed to melee range, he pulled out a dagger to try to defend himself. I took a few glancing blows before my spear went clean through the Orc's leg giving him a crippled debuff and a captured debuff a moment later.

I looked to help Olaf and Micaela, but they already captured the mage.

Finally, I looked back toward Rose fighting the <Ogre Bruiser Lvl 6>. Every time he struck, a third of her health would disappear, only to be healed back to full a moment later, compliments of Baby. I looked at Baby's status bars in my UI to see she was almost out of mana.

"Baby, start replenishing mana. I'll heal her," I called out.

"Can you keep up?" Baby asked, casting another heal.

"Not forever, but long enough for you to replenish some of your mana," I answered. I started chain casting my 'Lesser Heal'. It barely made a dent, but I could cast it a few times before the ogre's next attack landed. I couldn't quite get her health back to full with my heal only doing +71-90-HP per cast, but it bought Baby the time she needed.

I was also watching as the bruiser began to steadily lose health, now with Micaela and Olaf beginning to attack. Then it lost a sudden chunk of health when one of Olaf's bullets got a critical hit.

"What was that?" asked Rose, straining to block.

"My subskill," answered Olaf, sounding overly pleased with himself. "I'll be using it again in two minutes."

"Hopefully this fight will be over in one," laughed Rose, grinning as she fought toe to toe with the towering aggressor.

"Okay, Bye-bye, I've got the healing from here, start helping to whittle this guy down," said Baby, her mana back up over 50%.

I didn't hesitate. I ran forward, stabbing my spear into the back of the ogre's knee, causing it to drop to the ground, the leg no longer holding the weight. I also saw a new debuff, 'Hamstrung'. That wasn't my goal when I struck the leg, but I wasn't going to complain. Especially as my next attack was able to reach the ogre's neck for a critical strike.

With the bruiser temporarily down on one knee, he seemed to suddenly take a higher amount of damage from the group.

"Surrender," I requested of the ogre, not sure if it could understand me. Whether it did or not I would never know, he just kept fighting until, with the last-gasp, he dropped to his other knee, falling face down, dead.

"Everyone still alive?" asked Rose, panting and trying to catch her breath. Her stamina bar was almost zero.

"Looks like it. Okay everyone, let's take a five-minute break to recover. Eat and drink, you know the routine," I said.

Olaf and Micaela sat down back to back, leaning against each other. I guessed it was something they had done many times before, probably something from their military days. Rose sat against one of the cave walls with Baby sitting right next to her.

I chose to sit down on one of the crates by the barricade, appreciating the soft wood of the crate versus the rock-hard cave floor. Well, not exactly soft, but more forgiving than the stone floor at the very least. I didn't expect to hear a conversation taking place on the other side of the barricade.

"Two of my men are dead. Mind explaining why that is? I thought we had a deal," complained a man.

"We do have a deal," replied a much more guttural voice, more animalistic. "But I am not going to risk my position for two of your underlings. Besides, does this not mean more money for you?"

"Heh, you may have a point," said the first voice.

"And they failed, Duke Johnson did not die," added the second voice.

"I thought you said destroying the Moonshine and the still, was more important," argued the first voice.

"It was, and I am glad they at least did that right," agreed the second voice.

"Can I ask, why was it so important?" the first asked.

"You can ask, and I will even answer. It is none of your business," snapped the second voice.

"Fine, fine," said the first voice placatingly. "Just pay me my money."

I heard the sound of something jangling briefly, followed by a thump, and louder jangling against wood, probably a table or desk.

"Any other work you want to hire us for?" asked the first voice.

"No, I am leaving," said the second voice.

For a moment I panicked thinking the door was about to open but it never did.

"Creepy bastard, glad he is gone," complained the first voice.

Quest Alert: Shiny Delivery Service 4 (Recommended Level 4-5) - Completed
Conspiracy? Who hired the trolls to attack the Johnson's Farm and why?
Reward: +500-Experience

"Hey, what's this quest?" asked Rose.

Quest Alert: Shiny Delivery Service 5 (Recommended Level 4-5)		
You have confirmed the trolls were indeed hired to kill Duke Johnson but more importantly to destroy the Moonshine and the still that made it. Question the leader of the Bandits to find out who hired him.		
Reward: Experience		
Do you accept this quest?	Yes	No

429

"It's a chain I've been working on for a while. It would seem, you just got added to it," I answered, intrigued by the next step of the quest.

"It also just gave me level 4," said Rose, grinning.

"So, is this normal?" asked Baby, looking to Olaf and Micaela.

"Pretty much," said Olaf, grinning to match Rose.

"But how did you complete it?" asked Rose.

"Uh, I kind of just overheard a conversation," I answered honestly, pointing with my thumb over my shoulder toward the barricade.

"Hey, intruders, get them!" shouted a voice from up the tunnel we came from drawing our full attention.

"It's a patrol," shouted Rose in warning as she got back to her feet quickly and rushed to attack.

I was the furthest back but was fast enough to catch up and run past Rose and the two she engaged with. The last one turned tail and ran, he was a <Bandit Rogue Lvl 5>, bearing two sheathed daggers on his belt, neither of which he bothered drawing. I knew I had to catch up to him before he could get help. I caught up to him about halfway out of the tunnel, severely depleting my stamina from the effort. Even when I caught up to him and attacked, he wasn't slowing down or stopping to fight me.

I kept attacking, slowly sapping his HP but not fast enough. He would escape if I didn't slow him down in a more meaningful way. I tried to attack the leg just as I had against the ogre, hoping it would give him the 'Hamstrung' debuff. My spear struck hard, piercing the back of his leg causing him to howl in pain for a brief moment. He tried to continue running, but right away I could see the leg I had stabbed no longer wanted to keep moving. The bandit didn't drop to a knee the way the ogre had, but he was left dragging the useless limb behind him, the 'Hamstrung' debuff had indeed appeared.

The attack gave me the time I needed to stop him. I struck as hard as I could, unrelentingly, despite my already low stamina dropping even faster. Eventually, I had to resort to casting 'Holy Smite' repeatedly until he finally perished. I was exhausted when it was done, and the bandit laid dead. I also felt regret, I didn't even try to capture him.

I was so worried about him escaping and getting help, I just attacked until it was over. After sitting for a few minutes catching my breath and replenishing my stamina and mana, I began the walk back toward my companions.

While I walked, in an effort to distract myself from my guilt, I reflected on the fight itself. I wondered if I had discovered a new skill or rather a subskill. I opened the blinking exclamation points at the bottom of my UI and was greeted by a wall of text. Many of my skills had gained levels. But the one I was hoping to find was at the very bottom.

Two-Handed Polearms	Level: 27	Experience: 6.38%
Current Damage Modifiers	Damage: +13.00	Critical Strike Chance: +1.30%
Subskill: Hamstring	Reduce Enemy Movement Speed: 50% Duration: 15 Seconds Enemy Receives Increased Damage: +6.75%	Skill Stamina Cost: 47

I learned a new subskill 'Hamstring'. It also explained why the ogre took extra damage. And I learned it by accident, which was kind of awesome. I learned 'Stealth' skill by doing something specific. It was good to know I could also learn subskills this way, considering all of my subskills so far, had been taught to me either by trainers or from reading books.

When I returned to my group, I saw there was now one more captured bandit. They also appeared to have already replenished their mana and stamina and were just waiting for me.

"I hope there is a wagon down the last tunnel, hauling the prisoners and . . . well, it won't be easy without one," stated Olaf, closing the chamber of his hand-cannon.

"We'll need a team of wagons. Not all of those merchants will be strong enough to walk under their own power," I replied. Logistics were never something I had to worry about before, but right now, they were a great deal of concern to me.

"Let's hope the last tunnel has what we need. For now, we need to deal with the self-proclaimed Bandit King," said Rose, standing up and walking toward the door.

"I wonder if that will be his actual title when we see him?" wondered Olaf aloud.

"Should we knock?" asked Baby.

"It's only polite," said Rose, a mischievous grin etched on her face. It wasn't so much a knock on the door, as it was a mail booted foot, kicking it open. She was first through the door, followed by me then Baby with Olaf and Micaela coming through last.

A quick look around the room revealed a few treasure chests sitting against the back wall, but otherwise, was only occupied by a single desk and a few chairs. Standing behind the desk was a male dark elf. He really was called the <Self-Proclaimed Bandit King Lvl

6> by the game. Not much of him was actually visible. He was covered from head to toe in brown leather with a few red accents, including a dark red mask covering his face. He held a short-curved sword in each hand and each blade had a green sheen to them.

"Watch for poison," warned Rose, moving toward the bandit cautiously.

"How dare you invade my base! You will all die for this . . . well, the man and ogres will die. My men will enjoy the ladies a little first. I have never had a fairy before," the Self-Proclaimed Bandit King said disgustingly. I could almost feel him leering behind his mask as he looked at Rose and Baby.

"Over my dead body," snarled Rose, moving fast to start the attack. She opened the fight with a 'Shield Slam' knocking the bandit back a step, preventing the double overhand strike he had aimed at her.

Once Rose had started the fight, I flipped over the desk to begin my own. I hit him with my first stack of 'Lesser Holy Fire' then tried to 'Hamstring' him immediately only for him to dodge with a flip sideways up on to the desk. He was knocked right off again, when he took a shot to the small of his back from one of Olaf's hand-cannons, taking a big chunk out of his health. More importantly, it told me he probably knew the 'Acrobatics' skill.

Rose took the opportunity to hit him with another 'Shield Slam' while he was on the ground, then followed up with a quick stab, piercing into his shoulder between the leather armor pieces. I figured it must have been the 'Pierce Defense' skill she learned this morning. The elf screaming in a combination of pain and anger suggested it worked. Further evidenced when the elf ignored Olaf, despite my fear he would pull aggro from Rose, instead the bandit attacked Rose with a renewed voracity.

I hit him with another stack of 'Lesser Holy Fire', then tried to 'Hamstring' him again, he rolled instinctively out of my way, much to my frustration. I was pleased though that when he rolled back to his feet he got a ball of fire to the face from Micaela's ax, Sundance.

"Fighting him in melee is no good," warned Rose. "Stay at range and burn him down with magic. I can barely hit him as it is."

I understood and took a step back. I renewed my stack of 'Lesser Holy Fire' on him then started casting 'Holy Smite'. I was able to get almost six casts before I had to renew 'Lesser Holy Fire'.

The fight appeared to be going well. Rose seemed to have him fully under control. So, obviously, I wasn't expecting to pull aggro. It came as a shock to me, when the bandit vanished, only to reappear behind me. He stabbed both of his blades into my back, sending my HP plummeting and rewarding me with two different poisons. One reducing healing received by 50% and the other preventing wounds from closing which increased bleed damage by 25%.

Thankfully, Olaf shot true, knocking the Self-Proclaimed Bandit King away. Less thankfully, he jerked the blades free.

"If you die, run back fast," shouted Baby, her focus on healing her sister. I took a second to glance at the party bars and Baby's mana bar was getting lower by the second.

Seeing the rate my HP was ticking down, it was probably inevitable I was going to die in this fight. If Rose was afflicted with the same poisons I was, then Baby couldn't afford to heal us both.

It also made me realize how stupid I was to have gone after bandits without preparing better. I should have bought antidotes to deal with poisons, as well as some potions.

I was arrogant to think this would be easy.

I cast a heal on myself to see how effective or ineffective it would be. Less than +50-HP. I was bleeding -35-HP per second and 'Lesser Heal' took 2.00 seconds to cast. If I did nothing but heal myself, I would still die.

Accepting my trip to respawn was inevitable, I did the only thing I could. I burned as much mana as possible as fast as possible on the guy before my inevitable death. Between my 'Lesser Holy Fire' and 'Holy Smite', I wrought a considerable amount of damage in the short time I had before death. He only had 3% of his total HP remaining, when death claimed me, but he was low enough, I knew my team would prevail.

<Self-Proclaimed Bandit King Lvl 6> does -35-HP damage to you with Bleeding Wounds.

<Self-Proclaimed Bandit King Lvl 6> has murdered you.

I wasn't instantly sent to respawn like I expected. Instead, I was now a ghost watching the end of the fight in muted greyscale. It was odd, I couldn't move or feel my limbs, I just, kind of, was.

I watched fascinated as the bandit's health continued to drop all the way to the 1% mark. I could hardly believe it when he moved to dodge a swing from Rose, his feet slipped. His head bounced off the table and he hit the ground unmoving, but with his health still showing 1%. I saw Rose's lips moving but heard nothing.

I was then greeted with another system message.

Combat has ended with no one in your party capable of reviving you. You will be automatically transported and revived at the nearest graveyard.

CHAPTER 23

It took me almost thirty minutes to run back to the caves to meet my friends again. A few wolves died along the way for a single point of experience each and a few more paws in my collection. The boar charm was also now at 96/100, just four more wolves to completion.

"You finished him okay?" I asked, reentering the room, even though I got to watch the fight to 1% I didn't get to see them actually win.

"Yeah, we got him," said Rose, looking rather proud of herself. "He did some weird cutscene at 1%, where he slipped and hit his head on the table, gaining a knocked out and captured status. It was weird, and felt kind of forced, to be honest," she explained. Then she pointed toward the rest of the waiting group, "Anyway, they decided we should wait for you before talking to him."

"You didn't exactly argue against it," added Olaf.

Rose simply shrugged, then walked over to the chained man. She nudged him with her boot and when he didn't respond, she kicked him in the gut, getting a gasping cough from the captured bandit, who seemed to be wide awake now.

"Wha . . . what is this?" the bandit asked slightly dazed at first but was quick to realize he was chained up. Suddenly much more awake, he began wildly thrashing against his bonds.

"You've been captured," I told him plainly. "Now, you're going to tell me who hired you to kill the Johnson's."

"I am not telling you a thing," the bandit protested defiantly, glaring at me. The effect was somewhat ruined by his lack of armor and mask or anything that would have been remotely threatening.

"Baby, do you have any more of that slow rot potion left?" I asked, looking at the floating fairy and winking.

"I'm out, but I do have some animal sterilization potion I made for that farmer a few months ago. Those poor bulls, I have never heard such pain from an animal before," Baby replied.

"That should work," I said, looking back at the bandit who was now pale as a ghost and sweating bullets. "What do you think? Will that work for you?"

"I do not know who hired me, not exactly anyway. He was always cloaked. All I know is that he has money, a lot of it. He paid us 10-gold to destroy the moonshine factory and kill the man who ran it," the bandit answered. It seemed he was more than happy to sing.

"That's a start, what else? Any detail would help," I prompted him.

"He wore armor . . . and . . . okay, maybe you will not believe me, but he had very sharp teeth, I only saw a reflection once but . . . I do not know anything else. Now let me go," the captured bandit pleaded.

"No, you're going with us back to town along with the rest of your captured men," I said clearly and with as much authority as my voice could muster.

"Not that, anything but that. He will kill me, he killed my men, the ones that were captured before. I will not stand a chance," the bandit pleaded.

"That won't happen again. You and your men will be better protected this time," I said, believing it to be true. I just couldn't see Sergeant Butters allowing that to happen again.

"I would rather die on my own terms," said the bandit, he chomped his mouth closed hard then clenched his jaw so hard I could see the muscles flex with effort. Then I heard a cracking sound and saw a poisoned debuff appear on the man followed by him dying a second later.

"Suicide?" I asked in disbelief.

Quest Alert: Shiny Delivery Service 5 (Recommended Level 4-5) - Completed
You have confirmed the trolls were indeed hired to kill Duke Johnson but more importantly to destroy the Moonshine. Question the leader of the Bandits to find out who hired him.
Reward: +500-Experience

"We didn't get any answers, how is that completed?" asked Micaela, her arms crossed and looking annoyed. Everyone looked annoyed, even as the next quest popped up.

Quest Alert: Shiny Delivery Service 6 (Recommended Level 4-5)		
Time to widen your search. Questioning the leader of the bandits revealed the presence of a shadowy figure behind everything. Perhaps it is time to speak to the Johnson's directly and find out what they know, after all, it was the Johnson's still the shadowy figure wanted to be destroyed.		
Reward: Experience		
Do you accept this quest?	Yes	No

"Of course, we accept," said Rose. "I want to know what is going on here."

"It is one big bloody mystery, isn't it?" asked Olaf, unable to keep the silly grin off his face.

"A real life, whodunnit," said Baby. "Is it wrong to be excited about this? I know the guy just killed himself, but this is one heck of a mystery."

"It's not wrong to enjoy the game, it's why we're all here. Yeah, it sucks this guy killed himself, but I have to agree, this is getting interesting," I agreed with the sentiment. I had my theories about who was behind this, but they were just theories, nothing I could prove yet.

"Alright, that's enough lollygagging around here. Let's deal with the last tunnel and see about getting everyone and everything out of here," Rose stated before turning back the way we came to lead us back out. There was nothing more to be accomplished here, so I followed her as did everyone else.

The last tunnel was as narrow as the first, but not nearly as long. We found the last three bandits guarding the entrance to a large cavern. They were nothing special and were easily taken out. The room behind them was their stash room. On the left side of the cavern were half a dozen carts and penned oxen to go with them. The rest of the cavern was filled with crates of stolen merchandise, far too much to transport with just six carts.

"Okay, Olaf and Micaela, can you take two of the carts and oxen down the left passage, free the citizens, load anyone who can't walk into the cart," I said.

"We can do that, I've got the key. Baby, why don't you come with us, maybe you can heal them some more," suggested Olaf.

"Rose, you and I will take a cart and start collecting the bodies and captured bandits," I said.

Rose only nodded her agreement.

It took almost an hour for Rose and me to collect and load the dead and the prisoners. Some of them decided they wanted to be uncooperative and had to be subdued again. Thankfully, they were easy to subdue as they were still fairly beaten down.

Shockingly, the Self-Proclaimed Bandit King's body was missing, as was the bag of gold we had been left sitting on the desk. Rose was definitely peeved to have been played so well by the bandit. I thought he might have actually deserved his title of 'Bandit King' if he was willing to fake his own death to escape.

After that, we used the last three carts to load up as much of the goods as we could, including the three treasure chests from the room of the Self-Proclaimed Bandit King.

Returning to town was slow and required frequent rest breaks for the former captives but eventually, we returned to town, causing a massive uproar in the process.

"What is the meaning of all this?" demanded Lieutenant Graves, he was stomping down the street toward us at the main gate.

"Run, go get Sergeant Butter," I whispered to Gavin, who nodded and took off at a run.

"I said, what is the meaning of all this?" Graves demanded louder.

"The end of your bandit problem," I answered, meeting the glare of Graves. He was just as ornery as the first time I had met him, maybe more so.

"We do not have a bandit problem," Graves insisted, glaring right back at me.

"Not anymore you don't," Rose stood next to me, adding her own glare at Graves.

"We were asked by Mayor Semper to look into the missing caravans and merchants. If there isn't a bandit problem, why would he ask us to look into it?" asked Olaf, adding his own glare at the lieutenant.

The lieutenant snarled and seemed to consider what he'd say next. After a moment of glaring at me, he relented. "I see, very well. Guards, execute the bandits immediately. I will not have such unlawful men running rampant in my province."

"Sergeant Butters," I yelled loudly, seeing him coming down the road, he was wearing full armor, which was unusual for him. For that matter, there was something off about this entire situation.

"What are you yelling for?" Sergeant Butters asked, coming closer. He took a moment to observe the situation before grinning. "I knew it was a good idea when I recommended it to the mayor, having you look into the bandit issue certainly worked out. I take it the dead men and those in shackles are the ones responsible?"

"Yes, they are Sergeant Butters. I was just informing Lieutenant Graves here about the quest the mayor set us. He just ordered they all be executed," I explained.

"That does not sound right. The procedure is to bind them in the stocks and for a magistrate to be summoned from Root City, so he can issue sentencing. It also gives a runner time to go to all the various districts in Root City, to check all the bounty offices," said Sergeant Butters, rubbing his chin.

"I am in charge of this garrison. I have to say when we do not have sufficient resources to hold so many prisoners," Graves stated, sounding angrier if that was even possible.

"It's eleven men, we can easily manage so few," countered the sergeant easily. I could see he was also getting the feeling was something off.

"As an officer, if Graves ignores the law, wouldn't that be considered treason?" asked Olaf.

"I do believe that is an offense worthy of a court-martial," added Micaela.

I felt a shift in the air. Something felt dark and sinister. I looked again at the Lieutenant, his head was lowered, and his eyes shadowed. He looked to be straining physically. "Heh," he chuckled hollowly. "You insignificant meat sacks. You all would have shared in my immortality, now, I will kill you all, slowly, painfully. Tonight, I shall feast upon your corpses."

That deep guttural voice sounded all too familiar, the shadowy figure from the cave.

I attacked, leaping forward and thrusting my spear toward his throat. Graves didn't flinch. He simply sidestepped my attack, his clawed hand striking out, rending through my flesh from hip to shoulder, my HP bar plummeted by half from just one attack, while my body was sent flying. When I hit the side of a building another chunk of my HP dropped, and I received a 'Dazed' debuff.

"Stop him!" someone shouted from nearby. I saw Rose, at least I think it was Rose. Anyway, I saw someone run forward and swing a shield, only for the Lieutenant to kick him or her and send him or her sprawling across the dirt.

My HP was restored a moment later and the stun cleared up a moment after that. It was chaos. The sergeant and his men were trying and failing to fight off the Lieutenant, which was odd, as they were all higher level than him.

And then there was the lieutenant. Graves had transformed, no longer was he a man but a combination of wolf and man. He had to be at least 10-feet tall now with the way he towered over even Olaf and Micaela. The armor he previously wore on his torso and arms laid broken at his feet. His armor was replaced by thick fur, black as night covering arms and chest, while his snout was filled with razor-sharp teeth. I finally realized what he was, a werewolf and a powerful one it seemed with how he was tossing the men around. Watching even briefly, I saw his HP drop slightly only to refill near instantly. No matter how they hurt him, he continued to regenerate any damage.

I was quick to rejoin the fight, lighting him up with 'Lesser Holy Fire' and charging ahead with my spear enhanced with 'Lesser Holy Imbuement' at the ready.

"Insignificant worms!" Graves shouted angrily, as he sent another guard rolling across the ground.

I slid past one of his large arcing cleaves, popping up behind Graves and attacking with a 'Hamstring' hoping to slow him down at least a little. It seemed to be working. Then two-seconds later the debuff fell off with the damage healed. Then Rose died followed by Olaf and Micaela a minute later, they were almost at full health, then they weren't. Still, I attacked, stabbing and using 'Hamstring' as much as I could. This guy was probably going to wipe us all out and we weren't making a dent on him.

I was caught by a backhand a moment later from the beast hitting me for -453-HP damage but that didn't stop me for long. I was back to attacking as hard as I could.

Suddenly, the Lieutenant froze and sniffed the air, ignoring everyone attacking him. I heard something shatter overhead drawing my gaze. Liquid began showering over everyone. It did nothing to me or any of the guards, but the Lieutenant, he yelped painfully. He immediately barreled through the soldiers, knocking them from his path as he fled fast past the gates and into the forest, quickly vanishing from sight.

"Werewolves, a bunch of wimps," said the voice of someone I just wasn't expecting to see. It was Mary Johnson, the farmer's wife. She was holding a jar of moonshine in one hand and a pistol in the other while her husband held the open crate just behind her. She put the unopened bottle back in the crate and tucked the pistol into her belt behind her back. "Bye-bye, you and your friends, come meet us in the Town hall once you get everything sorted here."

Her statement left me completely perplexed, but I couldn't find a reason to argue with her.

"What did we miss?" asked Rose running toward us from the direction of the graveyard with Olaf and Micaela right next to her.

"Rosie," cried Baby, the little missile crashed into her sister. "I'm so sorry! I tried to get a heal on you, but you just dropped so fast."

"It's fine Sis, no harm, no foul. I'm alive see," Rose reassured her sister.

"But I failed," protested Baby. "I'm a terrible healer."

"Baby, you're a great healer, that was just an unfair situation. Whatever that event was, it was meant to be unwinnable," I said, trying to help reassure the childlike healer. And it probably was. I quickly explained everything to my friends regarding the Johnson's farm, the moonshine quest series, the murdered guard and how it all fit together.

"Talk about a complex quest chain. And so many varied paths all leading to the same conclusion," said Olaf thoughtfully before exclaiming, "God, I love this game."

"No kidding," said Micaela. "And to think, the forums say nothing about any grand quests, at least none of them we've been reading."

"And when you turn in these quests you're going to get a huge dump of experience points too," said Baby.

"We all will," said Rose, sounding a little giddy and excited.

"Probably. I imagine we'll also get another quest for each of the chains to stop Lieutenant Graves," I added.

"Okay, let's hurry up and get everything here sorted out," said Rose.

It took a while for everything to get settled. Sergeant Butters and his men took the bandits into custody as well as the stolen property while Trinico looked after the injured merchants and guards alike, many of their families had emerged to bring their loved one's home. Once all the people were sorted and Trinico was busy seeing to the wounded, the sergeant led us to the Town hall.

"What is going on here?" asked Rose first, entering the mayor's office. The mayor and his wife were there as were Duke and Mary Johnson.

Rose was answered by Mary shoving the bottle of moonshine into her hands. "Have a sip. It should calm you down."

Rose looked confused then looked at me for some reason. "What?" I asked with a shrug of my shoulders.

Rose rolled her eyes and took a sip only to cough viciously afterward. She then passed the jar on.

"I suppose we owe you an explanation," said the mayor, sounding a little guilty. "This town is cursed."

"How do you mean?" I asked. Was he referring to the wolves?

"Every few generations a werewolf comes to this town, we do not know why but one always comes. He brings chaos and danger to all of us then disappears suddenly and without explanation," explained Homer solemnly. "When that troll died, rather when the moonshine distillery was burned we suspected one may have returned. It was only confirmed after Guard Davies was killed."

"So, you knew he was killed by a werewolf?" I asked, looking at Sergeant Butters.

"Yes," the mayor nodded solemnly. "But we didn't know who. There was no sense in creating a panic."

"And the plan, to bring back Guard Davies and question him, was to find out who did it?" I asked.

"Yes, but we also needed to know why he allowed himself to be killed," added the sergeant. "Still need to know, as a matter of fact. We also need to find out if he has any other information we can use."

"I see, but he fled, does that mean he's gone for a few generations again?" I asked.

"I hope so," said Mary. "If not, I can only hope we have enough moonshine to encourage him to stay away."

"Why moonshine?" asked Rose curiously.

"We do not know the exact reason. All we know, is it works. It hurts him and that is enough for us," explained Mary, causing me more confusion. The way she was acting now, was much different from the kind, matronly woman, I had gotten to know.

"Okay, second, Lieutenant Graves was acting fishy about the alcohol from the start from what we gathered in town. How did no one put together he might be this werewolf?" asked Olaf, taking a small sip of the moonshine then passing it along.

"We suspected, but there was no proof. Why do you think I asked you all to look into him once you realized he was missing during the raid on the town?" asked Sergeant Butters. "Still, you did an excellent job getting him to reveal himself."

"So now what?" asked Baby.

"We still need more information. I am hoping Guard Davies will know more and can share with us. As for Graves, hopefully, he's gone, but I do not particularly like his parting threat, saying he was going to share his immortality with us," the mayor answered, worry evident in his voice.

446

"It will be another week before Davies can tell us anything," added the sergeant. "Nothing to do but wait."

"I don't care for long waits," growled Rose.

"Don't worry too much Rose. I'm sure Bye-bye will find plenty of trouble for us to get into over the next week," said Micaela, grinning mischievously.

"Anyway, I am afraid we do not know much more. I am truly sorry we did not warn you of the danger sooner," said the mayor contritely, his head bowed.

I frowned, it wasn't exactly what I suspected, but I definitely felt Graves was involved. "I understand why you didn't. I don't think I would have done the same, but I understand."

I turned to leave when I was called back by Duke. "Wait a moment, all of you. My wife and I owe you a great debt of gratitude. You found the beast threatening this town, something my wife's family has always been responsible for. The least we can do is repay you for your help."

Quest Alert: Shiny Delivery Service 5-7 (Recommended Level 4-5) - Completed
Time to widen your search. Questioning the leader of the bandits revealed the presence of a shadowy figure behind everything. Perhaps it is time to speak to the Johnson's directly and find out what they know.
Reward: +1,500-Experience

"And if you would be willing. Can we ask you to find Graves and destroy him once and for all?" requested Duke.

Quest Alert: Shiny Delivery Service 8 (Recommended Level 5-7)		
Hunt down and stop Graves . . . permanently.		
Reward: Experience, 5-Gold, Hidden		
Do you accept this Quest?	Yes	No

"You bet we will," said Micaela, happy to accept the quest.

"Regarding my request," started Mayor Simper. "I saw you returned with a large amount of the stolen goods. Did you want to submit that as the end of it?"

"Not yet, we're going back tomorrow for the rest of it," answered Olaf.

"Very well," said the mayor.

"It has been a busy day for you, I imagine you want to clean up and get some dinner," said Margie.

"Best idea ever," said Micaela excitedly.

"I overheard some of the people you rescued say they wanted to speak with you," added the sergeant.

"We'll check in with them now," I volunteered, it was more quests to be turned in.

We were actually greeted as soon as we stepped out of the Town hall. It was the Taylor family, mother, and son supporting a rather frail-looking man, I assumed was her missing husband. Standing next to them was the old man with the blue eyes and dirty beard, who asked us to rescue them all.

"Bye-bye," said Mrs. Taylor, fresh tears in her eyes.

"Mrs. Taylor, I'm glad to see your husband was one of those we rescued," I started before focusing on Mr. Taylor. "Will you be alright?"

"With time and some of the wife's cooking I will be," Mr. Taylor replied. "We want to thank you, all of you. Please take these cloaks and use them to protect others and yourselves."

Mrs. Taylor then handed each of us a cloak, mine was white, as was Baby's. Micaela got a pink cloak, matching her hair, while Olaf's was mottled greens and browns. And finally, Rose's was blood red, matching her hair.

Quest Alert: Find the Missing Taylor (Recommended Level 4-6) - Completed
Mrs. Taylor has requested your help in finding her missing husband.
Reward: +200-Experience, All-Weather Cloak

Not much experience but the cloak was the real prize for this quest.

All-Weather Cloak (White) – A cloak designed to protect from the elements. Provides warmth in cold climates. Provides cooling in hot climates. Provides dryness in wet climates.

No armor but it didn't need it. This was actually a very useful item. While I haven't experienced any inclement weather of concern yet, I knew I would. The World Tree was far too big not to experience it at some point.

"Thank you, it's very generous of you," I said. My thanks were quickly echoed by the others. They departed right after, eager to get Mr. Taylor home to rest and recover.

"Now then, I also want to thank you for your help. Name's Barnum, I own the 'Leather Emporium' across from the butchers," he pointed down the street. I couldn't help but notice it was in the direction of the closed leatherworker's shop. "Come by tomorrow and I'll make you each something special."

"We'll be sure to stop by," I replied.

"Definitely," added Micaela grinning.

"See you then. For now, I have a razor and a hot bath calling my name," Barnum said, giving us a nod of acknowledgment before going.

"Okay, so that's one more quest turned in. What else have we got?" asked Olaf.

"We still have 'Missing in Action 3', but it can't be done for another week. That's the quest Sergeant Butters mentioned. 'Breaking the Curse of the Wolves 1', I haven't even started yet, but I'm sure is related to everything going on. I need to read through the town history. 'Bandit Round-up', we'll turn in after we finish clearing out those caves tomorrow. And 'The investigation of Lieutenant Graves 1', which I thought we would have completed after tonight's events. We still need to do some more digging, I guess we still need to break into his home," I listed off the pending quests.

"Plus, all the training we can do, it's going to be a busy week," said Rose thoughtfully.

"Okay, so Mic and I are with you. I know I said I wanted to try to mine every other day, but this quest chain is just too good to pass up. So, let's get through this week. We can mine all next week after this chain is resolved," Olaf added.

"Rose and I are in too," said Baby, taking a nervous glance at her sister. She looked to be checking if Rose would agree, who nodded subtly, causing Baby's shoulders to sag in relief.

"So, dinner then reading. I have to finish one of those books tonight," I said.

"Hey Baby, I thought fairies could only wear a dress. How come you got a cloak?" asked Micaela, shifting the conversation.

"That's the only armor I can wear. Cloaks aren't armor, they are considered an accessory. I can wear accessories and charms, no problem. It would be too cruel, if a lady couldn't accessorize to her heart's content. Just no armor, except for the dress, which doesn't offer much armor, to be honest. Not that I need it since I can fly, and my magic shielding gets to be powerful too," Baby explained.

"How come you never cast any shields on me then?" asked Rose, looking indignantly at her sister.

Baby blushed then mumbled. "I haven't learned one yet."

"Why not?" asked Rose.

"I get my first one at level 10," Baby replied sheepishly.

"How do you know that?" Rose asked.

"It's what the forums said," Baby replied.

"And you believed them?" asked Rose. "If you hadn't noticed, they lie a lot."

"Ask Trini tomorrow," I interrupted before things could escalate. Apparently, it was my turn to play peacekeeper.

"I will," said Baby, immediately agreeing and trying to avoid an argument with her sister. I was starting to get the impression, Rose got a kick out of arguing, regardless of the reason.

Dogson welcomed us back with a pint and a healthy plate of food, much to our enjoyment. Dinner was quiet, but now that all the adrenaline had worn off, and we had time to think about the day, we just didn't feel up to talking much.

"I'm going to go get my shower and call it an early night," I said, excusing myself first.

"Night, Bye-bye, see you tomorrow, mate," said Olaf.

"Don't drown," said Rose, earning a strange look from our friends.

"You do care," said Baby teasingly.

Rose blushed and protested. "Not even."

I could only roll my eyes. "See you all tomorrow."

I took my shower and returned to my room. I know I had to read and finish one of those books tonight, but I also knew I wasn't going to be able to concentrate on it. Instead, I pulled out my journal and writing tools and began to write. Filling in the details and drawing the pictures. Letting what I had found to be cathartic, take shape.

When it was done I felt better, just as I had before. I took a few minutes afterward to draw a map of the caves we'd explored gaining another level to my cartography skill. I don't think it's normal for crafting skills to level as easily as mine have, but then again, they weren't the most complex skills. I suppose I shouldn't complain about it not being harder, as that would be foolish.

Finally, I took out the book 'Surviving the Greater Outdoors', sitting down to read. It was actually a pleasant book to get through. It was a firsthand account of a man camping and surviving for a year, away from people. It went through his trials, creating a new tent from tree branches and leaves, cooking food over a campfire and some of the seasonings he collected in nature. Before I knew it, it was nearly midnight and the book was finished. I also got an interesting skill and several subskills.

Campsite Management	Level: 1	Experience: 0.00%
Subskill: Tent Construction	Skill Effect (Passive): Enables you to construct a rudimentary tent.	
Subskill: Campfire Construction	Skill Effect (Passive): Enables you to start a safe campfire.	
Subskill: Campfire Cooking	Skill Effect (Passive): Enables you to cook food over a campfire and add 1 seasoning.	
Subskill: Campsite Perimeter	Skill Effect (Passive): Enables you to establish a campsite perimeter with a rudimentary warning system.	

CHAPTER 24

"Morning Sergeant Butters," I greeted him as I arrived at the training ring.

"Bye-bye, last to arrive today. Not getting lazy on me, are you?" he asked.

"Not at all, I was up late reading, so I slept in this morning," I explained myself. No rooster today thankfully, and hopefully, it wouldn't be the last time.

"So, what do you want to work on today?" the sergeant asked.

"I need a skill or two for 'Two-Handed Polearms'," I answered.

"Come with me," the sergeant ordered.

I was quick to follow him, first to his weapons rack where he grabbed his spear, then to a set of practice dummies.

"Okay, the 'Power Thrust' is a power attack. You are going to thrust your spear forward with as much power as you can muster. Your goal is to knock over the dummy," Sergeant Butters explained.

I watched then as he took just a step forward thrust the spear hard into the center of the dummy causing it to bend back hitting the ground then spring back up. The sergeant dodged the spring back moving away quickly.

"That's step one. This is step two," Sergeant Butters instructed. He attacked again, thrusting hard into the chest of dummy knocking it over, he then flipped over the downed dummy before it could spring back up. He attacked again, this time rolling away from the springy dummy as it came back. There was no order or pattern, just attack then use 'Acrobatics' to dodge the counterattack.

"That is the first thing I have got for you today," the sergeant said, then motioned for me to follow him. He led me to a series of hanging sandbags suspended from a metal bar.

"Next is 'Impale', it is pretty simple, stab and twist to inflict a bleeding wound." Sergeant Butters explained before stabbing one of the bags, the spear moved very fast to penetrate the bag, easily cutting into it. He then twisted the spear and jerked it back, sand came pouring out of the wound in the bag.

"I will leave you to it," said Sergeant Butters. "I should go check on the others."

"Thank you," I said. Since I was already here, I started with the 'Impale'. It wasn't as easy as it looked and as sharp as my spear was, I just wasn't piercing the sandbag. I would hit the bag causing it to swing backward. If the sergeant was teaching me this, I was strong enough to do it or he wouldn't bother, same for speed.

That meant it was in my technique.

I took a moment to reflect on his attack, it was fast, really fast. I had been trying to attack normally, which was fast, but not as fast as what the sergeant just showed me.

I tried attacking again, this time focusing on speed. A small hole in the sandbag was my reward. The bag swung back but it had a tiny hole in it now. It meant I was on the right path.

I struck again, a slightly larger hole. I struck a third time, focusing on my initial movement, where speed began. Success! My spear penetrated into the bag, I twisted the spear and yanked it back causing sand to pour from the wound. The hole wasn't as big as the one the sergeant made, but it was a good start.

Ten tries later I saw an Exclamation point appear in my peripheral, so I checked the system message.

You've learned 'Two-Handed Polearm' subskill 'Impale'.

454

Two-Handed Polearms	Level: 33	Experience: 6.38%
Current Damage Modifiers	Damage: +16.50	Critical Strike Chance: +1.65%
Subskill: Hamstring	Reduce Enemy Movement and Attack Speed: 50% Duration: 15 Seconds Enemy Receives Increased Damage: +8.25%	Skill Stamina Cost: 48
Subskill: Impale	Damage: 10-15 Bleed Effect: 2 Damage per Second Duration: 10 Seconds	Skill Stamina Cost: 51

Nice! I pulled out my canteen and took a few drinks to top off my stamina, as I walked back to the first dummy the sergeant showed me.

The dummy seemed to be set atop a large metal spring which explained why it would bounce back. The next question was how much strength I would need to knock it over. I gave it a tentative poke, but it didn't budge. I pushed a little harder, still getting nowhere. I struck it with a normal attack and it finally moved about an inch backward.

Power seemed to be the operative word for this skill. I struck again, this time trying to put more muscle behind it, causing it to rock back a good six inches. I needed more power. Not quite a running start but I needed to put more of my body into the strike. I took a step away from the dummy, gripped my spear with both hands, my right hand across my body and gripping the spear from below and closest to the spear tip while my left hand, my dominant hand, was cocked back gripping from the top closer to the butt of the shaft. I tried to visualize how the sergeant had done it, trying to mentally mirror his body. His knees were slightly bent, his right leg was back, ready to explode forward. I stepped my left leg back. When he attacked, his right leg stepped forward, not exactly lunging but it started the movement. The rest of his body followed that step, twisting slightly at the hips as his arms stabbed the spear forward.

I stepped forward with my left leg and the rest of me followed. My spear struck with such force I thought I was going to drop it for a second. There was second popping sound as the dummy hit the dirt. I was so preoccupied with my success I forgot about the counterstrike right up until the dummy was an inch away from head-butting me. My eyes closed on reflex in anticipation of the strike.

I opened my eyes sometime later, staring at the sky above me and my forehead throbbing in pain. Rotten dummy, rotten dazed debuff.

Eventually, I clambered back to my feet to face the dummy again. I tried the attack again, this time I remembered to get away before the counterstrike got to me. I did this a few more times before I attempted adding in the 'Acrobatics' aspect.

I flipped over it successfully my first try. The thing about the springs though is they bend back, even though it wasn't as far on the second recoil, it was enough to ring my bell again. Rotten dummy, rotten daze debuff . . . wait, I just thought that didn't I? Rotten dummy, rotten daze debuff.

When my head cleared I tried again. Strike, flip over, strike, dive to the left, strike, roll to the left. It took a while to get used to it, especially when my strike wasn't always powerful enough to knock the thing over, Usually, it was because I didn't step into the attack properly. Once I got into the habit, it became considerably easier.

Eventually, the game was satisfied I had learned the skill and rewarded me with a waiting system message, advising me of a few more skill levels and the new subskill.

Two-Handed Polearms	Level: 35	Experience: 57.32%
Current Damage Modifiers	Damage: +17.50	Critical Strike Chance: +1.75%
Subskill: Hamstring	Reduce Enemy Movement and Attack Speed: 50% Enemy Receives Increased Damage: +8.75% Duration: 15 Seconds	Skill Stamina Cost: 50
Subskill: Impale	Damage: 10-15 Bleed Effect: 2 Damage per Second Duration: 10 Seconds	Skill Stamina Cost: 55
Subskill: Power Thrust	Damage: +35.00 Chance to Stun: 10%	Skill Stamina Cost: 85

That was an expensive skill but so much extra damage. I checked the game clock, I had barely been here an hour and already I learned two skills, or rather subskills. I don't know if that surprised me more or the fact that Sergeant Butters didn't show up as soon as I finished learning them.

I looked around and found him working with Rose on something without any weapons or even a stance of any kind I could see. Were they just talking?

"If you do not believe what you are saying, no one else will either," instructed the sergeant.

"I do believe them," Rose protested.

"But you have yet to make me believe them," Sergeant Butters replied. "Take a break, clear your head. You can do this. I know you can."

"Fine," Rose said hotly, turning and stalking off.

"Everything okay?" I asked.

"Just fine," replied the sergeant smiling. "Miss Rose asked to learn more of the 'Command' warrior spells."

"What's that?" I asked.

"All classes, including warriors, have their own unique magic spells and abilities. They fall under a magical subclass called 'Command'," the sergeant explained.

"Can I learn?" I asked. I am a Warrior Priest, doesn't the warrior part make me eligible?

"You can try but I doubt it. Your ability as a warrior is more akin to that of a paladin. Still, if you want to try, I am sure Rose would appreciate the company," suggested the sergeant.

"Clearly, you don't know her very well," I joked. Truthfully, I had yet to figure her out. The skills I had applied in the game to make friends with the NPC's and even Olaf and Micaela to an extent didn't seem to work on her. Plus, we seemed to regularly rub each other the wrong way, somehow getting under each other's skin without much effort. "As long as she's okay with it, I don't mind trying."

"Well, have a seat. I will go check on the others and come back. Let Rose know for me," requested the sergeant, moving off to check on the others.

I ended up laying down in the grass and looking up at the clouds. The environmental settings were pleasant in this province. It seemed every day was sunny and warm. I had yet to encounter rain or heavy winds. That might have been because it was a starter province or maybe it was just the time of year for this kind of weather.

"What are you doing here?" asked Rose, sounding clearly frustrated.

"I asked Sergeant Butters if I could try to learn 'Command' too," I replied without getting up.

"And why do you want to learn 'Command' spells?" Rose questioned.

"Well, I figure, even just learning taunt might make things easier for our group," I answered, seeing and hearing the tension in Rose. She clicked her tongue in annoyance but didn't argue against it.

"It's hard," Rose said after a minute of silence.

"Why's that?" I asked.

"You channel mana to your throat, then speak. Your intent behind the words make them work," she explained. "But if your intent isn't clear then you get nothing."

"So, how did you learn to 'taunt'?" I asked. She said she taught herself, I was curious how.

"I just had to," Rose answered as if it would explain everything.

"Why?" I asked, prodding her to explain more about it, to which Rose growled in response.

"You don't have to get angry with me. I'm just curious. If you don't want to tell me, then don't," I stated.

"My sister was about to be chomped by one of those condors. Even though she is levels above me, she is physically weak. Weak enough that one of those birds could easily make a snack out of her, despite her level. She would have died, so I tried to use it, tried what I read in the forums and it worked," Rose explained.

"That's cool," I said honestly.

"Anyway, now I'm struggling to learn another 'Command' skill," she admitted.

"Which one are you trying to learn?" I asked.

"It's called 'Courage', it can remove mental effects from my group, effects like 'Fear' or 'Daze'," she explained.

"I wonder if someone can put a 'Fear' or 'Daze' on Baby for you," I suggested.

"Don't you dare," threatened Rose.

"I was just an idea. You learned it before because you wanted to protect your sister, right?" I asked.

"I'm not putting her in danger, just so I can learn a new 'Command' spell," replied Rose.

"Okay," I replied. "Maybe you need a reason to use it, not just the intent of what you want to do."

"That is a good idea," interrupted Sergeant Butters, returning from his rounds.

"Whatever, let's just try it," said Rose reluctantly.

"Focus your mana to your throat," coached the sergeant. "Now, think about what you want to do. Think about who you want to give 'Courage' to. Now, speak."

"Courage," Rose said plainly, but I felt a wave of something wash over me, somehow making me feel braver as if nothing could hurt me.

"Perfect, well done," said the sergeant.

"I . . . I learned it," whispered Rose stunned. Then a little louder, "I actually learned it. I've been struggling with that spell for two hours and I finally learned it. Yes!"

Then Rose stunned me. She gave me a hug. When she realized what she did, she punched me. "Don't touch me ever again," she warned me before stalking off.

"What was that?" I complained, rubbing my now sore jaw.

"Women, son, women," answered the sergeant. "Anyway, you want to try?"

"Sure," I replied. I knew what I wanted and had an idea how to do it. I channeled mana to my throat then I pictured Sergeant Butters attacking me and no one else.

"Taunt," I said.

Hindsight being what it was, I should have known better than to 'Taunt' a level 38 Knight.

<Sergeant Butters Lvl 38> does -3527-HP damage to you with a Punch.

<Sergeant Butters Lvl 38> has killed you in a training area. You will be resurrected momentarily.

"Well that was stupid," I said as soon as I was revived.

"Yes, it was stupid, what were you thinking," demanded the sergeant.

"That you would resist," I snarked back.

"Moron. Did you at least learn the spell?" the sergeant asked. "It does not always take even if you are successful."

I checked my system messages.

You've learned the Law and Order spell 'Order: Taunt'

Order: Taunt	Level: N/A	Experience: N/A
Spell Duration: 30 seconds	Spell Cast Speed: Instant	Spell Mana Cost: 10
Spell Effect (Active): For the next thirty seconds the target of your taunt will attack only you.		

"Yes, I learned it . . . sort of," I replied.

"What do you mean 'sort of?'" asked the sergeant.

"It is called a 'Law and Order' spell, specifically 'Order: Taunt'," I explained.

"Interesting, very interesting. We will have to experiment and see if you can learn any other 'Command' spells that fall within your spell subclass," the sergeant added.

"Who resurrected me?" I asked, as an afterthought.

"Guard Pickler, he is a Squire Paladin of the Goddess Freya," Sergeant Butters answered. "You are lucky he had just arrived for training."

That was interesting. I didn't realize the guards were anything but warriors. I guess it made sense. You needed archers and healers or medics as much as you needed warriors.

"Anyway, Olaf will probably stay in the firing range all day. I gave him a few different skills to work on, one more for 'One-Handed Artillery' and one for 'Duel-wielding Artillery' skills. Micaela said something about going out for another spirit or two. Baby has been training with Trini all morning. Rose disappeared, not sure where she went. Also, my men are here for their daily training, so you had best get moving to see Trini or she will tan both of our hides," warned Sergeant Butters.

"Sure thing, Sergeant Butters, I'll see you tomorrow for more of . . . whatever," I said.

"Think about what else you want to learn from me. I have taught you all I can for 'One-Handed Polearms', 'Two-Handed Polearms', and 'Phalanx Shield'. Anything else, you will need a higher-level trainer than me," stated the sergeant.

Wait, what was that? Did he just cut me off? Did the game put a limiter on the skills to two per weapon from the starting province trainer? What about Trinico then? Could she only teach two spells? If that was the case, then the only thing left in this town for me to learn was the skill books.

I'd definitely be asking Trini.

462

"Do not lose faith though, I can still teach you warrior skills, if you are able to," Sergeant Butters must have seen the frown I now felt on my face. "Anyway, get a move on," he ushered me off, then turned to his assembled guards and started barking orders.

I could only shake my head, feeling a little sympathy for them. They had lost three of their number last night, from the events with Graves. I am sure the sergeant would be putting them through their paces today.

I stopped in quickly to return the book to the mayor, then quickly headed to meet Trinico only to find the Temple empty, aside from a meditating Micaela. I say meditating because that's what it looks like, but it was actually just her, being off in the spirit world doing who knows what.

Having a little time on my hands, I went to Issara's altar again, dropping to a knee, I looked at her visage. I was struck by how much her image resonated with me. Since the first time I spoke with her, I have felt a connection to this being I've never felt before. I've never been a religious person in the real world, and I don't know if I'm religious in this one. I know the Goddess Issara is a computer program playing the role of a Goddess. But, after a rocky start, she had earned my loyalty in this world, not absolute loyalty but . . .

"Hello," I said, sort of expecting an answer, but not counting on it. I wasn't surprised when she stayed silent. "Yesterday was tough. I know this world is . . . different, but I'm struggling with what we had to do yesterday. Yes, it was justice, absolutely, but it still felt . . . wrong to end so many lives."

"I know there is nothing you can do about it, and I guess I'm not sure why I'm telling you, but . . . I don't know, I just wanted to say something to you. I wanted to know if you were okay with what I did or if you were disappointed in me or if you even cared," I stated.

"I know it was necessary and I did what was right, but I'm still struggling with it," I stated, feeling uncomfortable talking like that. I didn't usually express my feelings to anyone.

Our world is not your world. Justice is much more elusive and often must be obtained at the tip of the sword or spear, as in your case. I appreciate that you struggle with your actions, it makes me more certain than ever, you were the right choice. Continue to defend life and Justice, and I will never be disappointed in you, my one and only servant.

Okay, so she was listening, and I felt better that she empathized with my struggles. This was a good decision, taking a moment to speak to her.

"Thank you," I said, after a moment of silence. I then stood and headed for the exit.

"Ah, Bye-bye, finally arrived, have you?" asked Trinico, entering the temple with an exhausted-looking Baby, floating wobbly behind her.

"I wasn't late this time," I defended instantly. I was on time, less than ten minutes from the time I left the training ring.

"And yet, you took time to pray, instead of coming around back to find me," said Trinico, her ever serene smile in place.

I wanted to snark back but held my tongue. I had things to do today if I was going to get everything accomplished, I couldn't waste time arguing with Trinico over something so minute.

"So, what can I do for you?" Trinico asked.

"I was hoping you might be able to teach me a new spell or two," I answered.

"And do you know what you want to learn?" asked the priestess.

"I died to poison yesterday. I need a spell to deal with such things," I replied. That was only the second time I had died, since

464

coming to the game. Worse, it was completely avoidable. None of us thought to bring antidotes and a number of other useful supplies. There is no one person to blame for this oversight as we were all guilty of it. Now, we had to remedy the situation.

"Hmm, a 'Holy Cleanse' spell should suit you, assuming you are capable of learning," said Trinico thoughtfully. "I will return in a moment. Baby, would you benefit from this spell, too?"

"Yes, thank you," said the tired fairy. As Trinico walked away Baby fluttered over to one of the pews and dropped unceremoniously onto it. "So tired," she complained.

"Been there before," I commented. Then I took a seat next to her.

"How was your training?" asked Baby. "And where is my sister?"

"Training was fine, I learned a couple skills," I answered. "And your sister stormed off, I have no idea where she went."

"What did you do?" asked Baby, giving me a look of exasperation.

"Why did I have to do anything?" I asked. "How do you know it wasn't her fault? Which it was."

"Okay, what did she do?" Baby asked.

I could see Baby didn't believe me, but I answered her anyway. "She was struggling with a new 'Command' spell. I talked it through with her and made a suggestion."

"It didn't work?" asked Baby.

"No, it worked fine, and she learned the spell. Anyway, in her joy, she hugged me, then punched me and warned me to never touch her again. Then she stormed off," I answered, explaining what happened. Despite knowing what happened, I still could not puzzle out why it happened.

Baby just giggled, confusing me even more.

"I'll never understand women. I never understood them when I was in school either," I groused. "And stop laughing at me."

Baby's giggle morphed into peels of childlike laughter. Ugh, that cuteness was quite the ruthless weapon.

"Bye-bye, stop torturing that poor fairy and read this," said Trinico, walking toward us with two scrolls in hand.

Spell: Holy Cleanse – Teaches the Holy Cleanse spell		
Would you like to learn 'Holy Cleanse'?	Yes	No

"Thank you," I said, accepting the spell scroll which crumbled to dust a moment later. I checked my system message

You've learned the Holy Spell 'Holy Cleanse'

Holy Cleanse	Level: 1	Experience: 0.00%
Conditions Removed: 1	Spell Cast Speed: Instant	Spell Mana Cost: 50
Spell Effect (Active): Remove 1 poison or disease from afflicted target.		

"Is there anything else I can assist you with today?" asked Trinico.

"No, I'm good," groaned Baby, not moving from her spot on the pew.

"Actually, I could use a little more assistance. Sergeant Butters and I have been discussing how to improve my combat abilities. He said my magic can be used to boost my physical combat skills, which I already know how to do. He also said that as a warrior, pseudo paladin, I should be able to learn either skills or spells to increase my magic damage. Is that something you would be able to help with or do I need to find a paladin trainer?" I asked, spelling out my reasoning to the best of my ability.

"Interesting," said Trinico, rubbing her chin. "Just so you know, we do not have a paladin trainer in town, nor will you find one in any town or even in Root City. A paladin is granted his or her abilities directly by their God or Goddess."

"So, I need to pray to Issara for more skills?" I asked.

"Goddess Issara," Trinico corrected, "But, in short, yes."

I could only groan in frustration. I had spoken to my Goddess twice now and she had yet to mention it.

As if reading my thoughts Trinico added, "It is not her fault you did not ask."

"I suppose I should go pray . . . again," I added.

Trinico only nodded and waved me along.

Once again, I was before the altar, and once again, I took a knee.

"Hello . . . again," I said, trying not to let any resentment leak into my voice. "I have just been informed, I should be asking you for more spells and skills to fit the unique class you bestowed upon me. I don't suppose you would be willing to help me out."

Your prayer has been heard.

You've learned the 'Law and Order' skill 'Justice Strike'

Justice Strike	Level: 1	Experience: 0.00%
Current Damage Modifier	Damage: +0.50 Cooldown: 30 seconds	Skill Stamina Cost: 50
Skill Effect (Active): A righteous strike in the name of Justice. Increases damage or healing of next spell cast by 10.		

It was only one skill, but it was powerful. This is exactly what the Sergeant was talking about before. This skill would boost my spell damage, while my spells boosted my physical damage. Well, 'Lesser Holy Imbuement' increased my physical damage . . . no, that was also spell damage. 'Lesser Combat Blessing' increased my strength and dexterity, increasing my physical damage. Okay, so it wasn't much but I'm sure more spells will come.

"Thank you, Goddess Issara. I don't mean to sound greedy, but I could use a spell that increases my physical damage. Something to balance with 'Justice Strike'," I requested. I knew it was a long shot, but it couldn't hurt to ask.

Your prayer has been heard.

You've learned the 'Law and Order' holy spell 'Lesser Holy Shock'

Lesser Holy Shock	Level: 1	Experience: 0.00%
Spell Damage: 10-15	Spell Cast Speed: Instant **Cooldown**: 30 seconds	Spell Mana Cost: 100
Spell Effect (Active): *A shock of holy energy attacks the nervous system of your target stunning it and increasing physical damage received by 10 for 5 seconds.*		

That was an expensive spell, but the effect was nice, especially if it increased my parties damage as well. And what was with this 'Law and Order' category that just started popping up. Shouldn't I have had this all along? Or was it that these spells and skill would only ever be available to me and my class?

Regardless, I gave my thanks, "Thank you, Goddess Issara, you're awesome." I swear I heard a giggle of laughter after that but couldn't be sure.

I would need to practice both of these new abilities, but I was feeling much more comfortable with my current skills. I had a good balance of spells and skills, now I just needed to find the right combinations for them to maximize my damage output and minimize my resource use.

I retrieved Micaela from her spirit walk and sent her to get her husband, and I sent Baby to get Rose, agreeing we would all meet in front of the barracks.

"So, what's up?" asked Rose, arriving with Baby first.

"We need to go to the Leather Emporium and then finish clearing out the caves. There are five wagons and oxen waiting at the gates for us. After that, we're all free to do whatever we need to do," I answered.

Rose nodded then started talking to her sister about some dress she saw at which point I tuned them out.

I had to explain the same thing to Olaf and Micaela when they arrived a few minutes later. After that, it was a short walk to the shop.

"Welcome, welcome," said the old man when we entered, except he wasn't old, or at least didn't seem as old as he had the day before. With his beard shaved and his hair cut he looked much younger, probably in his forties, maybe fifties.

"You're doing better, Barnum," I greeted the much healthier looking man, his health bar alone told me as much.

"So much better, you would not believe how much a bath, a shave, and a haircut can do to revitalize the body and soul. Now, I promised you all a reward for my rescue and I intend to deliver," said Barnum energetically.

"First, for you Bye-bye, these have been collecting dust in my back room for years but as I understand it you might find a use for them," said Barnum, handing me leather armor dyed white.

Quest Alert: A self-proclaimed Bandit King (Recommended Level 5-7) - Completed
Stop the self-proclaimed Bandit King and use his key to free the captured merchants.

Now, I was intrigued, but I would check them in a minute. I was always interested to see what my friends would get as well.

Rose was handed a small chest. "Those are blood samples from some of the rarer beasts I have slain over the years in my pursuit of higher quality leather. I hope you find them useful," said Barnum.

"I'm sure I will, thank you," said Rose, already having opened the small chest and looking at the vials within.

"For you, Miss Babies, I believe this bag will be very useful as it will reduce the weight of anything within by a factor of 10," said the leatherworker.

"So, ten pounds will carry as one pound?" asked Baby.

"Yes, indeed," he replied with a kind smile. Then he turned to Micaela. "For you, a new belt. It should be better able to carry your totems."

"Thanks, this is perfect," cheered Micaela, quickly equipping it. She then pulled two more gourds from her bag, each now able to be secured to her belt. I made a mental note to ask her about her two new gourds later.

"And for you Olaf, I thought you may appreciate these," Barnum handed the man a large pair of pants, mottled black and green, reminding me of older style camouflage and matching the cloak he received the night before.

"Artillery Leg-guards," said Olaf aloud

I had to guess he was reading the description.

"Thank you," the ogre added as an afterthought.

"No, thank you," said Barnum gratefully. "Thank you all so much. I am not ready to die, not yet at least. I still wish to see so

470

many of the rare and legendary leathers the World Tree has to offer. It would have been a real travesty to have died before then."

"Are there any rare or legendary leathers in this province you wish to have us collect for you?" I asked. I knew none of us were able to harvest leather, but we could always drag a corpse back here for him.

"As a matter of fact, there is a rather elusive <Ridge Lion King> I've been hunting for years. That's how I was captured you know. He is said to stalk the highest ridge to the far north of town. If you could bring him back to me, I would reward you all very well," requested Barnum.

Quest Alert: Hunt the Elusive <Ridge Lion King> (Recommended Level 5-8, 3 or more Adventurers)		
Barnum has challenged you to hunt the elusive and very dangerous <Ridge Lion King>. Return with the body of the beast for him so he can work the leather and you will be well rewarded.		
Reward: Experience, Good Variable Piece of Gear, Collectable Trophy		
Do you accept this Quest?	Yes	No

"Yes, we'll do it," said Rose, grinning excitedly and accepting the quest for all of us.

"You just can't help it, can you?" asked Baby, looking at me.

I shrugged but grinned a little anyway. "What can I say? When you're good, you're good."

"We're definitely forming an Order," said Olaf, a finality in his voice. "No more doubt about it. We are forming an Order and Bye-bye will be our secret weapon."

"I still think we should make a rank for him called 'Cool Stuff Finder'," added Micaela.

"What do you think, Sis? Should we join this Order?" asked Rose, looking at Baby.

"Yes, yes, we should," said Baby with a firm and serious demeanor. It was out of place on her childlike face, but I could see a small upturn at the corner of her lips, betraying her seriousness. I kept it to myself. She was having fun. We all seemed to be having fun.

"So, Mr. Cool Stuff Finder, where to next?" asked Rose, grinning excitedly.

CHAPTER 25

Nothing could get me down right now. You may ask, 'Bye-bye, why can nothing get you down right now?' My answer can be summed up in a few simple words, 'Holy Order Light Leg-guards'. What are the 'Holy Order Light Leg-guards', you ask? They are light leather armor for my legs that are simply awesome. Like, really awesome. First, they are of Good quality.

I don't remember if I have mentioned the various levels of gear quality, but it goes something like this. Poor quality is the worst you can get, this gear will usually have very little durability and provide almost no protection of any kind. Normal quality is what most starter gear consists of, this has okay defense and durability, but almost never offers more than that. Good quality is a considerable step up from there. This gear has solid defense or offense bonuses and durability, in addition to giving some nice stat bonuses. After that is High quality, another step-up in all aspects, some even give unique abilities only usable while equipped.

As far as the forums are concerned, there have only been a few dozen pieces found or made, but as we know, the forums lie so much right now. After High quality is Mystic quality, forged with magic as well as tremendous skill, the stuff is currently the highest discovered level of gear, but again, that's per the forums. Also, per the forums, there are supposedly two or three higher gear qualities, but nothing has been confirmed.

So, again, for a beginner province, getting Good quality gear is a huge bonus. 'Holy Order Light Leg-guards' are good quality, making me so unbelievably happy to have them.

Holy Order Light Leg-guards – Light Leather - +20-Armor, +5-Endurance, +10 Intellect, +5 Wisdom, +10-Holy Damage, and Healing, Durability 35/35

They were considerably heavier than any other piece of gear I've gotten so far at 5-lbs but wow, such great boosts.

"I still say they clash with your vest, you should replace it," said Micaela, giving me unwanted and unneeded fashion advise. I was well aware that my gear appearance clashed, but who cares, they work and have awesome stats.

"Babe, it's only starter gear," said Olaf.

"And you, Olaf, totally need a shirt, you're a giant Sergeant Butters now, except with camouflage pants instead of armor. When did you buy that tank-top anyway?" asked Micaela.

"A while ago," answered Olaf, his single eye eye-rolling at his wife's antics.

"I think he looks good," said Rose, grinning and staring at Olaf's exposed arms. "Real eye-candy. I mean, just look at those muscles."

"Hey, you look away, my eye candy only," warned Micaela, stepping in between the two, blocking Rose's view.

I could only shake my head. We'd been having this same conversation for the last two hours. That's how long it took to get to the caves, loot them, and return to town with four and a half carts filled with stolen goods.

But I was still in a good mood, nothing could ruin that.

Entering the Town hall with the ongoing conversation still jabbering on I went straight to the Mayor's office door and knocked.

Homer emerged a minute later. "Welcome back, Bye-bye, how can I help you?"

"We have returned with the last of the stolen goods. Thought you might want to know," I answered.

"Excellent, well done, all of you," said Homer gratefully.

Quest Alert: Bandit Round-up (Recommended Level 4-6) - Completed
Mayor Simper has tasked you with eliminating the bandits ambushing local merchants going to and from the World Tree portal and recover any of the stolen goods or money.
Reward: +500-Experience, 5% of recovered goods to be paid in 5 days hence

I hadn't been paying much attention to my experience totals, so I was surprised when I saw the next announcement.

Congratulations! You've reached Level 6!
+1 to bonus Holy Spells, +1 Intellect, +1 Charisma

I hadn't been paying much attention to my stats, except to make sure that I capped them with every level. But now I was level 6. I passed the level 5 threshold. Now my stats would gain experience differently. Some would grow quicker than others, but because of my unique class, I would need to spend time training all of them. I pulled up my character screen to see where I was with all my gear boosts.

Level:	6	Experience:	2.29%
Class:		Novice Warrior Priest of Issara	
HP (Health Points):			1250/1250
MP (Mana Points):			860/860
SP (Stamina Points):			690/690
Strength:			50
- Melee Damage Modifier			+50
Dexterity:			55

- Melee Critical Strike Chance	5.50%
- Hit Chance	62.75%
- Dodge Chance	5.50%
Endurance:	125
Stamina:	69
Intellect:	86
- Spell Critical Strike Chance	8.60%
Wisdom:	55
Charisma:	79
Health Regeneration per minute:	63
Mana Regeneration per minute:	28
Stamina Regeneration per minute:	39
Holy Spell Damage Bonus:	58
Holy Spell Healing Bonus:	38
Carrying Capacity in Lbs.:	250

All told, I was in a good place for the start of level 6. I had the skills necessary to train my stats due to 'Acrobatics' and 'Meditation'. I would have to test 'Acrobatics' to see how well it did, but 'Meditation' would be a last resort just because of the time constraints.

"Hey, congrats on level 6, mate," said Olaf, clapping me on the back and nearly planting me in the floor. "You're officially over-leveled for this province."

I shrugged nonchalantly. I didn't care if I was above the recommended level, I still had things to do in this province and I had no intention of leaving until I was satisfied. I had told my friends as much a few times.

"Back to the grind you go," joked Micaela.

Why? Just why did she have to remind me? Much as I accepted the necessity of the evil that was grinding, I didn't much care for it.

"Yeah, yeah, Jack got a level, what's next?" asked Rose, quickly moving the subject away from me. While I know she did it in an effort to tease me, I was actually grateful for it. No matter how comfortable I may have gotten in dealing with an audience, I still didn't enjoy it.

"Hunting down the lion?" asked Micaela excitedly.

"Nope," I said with a small grin, happy for her enthusiasm. While it was a good idea, there was no rush for it. We could do it tomorrow when we had more time. "I want a crack at breaking into Lieutenant Graves home."

"If that's the case, I'm overdue to start training to become a professional Engineer with Giggle-Ana and Mic needs to buckle down and work on becoming a professional Builder. You good on your own?" Olaf explained and asked.

"Of course, I can't imagine running into too much trouble with Graves fleeing the town. How about you two?" I asked looking toward Rose and Baby.

"I am going to work on my professions too. But to do that, I need to get more herbs, and with this new handy dandy bag, I can carry a whole lot of herbs," said the happily floating fairy. "So, I will be venturing outside town to do a bit of herb harvesting."

"I was thinking about becoming a professional 'Enchanter', but you have to learn writing first," replied Rose.

"Writing is pretty easy. Just go to 'Ned's Sundry', buy a blank book and something to write with. Then you just start writing whatever you want, and you should get writing pretty quickly. Just a word of warning, as soon as you hit level 10, make sure you stop and go learn the evolution. Any levels past 10 will be reset back to 10 when you evolve it to 'Enchantment'," I volunteered.

"Then I guess I know where I'm going, see you all later," said Rose, leaving with Baby to manage their business. I wanted to ask her about her second profession, but she was gone so quickly, I didn't get a chance to ask.

After a few more farewells, I was on my own again. The mayor had been kind enough to mark Graves's home on my map for me earlier, so finding it wasn't difficult.

The ex-lieutenant's home was larger than most of those surrounding it and didn't seem to fit in with the rest of the town. It was two stories, painted gray with black trim and a blood red door, a creepy blood-red door. I had to ask myself, how no one in town figured this guy for evil from the start?

Nothing appeared to be out of the ordinary as I approached. The porch extended the entire length of the house and the single deck chair looked unused. I tried to peek inside the windows, but the curtains were all drawn shut.

I went to the door and gave the doorknob a little jiggle to see if it was unlocked. It wasn't. I took out my lock picking tools and dropped to a knee to put the lock to eye level. I inserted my picks and immediately heard an odd clicking sound and a little snigger of laughter just behind me.

I barely turned to look for the source of the laughter, when suddenly there was no porch below me and I was falling. My first thought was I would be falling toward a pit filled with spikes so when I splashed into liquid I was relieved. That relief quickly vanished, as I realized I'd just fallen into a pit of acid, which rapidly and painfully devoured me.

Acid Pit Trap does 25-damage to you with 'Acid Burn'.

478

Acid Pit Trap has murdered you. You will be automatically transported and revived at the nearest graveyard.

Well, that was horrible, what a slow and painful death. Okay, so not too painful, maybe equal to a constant sunburn or standing too close to a bonfire, painful, but not unmanageable. Still, to take so many ticks of -25-HP until it slowly killed me should be considered torture, something strictly forbidden in this game.

I'd have to complain about it later.

It turned out I was wrong about my earlier belief, that nothing could take away my good mood. My return to Graves's home was made with each stride taken in anger. This time I didn't bother with the trying to pick the lock, I just kicked in the door and jumped through. I looked behind me to see the trap door slowly closing.

I 'hmphed' in triumph then stood. I looked around briefly before I felt a strange breeze blow past me. A moment later, my head rolled backward, disconnected from my body before my vision went black again.

Decapitator 3000 does 1,250-damage to you with 'Decapitation'.

Decapitator 3000 has murdered you. You will be automatically transported and revived at the nearest graveyard.

The line of explicative statements following my resurrection could have made an orc blush. For a guy who wants to hunt down hidden treasures and has made a list of skills that will probably be necessary, I was being really dumb about this. I think I was angrier with myself now than I was with the traps or even Graves. I should have figured Graves would have booby-trapped his home.

"Calm down, Bye-bye," I voiced to myself. I needed to be smarter about this. The home is trapped. I need to learn more about traps. Thankfully I have just the book to do it. I was tempted to sit on the singular unused deck chair in front of Graves's home, but with the recent run of bad luck with traps, the chair would undoubtedly kill me. It would probably end up being a mimic and eating me whole.

Instead, I returned to the Inn, beaten by the house, but not defeated. I would re-arm and try again soon enough. I sat in my favorite chair by the fire, ordered some lunch from Trish and cracked open 'Trapology'.

I barely started reading, when Trish dropped off a sandwich for me. I set my book aside and ate. It was probably good I did, as, by the time I finished eating, I had calmed down considerably.

Calmer now, I reopened the booked and began to read. The book was broken into two halves. The first half was all about trap construction which covered building rudimentary traps and snares. It was mostly focused on the triggers to set traps off, it also had a small section on trap placement.

The second half, which ended up being the half I was interested in, was all about trap disarmament. It built off the first half portion concerning triggers but disarming them instead of arming them. It also had a small section about how to spot traps and finding the hidden triggers. I was surprisingly intrigued by the subject. It also went into a bunch of details from ancient traps to modern traps, even touching briefly on magical traps which were so much more complicated as well as significantly more dangerous.

I was so engrossed in the book, that when I closed it after reading the last page, I was surprised to see Olaf and Micaela sitting on the couch and Baby and Rose sitting on the other two chairs similar to mine. They each had a drink in their hands and were happily chatting. I was shocked they had arrived, and I hadn't taken note of it. I also felt guilty, I was worried I'd been ignoring them. I also took note of music playing in the background, something I don't remember occurring before now.

"All done then?" asked Olaf. "I hope we didn't distract you. One of the guards mentioned he saw you coming from the graveyard a few times today, looking mighty unhappy."

"No, I didn't even know you guys were here already," I answered quickly. "I hope I didn't ignore you, I was deep into the book."

"Nah, you're fine Jack. We were having a nice talk all about you. Who knows when I'll next get dirt on you from Micaela," Rose replied, a wicked grin on her face.

I felt my eyes narrow, first at Rose, then at Micaela. Any guilt I may have felt for ignoring them quickly vanished.

"What happened to you anyway?" asked Baby.

"Acid Pit Trap and the Decapitator 3000," I answered Baby, she was just too cute to ignore or be mad at.

Rose choked on her beer, then once she cleared her throat cackled in laughter. "Decapitator 3000, for real?"

"Yes, and let me tell you, it works quite well," I said frostily. My hand subconsciously rubbing my throat.

"Blimey mate, bad luck that is," said Olaf, rubbing his own throat.

"Was that the trap book you were reading then?" asked Baby.

"Yeah, it was. It was actually an interesting read too," I added.

"So, did you learn any skills from it?" asked Micaela.

"Let me check," I said, opening my system messages to be greeted by a wall of text.

You've learned the skill 'Trap' and subskills 'Create Snare', 'Create Spike Trap' & 'Disarm Trap'

Trap	Level: 1	Experience: 0.00%
Skill Effect (Passive): *Knowledge and understanding of traps.*		
Subskill: Create Snare	**Skill Effect (20 Stamina + Materials):** *Allows for the construction of a basic trap to catch small game. Chance to capture 25%*	
Subskill: Create Spike Trap	**Skill Effect (20 Stamina + Materials):** *Allows for the creation of a basic trap to wound and slow. Damage 5-10 Chance to Slow 20%*	
Subskill: Disarm Trap	**Skill Effect (20+ Stamina + Tools):** *Enables you to disarm a trap, more complex traps will require more Stamina.*	

You've learned 'Perception' subskill 'Spot Trap'

Perception	Level: 9	Experience: 44.21%
Skill Range: 10.90 yards	**Chance to See:** 12.25%	**Chance to Identify/Track:** 14.50%
Subskill: Beast Tracking	**Skill Effect (Passive):** *Enables you to see animal tracks to better hunt them.*	
Subskill: Humanoid Tracking	**Skill Effect (Passive):** *Enables you to track humanoids.*	
Subskill: Eye for Detail	**Skill Effect (Passive):** *Enables you to see details that would be missed otherwise.*	
Subskill: Spot Trap	**Skill Effect (Passive):** *Enables you to see hidden traps.*	

In addition to all of that, I was informed I had gained +3-Intellect and +2-Wisdom from reading the book, as well as 2 levels to 'Lore'. Checking the clock, it took me about three hours to gain those 5-points, where it would have taken me 5-hours if I had just used 'Meditation'. So, reading was still the faster method of gaining skill points, at least for now. That could always change in the future, but for now, I was pleased with it.

I whistled in appreciation for the gains and shared them with my friends.

"I got next," said Olaf before anyone else could lay claim to it. I tossed the book to him.

"Just let the mayor know, I don't want him to come after me for it," I said.

"Will, do. I'm actually looking forward to reading this one. Giggle-Ana even said this book would be big for me with engineering. She said I would be able to build traps that would go to waste if I didn't know how to use them," explained Olaf.

"Did you finish a book last night?" asked Baby.

"Yeah, I turned in 'The Greater Outdoors' this morning," I answered.

"Which I've got right here," said Rose, removing the book from her inventory and showing Baby. "I'll let you read it when I'm done."

Baby pouted but didn't fight it.

"What's the plan for tomorrow?" asked Micaela.

"Training in the morning, Lion in the afternoon?" I half stated, half asked.

"I'm in," said Rose.

"Works for us," said Olaf, answering for himself and his wife.

"I suppose I'll have to keep you all alive," added Baby, trying to sound reluctant, but failing spectacularly. That baby face of hers would forever prevent anyone from taking her seriously.

"Okay, so we have a plan. Now, there is something more serious I want to talk to all of you about," started Olaf.

"Sure," I replied without hesitating.

Rose studied Olaf for a moment before setting down her beer and focusing on him. It gave me the idea that I should set mine down as well, while Baby set down her tiny mug too.

"Go ahead, babe, we're all listening," said Micaela, encouraging her husband to speak.

Olaf cleared his throat nervously. "So, I know I've mentioned a few times, I want us to form an Order. You all sounded receptive to the idea, but I wanted to discuss it with you all in more detail. Now, I won't be offended if you're not interested and were just being nice about it before, but I'm serious about this. So, if you're not interested, please let me know now. I don't want to put in the money and effort if you're not truly interested." He paused here to give each of us a measured look except for Micaela.

"I can't say for sure," answered Rose. "I'm interested, but I'm not signing up for anything until I read the fine print. Also, don't take this the wrong way, but I hardly know you. We've only known each other for a few days, not much to build the kind of trust I would want in guildmates."

"That's perfectly fair," replied Olaf. "I appreciate the honesty too. And you're right, we don't know each other that well yet, but I think we've built enough trust to at least discuss this. I hope you'll stick around with us long enough to build more trust."

"I'm with my sister," said Baby, not needing to elaborate further. Where her sister went so too did she.

"Bye-bye?" Olaf asked, specifically looking at me.

I had truthfully been on the fence with the idea of creating an Order in the game or even joining one. I didn't want to be beholden to an Order if they ever went to war with another Order. I didn't want to be taxed on anything I earned, in addition to the taxes Seed

Inc already levied in the game, in addition to the taxes I'd pay to the government for any money I earned while playing.

But it wasn't all bad either.

I did like the idea that I would have a group of people I could call on to help me when I found something too difficult for me to manage on my own. I felt it wouldn't be so bad, if Olaf, a person I considered a friend, would be running it. And most importantly, I loved this group, even with Rose, despite the constant verbal sparring or maybe because of it. If every one of us joined, it was a solid start to an Order.

Rose might be . . . difficult to work with sometimes, but she was already proving to be a capable tank and she was a rare class. Baby was all kinds of awesome cuteness and OP heals, her magic would only get stronger. Micaela was a shaman and seemed to be a good one from what I could tell, her totems seemed powerful too and would only get more so. And Olaf would be ridiculously powerful as a damage dealer, his hand-cannons were already stupid powerful and would only get more so as he improved them and his ammo with his engineering.

Which left me, I don't know how powerful I'll become in the end, but I was a great tweener class. A tweener class is one that fits somewhere between categories. I can tank a little, I can DPS, and I can heal too, though my ability to deal damage per second (DPS) is probably my strongest specialization.

I was getting off topic. I had to answer the question, do I really want to join, to help found an Order. No, I don't. But I want to help my friends and continue to adventure with them, so yes.

"Yes, I'm in. But, I don't want any responsibility. I'll help out with Order quests when I can, but I want to be able to freely explore and find whatever Easter Eggs this game has hidden away," I stated,

I may have taken a little longer to answer, but I felt I had to be clear about my intentions.

Olaf sagged in relief.

"Told you he would," said Micaela with a light laugh.

"You were right, I was wrong," said Olaf, looking to his wife. He then looked back at me. "I'm glad you're willing, and I am perfectly fine with that. That's exactly what I want you to do anyway."

"It sounds as though you're planning to build this guild around him. Is Jack here truly that valuable?" asked Rose, eyeing me up and down, trying to see what Olaf saw.

"I hope he is," said Olaf. "In the short time I've known Bye-bye, he's proven invaluable to me and Micaela. He helped me get my class, something the forums said wasn't possible until level 30, and only if I remained un-classed. He introduced us to Sergeant Butters and Trinico. Before then, we didn't know there were any trainers of any kind in this province, beyond a few profession trainers. Then there are all the quests, I've never heard of a starting province offering so many quests. I know it's a risk, but with his track record thus far, I think it's a risk worth taking."

"He's not wrong, Sis," said Baby. "Starting provinces are notoriously low on quests. It's easier in the higher provinces because it's usually a campaign-style, where you're reporting to one guy and he starts you on a long quest chain. But even there, the side quests are rare."

"I see," said Rose thoughtfully. "I'll reserve judgment for now. You've got about two weeks left before your first log out right? I'll be watching."

I'm not sure if that was a good thing or a bad thing.

"Anyway, Bye-bye may be a big part of my plans, mostly for making the Order famous. I have more things in mind. I stopped at the Town hall after getting my first engineering lesson with Giggle-Ana and picked up this little booklet." At this, Olaf showed us a small book, less than a hundred pages to it, if my guess was right.

Olaf continued, "This is the 'Guide to Order', it goes over all the details of forming an Order and the different types of Orders we can form, as well as some of the benefits," explained Olaf. "I know what kind of Order I'm leaning towards, but I do want some input, so I'll try to lay out the options available to us."

"First, to form an Order we either need to have a citizen of rank equivalent to Knight, to sponsor us or a player of the same equivalent rank, to form the Order. Right now, I'm ranked an Ensign Ogre Artillery, I need to earn the rank of Captain, which is two ranks away. However, I'm a Miner Rank IV, which is actually a rank above the Knight equivalent, unfortunately, professional rank limits the choice of Order severely. So, we have options available to us," Olaf explained the first option.

"Second," started Olaf, pausing to take a sip of his beer. "If we form an order, we have the option to rent space in Root City for an Order Room, according to this, the room wouldn't be much bigger than the mayor's office. We also have the option to build an Order Manor in a province of our choosing."

"What's the difference?" asked Baby curiously.

"The Order Room is just a room, large enough for a handful of officers to meet and discuss Order business. The forums say, most Order's just have their favorite bars in Root City and anyone looking to join can find them there. I guess they also have their meetings and such in the bars. The downside, it isn't private, so people can eavesdrop and share your plans if you aren't careful. Still, it's super cheap, just 1-gold per month," explained the Olaf.

"The Order Manor is much more complicated. First, you have to have a certain reputation with the province you want to build in, so far, no one has reached such a level," Olaf continued.

"How do you know your reputation?" I asked. I don't remember seeing a reputation menu anywhere.

"Exactly," said Olaf. "Moving on. Second, it's expensive. You have to buy the land for the manor, then you have to pay to build the bloody thing. Third, your Order Manor can be attacked by other Orders, and you are also partly responsible for protecting the town or village, in which you establish your Order Manor. Fourth, and most importantly, Order Manors open up all kind of special guild quests and events, as well as giving you the option to annex the village or town and take over management of it."

"They even put in city building?" I asked, slightly astounded. There was nothing about it on the forums.

"I didn't know about it either until I read this fellow," said Olaf, tapping the booklet again. "That's the gist of how to form an Order. Any questions? Preferences?"

"I'd love to build a Manor," said Micaela. "Between our combined mining and my new 'Construction' profession the cost of building would be significantly reduced."

"I'm not preferential," I added. And I wasn't. But then I thought about it, how nice would it be to build an Order Manor here? We know the people, we've already befriended most of them. Plus, it would make for one heck of a recruiting tool to have an Order Manor in one of the starter provinces, more so if we advertised on the forums. I imagine it would be easier for us to establish our Order here too because we have the 'Local Hero' title already.

"Hmm," I hummed thoughtfully at that.

"What is it?" asked Olaf, I could almost hear the sudden excitement in his voice. "What did you figure out?"

"Well . . . I don't know if I figured anything out but . . . well, we've already earned the title 'Local Hero' here. I would think that would meet whatever reputation criteria there may be," I answered.

"Pure bloody brilliance," Olaf nearly shouted. "I'll talk to the mayor about it tomorrow. See what he says."

"What's this? What title?" asked Rose, looking askance of us.

"Remember that raid on the town?" I asked, grinning at the chance to get one up on her. "Those of us who stayed and fought were awarded a hidden quest awarding us the title 'Local Hero' and 5-gold. It was pretty awesome."

Rose ground her teeth before smirking. That smirk was dangerous and continued to prove as much every time I saw it on her face. "I would have thought 'Local Zero' fit you better, but you can't account for some people's tastes. Besides, it's just a title, not like it does anything."

My turn to smirk. "Triple's Charisma in Hurlig Ridge," I added smugly. "And reduces the costs of goods and services by 20%." I knew the smug grin on my face was mean, but I couldn't help it. Rose brought it on herself.

"Hax," Rose grumbled, crossing her arms and sulking in her chair, pretending I was no longer there.

Point for me.

"Anyway, we can worry about that later. I have one more topic to cover. The Order types," said Olaf, taking control of the conversation back.

"There are types of Orders?" asked Micaela, perking up.

"Yeah, yet another surprise from the book. Apparently, there are a few different types of Orders. I'll start with the two I have rank enough to start. First is an Order of Mercantilism. These Orders get quests focusing on creating trade routes, opening stores or shops, and the buying and selling of goods. They get bonuses to pricing and increased experience for Charisma, Intellect, and Wisdom," explained Olaf.

That wasn't too bad at all. Though I had no interest in managing trade routes or a store, the bonus experience was nice.

"I can also create an Order of Craftsmen, which is for professions. It gives increased experience to all professions and whichever stat is most affected by your profession. So, for me, I use Strength for mining and Dexterity and Intellect for engineering, so I would get bonus experience for those," Olaf continued.

Also, not bad, but kind of dull. I have an appreciation for crafting armor and weapons, but it's so much time in front of a forge or cauldron or some other crafting tool, instead of being out there and seeing everything there is to be seen.

"I'm not interested in either of those," I said.

"Me neither," said Rose.

"Meh," said Micaela with a shrug of her shoulders.

"Yeah, what she said," said Olaf, nodding to his wife. "I personally find them boring, but I had to bring them up as it is something we could do now. I'd rather wait until one of us hits the equivalent rank of Knight."

"How do we rank up?" I asked. There hadn't been much on the forums about it. In fact, it was hardly mentioned at all.

"Forums suck," griped Micaela.

"Yeah, we don't know that either. At least not yet. It could be level related, it could be merit-based, or even a combination of both," explained Olaf.

"Okay, what else? I think we all agree we'd rather wait than settle," said Rose, who seemed much more interested than before.

"Okay, next is the Order of War, this is a ranked Player versus Player Order," started Olaf.

I cut him off immediately. "No, just no."

Olaf blinked in surprise at my small outburst. "Okay, that's off the table."

"Awe, but I love PvP," said Baby pouting for a moment then grinning mischievously. "Said no one ever. I hate PvP. It's why I picked a race better built for PvE."

Player versus Environment or PvE would be the opposite of PvP. This is more you versus the game, rather than you versus other players. Personally, I was in total agreement with her.

"While I'm not into PvP, I do find it fun on occasion. I don't think an Order focused on PvP will make or break me so that's fine," added Rose.

"I'm kind of the same way, Rose," said Olaf. "But the missus here is more akin to your sister and Bye-bye, so it suits me just fine to eliminate that one."

"What's next?" I asked.

"Order of Knights," Olaf started. "This is a royal order, so it has to be approved by one of the Kings or Queens of the various races. You are also then beholden to that King or Queen, you become part of their army. That said, you get significantly more for it. Reduced costs on just about everything. Experience boosts to your primary stats for your class. But its super strict. You are subject to military order, so saluting or bowing depending on your new King or

Queen's cultural preferences. Rank within the guild becomes super important too. Now, this is one I would personally prefer to eliminate. I was in the British Army once, I would prefer to never be in one again. Unfortunately, I do recognize this one gives us a ton of benefits."

"Yeah, I'm not taking orders," said Rose, crossing her arms, daring anyone to try.

I chuckled a little. "I'm gonna pass too."

"Thanks, guys," said Olaf with a friendly smile.

"Next is the Order of Service. This one might be a good fit for us. This a pretty generic type of Order. It gives increased provincial rewards, meaning quests completed in provinces give more and better rewards. It also makes it easier to obtain quests and side quests specific to the province you're currently working in," Olaf explained.

"That doesn't sound bad at all," said Baby. "Any experience bonuses?"

"Only as part of the quest completions. But I imagine many of those quests will give you +1 to a random stat too," added Olaf.

"I'm not against this one either," I said. That would make hunting a province to completion much more worthwhile all the way around.

"Like I said, I think it could be a good fit for us. It will let Bye-bye hunt his Easter Eggs to his heart's content, while also giving our members access to quests and leveling opportunities. The only downside I can see, is once we get to the highest levels those extra quests won't do us much good. It will help us level up new members, but long-term could have sustainability problems," Olaf explained.

Olaf made a very good point there. While the game had no level cap to speak of, it did have problems with return on investment.

Eventually, players will get to a point where it will require thousands of quests and tens of thousands of monster-kills to level, you might only level once every two or three months.

"It's still worth considering," said Baby. "What else have you got?"

"Okay, next and last up and the one I personally think is the best fit for my plans regarding our Order. The Order of Adventurers. This one doesn't have much for benefits except for one big one. One, I think, makes it the only logical choice. Adventurer Level Quests. Big, grand quests encompassing multiple provinces, taking months to complete, giving rewards beyond anything else in the game. Now, from what the booklet says, these quests are hard, harder than anything else given by the game, but again, the rewards are commensurate with the difficulty. Not just combat quests, there are crafting, exploration, dungeon and even raid quests," Olaf finished his pitch.

If the previous sounded good to me, then this one had me drooling, daydreaming about all the hidden mysteries and adventures there were out there for me to find and explore.

"That one," I said excitedly.

"I thought you might love that one. I like the sound of it myself but it's risky again. Great in the higher levels but leveling wise probably not as beneficial," explained Olaf.

"Can we change the type of Order later? Can we start as an Order of Service then change later to an Order of Adventurers?" asked Baby.

"Sadly no. You can disband your order, but you lose everything. Any trophies, your Order Manor, any related titles, all of it gone," explained Olaf.

"Ouch," I sympathized. "That would not be cool."

"Yeah, so we have to be sure about what we choose to do. I know my vote goes to the Order of Adventurers. So, with me and Bye-bye, that's 2 votes. Rose? Baby? Mic?"

"If we choose to join you, I would have to go with the Adventurers, myself," said Rose. "I know it's more practical to go with the Order of Service but I'm not here to be practical. I'm here to cut loose and have fun. To go on adventures and see all this world has to offer and more. I can't do that if I'm always playing it safe. Playing it safe is for out there, in here there is no holding back. Anyway, that's just my two cents."

I found myself slightly in awe of Rose, perhaps for the first time since we met. I saw her as more than just a pretty girl with attitude for days. I looked away before she caught me staring but it left me looking at her in a new light.

"I am more comfortable with the Order of Service," said Baby, then she sighed. "But, my sister has a point, a small one, but still. So, Order of Adventurers it is." Rose playfully glared at her sister for the small dig but laughed a little anyway.

We all looked at Micaela. "What?" she asked. "As if I wouldn't agree with my husband. Adventurers we are and adventurers we'll stay."

"Then it's settled," said Olaf. "When we go to Root City, I'll get the last details we need in order. The only thing we have to do now is earn a class rank equivalent to a Knight."

With a plan for the next day in place and our plans for the future outlined, even roughly, we collectively decided to spend the evening socializing, we all needed to boost our Charisma stats, especially me even though I had the highest Charisma stat among us. Gamer greed said I needed more so I could get more quests, after all it was most likely my high Charisma score, earning us all these quests.

I could only imagine what a pure human could do with their Charisma maxed out every level.

CHAPTER 26

I was slow to wake up the next morning and the rooster wasn't helping my hangover any. Somehow, I managed to ignore the demon bird and make my way downstairs for breakfast and a pint.

I found Rose waiting by herself. She beat me and everyone else down to breakfast.

"Morning," I greeted Rose, taking the open chair across from her.

"Morning," she grumbled back, she seemed to be more hungover than I was, or she was just unhappy that I sat down across from her.

"How is the writing going?" I asked her, trying to make small talk.

"Fine, level 5," she answered in a short, clipped sentence.

"I found it beneficial myself. I tried journaling, it was cathartic, still is for that matter," I tried again to engage her in conversation.

Rose growled at me.

I sighed, accepting defeat, I started to stand. "I can see I'm bothering you, I'll go sit elsewhere."

She growled again. "You don't have to go, I'm just hungover."

"I see," I said, retaking my seat and waiting on breakfast and the hangover cure to arrive.

Eventually, salvation did arrive, and we settled into a companionable silence as we ate and drank our meals.

"I've been writing Poetry," said Rose, softly, a hint of blush on her face.

"Nice, I didn't know you liked that sort of thing," I said. I suddenly realized I knew almost nothing about Rose the person. I knew plenty about her as Rose the Vampiric Knight. I also knew the attitude she generally presented, and this was different. Was that just her being in character? Or was she just so hungover, she let her walls down?

"I'm not good or anything, but it works for the skill. I'll be glad when I get to level 10, then I can just focus on enchanting. So, journaling?" asked Rose.

"Yeah, I was struggling to find something to write about and before I knew it, I had just written the story of my first day here. I was doing 'Drawing' too, so I drew a few pictures to go with it. It worked pretty good to level both at the same time. Stupid me though, I leveled up way above level 10 and when I evolved the skills all those levels were lost," I explained.

"Thanks again for the warning," Rose said honestly. "I'm looking forward to 'Enchanting'. Panther has been telling me there are some enchantments only vampires can learn and use, so I'm looking forward to it."

"Hey, I never got to ask. What is your second profession?" I was ever the curious person.

Rose clicked her tongue and crossed her arms. "You'll just laugh."

Why would she be embarrassed by a profession choice? Professions aren't something to laugh at, at least I didn't think they were. "I won't," I replied, frowning.

Rose eyed me a moment before she mumbled. "Lore."

"Really?" I asked, a little excited. "Me too."

"What?" she asked. "But you said you have Drawing and Writing."

"And Lore. I'm half human, I get a third profession due to their racial ability, Versatility," I said excitedly.

Now Rose suddenly seemed eager to ask me questions. "What level are you? I'm only level 2 and I'm not sure how I got that far."

"I'm level 6, I think it is just reading anything related to the history of the World Tree. I think I got my first level after reading the bestiary, the part at the end of the book talked about a number of the legendary beasts in the World Tree. I got more from the 'Trapology' book section talking about ancient traps and where they were typically used," I answered.

"Do you know what we can use it for? The little bit of reading I did, said it was a junk profession, but I doubt that. I mean, why would they put in a useless profession?" Rose chattered, suddenly seeming to enjoy talking to me.

"As it was explained to me, Lore can lead you to ancient knowledge. For example, I can use it to find lost skills or spells. I bet you can find other things, schematics for weapons and armor, even potions, and enchantments too. If you have the patience for it," I said.

"And they called it useless," she griped. "That sounds awesome."

"Well, as you now know, the forums lie way too much. I bet you, people put that out there on purpose to keep such things to themselves. Either way, I think it's going to be super beneficial," I agreed with her.

"So why writing and drawing then?" Rose asked. "I mean, if Lore can give you schematics and such, why those two?"

I was happy to answer, excited even for the conversation. "I evolved my 'Writing' to 'Runology' and 'Drawing' to 'Cartography'. As Mayor Semper explained it to me, 'Runology' is words of power. With it, I can create spell or skill books and scrolls, meaning all the lost knowledge I can dig up with Lore can be put on paper and sold for a great deal of money or given to help a friend. It's super hard though and even more time-consuming. 'Cartography' is about maps, and one of the things you can find through 'Lore' is treasure maps. 'Cartography' lets you read the map. It's all pretty complimentary."

"No wonder Olaf thinks you're some kind of magnet for finding cool stuff. You've actually crafted your character to do exactly that," said Rose, looking somewhat impressed by me, possibly for the first time ever. I think I prefer this version of Rose much more than the abrasive girl with attitude for days.

"Thanks, I think," I joked.

"Stop, I mean that in a good way," Rose said, laughing lightly. "Have you learned any of the ancient languages yet?"

Now it was my turn to be puzzled. "What do you mean?"

"For instance, I picked up Vampin, the ancient vampire language, when I was blessed by the Goddess Lilith. It's now listed as a subskill under 'Lore'," she explained.

"I have not," I answered. "I will have to see about grabbing some language books from the Town hall if they have any."

"They have a few actually. I looked but didn't grab any. Too many other things going on right now. Speaking of, we should get over to see Sergeant Butters for training," said Rose.

I was surprised when I felt disappointed our conversation ended so abruptly.

"See you over there, slowpoke, try to keep up today. You're making the rest of us look bad," she said, her attitude and walls firmly back in place.

"See you there in a little while," I said, I needed a minute to clear my head before I joined her for training. I have generally enjoyed our banter to an extent, but that conversation was so much better. Why'd she have to go back to being . . . her. I guess I needed the minute to disassociate the two drastically different personas.

I gave her a head start as I'm still not sure I want to deal with the persona chock full of attitude just yet. Eventually, I sighed and reluctantly began a forced march to the barracks.

"Morning," I greeted the man in charge with as much enthusiasm as I could muster, which to be honest wasn't much.

"Who killed your cat?" the sergeant asked.

"I'm just having an off morning," I said, trying to muster up a little more energy for training.

"So, what do you want to learn today?" Sergeant Butters asked.

"I have no idea," I answer honestly. I could learn some more warrior skills I suppose. Or I could try and level up my current spear skills. I know I needed to level up 'Justice Strike'.

"Can I make a suggestion then?" offer the sergeant.

I readily agreed, "Yes, please do."

"You have skills for 'Two-Handed Polearms' and 'One-Handed Polearms', did you happen to notice I taught you different skills for both. Think about it," the sergeant suggested before walking away.

"Did he just say what I think he said?" I questioned aloud, there was no one to answer, but sometimes things just need to be said out loud. If he did say what I think he said, then he just told me that my subskills can be learned for both 'One-Handed Polearms' and 'Two-Handed Polearms', which actually makes sense. I just need to train them on my own and as I already knew the skills I would just need to adapt them accordingly. In short, my reluctance to come train this morning was forgotten.

Seeing as Rose was pretty much our tank for the time being, and I was doing more DPS, it made more sense to me to train the two subskills, 'Jab' and 'Rapid Striking' with my 'Two-Handed Polearms' skill first.

In short order, I found myself facing one of the dummies.

"Don't forget to practice your 'Acrobatics' at the same time," suggested the sergeant as he walked past me and toward the range, where I was sure Olaf was busy trying to blow up all the targets with a single shot. Looking where Sergeant Butters came from, I saw Rose and Micaela facing off with each other, sparring with the sergeant's blunted weapons. I was glad to see my friends were working so hard to improve. I hoped they were having as much fun as I was.

I shook my head to clear away the extraneous thoughts and focused on the dummy in front of me. 'Jab' first, I thought to myself. My arms both jutted forward, pushing as much speed as I could. There was a clang as my spear met metal and I jerked my arms back again. It almost felt right, except for being too slow, but the attack principal was right. I struck again, pushing myself to move faster. I attacked again and again, each attack trying to move faster than the one before. Eventually, I realized I had been standing still, something I wasn't ever going to be able to do in real combat. I began to slowly mix in some 'Acrobatics', steadily circling the dummy, striking quickly from the air and the ground. I found quickly 'Jab' was fairly effective in the air, it was fast and didn't require a ton of power, the way 'Power Thrust' did. I didn't notice, when I stopped focusing on the

501

attack and controlling my arms, I had started to use the mental command 'Jab', executing the attack as quickly as I did when I wore a shield, maybe even a little faster.

Assuming I had learned the subskill and ignoring the exclamation marks notifying me of it and probably a few +1 to stat notifications, I moved right into trying to use 'Rapid Striking'. I discovered quickly I was slightly slower, but felt more power behind the skill, or my attempts at learning the subskill did. I was also quick to realize, using it in the air didn't work well, I would barely start and have to move again.

I still tried a few more times, but eventually decided the skill was meant to be used while stationary, which meant I had to use the skill then move, not both at the same time. Once I figured that out, I was able to focus more on the attack, moving with speed and letting go of accuracy to spread the damage over a wider area. Just as with 'Jab', it didn't take long before I was mentally giving the command for 'Rapid Striking'.

Once I felt satisfied I had learned the subskill, I took a moment to get my notifications and as expected, I was greeted by a wall of text with multiple skill level gains for both 'Two-handed Polearms' and 'Acrobatics' as well as a handful of +1 to stats. I had gained +1-Strength, +2-Dexterity, +1-Endurance, and +1-Stamina. The real prize was the advancement of my 'Two-Handed Polearms'. I was beginning to think my skill leveling was broken. There is no way I should already have this skill up to level 42, or at least I didn't think so.

Two-Handed Polearms	Level: 42	Experience: 87.77%
Current Damage	Damage: +21.00	Critical Strike Chance: +2.10%

Modifiers		
Subskill: Hamstring	Reduce Enemy Movement and Attack Speed: 50% Target Receives Increased Damage: +10.50% Duration: 15 Seconds	Skill Stamina Cost: 58
Subskill: Impale	Damage: 21-22 Bleed Effect: 3 Damage per Second Duration: 10 Seconds	Skill Stamina Cost: 62
Subskill: Power Thrust	Damage: +42.00 Chance to Stun: 10%	Skill Stamina Cost: 92
Subskill: Jab	Damage: +21.00	Skill Stamina Cost: 62
Subskill: Rapid Striking	Damage: -4 Strikes: 18	Skill Stamina Cost: 142

Meanwhile, 'Acrobatics' gained five solid levels.

Acrobatics	Level: 22	Experience: 71.44%
Combat Movement	Dodge Chance: +11.00%	Skill Stamina Cost: 5 per second

Even if it was broken, I wasn't planning to tell anyone. Though I did plan to inquire with my friends, to see how fast their skills and spells were leveling.

Checking my game clock, I saw I still had an hour left before Sergeant Butters kicked us out, so I spent my time just practicing attacking the dummy. I decided to save learning the skills for my 'One-Handed Polearms' for another day. It was a good hour too. I got another handful of +1 stat bonuses, matching my earlier gains and getting my 'Two-Handed Polearms' level 48 and 'Acrobatics' to level 25.

After that, we all joined Baby at the temple for training with Trinico. When we arrived, Baby, Olaf, and Rose, all went into the

Puzzle Rooms. From talking to Olaf, he was only a few puzzles away from finishing. He was hoping to complete them today. Micaela meanwhile was quick to go on her spirit walk leaving me alone with Trinico.

"So, you are level six now, well done," Trinico said, kind as ever. She then opened the small bag she keeps at her hip and pulled out a spell scroll. "I think you will be able to learn this now, but I can never be sure with you." I accepted the scroll happily, hoping it would be one I could learn.

Holy Spell – Lesser Mental Fortification – Teaches the Holy spell 'Lesser Mental Fortification		
Would you like to learn 'Lesser Mental Fortification'?	Yes	No

Of course, I want to learn it.

You've learned the Holy Spell 'Lesser Mental Fortification'

Lesser Mental Fortification	*Level: 1*	*Experience:* 0.00%
Spell Duration: 10 minutes	*Spell Cast Speed:* Instant	*Spell Mana Cost: 50*
Spell Effect (Active): Increase Intellect +2, Increase Wisdom +2, Increase Resistance to Fear 1%, Increases Resistance to Mind Control 1%		

Very nice. I now had a complimentary spell to 'Lesser Combat Blessing'.

"Oh, I'm an idiot," I said suddenly.

"I am aware, but do you mind sharing, why you are an idiot this time?" Trinico asked.

"I've been forgetting to use 'Lesser Combat Blessing' on my friends, even when we're not in combat," I explained. So much lost experience. It also reminded me I haven't cast 'Justice Bringer' even once since it was nerfed. In case you were wondering, Nerf is an old toy company that made soft toy weapons and sports equipment. The toys were unlikely to cause real harm if hit or shot by one. The act of something being 'nerfed' is making it soft like those old toys. Basically, reducing its power and effectiveness. No gamer ever enjoyed being nerfed.

Justice Bringer	Level: 1		Experience: 0.00	
Spell Duration: 1 hour	Spell Cast Speed: Instant	Spell Charges: 1 / 1	Spell Mana Cost: 100	Recharge: 00h:00m:01s
Spell Effect (Active): *All Adventurers and Citizens within 20 yards have their effective level lowered or raised to match your own. Does not work on enemy Citizens, Beasts or Monsters.*				

It was the first time I had looked at it in a while, so I was slightly surprised by the Recharge showing an actual timer now and it was flashing at 1-second until recharge. If that was the case, then I could use it now and get my charge immediately, this would make leveling it considerably more feasible.

Meanwhile, Trinico could only sigh, I could hear the disappointment in her voice. "At this rate, you will never reach level 100 with even your Rank I spells. How do you ever expect to reach the next spell rank?"

"Sorry, could you run that by me again?" I requested, not fully understanding what she just said. "What was that about the next spell rank?" I asked before she could answer. "Are you saying I need to get my spell up to level 100 to unlock the next rank?"

Any more questions were forestalled by a solid knock to my noggin curtesy of Trinico's staff. "Honestly, so impatient. To answer your final question, yes. Once you get a spell with the rank of 'Lesser' to level 100, you will be able to rank up the spell. I would expect, most casters have achieved rank II of most of their spells by the time they reach level 10."

"I had no idea. What else don't I know?" I asked seriously.

"A great deal, I imagine," joked Trinico. I didn't appreciate the joke just then, but she was quick to placate me. "Please, ask your questions. I will do my best to educate you."

"Okay, so it's expected by level 10, most of my spells should be level 100 or rank II. Once I get a spell to rank II does it start the leveling process over again?" I asked.

"Yes, you are exactly correct," the priestess answered patiently.

"Okay, but won't some of my spells be overpowered if they keep leveling up?" I asked, pushing for more information.

"Let me counter with a question of my own, what is your highest-level attack spell?" she asked.

"My highest? 'Lesser Holy Fire' right now," I answered.

"And is your 'Lesser Holy Fire' capable of killing a <Wolf Lvl 1> by itself?" Trinico asked.

"No, not at the moment," I answered.

"Exactly, your most powerful spell, at the moment, cannot kill the lowest level aggressive beast by itself. What does that tell you?" prodded Trinico.

"Either I'm way behind on leveling my spells or I shouldn't expect to one-shot anything until I get my spells stronger," I stated.

"You are correct on both counts," she informed me, it wasn't said kindly. "Think of it like this. For each level you gain, you are able to gain 10 points to each stat, you should think of your spells in the same way."

"Okay, I think I understand. Now, I can't help but notice some of my spells do not have the qualifier 'Lesser', does this mean they don't have additional ranks?" I asked.

"Correct, 'Holy Smite', for example, will get to level 100 and grow no stronger, same for many others," Trinico explained, but before I could question it, she continued speaking. "It is only a starter spell, you will get many spells far more powerful. However, many of those more powerful attack spells require 'Holy Smite' at level 100 as a prerequisite.

That did indeed answer my concern.

"What about skills? Do they operate the same way?" I asked eagerly.

"Skills also rank up at level 100 though most people don't rank up their skills until they reach around level 20," she answered.

"Is it possible to rank up sooner?" I asked.

"It is possible but very difficult," Trinico answered.

"So, about what level should my strongest Skill be at for level 6?" I knew I shouldn't have asked but it was too late.

"For level six, most combat skills will be in the 20-30 range," she answered.

That actually wasn't bad. Except for 'Two-Handed Polearms', that was exactly where most of my skills were. So maybe I wasn't broken, just dedicated.

"Any other questions?" the priestess offered.

"What about professions?" I kept asking more questions.

"They also rank up at level 100," she answered.

"What rank are you?" I asked curiously. "I mean, what rank is your 'Runology'?"

"My Runology is Rank X, I am at master level. It is the only reason I can craft your Goddess-level spell."

I was confused. I was only Rank I, in my Runology, and yet I was able to craft the spell. I was missing something. I checked my skill again.

Runology (Evolved from Writing)	Level: 27	Experience: 48.47%
Professional Skill: Runology is the art of communicating power.		
Chance to Learn Rank I Unknown Rune: 13.50%	Chance to Craft Rank I Skill Book: +6.75%	Chance to Craft Lesser Spell Book: +3.375%
Professional Skill: Writing is the ability to communicate through the written word.		

Now, wait just a minute. My skill never said anything about 'Rank I' before or 'Lesser' anything either. "What's going on here?" I demanded. "My profession changed. It now has a qualifier 'Rank I' for skills and 'Lesser' for spells." I was answered not by Trinico but by a system message filling most of my screen.

Greetings, a patch was implemented 2 days ago improving a number of tooltips for the following evolved professions: Runology, Enchanting, Instrumentation, Acting, and Building. Full Patch details are available at WorldTree.com for you to review at your leisure.

Ah, that explained it. I wish they would have sent some kind of in-game mail or system message with all the patch notes at once. Now I had to wait a week and a half to log out of the game only to go online to check the website. What a pain.

Trinico stood there with her eyes glazed over until I closed the message box. And even when she was animated again she seemed to have forgotten the question. It was a little creepy but at least I understood what happened. I reviewed my other skills quickly to make sure I hadn't missed anything, but the rest looked much the same as before.

"So, if I'm understanding this right, once I get Runology to Rank II and level 100 of that, I'll have a 100% chance to craft a Rank I skill book?" I asked.

"Assuming you are Rank II in that skill, yes," Trinico answered.

"Ah, see, that makes more sense. I thought if I got to level 100 that was it, I'd only have at most a 75% chance to make a skill book and a 62.5% chance to make a spell book," I said.

"Then I am glad we were able to sort it out. Now, is there anything else I can help you with today?" asked the priestess.

"Seeing as I am way behind on my spells, do you have any recommendation for leveling them up faster?" I requested.

"The best way is to simply cast your spells on something or someone your level or higher," Trinico replied. "If you can tolerate the pain, you can even practice on yourself though I do not recommend it."

"What about the practice dummies? I can I use those?" I really didn't want to light myself on fire.

"You certainly can, but the experience will not be as high as it would be against a worthy opponent," Trinico advised me.

"That's okay, it gives me options. Anything else you can help me with today?" I asked hopefully. "Or anything I can do for you?"

"Not today, but thank you, Bye-bye. Why don't you go ahead and rest while you wait for your friends?" the priestess suggested.

Rest, who was she kidding, I had almost two free hours. I would definitely be taking advantage of the time. I have a number of books I am way behind on reading. It was past time that I got to reading them. I sat on the pew and opened 'Let NO-Thing Go to Waste' and started reading.

It was actually a pretty simple instruction manual for getting useful bits from critters and machines. From critters, it was about a good knife, capable of cutting through bone and tissue, and the basics of quartering an animal for the meat. There was a chapter dedicated entirely to the removal of viscera, as well as some information about which viscera were useful in crafting if you could successfully harvest them, without destroying them. Bones were mostly useless, but teeth had some value as did eyes and the brain. If I had to guess, at the lowest levels and ranks, you'd get meat and the occasional bit of crafting materials and common ones at that. For machines, you actually need a couple of tools, specifically two wrenches, and a screwdriver, then it was just a matter of taking them apart without stripping the bolts or breaking the gears. Parts were apparently quite valuable to engineers, too.

Thankfully, it wasn't a long book, as when I closed it, I only had a 15-minute wait for my friends to finish their training for the day.

I checked my system messages while I waited. I gained +2-Intellect and +1-Wisdom as well as the skill 'Scavenging'

You've learned the skill 'Scavenging'

Scavenging	*Level:* 1	*Experience:* 0.00%
Skill Effect (20 Stamina): Scavenge useful materials from dead animals and broken machines. Chance to successfully scavenge something useful 1.00%. Chance to successfully scavenge something more useful 0.05%.		

This was a good day so far, I learned some invaluable information, gained a new spell and a new skill in addition to gaining a few points of stats. And I had the <Ridge Lion King> to hunt this afternoon too.

"I am now one with the universe," said Olaf, walking out of the hallway, a barely suppressed smirk on his face.

I chuckled despite my best efforts, I wanted to make a joke, but the laugh ruined it. Thankfully Micaela was there to pick up the slack.

"Okay your oneness, make me one with everything, I'm hungry," ordered Micaela.

Olaf's smirk vanished, turned into a full-bellied laugh. "So, lunch before hunting?"

"Works for me," said Rose, coming out of the hall just behind him with Baby hovering near her shoulder.

"Alright, let's go eat. Then we've got a lion in need of killing," I said excitedly.

CHAPTER 27

The trip from the village, to the river north of it, was relatively quick and uneventful. Crossing the river proved to be a challenge. The water moved quickly and was pretty deep. Swimming was too much of a risk to even attempt it. Especially, considering we didn't know if it required a skill or how our armor would affect us. We ended up walking east along the river until we found a shallow run, it was much wider than downstream, but thankfully only knee deep.

As soon as we got to the other side of the river, we were set upon by three <Wolf Lvl 3> beasts and an <Alpha Wolf Lvl 5>. The attack patterns were the same as the lower level beasts surrounding the village, just more damaging. We made short work of them, having a full group of five. I also got the chance to use 'Scavenging' on the alpha wolf. I got a few rough looking chunks of meat and a 'Sharp Tooth'.

I also found out why Olaf hadn't been using his own 'Scavenging' skill this entire time. It took almost 30 minutes to scavenge just the one wolf. To say my party was not happy with me might have been an understatement. It was quickly agreed, any 'Scavenging' was to be done on my own time.

I was able to claim one of the bounty paws, leaving me just three paws shy of learning 'Boar Charge' whatever that was. Still, a free skill or spell was a free skill or spell.

It didn't take long to get those last three paws. As we walked, we were attacked every ten or so yards by another group of wolves. Then I got my last paw.

Boar Charge Charm has become fully charged and shatters. You learn the spell 'Boar Charge'

I wanted to cry when I saw that message. My charm was gone . . . forever gone. Even if I got a spell from it, it was gone. No more stamina or endurance bonus, just gone.

Then I read the skill.

"Yes!" I shouted excitedly.

Boar Charge	Level: 1	Experience: 0.00%
Spell Damage: 25-200 per second	Spell Cast Speed: 5.00 seconds Channeled Cooldown: 30 minutes	Spell Mana Cost: 150
Spell Effect (Active): Summon a stampede of spectral boars that will charge a targeted area dealing damage and knocking down anyone in the area of effect.		
Charm Earned Bonus (Passive): Blessing of the Boar Spirit - +10-Endurance, +10-Stamina		

"What?" asked Olaf, allowing me to share the news of my new spell.

"Lucky blighter," said Olaf, grinning.

"I hate you," complained Rose. "That is so unfair. I'm the tank, I need the stamina and endurance buffs."

"Yeah, but that is crazy expensive for a level 1 spell. And it's unranked," added Baby.

Rose clicked her tongue in annoyance. "I hate it when you're right." It seemed I was the only one that didn't know about spell and skill ranks, if the way they were all nodding was any indication.

Talk about a noob moment.

"Yeah, but it could be a prerequisite to something even stronger," added Micaela thoughtfully.

I knew there was a reason I liked the excitable ogre.

"You should keep an eye out for anything related to boars in the future Bye-bye. You might find something better," Micaela added.

"I will," I answered, and I would. Even with that, I was excited to try the spell out. I had my first AoE, area of effect spells were great for dealing with large groups, not so great for single target, but that was the point. Plus, this one had a knockdown effect, which was a pseudo crowd control ability.

Anyway, with my exciting moment passed, we resumed our trek north toward the base of the mountain. The further north we traveled, the more the land started gradually sloping upwards. Eventually, we reached a point where the slope became an impossible incline, we could no longer traverse easily. It looked climbable if you had climbing equipment, but we didn't.

"I suppose we should look for a path up," suggested Olaf, his gaze also directed to the top of the ridge.

"Do you think it will be so easy?" asked Rose.

"Probably," said Olaf. "Games are usually good about giving players a path to things. Just a suggestion though, keep an eye out for more of those damnable cats."

"Yeah, yeah," said Rose, waving him off. "East or west?" she asked as an afterthought, looking left then right.

"East," I volunteered. Call me greedy, but my map would be completed if it killed me.

We moved east, as I requested, finding the occasional path that would go a little higher, but lead to a deadend. It wasn't until we were about a hundred yards from the waterfall, at the northeastern most point of the province, we found a path up. It wound back and forth a few times before we found ourselves standing atop the ridgeline.

Talk about breathtaking.

I could see the forest south of us stretching for miles. I saw white smoke rising from various chimneys and cook fires from the town. I could even see the top of the Town hall and the Doghouse Inn, the two tallest buildings in town. Beyond that, I could see the forest thin and further still, the Rolling Hills of Evermore appeared emerald green and never-ending.

I turned and looked to the north, it was all mountains and valleys, as far as the eye could see. I even saw a couple of volcanoes puffing black smoke in the distance. Part of me wondered if a dragon might call one of those home. Or maybe those were Dwarven forges puffing black smoke from lava forges. My imagination might have conjured up more endless adventures if an impatient Rose hadn't called me back to reality.

"You still with us?" Rose asked, snapping her fingers in front of my face.

"Yeah," I answered after a moment. "What a view!"

"I know I'm something special to look at, but we're up here for a reason, let's get hunting," countered Rose, grinning.

"Like a car wreck," I retorted. "I know I should look away, but I can't help but wonder, what happened."

Olaf chortled a little but was quickly silenced by a look from Rose, and an elbow from his wife.

"If I pushed him off, you'd all stay quiet about it, right?" asked Rose, looking to the others.

"Honestly," complained Baby. "Let's just get going. We don't have a ton of time if we want to find this <Ridge Lion King> before we have to turn back. I don't know about the rest of you, but I don't particularly want to get stuck outside the village after dark."

I hadn't considered it before, but I wasn't too put out by the idea of camping out. I had the skills for it now. I could make a tent, cook the wolf meat I collected earlier, even set some traps to keep us safe. I was actually okay with us not getting back to town.

"We could camp out," I suggested.

"We've still got our tent and sleeping bags," added Rose.

"Ugh, I hate camping," whined Baby.

"We can camp if we have to, but we should focus on the lion," said Olaf, trying to herd us onward.

He was right, we all acknowledged it and started walking the ridge line west. The top of the mountain ridge line was mostly flat, wide enough for two humans to walk side by side, but Olaf and Micaela had to walk single file. We must have gone a few miles before the path on top of the ridge came to an abrupt end. A particularly jagged and tall rock preventing us from moving further forward. It did, however, have a path going down either side, north, and south. Given our quest was for 'Hurlig Ridge' province, we went south, though the north would be interesting, just to take a peek at on our way back . . . if we have time.

The south path zigzagged east then west a few times before ending on a small plateau. It was a mostly flat, circular area. The west end and around to the south, had a sheer drop off, promising death to anyone who fell off. To the north, the steep incline of the mountain was interrupted by a rounded cave entrance that seemed to be growling at us, probably an effect of the wind, but possibly the very thing we were here to hunt.

"I think this is it," said Micaela, stating the obvious.

"So, do we go in after it or try to get it to come out to us?" asked Rose with her back to the cave entrance.

I looked toward the cave in an attempt to study it, while the others discussed strategy. There was no telling how deep the cave was, but from what I could see, it was pitch black inside. Not an ideal place for someone without some kind of night vision. It was then I saw a slight waver of air, reminding me of heat on the pavement. I tried to focus on it only to realize what it was.

Without thinking it through too much, I urgently pushed Rose out of the way, just as the attack was about to hit her. I took the hit in her place, thankfully only a glancing blow, but it still reeved -433-HP from my health pool.

I didn't have time to think too much about the damage, as the now visible <Ridge Lion King Lvl 8>, didn't seem interested in stopping its assault on me. I flipped over the next swipe and rolled past the follow-up.

Thankfully there wasn't a fourth, as Rose saved me.

Rose slammed her shield into the side of the beast then taunted him. "Here kitty, kitty. I've got a ball of yarn with your name on it."

Thank goodness for that. Thank goodness too for Baby, her healing spell restoring my health in an instant.

We didn't have much chance to buff before the fight, so I took a minute to ensure everyone had 'Lesser Holy Barrier', Lesser Mental Fortification' and 'Lesser Combat Blessing', after which I renewed 'Lesser Holy Imbuement' on my spear.

"Slow DPS to start," called out Rose, her sword striking suddenly, followed by her shield interrupting the attack of the <Ridge Lion King Lvl 8>.

"Watch your stamina," warned Baby. "You don't have to stop every attack with your 'Shield Slam'. Target the double swipe attack if you can." Rose didn't nod or acknowledge the instruction but seemed to do as she was asked without hesitating.

I hit the beast with my first stack of 'Lesser Holy Fire' allowing it to tick for a few points of damage before I moved in to fight. Once I had a chance to truly look at the <Ridge Lion King Lvl 8>, I had to say it was an impressive beast. It easily stood four feet tall at the shoulders, probably would have been five to the top of the head if he weren't crouched in an attack stance. His fur was grey-white, except for the random splotches of reddish-brown in his mane, probably drying blood from his latest meal.

I struck once with my spear, no skills applied other than my 'Lesser Holy Imbuement'. I didn't crit, but I was pleased anyway by the -161-HP the floated up from the beast's body. I cast another 'Lesser Holy Fire' adding the second stack. Left it for a few seconds then struck again with my spear for -153-HP damage to him. A few seconds later, I dropped on the third stack of 'Lesser Holy Fire'.

"Okay, start ramping up your damage output," said Rose, feeling more confident in her ability to keep threat on the beast.

It was finally my chance to try out the combo, I'd been thinking about for a while now. I started with 'Hamstring', lowering its attack speed and increasing the damage it received by 12%. Then 'Justice Strike' triggered, dealing -183-HP damage. I followed it up with a 'Lesser Holy Shock', which stunned the <Ridge Lion King Lvl 8> and dealt -83-HP damage. And last, but certainly not least, 'Power Thrust' walloped it for -215-HP damage. I ended the combo with 'Impale', adding a bleed, then casting 'Lesser Holy Fire' just as my cooldown ended.

That combo would have killed most beasts close to my level, but I knew, this was a tougher customer. Still, to see my combo knock out around 5% of its total health didn't disappoint me.

Then Olaf got a critical strike taking out 12% in one shot.

"Oi, Olaf, take it easy" grunted Rose, as she used her shield to slam the beast and interrupt one of its double swipe attacks.

"Sorry," Olaf said from about seven or so yards away from me, facing the right flank of the target.

"Nice shot, love," added Micaela, her duel axes hacking away from just to my left.

Seeing as I didn't pull aggro nor did Olaf, I took that to mean it was safe to go a little wild with my attacks. It didn't take long for the <Ridge Lion King Lvl 8> to drop to nearly 51% health. It hadn't occurred to me, to be prepared for him to use a special ability, as so far, none of the beasts we had fought used anything of the sort. And yet, when the beast's HP dropped to the 50% mark, it halted its attack and bellowed out the loudest roar I've ever heard.

It wasn't only loud, but also, unlike anything I had ever heard before. Without realizing what I was doing, I turned and ran, much to my own confusion.

"Hold Fast," shouted Rose. I felt her words wash over me, and I was back in control of myself.

"What the bloody hell was that?" asked Micaela, rushing back to attack.

"Fear effect," answered Rose. "The idiot was stupid enough to attack me first, which broke me lose from the fear. I used my 'Command: Courage' spell to break you all free. Let's hope he doesn't do that again any time soon though. My spell has a 2-minute cooldown."

"Okay, stop DPS at 27%," ordered Baby. "We'll only push past that mark if Rose's spell is off cooldown."

It was a sound plan, I just had to hope it didn't trigger more frequently than 25%.

As it turned out, we didn't need to worry about another 'Fearsome Roar' from the lion because at the 25% mark, nothing happened. In fact, he didn't do anything different until 10%, when he soft enraged. Normally in games when a player or boss 'enrages,' the damage is doubled or even tripled, as is the speed of attacks or spells being cast. A 'soft enrage' is a less powerful version, the damage is increased and so is the attack speed, but not to the degree of a true enrage.

Still, I could see the beast started taking massive chunks of health from Rose, giving us a sense of urgency to kill it. It didn't last long as between me, Olaf and Micaela, it only took a few more hits to kill it.

The kill was worth +200-Experience points, the most anything I'd killed so far had awarded me.

"+500-Experience, sweet," said Rose, grinning. It wasn't uncommon for lower level players to get more experience than the higher-level players, a common balancing mechanic to help the lower-level players catch up to the higher-level players. It usually only affected killing things, as quests were generally fixed for experience rewards based on the level and difficulty of it.

"Yay, I got +20-Experience points," cheered Baby jokingly. "Those are the first experience points I've gotten since we fought and killed the <Greater Condor>." At level 9, it wasn't surprising.

"300 hundred for me," added Micaela.

"Me too," said Olaf.

"Now, the real question is, do we check out the cave?" asked Rose, grinning and pointing to the cave the beast snuck out of.

"Sure, but not too deep," said Olaf. "I want to get this guy back to town, so we can turn in the quest."

"I can't see in the dark," I said.

"Neither can we," said Olaf, reaching into his bag and pulling out a helmet painted yellow and covered in scratches. The important part was the candle mounted on top of it. "Mining would be a might difficult if we couldn't see where we were going or what we were hitting."

Olaf led the way with Micaela bringing up the rear with her own helmet and candle. The entrance to the cave was narrow, just wide enough and tall enough for Olaf to fit. I couldn't see too far ahead but it seemed to go on for a while.

"I'm surprised you're not leading the way, Rose," I commented, trying to be careful not to trip over the uneven cave floor.

"I can't see in the dark either. But I can see heat," Rose replied. "The Goddess Lilith grants me the ability to see heat, same way snakes do. If I had signed on with Dracula, I would have gotten an echolocation ability."

I could see where both had their uses.

The tunnel eventually opened into a slightly larger cavern. The inside was filled with bones, piled and fit together forming a demented bird's nest, made with the skulls of animals and humanoids alike. I was about to turn back around and leave when I caught a flash of light to my left.

As Olaf and Micaela's combined candles seemed to be enough to light the small cave nest, I wasn't worried about venturing away from the group. It was a good thing I did, too.

I found a pool of water beneath a stalactite, steadily dripping water from above. It wasn't the pool of water or the stalactite I found interesting. It was the bottom of the shallow pool below the dripping stalactite. It was filled with shiny metal disks of Copper, Silver and a few bright spots of Gold.

"Jackpot!" I called, getting the attention of the group. They rushed over to see what I'd found.

"Cha-ching," said Rose cheerfully, seeing all the shiny metal.

"Look, over there, another pool of water," said Olaf, pointing toward the back of the bone nest. It was another pool of water, metal flashing from within.

We found two more such pools. When we collected all the shiny metal coins, each of us ended up with 10-Gold, 4-Silver, and 56-Copper. A profitable endeavor indeed. After that, we collected the beast's corpse and made a strong effort to get off the mountain before the sun set.

We managed to get down, but not much further before we collectively decided to set up camp for the night. I finally got to use my 'Campsite Management' skills, building a tent and bedding for myself. I built a second tent for Olaf and Micaela, but they had sleeping bags, I made a mental note to pick one up as well. With the tents put up, I started a campfire and put the wolf meat on a spit to cook. And finally, while it cooked, I put up a perimeter and a few traps for game.

If we were lucky I'd catch us some breakfast.

When I finished and sat down to wait for the meat to finish cooking, I checked my system messages. I'd gained a few skill levels in all the spells, I had been using today as well as my 'Campsite Management' and 'Trap' skills. Somehow, even 'Lore' gained a level. I also gained +2-Strength, +3-Dexterity, +4-Endurance, and +2-Stamina. It was a darned good day.

Rose took a few tentative sniffs of the meet. "Smells edible," she commented.

"It is edible," I replied.

"No seasoning?" Rose commented.

"I didn't think to bring salt and pepper, sorry," I retorted.

"Did you happen to bring plates, forks, and knives?" Rose asked.

I hadn't even though about that.

"We've got you covered," said Micaela, pulling out a stack of tin plates and utensils. "We use these at the mines all the time."

Thank the Goddess for her and Olaf, thank the Goddess she had enough for all of us, and thank the Goddess for the look on Rose's face. Grumbling, Rose sat and quietly glared at her wolf steak until hunger won out.

With the meal done, Olaf and Micaela chose to retire first, saying they'd take the next watch. It was early but plenty dark enough to sleep. We agreed to split it into two 6-hour watches. Baby, Rose and I had first watch.

Rose and Baby were occupied talking to each other, so I took the opportunity to take out my journal and start writing about the day. It wasn't a super full day, and I was eager to work on my map, so I filled my journal for the day pretty quickly.

I finally pulled out my map and got to work, intent on finishing the area we explored today. I did my best to put more detail into the river, making sure to notate deeper water from shallow and slower from faster. I added a note about the <Wolf> and <Alpha Wolf> packs we ran into, as well as, the <Ridge Lion> beasts we encountered all along the mountain. I put more detail into the path up to the ridge. I added the path to the <Ridge Lion King> last, including the cave. I made note of the path to the north but had to leave a '?' next to it as it was decided we just didn't have enough time to go exploring.

"That's not bad," said a voice right next to my ear. I was so startled, I almost threw my map into the fire when I jumped to my feet and away from the sneak attack.

Instead of danger, I was greeted by a laughing Rose and Baby.

"That's not funny," I said, feeling embarrassed by their sneaking up on me, even more so that I didn't notice. If I had been the only one on watch, I'd already be dead.

"Oh, but it was funny, so very funny," said Rose, mirth still on her face and dancing in her eye.

I was about to retort when the world took on a red tint.

Enemies of Issara's justice are nearby and must be punished

"Shh," I hissed, suddenly looking around us. I found them, three targets. The jangling of my perimeter rope telling me they were getting closer.

"Damn, Whiz, you triggered a perimeter," complained one of them too loudly.

"Wake Olaf, and Mic, quietly," I warned Rose and Baby.

"Baby, go," whispered Rose, deciding to stand next to me and face the danger together. Baby didn't hesitate, flying silently into the makeshift tent to wake the other members of our party.

"Since when do noobs have the skill to set up a perimeter?" retorted another voice.

"I don't know, maybe they camp in RL," the first complainer replied.

"Both of you shut up!" shouted a third voice. Then softer I heard him speak again. "Why did I have to open my trap, now they know there are at least three of us."

Ah, the third one was trying to make it appear they had a bigger party. Not that they should have needed it. If he was an enemy of Issara then he was at least level 26 if not higher. On the other hand, maybe he didn't know what he was approaching and thought maybe we were PK'ers too.

"You may as well come out," I shouted. I needed to draw all three of them in closer, my spell just didn't have the range it used to.

"What are you doing?" hissed Rose.

"Trust me," I whispered to her. Then I yelled again, "Come on, I don't have all night. If I'm going to be sent for respawn I'd rather just get it done and over with."

"Huh, how about that?" said the first voice.

"I've never had a noob volunteer to die before," said the third.

A moment later, all three of them came in sight of the campfire. I also saw the outlines of two more enemies of Issara come into visual range, slowly creeping up from behind us. If not for the blessing of the Goddess, I would probably have believed the guy about their only being three of them. Now I knew better.

"You guys hungry?" I asked, motioning to the bit of meat still over the fire. "Might be a little dry by now, but it should still be edible."

"Don't mind if I do," said the guy in the middle, moving forward quickly, his dagger at the ready. <Shifty McSquigglebottom Lvl 27>, he had two daggers, maybe swords? They were bigger than daggers when compared with his short squat form. I think he was a dwarf, or maybe half-dwarf, half-gnome.

"It might be poisoned you idiot," warned the third voice, probably the leader. <Burnie Burns Lvl 32> appeared to be a mage carrying a gnarled wood staff and was wearing black robes, a large hood covering his head from view. With so much of him covered up, I couldn't tell what race he was.

"It's not poisoned," I replied, not expecting them to believe me.

"Even if it was, I'm resistant to poison," said Shifty, eagerly cutting off a piece. "Meh, a little dry and could use some seasoning but not too shabby. Shame we have to kill you and your friends."

Rose snarled at him, I did my best to hold her back with one arm. The other two seemed to be trying to sneak around behind us.

"Let's just kill them already," said the impatient voice of the second guy. <Wart Legz Lvl 29> looked the part of a barbarian, the massive battle ax held lightly in his two massive Orcish arms boasted a high strength stat.

Baby had yet to return with Micaela and Olaf, hopefully, they snuck out the back of the tent and were preparing an ambush of their own.

The other two were close enough now. "I suppose it would be rude of me, not to offer the five of you the chance to surrender," I said, a small smirk at the corner of my mouth, confidence oozing as best I could make it.

"Eh?" uttered a confused looking Burnie.

"Ha," laughed Wart loudly, it was completely fake. "You're a comedian, are you?"

"No, I'm a servant of the Goddess Issara," I replied.

"Issara, which God is that?" asked Shifty.

"Issara," mumbled Burnie a few times before his eyes went wide. "Oh, hell no! Run, run now!" Burnie suddenly turned and tried to flee.

"Justice Bringer," I chanted, a pulse of light burst forth from me.

A second later, Burnie's head exploded from a perfectly placed shot from Olaf. I turned to face the two who were trying to sneak up on us and smirked. I finally got to try my new spell.

"Boar Charge," I shouted, mentally targeting the area the two killers were trying to sneak through. I heard the charge before I saw it. It was beautiful to behold, as a drove of blue spectral swine plowed through the forest, stampeding through, gouging and knocking down the two dagger wielding men. I attacked the weakest man first, pouncing on him with 'Justice Strike', followed by 'Lesser Holy Shock' to stun him, then killing him with a 'Power Thrust'.

I looked to the next guy, who seemed to fair better than his dead friend. He attacked, leaping at me with both daggers high in the air. I simply dove forward, rolling past his attack and getting behind him. I struck with 'Hamstring' followed again by the rest of my favorite combo of skills. I added a pair of 'Jab' attacks, while he was still stunned, ending his life.

I looked back to my friends planning to help them, only to see the barbarian looking fellow on his knees, begging for his life only to be ruthlessly snuffed out by one of Olaf's hand-cannons.

"Now how the devil did that just happen?" asked Rose, looking at me with her piercing red eyes and a slightly amused grin.

I guess I had some explaining to do.

CHAPTER 28

"That explains why my healing magic got weaker suddenly. I almost panicked when I thought someone snuck a debuff on me, or something," complained Baby.

"Sorry Baby, I didn't have a chance to warn you or Rose," I apologized.

"I thought you said it went to the town priests," asked Rose sharply, looking at me accusingly.

I cringed. "In my defense, I didn't know either of you very well yet. The spell is new for the town priestess, but only because my Goddess, the Goddess Issara, gave me the spell so ultimately, so that I would give it to the World Tree. I think it was a test from her," I tried to explain. "One of many tests she has put before me actually," I added as an afterthought. "And, as soon as I did give it to Trini, Issara nerfed the thing nearly to death. It just happened to benefit us this time."

"Is that why that guy Bernie panicked?" asked Baby.

"I think so. I can only guess stories have started to spread about my ability. If they die while under the effect, it can knock them all the way back down to level 1."

"Woah, what the hax is that about?" asked Rose, clearly shocked. I explained the 'Judgement' mechanics which left Rose and Baby slightly stunned.

"Rose, I know you wanted to think about this, but we have to join their order. Can you imagine how nice it will be if we don't have to worry about player killers anymore?" Baby asked.

"I'm not a guaranteed instant win ticket," I warned quickly, the last thing I needed was them jumping to the wrong conclusion. "I can only even the playing field. I can only give us chance for it to be fair . . . well fairer. There are still going to be skills and spells that are seriously overpowered, just as there are in all games."

"Whatever you say, Mr. Fairplay," said Rose, her arms crossed.

"Ooh," said Olaf, perking up suddenly. "I like that."

"Like what?" Rose and I asked at the same time.

Please tell me he doesn't like the nickname.

"Mr. Fairplay is a pretty good nickname," commented Micaela, a playful smirk on her face.

"Not that," said Olaf to my relief and Rose's disappointment. "Fairplay. The Order of Fairplay, what do you guys think?"

"Could be worse, but it doesn't sound too adventurous," said Rose with a shrug.

"We'll put it on the maybe list," said Micaela, taking out a small pad of paper and flipping through a few pages then writing.

"Just how many order names have you come up with?" I asked curiously.

"With Fairplay, I have one-hundred and seventy-two possible names," chirped Micaela happily.

"Anyway, it's close enough to our shift, why don't you three try to get a little shuteye, sunrise will be here before you know it," suggested Olaf, ushering us off.

I didn't sleep well, the bedding of leaves I'd made was of poor quality and the darned things kept finding their way into places they didn't belong. Morning couldn't come soon enough as far as I was concerned.

So, when the first light of dawn broke, I was up and out of my makeshift tent. I gave a quick greeting to Micaela and Olaf then went to check my traps. Unfortunately, I was skunked, not a single critter to speak of. It didn't help that most of the traps had been destroyed by our late-night visitors.

We ended up eating rations for breakfast before breaking camp and continuing our march back to town. We had to deal with packs of beasts until we crossed the river then it was just the occasional wolf or alpha.

We were back through the gates a little after 8:00 AM according to my game clock.

"Any plans today?" asked Rose, once we were back through the village gates.

"Sergeant Butters, Trini, Barnum, B&E," I said shortly as possible.

"B&E?" asked Baby, confused.

"Breaking and Entering," I answered. "I intend to test my luck against that evil house again today."

"Do you know if anyone in town sells popcorn?" asked Rose, smirking.

I frowned and glared at her. "I am not here for your entertainment."

"Oh Jack, you say the silliest things," quipped Rose, sounding more than a little amused.

"Why me?" I grumbled.

Rather than engage her further, I started walking toward the barracks. I had a simple plan today, learn the three 'Two-Handed Polearms' subskills for my 'One-Handed Polearms' skill set. After that, I'd see if I couldn't use the practice dummies instead of going to Trinico's, so I could start leveling up my magic. Which reminded me, I recast my buffs on my friends and myself.

"Morning," I greeted the sergeant ahead of my friends. "I'll be working on the training dummies today," I told him. "Actually, do you mind if I continue to work with the dummies, instead of going to see Trinico today?"

"Sure, just give my men preference, if they need the dummies," the sergeant replied, waving me along. It didn't take long for me to learn all three subskills for 'One-Handed Polearms' and once I confirm I had learned them, I started working on my spells.

One-Handed Polearms	Level: 31	Experience: 45.88%
Current Damage Modifiers	Damage: +15.50	Critical Strike Chance: +1.55%
Subskill: Jab	Damage: +15.50	Skill Stamina Cost: 41
Subskill: Rapid Striking	Damage: -10 Strikes: 13	Skill Stamina Cost: 81
Subskill: Hamstring	Reduce Enemy Movement and Attack Speed: 50% Target Receives Increased Damage: +7.75% Duration: 15 Seconds	Skill Stamina Cost: 46
Subskill: Impale	Damage: 15-16 Bleed Effect: 2 Damage per Second Duration: 10 Seconds	Skill Stamina Cost: 51
Subskill: Power Thrust	Damage: +31.00 Chance to Stun: 10%	Skill Stamina Cost: 81

Well, spells and one skill, 'Justice Strike', which I needed to level as much as I could. I simply rotated through them, 'Justice Strike', 'Lesser Holy Shock', 'Holy Smite', 'Lesser Holy Fire' and 'Boar Charge', until I was out of mana. I sat, drank mana infused water and started again. Eventually, I ran out of water and called an end to my training for the day. I was only able to cast 'Boar Charge' a few times given its 30-minute cooldown, but it still gained a few levels. Everything else though gained several levels each, but 'Justice Strike' and 'Lesser Holy Shock' had the biggest gains, 12-levels each, which made sense as they were my weakest spells, still are, but they are getting steadily stronger.

Justice Strike	Level: 18	Experience: 4.51%
Current Damage Modifier	Damage: +9.00	Skill Stamina Cost: 68
Skill Effect (Active): A righteous strike in the name of Justice. Increases damage or healing of next spell cast by 28.		

Lesser Holy Shock	Level: 18	Experience: 4.51%
Spell Damage: 28-33	Spell Cash Speed: Instant Cooldown: 30 seconds	Spell Mana Cost: 136
Spell Effect (Active): A shock of holy energy attacks the nervous system of your target stunning it and increasing physical damage received by 38 for 5 seconds.		

I looked around to see my friends were gone, probably already off to see Trinico. Given, I had been training here for almost 4 hours, I figured they had another 2 until they were done at Trinico's. I decided I was overdue for a trip to Ned's sundry. My mana canteens were tapped, I was out of rations and still hadn't bought a better bag. I also needed to look into buying a sleeping bag and maybe a tent, if the price was right.

Ned's sundry was much the same as the first time I visited, though considerably busier than the last time I had seen it. There must have been 10 fresh level 1 adventurers in there. Poor Ned was drowning in demands and requests.

"Bye-bye, save me," Ned cried out upon seeing me. Suddenly all eyes were on me.

"Hey, he's level 6, I bet he can help us," said a young man, probably only eighteen or nineteen years old, if I had to guess. <Surfer Boi2 Lvl 1>, I read his name. He also appeared human. There were two young men and two young women with him, probably around the same age.

"Yo, bruh, hook us up," said one of his companions, a <Zurfer Dude Lvl 1>, also human looking.

"I'm sorry?" I replied, not sure what he was saying.

"Sorry for my idiot friends," stepped up one of the young women, <Arial Norenci Lvl 1>. She was a pure elf if the ears were anything to go by. "We were hoping you could help us out. The forums are abuzz, saying this province is a safe place for people to start playing. Could you give us some pointers?" she asked politely.

"Oh," I was shocked. I couldn't believe what she was saying. I was more confused by who on the forums was saying this place is safe to level. "Well, nothing is completely safe, get that out of your head now. There are still Player Killers roaming the wilds, but the village is safe, I suppose. As for giving you some tips . . . I suppose I could help out a little. First things first, get a room at one of the inns, you're going to want a safe place to sleep at night unless you want to camp outside of town. Second, go introduce yourself to Sergeant Butters, he can be found around the back of the barracks. He can offer you weapon training. Third, meet the mayor in the Town hall. You'll also find the job board there with some basic quests to get you started." As I was explaining, it dawned on me as I looked around, I suddenly had the attention of everyone in the shop, including Ned. "And fourth, this is the most important part. It will help you more than anything else. Get to know the people, the citizens as they are called, talk to them like they are normal people, you'll be amazed by the results. For example," I paused to look at Ned. "Ned, how's business been lately?"

"Oh, me, well Bye-bye, I have to tell you, things have really picked up lately. I have had so many requests and even some odd ones. Would you believe, someone came in here the other day asking for a submachine gun? I do not even know what that is, but it had the word gun in it, so I sent him to see Giggle-Ana. He had the nerve to get all huffy with me, saying he had already visited her then stormed off. Some people are just so rude. But, the Gods and Goddesses do not put anything before us, which we cannot weather, for that is the eternal test," Ned rattled on.

"Sounds rough, say, I don't suppose there is anything these new adventurers could do help you out?" I asked.

"Well, as a matter of fact, I'm running low on Adventurer Jerky. Rita said she'd be happy to make some, but she needs salt. I have plenty of salt, but I'm so busy, I just haven't had time to run some to her. If any of you would be interested, I would appreciate the help," Ned requested, spawning a low-level quest.

"And there you all go," I said, declining the level 1 quest. "One last thing about that, don't expect to talk to a citizen, demand a quest and get one."

"Wow, that was so realistic," said Arial. "Hey, what else do you know?"

"Figure out what profession you want and find out how to get it. Don't trust anything the forums told you, they lie. High

534

Priestess Trinico can help you with a number of healing spells if that's the path you want to take. The town mage, I can't remember his name, anyway, he's the local mages guild representative, he can teach you elemental spells. I don't know if he charges or not, you'll have to talk to him," I instructed.

"What about crafting?" asked another young man, this one a dwarf named <Hammer Tim Lvl 1>.

"What do you want to learn?" I asked.

"Blacksmithing and mining," Hammer replied.

"Go see Kirlan Dunkirk, he can teach you Blacksmithing. For mining, I think you have to go see the mining foreman at the mines to the southeast of the village. If there are any other crafting question, go see the mayor in the Town hall, he can direct you, same with any class questions," I tried to get ahead of being bombarded by more questions.

"Any other tips?" asked Arial.

I answered, "Buy yourselves a few canteens, fill half of them with the mana enriched water Ned sells, and the other half with the stamina water from the barrel behind the barracks. Other than that, I can only emphasize, talk to the citizens. They will give you hints when they talk to you if they need your help with something, which reminds me, don't underestimate the value of the Charisma stat." I didn't tell them everything I knew as there were just some things you needed to learn for yourself. Hopefully, I gave them enough to get them started.

"So, where are you staying?" asked Arial.

"Dog House Inn, it's just kitty-corner from the Town hall. It's very nice and the price is fair," I answered. "If you choose to stay there, he might give you a discount if you mention my name. Also, talk to his wife, they have an ongoing quest to gather blackberries to make pies, and they are quite delicious."

"Maybe I'll see you there later," said Arial, her hand brushing mine as she left.

It seemed most of the attention on me faded after that, as the new adventurers were now scrambling to get out of Ned's, and off to find an adventure.

"Well, that was intense," said Ned. "Now, how can I help you Bye-bye?"

"I need a new bag, something with more carrying capacity. I need a sleeping roll, and maybe a tent. And finally, I need a higher-level mana restorative and stamina restoratives if you've got any," I requested.

"I can certainly help you with all of that," said Ned, a friendly smile on his face.

He was quickly moving about his shop in a precise manner, moving from one shelf to the next and selecting a few items, then moving on to the next shelf. It took him a few minutes to return where he then set a line of items on the long counter, normally separating him from the rest of the shop.

"Here are two of our best bag options, 100-lbs Traveler's Satchel and the 200-lbs Traveler's Satchel," he motioned to two plain brown bags that looked exactly the same. I appreciated the bags where the typical game blackholes, where anything could fit in the bag as long as there was space or carrying capacity.

"2-Gold and 5-Gold," he added.

"The 2-Gold bag is plenty for me, at least for now," I said, happily taking the 100-lbs Traveler's Satchel and slipping the strap over my shoulder. I handed Ned his money then transferred the contents of my old bag, which wasn't much, to my new bag.

As I was moving stuff over, I found the 'Sharp Tooth' I had gotten the previous day and set it on the counter. "What is this worth?" I asked.

"10-Copper," Ned answered without even inspecting it.

I nodded accepting the price and in one smooth move from Ned the tooth was gone and in its place was 10-Copper.

"Sleeping rolls are pretty standard, 25-Copper each," Ned said, this time there was a single brown simple pad and blanket, rolled up and tied, which would work just fine. I paid Ned and put it straight into my new bag.

"You have a few options for tents ranging from 1 person triangular to a 10-person wall tent commonly used by soldiers," he offered a wide range but only had three on the countertop.

"How much?" I asked.

"The single person triangle tent is 50-Copper, the 10-person wall ten is 10-Gold," Ned answered.

The large wall tent was tempting but way too expensive.

"How about a simple 2-man triangular tent?" I asked.

"75-Copper," he answered.

"That would be perfect, thank you," I said, paying the shopkeeper.

"Last up, the waters, also, do you have canteens capable of holding more without having to be larger than this," I asked holding up one of the empty canteens.

"Sure, I have a few higher capacity canteens around the same size," Ned replied. He actually went into the back of the shop and returned a moment later with a few more canteens about the same size as the metal one I was still holding. These new ones were color-coded it seemed.

"The blue canteens are made for mana water, they are enchanted to make any water put in them into the basic mana enriched water, but if you put already mana enriched water in them they will make the water into improved mana enriched water," the shopkeeper explained.

"Will they improve other mana restoratives as well?" I asked.

"Absolutely, and they hold up to 20 drinks each," Ned answered.

"How much?" I asked, only so I would know how many I could buy.

"5-Gold each," Ned answered.

Ouch, so expensive.

"The green canteens have the same properties but for stamina replenishing," he added.

"How much for the next level of restorative?" I asked.

"Another Gold per filled canteen," Ned answered.

Okay, I didn't have enough for the canteen and the water. It was time to 'Barter' a better price. "That's awfully expensive," I started. "Let's say 6-Gold for two canteens and 1-Gold for the restorative."

"And here I thought you fought against banditry. I could not let two canteens go for less than 9-Gold and the price on the restorative is fixed, non-negotiable," the shopkeeper countered.

"I suppose I can accept the price on the restorative is fixed, but that is still way too much for the canteens. Let's call it 7-Gold, 5-Silver and I'll fill up my other canteens too," I offered.

Ned eyed me for a moment before speaking, "Deal."

I paid him and filled all my canteens include my old canteens with the next level restoratives. Manaberry Juice and Stamina Water Plus.

I wish I had the money to buy more but for now, I had to be satisfied with one of each. I'm sure on down the road I'll want to buy even better canteens.

| High-Capacity Canteen (20/20) - Filled with Improved Manaberry Juice, restores +125-MP per mouthful. |
| High-Capacity Canteen (20/20) - Filled with Improved Stamina Water Plus, restores +125-SP per mouthful. |

Now that my business was complete, and I was down to just under 2-Gold, it was time to go meet up with my friends at the temple.

"About time you showed up," Rose greeted me.

"Sorry, were you waiting long?" I asked.

"Only a few minutes," said Baby, cutting off Rose from giving me a hard time. "Where did you go anyway?"

"Oh, I had to pop into Ned's for a few supplies. You'll never believe what happened there," I added, not completely excited about it. Anyway, I shared my story with them.

"How did word get out? That's what I can't figure," I said, at the end.

"We weren't the only adventurers defending the town," said Olaf. "Probably one of them logged out recently and put it out there. That could prove to be a mistake though. You might as well be daring a PK order to come hunting."

"Not necessarily," said Baby, thoughtfully. "What if last night was a PK group testing the waters? When the rest of their guild finds out then this place will suddenly become a place for player killers to fear."

"If, only if. For now, it doesn't matter, does it," said Rose. "Let's go turn in that corpse for our loot and then I plan to find a good seat to watch the show."

"I think I'll be going back to see Giggle-Ana for more engineering training, as fun as watching Bye-bye get mauled by a house sounds," said Olaf, chuckling at my expense at the end.

"I'll be going for more herbs for the same reason," said Baby.

"I will be going to the show," said Micaela, smiling happily, her single eye dancing with glee.

Great, just what I wanted, an audience.

"Come on, let's go turn in this lion so we can get to the fun part," said Rose, trying to hurry us all along.

The 'Leather Emporium' was empty when we arrived aside from Barnum, who was just coming from the back room when he heard the door jingle with our arrival.

"Back so soon?" Barnum asked.

"Yes sir," said Olaf, approaching the counter and removing the body of the <Ridge Lion King> from his mining bag.

I was surprised it could hold that much weight even with his strength, but as he explained it, he had lightening enchantments, which allowed him to carry four times his actual carrying capacity. Olaf explained it was common for miners to do this, so they could carry back more ore.

Olaf set the large beast on the counter.

"My word, you actually got him," said Barnum, sounding astonished. "Help me carry him into the back, will you?"

Olaf picked up the beast and carried him to the back room, returning a moment later.

"Barnum asked us to wait a bit," Olaf explained without being asked.

"How long is a bit?" I asked. I still had things I wanted to accomplish today. Olaf could only shrug.

A bit turned out to be an hour and a half. When Barnum returned from the back room he at least didn't come empty-handed.

"Thank you for waiting so patiently. First, Mr. Olaf, for you," the old hunter said, handing Olaf a pair of gloves matching his pants.

"Thank you," said Olaf, sliding them on.

"Miss Micaela," Barnum said next. He handed her a pair of boots or rather frames for a pair of boots. "You should be able to mount a totem to these for the armoring, I've only provided you the framework and a padded sole, which I believe you will appreciate."

"Excellent!" cheered Micaela, hopping excitedly and shaking the entire shop.

"For you Miss Babies," Barnum addressed the fairy. He handed her a leather necklace with several claws dangling from it. "I do believe this necklace should help to keep you alive."

"Dodge is always welcome," said Baby, slipping the necklace over her head.

"Miss Rose," Barnum said next. He handed her two things, a vial of blood and a lion-shaped charm made from the lion's fangs.

"Excellent indeed," said Rose grinning, the charm vanishing from sight as she equipped it and then putting the vial in her bag.

Finally, he got to me, "I thought you might make use of this," Barnum said, handing me what could have been the lion's mane dyed white.

Quest Alert: Hunt the Elusive <Ridge Lion King> (Recommended Level 5-8, 3 or more Adventurers) - Completed
Barnum has challenged you to hunt the elusive and very dangerous <Ridge Lion King>. Return with the body of the beast for him work the leather and you will be well rewarded.
Reward: +1,500-Experience, Holy Lion Mane Shoulder-guards, Lion King's Pride

I took a closer look at the Holy Lion Mane Shoulder-guards.

> Holy Lion Mane Shoulder-guards – Light Leather - +15 Armor, +5-Strength, +10-Dexterity, +5 Intellect, +10-Holy Damage, and Healing, Durability 30/30

Equipped, so very nice. I love Good quality gear so much. Looking at myself in one of the shop's mirrors, I now appeared to have a great white lion's mane covering my shoulders and upper back and the white color matched my leg-guards perfectly. I just needed a new chest armor and maybe some gloves, to have a matching outfit.

"Now he's got some style," said Micaela, nodding in approval of the look. "Still need to do something about your vest, but your look is starting to come together."

"I owe you all great thanks for this," said Barnum. "I hope this small token of my appreciation is enough."

"We were happy to help," I jumped in before Rose could. I knew I was pushing my Charisma to the maximum, but I had to try anyway. "Is there anything else in the area we can hunt down for you?"

"Oh goodness no, you have all done enough for me," Barnum replied.

"Are you sure? We don't mind," I offered.

"I am always happy to take in whatever unusual or rare beasts you might collect, but there is nothing else in the area that I am aware of. However, if something does come along or if I catch wind of something rare, I promise to reach out to you all first," Barnum promised.

I suppose that was it for now. And I was fine with that.

"Oh, and before I forget, should you ever form an Order, come back and see me. That lion is a valuable bit of prestige for any Order to display in their hall."

"We will, we promise," said Olaf, grinning excitedly.

Once we were back outside. "See, this is why we have to form an Order together, all five of us."

"Stop pushing already love, most of us have already agreed," Micaela tried to temper her husband.

"You're right, sorry," said Olaf, apologizing mostly to Rose and Baby.

"Enough chit-chat, it's time for the show," said Rose, far too gleefully.

"You're a cruel woman, I hope you know that," I said flatly.

Rose only smiled back at me, seeming to enjoy my anguish.

CHAPTER 29

I grumbled the entire walk to Lieutenant Graves's home, while Micaela and Rose jabbered about who knows what. Arriving at the house, it somehow looked even eviler than before.

Standing before the front steps, I took a few deeps breaths, trying to tune out anything around me that might distract me. I could see the front door or rather the deck just in front of the door, glowing in my vision, there was a little line that drew away from where I knew the trapdoor to be. It led to the side of the porch. I followed the glowing line to some kind of trigger mechanism, or what I assumed was a trigger. I took out my utility knife and cut the flashing red cord. The glow from the trap faded completed. I think I just disarmed my first trap.

I went back around to the front of the house, the panel with the pitfall was no longer glowing. I think the deck was now safe. I climbed the steps cautiously. I took a few test steps on the pitfall trap, but it didn't budge, even stomped on it once and not even a shimmy.

Now, I was looking at the door, on the other side of which was the Decapitator 3000, just waiting to take my head off and send me to respawn. I couldn't see anything on the door or the lock, so I got to work picking the lock. It took about a minute before I heard the click of it unlocking. I turned the knob slowly, opening the door just slightly and saw a new glow on the floor and wall. I saw the line again, this one leading up across the entryway ceiling before turning back toward the door and out of view. I risked opening the door a little more and saw the line continue to the wall above the door frame. There was a little blue crystal mounted there, flashing red. I reach an arm up and plucked the crystal out of the wall.

The glow stopped, the trap seemed to be disarmed now.

I put the crystal in my bag, you never knew what would come in handy later. Games love to use things like this, to create a puzzle.

I let the door swing open the rest of the way but moved so the door frame acted as a shield. I peeked around the corner, looking for any unusual seams or out of place items. My vision lit up, just beyond the entrance hall. The next area floor was lit up, flooding my vision with light. There was so much of it, I didn't see any line leading to a switch to disarm it. What I did see, were safe spots. The squares were spread about a step apart, placed so I could safely use them to cross the room. I had to hope, the trail of steps would lead me to the disarmament point.

I took the first step, making sure I was safely inside the border of the safe spot. Then another step, and another. The path led me to a grandfather clock, the face of which, was flashing red. Do I smash it or set the time? I studied it closer. It was then, I noticed, the clock had the faces of the moon on the outer ring of the clock. I wound the minute hand forward and the faces of the moon slowly moved. I started spinning the minute hand faster, hours and days past until the moon reflected fully. I heard a clicking and the glow that had previously surrounded me faded to nothing. I breathed a sigh of relief. It seemed I had disarmed the first floor's traps.

"Well I'll be buggered, you figured out how to disarm the first floor," said an unfamiliar voice behind me.

I turned swiftly, to see a human male. He had dark black shoulder length hair which was completely untamed. He also wore a black leather jacket, and blue jean pants with tears in them which appeared deliberate. He had a single dagger at his hip, but otherwise, I saw no other weapons. <Heath Rickards Lvl 5> appeared to be my age or maybe a little older. I got the impression, he was confident in himself and his abilities, if his nonchalance about entering this house was anything to go by.

"What do you want?" I demanded my spear at the ready.

"Relax, I'm not here to fight. I just wanted to see who was breaking into the unbreakable house, mate," Heath replied, still looking around the room. "I've been trying to break into this place for almost a week. Bloody traps are everywhere in this bloody nightmare. How'd you manage it?"

"I disarmed the traps," I answered.

"Which thieves guild rep taught you that?" Heath asked.

I responded, "None of them, I'm not a thief."

"Ha, well how do you like that. Brilliant mate," he said in a British accent. Something about it sounded off though. Was he trying to force the accent?

"So, what is your interest in this house?" I asked, wondering if our quests had crossed paths or if he was just a thief.

"Me? I've broken into every house in this town at least twice, but this place has bloody killed me, every bloody time. It's bloody ridiculous, is what it is. Where did you learn to disarm traps?" Heath asked, clearly not taking me seriously or my spear being aimed at him.

"A book in the Town hall, called 'Trapology'," I answered.

"So, you've robbed everyone in this town then?"

"No, I didn't say anything about robbing anyone. I just picked the locks, snuck around, did a little eavesdropping, maybe checked a few pockets, but never took anything," Heath explained.

"Why would a thief, and I'm assuming you are a thief, not steal anything?" I asked.

"I'm only a thief out of necessity, not because I want to be," Heath replied.

"Same question, why not steal if you need to be a thief?" I asked.

"I have to get rank II, in all the thief skills to become a bard, mate," Heath answered.

"Who told you that?" I asked.

"The Thieves Guild," he answered. "Once I get my rank up in 'Stealth', 'Lockpicking', 'Pickpocketing' and 'Espionage', they let you choose a specialization. I'm going the Bard path."

Huh, this was a first for me. Someone who actually used the game for knowledge on advanced classes, instead of the forums.

"Mind if I ask what your interest is in this place?" asked Heath.

"Oh, a quest. I'm looking for information on the owner," I answered, relaxing a little. This guy didn't seem to be too threatening.

"And why are the guards outside gambling on this instead of arresting you?" he asked, grinning.

I blinked unsure how to respond to that. Not even sure if I believed him. So, I walked back toward the front door and low and behold, a crowd had indeed gathered to watch. I also saw Gavin running some kind of betting pool.

"Ah, that would be Gavin running the betting pool. I imagine Rose is probably responsible for some of this too," I added as I watch Rose and Gavin chatting before separating and working the crowd again.

I shook my head and sighed. "Why? Why me? What did I ever do to deserve this?"

"Not sure, mate," said Heath, patting me on the shoulder, surprising me. I forgot he was here.

"Are you gonna stay and watch me?" I asked.

"Might, might not," he replied, not moving.

Deciding I would just have to ignore the thief, I started exploring the first floor. The dining room, where I was with the clock, was empty with nothing behind any of the paintings or hidden under loose floorboards. I opened the kitchen door and nearly vomited. The room was covered in blood, and there appeared to be a rotting animal carcass on a butchers table in the center. I decided right then, the kitchen would be the last room searched, and only if I can't find what I'm looking for elsewhere.

I returned to the front entranceway, putting the dining room and kitchen behind me, the exit to my right and stairs going up on the left. Directly ahead of me was the living room. It was sparse, only a couch and end table, an oil lamp sitting on top of it. To my disappointment, there was nothing to be found after searching the room, even pulling off the couch cushions and searching the crevasses.

There was a door under the stairs that's lit up brightly with a small panel next to it flashing red. I looked at it carefully without touching it. There were two slots that appeared to be the perfect size to fit two crystals, the same size, and shape as the one I pulled from above the door.

"That kitchen is nasty, mate," commented Heath, having joined me in the living room.

I ignored him. I needed to find another crystal. The only place left to search was upstairs. I looked at the stairs carefully, trying to see if there were any trick steps or traps waiting, but nothing lit up on the steps or the walls around the steps. I stepped up the first stair tentatively and other than a little creaking, there were no sounds of imminent death and danger. About five steps up was a small landing, where the stairs turned back in the other direction.

I took another step and thankfully, same as the first step, nothing happened. It wasn't until I could see the landing at the top of the stairs, my vision was filled again with light, this time there was nowhere safe to step. That said, I could see the line of light leading up the wall at the far end of the hall, to a stone looking completely out of place. I understood though, I would need to press that stone to disarm the trap. I tried to cast 'Holy Smite' and 'Lesser Holy Shock' on it just in case it might work, but nothing happened, not even a twitch.

I needed someone who could shoot it or throw something accurately at it. Then I sighed as a thought occurred to me. There was a thief in the house and thieves usually picked up a throwing or bow skill.

"Heath," I called down the stair.

"Yeah, mate?" the thief answered.

"Can you throw accurately or shoot a bow?" I asked.

"Both actually, why?" Heath confirmed.

"Can you come up here?" I asked.

"Sure," I heard him climbing the steps without care, making me pray he didn't set off something I might have missed.

"So, what do you need me to shoot?" Heath asked.

"See that stone sticking out of the wall?" I asked pointing to the end of the hallway. "Can you hit it?"

"Sure," he said, pulling out a small stone from a pouch at his hip. He tossed it up once and caught it, then suddenly threw it. The stone shot from his hand, hitting the out of place stone at the end of the hall, with a loud crunch, as the stone switch slammed home. I was relieved he didn't break the trap with how hard he threw. Still, the floor was no longer glowing.

Now I had three doors to search. The first, right next to the top of the stairs was a bathroom, only a sink, and tub. I was cautious about exploring, carefully watching the floor ahead of me. I opened the only door on the left, in the middle of the hall. It was the bedroom. There was a large bed, it had been torn to shreds and covered in claw marks. And I'm pretty sure, the sheets were not naturally brownish-red. I checked under the bed and around the edges, even flipped the mattress off of it before finally checking the two shallow closets, just to make sure I didn't miss anything.

I returned to the hall to find Heath was kneeling before the last door, working with his lockpicks.

"Tricky bugger, this one is," Heath said, grinning a little, as he fiddled with the lock. Meanwhile, I was trying to see if there were any traps on the lock or door, but nothing was popping in my User Interface.

I heard a click of the lock coming free. "There we go, mate, all yours," Heath stood and backed away from the now unlocked door. I cracked the door slightly and just as I had with the other doors I had opened in this house so far. The wall to the right of the door and the floor were glowing brightly. I found the line again, running along the ceiling toward the door. I risked opening it a little further, to see the line run again to a little crystal. I reached up and popped the little crystal loose, causing the glow to vanish.

I let the door swing open now, careful to stand out of sight, using the wall to shield me from the room. I peeked around the door again, studying the room carefully. It was an office. The room had only a large desk and a comfortable looking chair sitting behind it. I didn't see any readily apparent traps, so I entered. I looked around again, now that I was in the room, but there were no traps as far as I could see.

"Well done," said Heath, striding in without a care.

Meanwhile, I was still being cautious. I carefully moved toward the desk, terrified something might be lurking, inside or underneath it.

"Relax mate, we're home free," said Heath, moving around the desk and pulling out the chair and sitting in it only to hear a click making both our stomachs drop. "Not again," he groaned, his British accent suddenly forgotten.

Now there was a visible glow coming from the bottom of the chair. "Don't move," I warned him. I slowly, carefully approached, dropping to the floor, and lying on my back. I scooted toward the trapped thief, to see what he was dealing with. I saw a metal casing with screws, pinning it to the bottom of the chair.

"Don't suppose you have a screwdriver?" I asked.

"Yeah, you need one?" Heath asked.

"If you do, yeah, just move slowly. This feels like one of those old movies, where the chair goes boom if you move too much or get off of it," I warned him.

"Yeah, sure," he replied, moving slowly. A minute later, I felt something drop onto my stomach. He actually did have a screwdriver, I had no idea why he had one, but I wasn't going to complain.

I slowly unscrewed the plate from the chair. As the plate dropped away I could see an old alarm clock and a couple of small sticks of what I could only guess was explosives. And worse, the clock was now ticking down. Please 'Disarm Trap' do not fail me now, I send a small prayer to my Goddess and get to work. My vision glows again, I followed the glowing line into the bomb until I found a glowing red wire. My utility knife cut the wire with ease, instantly causing the glow to stop.

I crept slowly away from the now disarmed bomb and the man who armed it.

"Hey, where are you going?" Heath asked.

"I gonna go get a drink, just . . . wait here. I'll be back," I said, my voice shaky, mostly because my nerves were still shaky from that experience. I literally, just disarmed, a freaking bomb. I cut the red wire. How awesome was that?

"Don't leave me here," Heath's voice pitched high in panic.

"You'll be fine, just . . . don't move," I said. Then I stomped loudly, "Boom!"

The girlish scream coming from Heath, as he jumped out of the chair and leaped over the desk in a single move, almost had me doubled over with laughter.

"Oh, you jerk," Heath said, breathing heavily and holding his chest, feeling his heart hammer in his chest.

"You should have seen the look on your face," I said, through my laughter.

Finally, Heath laughed a little too. "Okay, so I may have deserved that."

"You definitely deserved that. I can't help but notice you're not British anymore," I commented.

"Hey, it's a game mate, you can be whoever you want to be. Me, I want to be a British rocker," Heath said, slipping back into his bad British accent.

I couldn't disagree with him, but he still sounds ridiculous. "Anyway, I am actually here for a reason," I said, even as I began digging through the desk. Being careful as I open each drawer, to make sure there were no traps. I pulled the drawers completely free and dump the contents on the floor, making sure I shook the drawers to check for hidden compartments. The only draw I couldn't search, was the center, as it was locked tight.

Heath volunteered once again to open it, or rather, he just started to pick the lock, as soon as he saw it was locked.

Meanwhile, I was looking through everything in the other drawers. It was all guard reports and personnel files. Drunken disorderly citations for Gavin and a few other guards but nothing incriminating.

Eventually, only the central drawer remained, Heath was still working on. It took him a few minutes, but eventually, the lock clicked open. I started to slide the drawer back, stopping when I saw a glow right away. There were two lines leading to two different strings on opposite sides of the drawer.

"I think they have to be cut at the same time, can I borrow your knife?" I asked.

Heath handed it over to me. And with a simple flick of both wrists, at the same time, his knife and my utility knife cut the strings with ease causing the glow to fade.

Pulling the drawer back, there was a single large envelope. I dumped the contents onto the desk. There were land deeds for some land, to the northwest, if I read it correctly. They went back centuries, under dozens of names, but the handwriting of the owner was the same on all of them. Maybe Graves really was immortal. But this was definitive proof, the kind of proof I needed.

"I'd say that about does it," said Heath.

"Not quite," I said. I wouldn't have been sad to see Heath leave, but he had proven himself useful. "There is that door in the living room, still. I now have the two crystals needed to open it."

"Lead on, mate," said Heath, in his bad British accent. I could imagine Olaf and Micaela would hate the way this guy was butchering their natural accents.

I was considerably more relaxed, as I headed for the last door. I was a little nervous after I inserted the first crystal, but when nothing happened, I added the second, causing the glowing door to fade. I then tried the door, only to find out it was locked tight.

Again, without asking, Heath went to work on the lock, this one seemed to be easier than the desk because it clicked open in just seconds. I opened the door, but there was no glow of a trap to be seen. Inside the closet, the floor had been hacked out, revealing a hole in the ground. A ladder extended into darkness, below the house.

Heath appeared next to me moment later, holding a lit oil lamp, the same one that had been on the living room end table.

"After you," I said, motioning for him to go first.

"Nah, you got this mate, I'll hold the light," he replied.

I rolled my eyes but started descending the ladder anyway. It was maybe a twenty-foot climb down, about halfway, the tunnel changed from dirt to hard stone. At the bottom of the ladder was a small cavern. I couldn't see anything around me, there just wasn't enough light.

"Bring the light down, I can't see anything," I shouted up the hole.

"Is it safe?" Heath called back.

"I can't see anything, I don't know. Just climb down already," I shouted back up. If there was anything down here, I'm sure it would have attacked me by now.

Heath's footsteps sounded against the ladder as he climbed down, the sound filling the cavern easily. The closer he got to me, the more light filled the cavern. Eventually, he arrived. The oil lamp he carried, now illuminating the small cavern. There wasn't much to it. A large chest to the left, and to the right was what I thought was the acid pool responsible for killing me a few days ago. Last, there was a small altar straight ahead.

"Ooh, treasure," said Heath, moving straight to the chest.

"I thought you didn't steal?" I asked him.

"I don't steal from innocent people. Anyone that would boobytrap a chair to explode is not innocent," he retorted.

"I don't see any traps, so I think it's safe. Just remember, I get the first pick of gear and 75% of the money if there is any," I claimed.

"Now, wait just a tick, mate. Why do you get so much?" Heath asked.

"I've done most of the work. I disarmed the traps, and I saved you from getting blown to bits."

"I guess I've got to give it to you, mate," Heath said reluctantly, moving with more confidence now, working on opening the chest.

While Heath was working on opening the chest, I moved to study the altar. It was covered in symbols I've never seen before. On top, sat a small bowl, filled with what I believed to be dried blood. I couldn't make out anything from the writing, so I pulled out a sheet of drawing paper and sketched the altar and the symbols. I would need to take this to Trinico, hopefully, she would know more.

"Bugger," said Heath, from by the chest. It was open, but there was only a pile of robes inside.

I move to look closer, picking up one of the robes. They smelled musty, they must have been in that chest for a long, long time. 'Cult of Hellgrind Ceremonial Robes', the tooltip prompted.

That sounded bad to me. I put one of the robes in my bag, I'd have to ask Trinico about them too.

One more check of the chest revealed more of those robes, but nothing of value.

"Time to go," I said finally. I was half tempted to burn it to the ground, but I figured, it would be better if someone with real authority, decided what the best thing to do with this place was.

When I finally left the house behind, it was to a combination of cheers and boos, and even more, money changing hands. There were more when Heath emerged behind me.

"Come on, Jack. I was counting on you dying for me, at least once," said Rose, stomping up to me.

"Gee, thanks," I said sarcastically.

"Well hello, and who is this beautiful young woman?" asked Heath, moving in to get a closer look at Rose.

"Where?" I asked, getting punched in the arm, by a blushing Rose. For some reason, I had an irrational desire to pass that punch onto Heath.

"Shush, Jack, let the man adore me," said Rose. "Hello, I'm Rose."

"A beautiful name for a beautiful flower," said Heath.

It had to be the cheesiest thing I've ever heard, yet it reduced Rose to a blushing mess.

"Rose, we'd better go get the others. We need to see the sergeant and Trinico, to go over what I've found," I said, trying to steer her away from this Heath guy, for her own sake. The man was a menace.

"Now, now, no need to rush off. Rose and I were just getting to know each other," protested Heath.

"Yeah, we were just getting to know each other," added Rose.

"Heath, we'll be having dinner at Dog House Inn tonight, sometime after 6:00, why don't you meet us there? Right now, we need to get going," I said, trying harder to move us along.

"Oi, Bye-bye, I just made 5-Gold betting on you. Thanks," Micaela said, her accent as real as can be.

"Glad to see you had faith in me, unlike some people," I added glaring at Rose. "Anyway, we need to get the others, then go find Sergeant Butters and Priestess Trinico."

"I had plenty of faith in you," defended Rose. "Faith that you'd die at least once, and it seems, that faith was misplaced. You lived."

"You know, if he can't appreciate a delicate flower such as yourself, I'd be happy to keep you company," said Heath, subtly moving closer to her.

"What the bloody hell is that accent?" asked Micaela.

I could not help but thank my Goddess for Micaela's timely interruption, and for possibly, saving Rose from the wannabe rock'n'roller.

Micaela to the rescue. "Please tell me, your roleplaying behind, doesn't seriously think that's a decent British accent?" asked Micaela, staring at Heath in disapproval.

"Now Micaela, he did mention this is a game, and if he wants to be a British rocker, then who are we, to get in the way of that? Besides, Rose appears to be enjoying the company," I said, laying it on a little thick.

"Oh, Rosie, please say it ain't so," begged Micaela. "Don't fall for this wanker's bad accent and bad boy attitude."

"Really, it's fake?" asked Rose, looking at Micaela then at Heath and back again.

"Yes, my dear, completely false," said Micaela, assuring her.

"Alas, our love was not meant to be," said Heath, making a less than graceful departure.

"See, total wanker," said Micaela, watching Heath's rapid retreat.

"Too bad, he might have been fun for a night," said Rose before shrugging. "I suppose we'd best get to whatever urgent mission, Jack here, was complaining about before."

And once again, everything was right in the world.

CHAPTER 30

After agreeing to meet at the temple, we split up again. Micaela went to find Olaf, while Rose went outside of town to get Baby, and I went to get Sergeant Butters.

"Bye-bye, what can I do for you?" asked Sergeant Butters, seeing me approach. Given, I had just passed his tired looking soldiers, so it was safe to assume that he was done training them for the day.

"I was finally able to investigate Graves's house. We're all meeting up at the temple, as soon as possible. I was hoping you would come to hear what we've found," I explained.

"Alright, I'll meet you there shortly, need to clean up first," Sergeant Butters replied.

I could only nod before he was moving quickly into the barracks and out of sight. Rather than head back immediately, I decided to stop into the mayor's office, figuring he might be able to help me out or even join in on the conversation at the temple.

"Bye-bye, how are you doing, son?" the mayor asked with a friendly smile.

"Doing well. I don't mean to be rude, but I'm kind of in a hurry. Have you ever seen this writing before?" I asked him, showing him the sketch of the altar.

"No worries, no worries. Let us see what you have got there," Mayor Semper replied, studying the drawing. "Hmm, not sure, I'm afraid I can't read this. Trini would know more," he offered. "Why do you ask? Where did you find it?"

"Under Graves's house. He had an altar covered in it," I answered.

"Well now, that does pose a problem. I suppose we should go see Trini and see what she thinks," the mayor said.

"I was going there next, but I figured I'd see if I could get a book on this language first," I explained.

"I am afraid, I do not recognize this language, it may be written by one of the lost ones or their followers," the mayor said.

"Lost ones?" I asked.

"Lost Gods and Goddesses. Those who grew bitter and angry with their domains and revolted against their pantheons. They were cast out, shamed and stripped of their domains. But once a God, always a God, except now they have nothing to hold them back. All manner of cults and religions sprung up from them and caused all sorts of havoc," Mayor Simper explained.

"Was the Cult of Hellgrind one of them?" I asked.

"I could not say. Once again, we need to ask Trinico," he said again. I accepted the mayor's judgment and followed him to the temple. Everyone except for Rose and Baby had gathered.

"Just waiting for Baby and Rose," I said, wanting to wait for them to arrive before we got started.

"We're here," said a slightly winded Rose. With everyone present and accounted for, we moved into Trinico's office.

"Okay, so I finally got to investigate Graves's house. There were so many traps," I started, trying to lighten the mood, but it appeared none of the citizens were in the mood for it. "Right, first, I found these land titles going back to the founding of the village." I set the envelope on Trinico's desk.

The mayor took the envelope and emptied out the contents.

"It's all for a plot of land to the northwest of town. Each time the ownership has changed hands, there was a new deed printed. And while it changed ownership several times, the old owner and the new owner, have the same handwriting. I think it's all the same person, Graves," I explained.

"It lines up," said the mayor.

"What concerns me, is this land plot covers the entirety of the old ruins," added Sergeant Butters, looking at one of the deeds.

"I'm more concerned about this," I took out the robes. "Have any of you ever heard of the 'Cult of Hellgrind'?"

Sergeant Butters stood sharply and backed away, spitting at the robes.

Trinico immediately began chanting under her breath causing a bubble of light to surround the robes. When it faded, she spoke. "It is clean David. There is no magic present on these robes."

"Are we too late?" the sergeant asked, I could hear worry in his voice.

"No, there was never any magic on these," said Trinico.

Sergeant Butters visibly calmed, sagging in relief upon hearing those words.

"Mind explaining the overreaction?" asked Rose.

"Overreaction my grizzled hide," spat Sergeant Butters. "If anything, it was an underreaction. Getting old, bites."

"So, you've heard of the Cult of Hellgrind?" I asked, trying to get the conversation back on target.

"Remember the story of the demon incursion, we told you of?" asked Trinico. The thought instantly making me feel slightly sick at what I expected she was about to reveal.

I nodded slowly.

561

"The Cult of Hellgrind are the ones responsible," stated the priestess.

"Okay, so, I know I'm new here an all, but a demon incursion doesn't sound good," said a voice with a bad British accent. I recognized the voice but didn't understand what it was doing here.

"Heath?" I asked. I was confused even as I turned and saw the thief, leaning against the wall casually.

"Hey, mate," Heath greeted me. "So, demon incursion, bad thing yeah?"

"Heath?" I questioned again. When did he get here? How did he get here? Why the devil was he here?

"Yeah, you need something, mate?" Heath asked.

"What are you doing here?" I demanded, nearly shouting.

"Well, I saw that pretty thing running through town, and I thought to myself, Heath old son, that is one fine lass, wouldn't do you no harm to give her a second shot. So, I followed her. But when I saw she had a daughter, I was going to bugger off, don't need that drama, if you know what I mean. But then I saw all these important people, and it seemed kind of serious, and I thought there might be a pinch of excitement, so I just followed along," Heath explained.

Micaela snorted and tried hard not to laugh, but she couldn't help it. Poor Baby looked absolutely mortified. Olaf looked about as confused, as I felt. But Rose . . . Rose was bright red. I didn't know if she was embarrassed or blushing.

Then she pounced on Heath.

Her metal-clad fist making a resounding gong as it impacted with Heath's head, sending him on a quick trip to dreamland, an 'Unconscious' debuff now present. But she didn't stop there, kicking him hard, while he was down, a gasp and a squeak, escaping him. Ah, she was mad, I made a mental note of that shade of red, for future reference.

Finally, Rose turned back to the group. "What?" she snapped at all of us wide-eyed onlookers.

"Nothing, nothing at all," was the general reply, no one dared to look at her.

"She beat me to it," whispered Sergeant Butters softly, I could barely hear him, but apparently Micaela heard, and was once more laughing loudly.

"So . . . do we just leave him?" asked Olaf, now that Micaela had broken the tension.

"I hate to say this," started Trinico. "But a thief, of his skill, might prove useful to you. If he was able to sneak in here, past both David and I, then he has real talent. Even if he is scum. Perhaps one of the Gods or Goddesses will curse him with impotence for such behavior. We shall all have to pray, yes? But for now, perhaps, we should wake him." She then mumbled a spell causing a ball of water to form in the air above him and suddenly drop.

Heath was upright in an instant. "Anyone see a gorilla around here. I could have sworn, one just attacked me."

I moved quickly, attempting to hold Rose back, though I was mighty tempted to let her attack him. "Not the time," I said softly to her, it seemed to work as she backed off. She stood back and crossed her arms while glaring at him.

"We've gotten sidetracked here. Please, Trinico, tell us more," I tried to steer the conversation back on target.

"The demon incursion that hurt my David so badly, that nearly destroyed the World Tree, was instigated by the Cult of Hellgrind, believers in one of the fallen ones," explained Trinico sadly, glancing briefly at her husband.

"But which?" I asked.

"We do not know, we were never able to question any of their followers," answered Trinico. "When we found the cultist's base, when we moved to stop them and close the portals, they chose death. Every man, woman, and child either took their own life or died on the battlefield. They were truly dark times."

"Okay, so Graves is either a member of the cult or the fallen one himself. If so, what's his angle? Why does he keep coming back to this town? What is he looking to accomplish?" I asked, thinking aloud.

"He's lonely," said Micaela. "He said it before he fled. He said he was going to make us all immortal."

"Okay, so how would he do that?" I asked, then looking to the mayor. "You said you couldn't read the symbols on the altar, but do they look similar to those at the ruins?"

"Well . . . only similar in that they cannot be read. I see the symbols, and part of me recognizes them, but then it gets kind of blurry, and I cannot remember what they are. It is like having a word at the tip of your tongue. It is the same for all the citizens of the World Tree, I should think."

"I don't see a blur," I reply, the symbols or letters look clear to me, I just don't have a language to reference.

"You do not?" asked Trinico, surprise, clear in her voice. She rushed quickly across the room to a bookshelf, removing several tomes. She rushed back just as quickly, setting them down in front of me. "Look, which of these books does the language match?"

I frowned at how harried she seemed but did as she asked. I opened the first book and shook my head no. I opened the next and again no. The fifth book I checked was closest. "Does this look like it to you guys?" I asked, the symbols looked alike to me, but a second opinion never hurt.

Olaf looked over my shoulder. "No idea, it's all blurry to me."

"Me too," said Micaela.

"No clue, mate," said Heath.

"They look the same to me," said Rose, standing next to me.

I looked at Baby who only shook her head. It was only me and Rose able to read the symbols.

"Lore," Rose and I said at the same time.

"That's the only thing we both have in common. 'Lore' lets us see the writings of the lost ones, in their original language," I elaborated.

"Norse, you must learn Norse," said Trinico, picking up the book. She then took two blank scrolls from her drawer and began writing. I recognized the writing as Runes.

"She may be a while. A whole language is not exactly a small bit of knowledge," warned the sergeant.

"So, how does all this work?" asked Heath.

"How does what work?" I asked.

"Before that," said Olaf, sounding gravely serious. "Stop polluting my accent, you wanker."

"Relax, mate," replied Heath. "It's just a game, let me have my fun."

Olaf grimaced, as if hearing Heath speak was physically painful. "Please, just stop."

"No can do, mate," said Heath, grinning as if he'd won some giant victory.

"Troll," grumbled Micaela.

"Anyway, how is it you can read Norse, but not this Norse?" Heath asked, pointing from the book used to identify the language to the sketch I made earlier.

"The other Gods and Goddesses have cursed anything written by the fallen ones or a follower of a fallen one if written in the language of the fallen one's original pantheon," the mayor tried to explain.

"So, if he wrote in French instead of Norse you might be able to read it if you speak French?"

"I'm not sure what language French is, but yes," answered the mayor.

"How odd," said Heath. "How long do you figure this will take? Do I have time to pop over to Doc B's for a drink?"

"Sit down and shut up," Sergeant Butters finally snapped.

Heath seemed to finally get the hint and sat down in one of the open chairs next to Baby.

"So, Rose is your mummy, huh?" Heath asked, baby-talking Baby.

One of Baby's eyebrows rose slightly, but then I saw a glint in her eyes spelling mischief. "She's the bestest mommy on the whole planet." I nearly choked, when I heard that. The voice was perfectly childlike, as were her mannerisms. Even the smile was perfectly simulated.

I looked at Rose, who suddenly had a deer in headlights look on her face which was even more priceless.

"Well, aren't you just the luckiest little girl on the planet. I'm impressed your mom would let you play such a game, seeing as you're so young, forward-thinking of her," Heath cooed.

I looked at Rose again. She was turning red. Having seen the same shade just a short time ago, I now understood this angry red. I looked back at Heath, then realized I was directly in the path of destruction. I tried to be subtle about it, as I slid my chair back until I was no longer at risk of being caught in the crossfire.

Somehow, everyone else moved away from Heath as well, except for Baby, though I could see her wings were twitching slightly, in preparation to escape.

I looked to see that the sergeant was grinning a little, even he was struggling to keep a straight face.

"Raagh!" screamed Rose, suddenly blurring and appearing across the room, her shoulder lowered, and Heath went missing from his chair. He was now buried under a pile of books and broken bookshelf pieces, behind where he was sitting previously. I looked at him carefully to see the debuff 'Unconscious', again, there was no timer on it, but from earlier experience, Trinico would be able to remove it.

"Nice, well done, Miss Rose. I think you just learned 'Charge' without my help," cheered Sergeant Butters.

"I think we can leave him unconscious, for now," volunteered Olaf with a small grin and trying not to laugh.

I didn't bother to hold back, I was laughing hard. It was hilarious, especially watching as Rose was hopping around, trying to catch Baby, who was flying in circles near the office ceiling, trying and succeeding to avoid being captured by her irate sister.

"Sis, I won't hurt you, just come down already," said Rose, jumping again and swinging to capture Baby.

"You still look mad," said Baby, avoiding another swipe.

"I'm not mad," snapped Rose, sounding mad.

"You sound mad, too," Baby quipped.

"Baby, get down here now or so help me . . ." threatened Rose.

"No," she replied simply, then stuck out her tiny tongue and blew a raspberry at her before giggling and flying faster, to avoid capture.

Rose growled, seeming to have finally given up catching her sister. She grumbled something under her breath I couldn't make out, as she retook her seat and crossed her arms. She then switched focus, between glaring at Baby, and the heap that was Heath's unconscious form.

Eventually, Trinico came out of her writing trance.

"You are all children. Look at what you have done to my office," the priestess complained, a small frown marring her face. "Who was responsible for this?"

We all look at each other, then almost as one, pointed at Heath.

Trinico walked around her desk and handed me and Rose each a scroll. "Before you ask, no I do not know 'Lore', but I do have the skill 'Linguist'. That is why I am able to provide you with the subskills."

Rose and I shared a brief look before the scrolls crumbled to dust almost at the same time, granting the both of us the subskill 'Norse'.

Then Trinico continued walking until she hovered above Heath. She jabbed him with her staff a few times. "David, drag him out from under here. I do not want to get my books wet."

The sergeant complied, gripping the thief by his jacket collar and pulling him out not so gently.

Once Heath was clear of the books, Trinico doused Heath with water again, waking him up from his forced slumber.

"Seriously, does no one else see the bloody gorilla? It keeps attacking me." Heath asked as soon as he sat up, rubbing his head, where he was last struck.

This time, it takes both me and Olaf to restrain Rose.

"Anyway, you've all done as I've asked, gone above and beyond even. Please accept these with my gratitude," said the sergeant, notifying us of the completed quest and successfully distracting the group. He then handed each of us a cloth sack with our rewards.

Quest Alert: The investigation of Lieutenant Graves 1-3 (Recommended Level 4-6) - Completed
Sergeant Butters has asked you to look into the suspicious activities of Lieutenant Graves.
Reward: +1,500-Experience, Guard's Light Leather Bracers, Guard's Phalanx Shield, Holy Order Light Gloves

Now that was one spectacular distraction. Three completed quests at once and three pieces of gear, one of them of good quality.

Quest Alert: The investigation of Lieutenant Graves 4 (Recommended Level 5-7)		
Lieutenant Graves has been proven an enemy of not only the province but also an enemy of the World Tree. Put a stop to him before he unleashes something truly terrible.		
Reward: Experience, Good Variable Piece of Gear		
Do you accept this Quest?	Yes	No

"You can count on us," I said, accepting the quest without hesitating. This was another quest where the ultimate goal was to put a stop to Graves. That was two quests now asking us to put a stop to him. I had a feeling, the two quests I still had left would also be leading toward putting a stop to Graves.

"Do not forget, the ceremony to raise Guard Davies is in five days. I trust you will all be there," said Trinico. "Now, it is about time to sup, I suggest you all run along."

Knowing a dismissal when I heard one, my friends and I, plus Heath, departed the temple.

"You lot seem to get into the fun stuff," said Heath, as soon as we were outside.

I had no idea what to do about this guy. He'd literally forced his way into this quest line. And now, he probably had the quest to kill Graves. Thankfully, Olaf seemed to be thinking along the same lines, as I was.

"Okay, you wanker, here's the deal. You just won the bloody lottery of game quests. If you screw this up for us, I'll end you, and I promise it will hurt. Now, Trini says you might be useful, and she usually knows what she's talking about, so I'm willing to give you a chance. So, the real question becomes this, are you yanking us around here or are you actually going to help us?" Olaf stated seriously.

For just a moment, Heath's overconfident attitude and behavior faded. And then he spoke sans accent. "I'm in, seriously."

"Good enough for me," said Olaf, nodding. "Oh, and if you insist on speaking with that fake accent, at least learn to do it well. And one more thing, love the bloody name, Heath Rickards, classic."

Heath's attitude was back in place, and now he was humming a tune, as he walked with us, a little bit of a dance to his step. Yeah, this guy definitely had the attitude of an old-time rocker.

Back at the inn, we ate, laughed, and drank a little, but I was early to bed. Things were quickly coming to a head and I had some reading long overdue.

After a quick shower and putting my clothes in the basket to be mended, I returned to my room. I spent a few minutes doing some 'Maintenance' on my spear and shield, losing a few points of overall durability, but restoring the lost ones. I don't know why I bothered with the shield when I just got a new one, but I wasn't exactly in a hurry to equip the new shield, or even check it or any of the other new gear no matter how tempting. That could wait until morning. It would be my reward for reading the two town histories.

I sat in my desk chair, and propped my feet up on my bed, and open the first town history.

<u>Day 1</u>

My name is Homer Dobson. I'm proud to write this first history of our new village, Hurligville. I always liked the sound of a 'ville' and as this is my town, I figure I can name it whatever I want. We founded Hurligville on orders from King Leopold II, there are twenty families for a total of 52 men, women and children including my own family. We were supplied 30 wagons, 10 horses, 20 oxen, 20 chickens, 20 pigs and 5 hunting dogs and 2,000-lbs of grain and feed. We were additionally provided with tools, saws, hammers, nails, shovels, hoes and field tills.

We expect things will be difficult at first, settling new lands is never easy. But these untamed wilds promise the chance to build something with our own hands. It also promises us each land, something we couldn't dream of owning if we remained in Root City.

<u>Day 2</u>

The men and I have begun to chop back the forest in the area we have selected to build our first longhouse. We will need the lumber to build with, so it works to our advantage. The area we've chosen is about two miles south of the river and a bit elevated. I do not yet know what the rains will be here, nor do I know if the river floods, but best to be safe about it.

<u>Day 6</u>

The hunters had their first run-in with some of the local predators. A few wolves came sniffing around but were quick to run off.

Day 35

Pleased to announce the completion of our fifth longhouse. I can proudly say all of our settlers, officially, have a roof over their heads.

Day 198

Our first new settler arrived today. A man by the name of Tombs. He's young and seems energetic. He says he was a former soldier, sent late by the King to provide us some protection. He looks capable enough.

I set the book down for a moment and pull the envelope with the deeds from my bag. I check the oldest deed, it's a signed bill of sale from Homer Dobson to Manrock Tombs.

Year 1, Day 25

The local wolves have suddenly turned aggressive on us. One of the children has been killed by the beasts. Young Thomas was a bright boy, adventurous to a fault. I often caught the boy playing with the wolves, I cannot fathom it. Why would they have turned on him so?

Year 1, Day 99

We've had another death to the wolves, that makes seven dead. I've sent my eldest son, Davidson to ride to Root City and requisition a mage from the mage's guild. In the meantime, we've begun construction on a moat around the village. Ideally, we can use it to stop the wolves, Donna, the apothecary, says she can lace it with silver essence, to drive them back.

Year 1, Day 254

Still no word of my son or the other two riders I've sent out. I fear none made it.

Year 2, Day 3

At last, one of the riders has returned with a representative of the mage's guild, a serious man by the name of Balthazar. Alas, we also finally have confirmation, my son and four other riders never made it to the city.

Year 2, Day 15

I bear grave news. The mage has informed me that we have a werewolf problem. It is most likely the cause of the wolves turning so aggressive.

Year 2, Day 18

I announced to the village yesterday, the believed cause of our problems. Tombs packed up and fled. So much for being a soldier here to protect us.

Year 3, Day 25

While the wolves remain aggressive, it has been more than a year since we lost anyone to the beasts. It is our hope the werewolf has moved on.

Year 3, Day 151

There was an attack last night. The Travers Farmstead, the whole family was killed and mostly eaten, even little Sarah. It was the worst thing I have ever seen.

Year 3, Day 180

The mage believes this to be no normal werewolf after he and a number of our hunters encountered it last evening. He has been in talks with the Donald Maron, one of our farmers who happens to run a still on the side for medicinal purposes.

Year 4, Day 30

We have finally driven the beast off. It was a most unusual solution, but I could care not, for my people are safe. My town is saved after being terrorized by the beast for near 3 years. The mage enchanted the still, to distill the shine of the moon, into the grain alcohol. The combination of which reversed the effects of the light of the moon. As a result, this new 'Moonshine', as they have taken to calling it, weakens the werewolf significantly. It made him vulnerable.

Year 4, Day 31

Today, we found symbols carved into the earth and stained with blood, in front of the gates, along with the dead bodies of several wolves. I believe, it is a promise to return, and have his revenge. Many whisper, it is a curse by the werewolf. I say let him come, we will drive him off again. Still, knowledge should be preserved. Only one of my people could properly see the symbols, but he knew not the language.

Below it was a Norse inscription reading, 'By the will of the Betrayer, you shall be tormented for all time'.

Was the 'Betrayer' the name of the God?

The rest of the first book was uneventful, a number of grain reports, construction, wolf incursions and births, and deaths. Nothing alluding to the werewolf or the cause of the wolves to have become so aggressive.

I had just finished the first town history when there was a knock on my door. Figuring it was Dogson, I opened the door, wearing only my pajama bottoms.

I opened the door, but it wasn't Dogson, it was Rose.

"Hey," I greeted her, not sure what was going on.

"Hey," Rose said, trying to look anywhere but at me. "Mind putting a shirt on or something?"

I quickly grabbed the robe I had left hanging on the armoire door and slipped it on, hastily tying it closed. "Sorry, thought you might have been Dogson."

"No worries," Rose replied, sort of just standing there.

"Want to come in?" I offered, not sure why she was here.

"Sure," Rose answered, stepping in and walking around my little room. Stopping briefly to flip the pages of my journal, stopping on some of the pictures. "You draw well."

"I'm pretty sure it is game assisted," I replied, feeling more confused by the minute. "Was there something you needed?"

"Look, I'm not very good with this stuff but . . . thank you. You've made this game . . . fun. And you've . . . been a big help," Rose stammered.

"Sure," I replied, unsure why she was saying this now.

"Anyway, I hear the bath calling to me, so see you in the morning," she said, moving toward the door. She paused when she got to me, then did something I could never have predicted. She kissed me on the cheek, then rapidly fled. I never even had a chance to ask her why.

"I'll never understand women," I said, staring at the closed door she just left through.

I shook my head and sat down with the next book. After reading the first page 10 times, I gave it up as a lost cause and called it a night. "I'll never understand women," I said again, as I extinguish the candle lighting the room.

I brushed my cheek as I started to doze off, it felt warm.

CHAPTER 31

"Holy Smite," I chanted, blasting that cursed rooster to kingdom come.

"Not again, Bye-bye," howled Dogson.

I grumbled angrily. I took my time getting dressed before I headed downstairs. Before Dogson could berate me. "How much for the rooster?"

"2-Silver," the dogman answered.

I paid without a word of complaint.

Dogson accepted the money with a nod, then went back about his business. I turned away from him, finding an amused Rose.

"It deserved it," I said as I took a seat across from her.

"You'll get no argument from me," Rose said with a small grin. "Was it worth it?" she whispered conspiratorially.

"Best 2-Silver I ever spent," I replied in my own whisper, a satisfied smirk upon my face.

Baby joined us a few minutes later, looking sleepy, but happy.

"And how is Rose's daughter this fine morning?" I asked, laughing. I get a small glare from Rose but a giggle from Baby.

"How long are we going to keep this gag going?" demanded Rose, arms crossed and leaning back in her chair.

"Just a little more, you have to admit, it's really funny," I said, a small chuckle followed. Rose tried not to smile, but eventually gave it up as a lost cause, and grinned along with me and Baby.

"Here you are Bye-bye," said a voice, I didn't immediately recognize. I turned to see one of the level one players I had helped the day before. What was her name again? Aretha? Urita? I looked at her again and smiled in as friendly a manner as I could, I risked glancing up at her name, floating above her head, Arial.

"Hello again," I greeted her.

"Where were you last night? I looked all over for you," Arial pouted, coming closer to our table.

"I was here for a little while. I ended up calling it an early night. Have you settled in okay?" I asked.

"Oh, quite well. Mr. Dogson is very nice, and the room is comfortable. Thank you again for the recommendation," answered Arial.

"I'm glad it worked out," I said pleasantly.

"Jack, are you going to introduce us to your new friend here?" asked Rose. She sounded nice but for some reason, the hairs on my arms stood on end.

"Right, sorry. Arial, this is Rose Thorns and Babies Breath," I introduced.

"Arial Norenci, pleasure," she said, greeting them briefly before turning her attention back to me.

"And how do you know Jack?" asked Rose, drawing her attention again, and a small frown on the young woman's face.

"He was very kind to me yesterday. He gave me some wonderful advice, I can't thank him enough," Arial answered.

"It's not that hard, thank you, see. Anyway, Jack, we should probably get going. Training and all of that," said Rose, gripping my arm tightly, even a little painfully and starting to drag me toward the exit.

"Oh, but you must let me buy you breakfast," said Arial, gripping my other arm, also too tightly and halting my being dragged from the inn, also painful.

"We just finished eating, maybe some other time," said Rose, practically dragging me from the inn, and rather forcefully out of Arial's grip, which, if I'm honest, was rather unpleasant. Rose marched me the short walk from the inn to the barracks, stopping, just before we would have turned the corner.

Rose turned to face me, a serious expression on her face. "Look, Jack, I know you're a nice guy, but you've got to be careful."

"What are you talking about?" I asked, truly confused.

"That girl is not your friend. I don't know what her angle was, but you should be careful around her. I've got a bad feeling about her," Rose stated seriously.

"She seemed nice enough to me," I replied, not understanding what she was saying.

"Oh Jack, still so naïve. Trust me, that woman was a wolf in sheep's clothing," Rose warned.

I couldn't help but frown, she didn't seem so bad to me.

Rose finally turned away, continuing the trip to the training area. I looked to Baby, hoping she would provide me with some answers, but she appeared to be having a seizure, of silent giggles.

"What's that all about?" asked a voice, from behind me, making me jump out of my skin.

"Heath, I swear, I'm going to put a bell on you," I threatened, the man responsible for shaving years off my life. "Anyway, what are you doing here?"

"Oh, Olaf said I should come around here this morning. He mentioned something about weapons training, so here I am," Heath answered.

"Well, then go talk to the sergeant. He's the trainer you need to speak with." I said, leading him around the back and pointed out the sergeant who was talking to Rose.

"Cheers," Heath replied, walking ahead of me only to fade out of view. He reappeared behind Rose and got punched for it.

Now, it was my turn to giggle, serves him right.

"I actually do need training with the sergeant today," volunteered Baby. "There is supposedly a flying combat stance, according to Trinico. It's called 'Aerial Maneuvers'. She said it's similar to your 'Acrobatics' skill but performed in the air."

"Did you already learn 'Meditation'?" I asked.

"Huh, oh yeah, I learned it in a few days. Because I wasn't here training with the sergeant, and my time allotment in the puzzle room was double compared to most others, because of my race. I was able to clear it quickly. Trini also taught me a bunch of holy spells, but I have yet to go see Malcolm about any nature spells he might have," Baby explained. "Anyway, I better go get in line."

I didn't grasp what she meant about getting in line right away, not until I turned back to see Rose still chatting with the sergeant, and off to the side of her, was a line of 3 more players. I recognized them from Ned's the day before. They were all glaring at Rose, as she held them at bay with one arm, while she continued talking to Sergeant Butters. If I had to guess, she probably cut the line.

I shook my head. I know I should have just gone to one of the training dummies, working to hone my skills and spells. I had to prioritize my time for the next few days or however long it took to research the town history. That meant I had to get into the Town hall and start working on those town histories. I wasn't looking forward to it, but I knew it was necessary.

The Town hall wasn't open yet, but thanks to my handy-dandy key to the city, I was able to let myself in, and lock the door behind me.

After moving one of the wooden chairs to a spot, just in front of the stage, I sat down and propped my feet up on the stage. For as long as I expected to be reading, I had to try to get a little comfortable. I opened the second book in the series, hopefully, I could get past the first page this time. 'Hurligville Vol II: Years 5-10' was boring, filled with births, deaths, farming, construction, fires and all manner of mundane things. The only thing I tried hard to keep an eye out for, was any, and all, new immigrants to the village, just to compare them to the deeds. That first day passed slowly, reading the histories and working to understand the various shorthand writing styles of the different mayors. It was tedious and with every new mayor, I had to start over, learning a different style.

It was in 'Hurligville Vol IX: Years 81-90', on my second day buried in the histories of Hurligville, that I finally got a hit.

Mayor Trombly, the fourth mayor of Hurligville wrote:

Year 16 of the reign of King Randolph the IV, day 72

Had a friendly young man arrive in town today, by the name of Feuner Pyre. He said he'd bought the deed to some land in the province. I checked the deed, and it was legitimate. I gave him directions to his land and sent him along. He seems capable and strong, I wish him well.

Year 16 of the reign of King Randolph the IV, day 197

The Maron farmstead was attacked today. The farm remains intact, but James Maron was killed, defending his family. Thankfully, his wife and daughter were in town during the attack, but his son was there. Poor William is traumatized, we can hardly get a word from him, just howling and growling. He must have witnessed the wolves killing his father. We will hold services for him tomorrow.

Year 16 of the reign of King Randolph the IV, day 232

There has been another attack at the Maron farmstead. This time Marion Maron and her daughter, Daniella Maron, were taken from us. My wife and I have discussed it, and we've decided to bring William into our home, until he is well enough, and old enough, to take over the farm himself.

Year 16 of the reign of King Randolph the IV, day 254

William is settling in, but for some reason beyond me, he brought his family's still with him. The boy hardly lets it out of his sight. I suppose it is part of his family heritage.

The remainder of volume nine was more general updates. There were a few updates on William, mostly him starting to speak more, but refusing to talk about what happened to his family.

On the third day of study, I got my next clue. 'Hurligville Vol XII: years 111-120', the town confronted the werewolf. William saved the day, which was unbelievably brave, considering most of the entries from the time he turned 16 until this point, made him out to be a lunatic and a drunk. Granted, it was from the Mayor's perspective. William, also finally told his story too, witnessing the werewolf attack that killed his father. About the man who transformed into a giant wolf creature, the werewolf. William's obsession with the still and making sure to always have Moonshine at the ready. Apparently, drinking as much as he did, also acted as a kind of werewolf repellant, which kept him safe over the years.

Year 41 of the reign of King Randolph the IV, day 51

Thanks to the bravery of William and his mystic brew, our town is safe, and the werewolf has been driven off. And yet, just today we found dark tidings. Several wolves were slain, and their blood used to carve a message into the ground before our gates.

Again, there was a Norse inscription 'Curse of the Betrayer upon you all, none shall know peace.'

The next few years, spoke of a major bout of alcoholism for the entire town, followed by a brief period of prohibition, to tamp it down.

I continued to read, even as some of the level one players came inside, met with the mayor, picked up a book or two then went on their way, just as they did the last two days and for the most part, I ignored their presence. Most of them went on their anyway, except for one.

"Hello again, Bye-bye," greeted the young woman, Arial. "You rushed off so quickly the other day, I didn't have much chance to talk to you."

"Things are busy right now," I replied honestly. I was in the middle of a book when she interrupted me. Glancing at my game clock, I supposed I could use a short break. I have done little else but read for the last three days, breaking only for meal and to sleep at night.

"You don't look very busy to me," Arial pouted.

I smiled a little. I suppose sitting around reading, wouldn't look very busy to some. "Believe it or not, reading this, is part of a quest I'm working on."

"Oh, is it something I can help you with?" Arial asked.

"I'm afraid not. You need a few more levels for this particular quest," I explained, she was still only level 1, and I wouldn't be comfortable with her being on this quest before she was at least level 4.

"Awe, can't you make an exception, for little ol' me?" the young woman asked, batting her eyelashes.

"No can do," I replied with a friendly smile. "You should see about grouping up with some of the other level 1 players. Go out and do some quests, that sort of thing."

"Oh, but I'd much rather group with you," Ariel gently protested, breaching my personal space and making me a little uncomfortable.

"I appreciate the request, but I'm going to have to decline. My friends and I are deep into this quest, they are counting on me. Best of luck to you," I replied, trying to be as gentle as I can.

"But you could keep me safe and I could keep you . . . company," the elf tried again, invading my personal space even more. This time she pressed herself against me, one of her hands holding onto my arm.

Now, most of the time, I'm fairly oblivious to women. I've mentioned, several times, how I don't understand women at all. Never have, probably never will. But this, I understood clearly. It's not that she wasn't pretty because she was. From her platinum blond hair to her hourglass figure, and pouty ruby red lips, she rated highly.

No, the real turn off, her offer to trade her safety and protection in exchange for her company, like it was a business transaction. I was also turned off by her attitude. Why was she even playing the game, if she wasn't going to work hard at it? Why bother, if you're not going to play?

"That is very kind of you," I started, trying again to be gentle, even if she didn't deserve it. "But I feel you need to learn to protect yourself in this world. I wish you luck, but now I must get back to my work."

"God, you're an idiot," the girl finally snapped, an ugly frown marring her face. "Do I have to spell it out for you? Help me level and I'll sleep with you. Levels for me, fun for you. Win-win, you moron," shouted Arial, clearly angry.

"No, I got it, I just don't want it," I replied, any need to be kind evaporating with her sneer. "This world is not kind, if you can't stand on your own feet, then you don't belong here. Now, I've wasted enough time on you, please run along." The woman scowled, looking even uglier. She cursed under her breath then said some less than flattering things to and about me, before she stormed off.

I was about to return to my reading when some clapping stopped me from returning to my book. I looked to see Rose, leaning against the wall by the door.

"What?" I asked, confused by her presence.

"I'm . . . somewhat . . . maybe . . . but only just a little . . . like a tiny itty bit . . . impressed by how you handled her," said Rose.

"I may often have the patience of a saint, but, I'm not one," I replied, unsure of how to speak to her right now, she was being both teasing and kind of nice. How did this woman constantly keep me off balance?

"Okay Saint Jack, what are you working on?" Rose asked, walking up to me.

"Reading the town history. Trying to figure out what is going on with the wolves in the province. I know it's connected to Graves, but I'm having trouble figuring it out. The only thing I've gotten so far is why the Moonshine works and a couple of uses for it. The only thing important to the quest is two Norse messages." I showed her the two marked passages.

"Odd, is 'Betrayer' the name of the God or just a general description of the fallen one?" asked Rose.

"I don't know, I'm hoping one of the later histories will have more details, but the closer I get to the end, the more I doubt it. After three days I should have more information than this," I answered, frowning as I looked at the stack of finished books.

"Maybe it's not the town history you need then," suggested Rose.

"What are you thinking?" I asked.

"Well, this is about a God, right? Then wouldn't something on the Norse Gods, be a good place to look?" suggested Rose.

She made a good point.

But that would mean risking a visit with Trinico, and her moods were hard to predict. Especially when I hadn't been to train with her in several days. Not that I needed to at this time, but still, her staff hurt when it struck my head. Even though she said she didn't have anything to teach me at the moment, per her own words, I still could have come by just to chat.

Hopefully, she won't be too cross with me.

"Let's go see Trini then," I said reluctantly before putting away the books I had finished.

When I arrived in the temple, it was just like the training fields and the Town hall, there was a significant influx of level 1 players. Many of them kneeling before one altar or another, I even saw one of them bathed in golden light for a moment, and when the light faded, the player jumped up and cheered, then did a very strange hip thrust of celebration, it was uncomfortable to watch.

I saw Trinico standing at her pulpit with a line of four different level 1 players waiting to speak with her. Part of me wondered where all the level 1 players were coming from. First, all the players in Ned's yesterday, those at the training fields this morning, and now more here with Trinico.

"I guess we get in line," said Rose, motioning me to go ahead of her.

Rather than join me in line, she went and sat in one of the pews to wait. Interesting, how she said 'we' should get in line, and it ended up just being 'me'.

Still, as I looked at the level 1 players ahead of me, I let my curiosity get the best of me, and listened to some of the conversations.

"I want to be a fire and ice mage, combining the two, making burning ice," said an over enthusiastic player, wearing bright blue robes.

"Very creative, but not really possible. Fire and Ice cancel each other out, however, fire and water can be combined to form steam magic, which can be very powerful," suggested Trinico, in her normal, ever-patient manner.

"Ooh, can I use steam to power machines?" the enthusiastic player asked.

"I would not know about that, but you could always ask Giggle-Ana, the town engineer. As for learning elemental magic, you will want to seek out Malcolm, he is the local Mage's Guild Representative," Trinico responded.

"Thank you very much," said the enthusiastic player.

"You are most welcome, Mr. Icyhot. I wish you luck on your journey," Trinico said to the young wannabe mage.

<Icyhot Jelloshot Lvl 1> sped out of the building after that, smiling brightly. I almost wanted to follow him, to see if he succeeded.

Next was a young woman who looked to be carved from wood, rather than made of flesh.

"Hello, I'm a dryad, but I have no idea what I can do. I only know I get a bonus to nature magic," the dryad woman started. "Oh, and I'm Kimmie, nice to meet you."

"Nice to meet you as well Ms. Kimmie. You have a great many options available to you. Tell me, what do you enjoy?" asked Trinico.

"Well, I chose to be a dryad because I get to be a tree, and I love nature. I even have a small garden, in the other place."

"Ah, so you enjoy growing things. Do you see yourself as more of a healer or someone who prefers to fight?" the priestess continued to probe.

"I'm a fighter, no doubt about it, I'm an environmental activist at heart," Kimmie answered with a grin.

"Well then, I cannot tell you what class to choose, but I can, maybe, point you in the right direction. If you wish to fight, you must decide, if it is with magic or weapons, up close or from far away," Trinico explained.

"Well . . . I chose a bow for my weapon, I think it's pretty fun so far. But I want some magic too because that's super neat," Kimmie said, sounding like she wasn't sure what she wanted to do.

"Do you like animals?" Trinico asked.

"Very much so," the dryad replied.

"Well then, I suggest you visit Barnum, he is the town leatherworker, and once upon a time, he was a very good beast tamer," said Trini.

"Ick, do you mean skinning and stuff?" whined Kimmie.

Trinico smiled kindly and laughed a little. "Animals eat other animals, and what is left feeds the earth, and from the earth grows the plants you so love. Nothing says you have to become a skinner or leatherworker, but I feel a conversation with Barnum might suit you. As for learning some magic, Malcolm will also have a selection of nature magic available to you for you to try."

"I'll give him a chance, but no promises," said the Dryad.

I looked at her again as she left. She was literally, a little walking tree, maybe a foot shorter than me with rich dark wood for skin, and orange and red leaves for hair. <Kimmie Underwood Lvl

1> smiled as she passed by, I returned the smile and gave her a friendly nod.

The next person approached, he looked to be older, easily in his fifties, maybe even in his sixties.

"Afternoon ma'am," he nodded to Trinico, then stood with his legs slightly apart and his hands clasped behind his back. "Names Duncan Donut, I want to become a priest." <Duncan Donut Lvl 1> was a dwarf, short and stocky with a powerful looking physique. He spoke without the brogue the citizens did. Unlike the other Dwarves I've met, this one broke the mold for appearance. He had a military buzzcut, jet black hair with a few strands of grey, and a perfectly cut and trim mustache. It was a very militaristic appearance.

"Wonderful to meet you, Duncan. I am always so pleased when another chooses to join our order. Do you know who you wish to pledge to?" asked Trinico, sounding at least a little excited.

"I'll be honest, I'm not much on paganism, that said, I don't have much of a preference. I was a combat medic a long time ago. I patched men up, so they could keep on fighting. It's been a long time since then, but I want to feel the same sense of accomplishment again," Duncan explained.

"A fantastic goal. Might I suggest, you simply become a combat medic once more?" Trinico suggested.

"Is that an option?" Duncan asked, looking confused.

"Indeed. It is a more difficult path, than that of the priest, and requires considerably more training, but it is an option," explained Trinico.

"How do I start?" Duncan asked eagerly.

"Start with a visit to the Town hall. There, you will want to pick up a few books. 'Healing for the Non-Magical', 'Combat Triage' and 'Pain Management'. You might also want to pick up 'World Tree

588

Anatomy' for a better knowledge of the various races, who fill the World Tree with color and life," instructed Trinico.

"Skill books?" Duncan asked sounding confused.

Seeing I was next in line, I volunteered a little information to him. "Not true skill books. They are books, if you study them well enough, will reward you with skills."

"Good, wouldn't want something as easy as skill books anyway. A man has to earn his skill. Thank you for the intel, son," said Duncan, giving me a polite nod.

"Yes, thank you, Bye-bye, that was kind of you," said Trinico.

"Happy to help, good luck to you," I said to him genuinely.

"Thank you, maybe I can buy you a pint some time," Duncan offered. It didn't matter if he ever came through with the pint, I was genuinely happy to help the man. I didn't even know there was a combat medic class in the game. It would be interesting to see how a healer without magic worked.

"Seeing as you were kind enough to help that man, I shall forgive you for not coming to visit me for training or learning the last few days. How might I help you now?" Trinico asked, giving me a stern look.

"I was hoping to borrow a book on the Norse Gods and Goddesses," I answered plainly.

"Certainly," said Trinico. "I'll be back in a moment, please wait with Miss Rose."

I nodded then went join Rose on the pew.

"Dude, what did you say to her?" asked another player as I passed. "Is she coming back?"

I hadn't noticed there were several more people in line than before. "She's just grabbing a book for me, she'll be back in a minute.

"Oh, that's a relief," replied the same player, <Generalissimo Torrez Lvl 1>. That was a heck of a name.

"Hey, aren't you over-leveled for this province?" asked another player, a girl named <Genie Shotgirl Lvl 1>, an elf, not sure which race though.

"I guess I am. I've still got a few quests I'm finishing up with some friends, but when we're done with them, I think we'll all be moving on," I answered.

"Oh, you're one of those," said the girl.

"Yeah, I'm one of those," I replied. 'Those' being a completionist. Someone who can't leave an area or zone, or in this case a province, with an incomplete quest. Some people scoff at it because of the smaller returns from quests and experience, but I don't mind. It would bother me so much more, if I left an unfinished quest, and lost out on something hidden or unique.

"Here you are, Bye-bye, please return it when you've finished," requested Trinico, having snuck up on me, book in hand.

"Thank you again," I said accepting the book. Rose and I left the temple behind and headed for the inn for a late lunch.

During lunch, I was more animated than was probably necessary, telling Rose about the few level 1 players in the temple and their class plans. There were so many different classes out there to be played, I couldn't wait to see them all.

Rose even joined in, telling me about some of the people who came into the temple, while she was there earlier. "There was this gnome fellow, <Fitz Bangs Lvl 1>, when he talked to Trinico, he said 'I'm going to be an engineer.' Trini responds to him, 'That is a wonderful profession, but what class are you interested in? Can I help you, in any way, to find your path?' 'I'm going to be an engineer.' The gnome insisted. 'Engineering is a profession. What are you looking to be able to do?' Trini pressed him further. 'I want to make things explode or fall apart,' he replied. I just happened to look at Olaf, and I thought he was going to pull a Micaela, when she saw Baby for the first time, and tackle the poor little guy. Trini eventually suggested he look into becoming a demolitions expert. Last I saw, he and Olaf had become fast friends."

I couldn't help but laugh, that certainly sounded entertaining.

When we finished our late lunches, Rose and I went our separate ways, I went up to my room to read the book Trinico lent me, while Rose said she had an appointment to meet Malcolm for 'Enchanting' lessons.

I sat in my chair, propped up my feet as usual, and opened the book, 'Halls of Valhalla', and began to read, hoping after three days of reading with very little to show for it, this book would be my salvation.

CHAPTER 32

So many Gods and Goddesses, why did there have to be so many of them? Tell me, why? Odin, Thor, Freya, Frigga, Syf, Loki, and the list went on and on. And these were just the Norse Gods. How many pantheons did the World Tree represent? I know, I've heard of at least four of them so far, the Vampires, the Greeks, the Babylonians, and now, the Norse. But, how many more of them would I encounter? I thought about the temple again, the building was large and filled with so many altars to the various Gods and Goddess. They couldn't all possibly fit in there, could they?

As time-consuming as it was, reading about the Norse pantheon had paid off. When I was reading about the God Loki, it made mention of his sons, one of which was a giant wolf, the God Fenrir. That was my first hint at the fallen one. Unfortunately, the details pointed to him being a rebel, seeking to claim the God Odin's throne, as is the nature of wolves, to rise up as part of the pack hierarchy, but not one of a betrayer.

And then I read about the God Fenrir's sons. The God Hati and the God Skoll. The legend tells, the God Hati, sought to swallow the moon, and bring eternal daylight to all the realms. On the other side of the same coin, The God Skoll sought to swallow the sun, and bring eternal night. If both succeeded it would bring about Ragnarök or the end of the world. Enemy and Betrayer, the literal translation of their names. The words on the ground weren't just an epithet, but an actual signature. The God Skoll and the Betrayer were one and the same. Skoll was the fallen one we were after.

Graves was a servant of the God Skoll.

Quest Alert: Breaking the curse of the Wolves 1 (Recommended Level 4-5) - Completed		
Mayor Simper has suggested looking into the town history for the source of the wolf problem.		
Reward: +250-Experience		

Success!

Quest Alert: Breaking the curse of the Wolves 2 (Recommended Level 4-5)		
Your careful and diligent research has led you to the God Skoll and the God Hati, the sons of Fenrir. Hurry and bring your findings to Trinico.		
Reward: Experience		
Do you accept this Quest?	Yes	No

I was up and moving in short order, there was still plenty of daylight, I needed to see Trinico, the sooner, the better.

It was a quick trip to the temple. Thankfully the line of players seemed to have gotten what they wanted from Trinco. Or she finally got tired of them and sent them all away. Either way, she seemed to no longer be occupied.

"Hello Trinico," I greeted her, rushing up to her.

"Bye-bye, back again I see. Finished with my book already?" she asked.

"Yes, ma'am. I think I figured it out," I added.

Trinico sighed. "And what have you figured out?"

I quickly explained, what I found in the town journals, and about the threats, written with the blood of the wolves. "I think the fallen one is the God Skoll," I answered. "He is a wolf God, who wants to swallow the sun and bring about eternal darkness. His name actually means Betrayer."

Trinico gave me a look that reminded me, it was her book, and she had already read it, and probably knew as much. It also made me realize, I didn't need to read the book in the first place. I could have just told Trinico about the messages and saved myself a ton of time and effort.

"Something does not add up," Trinico commented thoughtfully, her hands steepled together. "If Graves wishes to turn the population into werewolves, then why set the wolves against us. Why kill the wolves and use their blood to write the threats?"

She was right. I was missing something. What if the wolves were the enemy of the God Skoll? What if the wolves were trying to kill the townspeople to stop whatever plan the God Skoll had in mind? It was extreme but plausible.

Quest Alert: Breaking the curse of the Wolves 2 (Recommended Level 4-5) - Completed
Your careful and diligent research has led you to the God Skoll and the God Hati, the sons of Fenrir. Hurry and bring your findings to Trinico.
Reward: +250-Experience

"There is only one way to find out," said Trinico. "Now that we know the pantheon and the fallen ones involved, we can ask the Norse Gods for their help. However, you will have a most dangerous task ahead of you, if we are to get to the bottom of this. I need a wolf, alive."

I felt the blood drain from my face. The wolves weren't much challenge at this point, and they didn't do a ton of damage either. But they were still dangerous. They could call for help, and even though they didn't do much damage anymore, their bites still hurt, as did their claws.

"I suggest, you start by visiting Barnum, you will want to purchase a sturdy net. Then go see my David and learn to use it. Then I want you to drag one of those beasts back here. Will you do this?" Trinico asked.

Quest Alert: Breaking the curse of the Wolves 3 (Recommended Level 4-5)		
In speaking to Trinico, you have determined there may yet be more to this curse. You have been tasked to capture one alive and bring it before the Norse Gods.		
Reward: Experience		
Do you accept this Quest?	Yes	No

"I have to," I answered, accepting the quest. I tried not to show it, but things were getting exciting.

Trinico gazed out the windows. "It is getting late, best hurry if you want to catch David before his shift tonight. I will expect you in the morning with your task completed."

"I'll be here," I answered.

"Oh, and finish the book, knowledge is power young man," suggested Trinico, holding out the book I had just returned to her. I took it back. She was right. I needed to know more about the Norse Gods.

I ran to the leatherworkers, intent to get a net and get to the training grounds before the sergeant departed for the evening.

The door to the Leather Emporium jingled, as I opened it. Barnum was there, talking enthusiastically with the dryad I had seen earlier that morning. I watched for a moment as the young woman was nodding along absentmindedly.

"Alas, a customer," said Barnum, sounding slightly remorseful, turning from the young woman. "Now do not go anywhere, I want to tell you all about the time I tamed a Nemean

Lion, who I named Hercules, he was such a good companion, a curse upon that dragon for eating him."

I looked at the girl who was now looking at me pleadingly as if begging for help to escape. "Ah, Kimmie, here you are. The Sergeant mentioned you were late for your archery lessons. Best hurry along or he'll be rather cross."

I saw the relief flood Kimmie's eyes. "Oh no, I'm so late. Sorry, Barnum, I have to run, but I promise I'll be back soon."

"I understand my young apprentice. Sergeant Butters is not known for his patience. It would be best you hurry along then," said Barnum, nodding in understanding.

"Thank you," Kimmie said, a little too enthusiastically, practically sprinting for the door.

"She is a fine young woman. She will be a heck of a tamer when I'm done with her," said Barnum, a little extra pep in his step. "Now, was giving Miss Kimmie an excuse to escape my old stories the only reason you came?"

It seemed I was caught. "Caught me, did you? Anyway, I am actually here to see about buying a net. I have a wolf to capture," I explained.

"Certainly, I have just the thing, wait right here," Barnum said before hurrying into his back room.

I half expected him to be in the back room for an hour, making the net from scratch, but when he returned a minute later with a bundle of leather straps, I was pleasantly surprised.

"This ought to do right by you. It is a standard capture net with a draw rope to close and trap your targets. However, the leather is tougher than your standard rope and I've reinforced each cross stitch with metal studs. This should easily hold any wolf the woods surrounding us have to offer," said Barnum, offering the net to me.

"How much?" I asked.

"Oh, I could never sell this. It was the first capture net I ever made. No, this is a loner. I expect you to return it to me once you've captured your wolf. If you intend to learn beast taming, you'll have to make your own eventually," explained Barnum.

"Oh, I'm not trying to become a beast tamer. We need one to question," I explained. It took a second for me to process what I just said. "I need to bring one before the Gods in the temple. It has to do with the werewolf business."

"Awful business, that beast is. Well, then, I hope this net serves you as well as it has me," he said, holding it out toward me, then added, "But I still want it back when you're done."

I chuckled, accepting the net. "I promise, I'll bring it back to you."

"Good," Barnum said.

A quick farewell and I was on the road again, running once more, trying and catch the sergeant before he left for his guard shift.

"Running late today, Bye-bye?" the sergeant greeted me. "I thought I would have seen you this morning."

"Research," I answered between breaths, I had run hard to get to the training circle in time. "I am trying to figure out how the wolves around town are related to Graves." I then relayed what I've uncovered and explained the task Trinico had assigned me.

"Well then, we'd better get to work," Sergeant Butters replied seriously. "We don't have much time, but we should, at the very least, be able to get you some kind of proficiency using a net."

"Great, how do we start?" I asked eagerly. I had forgotten a net was a possible weapon pairing for the spear. More importantly, it meant more skills for me to learn.

The sergeant grinned and moved into the storage shed attached to the back of the barracks, returning a moment later with what appeared to be a sheep.

"Meet the Sac-Lamb, as the boys call her," said the sergeant, setting down the sheep in front of me. It was actually a small barrel on four wooden legs covered in wool with a carved rams head attached to it.

"Let me guess, I have to catch it with my net?" I asked.

"Yeah, how did you know?" the sergeant asked sarcastically before laughing. "Anyway, your goal right now is two-fold, throwing the net with one hand so it opens wide and actually hitting your target."

I wasn't sure how hard it could be to throw a net, but I didn't imagine it was that hard. However I learned quickly that throwing with one hand was anything but easy. First, the sergeant showed me how to prepare the net. In fact, he showed me three different ways to prepare the net. The one I found easiest, involved rolling it such a way that it would unroll when thrown. Then came the actual throw, an underhanded lob, a sidearm or a shot put. I found the shot put worked best for me, I had better accuracy and the trap seemed to open better that way. After I was consistently getting the net to open wide, I worked on hitting the stationary sheep, then yanking on the tether, to draw the net closed.

"There, that was not so bad, was it?" asked the sergeant, seemingly pleased with my progress. "Now you just need to practice. You're welcome to stay to practice, but I need to get moving, my shift is starting soon."

"Thank you for all your help Sergeant Butters, I appreciate it." I was genuinely thankful to this man. He had given me so much without asking for anything in return.

"Just keep helping the people, and we'll call it even," said the sergeant, he gave me a small salute, then marched off to do his duty.

Before I resumed my practice, I decided it was time to check the flashing exclamation points in my peripheral. I was slightly shocked at my stat gains. Apparently, reading that much over a few days in a row was very beneficial. I gained +10-Intellect and +6-Wisdom. I also gained a new skill I hadn't expected, or thought would even exist in this game.

You've learned the skill 'Speed Reading'

Speed Reading	Level: 3	Experience: 87.41%
Skill Effect (Passive): *Read 8% faster.*		
Skill Effect (Passive): *Increases your Intellect and Wisdom Experience Gain by 3.00%*		

It was even better since I had already gained a few levels with it. I made a mental note to look for more skills giving passive bonuses.

At the end of the list, I found the new skill I had been working towards along with +1-Strength, +1-Dexterity, and +2-Stamina from the training to learn it.

You've learned the skill 'Net' and subskill 'Net Toss'

Net	Level: 1	Experience: 0.00%
Subskill: *Net Toss*	**Capture Target:** *Below 25% HP*	**Skill Stamina Cost:** *50*
Preparation Time: *10 minutes*	**Skill Effect (Active):** *Slow netted target by 50% for 30 Seconds*	

It was a costly skill, especially the preparation time, I would at most be able to use it only once per fight. I'm sure as I gained more levels with the skill, the time cost would drop, but for now, it was not the most useful of skills. It might never be. Especially, if I can only use it once every ten minutes.

I stayed and practiced for another hour, only gaining two skill levels and wiping off two whole seconds from the preparation time. Seeing the sun had just about set, it was time to return to the inn and see about dinner. I had a little more to read on the Norse pantheon tonight.

Olaf was the only one there when I arrived. He was tinkering with something, a small metal box in one hand and a tool I didn't recognize, in the other. He was also wearing some kind of magnifying glass over his one eye.

I wasn't sure if I should bother him right now, so I chose instead to sit and order a drink. I was dying of curiosity, but I also figured since he let me read the other day uninterrupted, I could show him the same courtesy. So, I sat and waited.

Thankfully, it wasn't a long wait.

"Evening mates," greeted Heath, loudly, clapping Olaf hard on the back, causing the big man to fumble the box he'd been working on. He juggled it a few times before finally catching it. "Sorry about that, didn't see you were working on something."

"You could have just killed us all," said Olaf, eyes wide and a drop of extra perspiration rolling from his brow. As he stared at the box in his hands.

"Are you playing with a bomb?" Heath asked, pointing at the box.

Olaf looked around nervously for a moment. "Maybe," he finally answered.

"Nice," said Heath, grinning widely, and giving Olaf a thumb's up.

"Not nice," I replied. "Are you telling me that box could have just blown up my home?" I hissed, questioning the Ogre.

Then he smirked.

"Oh, you jerk," I said, seeing the smirk. "So, what is it really?"

"Oh, it's an engineering puzzle Giggle-Ana assigned me. I have to figure out how to open it before she'll teach me more," Olaf answered.

I looked at the box and saw a little flashing red square partially covered by one of his meaty fingers. "Have you finished the 'Trapology' book yet?"

"Yeah, yesterday, why?" Olaf asked and answered.

"Did you learn the skill 'Spot Trap?'" I asked.

"No," Olaf replied, digging into his back and pulling the book out. "I swear, I've read this thing cover to cover, twice."

I looked at my skill list again, specifically 'Perception' where 'Spot Trap' was a subskill.

Perception	Level: 18	Experience: 12.35%
Skill Range: 11.80 yards	Chance to See: 14.50%	Chance to Identify/Track: 19.00%
Subskill: Beast Tracking	Skill Effect (Passive): Enables you to see animal tracks to better hunt them.	
Subskill: Humanoid Tracking	Skill Effect (Passive): Enables you to track humanoids.	
Subskill: Eye for Detail	Skill Effect (Passive): Enables you to see details that would be missed otherwise.	
Subskill: Spot Trap	Skill Effect (Passive): Enables you to see hidden traps.	

"How many eye skills have you learned?" I asked.

"Just Beast Tracking and Spot Ore Vein," Olaf replied.

"The only thing I can figure is it requires you develop 'Perception' first and the skill requires three ocular skills," I explained.

"Don't suppose I can borrow the book with the eye exercises from you?" Olaf requested.

I didn't want to. Call me greedy, but there were still so many skills I wanted to learn from it, but right now his need was greater. I pulled the book from my bag and held it out to him only for Heath to snatch it.

"So, visual skills eh?" Heath asked, flipping through it rapidly, blinking each time he turned the page. He then handed the book to Olaf without another word.

Olaf and I shared a brief look before staring at Heath.

"What?" the thief asked. "Something on my face?"

"What did you just do there?" asked Olaf.

"It almost looked like you were snapping photos of each page, and your eye was the shutter," I added, wondering if that wasn't exactly what he was doing. Except streaming and in-game screenshots hadn't been enabled in the game yet, unless they were part of the recent patch.

"Oh, you caught that, huh?" asked Heath.

"Yes, what was it?" I asked.

"Another thief skill. 'Espionage' allows me to steal information. Blueprints, important documents, anything able to fetch me a pretty penny, is mine for the taking . . . if I was into that kind of thing," Heath added as an afterthought.

"What good would that do you?" asked Olaf.

"First, knowledge can be sold. Battle plans are worth ridiculous amounts of money to the right buyer, mate. And, if you've got the advanced 'Drawing' profession 'Forgery', and I do, then you can recreate it. In the case of the book, I can just read it at my leisure later," Heath explained.

"Can you do that with any book?" I asked.

"Pretty much. But I can only store so many images. Right now, my capacity is just over three hundred pages, that book took up two-hundred and twelve of those pages. The rest of the pages are pretty much empty right now," Heath explained.

"I have to ask, why 'Forgery' if you plan to become a bard?" I asked curiously of my new forced companion.

"I took that more out of practicality, than anything. It's bloody useful to be able to create papers at a moment's notice. Originally, I was going to evolve 'Drawing' to 'Artistry', but 'Forgery' just seemed more useful," Heath answered.

"What are your other professions?" asked Olaf, he seemed more interested in getting to know Heath. Much as I didn't want to admit to it, so was I.

"I have 'Lumberjack', 'Woodworker' and 'Musician'," Heath answered proudly. "I'll be able to make my own instruments eventually. And 'Musician' is the prerequisite profession, to become a bard."

"So, why haven't you played for us, yet?" asked Olaf. "I would expect Heath Rickards to strum a mean lute."

I chuckled a little while Heath looked appalled. "Not a chance mate, this bard will never touch a lute, or may the Gods strike me down. I was playing my guitar in here the other day. Eventually, I'll be playing an Ax and nothing else. I just have to make one first. I bought a blueprint for my ax, but I can't learn it yet. Not until I get my 'Woodworker' profession to Rank II. For now, I've just been trying to stockpile lumber. I'm barely halfway to Rank II of my Thief skills, so I've got time."

"I've got a question," started Rose, as she sat and joined us, Baby coming in right behind her. Rose looked to be in a good mood, while Baby looked a little pale, to be honest.

"What's that?" asked Heath. "I promise I'll keep my answer clean for the little one."

Olaf and I snorted but were silenced by a glare from Rose.

"How does becoming a bard, require you to become a thief first?" asked Rose, choosing not to engage, though I was sure, she was mighty tempted.

"It doesn't, well, not exactly, anyway," Heath answered, grinning and confusing all of us more than a little.

"Okay, so maybe I haven't told you all the full story. Anyone can become a Bard, you only need the 'Musician' profession. They are good for buffing and debuffing, but otherwise pretty useless. They completely lack combat skills. I've heard some Bard's have gotten good at weapon swapping, going from an instrument to a bow or gun, and back again, or adding in some mage spells," Heath explained.

"So why the Thief class?" Rose asked.

"I'm actually trying for a Jack of All Trades, It's an advanced Bard class. I've already learned five spells from the Mage class and gotten to them to Rank II, which was so much easier than the Thief skills have been. Anyway, once I get the Rank II of the Thief skills, I'll get offered the chance to test with the Thieves Guild for the class Jack of All Trades. It's a massive grind but should be well worth it," Heath explained further.

"That's sounds overpowered," commented Olaf.

"Yeah, but it still doesn't explain how a Thief relates to becoming a Bard. And now, I'm wondering how a Mage relates," Rose pressed.

Heath laughed. "In ye olden times, Bards in court were often thieves too. Robbing from the rich lords, stealing jewelry and coin, while their music or stories distracted them. They would often steal daughters and wives too, if only for an evening. As for the Mage spells, it was more about learning illusions and simple cantrips, ways to make escape easier or to charm their way into places. Places they certainly should not have been."

"It's rather genius," I commented. "I think I may have underestimated you, Heath."

"Good," the thief said, grinning. "I want everyone to underestimate me, it makes them easier targets."

"So why tell us?" asked Rose suspiciously.

"I know I forced my way into your circle, but you're giving me an honest chance, and you're all showing me some trust. I figured I could try and show you all a little trust, too," Heath explained. I felt he was genuine too, but I was still cautious.

"I'll be watching you," said Rose, ending her interrogation of the thief, apparently agreeing with my unspoken thoughts.

"My goodness, your mommy is awfully protective of her friends, isn't she?" asked Heath, baby talking to Baby.

"It's mommy's job to protect us," said Baby, playing along, but not sounding as convincing as usual. I noticed a bit of color had returned to Baby, but she still seemed lethargic.

I looked again at Heath. He had a kind smile for Baby, but I was now suspecting, Heath knew it was an act and was simply playing along. The more I learned about him, the more I suspected, this man was more aware of everything going on than I originally thought.

It also made me feel nervous to be around him.

"Say, Heath, I don't suppose you were the laugh I heard, the first time I tried to break into Graves's home?" I asked.

"No idea what you're talking about, mate," Heath replied, not looking in my direction.

"I have news!" shouted Micaela, entering the inn causing us all to turn to look at her. Under her arms she had a bunch of metal and copper pieces, I couldn't make heads or tails out of.

"Whatcha got there, Babe?" asked Olaf.

"So, I spent some time today helping the Johnson's at their farmstead, mostly tearing down the old structures, and clearing away the debris. Anyway, while I was helping them, I found this stuff," Micaela explained, shrugging her shoulders and shifting the pieces she was holding.

"And what is that stuff?" asked Olaf.

"The remains of the still. I thought maybe we could fix it up for them, and by 'we', I mean you, Mr. Engineer," Micaela finished, looking at her husband.

"Happy to, I've never worked on a still before. This should be fun," said Olaf.

Meanwhile, I was feeling a little of extra excitement myself. If the magic on the still remained intact, then we could give this town back their weapon against Graves, if we fail to stop him.

Quest Alert: Be'still' my heart (Recommended Level 5-7)		
Repair the magical still that created the first 'Moonshine'.		
Reward: Experience, 5-Gold		
Do you accept this Quest?	Yes	No

"Bye-bye," was the collective call, as all eyes went to me, except for Heath who looked confused.

"What?" I asked with a shrug and a small grin.

I ended up giving them more background on the town history and got a few good laughs when I enlightened them to the creation of 'Moonshine'. I also took a minute to fill them in on the wolves and the Norse Gods involved.

After dinner, and a few drinks and some socializing, I called it an early night. I wanted to finish the 'Halls of Valhalla' book.

But first, I updated my journal, giving each of the level one player's I'd met, a bit of time to describe and draw, adding all my quest updates, level progression, and skill updates.

Then I sat to read. The remainder of the book went into more details of the various Gods, but I was trying to focus on anything relating to the children of the God Fenrir.

Sol was interesting, she was the actual sun. Sol's guard Svalinn was a Valkyrie, she helped to contain Sol's flames, so as not to burn the World Tree, as well as defend her from Skoll. The moon was named Mani, who was Sol's twin brother. He had no need of a guard to protect the World Tree from the light he gave, I almost snorted at that because, at the moment, that is exactly what we needed, moonshine.

When I closed the last page, I looked again at my system messages, I gained +2-Intellect, +1-Wisdom, and +2-Charisma, which was nice. I was surprised, I was able to level cap my Wisdom and Intellect stats already, but then again, I had just basically spent a few days straight studying. The Charisma gains were obviously from socializing with my friends, even Heath.

The last surprise of the day was a change to my 'Lore' profession, or rather an evolution of my subskill. I had also gained a bunch of levels in the profession as well.

Your subskill 'Ancient Norse' has evolved to 'Norse Mysticism I'

Lore	*Level:* 19	*Experience:* 1.11%
Professional Skill: Lore is the study of the history of the World Tree and its denizens.		
Subskill: Norse Mysticism I	*Your knowledge of both the Ancient Norse language and their Mythos has granted you a level of mastery.*	

| | Knowledge of Norse Skills and Spells is improved. | |

That left me with a whole new set of questions. What are Norse Skills and Spells? How much was improved? What was improved about my knowledge? I had questions and no immediate answers. It was one more mystery on my growing list, but rather than frustrate me, I just got more and more excited.

I also remembered my promise to myself, to check out the new equipment Sergeant Butters awarded me. I was a little late I suppose, three days late, but now seemed to be a good time to take a look. I opened my bag, removing the three new pieces of equipment.

Guard's Light Leather Bracers – Light Leather - +4-Armor, +5-Endurance, +2-Stamina, Durability 15/15
Guard's Phalanx Shield - +20-Armor, +10-Endurance, +5-Stamina, Durability 40/40
Holy Order Light Gloves – Light Leather - +10-Armor, +5-Strength, +5-Dexterity, +5-Intellect, +5-Holy Damage, and Healing, Durability 20/20

All nice upgrades to my equipment. I think I was just lacking a helm, a new chest armor piece, and an upgraded spear as far as major equipment pieces go. I was also in need of a new charm and several accessories.

Equipment Slot	Name	Armor/ Damage	Bonus Stats
Helm:	Empty		
Head Accessory:	Empty		
Shoulders:	Holy Lion Mane Shoulder-guards	+15 Armor	+5-Strength, +10-Dexterity, +5 Intellect, +10 Holy Spell Damage and Healing
Back:	All-		

	Weather Cloak (White)		
Chest Armor:	Light Vest	+5 Armor	
Chest Clothing:	White Cotton Shirt	+0 Armor	
Wrists:	Guard's Light Leather Bracers	+4 Armor	+5-Endurance, +2-Stamina
Hands:	Holy Order Light Gloves	+10 Armor	+5-Strength, +5-Dexterity, +5-Intellect, +5-Holy Spell Damage and Healing
Arm Accessory 1:	Empty		
Arm Accessory 2:	Empty		
Finger Accessory 1:	Farmer's Ring of Stamina		+2-Stamina, +4-Stamina Regeneration
Finger Accessory 2:	Empty		
Waist:	Guard's Light Leather Belt	+6 Armor	+5-Endurance, +2-Stamina
Leg Clothing:	Cotton Jeans	+0 Armor	
Leg Armor:	Holy Order	+20 Armor	+5-Endurance, +10-Intellect, +5-Wisdom,

	Light Leg-guards		+10 Holy Spell Damage and Healing
Feet Clothing	Silk Socks	+0 Armor	
Feet:	Well Tread Boots	+10 Armor	+5-Dexterity, +5-Endurance, +5-Stamina
Weapon:	Hasta	7-8 1h Dmg, 14-26 2h Dmg	
Off-Hand:	Guard's Phalanx Shield	+20 Armor	+20-Armor, +10-Endurance, +5-Stamina
Charm:	Empty		
Bag:	100 lbs. Traveler's Satchel		

CHAPTER 33

Morning came, and I was early to rise. The rooster I killed the previous day had yet to be replaced, so it was a quiet awakening and one I was thankful for. I looked out my window and could see the first rays of sunshine creeping over the rooftops lining the street outside my window.

I stretched a little, not because I needed to, but because it felt good. I didn't stop to appreciate it very often, but this body, this avatar, was kind of amazing. I was strong, agile and capable. Efforts that would have left me gasping for breath in the RL, or real life, were now so effortless. I hoped, when I finally logged out, it would be just as effortless. I also knew I had to temper my expectations. It would take at least one more session to truly repair my body. I say repair, even though it's not actually broken, but the years of bad food habits and lack of exercise certainly had a negative effect on my health. Still, that was a worry for next week. Today, I had things to accomplish.

I dressed and made my way downstairs where I found Micaela, Olaf, and Heath all waiting.

"Morning, Cool Stuff Finder," greeted Heath. "Olaf and Mic have just been giving me their pitch for forming an order. I've got to say, it sounds bloody brilliant. If you can find the sort of things these two say you can, then I just might be inclined to join up."

I looked to Olaf and Micaela, who nodded to me. "I see, and it had better not be 'Cool Stuff Finder'," I warned them, sending a glare specifically toward Micaela.

"Awe, but I like that rank idea," Micaela pouted. "It fits you so well."

"Never happening," I replied flatly, taking a seat and waving to Dogson for my breakfast. A few minutes later, a tired looking Baby floated down the stairs.

"Morning, Baby, not get much sleep?" I asked.

"No, Rosie was up late hissing back and forth with Panther, working on her enchanting. I could have dealt with the candlelight, but her hissing was just too creepy. It gave me nightmares about being eaten by snakes and snakemen," Baby answered, finishing with a big yawn, looking super cute.

"Aw, poor little girl, I'll have a word with your mommy. Little girls need their sleep," said Heath.

"Oh, stuff that," said Baby. "Look, Rose is my baby sister. I'm just playing a character that has the body of a child."

"So, you're saying, she doesn't have any baggage?" asked Heath, a lecherous grin forming on his face. I felt a strong urge to wipe that look right back off.

"My sister has plenty of baggage, but having a small child, is not a part of that," Baby replied. "However, if you want to continue to work with us, then I need it to be clear up front, my sister is permanently off your radar. There are plenty of other women around here, I'm sure are more than willing to give you time and attention. Maybe you should stick with the one you left with last night, that Arial girl, the one that was hitting on Bye-bye, seems more appropriate. Am I clear?"

I was suddenly looking at Baby in a new light. She had always been so compliant and kind. Always playing peacemaker. Maybe, that was why I had always associated her with just being a super cute and kind person. Something about her right now, looked neither cute nor kind. She looked fierce and strong.

"Baby is right," said Micaela. "We're happy to have you along but we won't tolerate any nonsense. If you're going to pursue Rose, then you had better be serious about it, or I'll make you hurt in ways you can only imagine."

Heath sobered up or rather just became more serious before he spoke next. "You make a perfectly valid point. One should not dip their pen in company ink, as they say. I understand your reasoning, and to be honest, I'm not looking for anything serious, so I'll abide and keep clear. Just keep in mind, she might not keep clear of me."

"Oh please," chortled Micaela. "The only reason, Rose would pay you any mind, is if she was trying to make someone else jealous."

Who was Rose trying to make jealous? Did that mean there was someone Rose liked? I know she kissed me on the cheek before, but that was just a friendly thank you, wasn't it? The idea that Rose was interested in someone made me feel a little sad for some reason.

"Morning, all," greeted Rose, distracting me from my thoughts as her armor clanked with each step down the stairs. I hadn't paid much attention, but her armoring looked so much different. A large portion of her orange copper armor had been replaced with dark red and black pieces.

It also made me realize, I hadn't paid much attention to any changes in my friends' armor and gear.

Micaela still wore the mining overalls but now she had stone plated boots and stone plated gauntlets, I assumed they were totems, but I hadn't asked about them or even noticed.

Olaf wore several pieces of camouflaged armor covering his hands and legs, even his artillery pack was now camouflaged. He also had a bandoleer across his chest, some kind of bombs hung from it.

Baby's appearance hadn't changed much, but I did notice she now had a few rings on her fingers, and a bracelet around her left upper arm. Also, the wand, usually hovering at her hip, was different. The previous wand was little more than a gnarled tree branch, this one was smooth, straight, and polished to a nice luster.

Heath hadn't changed at all, but I'd only known him a few days.

Looking at my friends, it made me realize just how much we had all changed. I doubt I'd even recognize myself from my first day.

"So, what's the plan today? Seeing the sergeant first or right out to capture the wolf?" asked Rose, sitting down next to me.

"I think we need to get the wolf first, just in case there is another step in the quest chain. The questioning of the dead guard is scheduled to start at 8:00 tonight, according to my quest timer," I answered.

"Works for me," said Rose, signaling Dogson for her breakfast.

Breakfast was eaten quickly now that we were all here and ready for adventure.

We found our first <Wolf Lvl 1> not too far outside of town. I hit it once, just once and it died.

"That could be a problem," commented Olaf.

"Yes, yes it could be," I replied, still not believing I just one shot the wolf. I did the math on my damage and I guess I shouldn't have been surprised. The base damage on my spear while equipped one-handed, was only 7-8 damage. But then, I had 66-Strength with all my gear, each point adding 1-point of damage. 'One-Handed Polearms', at level 31, added another 15.50-damage and finally 'Lesser Holy Imbuement' added 7-8 base damage, plus my holy spell damage bonus of 94. I don't know why I was so surprised when the <Wolf Lvl 1> died in one hit, considering they only have about 75-HP total. Still, -205-HP from one hit was a beautiful sight to see.

"Can anyone hit a wolf just hard enough to drop it down to 25% health?" I asked.

"I might be able to with just 'Shield Slam'," offered Rose.

"Can we try?" I requested.

It took a few minutes for me to spot another set of tracks and another minute to find the <Wolf Lvl 2>.

"Ladies first," I motioned for Rose to go ahead. She struck hard and fast, charging in and knocking the <Wolf Lvl 2> to the ground, she then struck it with her 'Shield Slam'. With just those two hits the beast dropped to half health.

"Just one more hit I think," I said, watching the enemy health bar closely. I had my net ready to capture the beast the moment I was able to.

"Right," said Rose, smacking it one more time with her shield. Seeing 45% of the beast's health vanish almost made me panic. It was now down to just 2% health. "Oops," she laughed. "Critical strike," she explained.

Thankfully it was still alive, I used my 'Net Toss' skill. The net enveloped the wolf and I yanked back on the tether drawing the net closed around the wolf. It continued to thrash but reflected a 'Captured' debuff all the same.

"Nice, now we just have to drag it back to town," said Heath. "Not bad work everyone, well done."

"What exactly did you do, Heath?" asked Rose, a small glare aimed at him.

"I was instrumental in this capture. I gave you the courage you needed to face such a fierce animal," Heath answered.

Rose tried to continue glaring but gave up and laughed. "Just keep telling yourself that."

"I do every day," the thief retorted, a grin of his own in place.

"Alright, folks, let's get this brute back to town," I said, trying to move the group along.

I end up having to manage the brunt of the work. No one could approach the captured wolf without risking the beast snapping at them. As a result, I had to drag the netted and captured beast along the ground behind me, steadily draining my stamina.

"Oi, what's the big idea?" asked the guard on duty, his sword drawn, while he glared at the wolf.

He looked familiar to me, but I haven't met all the different guards yet.

"Kill that rotten beast. How dare you bring it into our town?" the guard demanded.

Now I recognized him. He was one of the guards with the sergeant when I found Davies' body. He had a strong dislike of the wolves. It seemed, nothing had changed.

"No can do," I replied. "I've been ordered to bring a captured wolf to High Priestess Trinico."

The guard huffed and glared, but eventually relented. "Fine, go on."

"Not the nicest fellow, is he?" asked Heath.

"Seems to have a personal grudge against wolves," I replied.

"As I understand it," started Olaf. "The wolves have been tormenting this town for generations."

"Nearly three centuries," I added. I had read the town history, or at least the first 100 years of it, and I knew there still several volumes of it to go. I doubted, I would read any more of it, unless I was really bored.

We got plenty of looks from players and citizens alike as I continued to drag the netted wolf through the streets.

Inside, Trinico was once again standing at her pulpit, a line of players waiting to speak with her.

"Morning Trinico," I greeted, struggling with the now very agitated wolf. "Sorry to interrupt but I brought the wolf and he is most unhappy to be here."

"Apologies, everyone, I'm afraid this is urgent business I have to address," Trinico said to the waiting line, getting several groans of disappointment. She then turned to me and my friends. "Follow me," she ordered.

The priestess led us through the temple to one of the many alcoves. This one though was covered in Norse symbols and the depictions of the many Gods, all of which, I recognized from my research.

"Place the beast in the center of the alcove," Trinico instructed.

I dragged the beast in, carefully maneuvering so the beast wouldn't bite me through the net.

"Very good, step back," Trinico warned. Then she began to pray in Ancient Norse. After a moment, I felt something shift as a shadow fell over us. I turned to look for the source of the shadow, only to see, possibly the largest wolf ever towering over us and filling most of the temple.

"Show me," the giant wolf, God Fenrir ordered.

We parted to either side of the alcove to allow the God better access to see the cowering, trapped wolf. It was clearly terrified of the being standing over it.

"Lord Fenrir, we are grateful to you for your assistance," said Trinico, bowing formally to the God, now standing in our presence. "Please, guide us in breaking the curse placed upon our village by one of the fallen."

"My sons cause nothing but heartache to me. Always striving to win, competing against each other, and not caring such a thing could end all of us, nor care for the damage they cause. It disappoints me so," stated the God, his voice sounding both angry and disappointed. The God Fenrir sounded remorseful to me, sad even. I felt for him.

The God Fenrir leaned his massive head closer to the trapped wolf, then breathed in deeply before exhaling a powerful breath, filling the temple and extinguishing candles all around us, blowing offerings away as well. But what I was interested in, was the white shadowy mist blown free from the trapped wolf.

"Hati!" the God Fenrir howled angrily, shaking the foundation of the building and rattling the glass. *"How dare that child corrupt my children, all to stop his twin from gaining power."*

"How can we serve you, great God Fenrir?" Rose asked, stepping forward and bowing.

"Hmm, a servant of Lilith seeks to help me, how odd. And what's this, a servant of Issara as well," the God Fenrir said looking from Rose to me. I was slightly worried we were both about to become a snack for this God.

Rose's Charisma was still not high enough if I had to guess. I stepped up next to her, bowing as well. "I serve the Goddess Issara, as an agent of her justice. Your children have placed a curse on this village, the people deserve justice. Please, tell us how we might break this curse and bring justice to these people. How can we serve to help your other children, those who have been tainted?"

"Hmm, these two fleshlings are interesting. I shall have to keep an eye on them," said the God Fenrir, sounding amused. *"Very well, if you wish to serve, then you shall. Find me the leader of this pack and bring him before me. The taint of Hati must be cleansed at its source."*

Quest Alert: Breaking the curse of the Wolves 3

(Recommended Level 4-5) - Completed
In speaking to Trinico, you have determined there may yet be more to this curse. You have been tasked to capture one alive and bring it before the Norse Gods.
Reward: +500-Experience

A moment later we got the next quest in the chain.

Quest Alert: Breaking the curse of the Wolves 4 (Recommended Level 5-7)		
The God Fenrir has charged you to put a stop to his children's squabble. Capture the leader of the wolf pack and bring it before Fenrir.		
Reward: Experience, Divine Favor		
Do you accept this Quest?	Yes	No

"We are honored," said Rose, accepting for all of us.

"Return before sundown, I shall wait no longer," said the God Fenrir, disappearing as if he'd never been there, along with the wolf, leaving behind an empty net.

"I never expected Lord Fenrir would show up himself," said Trinico, trying to straighten her robes. Then she looked around the temple and scoffed. "Look at this mess. You," she paused pointing to the shell-shocked, level one players who just witnessed the event. "All of you, clean this place up, relight the candles, set straight the offerings and altars. When it is complete, come to see me and I will reward your efforts," ordered Trinico, issuing a quest to everyone present except us. "What are you six still doing here? You'd better hurry," scolded the priestess, addressing my group.

"Just one question, where can we find the pack leader?" I asked.

"To the south is a quarry. It serves as the wolves' den. You will find the pack leader at the deepest point," Trinico answered.

"So much for it being a mine," groused Olaf.

"There is a great deal of tin and silver there, but the wolves tend to make it difficult to mine," advise Trinico, looking slightly impatient we were still standing there.

"We're going," I said, ushering our group out.

Thankfully, I knew exactly where the valley she spoke of was. It was the sole unmapped area in the south portion of the province.

"So, is no one going to point out how awesome that was?" asked Micaela once we were outside the village.

"I have no idea how to respond to what we just witnessed," said Heath, sans accent. "That might have been . . . no, that definitely, was the most amazing thing I've seen since my first dive."

"Yeah, Jack has a talent for getting us into interesting situations. That said, this might be the coolest yet," said Rose, not a hint of snark or sarcasm in her voice or on her face.

"Bye-bye is the gift that keeps on giving," added Baby with a giggle.

"I don't know if that's the most amazing thing I've seen him do, but I'll admit it was pretty impressive," said Micaela happily.

I turned quickly to glare at Micaela, hopefully, communicating my request to keep silent about certain events. I still wasn't sure what to think of Heath or if I could trust him with certain knowledge.

"If that isn't the most impressive thing you've seen, then I can't wait to see what he pulls off next," said Heath, grinning excitedly, and in that instant, I went straight from irritated to embarrassed.

"Alright, that's enough. Leave Jack alone, I think we've inflated his ego enough already," said Rose, coming to my rescue and teasing me, all in one breath. It surprised me she would do that, but I was grateful. I caught her looking at me, so I gave her a small smile and nod of thanks.

"So, this valley, how far away are we talking?" asked Rose.

"Not too far from where we fought the <Greater Condor> when we first met," I answered, stepping up next to her while the rest of the party followed behind us.

We encountered a few wolves along the way easily dispatching them, eventually turning it into a game to see who could get the strongest one hit kill shot. Olaf won by a mile, with his stupid guaranteed critical hit skill.

"Anyone have any idea what we'll see down there?" asked Rose.

"If you all can wait a minute, I can go scout it out," offered Heath.

Time to trust him or not. "Do it, but be careful," I warned.

Heath smiled confidently and vanished from view. He didn't even leave any footprints.

"I'll say this, Heath has some ridiculous stealth skills," commented Olaf. "If only his British accent was as good."

"He's trying to improve at least," added Micaela.

It took about twenty minutes before Heath reappeared.

"And here I was hoping to catch you all talking about me," Heath said in his usual overconfident manner.

"No such luck," said Olaf.

"What's the verdict?" asked Rose, motioning toward the Valley of Wolves, as I now called it on my map.

"Right, there were several side caves carved into the rock. The caves aren't deep, ten feet at most. Each cave houses three to four wolves, going all the way down to the cul-de-sac at the bottom. There were five caves there, and sitting out in the open, right in the middle, appears to be our target. I don't think this will be an easy fight down. Everything down there is at least <Alpha Wolf Lvl 4> or higher. There were several <Matriarch Wolf Lvl 5> and up. The guy at the bottom was called the <Alpha Wolf Primus Lvl 8>," Heath reported.

"Okay, so, slow and methodical, just like the bandit hideout," I started. "We clear every side tunnel, I don't want any extra wolves being called out when we get to the last one."

"Make sure you give me a chance to get aggro before you ramp up your damage," warmed Rose. "If we are fighting multiple targets, it will take a few to get proper threat. That also means you need to hold on before healing too soon, Baby. Jack will call out the kill targets. Everyone good?"

Everyone agreed, and Rose took the lead in with the rest of us following just behind her. As we entered the valley I could see the cave lining either side, starting at about twenty feet below the surface. They also appeared to be staggered positioning, one on the left then one on the right further in then back to the left.

"Left side first," said Rose, approaching the cave.

The good news is, we didn't have to enter the cave. Three wolves came out to greet us, or rather, to greet Rose. Rose was faster, she used 'Charge' on the matriarch, then used 'Shield Slam' on an alpha, and struck the last alpha with a jab of her sword, causing the beast to yelp in pain. Then she struck it again, making it angrier. I decided that one died first.

"Left first," I said as I moved in to attack. I cast a 'Lesser Holy Fire' as I moved in with Micaela right next to me. I couldn't see Heath, but I assumed he was there, moving about while hidden from view. I attacked first with 'Hamstring' and follow up with 'Justice Strike' and 'Lesser Holy Shock' but before I could finish my combination it was already dead.

"Alpha next," I called out. Once again, it was dead before I could finish my combination. As I turned to fight the <Matriarch Wolf Lvl 6> her fur bristled, and a growl tore from her throat, answered by howling from the two closest caves. We were suddenly set upon by six more beasts.

"From now on, momma wolf dies first," shouted Rose, trying to grab up aggro on the new threats.

I quickly equipped my shield, then taunted the four new alphas. "Focus on those. I can hold these for a little bit."

"I'll start taking them from you as the matriarchs die off," said Rose, grunting as she blocked another attack.

I felt rusty fighting these guys.

I haven't used my shield in a while, so my timing was a little off, but my footwork was spot on. I kept up 'Lesser Holy Fire' to the best of my ability and used 'Justice Strike' and 'Lesser Holy Shock' to keep my own threat up, while Baby was working double duty healing me and Rose.

"Taking two," said Rose, warning me she was taunting two of the wolves away from me. "Oi, kibbles and bits, come get me."

Two of the wolves I'd been tanking, left to fight Rose. With only two to tank, I returned my shield to my bag and started to lay into them. I smiled a little, I was now free to move. I jumped, easily flipping over one of the lunging wolves. When I landed I triggered my 'Rapid Striking' skill, striking out at the two wolves in front of me without holding back. It was fun, watching each strike hit for almost - 120-HP. I took some damage for not moving, but the two alpha wolves were all but dead. I was quick to move, as they were still intent on turning me into dinner.

I hit the one with lowest remaining health with 'Justice Strike' then 'Lesser Holy Shock' and finally got to follow through with

'Power Thrust', killing it. My last strike was a critical, which left me facing just one alpha. It was relatively simple to avoid and dodge a single wolf with my 'Acrobatics' skill. Within a minute, I wrecked the beast. Even though I was breathing heavily when it died, I knew I had to help with the rest of the beasts. However, when I turned to help my friends, they appeared to have just killed their last wolf as well.

"Alright, now that is what I call good fun," said Heath, his dagger slipping back into the sheath on his belt.

"Nice work everyone, take a minute to drink and eat if you need it," said Baby, casting another heal on me, then Rose bringing us both back to full.

I sat down on one of the larger boulders littering the quarry. I took out my two canteens and started to drink. I was slightly surprised when Rose sat down next to me.

"Not bad, Jack. Not as good as me, but not bad," Rose joked tiredly. "Thanks for jumping in to help tank those. I might have been in trouble if I had to manage all of those at once."

"Sure, it's why I learned taunt. You were pretty awesome on that initial pull. Really nice job getting aggro so fast," I complimented her.

"Thanks," said Rose softly, taking a sip from her own canteen. Eventually, Rose sighed and stood. "Okay, enough laying around. We've got more work to do."

We systematically exterminated the wolf population residing in the mine quarry. We actually got decent experience for all of them as well. I think I gained around +250-Experience, give or take a few points. I also figured out how to scavenge in a way that targeted specific parts, in this case, the teeth. Olaf and the others with the skill joined in as well. Before we knew it, we were at the bottom, or near enough to see the <Alpha Wolf Primus Lvl 8>. He was big, abnormally so, not as big as the God Fenrir, not even close, but he had size on Graves for sure.

"That's a big puppy," said Micaela, staring wide-eyed at the beast. "Can I keep him for a pet after we capture him?"

"No . . . maybe . . . I don't know," were Olaf's answers as he studied the beast. "You're not a beast tamer. How would you even make him your pet? Plus, with all your totems, don't you think you have enough pets?"

Micaela could only shrug.

"Are there wolves in those caves?" I asked, looking at Heath.

"I couldn't get close enough. The big fella seems to be able to see through my stealth and illusions," Heath answered.

"I think Jack will have to tank anything coming out of those caves. I'll handle the big guy. Priority has to be killing whatever adds spawn though," said Rose thoughtfully. Adds or additional enemy spawns could really complicate a fight if they aren't controlled quickly. I couldn't help but agree, already equipping my shield in preparation for the fight to come.

"On you Rosie," said Baby, floating up above us, a good five feet, to take herself out of range of danger, or at least most of it.

Rose clapped her sword against her shield twice before she roared loudly, then suddenly blurred, her body surging forward until her shoulder impacted the giant wolf. She followed up with 'Shield Slam' and a few precise strikes, each met with a yelp and a growl of anger.

Micaela was next to me as we moved in to attack, but this time, she was using Sundance to throw fireballs as she went. Not to be outdone, I was hitting the beast with 'Lesser Holy Fire' and

'Lesser Holy Shock' and I hit with 'Justice Strike' as soon as I got into melee range.

Everything was going smoothly, it was a tank and spank fight for the first 10% of his health. Then the Primus just had to go and light himself on fire before exploding in a wave of fiery death, burning everything in its path, including us. It was honestly rather painful, even with the pain muted.

"Bye-bye, help me heal," called Baby, working overtime to get Rose back up.

I set about trying to heal Baby up first, before I started dropping heals on the rest of us.

"Wolves incoming," warned Heath, causing me to stop my healing. Three wolves emerged, each coming from a different tunnel. <Frenzied Wolf Lvl 3> the nameplates stated. One headed for me, so I didn't worry about it. The other two went for different targets, one for Micaela and one for Heath.

"Come get me," I tried to taunt the one headed toward Micaela only to get an 'Immune' message pop up. "You can't taunt them," I warned everyone.

"Everyone, kill your target, then help with the others," called Rose. "Olaf, help out."

I might have grinned a little as I put my shield away. 'Lesser Holy Fire', flip over the target, 'Hamstring', roll to the left, 'Justice Strike', cartwheel to the left, 'Lesser Holy Shock', flip back away, 'Power Thrust', and the wolf died. I looked back to my group and was shocked. Micaela was dead.

"What happened?" I asked.

"If they hit you, they exploded and instantly kill you," explained Olaf. "Or rather, they did just enough damage to kill Mic.

626

We have to be topped off when they come out. You and Heath seemed to do alright with the flipping around thing."

"Well, then shoot something," I complained. I didn't have time to stand around and worry. I had to get back to capturing the wolf boss.

"10% mark coming, brace," warned Baby.

The wolf didn't explode this time. Instead, he breathed fire and started slowing rotating. It caused those of us not directly in front of him to start running, trying to stay ahead of the flames, which were steadily getting faster.

"Must move faster," commented Heath trying to get away from the wall of flames.

The wolf stopped when he got back to his original position then resumed attacking Rose.

"Wolves," warned Heath.

Thankfully, everyone made it through the previous round of attacks without significant damage, other than Rose. And Baby had plenty of time to heal Rose once she was out of the flames.

I took out my <Frenzied Wolf Lvl 3> quickly, avoiding being hit by it, but there was a moment when I thought I had mistimed my dodge. When the next 10% of the boss's health dropped, we didn't know what to expect, so we were pleasantly surprised when he did his flame breathe again. Then at 60% health, he exploded again. This time, Baby and I pushed out as much healing as we could to get everyone topped off, before the wolves came out.

It was a slow fight and transitioned so many times. At 50% health, the boss called out six wolves instead of making us die in a fire. The wolf targeting Rose detonated when it hit her, but her armor protected her better than the rest of us. I finally ate a detonation, but I did it intentionally, so I'd only have to face one wolf instead of two.

It actually worked better than I had hoped, because it killed the second wolf. Thank you, friendly fire, for working to my advantage for a change.

"Fight them right up next to the boss, if they do hit you the detonation does friendly fire damage," I called out the warning to my group.

"I know," snapped Rose, straining to block an attack from the Primus.

I guess I didn't check the boss's health before I said it, but he'd already lost 5% of his health since I last looked, my guess would be the one that detonated on Rose did that.

The next 10% the boss exploded again and the 10% after that, the Primus called extra wolves again. Finally, he was down to the 24% mark. I equipped my net and prayed this would work. I activated my 'Net Toss'.

"Captured!" cheered Baby.

"Bloody hell, I just missed it," complained Micaela, running down the hewn stone ramp, she was sweating and gasping for breath, but she'd made it.

"Sorry, Babe, we didn't know how close you were," said Olaf.

"It's alright love. At least we didn't wipe on big ugly here. How does your net fit exactly? I was sure it wasn't that big before," Micaela commented, even though I was sure she understood the game had a natural tendency to make things fit.

"It's a game, love, it fits because we need it to fit," said Olaf, grinning excitedly.

"Oh well, let's get this big puppy back to the temple." Turning to start the trek back, Micaela paused and added, "I wonder if he'll even fit through the door?"

"It should squeeze through," I said, tugging on the tether, making sure it was tightly drawn.

Looking at the trapped wolf I was surprised that it fit too. The net was drawn so tightly around it, the <Alpha Wolf Primus Lvl 8> didn't have room the thrash around or snap at me when I got close. He had to settle for glaring balefully at me.

"Okay, I think all of us, but Rose and Baby will have to carry this guy. I'm not strong enough to do it on my own." I stated.

"You heard Jack, get to work. We've only got two hours to get this guy back to the temple," ordered Rose, clapping her hands as if it would get us moving faster.

CHAPTER 34

"Oh no, not again!" shouted the same guard as we approached the gates. I sighed, I didn't want to deal with this guy, but Rose had no such qualms.

"Listen here grunt, we're working to remove the curse, to put an end to the danger of these wolves. Are you really going to interfere?" Rose asked.

"But it's the pack leader," the guard protested.

"Yeah, and if we can cure him, the problem is resolved forever. Now let us through, or do I have to go get your boss. You know, Sergeant Butters, the guy who likes us."

The guard growled angrily. "Just go already."

"That's what I thought," said Rose, smirking superiorly.

If the walk through town the first time dragging a wolf got us odd looks, then this time completely stopped traffic. As if that weren't enough, people didn't just stop and stare but started to follow along behind us. I couldn't help but notice there must have been at least 20 players ranging from level 1 to level 2, some of which I even recognized.

When we got to the temple, a few people jogged ahead and opened the doors wide for us, granting us passage inside. Once again, we dragged the wolf to the Norse alcove, placing it in the center, while Baby flew ahead to retrieve Trinico.

"That is a big wolf," commented one of the audience members, that's right, we now had an audience of Citizens and players alike.

"Stand clear," warned Trinico. "When Lord Fenrir appears, if you do not wish to be squashed like an insect, you will stand back."

The woman gave me and the others a brief acknowledgment before she began to pray. Similar to the first time he appeared, we were covered by a large shadow, marking the arrival of the God Fenrir.

"So, you have succeeded," the God Fenrir said, sounding slightly amused. He stared at the shivering bundle of a wolf, it was almost amusing if you consider just a little while ago, it came close to decimating us.

The God Fenrir stared down at the bundle. *"Show yourself, son, make your presence known to me. If I have to force you from this vessel, Hati, you will not like the consequences."*

A white mist rose from the captured wolf, this time taking the form of a smoky ghost in the shape of a wolfman, strikingly similar to Graves. *"Father,"* the fallen God, Hati hissed angrily. *"Why do you interfere in my business?"*

"The Fallen are the business of all the Gods," howled the God Fenrir angrily, shaking the building in the process.

"Fallen? Why? Because I worked to do what I was born for? How hypocritical of you. How very . . . Norse," scoffed the Fallen God Hati.

"Your divinity was to hunt the moon through the skies until the end of days, to always push the cycle of life forward and to mark the passage of time," argued the God Fenrir

"No, that is what you wanted. I want the power that comes from absorbing the moon and becoming the God of light. I will take that fool Sol's domain from her by destroying that which she never could. Besides, you should be

631

grateful I am here. If it were not for me, then my . . . brother . . . the traitor would have already plunged the world into darkness and become the God of darkness," stated the Fallen God Hati.

"And now I am telling you, you are not welcome here. I will deal with your brother and he too shall be expelled from this place," ordered Lord Fenrir, shaking the building.

"I will give you 48-hours to expel him. If you fail, I shall return, and our war shall proceed until either one of us wins or we both die. And be warned, any who stand in our way shall be torn asunder," threatened the Fallen God Hati.

"So be it, I accept your terms," said the God Fenrir. *"Now, begone."*

The white mist that formed the Fallen God Hati became little more than smoke in the wind as he vanished.

Quest Alert: Breaking the curse of the Wolves 4 (Recommended Level 5-7) - Completed
The God Fenrir has charged you to put a stop to his children's squabble. Capture the leader of the wolf pack and bring it before Fenrir.
Reward: +2000-Experience, Blessing of Fenrir

"You have done well, fleshlings. You have earned a modicum of my respect, take these gifts with my gratitude," said the God Fenrir, an orb of light floated from the God to each of us.

When I touched the orb, it burst in a shower of sparks.

You have learned the Norse runes of 'Strength', 'Healing', 'Gladness', 'Victory', and 'Justice'

Lore	**Level:** *19*	**Experience:** *1.11%*
Professional Skill: *Lore is the study of the history of the World Tree and its denizens.*		
Subskill: *Mysticism II* Norse	*Your knowledge of both the Ancient Norse language, runes and their Mythos has granted you a higher level of mastery. Knowledge of Norse Skills and Spells is greatly improved.*	

Runology (Evolved from Writing)	Level: 35	Experience: 4.15%
Professional Skill: Runology is the art of communicating power.		
Chance to Learn Rank I Unknown Rune: 13.50%	**Chance to Craft Rank I Skill Book:** +6.75%	**Chance to Craft Lesser Spell Book:** +3.375%
Professional Skill: *Writing is the ability to communicate through the written word.*		
Norse Expertise: *+100% to craft any known Norse spell or skill book of Rank I regardless of level.*		

Wow! That was so much upgrading, now if only I knew a Norse skill or spell.

"Now, I must ask one more favor of you. Find my other son, Skoll and stop him," ordered the God Fenrir, offering us the next quest in the chain.

Quest Alert: Breaking the curse of the Wolves 5 (Recommended Level 5-7)		
The God Fenrir has charged you to put a stop to his children's squabble. Stop the Fallen God Skoll before the Fallen God Hati returns in 47:57:43		
Reward: Experience, Hidden		
Do you accept this Quest?	Yes	No

"We will see it done," I answered, accepting the quest.

In an instant, the God Fenrir was gone as was the captured wolf, my net laid empty on the temple floor.

"Well done young ones," said Trinico, smiling at us proudly. Then she looked at the crowd, beginning to chatter loudly. "All of you have business to attend, disperse."

"So, am I the only one who noticed Graves's werewolf form and that shade were almost identical?" asked Micaela.

"Yeah, we noticed," said Rose. "I bet Graves is inhabited by Skoll the same way that wolf was inhabited by Hati."

"So, now what?" asked Heath.

"We have one more task tonight. I think it will give us the last piece we need," I started. "Everyone be back here in four hours."

"What are you going to be doing?" asked Rose.

"I have to return the net to Barnum and then I think dinner at the Doghouse Inn," I answered.

"I think I'm going to get started working on repairing that still for the quest," said Olaf.

"I should probably get back to the apothecary, I want to brew some more potions for us," said Baby.

"I think I've got a stockpile of lumber in need of working," said Heath, vanishing a second later without a goodbye.

"I have got some new training for Butch and Sundance thanks to Grandpa Fen," chirruped Micaela excitedly.

"Grandpa Fen?" a few of us questioned at the same time while Olaf could only bury his face in his hands.

Micaela just grinned and nodded before she turned and skipped off. The sight of a grinning, skipping, and unless my hearing suddenly went bad, humming ogre, would forever be burned in my memory.

"I got nothing," said Rose with a shake of the head. "I suppose I'll keep Jack out of trouble for the next little bit."

"See you later, Sis," said Baby with a little giggle, before she was off, flying down the street.

"Good luck," said Olaf, clapping me on the shoulder, before he too departed on his task.

"Lead the way, Jack," Rose seemed to be in a good mood, so I wasn't going to argue.

We walked slowly down the street, no need to rush at this point. "So, did Fenrir give you a bunch of Lore?" Rose asked.

"Yeah, he taught me a bunch of new runes too. Ones unique to the Norse skills and spells not that I have any idea what those are," I replied

"Same, but like you I have no Norse enchants," Rose added.

"So, for your Lore, do you have a subskill Norse Mysticism?" I asked, hoping maybe Rose knew more than I did.

"Yeah, rank I. Do you know how much the boost is?" she asked.

"No idea, I've actually got rank II though. I think it was from reading this," I said, removing the book 'Halls of Valhalla' from my bag and holding it out to her. "It's Trini's book, but I'm sure she'd be okay with you reading it."

"Thanks," she said, accepting the book and putting it in her own bag. "So, that net skill of yours was pretty handy."

"Yeah, it wasn't bad at all. I wonder what else I can do with it," I said.

"In old gladiator movies, they would use them kind of like whips if they failed to net their target. I think they also used them to bind up weapons." Rose was smiling as she described it.

"Do you like history?" I asked.

"I love history. But . . . well . . . you know how things are out there," she said a little sadly.

I could only nod in agreement. "I was an archeology student once. When the school cut the program, I was . . . so disappointed. The idea that there was nothing left to discover. That there was no adventure left," I said, still feeling sad about the whole event.

"Unless you want to go into space, spend a dozen or more years in deep cryo-sleep. Meanwhile, everyone you know, and love gets older, possibly dies, and that's assuming the world we know even still exists when you wake up," added Rose, sounding as disillusioned with the whole thing as I was.

"No, thank you," I commented.

"Couldn't pay me enough," Rose added her agreement.

Before we knew it, we arrived at the shop. I found the same poor dryad girl being bored to death by Barnum.

"Ah, Bye-bye and Ms. Rose, welcome back. I suppose you are here to tell Ms. Kimmie she is late for archery lessons again?" asked Barnum.

Kimmie looked at us both pleadingly.

"Sorry Kimmie, I saved you once. You came back for more on your own," I stated.

Kimmie looked crestfallen.

"Oh, let her go play Barnum, I'm sure she'll be back for more lessons tomorrow," said Rose, saving the young woman.

"Fine, fine, run along Ms. Kimmie, and take Hunter with you, such a lazy little mutt," ordered Barnum.

"Come on Hunter, let's go," said Kimmie, turning away from Barnum.

As she left, I saw a small wolf with the name <Hunter Lvl 1> jump over the counter and run after her.

"Tamed her first pet, huh?" I asked.

"Hmm, yes, a little fellow, but loyal. He'll grow, but he'll never be the most powerful beast. But no need to worry, her menagerie will grow, and before you know it, she'll have a dozen beasts obeying her every whim.," laughed Barnum. He calmed and looked more serious before he spoke again. "Now, what can I do for you two?"

"Well, I came to return the net you loaned me," I replied, setting the net on the counter. "I was also hoping to buy one."

"Certainly," Barnum said, taking the net and then going into the back room with it. He returned a moment later with another net, that looked almost exactly the same, but made of black leather and much shinier, probably new. "I started making this as soon as you left yesterday. I knew you would be interested in getting one of your own after you had the chance to use my old faithful."

"Thank you, how much?" I asked, feeling slightly afraid of the price tag for a such a nice piece of equipment.

"2-Gold," the leatherworker answered.

"That's too much, the leather isn't even worth that much, 1-Gold," I haggled, rejecting the first price immediately.

"I will have you know this is fine quality leather, very sturdy. 1-Gold, 9-Silver," Barnum countered high.

"1-Gold, 2-Silver," I returned.

"Honestly, we could argue this all day, let us save us both some time and simply agree to 1-Gold, 5-Silver. Deal?"

"Deal," I said, paying Barnum and accepting my new net.

Barnum's Patented Capture Net – A well-constructed net for use in combat. Durability 50/50 (Cannot be Repaired)

"Got anything I might find useful?" asked Rose, looking around at the various leather pieces.

"I am afraid the only things I carry that you might find useful, are improved grips for your sword and shield," Barnum said sadly.

However, to Rose and me, an angels' song filled the small shop. Small upgrades could have big effects.

"Please, tell us more," said Rose, looking dangerous with her fang filled grin.

"Well, most adventurers aren't interested in such minor accouterments, so I hardly ever mention it," said Barnum, surprised by our interest.

"Does it interfere with enchanting a weapon or shield?" asked Rose.

"Not at all," answered Barnum.

"What can an improved weapon or shield grip do?" I asked next.

"Well, depending on the quality, they can do many things. Most have the ability to prevent disarming skills. The highest end one I make for shields improves your grip and control, so you gain a bonus to your ability to block as well as preventing disarming skills. For swords, the better ones will increase control and accuracy," Barnum explained.

Rose had her sword and shield on the counter a moment later. "How much for both?"

Barnum blinked in surprise. "Really? You want both?"

"Yes, best you've got. How much?" asked Rose.

"5-Silver for the shield, 3-Silver for the sword," Barnum answered.

Rose cringed. "Eh, Jack, can I borrow a few Silver, I'm short."

"I'm down to just 3-Silver myself, will that cover the difference?"

"It should be just enough," Rose said, smiling gratefully.

I put the silver on the counter. I was now down to just 13-Copper. Hopefully, nothing expensive comes up soon.

"Thanks, when will they be ready for pick up?" asked Rose.

"You can wait here if you want, I'll have them ready in about 30-minutes," Barnum answered, collecting the money and the weapon and rushing into the back.

"How does no one know about this?" asked Rose the moment Barnum was out of earshot.

"I have no idea. But it's awesome. I mean, come on, a weapon or shield upgrade that doesn't take up the enchanting slot. How overpowered is that?" I asked.

"And so cheap. I wonder how much of an upgrade to accuracy or shield block?" asked Rose curiously.

"Even if it's just 1%, that's huge," I replied. "I wish I could do something for my spear."

"I'm sure you've got a good grip on your spear," said Rose with a slight giggle.

"Really? Really Rose? I expect those kinds of jokes from my brother or Olaf but you . . . I just don't know what to say," I teased in mock shock.

"I'm sorry, it was just too perfect," Rose laughed loudly and happily. It was kind of infectious, her laugh, and despite my best efforts to the contrary, I smiled. When she caught me and laughed harder, I could only shake my head feeling chagrined.

"Feeling better now?" I asked once she finally stopped laughing.

"Much, thanks, Jack. I needed the laugh," Rose said lightly.

"I'm glad to have amused you so," I reply flatly.

"Oh, don't be such a sourpuss, it was funny, even you smiled," said Rose, smiling.

"I smiled?" I asked, feigning innocence. "I know not what you speak of."

Rose rolled her eyes at me, but the smile never left her face, it somehow made me feel happier to see her smile.

"Tell me a little about you. It doesn't have to be anything specific," I requested.

"Well, Baby is actually my cousin. When I was little, I went to live with her and my aunt. After a rocky start, we've been as close as sisters since. College never held much interest for me, I was never interested in becoming a starving artist. I'm a gamer chick at heart, but math and programming were never my things. I guess the money situation should be a concern, but it's not," Rose confided in me. "Which reminds me, you don't seem to be a stuck-up snob, how is it you can play?"

"Oh, uh, have you ever heard of 'Puzzle Box'?" I asked.

"The phone app, yeah, Baby loves that rotten infuriating game. Drives me nuts," Rose huffed.

"What level are you stuck on?" I asked, grinning a little.

"I'm stuck on level 82, how'd you know I was stuck?" Rose asked.

"Only someone who actually loves it, would get so angry when describing it," I replied with a laugh.

"So, what about the 'Puzzle Box'? Why did you bring it up?" she asked.

"I kind of invented it when I was in high school, then sold it. Anyway, that pretty much has me covered for money," I answered.

"I knew there was something familiar about you. You infuriate me about as much as your game does," said Rose.

"Hey, who's the infuriating one here? From day one you've given me nothing but grief," I retorted.

"And you've given right back, I'd say we're pretty evenly scored at this point," replied Rose.

"You are so infuriating, you know that, right?" I asked.

Rose grinned a little and shrugged. See, infuriating.

We talked a little more about ancient war movies we enjoyed and books we'd read. Barnum returned as promised with the upgraded shield and sword.

"So, how much?" I asked.

"A flat 1% to Hit Chance and 1% to Shield Block," Rose answered giddily. "I almost want to go right out and try it."

"We've got time," I said, checking my clock. It was just past sundown and we weren't expected back at the temple for another three hours.

"Nah, I'm actually getting hungry. We skipped lunch today," said Rose, patting her armored belly.

Dinner was fun. We ate, had a few drinks and shared a few laughs but I kept looking around for our friends.

"Who do you keep looking for?" asked Rose.

"Huh, oh, I thought your sister and our friends would have shown up by now," I explained.

Rose's smile faded a little sadly.

"Don't get me wrong. I'm really enjoying talking to you and sharing dinner with you. I'm glad we did. But I'm worried about them. They usually show up by now. What if Graves figured out what we're up to, or another PK Order showed up and is graveyard camping them," I said.

Rose's smile returned but only slightly. "I'm sure they're fine. They probably just lost track of time and for all we know, Heath is sitting in the open chair next to one of us just because he can."

Rose was right. Of course, she was right, and I suppose if she wasn't worried then I shouldn't be either. I took a swing at the open chair next to me just to be safe. Confirming it was empty, I relaxed, and our conversation resumed.

It was just past 8:00 when Olaf and Micaela arrived, followed shortly after by Baby. Heath simply appeared in the chair next to me scaring me half to death. We left a few minutes later and arrived at the temple almost 30-minutes before the timer expired.

"About time you showed up," complained Sergeant Butters. "Let's hurry downstairs. Trini just about has everything set up."

We followed the sergeant into the basement and to the rotting corpse. I was surprised when instead of an even more rotted corpse, there was now a mummy, freshly wrapped and sitting on the table. Guard Davies face was uncovered, it seemed he hadn't begun to rot yet, or the embalming was just that good.

Trinico bustled around the stone table holding the mummified guard. She was lighting incense and drawing lines in chalk all around the table and around four small clay jars. I couldn't translate the symbols but recognized them from one of my archeology courses in college, they were Egyptian hieroglyphs.

"Egyptian?" Rose asked.

"I think so," I replied.

"Anubis is usually easier to work with for these things," stated Trinico, answering the unasked question.

"Wait, are you actually turning him into a mummy?" I asked.

"I have already mummified him, now I intend to call him up," explained Trinico.

"Could be worse, she could be raising him as a zombie," commented Olaf.

"No zombies," stated Trinico fiercely, glaring at Olaf for even suggesting. "Zombies are a hellish plague. They would consume the entire province in a matter of days. I will not risk it."

"I repeat, could be worse," repeated Olaf, swallowing nervously with the way Trinico was glaring at him.

Trinico eventually relented and resumed preparing for the ceremony.

"It is time," said Trinico once all her preparation had been completed. "Do not cross the barrier marked on the floor."

I looked at the ground and saw there was a line of hieroglyphs written on the floor surrounding the stone slab.

Trinico stepped inside the line and began to pray. I only recognized one word, 'Anubis' the Egyptian God of the underworld and mummies. I didn't understand what she was saying but it was fascinating to listen to. The woman spoke the ancient language seemingly fluently. It must have worked because the mummy twitched, then spasmed, then groaned and finally guard Davies screamed. Smoke rose from the four jars and wafted toward Davies' face before he breathed them in. When the last of the smoke vanished, he calmed, only for an instant, before he let loose a pathetic whimper, then wailed woefully. I felt sympathy for him, but only for a moment.

Trinico spoke a final verse then sagged, looking completely drained. She motioned to David.

"Guard Davies," started the sergeant once the wailing had subsided. "Do you know where you are?"

"I'm in hell," the mummified man took a moment to respond, his eyes vacant, but still tears leaked from the corners of his eyes.

"Do you know why?" asked the sergeant.

"I made a deal with a Fallen One," Davies replied.

"What was your deal?" asked Sergeant Butters.

"If I eliminated the Troll, then I would be granted immortality," answered Guard Davies.

"Who was this deal with?" asked the sergeant.

"The Lieutenant," the guard answered.

"Why did you allow the Lieutenant to kill you?" asked the sergeant.

"He wasn't supposed to kill me. He promised to turn me, to make me powerful, an immortal, it was just supposed to be a scratch, and then a long and painful change. Why did he kill me?" asked Guard Davies.

"Do you know where the Lieutenant can be found?" asked the sergeant.

"His home, the barracks . . ." the mummy hesitated, a look of pain crossed his face.

"Where? What are you not saying?" insisted Sergeant Butters.

"I . . . I cannot . . . please, the fallen one is hurting me," Davies stated as he started to writhe.

"Tell me," ordered the sergeant.

"In the . . . ruins . . . there is . . . a door . . . hidden," finally, the mummified guard screamed in pain, his body catching fire, black shadowy flames quickly consumed the corpse.

Trinico shuddered and fell backward. Sergeant Butters moved faster than I've ever seen and caught Trinico before she could hit the ground.

"Such . . . darkness," whispered Trinico.

"I'll look after Trini," said the sergeant, "Wait for me in the main temple, I will join you shortly."

We nodded and walked up the stairs in silence. We sat in the pews to wait, we all worried for Trinico, but mostly we were angry with Graves and Skoll, they must have burned Davies.

644

"Graves is going to die for this," said Rose angrily, her fist slamming into an open palm.

"Tomorrow, we go to the ruins. We find the hidden door and then we kill him," I said, feeling just as angry for the state Trinico was now in.

"I don't care if we have to level the place," said Olaf. "I've been learning about explosives lately. I'm sure I could whip up enough to do the job."

"I hope Trini will be okay," said Micaela, morosely.

"She should be fine with some rest," said Baby, trying to reassure us. "She only looked to be mana and stamina depleted. You get a pretty nasty debuff if you ever completely drain both."

David joined us a moment later, his arms full of stuff. "Trini is resting now. She'll be fine though. She wanted me to give you these," he said, handing each of us a piece of equipment and giving us the quest completion notice.

Quest Alert: Missing in Action 3 (Recommended Level 4-6) - Completed
Guard Davies has been murdered. Details at the scene suggest the murderer is somehow related to the nearby ruins. Unfortunately, the Priestess Trinico found no signs of magic or poison on or in the dead guard leaving her no choice but to call back the man's spirit from the nether. Return in 14 days.
Reward: +500-Experience, Holy Order Light Jerkin

"Do me a favor now. You know where to find this flea infested mongrel. Hunt him down and kill him," requested David.

Quest Alert: Missing in Action 4 (Recommended Level 5-7)		
Guard Davies has confirmed the involvement of Graves and given you a clue where to find him. David has asked you to hunt down Graves and put an end to his evil machinations.		
Reward: Experience, Hidden		
Do you accept this	Yes	No

"You bet we will," I said, just as eager as everyone to finally put an end to this guy.

"One more piece of advice. You may want to check in with the Johnson's, see if you can't acquire some of their Moonshine. You'll need it if you intend to succeed," warned the sergeant.

"They are staying back out at the farm," volunteered Micaela. "Their house is mostly rebuilt. We'll go see them first thing in the morning."

"Good luck," said Sergeant Butter, leaving us and returning to his wife's side.

CHAPTER 35

I awoke early the next morning when the newest rooster decided it was time for me to rise. While tempted to smite the bird, I had too many things to do today.

Plus, I didn't have another 2-Silver to pay for it.

But before that. I opened my bag and pulled out my new chest piece, partly to admire it but mostly to equip it.

> Holy Order Light Jerkin – Light Leather - +20-Armor, +5-Endurance, +5-Stamina, +10-Intellect, +10-Holy Spell Damage, and Healing, Durability 35/35

The white leather, sleeveless jacket matched perfectly with the rest of the gear of the same name. Too bad it wasn't an actual set of gear with bonuses for equipping multiple pieces. It occurred to me, the game may not even have such a thing implemented, but that was a worry for another day. I smiled a moment before I put on my black shirt and black jeans. Then I started putting on my armor, one piece at a time, the leg-guards and belt, then the vest, followed by the shoulder-guards. I put on my socks and boots before finally putting on my gloves to finish the ensemble.

I was the first downstairs that morning, but was quickly joined by Micaela and Olaf, who were excited about everything set to happen today. And yet, when they sat down, nothing was said, just a nod and a grin of excitement.

Baby and Rose came down about twenty minutes later, joining us in companionable silence. Only knives and forks against plates occasionally broke the silence as we ate wordlessly. Even Heath, apparently, decided to keep quiet as he appeared in the chair next to me. His sudden appearances were becoming a regular thing, so I wasn't startled when he did it this time. Okay, so maybe I was a little startled, but it was an improvement as far as I was concerned.

When the meal was finished, and we were ready to go, we stood as one and walked out in silence.

"Everyone ready?" I asked, looking to my friends and breaking the building tension. "Potions, water, foodstuffs, whatever else you might need or want, make sure you have it now because I have no intention of returning to this town until we've finished the quest."

"I know how expensive potions can be, but in the process of upgrading my craft, I've made so many . . . way more than I could ever use," Baby started. "They aren't very high-level potions, as the ingredients in this province don't support the higher end stuff, but these should more than suffice for our purposes." She then flew between us passing out potions. She gave each of us ten small vials of 'Lesser Mana Potion', 'Rank I Health Potion' and 'Rank I Stamina Potion', and five small vials of 'Lesser Antidote Potion'. Each vial contained just one mouthful of potion, restoring 150-250 points of either MP, HP or SP. It was generous of her to share.

"I remember the days of grinding out low-end products to level crafting," said Olaf, happily accepting the gift. "So, thank you for this. I know this game has mostly moved crafting away from such things, but I also understand there are a few professions unable to get around the grind."

"It wasn't too bad," said Baby. "With alchemy, you can actually use the entire cauldron to its capacity, so you can make more than one dose at a time. I only had to make 4 different batches and the experience was awarded, based on the actual actions in preparing the potions. Still, it took so long to grind so many herbs into powder or paste."

"Well, I appreciate it all the same," said Olaf.

"Thanks, Sis, but we're burning daylight here," said Rose, trying to get us moving.

I was just as eager as she was to get moving. "Let's go everyone."

The trek to the Johnson Farmstead was quick enough. The wolves seemed to have gone neutral, running from us instead of attacking on sight.

When we came in sight of the farm I was impressed by how much had been rebuilt. The house was slightly larger than the one that burned down, coming out a good 10-feet longer. I could see Micaela's handiwork from the stone walls built up all around it. I could also see large wood beams for the framework of the roof were in place, but yet to be covered.

"Who did the woodwork?" I asked.

"There is a civilian named Reed Fir, he's the town woodworker. He did all of the framing and flooring. I imagine he'll do the roof too," answered Micaela.

"The stonework looks good, babe," added Olaf.

I also saw a tent set up next to the house, I guessed that was where Duke and Mary were staying for the time being.

When we got closer, Duke must have heard us talking because he came out of his tent, armed with a pitchfork aimed in our direction.

"Morning Duke," I greeted him.

"Bye-bye," Duke nodded in return, relaxing slightly, then jabbing his pitchfork into the dirt. "What are you doing here so early?

If you have come to help with the construction, I am afraid you are too late to help with clearing away the refuse."

"Morning, D," chirped Micaela, waving excitedly at the farmer.

"Honestly Ms. Micaela, my name is Duke, not 'D'," the farmer grumbled.

"Oh, leave her be," said Mary, emerging from the tent. She looked ruffled and flushed but otherwise perfectly normal. "Morning to you too, Ms. Micaela."

"Morning Mary," said Micaela.

"Yes, yes, morning everyone, now what do you want?" asked Duke, sounding impatient. It was about this time I noticed how ruffled and flushed he also looked.

"Did we interrupt?" asked Heath, grinning lecherously.

"Yes, you did, now what do you want?" asked Duke, now glaring at Heath.

"We need Moonshine," I stated, feeling embarrassed as I put two and two together.

"Having a party?" asked Mary.

"A hunting party," answered Rose, grinning ferally.

"We found where Graves is hiding. We intend to hunt him down and finish him, but we need some of your Moonshine to take away his protection," I elaborated.

"We have only four jars left," said Mary, looking a little worried.

"It'll have to be enough," I said, hoping it would indeed be enough.

Mary ducked back into her tent and pulled out the wooden crate holding the last of their Moonshine. She set the crate on the ground and opened the lid revealing four corked jars. "You are welcome to them. I hope you can stop him once and for all."

"We'll do our best," I replied as I reached down and retrieved one of the jars.

Moonshine – Grain alcohol with distilled Moonlight.

The description was as I hoped. I placed it in my inventory then gave one to Micaela and Olaf and the last one to Heath much to the surprise of the group.

"Heath has the element of surprise, he can probably get in closer than any of us and douse Graves much easier," I explained myself.

"Good luck to you all, now get lost," said Duke kindly then rather harshly.

A few quick goodbyes and we on our way again. It was actually fortuitous, we went East toward the Johnson Farmstead, as the river crossing was a little further east and north. On the other side of the river, we encountered the same wolf packs, but for the most part they ignored us unless we got too close, then they would defend themselves.

We followed the river west and past the town until the trees thinned and the river started to dry up. When the river finally disappeared a system, a message popped up.

You've entered 'Hurlig Flatlands' province.

Hurlig Flatlands – Level 25-30

The Hurlig Flatlands is a rocky and desolate territory, rendered dead centuries ago by the dragon Reksoni. Now only death lives here but to those brave enough to challenge this area, there are rich minerals and rare herbs to be found as well as a multitude of dragonlings whose leather will fetch a high price.

"Ooh," said Olaf, Micaela and I in one voice.

"Dragons . . . real dragons," said Olaf excitedly. "We're coming back to this place when our level is high enough."

"Right, as exciting as finding 'Hurlig Flatlands' is, what do we do now. We didn't find the ruins?" asked Rose.

"Give me a few minutes to update my map and get our position," I requested. I took out my map and began to fill in our journey along the river. "Okay, we're about 4-miles west of the quarry entrance if you look on a parallel line. The ruins are going to be somewhere in this area," I explained showing my map to Rose and the others, pointing to the large blank area north of the river.

"It won't be too far from the river as I'm sure they needed water to be accessible," I added.

"So, we go a mile or two north then work back east?" asked Rose.

"That should work," I replied.

"Great, breaks over, let's get moving people," Rose called out loudly.

We went north as planned and back east but found nothing. North again and west to Hurlig Flatlands border and finally north, until we hit the base of the mountain ridge.

"It has to be along the ridge. I can't believe they would build so far away from water," I said, part of me still thought we had to have missed it.

"Maybe that's why they're ruins and not a prosperous city," offered Baby.

"I doubt it. I would bet the city's patron was the God Skoll and when he fell, so did they," Rose countered, she was probably right. The Cult of Hellgrind didn't just appear one day, they had to come from somewhere.

"What kind of city would worship a God who wants to bring eternal darkness?" asked Micaela.

"Remember what Lord Fenrir said, they weren't meant to bring eternal darkness. Skoll and Hati were meant to keep time moving forward. The risk if they succeeded was meant to keep Sol and Mani motivated to keep moving. To prevent Ragnarök from ever happening. At some point, someone or something twisted them, made them see it as a challenge to beat the other and from there they not only were trying to win but they started to work against each other," I explained.

"But why?" asked Micaela.

"Someone or something wanted the World Tree to end, to see Ragnarök," I added. "Of course, this is only speculation but if I'm right, then just . . . wow. The game developers put in a ton of work into making such a fantastic storyline."

Olaf chuckled. "And to think, we'd probably never have found any of this without you."

"Oh, I'm sure you would have found it eventually. Remember, the game is still in its infancy," I said, trying to pass the unwanted attention.

"Once they start to allow streaming and posting screenshots and videos, things will improve. You'll get more people taking advantage of the 'Lore' profession and more quest chains will get unlocked," Heath chimed in. It was often easy to forget he was there, he was almost silent at all times and always using his 'Stealth' skill or hidden by one of his illusion spells. The thief was truly dedicated to trying to train up his skills, which I applauded him for, but at the same time, I kind of wish he'd socialize more outside of the pub.

Trekking East again and following the base of the ridge was slower going, the land was uneven, and we occasionally had to divert around a rock formation. Eventually, we did find the ruins, though there wasn't much there to call ruins.

There were some large, brown stones sparkling a little, my guess would be the Crystal Sandstone, the sergeant mentioned when we found Davies body. They formed a part of a wall and just beyond were a few more stones that seemed to form the base of buildings, but nothing substantial remained.

"So now what?" asked Olaf, looking around the barren ruins.

"Now, we search for the hidden door," I answered, sitting down on one of the remaining large stones. I wasn't not searching, I just needed to think this through. There was nothing large enough left standing to be a door, hidden or otherwise, at least nothing in these ruins.

We were only left with a couple options.

"Look for a trap door of some kind or out of place or recently disturbed ground," I hoped I was right. I wasn't looking forward to the other possibility as I gazed up at the mountains looming over us.

"Over here," called Olaf from near one of the broken walls.

I ran to him, hoping he'd found the entrance.

"What did you find?" I asked.

"An inscription," Olaf said, motioning at the wall.

I looked at the faded inscription carved into the wall and sighed disappointedly. "Praise be to Skoll, may he forever mark time and speed through the skies," I read the inscription aloud. I was not expecting it to do something.

Another inscription became visible below it.

"Praise be to Hati, may he hunt with patience through the night," read Rose, joining us with Baby right at her side, another inscription appeared.

"Light and Dark, two as one, strike true," I read the final inscription.

You've learned the Norse spell 'Edda of Light and Dark'

Edda of Light and Dark	Level: 1	Experience: 0.00%
Spell Duration: 10 minutes	Spell Cast Speed: Instant	Spell Mana Cost: 250
Spell Effect (Active): Your next attack will slow your target's attack speed 1% and increase your attack speed 1% for 5-seconds. (Stackable x10)		

"Oh, my Goddess!" I exclaimed, seeing the effects and cost of the spell. That was ridiculous, 250-MP for 10 minutes . . . but the effect was even more ridiculous.

"What? Holy what?" asked Olaf.

"You didn't get it?" asked Rose.

"Get what?" Olaf asked, looking rapidly between the two of us. I looked at the others and aside from me and Rose they just looked confused.

"Lore strikes again," said Rose, grinning. "I think me, and Jack here just got a new Norse spell. 'Edda of Light and Dark'. It's a buff I think." She looked to me to verify.

"I'm pretty sure it's a buff. The description says it gives 1% slowing to my target and 1% haste to me upon striking and it stacks up to 10 times. But it costs 250-MP to use it," I explained.

"That would be great for me," pouted Micaela. And it would be great for her. She doesn't use much mana in a fight since her shamanistic abilities work off of a global cooldown system.

"Wait a second, I can actually give you the skill," I said, remembering my recent improvement to my 'Runology'. I generally kept all my stuff on me out of habit despite knowing it was perfectly safe at the inn. As such, I had paper and my writing supplies. "Do you all mind waiting, it might take a little while?"

"You do that, we'll keep searching. Maybe we'll find another inscription," Rose volunteered, smiling a little.

I found myself a flat stone and sat down to start inscribing the spell. I'm sure I'll be doing it again soon for the rest of our party but for now, Micaela would benefit the most from such a spell.

I focused on the paper and cast the spell. My hand began writing automatically and stopped about twenty-minutes later according to my game clock.

"Done," I said proudly, rolling up the paper. When I looked up, everyone seemed to be looking over every nook and cranny of the ruins but finding nothing. They barely looked up at me when I spoke, except for Micaela who was almost skipping as she came to get her new spell.

"Is it done? Does it work?" asked Micaela eagerly.

"Try it and find out," I said, offering her the rolled-up parchment.

She took it in hand and it crumbled to dust an instant later. "Yes, I learned it. Thank you, Bye-bye," Micaela shouted, then gave me a bone-crushing hug leaving me gasping for breath.

We searched for another 20-minutes but found nothing in the ruins.

"I seem to ask this a lot," started Rose. "But, now what?"

I sighed and look up the mountain slope. This section of the mountain above us was in rough shape. There were gaping holes and jagged rock formation all over it. "It's probably hidden up there then."

Everyone grimaced as they followed my gaze and looked at the mountainside.

"Everyone, pair off," ordered Rose, "Baby, you're with me."

"I guess it's you and me, mate," said Heath, appearing next to me and putting an arm around my shoulders.

"We'll go right," volunteered Olaf for himself and Micaela.

"We've got middle then," said Rose.

"I guess that leaves us with the left," I said, looking at the path ahead of us. But then I stopped.

"Wait," I called, halting my friends.

"What is it?" asked Heath.

"I see tracks," I answered. "Boot tracks, the same style of boot as I saw by where Davies was killed."

"Can you follow them?" asked Olaf, hopefully.

"Yeah, there are a lot of them coming and going from the same path," I said. Right there on the left side, where we were about to ascend, were the highlighted boot prints. So many boot prints, but they all followed the same path.

"Lead the way," said Rose excitedly.

The path up wound between jagged spikes of rock and through loose rock and dirt. I even lost the tracks a few times when they went over hard rock only to pick them up again a few yards later. Eventually, they led us to a small cave we would never have seen from below and probably never would have found up here if not for the tracks to follow. The entrance was large enough but the rock outcropping around it almost created a maze.

About five-yards inside the cave was a large stone door with the glowing image of the moon inside a glowing yellow sun, both engraved on it and surrounded by Norse writing.

"Open in the name of the Forefathers, who keep time moving forward," Rose read the inscription aloud. A grinding noise followed by the door sinking into the floor. Just behind the door was a grey mist we couldn't see through and if not for the system message we would never have known what laid beyond.

You've discovered 'Hidden Norse Temple'

Hidden Norse Temple – Dungeon – Level 5-7
The Hidden Norse Temple was lost in the annals of history, thought to be destroyed long ago this temple houses many mysteries and grave dangers for any who enter.

"He actually found a dungeon," said Baby in disbelief, her eyes wide as she looked at the mists before us.

Olaf though held out a hand toward Baby and made a pay up motion. Baby sighed but fluttered over and dropped a few Silver into the waiting mitt.

"Pleasure doing business with you," said Olaf, adding the money to his bag.

"Did we really just find a starter dungeon?" asked Rose, not quite believing what she was seeing.

"Yes, we did," said Heath, sounding slightly awestruck, his accent forgotten again.

"What are we waiting around out here for?" asked Micaela, snapping us all out of our slightly dumbfounded states. "Let's get in there already."

The woman was infectious, her excitement spread to us all.

"Rose is in first followed by Baby. Dungeons don't usually have enemies right by the entrance but better safe than sorry," I ordered, just as excited as everyone else but trying to temper it with a sense of caution.

Rose stepped inside followed closely by Baby.

I went next. When I stepped into the mist I wasn't sure what to expect. I suppose I expected something to happen, but it didn't. I took two more steps forward and then I was out of the mist facing a stone hallway with luminescent blue light glowing from the ceiling. It wasn't bright, but it gave just enough light to see everything without being able to see much in the way details. It was slightly better than torchlight, it was constant and didn't flicker.

"Yeah, this light is going to give me a headache," complained Rose, a few feet ahead of me.

Someone bumped into me from behind, jostling me forward a few steps. I didn't think about the people coming through behind me. I looked back to see Olaf who was then bumped by Micaela as she entered.

I took a few more steps forward just to clear the doorway and give them enough room to enter properly as well. I looked at the stone hall again. It was as wide and as tall as the door outside was and must have been about fifty-yards long. I could see a larger room beyond that but couldn't make out any details.

"Should we worry about traps?" asked Rose, as she stepped forward to lead the way.

"Don't know yet," I answered.

"Okay, then, for now, I'll lead, Jack, stay on my hip for now, if you see a trap call it out. Baby, then Heath and Mic, Olaf, you've got the rear," ordered Rose, giving us a basic formation.

We moved slowly down that first hall, not sure what to expect. When we got to the end of the hall the room was less a room and more of an intersection. There were tattered wall hangings with illegible Norse writing, a rotted corner table and broken vase but nothing else of note. From the intersection there were three paths, or rather should have been three paths, one of them was completely caved in.

"Which way do we go?" asked Rose, she looked tightly wound right then.

I put a hand on her shoulder getting her to look sharply at me. I smiled at her and took an exaggerated deep breath and let it out slowly. She took the hint and did the same. It seemed to calm her.

"Well, the middle path usually leads to the last boss, so I'm saying we take the tunnel on the right," said Olaf. "I want to see what all this place has to offer."

I was going to agree, but something about that collapsed tunnel had me curious. "Say, Olaf, Mic, would you guys be able to clear that cave-in with your mining skills?"

Olaf blinked in surprise but then grinned. "You bet your mystery finding behind we can."

It didn't take long for them to clear the path. It turned out the collapse only went a few feet deep. The hall beyond was lit similarly with the same glowing blue light. But before we entered the tunnel, I renewed everyone's buffs including my own.

This hall was narrower, so we had to move single file. About ten-yards in, the path turned right and then opened to small armory, ten feet further in. The room appeared to have been mostly looted, except for a few pieces of rusting armor. It made no sense to me. Games don't put in hidden rooms unless there was something to be found.

"Look around, we're missing something," I requested. As I was searching I didn't notice as Heath and Olaf took up position on either side of me until I bumped into Olaf causing me to pause.

"So, how was it?" Olaf asked softly.

"How was what?" I asked.

"Your date, mate?" asked Heath, also quietly.

"What date?" I asked. When did I go on a date?

660

"With Rose?" asked Olaf, looking at me in slight disbelief.

"When?" I asked.

"Last night," added Heath, giving me a similar look.

That was a date? I was about to question them both rather loudly when Olaf warned me off with a finger to his lips. "That was a date?" I asked softly.

"Did you really not know it was a date?" asked Heath.

"How would I know that was a date? I didn't ask her out and she didn't ask me out. We just . . . kind of went about our business." Now, I was feeling a little self-conscious. If that was a date, then was it a good date? If you couldn't already tell, I don't have much experience with dating. My ignorance of it being a date is ample proof of that fact. "Wait, did Rose know that was a date?"

Heath and Olaf shared a look for a moment before they shook their heads and simply walked away leaving me confused. Was that really a date? I sighed and tried to refocus on the task at hand.

After 10-minutes of searching, we found nothing. In my frustration from a combination of not finding anything and feeling confused about the whole Rose-date situation, I kicked a rusted helmet. It clattered along the floor until it went unimpeded through a wall without leaving a mark. It made the sound of metal clanging against metal a second later.

"Did everyone else just see that?" I asked.

"The helmet going through the wall?" asked Heath. "Nope, didn't see a thing."

I chuckled in spite of myself. I followed the path of the helmet to the wall. It was completely solid at chest level. I started feeling downward until my hand went through the wall near my knees. "It's a small opening," I said, kneeling down to poke my head through. When I did, it hit wood rather painfully, causing me to jerk back and rub my head as if it would sooth the pain.

Rose was in front of me in a second with her sword drawn and shield ready to protect me. "What was it?"

"Not a monster," I answered, calming her down. "I think I hit my head on a chest. Olaf, think you could reach inside and pull it out. That thing didn't even budge when my head hit it."

"Consider it done," said Olaf. His big meaty arm reached through the illusion hiding the treasure chest and with a grunt of effort pulled it through for us to all see.

It was a treasure chest made with rusting steel bands and dark wood clearly starting to rot. I even saw a crack where my head hit it, even though I felt I took more damage.

"Shall we break it open?" asked Micaela excitedly. We were all excited. It was our first treasure chest.

"Leave it to me," said Heath, slipping in front of the chest and kneeling before the lock, his picks going to work deftly. "This thing is a rusted bloody mess. Olaf, mate, got any oil on you?" I was surprised when Olaf was actually able to present a small oil can.

"I use it for some of my engineering projects," Olaf answered the unasked question.

A few seconds later there was a clicking of the lock giving way followed by an angry screech of the chest lid opening.

It was filled with dust and scraps of leather.

"Rotted books," I said softly, feeling disappointed.

"Only on top," said Heath, as he dug through it. He pulled out an intact book which he passed to Olaf who was closest. He then dove back in and started pulling out fist-sized gemstones, three of them. "That's all folks."

"What's the book, Olaf?" I asked.

"Don't know, can't read it. My UI reports as 'Unknown Text'," he answered, holding it out to me.

I accepted the book. It was covered in Norse runes but there were some I just didn't know. As a result, all I got for a description was 'Spear of (Unknown Rune, cannot translate)'

"I can only read part of it. Rose?" I offered the book to her.

Rose took it and took a look as well but quickly passed it back to me. "Same."

"Should I hold onto it then?" I asked the group.

"Might as well. You're more likely to be able to translate it in the future than the rest of us," said Olaf.

Rose coughed.

"You and Rose that is," clarified Olaf.

I rolled my eyes at Rose but put the book into my bag.

"What are the stones?" asked Baby, as Heath seemed to study them.

"Description says Mana Crystal 0/1,000," Heath answered.

"May I see one?" asked Baby, excitement in her voice.

"Sure," said Heath, tossing one of them to her.

Baby caught it with both hands and sagged in the air from the weight of it. She then focused on it and it started to glow blue. "Yes, it's what I thought. You can charge this with mana and use them to recharge your own mana later. Can I keep this one?" she requested.

"Yeah, mind if I keep one of them?" asked Heath.

I looked to the others, but none of them seemed to mind so I shrugged. "That leaves one, who wants it?"

"I think we should give it to Baby also," said Rose. "I know you and I both use mana, but not to the extent she does."

"I'm fine with that," I replied. I truly was fine with it. Hopefully, we'd come back to this dungeon a few more times before we left this province now that we knew it was here.

"Thanks, guys," said Baby, putting the second stone into her bag. "Next time we take a break, I'll try charging them up."

"That's fine," said Rose. "Anyway, let's get moving."

When we returned to the intersection there was an extra glow not there before.

<Ghostly Cultist Lvl 6> and <Reanimated Cultist Lvl 7> had taken up residence in the room. I counted 6 of them, two ghosts and four zombies.

"Where did they come from?" whispered Rose.

"Probably spawned because we opened that chest," suggested Heath.

"I didn't see any traps on the chest," I defended.

"Then maybe when we pulled it from its hiding spot," Heath countered.

"Look, it doesn't matter what caused them to spawn. What matters is how we're going to deal them," interrupted Rose. "Now, Jack, see the one standing by himself?" she asked pointing to one of the <Reanimated Cultist Lvl 7>. "I want you to try and pull him to us by himself."

"And if he brings the others?" I asked.

"Then it's a good thing the hallway is narrow," Rose replied as she readied her sword and shield.

CHAPTER 36

'Holy Smite' should have been the perfect spell to pull one of the monsters to us. I thought it was a good idea at the time. I hit the lonesome <Reanimated Cultist Lvl 7> as planned. I didn't plan for it to get a critical strike or for it to be weak to Holy magic . . . really weak to Holy magic, like 53% of its health gone in one hit weak to Holy magic. Unfortunately, it only had eyes for me and completely ignored Rose's attempts to taunt it. That left me flipping around and bouncing off walls to avoid the deranged zombie cultist, while my friends did their best to kill it without accidentally killing me. As if that wasn't enough, we learned it was resistant to all physical damage. Long story short, my trying not to die, ended with me doing about 90% of the damage to kill the thing, and ending up with just 11% of my health remaining, because when it hit, it hit hard.

"Okay, so, any suggestions?" asked Rose, looking at the remaining five undead enemies.

"Just one," I said. "Hold out your weapons, let's see if this works."

Rose held out her sword and I put my hand on the blade then chanted for my spell 'Lesser Holy Imbuement'. It seemed to work when her sword took on a white glow.

"Does it hurt you?" I asked, slightly worried because she was a half-vampire and holy and vampire generally don't get along very well.

"Not at all, I think we're good," Rose replied.

"Good, next," I said, looking to my friends. Heath was easy, Baby passed because she was more worried about healing. Micaela and Olaf both require the spell be cast twice, once for each weapon. It hurt my mana pool, but it would be worth it. Especially, if we could actually damage these guys.

"Okay, let's try this again. This time . . . don't crit, Jack," warned Rose.

This time I avoided using 'Holy Smite' and instead lit the next one on fire. It came with a friend too, so we got one ghost and one zombie. I tried to give Rose plenty of time to get aggro and she seemed to have them down. Then Olaf let the zombie have it with both barrels. Critical strikes taking off 75% percent of the health, was probably not what he had in mind. Suddenly, it was a scramble to kill the one he pulled. Thankfully, my combo, which was pretty much all Holy damage, was enough to wipe it out in short order.

"I hate this guy," complained Rose as she fought the ghost. "It's ignoring my shield, just goes right through it."

I cringed, I didn't think about putting 'Lesser Holy Imbuement' on her shield. I was well aware, I'd be getting an earful about it soon.

With the zombie dead, our DPS turned to the ghost. We tried to be careful but one of us still pulled aggro from Rose.

"Screw the undead, this is ridiculous," Rose complained loudly as she waited for Baby to finish healing her.

"I have a suggestion," said Olaf. "We're not going to be able to prevent taking aggro from you. But if we do it one at a time and kite them, we should be able to kill it before it gets to one of us." Kiting wasn't a bad idea. It was risky trying to drag an enemy around on a string the way you would a kite in the air, but it was doable if you had enough space to work with. As it was, we had enough space and I knew I would be able to generate plenty of threat to make it chase me.

"We can try it," I said, then I cringed for what was coming next. "But first, let me see your shield, Rose." She started to hold it out to me, then paused halfway. Her eyes narrowed. Yep, she figured it out.

"We'll have words later," Rose said as she finished holding the shield out toward me.

It took only a moment for the 'Lesser Holy Imbuement' to take hold on her shield.

"Okay, take three," said Rose, looking into the enlarged intersection and the three grouped up undead cultists.

"Let's get the ghost first," I said. Rose would have an easier time with the zombies than she would the ghost, and it best to make her life easier right now.

"Charging in," warned Rose before she blurred from view and reappeared, slamming into one of the zombies, then bashing the other with her shield and taking a large chunk of its HP away.

I cast my 'Holy Smite' and 'Lesser Holy Fire' getting full aggro and knocking out almost a quarter of the HP from the <Ghostly Cultist Lvl 6>. Olaf fired next taking another 20% and his second shot taking 22%. My second 'Holy Smite' hit right after and got a critical strike, taking out the rest of its health. It didn't even make it halfway across the room before it died.

We looked back at the two zombies Rose was fighting and both were down a fair bit of HP, both hovering around 80% remaining.

"Okay, get the zombie on the right next," I shouted the warning.

Rose slammed her shield into then jabbed her sword into it knocking off another 6% of its health.

Since we were trying to kite it we pulled aggro, we all stayed at range. Micaela threw a fireball from Sundance, except the fireball had a white aura that exploded when it hit the zombie, stripping away 19% of its health. My 'Holy Smite' landed next for another 24% and Olaf finished it off, each of his shots popping for around 20% each. And, we never pulled aggro.

"That was great," said Rose. "Now, do it again."

So, we did, and the last zombie fell.

"Not a bad bit of work," said Heath, leaning against the wall.

Heath had to stay out of the way for this fight since we were trying to fight at range and to my knowledge, he didn't have much in the way of range damage abilities . . . unless he was hiding something.

"Okay, we have a working strategy if we run into any more of those," said Rose, sounding more confident then she had after our first couple of pulls.

"Lead on," said Olaf, motioning to the path straight ahead of us.

The path on the left was the one we assumed led to Graves, but as he said earlier. We want to see everything this dungeon has to offer.

We followed the hallway. It mirrored the one just opposite of it, except instead of an armory we found a large room with a few workbenches. Unlike the armory, these workbenches were occupied with an assortment of the undead. Walking among them, occasionally stopping to check their work, was an ethereal woman, garbed similarly to Trinico's high priestess outfit. This made sense when I saw her name, <High Priestess of Hati Lvl 9>. The fact she was a priestess of Hati confused me, really confused me. Why would a priestess of Hati be in a temple of Skoll? Or was this even a temple of Skoll? The dungeon was simply called the 'Hidden Norse Temple'.

"Okay, we need to time our pulls," said Rose, interrupting my thoughts about the temple. Then, she started laying out a strategy, "I don't think we want to pull the High Priestess until we've cleared the rest of the room."

I looked again though. Something about this felt wrong to me. I looked at one of the workers. <Trapped Soul Lvl 6> and <Conscripted Spirit Lvl 7>, they were forced to be here.

"Wait," I said before Rose started attacking.

"What is it?" Rose asked, a little impatiently.

"Look at the names on the mobs. They are all forced to be here," I said. "Even the High Priestess," I motioned to the shackles around her ankles. They all had shackles. "I don't think we're supposed to kill them, I think we have to set them free."

Rose looked to be contemplating what I said for a moment before nodding. "I trust you."

"So, how do we do this?" asked Heath.

I turned and looked at Heath and grinned. "You, my friend, are just the man we need."

"Why do I get the feeling I'm not gonna enjoy this?" asked Heath.

"It won't be so bad, now let me see your lockpicks," I said, "I have a plan."

Heath vanished a minute later, off to work on his part of the plan. All we could do was wait to see if it worked. Suddenly, there was a clicking sound and the shackles on one of the chained ghosts clicked open and evaporated. The name of the unshackled prisoner changed from <Trapped Soul Lvl 6> to <Freed Soul Lvl 6> and a notification of +100-Experience appeared. A moment later there was another being, a woman in shining silver armor with golden wings, <Valkyrie Lvl ?>. She took the arm of the freed ghost and together they flew upwards through the ceiling.

"That was awesome," commented Micaela, grinning wildly.

"So pretty too," added Baby.

The Valkyrie was indeed beautiful, with long blond hair, pouty lips and an athletic figure most men would find attractive, I certainly did.

"One down, a dozen more to go," said Rose, drawing our attention away from the space previously occupied by the Valkyrie. It was hardly a moment later, the next shackle fell away granting another +100-Experience. And another Valkyrie arrived to take the soul into the afterlife.

"Eleven to go," counted Rose, watching closely. Ready at a moment's notice to charge in.

It took a while and I had to reapply 'Lesser Holy Imbuement' on the lockpicks twice, but Heath was able to free every one of the undead ghosts.

Then came the High Priestess. Unfortunately, she never stopped moving, even though there was no one left for her to oversee she never stopped moving.

"Oh," I said, figuring it out. "We need to stop the High Priestess from moving . . . or slow her down." I shared a look with the group and understanding passed.

"So, you need to make three more scrolls, even for you Sis, we need all of us putting those slowing stacks on her so Heath can undo her shackles," ordered Rose.

"I'll get started," I said, walking back into the hall and sitting down. That was another hour gone making three more scrolls, one for each Olaf, Micaela, and Baby. Then time for everyone to use the spell, renew all the other buffs then regenerated mana back to full.

"Okay, charging in," said Rose, once everyone was ready.

"You fools, run while you still can," pleaded the High Priestess as she cast a protective barrier around herself.

The High Priestess looked so sad, I could see she didn't want to fight us, but she had no choice it seemed.

"Can't do that sister," quipped Rose. "Minimal heals, Sis, focus on getting those stacks."

I rushed in to attack as did Micaela, while Olaf found a good angle to shoot from.

"Heath, stay hidden until High Priestess has fifty stacks of slowing, it should show as five different debuffs with ten stacks apiece," I ordered.

Heath didn't say anything, so I had to hope he got the message.

As far as building up stacks of the debuff went, it revealed a whole other issue. We were taking out huge chunks of her health due to the 'Lesser Holy Imbuement' on everyone's weapons.

"Damn woman, heal yourself," I shouted at the High Priestess, worried we'd kill her before we slowed her down enough to actually set her free.

The High Priestess blinked at me in surprise. "Foolish mortal, why? Why would you wish me to heal myself? Am I not your enemy?"

"Not as far as I can see. You are just trapped here, we cannot free you if you die," I argued back. I didn't know if it would do any good, most boss or sub-boss fights were kind of scripted. I didn't expect much of an AI to be present in this one, but I had to hope.

And she did, she healed herself once, bringing her health up a big chunk then resumed dealing damage to Rose.

I don't know why she healed herself, but that little bit of healing seemed to be just enough. "Heath, now!" I shouted. It turned out it wasn't necessary because the words barely left my mouth and the chains unlocked and disappeared. The High Priestess didn't change names, but she did stop fighting and the sadness previously marring her ethereal face vanished, replaced by a grateful smile and tears of joy.

"Thank you," The High Priestess said, taking the hand of the Valkyrie that appeared to take her to the afterlife. She then flew upwards, guided by the Valkyrie and vanished. However, unlike the others, when she vanished, she let loose a rain of loot. We were all pelted with coins and equipment. I almost lost a toe when a dagger landed right next to my foot, another inch and left pinky would be gone forever . . . or until it grew back . . . was healed back? Whatever, point is, raining loot is not as fun as it should be.

"That was different," said Heath with a laugh.

"Crazy fun is what that was," said Micaela, giggling happily.

"Alright, let's see what all this loot is," I said, looking around at all the shiny money and shinier equipment.

"Gather everything into one place first, then we can sort who gets what," ordered Rose, picking up a handful of coins and setting them on one of the work tables that had something cloth piled on top of it already.

I reached down and picked up the dagger and handful of coins before adding them to the pile. The coins were the hardest thing to collect, they seemed to be scattered everywhere. It was in reaching for one such coin, I found another illusionary wall with a chest inside.

"Olaf, need your muscles again. Found another chest," I called to him.

That set everyone grinning a little more, loot and a chest. I hoped this one would be in better shape than the last one but alas, it was not to be. It almost looked worse.

"I'll get to work on this while you all sort that out," said Heath, looking at the chest eagerly. He took the oil Olaf held out and went to work.

"Okay, a dagger with a golden blade, a glowing yellow wolf-shaped charm and a dress. Coins too but Baby is still counting them," said Rose, listing off the spoils of our success.

"That dress looks tiny," commented Micaela, lifting up the dress. "I'm pretty sure this is a fairy dress unless you planned on using it as a nightie, Rose. What do you think Bye-bye, would Rose look good in this?"

Rose and I both blushed. "Right, that will go to Baby then," ordered Rose quickly.

Baby looked up and looked at the dress. Unlike the poufy white dress, she wore now, this one was much slimmer and considerably more elegant, it also had a golden sheen to it that drew the eye. She was happy to accept the dress then quickly flew out of sight only to return a minute later in her new dress.

"Ah, I feel so much better," Baby sighed in relief. "And this one even has stats, bonus to all healing, not just nature or holy healing."

"Congrats Sis, it looks good on you too," said Rose, nodding in approval.

"Ooh la la," said Micaela. "Very sheik, my darling."

"Thank you," said Baby, looking rather puffed up about it. The cuteness of her childlike features defeated the effort, but the meaning was understood.

"Next up, Dagger of the Sun," said Rose, reading the description. "Heath, as the only dagger user, do you want this?"

"I'll take it. Even when I finally make my ax it will be good to have a backup," he spoke, not looking away from the lock he was still trying to pick.

Rose shrugged and stabbed it into the work table. "And last, we have a Sunlight Wolf Charm. Grants a spell or skill called 'Call of the Sun Pack', adds Dexterity and Spirit. What the heck is Spirit?"

"It's a shaman only stat," I answered, looking at Micaela who appeared to be ready to explode with glee.

Rose tossed the charm to her and Micaela quickly equipped it, the charm appeared dangling from Sundance a moment later.

"So, what's the gold count?" I asked, looking at Baby who was having fun fluttering around in her new dress.

"Huh?" Baby asked, seeing both Rose and I staring at her. "Oh, I . . . uh . . . kind of forgot."

Rose and I ended up counting the gold. We counted a grand total of 13-Gold, 9-Silver and 68-Copper which resulted in each of us getting 2-Gold, 3-Silver and 28-Copper. Most of what dropped were copper coins so while it looked like it should have been a small fortune, it actually wasn't that much all together. The game needed to find a better way of dealing with money drops or at least a better way of dividing it up automatically. Still, at about a dollar per 10-Copper, ten dollars per Silver and a hundred dollars per Gold we just made a nice little profit from just this one boss.

"Got it," said Heath, finally popping the top on the trunk.

Once again, filled with dust from disintegrated tomes. He pulled out a book and two gems. Rose and I each took one of the gems this time. The book was handed directly to me.

Norse Skill – Valkyrie Strike – Teaches the Norse Skill – Valkyrie Strike		
Would you like to learn 'Valkyrie Strike'?	**Yes**	**No**

"It's called Valkyrie Strike," I answered before they could ask what it was.

"Ooh, another Norse skill," said Rose excitedly. "Hurry up and learn it, so if it's any good you can teach it to me."

"Okay," I replied, trying to placate her. "Just give me a second."

You've learned the Norse Skill 'Valkyrie Strike'

Valkyrie Strike	*Level: 1*	*Experience: 0.00%*
Current Damage Modifier	*Damage: +1.00*	*Skill Stamina Cost: 50*
Skill Effect (Active): A combat skill of the Valkyrie of Valhalla, used to keep their charges in line on their trip to the afterlife. Physical Damage is converted to Holy Damage. (May only be used by Female Characters)		

"Hax!" I exclaimed, not wanting to believe what I just read or what just occurred.

"What happened?" asked Micaela, "Did it not work?"

"No, it worked," I answered, not sure how to explain the next part. "I am just not permitted to use it."

"Why not?" asked Rose.

"It can only be used by a Female Character." I answered quietly, hearing peals of laughter right after. I didn't think it was that funny. I only learned it, so I could make skill scrolls for Rose and Micaela. Both of whom, were being rude and greedy.

"Something you want to share with the rest of us?" asked Olaf.

"No, nothing to share. It just says I can't use it," I replied, trying not to step into his trap. "Anyway, do you want it now or later?"

"What does it do?" asked Rose as she finally stopped giggling at me.

"Converts physical damage to holy damage," I answered.

"That would be extremely useful to me right now," said Rose, her laughter forgotten.

I could only sigh. "I'll start writing, again. Hopefully, it won't take too long."

Forty-seven minutes. That's how long it took to make just one copy for Rose. Micaela's kicked puppy act almost cost us another 47-minutes, thank Olaf for preventing that time waste, but I had to promise to make her one later.

At last we were moving again. The intersection had a new group of undead for us, one ghost and two zombies. We still had our strategy, so we made short work of them. The last hallway was straightforward for about twenty-yards, then it slopped downwards for about two-stories. At the bottom of the first ramp was a pack of six undead, split into two groups of three. The same strategy worked, we just had to pull the first group back before managing the second in the normal manner. The landing was actually a switchback for another ramp going down again.

We found another pack of undead and managed them with ease by this point. One more switch back and we were standing before a large door bearing the same symbols found on the entrance to the dungeon, except this door was cracked open, half of it lying in pieces scattered around the entry.

As we got closer to the damaged door, the sound of rushing water came from the other side of the opening and the new moisture in the air wet our skin.

"Everyone ready?" I asked before we went in. One more check of buffs and we were set.

Rose went in first with Baby and me just behind her.

The room was less a room and more a giant underground reservoir.

"This explains why they didn't build closer to the river," commented Olaf.

"Why build near a river when the mountains provide so much better protection," growled an all too familiar voice.

"Graves," I hissed, turning to see him sitting on a throne. The throne made me uncomfortable to even look at it, it was made with animal bones, wolf bones if I had to guess.

"Meat sacks," Graves nodded, not moving or even reacting much to our presence.

"Isn't this the part where we fight?" whispered Micaela very loudly. It occurred to me, she definitely intended for Graves to hear her.

"He doesn't look ready to fight yet," Olaf whispered back just as loudly.

"You will all die soon enough," said Graves unconcerned. "I am curious though. You are the first in millennia to have come this far, you have earned a modicum of my respect. Tell me, how did you find your way in?"

"Your boots left a pretty clear trail from all of your comings and goings," I answered.

"I see. That was a mistake on my part, one I shall not make again. Any final words before you die?" Graves asked.

"Who are you? Really?" I asked.

"Have you not figured it out? I am Skoll," Graves howled proudly.

"No, I didn't ask which God you brought into your body. I asked who you are," I clarified.

Graves narrowed his eyes, glaring at me before smirking and snorting in amusement. "Now I see. You have become quite the thorn in my side, I will be glad to pluck you, but I suppose . . . I could entertain your . . . query."

"I am Hellgrid, son of Brun, son of Leif, High Priest of Skoll the sun chaser and yes, I have trapped Skoll within my body and become a true immortal," Graves boasted.

"Are you the Betrayer?" I asked.

Graves laughed maliciously. "Yes! Now you see it. I am the Betrayer. I set brother against brother with honeyed words and plots within plots. And when Skoll was weakened by the other Gods, I offered him refuge within, a place to hide and recover. I fooled him so easily, after all, this body is not strong, I am no great warrior, none would suspect a lowly priest. But he did not know how meticulously I plotted his downfall. How carefully I crafted his cage. I have lived for millennia because of his ignorance, stupid mutt knew no better until it was too late for him."

"So, Hati and Skoll, becoming fallen ones were your doing?" I asked, eager to know more.

"Never in my wildest dreams did I think, I could make not one, but two Gods fall at once . . . my master was more than pleased," bragged the would-be God.

"Your master?" I asked.

Now Graves, no Hellgrid, looked startled as if he'd let something slip he was not meant to. "Enough of this talk, it is time for you to die."

"Wait, one more question," I requested.

Graves narrowed his eyes and relented with a nod.

"The Demon Incursion? Why?" I asked.

"My slip will already cost me so why not, I was ordered to. Ragnarök was not happening fast enough for my master's liking, so the Demon Incursion was instigated. Anything else before you die?" asked Hellgrid.

"Just one more question, are you thirsty?" I asked.

"What?" Hellgrid asked, confused by my question.

"Have a drink," I said.

Heath appeared standing on top of the throne causing Hellgrid to look up. Heath then promptly smashed the entire jar of Moonshine across the werewolf's face, inevitably forcing some of the toxic liquid into the beast's mouth and nose.

Hellgrid coughed and hacked and even tried to vomit the little moonshine that slipped through but to no avail. His immortality was taken away, 'Vulnerable' debuff clear as day to us. Now we just had to kill him before he either burned it out of his system or killed us.

"I can't believe your crazy plan just worked," said Rose, wide-eyed.

"I figured our chances were 50/50 depending on if Heath got caught sneaking up on him," I said with a shrug.

"Stop standing around and kill him already," shouted Heath, flipping away from a wild swing.

Hellgrid's black fur bristled with anger. He snarled but winced when he disturbed the fresh cuts on his face.

"Charging," shouted Rose, blurring from view only to reappear as her shoulder slammed into the towering monster. She struck with her shield, then shifted back to dodge an overhead attack from Hellgrid. She shifted back in, jabbing at him with her sword, its tip finding a spot between the werewolf's chest piece and shoulder guard. He swung his own counterattack, striking her shield hard. Even with the shield block, she took a healthy bit of damage.

I was waiting patiently as were Olaf and Micaela. We needed to be sure Rose had aggro before we attacked.

"Okay, start slowly," Rose called out, feeling confident in her threat levels.

Micaela and I started walking forward with a measured pace, her throwing a fireball from Sundance whenever the cooldown expired while I worked on building up stacks of 'Lesser Holy Fire'.

When we finally got into melee range we looked to Rose for permission to start heavier DPS. A subtle nod was all she gave us.

I started with a 'Hamstring', both increasing the damage he takes and slowing him down by half. I then added an 'Impale' to him. We had agreed before the fight, we would go slow until we made it past the first 10% of his health. I added my third stack of 'Lesser Holy Fire' and started to attack him with my spear, base damage only or rather base damage plus 'Lesser Holy Imbuement'. I also still had the 'Edda of Light and Dark' buff so I was adding more slowing effects and increasing my own haste.

"10% incoming," called Baby, as she topped off all our health pools.

Hellgrid suddenly spun in a circle knocking all three of us back from him. His powerful legs coiled before he sprung upwards toward the ceiling of the cavern. His large hand grasping one of the stalactites. "You will all die here," he shouted, his other hand reached for another stalactite and broke it free of the ceiling. His arm reared back to throw.

"Take cover," shouted Olaf, figuring out what was coming next.

The stalactite was launched like a missile right at me. I dived out of the path and was back on my feet. It was a mistake to assume I was safe from just dodging the projectile. I should have expected stone shrapnel from the rock exploding when it hit. It pelted me and tore through me and my armor doing significant damage along the way and leaving behind a very unpleasant bleed effect.

His next throw was toward Olaf, who had taken cover behind a large rock, one of the many perforating the landscape. The missile hit and exploded but no damage was suffered by the big ogre.

"Everyone find a rock and take cover behind it," ordered Rose, finding her own rock along with Baby.

Heath was invisible somewhere around here doing who knows what and Micaela had already found a rock to hide behind. That left me as the only one not hidden, as well as Hellgrid's favorite target, even as I ran for cover, I prayed the bleed didn't kill me before I could heal myself.

Finally getting to cover, I started healing myself, spamming my 'Lesser Heal' for all it was worth until the debuff faded and my health was somewhat restored. I also used one of the Lesser Mana Potion's Baby had given me. It wouldn't restore all my mana, but it did give me some to work with.

"Is he ever going to run out of these things?" asked Rose loudly, drawing his attention and another missile was thrown her way.

"I don't know," I shouted, drawing a missile back toward me.

"Why hasn't he stopped?" shouted Micaela.

I risked peaking around the rock to see what Hellgrid was doing. He was still moving from stalactite to stalactite, breaking off spears of stone and hurling them at random. I tried to focus in on his health, which was holding steady at 89.5% and the 'Vulnerable' debuff hadn't gone anywhere. I needed to see his stamina, but it wasn't a visible stat, so I tried instead to focus on his breathing and perspiration, hoping to glean whether or not he was sweating more or breathing harder. I wasn't expecting to see a stamina bar appear under his health bar an instant later. I was half-tempted to look at the flashing exclamation points at the bottom of my view, but I couldn't afford to lose focus right now.

His stamina bar was draining fast.

"He'll drop soon, he's almost out of stamina," I called to my friends over the sound of exploding rocks.

"How do you know?" asked Rose loudly.

"I can see his stamina bar now, I'll explain later," I called back. Seeing the stamina dwindling fast.

Hellgrid swung to grab another stalactite only for his grip to slip and for him to tumble from the ceiling and land with a loud crunch, eating 10% of his health in an instant. I looked at him, he was down with a dazed debuff flashing steadily faster as his stamina began to refill.

"Attack now, hard as you can while he's dazed," I called, charging out to attack the beast.

I renewed my 'Lesser Holy Fire' as I ran toward him. As soon as I got into melee range I started my combination anew. 'Hamstring', 'Impale', 'Justice Strike', 'Lesser Holy Shock', 'Power Thrust', 'Power Thrust' and 'Power Thrust'. I didn't pay much attention, as my friends unleashed as much damage as they could manage.

Heath appeared next to me stabbing into Hellgrid's back just below the armor then vanished from view only to reappear and repeat the same action. Vanishing and attacking repeatedly, I could only imagine he was getting some impressive critical strikes from doing so.

I should have paid more attention to the 'Dazed' debuff he had suffered when he fell as it vanished suddenly, once 70% of his stamina was restored.

"I'll kill you all," Hellgrid howled, starting to look worse for wear. His health was hovering just at 62%. But it didn't seem to deter him as he went back to viciously attacking Rose.

"Get ready for another transition," warned Baby loudly.

"Everyone get to cover now," shouted Rose just before his health actually ticked down to the 60% mark.

I ran quickly to find a rock to take cover behind. When you don't know exactly what will happen, you have to assume he'll repeat the same attack he did last time.

"Oh, God, get him off," howled Olaf in pain.

I looked to see Hellgrid was standing on top of Olaf, mauling him, eating him and regaining health.

"Charge and stun him," I shouted to Rose. I used my own 'Lesser Holy Shock' as I ran.

"Baby, big heals, keep Olaf alive," shouted Rose, even as she slammed into the werewolf, damaging both him and Olaf. "Sorry Olaf," she said, seeing him hurt too.

"Just get this guy off of me," Olaf pleaded.

I attacked without holding back as did Micaela. I'd never seen her look so furious as she did then, every swing of her axes cleaving into the being who was trying his hardest to take her husband's life. Then Butch swung forward, the ax actually howled as it moved, and with a meaty hack into the werewolf's back, I saw 8% of Hellgrid's health bar vanish.

I glanced up to see Baby was working feverishly to heal Olaf, while we tried to knock Hellgrid off of him. I was worried slightly about the next transition, which was less than 1% away.

At 50% health, the beast finally rolled off Olaf looking even more pitiful. I'm not sure it was just the punishment he'd taken from our attacks, but he looked smaller, significantly smaller and his muscle mass looked thinner than before.

"No," Hellgrid groaned pitifully. "You will not defeat me here," he growled as he clawed the ground away from us.

"Be careful, I smell a trap," I warned my friends. He was still at 50% health, there was no way was he defeated so easily. Then I saw it, the vulnerable debuff was flashing rapidly, as if it was about to fade. I ran forward as fast as I could, pulling the jar of Moonshine from my bag as I went. I flipped over the werewolf and twisted in the air, so I landed facing Hellgrid. I slammed my jar down on his head, shattering it and dousing him inside and out again with another dose of 'Vulnerable' debuff.

"No!" Hellgrid howled, suddenly springing up, his razor-sharp claws tearing across my face, blinding me in one eye.

I rolled back in pain, albeit slightly muted thanks to the game but still awful. I couldn't even focus enough to heal myself. Thank the Goddess Baby was there to heal me, or I'd never have been able to rejoin the fight.

I climbed shakily back to my feet, blinking several times to make sure I could see again. I looked at Hellgrid, fighting Rose. His speed increased massively, even from when the fight first began but the damage seemed to have dropped off significantly. It was less damage per hit, but he hit considerably more often, which made it very difficult for Rose to interrupt him with her 'Shield Slam' skill.

I recast 'Lesser Holy Fire' as I charged in again, lancing through the back of his leg with my 'Hamstring' but instead of pulling my spear back out I twisted the vertical blade of the spear tip and ripped it horizontally out the side of his leg causing a gush of blood to leak from the wound. Hellgrid also didn't receive a 'Hamstrung' debuff, instead, he had a debuff 'Torn Ligament'.

If I didn't know any better, I'd say I just found a new skill, but I'd have to worry about that later.

"40% incoming," warned Baby from above us. More than ever, I was appreciating the fact that she could fly and heal so well.

"Hide or stay?" asked Olaf.

"Wait to see what he does," ordered Rose, not stopping her attack as she whittled away the last little bit of his health before the 40% mark.

"No, I cannot be defeated here," Hellgrid growled, jumping back to the water's edge. "Rise oh servants of Skoll, rise and defend his vessel," he called out before he began chanting and the water of the reservoir began to steam as the room turned cold, I could see the water turning white and start to freeze over. Within seconds the reservoir was frozen solid. That's when the ice cracked and cracked again and again until there was a layer of ice shards like broken glass. "Rise and defend," he ordered again. This time the ice shards rose into the air and began to collect, forming into wolf-like creatures made of jagged edges and sharp, pointy, ice shards.

"Any suggestions?" asked Rose, not liking the numbers Hellgrid now sported.

I was patient, watching carefully as the ice wolves were all gathering together behind Hellgrid. They seemed to be gathering as if they intended to attack all at once. When the last wolf joined the others, I couldn't help but grin a little. "Boar Charge," I shouted, targeting the area all the wolves had gathered.

Olaf shouted, "Fire in the hole," then chucked the bombs he'd had on the bandoleer into the knocked down wolves absolutely decimating them. Only two of the wolves escaped the carnage and Olaf was able to finish them both with a well-placed shot to each causing them to burst in a shower of ice shards.

Hellgrid didn't look too good either, his fur lost some of its luster, the skin you could see looked paler too. I wondered if he spent all his mana on one attack. I wasn't going to wait to find out, he had only 20% of his HP left and I was going to do everything in my power to kill him before his 'Dazed' debuff faded.

"Attack while he's drained," I shouted, already running for him. I saw Rose blur past me, her 'Charge' skill was getting a workout.

Heath appeared a moment later, stabbing and vanishing once again, I would have to ask him about it later but for now, I had to focus on killing Hellgrid. Once in range, I launched my attack combo again, 'Hamstring', 'Impale', 'Justice Strike', 'Lesser Holy Shock', 'Power Thrust' repeatedly until my 'Justice Strike' was nearly off cooldown then I began again.

We got him all the way to 6% HP when everything went mad. Hellgrid's skin bubbled and cracked, black smoke began to waft from the wounds in a way I didn't like the look of.

"More damage, kill him faster," I shouted urgently.

"Hehe," chuckled Hellgrid at 3%, sounding strained but also as if he had already accepted his death. "I may die here, but I'll take all of you with me." His body started ballooning in odd places, more cracks formed, and more black smoke began to pour out of him.

"Push harder!" Rose shouted, hacking as hard as she could.

I looked to see even baby had stopped healing and was now focused solely and doing damage, her wand firing bolts of magic as fast as she could.

1% ticked and more cracks appeared. I was starting to worry we wouldn't make it in time. 'Justice Strike' hit and everything seemed to freeze for a moment. Hellgrid's eyes rolled back and he fell backward with his mouth wide open, his tongue lolled lifelessly out the side. When he hit the rock-hard ground, smoke began to rush out of his open mouth rapidly deflating his body until a shadow of the werewolf stood atop the body.

"Free," the shadow werewolf growled, his body arched back and breathed deeply. *"You have freed me,"* he said looking at us now.

"You are Skoll?" I asked, just wanting to be sure.

"I am," the Fallen God Skoll answered.

"Yes, we didn't die," cheered Micaela breaking the tension in her usual way.

"Atmosphere babe, you've got to work on reading the atmosphere," chided Olaf with a shake of his head.

The Fallen God Skoll only chuckled. *"You have all done well. Take what you will from this wretched corpse and his treasure. I will await you in the temple in Hurligville. There is much to be decided."* The smoky form vanished, fading into nothingness, leaving no trace.

I looked again at the body of Hellgrid which started to desiccate rapidly until the skin flaked away and the bones crumbled until all that remained was a few pieces of equipment and a large sack.

"Now that was a boss fight," cheered Heath, appearing next to me and successfully startling me.

Once my heart calmed, I couldn't help but smile. That was one heck of a boss fight.

"Do you think they will all be so complex?" asked Rose. "Because I sure hope they are."

"Me too," I added.

"Loot time," sang Olaf, grinning at the pile just waiting to be divvied up.

CHAPTER 37

There were three pieces of armor remaining, all chainmail and they went to Rose since the rest of us couldn't use that level of armor. So, Rose got a new helm, chest armor, and gauntlets, all of which she refused to equip until she had them fully cleaned and checked for curses. The bag was a little more interesting. Once again, a good number of coins. There was also a necklace, a pair of earrings, a ring and a charm.

"Seeing as I just got three big upgrades, I'm going to pass on the rest of this stuff unless it is something blatantly tanky," started Rose. "So, I'll handle passing out the rest of the loot."

"So, what have we got?" asked Olaf.

"Skoll Band, +20-Dexterity and +1%-Critical Strike," Rose started, holding up the only ring for us to see.

"I would happily take it, but I think it will do Olaf or Heath more good," I said, taking myself out of the bidding.

"I am happy with both of my rings at the moment," said Heath, getting a look from each of us, questioning just how good his rings could be. "My rings give me bonuses to my thief skill experience gains. While that ring would be a great upgrade, it will be a long while before I can actually use it. I figure Olaf can use it now."

Rose shrugged and flipped the ring toward Olaf who happily caught it in his massive mitt. Despite the ring being normal-size, it magically enlarged to fit his meaty finger. The ring was a silver band with the engraving of a wolf chasing the sun with the moon behind it.

"Moonlight Choker, bonus to spirit again," said Rose, holding out the necklace to Micaela.

Micaela happily accepted it and put it around her neck, the silver band glowing softly.

"Earrings of the Sun-chaser, +5-Intellect, +5-Wisdom, and +10-Healing, no alignment listed. I believe these should go to Baby," Rose continued, sorting through the various loot pieces.

None of us disagreed. Baby took them and remove her necklace before they were clipped to her tiny ears, they were simple stud earring in the shape of a crescent moon, also with a subtle glow.

"Last up, the charm," said Rose, studying the small black wolf-shaped object. "Night Wolf Charm, no stats but has a skill or spell 'Lycanthropy'."

"No thanks," most of us said, myself included, at the same time.

Heath, however, appeared to be studying the charm and weighing his options. "Anyone know the weakness of a werewolf?" he asked.

"Silver," said Olaf.

"Probably holy magic as well," I added. "Oh, and don't forget moonshine."

"Strengths?" Heath asked.

"Regeneration and strength," said Rose. "I should know after we just fought that monster."

"Then I'll take it," Heath said.

I was surprised Heath was so willing to become a werewolf. But then again, it didn't do him any harm from the little bit of class progression I had discussed with him. In fact, it probably gave him a large number of benefits, as long as it didn't prevent him from becoming the bard he wanted to be. It seemed to me, he was intent on becoming a jack of all trades.

That left us with just the money to be divided up into 6 equal shares. We each walked away with 5-Gold, 7-Silver, and 42-Copper. Talk about a profitable day.

I checked my waiting system messages and gained a ton of stats, and skill and spell levels as well as a few new subskills. For stats, I gained +4-Strenght, +11-Endurance, +4-Stamina, and +2-Intellect. Skill levels and spell levels are too numerous to name, but the new subskills are a nice addition.

Perception	Level: 18	Experience: 12.35%
Skill Range: 11.80 yards	Chance to See: 14.50%	Chance to Identify/Track: 19.00%
Subskill: Analyze Stamina	Skill Effect (Passive): Enables you to see target Stamina	

And 'Hamstring' evolved into a subskill called 'Ligament Rip', which added a bleed effect mirroring 'Impale'.

Two-Handed Polearms	Level: 61	Experience: 15.63%
Current Damage Modifiers	Damage: +30.50	Critical Strike Chance: +3.05%
Subskill: Ligament Rip	Reduce Enemy Movement and Attack Speed: 50% Target Receives Increased Damage: +15.25% Duration: 15 Seconds Bleed Effect: 4 Damage per Second	Skill Stamina Cost: 86

"Let's get back to town, I want to turn in all these completed quests," said Rose, eagerly.

"We should also stop by the Johnson Farmstead too, turn in that quest or get them to come with us to town," I suggested.

Our departure from the dungeon was filled with laughter and joking as was the walk back to the Johnson Farmstead. We could hear activity going on at the farmstead before we could see it, the sound of banging hammers welcomed us back, each bang creating a marching cadence moving us onward. I could immediately see Duke up on the roof hammering boards into place along with two other men I didn't know. I also saw a few men on the ground sawing at logs and turning them into boards, which was kind of interesting, but not all too important at the moment.

"Duke," I shouted up to the man as we approached causing him to turn to look at us.

He said something to the other two men, making them laugh as he moved to the ladder to come down and meet with us.

Mary also came around from the front of the house, waving to us as we approached.

"So, did you succeed?" asked Duke.

"We did," I answered.

"Where is your proof?" the farmer asked, stopping all of us in our tracks. Hellgrid literally disintegrated due to his age once Skoll had been freed. His loot probably wouldn't suffice as proof.

"We're to meet with the fallen God Skoll in town at the temple soon, he's the proof," volunteered Olaf, thinking quickly and probably saving us.

"You are meeting a fallen God?" Duke asked in disbelief. "This I have to see. Come on Mary, let us join these adventurers in town for this meeting."

"I have always wanted to meet a fallen God," laughed Mary, also not believing us either.

The trip from there back to town was less pleasant as Duke and Mary kept poking fun at us. We had no choice but to grin and bear.

"I'll go get the mayor," volunteered Baby.

"I'll go with her," said Rose, speeding off with her sister and away from the Johnsons.

"We'll go get David," said Micaela dragging Olaf off without another word.

"Was it something we said?" asked Duke.

"You have been quite rude about this whole thing. I would have thought we at least warranted the benefit of the doubt," I explained.

Both of them suddenly looked abashed and a little shameful.

"You are right," said Mary first. "We should have given you the benefit of the doubt but try to see if from our perspective. The fallen Gods are our horror stories, any time one is ever seen it is followed by death and destruction."

"Which is exactly what Hellgrid . . . Graves wrought on this town over its three hundred plus year history, is it not?" I asked, trying to not let my temper get the best of me.

"Then why would we be meeting with a fallen God?" asked Duke, looking a little defiant once more.

"That will be explained in full once we get to the temple," I answered. I had no intention of telling the same story two or three times.

Inside the temple, I saw a few players in line waiting to speak with Trinico once again, as well as a number of players praying at various altars. It was not nearly as crowded as the last few times I'd been here, which was a good sign the rush of players into this province had slowed a little. I also knew everything was about to change drastically with the announcement of a beginner dungeon being in the province. I made a note to mention it to the mayor, he may need to see about hiring additional guards, and perhaps another priest or priestess to help Trinico, and a second sergeant or a proper lieutenant to help David.

Trinico waved to me once she saw me. "I'll be with you shortly Bye-bye, I assume the others are collecting David and the mayor?"

"Yes ma'am," I answered.

"Then please, wait by the Norse enclave and I'll join you there shortly," Trinico instructed.

I accepted and led Duke and Mary to the Norse enclave to wait.

It wasn't long before Baby and Rose arrived with the mayor, who was asking a long litany of questions, to which we gave the generic answer that all would be explained shortly. A few minutes later Olaf and Micaela arrived with Sergeant Butters, who was thankfully silent and not pestering anyone with questions.

Finally, Trinico joined us.

"Well, did you succeed?" asked the mayor, his patience at its limit.

"Yes, I believe we did," I answered. "Trinico, please call on Lord Fenrir, we will need his help."

Trinico complied and within moments, the Wolf God Fenrir, filled most of the temple with his massive frame.

"Have you succeeded?" the God Fenrir asked, looking at me and my group.

"We have," Rose answered, eager to be involved as usual.

"Please Lord Fenrir, call on your sons," I requested.

"*Skoll, Hati, show yourselves,*" ordered the God Fenrir loudly, loud enough to shake the temple and all within it.

The Fallen God Skoll appeared first, a black shadow in the form of a werewolf. "*Father,*" he said respectfully before bowing to him. If I didn't know any better, I'd say Lord Fenrir was surprised by the action. After a minute Fenrir nodded slightly to his son who stood straight again.

"*Hehe,*" chuckled a malevolent voice as a grey-white mist in the same shape stepped into view. "*What's this brother? Since when do you care to show anyone or anything respect?*"

"*Much has occurred,*" the Fallen God Skoll answered, I could hear the shame in his voice, and apparently so could Hati and Fenrir.

"*Tell us,*" ordered the God Fenrir.

I expected a long story to be told about how they were tricked, how Hellgrid arranged everything and even mentioning Hellgrid's mysterious master. Instead, Skoll just howled. A long mournful howl filled the temple, carrying so much pain, it brought me to my knees. When the howl finally ended, I saw everyone was on their knees, some with tears in their eyes. All except for the Fallen God Hati and the God Fenrir.

The Fallen God Hati moved to stand beside the Fallen God Skoll and as one they both bowed again, requesting "*Forgive us, father, we beg you.*"

The God Fenrir studied the pair for a moment before speaking. "*All-father, great Lord Odin, grandfather,*" he addressed to no one. "*I beg your mercy upon these two children. I beg you, restore them their pantheon and let them resume their duties. I beg you, allow them the chance to atone.*"

There was a rumbling all around us before the room was engulfed in golden light and when it faded the Gods Hati and Skoll were gone and only the God Fenrir remained.

"What happened? Where'd they go?" asked Micaela.

"My request has been accepted. The fallen have risen and are fallen no more," said the God Fenrir, he sounded joyous. *"Never before has a fallen God been restored. For this, you all have my deepest gratitude. In addition to the rewards for completing my quest to you, I shall grant you each a boon. You may call upon me once in any battle to aid you, but I warn you, do not do so lightly.*

You've been granted a one-use spell 'Summon God: Fenrir'

Summon God: Fenrir	Level: ∞	Experience: ∞
Spell Effect (Active): Call upon the wolf God Fenrir to aid you in battle		

"Thank you," I said first, which was quickly echoed by the others, this was a huge boon.

"Now, you have done as I've asked, put an end to the madness of my sons, and I thank you. You have also killed Hellgrid the Betrayer, but one death will never be enough punishment for what he has done. I have bound his spirit and those of his followers to the 'Hidden Norse Temple'. I charge all adventurers to hunt his dungeon for all time, may he suffer a million deaths. And for each death, he and his followers suffer, the adventurers who bring on this death, shall be rewarded," proclaimed the God Fenrir.

'Hidden Norse Temple – Dungeon – Level 4-6' has been unlocked in the 'Hurlig Ridge' province.

So, that was how the dungeon became repeatable. Did all dungeons have this feature? Did they all require being unlocked? And why did the level requirement drop from the 5-7 the first time we went in? Did that mean that without the God Skoll, Hellgrid was weaker? We'd definitely be going back there soon, I wanted another run at that place just to see how different it was.

"You are the leader of this town?" asked Lord Fenrir, leaning down and looking at Mayor Semper closer.

"Yes, Lord Fenrir, I am," the mayor replied, stuttering slightly.

"When you feel the adventurers are ready, you may offer them a quest to attack the 'Hidden Norse Temple', I shall provide you compensation of course. Is this agreeable?" asked the God, he wasn't asking.

"Of course, your Lordship," replied Mayor Semper, bowing deeply to the God.

And finally, the God Fenrir looked at us. *"Now for your rewards."*

"Before that Lord Fenrir," I interrupted, pulling the book with the unknown symbols out of my bag. "Can you tell me what this means?"

The God Fenrir peered closer, then reared back his head and laughed loudly. *"You continue to surprise me fleshling. Your Goddess was wise to choose you as her warrior. That book was lost to time, and yet here you have found it. It contains the blueprints for the 'Spear of Gungnir I', the first form for crafting the weapon of a God. I suppose I shall reward you first then."* The God Fenrir looked to be straining slightly, then bared his teeth in pain. Suddenly one of his fangs popped free of his mouth, stabbing into the ground in front of me, it was easily taller than I was by half. There were even bits of golden blood from where the tooth popped free. I looked back at Lord Fenrir who was still straining, another tooth already growing to replace the one he'd just gifted me.

Quest Alert: Breaking the curse of the Wolves 5 (Recommended Level 5-7) - Completed
The God Fenrir has charged you to put a stop to his children's squabble. Stop Skoll before Hati returns in 8:14:67
Reward: +2,000-Experience, Fang of the God Fenrir

"Be careful with that fang of mine, be sure you preserve all of it as it is, or its power will be lost," warned Lord Fenrir. *"Now, for the second part of your reward. Take my fang and that blueprint to the temple of the God Ivaldi, the dwarven God of smiths, in Root City, then place them upon his altar."*

I was waiting for him to tell me what would happen or what to do after that, but nothing came, just a quest box.

Legendary Quest: Spear of Gungnir I
Bring the Fang of the God Fenrir and the blueprints for the 'Spear of Gungnir I' to the temple of the God Ivaldi and place them upon his altar.
Reward: Experience, Unknown

Certainly intriguing, if nothing else. I carefully lifted the fang from where it was stabbed into the temple floor and placed it in my bag, eating up the majority of my carrying capacity.

The others each received their reward from the God Fenrir. A jacket for Olaf, a leather upper body armor frame for Micaela, a sword for Rose, a block of wood for Heath, which confused pretty much everyone, and a bracelet for Baby.

"Meat sacks, I wish you all well, but I have stayed too long in the mortal realm already." Just as suddenly as he appeared, the God Fenrir, was gone.

"Okay, now I believe you," said Duke with his arms crossed angrily.

"Oh, stop that, Duke," said Mary. "They have earned their reward."

"But . . . farming just does not pay much these days and without our still to supplement our income, we will be rather poor," the farmer complained.

"Actually," interrupted Olaf. "I'm working on fixing your still. I should have it ready in a few days."

Duke turned sharply to look at Olaf. "You can repair it?"

"Well, me and Giggle-Ana, but yeah, I think so," Olaf answered.

"That is a different story then," Duke said, pulling out a coin pouch.

Quest Alert: Shiny Delivery Service 8 (Recommended Level 5-7) – Completed
Hunt down and stop Graves . . . permanently.
Reward: +2,000-Experience, 5-Gold, Title: Hunter

I was quickly checking to see what the new title did, as I assume everyone else was, and I was not disappointed.

Title: Hunter (Increases Tracking skills effects by 15%, increases damage against beasts by 5%)

That would be super helpful in the future.

"I suppose I'm next," said Sergeant Butters. He handed me a helmet, Rose received a pair of sabatons, Heath got a garish leather chest piece, Micaela excitedly took a leather frame for leg-guards, Olaf was handed some kind of mechanical contraption I wasn't familiar with, and Baby got another bracelet or was this one an armlet?

Quest Alert: Missing in Action 4 (Recommended Level 5-7) - Completed
Guard Davies has confirmed the involvement of Graves and given you a clue where to find him. David has asked you to hunt down Graves and put an end to his evil machinations.
Reward: +2.000-Experience, Holy Order Light Helmet

I was notified a moment later by my level advancement.

Congratulations! You've reached Level 7!
+1 to bonus Holy Spells, +1 Intellect, +1 Charisma

"Congrats, mate," said Heath first followed by the others. As I looked around, it seemed everyone had gained a level except for Baby from all the quest turn ins.

"Congratulations everyone on their levels," I said. I should have been paying more attention to everyone else.

"Now hold on just a minute, we've still got one more," said the Mayor. He stepped up this time everyone received a ring, just a ring.

Quest Alert: The investigation of Lieutenant Graves 4 (Recommended Level 4-6)
Lieutenant Graves has been proven any enemy of not only the province but also an enemy of the World Tree. Put a stop to him before he unleashes something truly terrible.
Reward: +2,000-Experience, Holy Order Ring of Justice

Okay, this wasn't just a ring, it was a really nice ring. It was also High quality, far and away the best piece of gear I've received yet.

Holy Order Ring of Justice - +5-Strength, +5-Dexterity, +5-Endurance, +5-Stamina, +5 Intellect, +5 Wisdom, +5-Holy Damage and Healing, Increased experience gains for all Goddess granted skills by 50%

That plus the new helmet and I was in good shape as far as gear went.

Holy Order Light Helmet – Light Leather – +15-Armor, +10-Intellect, +10-Wisdom, +10-Holy Spell Damage, and Healing, Durability 30/30

I could only hope the rest of my group was as happy with their upgrades.

"And I'm spent," said Heath with a chuckle. "That was some fun times my friends, and just in time too."

"In time for what?" I asked.

"I have to log out tomorrow," Heath answered. "I'm glad we got this done before then. I'm glad I got to be a part of it. It felt good to do something worthwhile again."

"We probably wouldn't have succeeded without you, so we're glad you were here for it, too," said Olaf.

"Well now, I do believe it is time we celebrate," said the mayor, interrupting any further conversation. "Come tonight we will throw one heck of a party to celebrate. For now, I suggest you all go and rest. You have once again done us all a great service. We cannot thank you enough for all you have accomplished."

EPILOGUE

The last week in game blurred past us, all of us training and working on our skills. There wasn't much in the way of questing left for us to do, not that we had much interest other than Olaf and Giggle-Ana repairing the Moonshine Still.

We did run the 'Hidden Norse Temple' a few times, mostly because it was still fun, but also because we got a few more pieces of usable gear and a few pieces to sell and pad our bank accounts with.

There were a number of changes to the dungeon. For starters, the High Priestess was replaced by a High Cultist and there was no need to free anyone or pick any locks. And Hellgrid became the <Shade of Hellgrid Lvl 8>, it was the same fight otherwise, but he didn't drop nearly as much loot or as good of quality.

Heath logged out just as he said he would, but promised to log back in on the same day the rest of us planned on logging back in.

Now here we were on logout day, staring at the portal to the World Tree. Our plan was to travel to Root City and log out there. We all had business in Root City but had agreed it would wait until we logged back into the game in a week. Plus, Root City had the logout portals, so you could exit the game whenever you chose, instead of being forced out when your 30-days expired.

"The good news is, the logout portal is right across the street from the Hurlig Ridge portal," said Olaf leading us forward.

"It's partly why we chose this province," added Micaela. "The first time we logged back into the game, it put us in Root City instead of the province we were in before. We couldn't find the portal back to where we were before, so we ended up choosing the closest low-level province we could find."

"So, the portals don't tell you about the province before you enter?" I asked. I hadn't heard about this.

"Nope, you have to travel there to see what's what and then come back and try another until you find what you're looking for. I've heard rumors that on the higher branches, the portals move around too. So, it might lead you one place today, and the same portal will lead you somewhere else tomorrow. It certainly, makes things exciting," explained Micaela.

"Anyway, you ready to get your first glimpse of Root City?" asked Olaf, grinning.

"Noobs first," said Micaela excitedly.

"That would be you and me," said Rose, taking my arm in hand.

I was still confused about this situation. I had tried to talk to Rose about it a few times, but someone seemed to interrupt every time, whether it was one of our friends or one of the other players asking for advice on the dungeon or some quest or other. It was confounding how often it occurred.

Anyway, I walked forward with Rose at my side and we stepped through.

"Hey, watch where you're walking, noobs," shouted a man on horseback, tearing past us after almost running us over.

"Grilled Tolecki lizard, get your grilled meat on a stick!" shouted a vendor to my left. He had a small wooden cart he was pushing along the cobblestone street, barking his food for sale.

"Figs, sugar dates, and figs, get your figs," shouted another man. This one had barrels of figs and a simple canopy over his goods and himself.

I also noticed, it seemed rather dark, but I was sure it was morning when we left. One look at the sky and I understood. Above me, any chance of seeing the sky was overwhelmed by the massive tree and its branches looming over me, over the entirety of Root City. At the tip of each branch, I could see a portal glowing softly, it could just as easily have been fruit or berries I suppose. There was no sign of the sun through those branches as far as I could see. The street was lined with lampposts and oil lamps glowing softly.

Rose and I turned as one, to look at the portal we just came through, it hovered in the air just above a terminating root of the World Tree.

"That's a big tree," I commented.

"How big do you think it is?" asked Rose, looking at it in awe, right next to me.

"It's been measured," said Olaf, stepping through the portal followed by Micaela and Baby. "Fifty-four kilometers around or a little more than 33 miles for you Yanks. It stands at least ten times as tall. There is a winding staircase in the trunk going up about a mile before it starts opening to various branches. There is a canopy about fifty miles up, but no one has gotten so high yet, or rather no one has unlocked that high yet. People have tried to climb up, but the stairway hasn't finished growing. It's a neat game mechanic actually, limiting players from entering provinces they weren't ready for yet by stating the tree was still growing. Anyway, plenty of time for that later, Mic and I should get going, it'll be nearly 5:00 pm when we finish the logout process."

"It's been fun," said Micaela, giving each of us a hug while Olaf exchanged a few hugs and a handshake with me.

"See you in a week," Olaf said as his final goodbye and stepped into the multi-color logout portal.

"I always hate this part," complained Baby. "It will take me a week to get used to being big again only to get small all over again. Oh well, see you in a week, come on Sis." The diminutive fairy flew ahead into the portal vanishing.

"I had fun Jack, see you in a week," said Rose with a grin. Then she surprised me yet again.

She kissed me like truly kissed me and I kissed back lost in the moment. And when it ended, Rose practically sprinted into the logout portal leaving me dazed and then embarrassed, when the citizens and players alike, began catcalling and whistling at me.

I could only mutter, "I'll never understand women."

I sighed, I know I should just walk through the portal and logout, but I had some quests with the promise of nine rewards begging to be turned in at the temple of Issara and she promised me a conversation.

So, the first thing I did was look for a guard to point me in the right direction.

"Excuse me," I said to the first guard I'd found, a burly, unkempt looking human.

"What do you want?" the guard asked gruffly.

"I'm looking for the Temple of the Goddess Issara, can you point me in the right direction?" I asked.

The guard tilted his head from side to side, his eyes' studying me closely as if looking for something. "For a price," he finally said with a grin.

Did he just ask me for a bribe? I turned and started to walk away before he put one of his hands on my shoulder, his grip clamped down tightly.

"Now that was rather rude," the guard said calmly, but I could still hear the venom in his voice. "Here I was, being magnanimous and offering to help you for a fair price and you turn your back to me. That's a quick way to get a knife in the back sonny."

I took a deep calming breath. I had a feeling I knew what it was going to take to deal with this guy, but I certainly didn't appreciate it. "I suggest you release me now or you will lose your hand."

"Oh, threatening a guard of Root City, now are you?" he asked, almost sounding impressed. "And just what is a new adventurer such as yourself going to do against a seasoned veteran such as myself?"

I jerked my shoulder from his grip and turned to face him, my eyes narrowed. "Did you think to ask why I would be looking for the Temple of the Goddess Issara?"

"I figured you for an idiot, everyone knows the Gods of justice do not get priests or paladins," the guard answered.

"You're right, they don't and I'm well aware of this fact. Now, think again. Why? Why would I be going there if I already know the Goddess Issara does not take on priests or paladins?" I asked.

The guard's eyes widened slightly before he all but prostrated himself before me. "Begging your pardon my Lord, I did not expect . . . I am truly sorry. Please, beg the Great Goddess Issara to forgive me my rudeness."

"If you serve justice as a guard should then there is no forgiveness required. However, extorting coin from adventurers asking for assistance is a grave injustice," I stated.

"Please sir, I beg you, it will never happen again," the guard pleaded.

I frowned. There was no telling just how many this man had extorted already if he was only pleading now out of fear. "I will speak to her, but actions speak louder than words. I suggest you find a way to prove you serve justice."

"I will, I will prove it, I promise," he said solemnly, he looked truly embarrassed.

"Now, the way to the temple," I requested.

He gave me quick directions. It turned out, all of the temples to Gods and Goddesses surround the base of the World Tree closest to the trunk itself as a kind of last line of defense. As luck would have it, the Babylonian contingent was directly ahead of me.

It would have taken several hours to walk so I ended up shelling out the coin to a mage who looked less than reputable for a portal to the temple district. I made sure to note the cross streets, so I would know how to get back here.

Thankfully, he turned out to be a fairly reputable guy, even if the price he charged me was ridiculous, 6-Gold for a one-way trip was exorbitant and worse, I'd probably have to pay the same to get back.

When I stepped through the portal I was amazed at how different everything was. It was all bright as if the sun was shining without a cloud in the sky except there was no sun or sky to be seen, only the massive branches of the World Tree.

Focusing on my task, I took in my surroundings, the temples were all small Ziggurats, mostly indistinguishable from one another.

If not for a pull I felt from one of them, it might have taken me a while to find the right temple.

I entered without trepidation or fear, more excited than anything. The first room was fairly large and very clean but not well ornamented. No giant statues of solid gold or grand sconces carved into the walls. Just a simple square room, two square pools to either side of the entrance absent of fish or water plants. There were no worshipers to be seen, there didn't even appear to be an altar or offering area.

"What can I do for you, young man?" asked a voice from behind me and startling me rather effectively.

I turned to face the source to find an old man. He had silvery hair on his head though that was mostly dominated by a large bald spot. He wore simple brown robes and was leaning on a broom like it was a cane.

"Sorry for startling you," he said. "I am Hami, the caretaker of this temple."

"Nice to meet you Hami, I'm Bye-bye," I introduced myself.

"Pleasure young man. But I ask again, what can I do for you? I am sorry there is no priest or paladin to greet you but the Godly laws being what they are I am afraid none will be coming," Hami stated.

"That's alright," I replied. "I'm here to speak with the Goddess."

"I am sorry Bye-bye, but the Goddess Issara does not accept priests or paladins into her service," he insisted.

"I am already in her service," I replied.

"Then, by all means, proceed into the inner cloister. Only one in service to the Goddess Issara may enter," Hami replied. "But you should know, anyone not in service will be summarily smote."

"Thank you," I said with a small smile. "Please, show me to the entrance to the inner cloister."

Hami sighed in resignation. "Are all adventurers so stubborn and foolish?" he grumbled under his breath, but I heard him just the same.

"Through these doors," he said, bowing before a set of arched double doors easily ten-feet tall.

"Thank you," I said, opening the doors with ease and stepping through. When nothing struck me down I could hear Hami gasping behind me, it made me smile a little. But I paid him no mind, it was a short hallway leading to another set of arched doors. These also opened with ease.

The next room was the opulence I had expected . . . well, not opulent but considerably more decorative. All around the room were large marble columns from floor to ceiling. The ceiling was stepped and in the center was a large round crystal filling the room with light. The back wall of the room was dominated by a statue of the Goddess Issara, presented much the same as she had been in Trinico's temple back in Hurligville.

I don't know what I expected, but I was not prepared for the giant statue to come to life before my eyes.

"Took you long enough to get here," she complained, as she stepped toward me. And with each step she began to shrink until she was standing in front of me, just a few inches shorter than me. *"I thought you would be taller."*

"Eh?" was my eloquent reply.

"Well, no matter, you are finally here. My one and only servant and I must say, I did a good job choosing you too. To think, my servant, after just one month in this world would have found and saved, not one, but two fallen Gods.

The others are so jealous of me, I cannot thank you enough for that," the Goddess Issara started.

I finally got a chance to look at her, really look at her. The Goddess Issara was a teenager, maybe thirteen or fourteen years old, hardly more than a child. But she was also a Goddess, I reminded myself. Looks could be deceiving.

"You should have heard the way Nemesis was whining about having to dismiss her fifth champion already. As if it is my fault she has no taste in adventurers. And oh, you should have seen Tyr, she was so angry it was my champion that freed Gods from her pantheon and not her little favorite, though with a name like Freja Lov, I am not sure just how much you could expect," the Goddess gossiped.

I suppose it didn't help she was chattering the way I imagined a teenage girl would.

"Anyway, I know you are short on time, but you would not believe how lonely it gets being a God when you only have other Gods to talk to and most of them are so old that they are just boring as can be," she whined.

"I thought the Babylonian Gods were . . . you know ancient?" I asked.

"Oh, they are. Me, not so much. See, when the laws about Justice were passed, my dear mother refused to accept such a burden, her power represented too many domains. A lack of priests would have real consequences on the entire pantheon. So, she gave birth to me. I say birth, but it was her plucking a strand of hair from her head and breathing life into me. After that, she gave me the domain of Justice. Uncle Shamash also gave his dominion over justice to me, so I am the only Goddess of justice now for the Babylonian pantheon," the Goddess Issara explained.

"Anyway, I was all on my own fighting a losing battle against the criminal element until you came along. I have to admit, your plea, while a little silly, caught my attention. After I had a little peek inside at what was going on in

your head, I took a chance on you and boy did you ever come through for me," the Goddess confessed.

Does she ever stop talking?

"Right, time limit. First, your rewards for completing my quests, I believe you have accumulated nine rewards, yes?" she asked but didn't wait for an answer. In the air, in front of her, there was a slight shimmer before nine identical stone tokens, a little larger than a coin came into being. *"These sigils are your reward."*

"What do they do?" I asked, finally getting the chance to speak again.

"Lots of things, but it can wait until you return to me in a week. I do not want your mind spinning while you are supposed to be resting. And, in recognition of your service, I hereby promote you to Initiate Warrior Priest. Congratulations!" she cheered.

Class: Initiate Warrior Priest of Issara
Initiate Class Effects: +25% to holy or light bonus spell damage, -20% to bonus spell healing

That was not what I expected.

"I have questions-" I started.

"Questions that will wait a week. You will need your rest when you return you will be quite busy. I have much for you to learn and even more for you to do. Now go rest, that is an order from your Goddess," the young Goddess ordered.

I would have sighed in resignation, except I was no longer in the temple. In fact, I was looking at a logout portal again. A quick look around told me it was the logout portal my friends had left through not even an hour prior. All I could do was sigh in exasperation, my Goddess was almost as confusing as Rose . . . almost. With that, I stepped into the portal and the world faded to black.

"Welcome back, Mr. Jacobs," said a slightly familiar voice.

I blinked several times as I adjusted to the new setting. Fully opening my eyes, I saw Maggie sitting across from me in the same armchair she sat in when I first created my character. I looked around confused before I realized I was back in that same room except I was now sitting in a matching armchair except without any armor, just my jeans and shirt.

"I do hope you enjoyed your time in the World Tree," Maggie added.

"Very much so," I replied. The disoriented feeling was fading pretty quickly.

"I do wonder, was there a reason you chose to log out a day early? Nothing wrong I hope," said Maggie.

"Not at all, I just made some amazing new friends and we all agreed to log out together and back in on the same day," I explained.

"Wonderful," replied Maggie. "As this is your first logout, there are a few things to review. Before that, do you have any questions for me?"

"A few actually. I guess there was a patch, but no in-game message was sent with the details, only a system message when I discovered a change. Why was that?" I asked.

"The portion of the update that affected you was minor. The full update was rather significant and was not able to go live while you are in the game, and as such will not be applied until your next login. We did not want to distract you with the full details of the patch while you were in the game. That said, it is strongly suggested you review the full patch notes before your next login," Maggie explained.

I nodded, that made sense. I still thought they should have sent an in-game mail or something with notification of the portion of the patch that did affect me but what was done was done.

"I fell into an inescapable acid pit that killed me slowly, it probably should be considered torture and changed. It was an unpleasant experience to die that way even with the muted pain," I said.

"This issue has been logged and will be escalated immediately. The company sincerely apologizes for this incident and hopes it will not deter you from playing in the future," Maggie stated.

"Oh, and the walls of text for stat gains, that needs to stop, sure they can be funny, but so annoying. You should at least have a summary option," I added as a final thought.

"This request has been logged and will be sent to the proper channels," Maggie stated.

"I guess that is all I have for now," I said, there wasn't much else I could think of.

"Wonderful, now for the final details of your log out," she started. "First, when you emerge from the Seedpod be aware, you have been contained in a hermetically sealed capsule for nearly 30 days. You have not been washed or bathed nor has your hair been cut. You will probably want to immediately see to your personal hygiene. Second, you have not had solid food in 30 days, your first two days outside of the seedpod you are to restrict yourself to broth only and may add bread to dinner on the second day. Assuming all goes well, you may resume eating regular food though it is recommended you take it easy. Once again you must fast for 24-hours prior to login. Third, be mindful, that though you feel as if you have been moving and exercising the last 30 days, you have not actually been moving. Your skin will be slightly sensitive to pressure and your body may protest moving, too much, too quickly, so take things slowly at first. Remember to stretch three times per day, it is very important to maintaining your health. Do you have any questions about the above instructions and warnings? If you say yes and fail to comply with any of the aforementioned instructions, Seed Inc. will not be liable for any health-related problems that may occur."

Them refusing liability if I failed to follow instructions didn't sound good, however, none of what they spelled out was unreasonable. I responded, "I have no questions and will comply with the aforementioned instructions."

"Excellent, then we will see you in a week." Then everything faded to black once more.

STATS, EQUIPMENT, SKILLS AND SPELLS

Level:	7	Experience:	10.93%
Class:	Initiate Warrior Priest of Issara		
HP (Health Points):			1,900/1,900
MP (Mana Points):			1,600/1,600
SP (Stamina Points):			1,060/1,060
Strength:			85
- Melee Damage Modifier			+85
Dexterity:			95
- Melee Critical Strike Chance			9.50%
- Hit Chance			64.75%
- Dodge Chance			9.50%
Endurance:			190
Stamina:			106
Intellect:			160
- Spell Critical Strike Chance			16.00%
Wisdom:			100
Charisma:			110
Health Regeneration per minute:			105
Mana Regeneration per minute:			60
Stamina Regeneration per minute:			57
Holy Spell Damage Bonus:			157
Holy Spell Healing Bonus:			121
Carrying Capacity in Lbs.:			425

Quantity	Item
1	2-Person Tent
3	Full Water Canteen (5/5) - Filled with Manaberry Juice, restores +100-MP per mouthful.
3	Full Water Canteen (5/5) - Filled with Stamina Water Plus, restores +100-SP per mouthful.
1	Full High-Capacity Canteen (20/20) - Filled with Improved Manaberry Juice, restores +125-MP per mouthful.
1	Full High-Capacity Canteen (20/20) - Filled with Improved Stamina Water Plus, restores +125-SP per mouthful.
2	Adventurer's Jerky - Restores +100-HP
2	Pair of Silk Socks
1	Cotton Jeans
1	Black Cotton Shirt
1	Barnum's Patented Capture Net – A well-constructed net for use in combat. Durability 50/50 (Cannot be Repaired)
1	Spear of Gungnir I Blueprint
1	Mana Crystal (0/1000) - A crystal capable of storing mana for later use.
1	Fang of Fenrir - Legendary Crafting Material
1	Lockpicks
1	Screw Driver
2	Wrench

Equipment Slot	Name	Armor/ Damage	Bonus Stats
Helm:	Holy Order Light Helmet	+15 Armor	+10-Intellect, +10-Wisdom, +10-Holy Spell Damage and Healing
Head Accessory:	Empty		
Shoulders:	Holy Lion	+15	+5-Strength, +10-

	Mane Shoulder-guards	Armor	Dexterity, +5 Intellect, +10 Holy Spell Damage and Healing
Back:	All-Weather Cloak (White)		
Chest Armor:	Holy Order Light Jerkin	+20 Armor	+5-Endurance, +5-Stamina, +10-Intellect, +10 Holy Spell Damage and Healing
Chest Clothing:	White Cotton Shirt	+0 Armor	
Wrists:	Guard's Light Leather Bracers	+4 Armor	+5-Endurance, +2-Stamina
Hands:	Holy Order Light Gloves	+10 Armor	+5-Strength, +5-Dexterity, +5-Intellect, +5-Holy Spell Damage and Healing
Arm Accessory 1:	Empty		
Arm Accessory 2:	Empty		
Finger Accessory 1:	Farmer's Ring of Stamina		+2-Stamina, +4-Stamina Regeneration
Finger Accessory 2:	Holy Order Ring of Justice		+5-Strength, +5-Dexterity, +5-Endurance, +5-Stamina, +5 Intellect, +5 Wisdom, +5-Holy

717

			Damage and Healing, Increased experience gains for all Goddess granted skills by 50%
Waist:	Guard's Light Leather Belt	+6 Armor	+5-Endurance, +2-Stamina
Leg Clothing:	Cotton Jeans	+0 Armor	
Leg Armor:	Holy Order Light Leg-guards	+20 Armor	+5-Endurance, +10-Intellect, +5-Wisdom, +10 Holy Spell Damage and Healing
Feet Clothing	Silk Socks	+0 Armor	
Feet:	Well Tread Boots	+10 Armor	+5-Dexterity, +5-Endurance, +5-Stamina
Weapon:	Hasta	7-8 1h Dmg, 14-16 2h Dmg	
Off-Hand:	Guard's Phalanx Shield	+20 Armor	+20-Defense, +10-Endurance, +5-Stamina
Charm:	Empty		
Bag:	100 lbs. Traveler's Satchel		

One-Handed Polearms	Level: 31	Experience: 45.88%
Current Damage Modifiers	Damage: +15.50	Critical Strike Chance: +1.55%

718

Subskill: *Jab*	**Damage:** +15.50	**Skill Stamina Cost:** *41*
Subskill: *Rapid Striking*	**Damage:** -10 **Strikes:** *13* **Cone:** *30 0*	**Skill Stamina Cost:** *81*
Subskill: *Ligament Rip*	**Reduce Enemy Movement and Attack Speed:** *50%* **Target Receives Increased Damage:** +7.75% **Duration:** *15 Seconds* **Bleed Effect:** *2 Damage per Second*	**Skill Stamina Cost:** *56*
Subskill: *Impale*	**Damage:** *15-16* **Bleed Effect:** *2 Damage per Second* **Duration:** *10 Seconds*	**Skill Stamina Cost:** *51*
Subskill: *Power Thrust*	**Damage:** +31.00 **Chance to Stun:** *10%*	**Skill Stamina Cost:** *81*

Two-Handed Polearms	**Level:** *69*	**Experience:** *99.09%*
Current Damage Modifiers	**Damage:** +34.50	**Critical Strike Chance:** +3.45%
Subskill: *Ligament Rip*	**Reduce Enemy Movement and Attack Speed:** *50%* **Target Receives Increased Damage:** +15.25% **Duration:** *15 Seconds* **Bleed**	**Skill Stamina Cost:** *94*

	Effect: 4 Damage per Second	
Subskill: Impale	Damage: 34-35 Bleed Effect: 4 Damage per Second Duration: 15 Seconds	Skill Stamina Cost: 89
Subskill: Power Thrust	Damage: +69.00 Chance to Stun: 10%	Skill Stamina Cost: 119
Subskill: Jab	Damage: +34.50	Skill Stamina Cost: 89
Subskill: Rapid Striking	Damage: -2 Strikes: 29	Skill Stamina Cost: 169

Phalanx Shield	Level: 20	Experience: 66.55%
Current Defense Modifiers	Block Chance: +1.00%	Critical Block Chance: +0.50%
Subskill: Shield Slam	Damage: 7-8 Effect: Interrupt Chance to Stun on Critical Strike: 10%	Skill Stamina Cost: 30
Subskill: Shield-Counter	Block Chance: +30.00% Cooldown: 30 seconds	Skill Stamina Cost: 45

Net	Level: 3	Experience: 16.68%
Subskill: Net Toss	Capture Target: Below 25% HP	Skill Stamina Cost: 53

Preparation Time: 4 minutes 58 seconds	Skill Effect (Active): Slow netted target by 50% for 30 Seconds

Shift	Level: 10	Experience: 47.25%
Combat Movement	Range: 1.10 yards	Skill Stamina Cost: 5 per move

Acrobatics	Level: 39	Experience: 52.43%
Combat Movement	Dodge Chance: +19.50%	Skill Stamina Cost: 5 per second

Meditation	Level: 1	Experience: 0.00%
Skill Effect (Active): Enter the Meditation Mind Temple		
Intellect: +1 per 30 minutes	Wisdom: +1 per 30 minutes	Charisma: +1 per 30 minutes

Stealth	Level: 7	Experience: 8.93%
Non-Combat Movement: Speed Reduced by 78.25%	Chance of Being Revealed: 59.30%	Skill Stamina Cost: 2 per second
Subskill: Ambush	Critical Strike Chance: 100.00%	Skill Stamina Cost: 20

Justice Strike	Level: 27	Experience: 4.51%
Current Damage Modifier	Damage: +13.50 Cooldown: 30 seconds	Skill Stamina Cost: 77
Skill Effect (Active): A righteous strike in the name of Justice. Increases damage or healing of next spell cast by 37.		

Valkyrie Strike	Level: 1	Experience: 0.00%
Current Damage Modifier	Damage: +1.00	Skill Stamina Cost: 50

Justice Bringer	Level: 2			Experience: 0.00	
Spell Duration: 1 hour	Spell Cast Speed: Instant	Spell Charges: 1 / 1	Spell Mana Cost: 100	Recharge: 24 hours	

Spell Effect (Active): All Adventurers and Citizens within 21 yards have their effective level lowered or raised to match your own. Does not work on enemy Citizens, Beasts or Monsters.

Holy Smite	Level: 23	Experience: 19.09%
Spell Damage: 33-38	Spell Cast Speed: 1.50 seconds	Spell Mana Cost: 56

Spell Effect (Active): Smite a single target with holy damage

Lesser Holy Fire	Level: 38	Experience: 12.33%
Spell Damage: 21-23 per second	Spell Cast Speed: Instant Cooldown: 10 seconds	Spell Mana Cost: 116
Spell Duration: 30 seconds	Spell Effect (Active): Burn a single target with Holy fire. (Stackable x3)	

Lesser Holy Shock	Level: 22	Experience: 4.51%
Spell Damage: 32-37	Spell Cash Speed: Instant Cooldown: 30 seconds	Spell Mana Cost: 144

Spell Effect (Active): A shock of holy energy attacks the nervous system of your target stunning it and increasing physical damage received by 32 for 5 seconds.

Lesser Heal	*Level:* 19	*Experience:* 41.57%
Spell Heal: 45-55	*Spell Cast Speed:* 2.00 seconds	*Spell Mana Cost:* 38
Spell Effect (Active): Heal a single target		

Holy Cleanse	*Level:* 1	*Experience:* 0.00%
Conditions Removed: 1	*Spell Cast Speed:* Instant	*Spell Mana Cost:* 50
Spell Effect (Active): Remove 1 poison or disease from afflicted target.		

Lesser Holy Barrier	*Level:* 31	*Experience:* 69.06%
Spell Duration: 10 minutes	*Spell Cast Speed:* Instant	*Spell Mana Cost:* 81
Spell Effect (Active): Create a thin barrier of Holy energy around a target that absorbs 31-points of incoming damage.		

Lesser Mental Fortification	*Level:* 22	*Experience:* 55.50%
Spell Duration: 10 minutes	*Spell Cast Speed:* Instant	*Spell Mana Cost:* 50
Spell Effect (Active): Increase Intellect +7, Increase Wisdom +7, Increase Resistance to Fear 5%, Increases Resistance to Mind Control 5%		

Lesser Holy Imbuement	*Level:* 22	*Experience:* 13.36%
Spell Duration: 10 minutes	*Spell Cast Speed:* Instant	*Spell Mana Cost:* 50
Spell Effect (Active): Imbued Weapon now deals holy damage causing an additional 11-12 damage per hit		
Spell Effect (Active): Imbued Shield now deals holy damage causing 12-13 damage per block		

Lesser Combat Blessing	Level: 25	Experience: 5.76%
Spell Duration: 10 minutes	Spell Cast Speed: Instant	Spell Mana Cost: 50
Spell Effect (Active): Increase Stamina +8, Increase Strength +8, Increase Dexterity +8, increase Endurance +8		

Edda of Light and Dark	Level: 3	Experience: 25.00%
Spell Duration: 10 minutes	Spell Cast Speed: Instant	Spell Mana Cost: 300
Spell Effect (Active): Your next attack will slow your target's attack speed 1.1% and increase your attack speed 1.1%. (Stackable x10) (Personal use only).		

Order: Taunt	Level: N/A	Experience: N/A
Spell Duration: 30 seconds	Spell Cast Speed: Instant	Spell Mana Cost: 10
Spell Effect (Active): For the next thirty seconds the target of your taunt will attack only you.		

Boar Charge	Level: 5	Experience: 0.00%
Spell Damage: 125-300 per second	Spell Cast Speed: 5.00 Channeled Cooldown: 30 minutes	Spell Mana Cost: 250
Spell Effect (Active): Summon a stampede of spectral boars that will charge a targeted area dealing damage and knocking down anyone in the area of effect.		
Charm Earned Bonus (Passive): Blessing of the Boar Spirit - +10-Endurance, +10-Stamina		

Lore	Level: 27	Experience: 82.13%
Professional Skill: Lore is the study of the history of the World Tree and its denizens.		

Subskill: Norse Mysticism II	Your knowledge of both the Ancient Norse language, runes and their Mythos has granted you a higher level of mastery. Knowledge of Norse Skills and Spells is greatly improved.

Runology (Evolved from Writing)	Level: 44	Experience: 4.15%
Professional Skill: Runology is the art of communicating power.		
Chance to Learn Rank I Unknown Rune: 22.00%	Chance to Craft Rank I Skill Book: +11.00%	Chance to Craft Lesser Spell Book: +5.50%
Professional Skill: Writing is the ability to communicate through the written word.		
Norse Expertise: +100% to craft any known Norse spell or skill book of Rank I regardless of level.		

Cartography (Evolved from Drawing)	Level: 40	Experience: 15.55%
Professional Skill: Cartography is the ability to read and draw maps of varying detail.		
Professional Skill: Drawing is the ability to communicate through drawn images.		

Perception	Level: 24	Experience: 85.62%
Skill Range: 12.40 yards	Chance to See: 16.00%	Chance to Identify/Track: 22.00%
Subskill: Beast Tracking	**Skill Effect (Passive):** Enables you to see animal tracks to better hunt them.	
Subskill: Humanoid Tracking	**Skill Effect (Passive):** Enables you to track humanoids.	
Subskill: Eye for Detail	**Skill Effect (Passive):** Enables you to see details that would be missed otherwise.	

Subskill: *Spot Trap*	**Skill Effect (Passive):** *Enables you to see hidden traps.*
Subskill: *Analyze Stamina*	**Skill Effect (Passive):** *Enables you to see target Stamina*
Subskill: *Analyze Mana*	**Skill Effect (Passive):** *Enables you to see target Mana*

Trap	Level: 2	Experience: 25.00%
Skill Effect (Passive): *Knowledge and understanding of traps.*		
Subskill: *Create Snare*	**Skill Effect (20 Stamina + Materials):** *Allows for the construction of a basic trap to catch small game. Chance to capture 25%*	
Subskill: *Create Spike Trap*	**Skill Effect (20 Stamina + Materials):** *Allows for the creation of a basic trap to wound and slow. Damage 5-10 Chance to Slow 20%*	
Subskill: *Disarm Trap*	**Skill Effect (20+ Stamina + Tools):** *Enables you to disarm a trap, more complex traps will require more Stamina.*	

Campsite Management	Level: 4	Experience: 50.00%
Subskill: *Tent Construction*	**Skill Effect (Passive):** *Enables you to construct a rudimentary tent.*	
Subskill: *Campfire Construction*	**Skill Effect (Passive):** *Enables you to start a safe campfire.*	
Subskill: *Campfire Cooking*	**Skill Effect (Passive):** *Enables you to cook food over a campfire and add 1 seasoning.*	
Subskill: *Campsite Perimeter*	**Skill Effect (Passive):** *Enables you to establish a campsite perimeter with a rudimentary warning system.*	

Scavenging	Level: 1	Experience: 20.00%
Skill Effect (20 Stamina): *Scavenge useful materials from dead animals and broken machines. Chance to successfully scavenge something useful*		

1.00%. Chance to successfully scavenge something more useful 0.05%.

Lockpicking	Level: 3	Experience: 87.45%
Skill Effect (Active): *You have a 3% chance to pick a simple lock.*		

Maintenance	Level: 8	Experience: 51.33%
Skill Effect (Active): *Allows basic repair of equipment restoring 5 points of durability at the cost of 2 durability capacity.*		

Influence	Level: 5	Experience: 16.77%
Skill Effect (Passive): *Increases your Charisma by 0.50%*		
Skill Effect (Passive): *Increases your Charisma Experience Gain by 5.00%*		

Barter	Level: 3	Experience: 19.54%
Skill Effect (Passive): *Reduce purchase cost by 0.15% (0.15% Charisma)*		
Skill Effect (Passive): *Increases your Charisma Experience Gain by 3.00%*		

Speed Reading	Level: 3	Experience: 87.41%
Skill Effect (Passive): *Read 8% faster.*		
Skill Effect (Passive): *Increases your Intellect and Wisdom Experience Gain by 3.00%*		

Summon God: Fenrir	Level: ∞	Experience: ∞
Spell Effect (Active): *Call upon the wolf God Fenrir to aid you in battle*		

AUTHOR'S NOTE

Thank you all very much and I hope you have enjoyed this adventure. Bye-bye will return soon so keep an eye out for updates.

Please visit my website at M.A. Carlson
or Patreon - M.A. Carlson

To find similar stories and connect with authors, check out:
GameLit Society

20751907R00404

Made in the USA
Lexington, KY
07 December 2018